The Hoax

Adrienne Jones

Mundania Press

A Mundania Press Production

Mundania Press LLC
6470A Glenway Avenue, #109
Cincinnati, Ohio 45211-5222

To order additional copies of this book, contact:
books@mundania.com
www.mundania.com

Cover Art © 2006 by Trace Edward Zaber
Book Design, Production, and Layout by Daniel J. Reitz, Sr.
Marketing and Promotion by Bob Sanders

Trade Paperback ISBN-10: 1-59426-221-7
Trade PaperbackISBN-13: 978-1-59426-221-0

eBook ISBN-10: 1-59426-220-9
eBook ISBN-13: 978-1-59426-220-3

First Edition • July 2006

Library of Congress Catalog Card Number 2006927879

Production by Mundania Press LLC
Printed in the United States of America

10 9 8 7 6 5 4 3 2 1

Prologue

Alcoholics define rock bottom as that hellish yet divine moment when they can sink no lower into the pit of poisoned madness. At this point there are two choices. One is to let the hole collapse, and suffocate in the self-dug grave. The other is to begin a painful escalation upward. Charles Duvaine did neither. Though he had given up the bottle weeks before, he still lingered midway down, wedged between the walls of the pit, daring it one last chance to suck him into the molten core and incinerate him. While free of intoxicants, he was prisoner to his despair, leaving his bed only when his biological functions demanded it.

But rock bottom found Charles despite his indifference. It rose to greet him that morning in the form of a tiny clawed foot pressing against his lower lip. As slumber's grip loosened, he felt the trail of fur on his cheek, a brush of silken pelt. His eyelids fluttered. In a tumble of sheets he launched himself out of bed, swatting the rat off of his face with a yelp. The creature hit the floor and broke into a panicked scuttle, running in circles until it finally took refuge under a pile of dirty laundry. Charles looked down at the rumpled bed, where black pellets dotted his white sheets. "Oh, that does it," he said, wincing. "This has got to end today."

He examined the rest of his bedroom, repulsed. The previously beige carpet was now a blotchy abstract of curious stains. Laundry formed misshapen mountains across the floor, eclipsed only by six months of neglected trash. His eyes were drawn back to the rat droppings on his sheets and his jaw stiffened. It was bad enough that he'd let his once lovely beach house fall to hovel. But now he had rats, the token representatives of degeneracy.

He'd seen them in the house lately, phantom dust bunnies disappearing into corners as he glanced their way. He'd tolerated the random sightings, telling himself that he'd hire an exterminator when he was fully recovered. It seemed he'd have to bump up that deadline. His tolerance did not stretch to waking up with one of the damn things on his head.

He managed a sleepy grin as he tugged his bathrobe on. Part of him relished the disgust he felt. It was an indication that he was returning to normal. Two weeks ago he would have barely flinched upon waking with a rodent on his head. But he hadn't been sober then. An army of rats could have marched across his face, waving banners and beating tiny war drums. He either wouldn't have noticed or wouldn't have cared.

His bare feet padded the carpet as he moved from his bedroom to the outer hall, dodging empty rum bottles and pyramids of trash along the way. Morning sun streamed through the skylights, serving only to better display the filth he'd created. There was barely a square foot not soiled with some manner of garbage. The beach house had three floors and more rooms than he could count, and he'd succeeded in shitting up all of it. Bravo for consistency.

Clinging to the railing, he moved down the flight of steps that spiraled into the first floor. To his delight, his legs were free of the tremors he'd experienced when he'd first given up the bottle. Pausing, he surveyed the squalor below. The anesthetic shield of drunkenness had been lifted and he could now clearly view the mess he'd made of his house. And his life. He flinched, watching a rat exit a pizza box. Again, his revulsion comforted him, validating his return to the world of the living. *I cringe, therefore I am.*

In the kitchen he counted thirteen red lines drawn through the previous days on the calendar. He picked up the marker and made another triumphant slash. He'd been sober for two weeks. It might not sound like much to an outsider, but having been drunk for six months, Charles viewed it as quite an accomplishment. Flipping through the phone book, he chose a cleaning service called 'Fresh Start'. The name seemed to correlate with his current mission. He wondered if they could get the house back to its original splendor, the way it had been before he'd gone into a state of drunken recluse.

Charles hadn't planned on becoming a drunk, but he supposed no one ever did. He didn't wake one morning and randomly decide to kill enough brain cells to devolve him on the evolutionary scale. He glanced at the empty rum bottle in the kitchen sink, with its colorful illustration of the virile Captain Morgan. They should change the label, he thought, and replace the jolly pirate with a drawing of Cro-Magnon man. It would more accurately depict the liquor's effect on modern man. But that wasn't fair to the rum company. Nobody told Charles to drink a bottle a day for six months. He'd written that prescription himself.

In his meager defense, his list of gripes was a long one. Tragedy had walloped him twice in under a year. They'd never found the culprit that hit his wife Marie's car, sending her over a guardrail to her death. An accident, the police had said. He hated the word. Accident. It made it all sound so simple, like spilling a glass of milk.

It was a mere three months later that Jeffrey was speared in the throat on a hunting trip. Mistaken for a deer, the police had said to Charles. His vibrant twenty-one year old son, mistaken for a piece of venison steak. Marie's death had been shattering enough, but hearing the news about his son had been like swallowing poison. He knew that once it sank in, it would slowly kill him. And since he'd always felt that quicker was better, he determined to help the process along with a little poison of his own. Captain Morgan was glad to oblige.

So Charles became a cliché, crawling inside of a bottle to escape the pain. He'd turned easily to the bitterness, like one of those 'life done me wrong' characters in a tough guy movie. Of course those guys were always portrayed as deep romantic figures sitting in darkened rooms, swilling Scotch from short crystal glasses. You never saw Mel Gibson passing out on the kitchen floor or urinating into a four thousand-dollar vase, as Charles had done one night. Talk about pissing your money away.

During his binge, he'd convinced himself that his family had been cursed. He realized now that this was ridiculous. No family was cursed. Except maybe the Kennedys. It was fear of this imagined curse that prompted his retreat from his oldest son Joey, his last living child. He had abandoned Joey, thinking it in his best interest to steer clear of his cursed father, lest he have an accident too. Perhaps 'abandoned' was not the right word. Joey was twenty-eight years old, hardly a child. Still, Joey had needed his father and Charles had not been there for him.

His heart was heavy as he recalled Joey pounding on the beach house door, begging his father to come out of seclusion. He would make his amends to Joey, but not before he got himself and his surroundings cleaned up. Joey had been through enough without having to witness the disgrace his father had allowed himself to become.

With this thought, he dialed the number of the cleaning service and spoke briefly with a man who agreed to send someone out for an assessment. Charles imagined their reaction upon entering the house, which looked so well kept from the outside. He'd mentioned the horrendous condition of the rugs, but the man insisted that his service could clean any carpet. He probably figured Charles was some uptight cad from the rich neighborhood, belly aching about a little spilled caviar. They were in for a shocker.

A cockroach scuttled into the rum bottle in the sink, reminding Charles that he also had to call an exterminator. He was reaching for the phone when the doorbell rang.

The sound startled him. He certainly wasn't expecting company. Up until two weeks ago the sound of the doorbell meant that the booze had arrived. For months he'd survived, if one could call it that, by having sausage pizzas delivered daily, along with a bottle of spiced rum. Rum and pizza. What more could a man want? Quite a bit more, he'd finally decided, which was why he'd cancelled all further deliveries from the liquor store.

The doorbell buzzed again.

"I'll be right there!" he called out, pulling his filthy bathrobe together to hide his even filthier tee shirt. He stopped at the gold rimmed mirror and gave himself a once over. All of his life he'd been hearing about how handsome he was. *If my friends could see me now!* His black hair was arranged in greasy points. The tufts of gray at each temple, which had once given him a distinguished air, now stuck out on either side of his head lending him a mad scientist look. His pale blue eyes had turned an ominous gray, just a shade lighter than the circles beneath them. The doorbell persisted. Charles decided that whatever asshole was at the door deserved to see him looking this way, for showing up at nine in the morning on a Saturday.

When he opened the door he thought he had begun hallucinating. The young man on the porch was dressed in a red naval jacket, with gold trim and a double run of gold buttons down the front. He wore a matching red pirate style hat and a large gold hoop in one ear. The hair was definitely a wig. Thick black curls ran down the stranger's shoulders nearly to his waist. The face make up was as white as his gloves. He looked ready for a stage performance. The eyes were over done as well, with thick black liner and lashes that had to be false. Charles blinked, shaking his head in an attempt to clear his vision. The Captain Hook drag queen was still there.

"May I, um, may I help you?"

The thing smiled. "Mr. Duvaine?"

"Yes, I'm Charles Duvaine. What can I do for you?"

"Hello, Mr. Duvaine. I'm Kenny from Forest Bluffs Liquors. I have a special delivery for you."

Charles shook his head. "There must be some mistake. I cancelled all deliveries from your store two weeks ago."

The oddity put one gloved hand to his mouth. "Oh I am so sorry! I don't know how this could have happened!" His vocal inflection was so sing-song that either he was openly gay or he was putting it on.

Charles gave the young man a look. "That's okay. Don't worry about it. Why are you dressed like that?"

"Oh this?" he said, doing a little spin. "It's Forest Bluffs Liquors twentieth anniversary. It was the boss's idea that we dress up for deliveries. I'm Captain Morgan. Get it?"

Charles forced an awkward smile. "Yeah, I get it."

"It is your drink of choice, isn't it?" the pirate asked as he pulled a bottle out of a velvet sack on his waistcoat. Charles stared at the tall thin bottle with its enticing amber liquid and miniature picture of Captain Morgan, which looked eerily like the stranger at his door. He felt his resolve stumble a bit as the liquid in the bottle swished back and forth in the stranger's gloved hand. A wave of dizziness overtook him and he clung to the door for support.

The pirate's smile dropped. "Hey, are you okay?" he asked, taking Charles's arm and leading him inside to the nearest chair. Charles put his head between his knees, forcing long full breaths until the tremor passed. He sat up finally, embarrassed. The delivery boy glanced around the room and wrinkled his nose at the trash. He tried to hide the gesture by coughing, but Charles had seen it.

"Thanks. You can go now. I'm fine," he said.

"Are you sure?" the stranger asked, with concern that seemed genuine.

"I'm sure. I haven't been feeling well lately, but I'm fine now. Really."

The Captain Morgan thing nodded. "I understand. I have just the thing." To Charles's amazement, the kid swished over to the dry bar and grabbed a glass from the display. He unscrewed the cap of the bottle and poured a few ounces of the golden liquid into it. Charles watched stunned as the boy returned with the glass and knelt down, waving it under his nose. "This is what you need, isn't it? This will make you feel much better."

The fumes invaded Charles's nostrils and his mouth began to water. It had to be a bad dream. Was he still sleeping? Asleep or awake, it was time to order Kenny the delivery boy out of his house. "Please go," Charles said, his voice strained. "I don't want a drink. I've canceled my orders with your store. Go back and take me out of your computer."

The pirate stranger remained kneeling before him, grinning like an overgrown theatre puppet. "But this *will* make you feel better. Won't it Charles?"

Charles couldn't believe the kid's brazenness. And when did he say the little punk could call him by his first name? He lashed out and knocked the glass out of the stranger's gloved hand. It bounced onto the rug and liquor shot out in a spray of amber. The pirate stared down at the spilled rum, scratching his chin. Black-rimmed eyes looked up at Charles with mock concern.

"That's going to leave a stain," he said, suppressing a smirk.

Charles leaned forward in his chair. "Maybe you don't hear so well. I asked you to leave. Can't you see that I'm detoxing here? Now take your bottle and get out before I call the police."

The kid stood finally. He went back across the room and snatched the open bottle off the dry bar. Charles was sure he would leave immediately, after the way he'd been berated. Instead, he sighed deeply and walked back to the middle of the room. "You're not being very cooperative, Charles. After all, I've come to give you what you want."

Charles stared at the costumed stranger, the first shivers of fear tightening his stance as he realized that something was very wrong here. "That's ridiculous," he said. "I don't even know you. How the hell would you know what I want?"

The pirate chuckled. "Well it's obvious isn't it? Just look at this place." He did a little twirl, gesturing at the mess with his hand. "You've been holed up here for months, Charles. You quit your job. You've cut yourself off from your friends," he hesitated, "from your son."

The words slapped Charles. "How do you know about my son? Who are you?"

The stranger took a step closer. His painted face had gone blank. "You want to disappear, Charles. I'm here to help you do that. That is what you want, isn't it? To disappear?"

He continued toward Charles, swinging the bottle rhythmically from side to side. Instinct told Charles to run for the door, but he didn't trust his trembling legs. The stranger stopped before the chair and offered the bottle. Charles glared at him, waiting for his strength to return so he could either escape or beat the little son of a bitch to a pulp. Closing the distance, he pushed the rum bottle nearer until it was mere inches from Charles's lips.

"I quit drinking!" Charles said through clenched teeth.

The kid shook his head. "Not today."

Charles made his face as hateful as possible. "Get the hell out of my house."

The kid studied him a moment, then turned away, circling the room as he spoke. "Okay, Charles. Enough with the pleasantries. You have been an enormous pain in the ass to me. Do you know that? I've had to readjust my entire schedule to accommodate your little whims."

"What? I don't even know you. What the hell do you want from me?"

He shrugged. "What do I want? Well, that's a long story. I wouldn't want to bore you with the details. Actually, that's a lie. The truth is I don't want to bore myself telling you the details. So I'll put it to you frankly. I need your blood, Charles. Your blood. Trust me when I tell you that it is very important."

Charles frowned, confused in spite of his fear. "My blood? So you mean to kill me?"

The pirate raised an eyebrow. "Kill you? You see, that's interesting. The thing is, you were supposed to kill yourself, Charles. It would have been so easy. One of those drunken nights, I could have slit your wrists with your own razor while you were passed out. Nobody would have known the difference. They all would have assumed you did it to yourself, what with your being a basket case and all. But no. You had to quit drinking and fuck it all up!" The painted face flared with anger for an instant, then the maddened smile returned.

"What on earth are you talking about?" Charles asked.

"Don't you get it, Charles? Nobody is going to believe that you killed yourself if you're suddenly stone cold sober and calling cleaning services to come to your house. Now I'm a patient man, Charles, but your little recovery has thrown quite a monkey wrench into my plans. So take the bottle, and drink the damn rum."

Charles narrowed his eyes. "No."

The painted mouth went stiff. "Fine. If you won't take your medicine like a big boy, I'll have to force it on you." With one gloved hand, the costumed stranger thrust out and dragged him from the chair. Charles fought wildly but the kid ultimately toppled him to the floor and pinned his shoulders down with his knees. Charles worked to twist himself free but the sinewy youth had surprising strength, and held him firm. With a curl of his lip, he forced the bottle into Charles's mouth. "Drink it, damn you!"

Charles clenched his teeth, stopping the bottle's penetration just before his tongue. The mystery assailant grabbed his chin, and with a grimace of rage, squeezed his jawbone until sharp waves of pain forced his mouth open. He jammed the bottle into his mouth and down his throat, taking part of a tooth along with it. Charles tasted blood, warm and metallic on his tongue.

At first the rum trickled into his lungs and he choked. He tried spitting it out as quickly as it filled, but eventually he had to swallow to keep from drowning. When the bottle was empty save for an ounce or two, the painted stranger pulled it back and rolled off. Charles turned onto his side and coughed up the burning rum. When he could breathe again, he looked up at his attacker. "Who are you?" It came out as a whisper.

"I'm the answer to your prayers, Charles. I'm going to put you out of your misery."

Charles jerked back guardedly. The kid put his hands to his cheeks in an exaggerated gesture of despair. "Don't look so disappointed! You do want to see your wife again, don't you?"

The comment incensed Charles, and the emotion muscled down the fear. He lunged at the stranger, taking him by surprise. He had his hands gripped tightly around the pirate's neck when a pain ripped through his chest. His lungs seemed to freeze, unable to take in breath. He released his assailant and fell to the floor, gasping, clutching his left arm as agony shot through it in electric waves. Kenny, if that was his real name, stared down at him with a frown.

"Oh you've got to be kidding me. Are you having a heart attack?"

Through his pain and fear, Charles managed to stick his middle finger up. The pirate thing put his hands on his hips and shook his head. "No! You can't have a heart attack! Damn it, Charles. Is there no end to your insistence on screwing up my plans?"

Charles gasped as invisible cotton stuffed his lungs. In his blurring vision, he saw the visitor in the big red hat leaning down to take hold of him. The stranger lifted him to his feet, and Charles hung like a rag doll. "I need your blood, Charles. I thought we established that. How am I supposed to collect your blood if your heart stops pumping?" The stranger studied his surroundings then began dragging Charles toward the adjoining sitting room. The murderous Captain Morgan mumbled to himself as he made his way into the room. He seemed panicked now, which was odd since Charles was the one who was dying. By the time the assailant got Charles into the sitting room, his chest felt like it had a giant fireball burning inside of it.

The pirate bumped into an overstuffed chair, grunting as he maneuvered Charles's limp form toward the glass coffee table. Charles knew what was coming, but hadn't the strength or inclination to fight it. His pirate enemy turned him so that they faced each other, pressed so close Charles could feel his breath. "Don't worry, Mr. Duvaine," he said, the phony sing-song accent gone suddenly. He looked almost sad. "You're going to a better place. I promise. I'm doing you a favor."

That voice, Charles thought deliriously. Something familiar about the voice. Charles knew that voice. But from where? A haze was forming before his eyes and it was getting harder to think.

The young man shoved him. His back shattered the glass table as he plummeted through it. A thousand points of pain lit up on his flesh as he hit the floor, crunching the broken glass beneath him. He'd bought that table in Paris. Strange thoughts to have upon dying. He'd been on vacation with Marie at the time. Marie had loved Paris.

His killer leaned over him, pulling a quart-sized container out of his jacket. Charles couldn't imagine what he was going to do with that. Take his blood? What on earth for? He would never know. He felt the life draining out of him, spilling onto the floor along with his poorly pumping blood. His killer knelt down, moving in close. Charles forced himself to look up into those painted eyes. Just for an instant, he thought he recognized those eyes. Then, as the stranger moved even closer, he was sure that he did.

"You!" Charles gasped.

"Goodbye, Charles." He took the ridiculous red hat off in a gesture of respect.

"You!" Charles whispered again. Then the haze thickened, blotting out all light, and Charles was gone.

Chapter One

The locals called it Death Row. The street ran through one of those city side neighborhoods that insisted on calling itself a suburb, despite the silhouettes of the downtown buildings on the horizon. Trees caged in iron baskets sprouted from the sidewalk every five feet. Elderly women shuffled into antique shops, their brittle arms linked for support. All in all, Death Row wasn't a bad street. The unflattering nickname was derived from the glut of funeral homes that clogged the string of cafés and quaint specialty stores.

At the end of the road atop a rolling hill of manmade lawn, loomed the Shady Rest funeral home, where the wealthy serviced their dead. Like a palace in a village of huts, the polished colonial house looked grossly out of place and contradictory to its purpose. With its neon green lawn, white flagstone paths and fancy trim work, Shady Rest looked nothing at all like a funeral home, which was probably the idea. Silly really. No patron was going to forget why they were there, no matter how welcoming the place looked from the outside.

Out behind the Shady Rest, well hidden by a lilac bush, Patrick Obrien fell to his knees and lost his breakfast all over the neatly groomed lawn. His friend Shep stood over him. "Jesus Obrien," he said, his face pulled into a sour grimace. "Are you okay?" Shep's tone tried for concern but was closer to disgust. Patrick lifted his head just enough to sneer over his shoulder.

"I just vomited behind a funeral home, Shepherd. Does that sound okay to you?"

"Again," Shep corrected. "You just vomited behind a funeral home again. This is the third time you've done this in under a year, pal."

Patrick could have done without the reminder. His unnatural dread of funeral homes was not his proudest attribute. A towering redhead with an athletic build, he rather enjoyed the tough guy image his appearance evoked. Six foot three and full of muscles, yet he was reduced to a sick, quivering mess before every funeral wake. As an Irish Catholic, he understood the need for a church ceremony, but the purpose of the wake was beyond him. He'd never understood how displaying the cold, shriveled remains of a loved one should assist the grieving process. His stomach lurched at the thought of going inside, where death waited, spread out on a bed of satin.

"Get up, Obrien. You're ruining your suit," Shep said. Patrick wasn't used to looking up at Shep, who was a good five inches shorter than he was. Contrary to Patrick, Shep was small and wiry, with smooth boyish features that made him look far younger than his twenty-eight years. With his sandy, chin-length curls, and a strand of beads around his neck in lieu of a tie, one would never guess that Shep was independently wealthy. Patrick wondered fleetingly if he himself would look more like Shep if he didn't have to work in an office. Not likely. The hippie surfer thing just didn't look right on men Patrick's size.

Patrick shook his head, still fighting the nausea. "I'm not going inside. I can't."

"You have to," Shep said.

"I can't, Shepherd! Look at me. I can't even stand up. Go on without me. I'll meet you outside after the service."

Shep frowned down at him. "Don't be a tool, Obrien. Joey's our best friend. Don't you want to pay your respects to his dead father?"

"Can't I pay my respects from out here?" he asked hopefully.

Shep shook his head. "You have to go in and kneel before the coffin. You know the drill."

Shep's mention of the coffin sent a toxic shudder through Patrick and he doubled over, gagging. Shep shook his head like a disappointed parent. "Here, smoke this." Shep handed him a thin white cigarette shaped like a broken finger.

Patrick looked up at him, incredulous. "You want me to smoke pot before going into Joey's father's wake? Are you nuts?"

"It will soothe your stomach and it will relax you."

Patrick shook his head. "No way."

With hands on his hips, Shep scowled down at him. He was trying to look forceful, but with his cherubic curls and boyish face, it wasn't a look he could pull off easily. Only Shep's true friends knew the weight behind his seemingly innocent gaze. Shep's docile appearance was a guise for the ruthlessly manipulative little bastard he could be. "Obrien, it's a proven fact that marijuana cures nausea. Hospitals use it to help chemotherapy patients. A couple hits of this and your gut will feel good as new."

Patrick gaped at him. "Sure, good as new. I'll also be stoned at a damned wake! You know I have a phobia. The weed will only intensify it." Another cramp groped him and he doubled over, holding his gut.

Kneeling down, Shep rubbed Patrick's back, waving the joint under his nose. "Joey needs us, Obrien. We have to go inside. We're all he has left now." Patrick looked miserably up at Shep.

"We have to go inside," he said again.

Patrick nodded grudgingly. Unfortunately, Shep was right. Their friend Joey had hit a patch of bad luck. His father, Charles Duvaine was the third and final family member to croak on him in under a year. Some whispered of a curse, as they always did when multiple tragedies struck one family. Joey seemed to be handling the deaths well, however. Too well, in Patrick's opinion. His demeanor, when not cold and robotic, was light and cheerful. Patrick supposed it was a defense of some sort, but he couldn't be sure. He knew nothing about death personally. All of his grandparents were still alive and he'd never even lost a pet. Still, there was something inordinately peculiar about Joey's lack of emotion in the face of all this death.

Patrick remembered studying Joey at his mother's funeral, then at his brother's funeral three months later. It was the same show at both, Joey standing blank-faced with his hands linked at his waist, smiling easily as if attending a garden party. Three dead in a year and Patrick had yet to see him shed a tear. To each his own, he supposed. Peculiar or not, Joey was his friend, and Patrick needed to be there for him. Damn it. He loved Joey, but he sincerely wished his family members would stop dropping like flies in a freezer. He found the wakes excruciating, physically and mentally. But he supposed that was what true friendship was all about, the willingness to suffer for the other's comfort.

Screw it. He took the joint from Shep and lit it, inhaling the sweet, skunky aroma. With the second hit, his stomach was instantaneously soothed. A dreamy relaxation spread through his limbs and the morning sun seemed a tad brighter, the grass a shade greener. Shep stood patiently behind him, a satisfied smile edging his lips.

Patrick was eventually able to stand, pleased that he could once again look down at Shep. Shep smirked up at him, a hint of restrained mischief in his wide green eyes. Shep tried to be a good friend, but he had an obsessive inclination to taunt Patrick at any given opportunity. It was part of his person-ality, one of the many things that made Patrick want to strangle him. Patrick leaned in to Shep's smirking face and narrowed his eyes. "Just promise that you won't mess with my mind when we get inside," he said. "Promise me, Shep, or I'm not going in."

Shep grinned. "Obrien, you wound me. I would never do such a thing."

Patrick was tempted to reiterate, but he knew it would make no differ-ence. If Shep decided to play on his hindered mental condition, then nothing Patrick could say now would stop it. It was a gamble either way. Shep had a disturbing ability to talk Patrick into things that under normal circumstances he'd never agree to. In his private mind, he called it 'The Shep Factor'. If Shep jumped off of a bridge, would Patrick follow? He supposed it would depend on how skillfully Shep argued in favor of the act.

꧁꧂

The wake was in one of the larger viewing rooms, which pleased Patrick since he didn't have to walk past the corpse right away. He and Shep mixed themselves in with the suits and black dresses that formed a slow parade toward the coffin. His eyes were drawn to the cocoon of flowers at the rear of the room, and he glimpsed a well-dressed cadaver resembling the late Charles Duvaine. He averted his eyes.

Joey stood to the right of the coffin, greeting the line of mourners as they came. He looked spectacular in a tailored suit, his short black hair slicked back, accentuating his pointed cheek bones and ice blue eyes. Joey had strange eyes, so light blue that they were almost white. The eerie pale eyes were in direct contrast with the dark lashes and tanned French skin. Joey Duvaine was the best looking man that Patrick had ever seen, and it played on his tender ego despite their ten-year friendship. The jealousy was unwarranted and unprovoked, but his mind concocted it against his will. Joey was per-haps the least vain person Patrick had ever met, which made it tough to justify the childish thoughts. Especially now that the poor sap had lost his entire family.

He watched his tragic friend shake hands with each new mourner that came down the line. Just before Joey's mother Marie died, the first in this series of horrors, Patrick had secretly wished something bad would happen to Joey. He hadn't had anything so gruesome in mind as the elimination of Joey's entire family. He was thinking more along the lines of Joey's wise mouth finally getting his ass kicked at the bar, or perhaps getting reprimanded at work for showing up late every morning. But that would never happen, he knew. It all came down to one thing. Joey was special. And Patrick was not. It was something he'd learned to live with. For the most part.

"Oh man. He's all alone," Shep said, following Patrick's gaze. The mourners approached Joey one by one, whispering tearful condolences in his ear. Joey smiled at them, patting them on the back as though they were the ones in need of comfort. He received them alone, a family of one. Joey had a couple of aunts and a cousin left in his dwindling family, but they were nowhere in sight. "Come on, Obrien," Shep said. "Let's go up there."

Joey's fake smile widened and became genuine when he saw his two friends walking toward him. "I'm so glad you guys are here," he said, reaching out to hug Patrick, then Shep. "This is about as much fun as a rectal probe."

"How are you holding up?" Shep asked.

Joey shrugged. "I'm okay. I'll be better when my father is in the ground and my ass is on a bar stool." Shep cackled and patted Joey's shoulder. Patrick didn't laugh. Joey's nonchalance about these tragic events was turning from slightly abnormal to downright disturbing. Shep didn't seem bothered by Joey's less than conventional grieving behavior.

"Do you want us to stand up here with you?" Shep asked, smoothing a misplaced lock of Joey's hair, a mothering gesture.

Joey shook his head. "No way. I wouldn't wish this duty on my worst enemy. I'm certainly not going to rope my best friends into it. You guys go on. I'll catch up to you at the reception at my Aunt's house. You guys will be there, right?"

Damn. Patrick had planned on skipping the reception. He looked into Joey's eyes and they were uncharacteristically sad. Patrick felt a stab of guilt for passing judgment on him. "We'll be there. I promise," he said.

The people gathered in the room wore matching, pinched expressions. They were waiting for it to be over so they could go get a vodka tonic, or some other denial-inducing drug. Speaking of denial, Patrick glanced back at Joey, who was telling an off color joke to a gray haired man in a plaid suit. The man threw his head back and laughed heartily.

"Do you think he's okay?" Shep asked, following his gaze.

Patrick considered the question. Was Joey okay? He wasn't so sure. "He seems a little *too* okay if you ask me."

As always, Shep came bounding to Joey's defense. "Well that's a shit thing to say! Joey handles grief in his own way, so lay off of him, Obrien."

"Is his own way not to handle it at all? Look at him, Shep. The man is an iceberg."

Shep's face tightened. Joey's family had taken Shep in as a foster child at age fifteen, saving him from years spent in a hellish social service system. In Shep's eyes, Joey could do no wrong. He leaned in to Patrick. "Who are you to judge how Joey handles grief? Huh? If your entire fucking family died, you'd get a little cold hearted too, Obrien."

"He's not right, Shep. You know he's not."

"Joey is fine. You're so negative, Obrien. You're always looking for the down side of things."

"Oh really? So what's the up side to all of this? That Joey has a nice short Christmas list this year?"

Their whispers were elevating, and a few people glanced their way. Shep pulled Patrick to an empty corner of the room. "Why do you keep harping on this?" Shep asked. "Would you rather see Joey snap?"

Patrick tugged his arm back from Shep's grip. "You want to know what I think? I wish he would snap, Shepherd. I wish he would. I'm more afraid of what will happen if he doesn't."

"Joey's fine. Cut him some slack. This really sucks for him. He's just not showy about it."

Patrick wanted to cut Joey some slack, but Shep hadn't been with them yesterday when he drove Joey out to his father's beach house in Forest Bluffs. Patrick had agreed to help pack the place up while Joey searched the closets for a burial suit. Charles had made the beach house his permanent home after he "went off the deep end" as Joey put it. It was roughly ten months ago that Joey's mother was killed in a hit and run accident. Save for a tiny scraping of red paint on the panel of her white Volvo, the driver responsible for the crash remained a mystery. For a time, it seemed Charles would carry on bravely.

Then Joey's brother Jeffrey was speared in the neck by a rogue arrow from some unknown hunter's bow in the deep woods of Maine. His young friends discovered him a half-hour later, unconscious and nearly bled out. By the time they got him to hospital, it was too late. Joey tried for months to draw his father out, but the once-dynamic business man had become a hermit. Charles ignored the phone and dead bolted the door, refusing to answer even when Joey drove out there from Boston and pounded on it. Some of the neighbors told Joey that his recluse father was having sausage pizzas and rum delivered to the house daily, but no one ever saw him in person. No one saw him, that is, until last week when two women from a cleaning service responded to a call Charles had made. When the doorbell brought no response, one of them peered through the front window and saw Charles sprawled amidst a shower of glass on the floor.

The autopsy showed that he'd had a heart attack, brought on by excessive alcohol abuse most likely. Joey's aunts blamed the heart attack on the stress of losing his wife and young son so suddenly. Shep, a devout vegetarian, blamed it on the high cholesterol content in the sausage pizzas. Patrick had thought the act of packing up his father's beach house would be therapeutic for Joey. He'd been mistaken.

The smell hit them as soon as they opened the door. The place was littered with rotting food, pizza boxes and empty rum bottles. Rodents scurried into corners, their free-for-all interrupted by Patrick and Joey's intrusion. In a stunned sleep walk, Joey stepped over debris, with Patrick trailing behind like an overgrown shadow. Joey said nothing. He simply stared at the hovel, his handsome face an expressionless mask save for a small, arrow shaped scowl between his eyebrows.

Patrick had followed as Joey glided like a ghost into the little sitting den off the front living room. He'd stopped before the destroyed coffee table and stared down at the deep maroon blood stain on the carpet. The police, having seen all the blood, had originally thought Charles was murdered. Ultimately they re-thought this, concluding instead that the wounds on his neck were caused by shards of glass broken away when he fell through the table. Murder was ruled out altogether after the hospital confirmed the heart attack. Murder or no murder, the rust colored stain was the most upsetting thing Patrick had ever seen.

Joey had torn himself away from the sight abruptly and stormed out of the house. On the front steps, he stared at the ground for a time, breathing deeply and rubbing his chin. Patrick thought this might go on forever, but finally Joey spoke. "Patrick, could you take care of this for me? I mean calling an exterminator and a cleaning service? I'd do it myself but I have all the funeral shit to deal with."

"I'll take care of it," Patrick had said. "I'll have his things packed up for you too."

"No!" Joey had shouted, making Patrick jump. "I want it all tossed. Clothes, furniture, everything. I want the carpets ripped up, and I want to be able to eat off of the fucking bathroom floor."

With this said, he'd bolted for the car. He was halfway down the driveway when Patrick called after him. "Joey, wait a minute! Don't you want to keep something that belonged to your father? A watch? A neck tie? Anything?"

Joey had stopped and turned back, his face blank once more. "What for?" he said. "The man was a fucking pig."

Patrick had let it drop. He was beyond forcing Joey to express feelings that either weren't there or were buried too deep to be summoned. But he still didn't share Shep's assessment that Joey was 'perfectly fine'.

❦

Shep tugged on his sleeve, startling him out of his memory. "Come on, Obrien. It's our turn." Oh yes. The wake. He'd been off on a mental tangent, which reminded him that he was completely stoned on pot. And now he had to go look at the dead body. What fun.

They knelt side by side in front of the coffin. Patrick tried to convince himself that he was viewing a wax imitation of Charles Duvaine, but his stomach knew it was a corpse. The marijuana was holding off the morning's nausea, but the subdued threat of sickness was still evident. He forced himself to look at Joey's father, and sadness welled inside of him. Charles had always been kind to him. He'd been a handsome man but it was apparent that he'd let himself go, even with the mortician's pancake make-up. Also, the hair was all wrong. Charles Duvaine never wore a side part. Apparently Joey hadn't even given the funeral home a picture to work from.

"Do you think they really sew the lips closed with thread?" Shep asked.

"Shut up, Shepherd. You're supposed to be praying."

He shrugged. "But I'm not Catholic."

"Well I am, so try to show some respect."

Shep raised an eyebrow at him. "Yeah, right. You're Catholic. That's why you're at my house every Sunday morning watching Three Stooges reruns."

"You don't have to go to church to be Catholic, Shep."

"Whatever. I know nothing about religion. Hey, I bet his skin feels cold. I dare you to touch it."

Patrick's stomach gurgled unpleasantly. "Damn it Shep! You promised you wouldn't do this to me."

Shep smiled slyly. "I think I saw his finger move. Did you see it, Obrien?"

"You bastard." Patrick blessed himself and darted from the room. Shep had just destroyed what little control he'd had over his phobia, and he was about to be sick again. He stumbled down a crowded hallway toward the bathroom. He was vaguely aware of pushing a young woman out of the way as he dove through the bathroom door. He caught a glimpse of her startled blue eyes and a wisp of long dark hair against a navy dress.

He knew that the people in the hall outside could hear him getting sick, and he wished he could crawl out of the tiny window over the toilet. He ran the water and splashed his face. His chalk white reflection stared back at him from the mirror. His features were unmistakably Irish, from his smooth, fair skin to his crop of wavy reddish hair. The hair wasn't carrot red like some Irish he knew, but more of a strawberry blond. His eyes were like blueberries, with a prominent chin and sharp cheek bones. His upper body was wide and muscular, tapering down to a smaller waist, with long solid legs. Women usually found him attractive if Joey wasn't around. It seemed that next to Joey, he looked like an old shoe. Even Shep had better luck with women than Patrick did. Some women were attracted to chaos, and Shep was like a bottled cyclone. Patrick couldn't compete with that either.

Relieved to find the hallway empty, he headed straight for the front door. He had paid his respects. Now he would wait on the front steps until Shep came out. They'd been through this routine before. It had been worse at Jeffrey's funeral. Patrick had nearly fainted on the coffin, and Shep had to all but carry him outside.

Seated on the steps outside, he took in a lung full of cool spring air. A musky perfume caressed the breeze, an artificial pleasure mingling with the earthy scent of new grass and lilacs. He turned to see a young woman with long chestnut hair moving toward him down the steps. She sat down beside him. "Hey, are you all right?" she asked.

To his horror he realized it was the pretty brunette he'd pushed out of the way on his mission to the bathroom. He wanted the steps to open up and swallow him. "I'm much better, thank you. If you could just shoot me now, I'd appreciate it," he said.

She laughed, revealing a dazzling smile. Her chocolate hair was parted in the middle and fell straight and sleek past her shoulders to her waist. She had a fresh, wholesome look, but she was not without sex appeal. Her lips were a bit too puffy, a look that made plastic surgeons rich, but hers was clearly a gift from God. Her blue eyes had little downward points at the corners, like she was just a bit sleepy. She was adorable. And he had shoved her into a wall.

"I'm really sorry about pushing you back there," he said. "I feel like an idiot."

She dismissed him with a wave. "Don't worry about it. I hate these things too. I didn't even go to the last two wakes. I was feeling guilty about it, so I forced myself to come to this one. It's such a tragedy." Her face grew solemn and she looked down at her knees. Her navy dress was short and silky, and he tried not to stare at her shapely legs.

"Are you a relative?" he asked, eager to discover her identity.

"No. I'm just a friend of the family."

"Me too," he said. She smiled at him and he was mesmerized. A car horn blew, and she stood.

"Oh, that's my ride. I have to go. It was nice meeting you."

"Yeah, same here." He was about to ask her name when she turned and made off toward the parking lot. He made a mental note to ask Joey about her. Would that be inappropriate? Asking Joey about women at his father's funeral? He recalled Joey's comment about wanting his father in the ground and his ass on a barstool. His inquiry about the girl would be mild by comparison.

While Patrick took in the air outside, Shep still lingered by the coffin, waiting for his chance to get Joey alone. The opportunity came as the last group of mourners cleared away to go acknowledge the deceased. Shep moved in and slung an arm around Joey, turning the two of them away from the eyes of the crowd. "Hey zombie boy. We need to talk. Just what the hell do you think you're doing?"

Joey scowled at him. "What do you mean?"

Shep gripped his elbow and leaned in close. "You need to start showing a little emotion there, genius. Obrien is getting freaked out."

Joey yanked his arm back. "Get out of my face, Shepherd. You reek of pot."

"Do you think this is a joke, Joey? What are you trying to do? Ruin everything we've worked for?"

"Give me break, Shep. What am I supposed to do? Stand up here and cry? I don't feel anything. You know that better than anyone."

"So fake it then! I know you can do that much. Obrien needs to think you're beside yourself with grief. He won't comply otherwise."

Joey raised his hands defensively. "Back off, Shepherd. I know what needs to be done, and I'll do it."

There was a long silence, before Shep finally said, "See that you do." He stepped gingerly back through the crowd of mourners, and went outside to find Patrick.

Chapter Two

It was the funeral party. That's how Shep kept referring to it on the drive over. When Patrick suggested it might be more appropriate to call it a reception, Shep laughed at him, insisting that if there was beer and food and people mingling, then it was a party, regardless of the occasion.

Joey's Aunt Betsy had a spacious ranch style house with a decent yard, just minutes from the Lady of Grace cemetery. She had therefore earned the gruesome task of hosting every post-wake gathering. Patrick had grown fond of Betsy over the years. She was Charles Duvaine's youngest sister, just turned forty. Betsy was normally adorned with beaded jewelry and outrageous gothic style clothing. This day she wore a modest black suit, which would have given her a conservative air if not for the yellow-tipped crew cut and multiple hoops that ran up the side of her ear like a zipper. Her home was a hodgepodge of candles and mystical looking crystals. Joey said she claimed to be a psychic, but Patrick had never seen any evidence of this.

Across the crowded kitchen, he caught sight of Joey, who remained magnetically handsome as he stuffed a seafood salad finger sandwich into his mouth. Shep had disappeared, and Patrick set off to find him and talk him into heading out to the nearest smoke filled bar room, where people wore colors other than black. Traveling from room to room, he scanned the crowd for his friend's familiar mop of dirty blond curls, but he was nowhere in sight.

Laughter erupted from somewhere outside. Patrick followed the sound, knowing instinctively that it would lead him to his friend. If anyone was the source of giggles at a funeral party, it was Shep. He found him in Betsy's back yard, with a couple of girls and an old man. They were drinking beer out of Shep's enormous cooler, and they all had cigars. "Obrien! Join us," Shep said.

The old man introduced himself as Joey's granduncle on his mother's side. Deep lines carved his face like one of those shrunken apple heads Patrick had made as a kid. "Care for a cigar?" the man asked. Patrick fought not to sneer at the man's filmy yellow fingernails as he offered the cigar.

"Oh, no thanks. I'll take one of those beers though."

Shep handed him a beer from the cooler, then turned to the blond at his left. "Do you want another one, Robin?"

Patrick noticed now that it was Joey's cousin Robin standing next to Shep. Robin and Shep had been dating on and off for six years, but Shep insisted that the relationship was not serious. This baffled Patrick. But that was Shep's business, a fact he reminded Patrick of whenever he dared comment on the subject.

"Slow down, Shepherd! You've had four beers in a half hour." Robin kicked the cooler shut with her tiny black shoe. Patrick flinched. Robin Duvaine made him uneasy, always had. She was a petit beauty with china doll features and pale blond waves that brushed her shoulders. As fetching as she was, Patrick swore she could spit fire if she wanted to. She was boisterous, insulting, and vulgar. In essence, she was just like Shep, deceptively sweet-looking with a snake-like demeanor. He wondered if Shep realized that he had chosen a woman who was exactly like him.

"Robin, you remember Obrien," Shep said.

Robin turned to Patrick and narrowed her pretty blue eyes. "Yes, I know Obrien. He doesn't like me."

"That's not true!" Patrick said, shocked that she had pegged his thoughts. "Why would you say that, Robin?"

"Because you always look at me like I'm some sort of fungus with legs."

A hot flush stung his cheeks. He turned away, unwilling to let Robin see his discomfort. He found himself looking into a pair of lovely almond shaped eyes. It was the brunette he'd met at the funeral home, the one he'd inadvertently pushed into a wall.

"Oh, yeah. This is Kelinda," Shep said, "Robin's friend, just moved back from Colorado."

The girl stuck her hand out and Patrick took it. "We've met," was all he managed to say. His eyes didn't want to leave her face. Afraid she'd think him insane, he forced himself to drop her hand and turn his attention to Shep. "Are you about ready to get out of here?"

"I'm way ahead of you buddy. These two lovely ladies have agreed to accompany us to the fine drinking establishment known as Monty's Bar and Grill."

Patrick grinned. Monty's was one of their favorite watering holes in Boston. He, Shep and Joey did happy hours there at least twice a month. He glanced at Kelinda, pleased with this turn of events. It had been a long time since he'd been out with a beautiful woman. It had been a long time since he'd been out with any woman.

They bid goodbye to the granduncle with the shrunken apple face, and went inside to find Joey. He was near the front door, holding onto his Aunt Carol, who was sobbing uncontrollably. Carol was Robin's mother, a frumpy middle aged woman with a poodle style cap of yellow hair.

"Oh, jeez. My mother's hysterical. Hang back a minute so Joey can get rid of her," Robin said. Patrick frowned. Apparently the Duvaine children were not a compassionate bunch. When Joey had effectively gotten rid of his aunt, he walked over to them and slung an arm around Patrick's wide shoulders.

"How you doing, Obrien? Had enough, I see."

Patrick forced an awkward smile. It was no secret that he found these functions unbearable. "We're going down to Monty's. Do you want to meet us there?" he asked.

Joey nodded. "Absolutely. Give me a half hour. I have to say goodbye to a few more people, and then I have to swing by the funeral home to give the guy a check. Hey, don't you think I should get a discount this time? My family has given them a lot of business after all."

Patrick and Shep laughed, accustomed to Joey's dark humor. Kelinda looked appalled though, and that was fine with Patrick. If Kelinda thought Joey was a cold-hearted freak, then maybe she wouldn't find him attractive. Every woman he'd ever been interested in had been secretly in love with Joey. It wasn't paranoia, it was a simple fact. Joey never said anything, but he knew. He went out of his way to avoid Patrick's girlfriends, but his nobility was equally enraging.

Shep and the girls went out ahead of him, but Aunt Betsy caught his arm before he could exit. "Hey, tough guy. Can't you say goodbye to your hostess?"

Patrick smiled and rubbed a hand over her crew cut. "You should come to the bar with us, Betsy. They'd love you at Monty's."

"You vex me, Patrick. Thanks anyway. I don't think they could handle the hair."

"Oh you'd be surprised what they can handle at Monty's."

Betsy's face darkened, and she leaned in close. "Take care of my nephew for me, Patrick. Watch him, will you?"

He was surprised to see tears glistening at the corners of her eyes. "Don't worry about Joey, Betsy. I'll take care of him," he said.

She grasped his shoulders, eyeing him with urgency. "Watch him, Patrick. Watch him real close. Especially when he's with…"

Betsy stopped talking when Shep appeared in the doorway. "Obrien, are you coming or what?" Betsy shot Shep a scathing look, and Shep glared hatefully back at her. Patrick looked back and forth between them, confused.

"Goodbye Patrick," Betsy said, giving him a quick kiss on the cheek. "Remember what I said."

Outside, Shep threw Patrick the keys and hopped into the passenger side of his Jeep. Patrick didn't question the driving arrangements. He'd had only one beer to Shep's five. They headed downtown with the girls following behind in Robin's red Mustang. "Hey, what was that look you just got from Betsy?" Patrick asked.

Shep made a sour face. "She doesn't like me. It goes way back to when Joey and I were in high school. She thinks I'm a bad influence. She needs to get over it, the bald bitch."

Patrick didn't push the matter, but he wondered what Shep could have done to make Betsy dislike him so much. Of course it wasn't a stretch to imagine someone disliking Shep. Patrick had ten years of history with him and still could only take him in small doses. He and Shep were good for about three hours, then they would start nipping at each other. It was rare that the two of them spent time together without Joey there to serve as a buffer. Patrick was the odd man out in this little triangle.

Logically, it should have been Patrick and Joey who were more alike. They were both short-haired corporate types with similar backgrounds. They even worked for the same investment company. Patrick had gotten Joey the job, and then Joey had proceeded to be better at it, but that was another story. But for whatever reason, Joey and Shep were the soul mates of the group. They seemed to share a secret view of the world that Patrick would never quite understand.

Shep reached behind him and pulled a knapsack out of the back seat. He unzipped it and pulled out a tie dye tee shirt and a pair of jeans. Tearing off his suit jacket, he began to change.

"You brought a change of clothes?" Patrick asked.

Shep raised his eyebrows. "Never hurts to be prepared."

Patrick laughed. "Oh, Mr. Spontaneous. You packed an overnight bag because you knew you would run into Robin today."

Shep pulled the tee shirt over his head, and smirked at Patrick as he wiggled into the sleeves. "You're just mad that you didn't think to pack a slut bag, and now you might need one."

"What the hell are you talking about?"

"Miss Kelinda. She's just your type, Obrien."

"Oh, is that right? And just what exactly is my type?"

Shep stretched back in his seat and pulled on his jeans. "You know. She's got that fresh as a daisy, pure as the driven snow thing you like so much. She's certainly not my type. She looks like a cartoon."

"Kelinda does not look like a cartoon!" he said.

Shep cackled. "She does! It's the pouty lips and the dreamy blue eyes. She looks like a Disney chick. She should be out in the woods, singing to squirrels or something."

"Well I think she's beautiful."

Shep finished dressing and patted Patrick on the shoulder. "Good. I'm glad you like her. Oh, and by the way, you're welcome."

Patrick glanced over at him, frowning. "I'm welcome for what?"

Shep threw his hands up. "For the set up, you idiot! I was thinking of you when I asked the girls to go to Monty's with us. Weren't you just bitching to me the other day that you hadn't had a date in...oh, what was it? Six to eight months?"

"Thanks for remembering so accurately."

Shep gave him an exaggerated smile. "And you think I don't listen."

A thought nagged Patrick, a thought better left silent. "What about Joey?" he heard himself ask.

Shep did a double take at him. "I'm sorry, what?"

"I said, what about Joey? You set us up on kind of a double date. Did you forget that Joey is meeting us at the bar?"

Shep laughed loudly at this, and dismissed Patrick with a wave. "Please, Obrien. Joey can find his own girls."

Monty's Bar and Grill was a sprawling, dimly lit room with dark wood walls and a shiny oak bar that ran the length of the building. A smoldering stone fireplace in the corner gave the space a cozy, rustic look. Tables and chairs took up one side of the room, while pool tables and other games like darts and foosball occupied the rest of the area. Musicians unpacked equipment on the ramshackle stage in the corner. A mix of young collegiate types and bikers with interesting facial hair dominated the pool tables.

"Obrien, if it's not a personal question, what is your first name?" Kelinda asked once they'd settled at a table near the stage. He and Shep looked at each other, and Shep laughed like a hyena.

"Oh, man. What a couple of rude bastards, huh Obrien? We never even told Kelinda your name."

Patrick offered her his hand for the second time that day. "My name is Patrick. It's nice to formally meet you."

She took his hand and laughed, a wonderful sound, like bells tinkling. "It's nice to formally meet you, Patrick."

"Can you believe that's his name?" Shep said to Kelinda. "I mean, look at him. Patrick Obrien. Could he get any more Irish? He's like a caricature of himself."

Patrick grinned and shook his head. "I can't believe that after ten years, you're still making fun of my name."

Shep cackled. "That's how Patrick and I met," he explained to Kelinda. "It was freshman economics class, back in college. I saw Patrick walk in, this brawny redhead with his lacrosse stick slung over his back. He looked like a Celtic warrior."

"Oh please," Patrick said.

"He did. He sat down right next to me, and when the teacher got to his name on the roster—"

"I hear this scrawny little punk next to me laughing," Patrick cut in. "I couldn't believe this little hippie looking scrub had the audacity to laugh at me. Then he asks me—"

"I asked him if Patrick Obrien was a fake name," Shep interrupted. "You should have seen his face. I couldn't stop laughing, and he was turning colors he was so mad."

"Yeah," Patrick said. "But then I got my chance to laugh when the teacher got to his name on the roster. Go ahead, Shep. Tell Kelinda what your full name is."

Robin giggled. "Yes," she urged. "Tell her, Shep."

Shep jumped to his feet and puffed out his chest. "I was born Melvin Eugene Shepherd." He took a little bow and sat down. Robin and Patrick clapped.

Kelinda smiled at Shep. "Are you kidding?"

"No," Patrick said. "That really is his name. I thought I was done with Melvin Eugene Shepherd after that, but fate had other plans, unfortunately."

They were laughing so raucously that no one noticed Joey standing beside the table until he spoke. "Well that's a welcome sound. I haven't heard anyone laugh all day. It must have been the story of how we first met Obrien." The four of them looked up, and shifted in their seats, guilty that Joey had found them whooping it up right after his father's funeral.

"Pull up a chair. I'll get you a beer," Shep said, and bounded up to the bar. Joey dragged a chair over and sat. Patrick looked at Joey and frowned. Something was wrong. Joey looked awful. And Joey never looked awful, even when he tried to. His pale blue eyes flicked back and forth like he was seeing things that weren't there. It seemed to be some sort of nervous tic. His black hair had come unslicked, and a few rogue strands hung like spikes over his left eye. He didn't seem to notice. He was still in his black suit, but it seemed he had pulled the jacket on upside down. His arms were in the sleeves, but the collar was down at his waist. A trail of mustard smeared his cheek, and his white dress shirt had come un-tucked on one side. He seemed heedless of his condition as he sat staring at his fingers as though they held some fascination.

Patrick turned to Kelinda. "Why don't you girls go start a dart game. We'll join you in a minute."

She nodded. As the girls left the table, Joey's cousin Robin leaned in and gave him a kiss on the cheek. Patrick saw his own concern mirrored in her eyes. Shep returned with Joey's beer in a frosted mug, and placed it in front of him. Joey immediately drank half of it down, then he looked at his two friends.

"Are you okay, buddy?" Patrick asked.

Joey shrugged. "Yeah. Why?"

Patrick frowned. His attention was diverted then by the sight of a short, stout bald man entering the bar. Patrick recognized him immediately. It was Henry Donnelly, Joey and Patrick's boss at Parker Investments. "Holy shit. Is that Donnelly?" Patrick said.

Joey glanced over his shoulder. "Oh, yeah. He showed up at my Aunt Betsy's house. He was talking my ear off. I was dying to get out of there, so I told him he could meet us down here if he wanted to. I was just kissing ass. I didn't think he'd really come."

Patrick felt his mood sink. They could feign cordiality, but Henry Donnelly was still their boss, no matter how many beers he drank with them. Joey and Patrick's eyes followed as their boss ordered a Manhattan at the bar. "Should we wave him over?" Patrick asked.

Joey laughed. "Oh, don't worry. He'll find us. He was like a leech on me at Betsy's, chewing my ear about work bullshit. The guy is shit faced. That's got to be like his fourth Manhattan. And you know what else? He never even said he was sorry for my loss."

"You're kidding me!" Shep said.

"Nope. The guy is such a pecker."

Patrick sneered, lifting his glass to his lips. "Unfortunately, we work for that pecker."

Their little bald boss had found them. He pulled up a chair without being invited. "Hey Henry," Joey said. "Shepherd, this is Henry Donnelly. Henry, this is our friend Shep."

Henry shook hands with Shep and slapped Patrick hard on the back. "Mr. Obrien!" He was visibly drunk. He pulled his chair in and focused all of his attention on Joey, his own personal little cash cow. Patrick glanced over at the dartboard. Robin was shooting. Kelinda caught his eye and waved. He wanted to go over there, but he couldn't leave Joey alone with Henry Donnelly. Unfortunately.

Henry babbled in Joey's ear about the evils of the stock market and the importance of planning for the future. "Let me tell you something, Duvaine," he slurred. "You kids today don't think about the future. You're all going to be left out in the cold, my boy. Out in the cold." He took a hearty swill of his Manhattan. Patrick could smell his liquor breath from across the table. It had to be just about killing Joey. But Joey didn't seem bothered. He calmly sipped his beer, nodding occasionally as Donnelly blew his toxic breath into his face. Patrick was amazed by Joey's control. Joey Duvaine, man of steel.

He had barely completed the thought when all hell broke loose. Joey slammed his beer mug onto the table with a resounding crash, causing the entire bar to go quiet for several seconds. The band stopped tuning their instruments to peer toward the sound. Shards of broken glass went everywhere and cold beer ran off the table onto Patrick's lap. Henry Donnelly's mouth was frozen into a perfect circle of surprise. "Shut up!" Joey screamed into Donnelly's face. "Shut up, shut up, just shut-the-fuck-up!"

Joey's voice bellowed through the bar. Patrick caught a glimpse of Robin's dart go too far to the right and bounce off the wall as she looked over her shoulder. A smile formed at the edges of Shep's lips. "Here we go," he whispered to Patrick.

Joey stood and grabbed his boss by the collar, lifting him until he was on the tips of his shoes. Sweat ran in streams down the drunk man's bright red face. "Joey, what are you doing?" Henry squeaked.

"You want to talk to me about the future?" Joey screamed in his face. "I'll tell you about the future. Thirty years! That's how long my dad worked his ass off. Thirty God damned years. Do you know what it got him, Henry? Dead! That's what it got him. Dead!"

With this said, Joey dragged his boss across the dirty floor. Donnelly was like a giant sweaty rag doll in Joey's arms. His shirt came un-tucked, exposing his chubby white belly. People cleared a path as Joey maneuvered his flopping body around bar stools and tables, finally stopping just inside the front door. He hoisted the frightened man up to his face, and looked him in the eye. Donnelly tried to turn away, but Joey grabbed his cheeks and forced him to meet his eyes. "My father is dead," Joey said. "You never even said you were sorry."

In a quivering voice, Henry said, "I'm sorry, Joey."

Joey smiled pleasantly. "You should be," he said, then promptly kicked open the swinging door and tossed Henry Donnelly out onto the sidewalk. The door swung shut with an echoing bang, followed by an unnatural silence in the crowded bar. After a moment of staring at the closed door, Joey turned and began to shuffle back toward their table. When he had nearly reached the pool tables, he stopped, running a hand across the top of his head in a clumsy attempt to smooth his fallen hair back. He took off his jacket, pulled off his tie, and tossed them both onto the floor like they were so much trash. He walked a few more steps then stopped again. He unbuttoned his white dress shirt, removed it, and threw that on the floor as well, leaving him naked from the waist up.

"What the hell is he doing?" Patrick asked, panicked.

Shep sat back smiling with his arms crossed in front of him. "I believe he is snapping, Obrien. That is what you wanted, isn't it?"

Patrick looked on, astounded. Shirtless now, Joey walked a few more feet and stopped just short of the last pool table. Two large bikers with full beards had stopped their game. They stared at Joey curiously. Joey looked at each one of them, then dropped his pants, kicking them off along with his black tasseled shoes. Dressed only in his clean white underpants and a pair of black socks, Joey tried to proceed on. One of the bikers blocked his path.

Patrick felt himself rise from the table. He looked down, somewhat surprised to see that he was standing. It seemed his loyalty to Joey outweighed his desire to see him in a fight. Joey was swiftly becoming a fruitcake, but he was their own fruitcake, and nobody was going to lay a hand on him as long as Patrick was around. He started to move when Shep grabbed his wrist.

"Hang back, Obrien. I think he's got this one." Shep sat back relaxing with a beer as though this sort of thing happened every day. It did not.

"Are you crazy, Shep? Those guys are gonna kill him!"

Shep pulled Patrick into his seat. "Let him be, Obrien. If he gets into trouble, you can jump in."

Joey stood face to face with the considerably thicker man. The biker's bulbous beer belly was nearly touching Joey's flattened abdominal muscles. Joey's perfectly sculpted form glistened in the hue of a giant Budweiser light. The biker shook his head at Joey then glanced over at his friend, a man in a leather vest with tattooed arms. "Little buddy, I just gotta ask," he said. "I just gotta ask what in the hell you think you're doin?"

"Yeah boy," the other biker said. "What in the hell are you standing there naked fer?"

"You want to know what I'm doing?" Joey asked sweetly. The bikers nodded. Joey jumped up onto the pool table, scattering the biker's game balls in all directions. Some fell into the pockets, while others rolled off the table onto the floor.

"Oh, Christ," Patrick said, and stood again. Shep pulled him back down. Standing in the center of the pool table, Joey had the full attention of the bar patrons. He looked around the room, pointing a finger at the curious crowd.

"Do you all want to know what in the hell I think I'm doing?" he asked, mimicking the biker's vocal inflection. He's dead, Patrick thought, and stood again.

"Sit down, Obrien!" Shep snapped.

Patrick remained standing, just in case he had to dive over the table to save Joey's crazy ass. Joey beckoned the crowd, louder this time. "I said do you all want to know what the fuck I'm doing?"

"Tell us!" came the shouts from the crowd. It became a chant. "Tell us! Tell us! Tell us!" They shouted in unison, tapping their drinks and clapping their hands. Joey held his hands up to quiet them, a half naked politician giving a speech.

When the bar volume dropped to near silence, he screamed, "I'll tell you what I'm doing! I'm never wearing a suit again! I'm never wearing a suit again! I'm never wearing a fucking suit again!"

The crowd went wild, clapping and cheering for Joey, who walked in a circle atop the pool table with his hands clasped above him like a prize fighter. Patrick looked at the two bikers, and to his shock, they were cheering and clapping with the rest of the crowd. He glanced down at Shep, who gave him a shrug. "Anyone else would have gotten their ass kicked," Patrick said.

"Sit down, Obrien. You're making me nervous."

Patrick made a face. "I'm making you nervous? Joey just stripped in the middle of Monty's!"

The band chose that moment to spring to life, and Joey jumped from of the pool table to dance in front of the stage. Patrick stared at him, shaking his head. Joey thrashed about like an underwear-clad maniac. Patrick looked around the bar, and his jaw dropped. A number of business men were ceremoniously stripping out of their own suits. It seemed the act was contagious. All around him, patrons were removing their clothing. At the pool table, the two bikers had resumed their game, clad only in leather boots and underpants. One of them was wearing boxer shorts with little cartoon pigs all over them.

Taken up by the moment, Shep tore his shirt off and ran out to dance with Robin, who had joined Joey on the suddenly crowded dance floor. Patrick spotted Kelinda ordering a drink at the bar, and went to join her. Like him, she had chosen to remain dressed. He wasn't sure if that pleased him or not.

They stood alongside each other, watching the lunatics dance. Kelinda pointed and laughed as Joey attempted to do an Irish jig. Her smile dropped suddenly, and she looked at Patrick.

"My God," she said. "What happened to Shep's back?"

Patrick glanced at the dance floor where Shep danced shirtless under the blue lights. Patrick was so used to Shep's enormous scar that he barely noticed it anymore. The terrible scar on Shep's upper back had been a gift from his birth father, whose name he'd inherited along with several million dollars when the bastard finally died. Shep had been eight years old when his mother left his father, a wealthy land owner in Texas. The man became bitter and hostile after his wife left him alone with their eight-year-old son, whom he'd never wanted in the first place.

According to Shep, his father beat him regularly for being 'bad luck'. He would tell Shep that his very existence was bad luck, and that since he'd been born, bad things had happened, including his mother's desertion. The final act came when his father tied him to a pole in the stable and branded his back with a red-hot horseshoe. He made sure the horseshoe was upside down so that "everyone would know the kid was bad luck."

Clearly not too bright, he sent little Shep to school the next day with his bleeding wound still oozing through the back of his shirt. Shep's teacher spotted the wound and sent him to the school nurse, who promptly called the authorities. Shep spent the next seven years in what he called 'foster home hell' until the Duvaines took him in at age fifteen. He still wore the horrible scar between his shoulder blades, a puffy, discolored mound of flesh in the shape of an upside down horseshoe.

Patrick explained all of this to Kelinda, urging her to be discreet and never bring it up to Shep.

"That is so sad," she said, her blue eyes solemn. "Robin never mentioned that."

"Yes, well, he doesn't like people talking about it, as you can imagine." Kelinda nodded and leaned in to him a little closer. Her hair smelled like musk, and Patrick found himself wishing he'd brought his own car. He turned to her, and she smiled up at him. He was about to say something grossly unoriginal, like 'can I take you to dinner sometime' when Robin came out of nowhere and shoved him into the bar. Patrick gave her a dismayed scowl. She glared back at him like a blond pixie from hell, her tiny nostrils flared with anger. "Hey!" he shouted. "What the hell did you do that for?"

"Why didn't you stop him, Obrien? You shouldn't have let Joey do that to Henry Donnelly. If he's lucky, he'll only get fired!"

"I wanted to stop him but Shep held me back. Why aren't you giving him hell?"

"Because Shep's an idiot. You're supposed to be the responsible one."

"Don't worry about it, Robin. Joey's fine," he lied.

"Joey is not fine," she said. "I wish everyone would stop saying that. Joey is all fucked up. And now he's probably going to have assault charges filed against him. Come on Kelinda. Let's go."

Robin stormed off toward the door, stopping to speak briefly with Shep. Kelinda looked at Patrick, her eyebrows raised. "I guess I have to leave."

He nodded. "I guess so. Can I call you?" To his delight, she wrote her number on a cocktail napkin and handed it to him. He watched her walk away, admiring the way her long brown hair swung back and forth with each stride.

At the pool table, Shep was kneeling before Robin in a humorous attempt at begging her to stay. It didn't work. She walked out the door with Kelinda in tow. Patrick grinned as he watched Shep pretend to stab himself in the heart with a pool stick, making the bikers laugh. It looked like Shep wouldn't be needing that bag he packed after all.

Chapter Three

In spite of its notorious pollution content, the Charles River was a vision at night with the city lights dancing on its glassy surface. Cambridge twinkled on the horizon, a hook of luminosity staring them down from across the watery lane. They sat out under the stars on Joey's balcony, sipping a disgusting concoction Shep had whipped up as a nightcap. It had been Joey's idea that they all stay the night at his apartment, since nobody was getting laid, and none of them were in any condition to drive. Patrick suspected he didn't want to be alone.

"I have no family," Joey said after a long silence. "That is so messed up." He swirled his nasty nightcap like it was fine cognac.

Shep leaned over Patrick to look at Joey. "That's not true, Joey. You do have family. You have us."

Joey stared down at the river, looking like he wanted to jump into it and drown himself. "No, you're just sugarcoating it, Shep. I appreciate all that you guys have done for me, but you're not family. My family is dead." Patrick thought then that perhaps he preferred the vacant, unfeeling Joey to this new voice of doom version.

"I am not sugarcoating it!" Shep said. "We are your family now. Isn't that right, Obrien?"

It was one o'clock in the morning. Patrick wasn't sure he was up to playing nursemaid, but he tried. "Shep's right, Joey. It might sound corny, but we're your family now."

Joey shook his head. He looked messy and waif-like in the oversized sweatshirt. When it came time to leave the bar, Joey had refused to put his suit back on, holding fast to his proclamation that he would never wear one again. Patrick had begged Trent the bartender to give them something out of his gym bag for Joey to wear. Trent didn't mind. He knew he'd see them again. "I appreciate the thought, guys," Joey said, "but things are bound to change between us. The beauty of family is they have to stay in touch no matter how much you piss them off."

"You piss us off all the time," Patrick said. "We're still here."

"Yeah. That doesn't give us much credit," Shep added.

Joey sighed. "I'm sorry. It's hard to be optimistic when you have nothing going for you."

He's got to be kidding, Patrick thought. "Joey, you're insane if that's what you think. Just look at what you did tonight. You had that whole bar following your lead like you were the Pied Piper or something."

"A naked Pied Piper," Shep said.

"Right. But that's not the only time I've seen you do that, Joey. You've always been able to influence people. It's like magic for you. That's why you're so much better at marketing than I am, and don't think it pleases me any to say it."

Joey raised a finger. "Hey, wait a minute, Obrien. I said I—"

"I know. You're never wearing a suit again. We all heard you, Joey. My point is that you can do whatever you want."

"He's right, Joey," Shep said, draining the last of his glass as he stood up. "You've got influence. People listen to you."

Joey sighed. "People. Not family."

Shep crossed his arms in front of his chest and gave Joey a dark stare. He walked over and snatched Joey's drink out of his hand, dumping its contents onto the cement floor of the balcony. Joey looked up at him, his jaw slack in surprise. "What the—"

"Stop wallowing in self pity, Joey! It's pathetic!" Shep said.

Patrick felt as though his universe had just taken an unexpected hard left turn. Shep never so much as breathed wrong around Joey. Joey scowled up at him. "Have I done something to offend you, Shepherd?"

"Yes! Yes, you selfish, arrogant little prick."

Patrick was baffled. Joey and Shep weren't supposed to fight. Sure, Patrick and Shep fought all the time. That was expected. Patrick had even fought with Joey a few times. But Joey and Shep never fought with each other. It just wasn't done.

"You think you have no family left?" Shep screamed. "You think nobody's going to be there for you? Well fuck you, Joey. Fuck you!" Patrick had been concerned earlier about the lack of sentiment being displayed by his friends. Now everyone around him was falling apart. His cup runneth over. Joey sat motionless, his fingers still curved around the glass that was no longer there. Shep turned his back to them, mumbling to himself. When he whirled back around he had tears in his eyes.

"How can you say that to me, Joey? How can you say that to me of all people? Do you think I don't know what it's like to feel orphaned? Do you think I know nothing about pain? Well, let me tell you something. If I ever forget, I have this to remind me." Shep tore his tee shirt off and tossed it aside. Then he gave them his bare back, displaying the horseshoe scar between his shoulder blades. "Take a good look, Joey. This scar is what family used to mean to me." He faced them again. "That all changed when your family took me in. You gave me a home. You treated me like a brother. I felt safe for the first time in my life! And now you look at me with those sad blue eyes and tell me that you've got no family left? Well fuck you, Joey Duvaine!"

Patrick felt a knot forming in his stomach. Shep had never voluntarily brought up his past, and he'd never spoken of it without jokes before. Joey stood. He moved toward Shep, stone faced. Patrick was sure that Joey was about to hug Shep. Instead, he wound up and slugged him square in the jaw. The blow sent Shep stumbling backward. He caught himself by grabbing the railing. Patrick gasped. They were on the third floor, and if Shep had gone over...well, he'd be road kill. "How dare you speak to me like that after what I've been through?" Joey screamed at Shep, heedless that he'd nearly sent him plummeting to his death. "You can't allow me five God damned minutes of self pity, Shepherd? You're the selfish one, not me. So you had a hard life, Shepherd. Well, guess what? We all have hard lives, so get over it, MELVIN!"

Patrick gasped. You could get away with a lot with Shep, but calling him Melvin was off limits. "You son of a bitch!" Shep launched himself at Joey and they went down, sending chairs flying as they tore at each other in a wild rage. The situation was so foreign to Patrick that for a moment he was frozen. He felt like a child caught between his warring parents. Shep was on his way to winning the scrap and pinning Joey's arms down with his knees. Shep's size had always been a deceiver of his strength. The little bastard was strong as an ox. That he was exhibiting this now was unsettling. His strength was a freak, a parlor trick that he usually went to great lengths to conceal.

Finally finding the will to move, Patrick jumped out of his chair. With considerable effort, he tore Shep off of Joey. "Both of you stop it! This is insane!"

They scrambled to their feet, glaring at each other through labored breathing. Joey's cheeks were smeared with dirt and Shep's lip was bleeding. He wiped his mouth with the back of his hand and stared at the sticky red stain. A strange smile curved his wounded mouth. "So it's blood you want. Huh, Joey?"

Joey shook his head. "Let it go, Shep."

Shep continued to grin, looking crazed in the dampened moonlight. Tiny chips of cement clung to his sandy curls. "I understand now," he said, "blood is family. Family is blood."

With this statement Shep turned and disappeared through the doorway into Joey's apartment. Moments later he stepped back onto the balcony with a short blunt dagger. It could have been a hunting knife, save for the fancy gold handle with imbedded jewels. Joey had some strange shit in his apartment. Patrick gaped at the dagger.

"Shep, what the hell are you doing with that knife?"

"I'm going to give Joey my blood," he said, and promptly sliced a half moon cut just above his wrist. Blood seeped sluggishly into the wound.

"Has everyone lost their minds?" Patrick shrieked.

Shep gave him an innocent stare. "Joey obviously doesn't consider someone to be family unless they share his blood, Obrien. So I'm going to share my blood with him."

"Shepherd, give me that knife."

"No, give me the knife," Joey said.

Patrick caught Joey's wrist as he reached for the dagger. "No offense, Joey, but you're not in any condition to be handling cutlery."

"It's his choice, Obrien," Shep said.

Patrick studied his two friends, covered in sweat and blood, eyes wide and feral. "Fine," he said. "Take the knife, Joey. Kill each other for all I care. I've had enough theatrics for one night. I'm going to bed." Patrick stepped into Joey's apartment, determined to pass out on the couch regardless of the consequences. His friends seemed to have gone stark raving mad in a matter of hours, but he was too tired and fed up to care. He was heading toward the bathroom when he realized that Shep was trailing him.

"Can I do something for you, Shepherd?" he asked impatiently.

"Obrien, you have to come back outside. You need to be a part of this."

Patrick scowled. "A part of what, exactly?"

"Making a pact. A blood pact. Don't you see? Joey is feeling orphaned. He wants family. He wants blood. It's symbolic."

Patrick's eyes widened. "Oh, no. Wait a minute. You don't mean cutting ourselves and rubbing our blood together, do you?"

"Yes."

"No."

"Why not?"

Patrick turned away and laughed. "Why not? Well for starters, this isn't summer camp, and we're not in the third grade. There is of course the lunacy issue, and don't even get me started on sanitation. Should I go on?"

"Obrien, listen to me. I really think this will help Joey. You saw him. He's all messed up. He's totally depressed. God knows what he might do. I know this sounds crazy, but if it will help Joey, I think it's worth trying."

"This is beyond crazy, Shepherd. Do not ask me to do this."

"Come on, Obrien. Please? You have to trust me on this. I know what I'm doing."

Famous last words. Patrick had heard them before, more times than he could count. Shep looked up at him, his boyish face pleading. Patrick felt his resolve weakening. The Shep Factor was kicking in. He was about to jump off another bridge after Shep. "Can't we just spit shake or something?"

Shep stepped in closer and took Patrick's face in his hands. "Joey needs this. Obrien, please. You're the responsible one. If you do this, he'll follow along. He looks up to you."

Oh, great. He had to pull that out of his bag of tricks, manipulative little rogue. Patrick stared at Shep for a long time. Finally he threw his hands up and sighed. "Fine. I'll do it. But I'm warning you, Shepherd. This is absolutely the last stupid thing I'll do in the name of friendship. I'm drawing the line after this. Are we clear?"

A wide smile warmed Shep's face. "Don't worry, Obrien. This is the last thing I'll ever need you to do for me. I promise."

He grabbed Patrick by the elbow and dragged him back onto the balcony, where Joey leaned against the railing, staring sadly out at the river. Shep handed Joey the knife. Without saying a word, Joey made a slice above his wrist, identical to the one Shep had made on his arm. This is so unsanitary, Patrick thought, and winced at Joey's freshly carved wound. Joey held the knife out to Patrick, who took it apprehensively. It was slick with Joey's blood.

He gripped the knife, hesitating, and sneered distastefully at the wet blade. Mixing his blood with Joey and Shep's was about dead last on his list of things to do. They'd both slept around unsolicitously. He tried to push that thought away. Looking at Joey's somber face, he saw the importance of this childish act reflected in his pale blue eyes. Holding in a deep breath, he made the cut on his own arm.

His skin burned with a stinging pain as the blood welled up like a red smile. He'd never felt more foolish. He was twenty-eight years old, and he was outside at one in the morning carving himself up with a dagger. Shep grabbed the knife from Patrick and placed it on the balcony floor. He seemed driven by an uncharacteristic urgency. "Form a circle around the knife," Shep said. Patrick complied, silently amused by the dramatics. The three of them surrounded the knife, then Shep closed his eyes and began to whisper. Shep was really playing this up. The words he mumbled weren't even in English. They weren't in any recognizable language, so Patrick surmised he was making them up. "Esk ul kalde ich hlada ich dar."

Patrick smirked at him. "What the hell does that mean?"

"It's a phrase spoken by the ancients to bond them together before battle," Shep said.

"Oh, I see. Are we going into battle then?" Shep shot him a scathing look. Patrick couldn't hold in his giggles. "Sorry, Shep." Patrick was trying to play along, but Shep was being so damned serious. It was funny.

"What do the words mean?" Joey asked. Patrick stopped laughing and stared at Joey. He was wide-eyed and serious, like he was really buying it. Patrick wondered if this might be a good time to sell Joey some swamp land, or a slab of the Brooklyn Bridge.

"It means unity and brotherhood," Shep answered. "It will bind us together."

Patrick bit down hard on his tongue to keep from laughing. It was impolite to laugh at mental illness after all. "Hold out your arms," Shep said. Patrick stopped laughing. He didn't want to do this part. He said a silent prayer that Joey and Shep had no communicable diseases. Shep placed his own arm over Joey's first and held it there, letting the blood mingle. He said more strange words. Then he took his arm off, and led Joey's arm over to Patrick's. Placing Joey's bloody wound directly onto Patrick's, he sandwiched their arms together.

Patrick flinched as Shep pressed Joey's arm down on his fresh knife wound. Holding their arms firm, Shep closed his eyes and uttered the strange words again. "Esk ul kalde ich hlada ich dar." A tingling sensation started at Patrick's finger tips, then a painful jolt coursed through his arm, like a powerful electric shock. He jerked his arm back.

"Ouch! Holy shit. Did you feel that?" he asked Joey.

Joey shrugged. "Feel what?"

Patrick stepped back, rubbing his throbbing arm. "What the hell!" he said. "I just...felt something. It was...never mind."

Shep did not attempt to put his arm on Patrick's, so apparently they were done. Patrick had a sudden, inexplicable urge to get the hell away from Joey and Shep. If it weren't so late, he would have left right then and gone to his own apartment. His arm was still tingling and pulsing uncomfortably. Shep stared at Patrick's wound, then met his eyes. "Come on," he said. "Let's all go get some sleep."

Shep lay on the twin bed in Joey's spare bedroom and invited sleep to enter his body. He was just on the cusp when he heard the bedroom door creak open. He lifted his heavy eyelids, but he already knew it was Robin. He'd smelled her as soon as she entered the apartment. "What are you doing here? I told you I'd come over later and you told me to fuck off," he mumbled.

She moved to the edge of the bed and sat, her blond hair luminous in the window's moonbeam. "I changed my mind," she whispered, and slid her dress over her head. She wore a matching set of black lace underwear.

Shep gave her body a disinterested glance. "Very snappy outfit, but you're too late. I'm exhausted now."

She slid her hand over him and found him erect. He silently cursed his physical attributes. He loathed not having control over everything in his life, the way he had with Obrien tonight. He smiled at the thought of that victory. Robin assumed the smile was for her, and she climbed on top of him. "You don't feel too tired," she said.

"Fine," he said. "But get a condom first."

She frowned at him, the way she always did when this came up. "I'm not ready for a condom yet. Just relax." She pulled off his shorts and explored his body with her tongue, circling his hip bones and teasing around his upper thigh. When she slid him into her mouth, he gently eased her head back.

"Get a condom, Robin."

She pouted. "Do you think I'm diseased or something?"

He was too tired to have this argument again. They'd had it a hundred times at least. "It's not you I'm worried about. We've been through this. It's late, and I'm tired. If you want to do this, then get a damned condom."

"Fine," she said, and crossed the room to dig through his knapsack. She returned with the little silver packet. "Okay, Mr. Safety. I have a condom."

"Put it on me."

"Not yet," she said, placing it on the bedside table. "I'm not done playing." She climbed on top of him again. They kissed deeply for a time, their bodies gliding together like an old and familiar dance. She was nuzzling the edge of his collar bone, making her way down his arm when she bolted upright. "What the...is that blood? Shep, did you cut yourself?"

She held his wounded wrist up in the darkness. It was stupid of him not to bandage the cut before bed. He must be more tired than he thought. "Oh, yeah. Joey broke a glass," he lied.

She wrinkled her nose up. "Another one?"

"Yeah. I guess he was on a roll. I'll go bandage it up."

"No! Not yet. I'm not afraid of a little blood."

"Robin..."

"No!" she said, pushing him onto his back. "You're so damned uptight. Just lay back and relax."

He spotted a sticky red blotch on the white skin of Robin's lower arm. He sat up, with her still straddling him. "Oh, shit! You've got my blood on you."

She looked down at her arm, and a sly grin edged her lips. "I don't mind," she said. "I bet your blood tastes good."

She started to bring her arm to her lips. "No!" he yelled, grabbing her wrist and twisting it away from her mouth.

"Ouch! What's wrong with you? Let go of my arm!"

He dragged her out of the bed, his heart racing. She struggled against him as he pulled her down the hallway toward the bathroom. "Let go of me! What are you doing?" she asked, wincing as he gripped her wrist tighter.

Inside the bathroom, he turned the water on and forced her arm under the faucet. A pump bottle of liquid soap sat on the back of the sink. He squeezed a large dollop onto Robin's arm and worked it into a sudsy lather. Then he got a sponge from under the sink. She cried out and tried to pull away as he scrubbed her skin feverishly with the rough side of the sponge. Watery blood ran down the white porcelain into the drain. He continued to scrub until the stream of water was clear, then he let her go.

She backed away from him, glaring at him like he was a stranger. "If you're done scrubbing the skin off my arm, mommy dearest, would you mind telling me what your problem is?"

He gave her his back, pulling out the first aid kit and tending to his own wound. "I just don't like blood, that's all."

Robin studied him a moment longer, then made out of the room. "I'm going home," she said. "Call me when you've decided to behave like a human, if that's possible. Fucking psycho."

"See ya," he said without looking up. When she was gone, he gazed at himself in the mirror and frowned. He'd almost infected her. It was careless of him. All Joey had ever asked of him was that he never infect Robin with his fluids. He'd given Joey his promise, and he'd nearly blown it. He had no way of knowing what an uncontrolled contamination would do. One way or another, it would have changed her. And he didn't want to change Robin. He liked her the way she was. She was one of the only people he could stand to spend extended periods of time with. Obrien always said it was because the two of them were so much alike. Shep always laughed silently at this. If Obrien only knew. Nobody was like Shep. Nobody.

His lips pursed at the thought of Patrick Obrien. There had been a few tense moments when it seemed Patrick might not agree to the blood ceremony. Joey hadn't believed they could talk him into it at all. But Shep was never really worried. Obrien was a born follower. That's why Shep had chosen him all those years ago. And now it was done. With the blood ceremony completed, he could finally set his concentrations on the execution of the plan. There was much to be done, but it was now a matter of letting the events he'd planned so carefully fall into place. He let his frown turn upward to a smile. It was his turn now. And it was his time. And soon, all the world would know it. All the world, and then some.

Chapter Four

Patrick had a spring in his step as he strolled with his briefcase toward the Parker building. He liked his job. Patrick enjoyed having structure in his life. All he wanted was some stability. But with Joey and Shep around, that was nearly impossible. With them he could count on craziness and eccentricity at every turn. He couldn't keep up anymore. He'd had enough of the nonstop chaos. He only hoped now that Joey's Friday night antics hadn't gotten his own ass fired as well. He paused to study the puffy, half moon scar just above his wrist. It was smooth and shiny, more like a burn than a cut. He'd been worried about the strange way it was healing, but he supposed it would hurt if it was infected, and it didn't hurt. It did tingle every now and then, as though seeking acknowledgment.

He gave the scar a final musing then moved on down the sidewalk. Blood pacts and bar room brawls. It might not be a bad idea to put some distance between himself and his friends, he thought as he stepped into the office building. It might not be a bad idea at all.

He took the back elevator to the side entrance to avoid the Monday morning coffee crew that congregated in the front offices. He did not want to chat about his weekend, and he especially did not want to run into Henry Donnelly. Keyboards tapped their familiar beat as he passed the financial offices with his head down. He was trying to go unnoticed, which was quite a task for a six-foot-three redhead. He rounded the second corner, expecting to be welcomed by an empty corridor. Henry Donnelly stood midway down the hall, speaking closely with Jerry Schweitzer, the vice president. Patrick's gut jumped at the sight of Henry's bald head. The two men stopped speaking and turned to look as Patrick passed by.

"Good morning, Mr. Obrien," Jerry Schweitzer said.

"Good morning, Sirs," he said and scooted past, but not without seeing the large purple bruise on Donnelly's temple.

He spent the morning tackling projects that weren't due for months. He avoided leaving his office, even skipping his second cup of coffee so he wouldn't have to use the bathroom. At around ten o'clock a cleaning crew went into the office across the hall, the office that had been Joey's. They packed everything into boxes, stripping the room down to the plant hangers. Then they took the plant hangers too.

Calvin White appeared in his doorway. "Hey buddy. How's it going?" Calvin was a scrawny computer programmer with wispy brown hair that always looked like it needed to be brushed. He had skin so white it was nearly clear, and teeth that were too big for his face. Patrick and Joey loved him. When they did midweek happy hours at Monty's, Calvin was usually with them. Patrick smiled at Calvin, who leaned against the doorway wearing a crooked grin.

"Hey, Cal. How was your weekend?"

Calvin stepped inside. "How was my weekend? My weekend was uneventful compared to yours, Obrien. At least that's what I've been hearing all morning."

Patrick got up and closed the door. When he sat back down, Calvin followed, planting his butt on the edge of the desk. "So? Is it true what I've been hearing about Joey?" he asked.

Patrick shrugged. "I guess that depends on what you've heard. Although I can't imagine the rumor being much worse than the truth."

Calvin's grinned widened and he leaned in close. "No shit? Okay, tell me if this is accurate. The word is that you guys went to Monty's after Joey's father's funeral. Sources claim that Joey tried to strangle Donnelly, then tossed him out onto the street. Thereafter, it is rumored that Joey got all Jim Morrison and dropped his pants in the bar."

Calvin eyed Patrick expectantly. Patrick scratched his chin. "Yeah, that's pretty much it, barring a few unsightly details."

Calvin slapped his thigh and laughed. "No way! I thought for sure it was an exaggeration!"

"I wish it was, Calvin. I'm worried about Joey. He's losing it."

Calvin grinned, a face full of teeth with eyes. "Losing it? I would say so."

The door opened and Henry Donnelly stepped inside. "Excuse me, Calvin. I need to speak with Patrick privately."

Calvin jumped off of Patrick's desk. "Patrick, I'll get those reports to you this afternoon," he said, trying to play it off like they were discussing work. Patrick was fairly sure Donnelly knew exactly what they'd been discussing. Calvin left and Donnelly closed the door behind him. Here it comes, Patrick thought. I'm going to be standing in unemployment lines and going on job interviews. God, he hated job interviews.

"Would you like to sit down, Sir?" he asked, offering Donnelly his chair.

Donnelly's face was unreadable. He paced before the desk, hands clasped behind his back. "No, Patrick. I'll stand. What I have to say won't take long." The puffy bruise on his temple seemed to scream at Patrick. *Look at me! You are so fired!* "I want you to take over Joey Duvaine's client list. That is if you don't think it's too much for you to handle." Donnelly raised his eyebrows.

A surge of emotions fought for dominance. There was relief, surprise, and of course, guilt. But hell, Joey didn't want the job anyway. He'd said so himself. "I'd be happy to, Sir," he said.

"Good. That's good to hear," Donnelly said as he picked up a photograph on Patrick's desk. The picture was taken on a hiking trip in Vermont. He, Joey and Shep stood on the peak of Mount Mansfield with their arms around each other. Donnelly frowned at the photo, then carefully replaced it. "Joey Duvaine is a disgrace to this organization. The problem is that the clients love him. I don't know how he does it. It's like he hypnotizes them." Donnelly gave his head a quick shake. "At any rate, I'll be telling the clients that Joey left on his own accord. To tell them otherwise would be to ruin the credibility of Parker Investments. Do we understand each other, Mr. Obrien?"

"Yes, Sir." Normally he'd be falling over himself to defend Joey. But Joey had made his choices. And Patrick needed this job. He had no trust funds or dead relatives to live off of.

"Your friend is a lunatic, Mr. Obrien. I will not have our clients knowing that Parker Investments entrusted their money to a lunatic."

"Of course, Sir."

Donnelly picked up another photo of a white water rafting trip he'd taken with Joey and Shep. In a disquieting moment it dawned on Patrick that he had no pictures of a wife or children on his desk, as the other men at Parker did. He had only Joey and Shep. Donnelly continued to scowl at the photograph, making Patrick uneasy. "Was there something else, Sir?"

His boss replaced the photograph, and leaned over, placing his palms on the desk. "You obviously choose to associate with this maniac, and that's your business. I can't tell you who to socialize with outside of the office. Let me be quite clear, however. I do not want the name Joey Duvaine associated with this company in any way. He is not to visit you at work, and he is not to call. Is that clear?"

Patrick tried not to stare at the bruise. "Absolutely, Sir."

"And that goes for the other one, too."

Patrick frowned. "The other one, Sir?"

"Yes, the other one. You know who I mean. That little Peter Frampton looking character."

Patrick bit his lip to stifle a laugh. "Peter...Frampton, Sir?"

Donnelly's chubby face flushed. "Don't be a wise ass, Obrien. You know who I mean. Your friend Shep. He gives me the creeps. Just keep them both away from here. You got that?"

Patrick nodded. "Yes Sir."

Donnelly stared into his eyes suspiciously. Patrick held a poker face. Finally, his boss nodded. "Carry on then."

Patrick managed to avoid contact with Joey and Shep for an entire week. Each time the little scar on his wrist tingled he was brought back to the strange feeling of dread he'd experienced on the balcony that night. This sensation kept him from picking up the phone.

It was the following Saturday that he received a message from Shep, requesting he stop by Joey's apartment as soon as possible. Patrick couldn't imagine what was so damned important. Neither one of them had jobs now. But he ultimately decided to swing by Joey's, mainly because the gossip monger inside of him was screaming to get out. He just had to tell Joey what Henry Donnelly had said about him. It was too good.

He climbed the stairs and knocked on the apartment door. Silence answered. Finding the door unlocked, he stepped inside. He didn't feel at all intrusive by doing this. There'd been many nights when he'd come home to his own place to find Joey sitting in front of his television eating his food. "Hello? Are you idiots home?" He moved into the empty living room where video tapes were strewn across the coffee table. He picked up a plastic tape case that read 'THE REVEREND THOMAS KEMP'. Odd choice of viewing material, he thought, and tossed it aside. He picked up another. THE REVEREND WILLIAM MILES. Patrick recognized that one. Miles was a crazy church leader from down south. He'd been in the news last year for using church funds to support a mistress with a cocaine habit. Patrick hit the play button and Reverend Miles' plastic looking head appeared on the television monitor, screaming about sinners and premarital sex like an evangelistic pro-wrestler.

Patrick shut it off. What the hell was Joey watching this shit for? He moved into the kitchen and helped himself to a beer from the fridge. A stack of books sat on the kitchen table. Patrick set his beer down and began to sift through them. The first book on the stack was titled, 'Don't Know Much about The Holy Bible'. He tore through the rest of the stack... *Prophecies of the New Millennium, The Teachings of Christ, Predictions of Peace...*

He was beginning to think Joey had suffered a religious awakening, when he picked up the final book in the stack, 'The Reverend Jim Jones, Profile of a Cult Leader'. Patrick smelled a Shep scheme cooking and he didn't like the ingredients. He nearly dropped the book, startled by the crash of the downstairs door slamming. Shep's hyena laugh echoed in the stairwell as feet trampled up the steps. Joey and Shep burst into the kitchen, carrying small green and white bags and paper coffee cups.

"Obrien!" Shep said, looking surprised. "You should have told us what time you were coming. We would have gotten you a cappuccino." Patrick did a double take at Shep's outfit, a red and white tie-dyed tee shirt, black and white striped shorts, with a pair of black and white checkered sneakers. It was amazing what the wealthy could get away with. Joey sat down at the table and pulled a giant chocolate cookie out of his paper bag.

"What the hell is this?" Patrick asked, holding up the book on Jonestown. "Are you guys planning to poison somebody's Kool-Aid?"

Shep glanced at the book, then shrugged. "That's what we wanted to tell you about. It's research material. For Joey's new career."

Patrick set the book down, smirking. "Okay. I'll play along. Just what exactly is Joey's new career?"

Joey took a sip of his coffee, leaving a whipped cream moustache. "I'm starting my own church. It's gonna be cool." Patrick looked over at Shep, who wore a devious smile as he chewed his muffin. "Shep thinks I'll be good at it," Joey continued. "Major tax breaks if you can pull it off. You want in, Obrien?"

Patrick laughed, a quick puff of air. "Well. This is by far the most asinine idea I've ever heard."

"Why?" Shep asked. "Church leaders can make a lot of money if they know how to work the system. I know you always hear about them embezzling money and going to jail, but those guys are stupid. Like that idiot from Virginia last year that used donation money to support his coke whore mistress. He left a trail a monkey could find."

"What is your point, exactly?" Patrick asked.

"My point is that Joey's not stupid. He's a financial genius. Joey understands the Internal Revenue Service better than they understand themselves."

"So what you're saying, Shepherd, is that you think Joey should form a church because he's good with money? That's insane."

"It's not just that, Obrien. Joey's prettier than all those guys. Have you ever seen a pretty evangelist? Most of them look like cancerous toads. Like it or not, society wants to look at attractive people. They want to listen to attractive people. Joey's got it all. He's smart, he's gorgeous, and he's a genius at marketing."

"Don't even think about getting serious about this, Shepherd," Patrick said.

"Too late. It's already in the works. You should be thanking me. I found Joey a job he can do without wearing a suit. What have you done besides taking over Joey's accounts at work?"

Patrick was about to ask how Shep knew about him taking over Joey's client list, when Joey spoke up. "What's the problem, Obrien? You seem upset."

"What's the problem? You as a church leader! You're not even remotely religious, Joey. Do you even believe in God?"

Joey took a bite of his cookie and looked up, chocolate smearing his mouth and chin. He shrugged. "I dunno."

Patrick turned to Shep. "Did you hear that, Shepherd? Joey doesn't even know if he believes in God. Can't you see that it would be unethical for him to pursue this?"

Shep laughed. "Ethics? Is it ethical for a priest to rape an altar boy? Is it ethical for a so-called minister of God to take money from the poor and then spend it on hookers and drugs? With all these corrupt church leaders out there, I say we could do a lot worse than Joey."

Patrick sighed, rubbing his temples. "Shepherd, you just heard him say he doesn't believe in God."

Shep shrugged. "So what? Do you believe in God, Obrien?"

"Of course I believe in God."

"I don't think you do. You're just like everyone else. You think that by going to church on Easter and Christmas, you're insured. You just want your name in that hat in case you find it's all true when you die. You think you're contributing to some divine 401K plan."

Patrick laughed as the futility of the argument dawned on him. "You don't just *start* a church, Shep. What's Joey going to do? Put an ad in the paper? 'Aspiring church leader seeks small cult of followers for possible tax evasion'. You're wasting your time, Shep. Even the cheesiest of ministers have to travel for years to gather up a following."

Shep nodded with exaggerated stoicism. "You're right, Obrien. You're absolutely right. It would take a miracle to pull this off."

Joey's mouth sprayed coffee all over the table as he fell into giggles. Shep laughed with him. Patrick looked back and forth between them. "Oh no. What are you guys planning?"

"Just a little divine intervention. You know. To get the ball rolling," Shep said.

Patrick narrowed his eyes. "What kind of divine intervention?"

Joey smiled up at him, his face painted with cookie. "A miracle's going to happen. It's gonna be cool."

That was the second time in minutes that he'd heard Joey use that phrase. 'It's gonna be cool'. Two days in Shep's world and he already sounded dumber. Patrick shook his head. "What are you guys telling me here? That you're going to...*fake* a miracle?"

There was a long pause. Joey and Shep looked at each other. Then Joey looked up. "Uh-huh."

Shep nodded. "Yeah, that's pretty much it."

Patrick opened his mouth to berate them, but then he paused, his curiosity getting the better of him. "What? Like a burning bush or something?"

"Something like that," Shep said, and drained his coffee. "I already spoke with Russell and Craig. They've agreed to help us."

Patrick's eyes widened. "Russell and Craig? The Hoax Patrol? Oh no. Shep, don't tell me you're funding those guys." Russell and Craig were a couple of video technicians they'd met in college. They were twin brothers, one gay, the other straight. Craig was the straight one, and he was an uptight pain in the ass. Russell was the gay one, and he was nice as pie. Russell seemed to think Shep was some kind of hero. Patrick always thought the twins looked like the defective clones of Buddy Holly, with their thick black glasses and wiry dark hair. Patrick hadn't known them all that well but Shep still kept in touch. They'd developed a sort of Mickey Mouse special effects company, an expensive hobby mostly. Most of their energy was spent faking bullshit U.F.O. sightings for the pure thrill of fooling people. Joey had fondly dubbed them 'The Hoax Patrol'. The goon platoon was more like it. Russell and Craig's services, however pointless, did not come cheap. So Shep was already dumping cash into this moronic endeavor.

"Russell has the design worked out already. We're meeting at my house tomorrow to set it up. Are you in, Obrien?" Shep looked at him hopefully.

"Am I in? No I am not in! This is completely irrational! Not to mention a monumental waste of time, not that that's ever concerned you, Shepherd."

"He may be right, Shepherd," Joey said. He was flipping through one of the prophecy books. "How do you expect me to learn all of this crap? I can barely remember my phone number."

"You don't have to memorize it all, Joey," Shep said. "Just enough to convince people that she spoke to you."

Patrick stiffened. "Convince people that *who* spoke to him?"

Shep eyed him innocently. "Why, the Virgin Mary, of course."

Patrick gasped. "What? Oh, no. You guys can't do that. The Virgin Mary? That's sacrilege, man." Patrick fingered the small gold cross that hung from his neck, a confirmation gift from his mother.

"Obrien is right, Shepherd," Joey said. "Look at me. Nobody is going to take religious advice from some small time ex yuppie. I'll be lucky if I can scare up a small cult."

"No, Joey. You're wrong. Don't you get it? That is exactly why they *will* listen to you! You're the average Joe, like them. You're not like those phonies who try preaching to them."

Patrick laughed. "He's not?"

"No, Obrien! Think about it. Whenever there's a U.F.O. sighting or something of that nature, it's always some toothless yahoo standing in a cornfield that reports it. Everyone figures the damn hick's been hitting the moonshine. By the same token, whenever the Virgin Mary appears, it's in some remote village in a postage stamp sized country half way across the world, and the only witnesses are a bunch of hooded peasants. Again, nobody pays attention."

Patrick cleared his throat deliberately. "Cairo," Patrick said.

Shep frowned. "What?"

"Cairo, Egypt. The Virgin Mary appeared on top of a church there. I think it was back in the nineteen seventies. Hundreds of people witnessed it. Cairo isn't exactly a one horse town, Shepherd."

Shep narrowed his eyes. "Thank you, Obrien. I know where fucking Cairo is. My point was that Joey is an intelligent urban professional, and he has all of his teeth to boot. This is Boston, a cultural modern city. This is the hub, man! It will be a whole different reaction if something like that happens here!"

Patrick took a seat at the table and sighed, rubbing his forehead. "Okay, for argument sake, let's say Russell and Craig create a masterpiece apparition. What makes you think people in this so-called modern cultural city would even care? Why would people in the information age give a shit about miracle apparitions?"

"Because, Obrien, people will always fear death, no matter how many computer chips we manufacture. It's human nature. And as long as people fear death, they'll keep an eye out for that small flicker of proof that there's something more to this dismal existence."

"But Shepherd—"

"The turn of the millennium has come and gone, Obrien. There were no signs from God. There was no second coming of the Messiah. There were no swarms of locusts. All we got was an economic recession and a war on terrorism. Quite frankly, I think people were a little disappointed. That's our trump card. We're going to give them back the magic."

Patrick shook his head. "Shepherd, people want reality, not magic."

"Exactly my point!" Shep said. "People want reality. That's why we're going to make Joey as real as it gets. He's going to be Mr. John Q. Public. He could be your neighbor, your brother, your friend, or your son."

"So then what? You think people are just going to accept him because he looks wholesome?"

"No. People are going to accept him because he's going to refuse to talk about the incident."

Joey looked up from his coffee cup. "Why do I refuse to talk?"

"Because after the apparition, everyone is going to assume it's a hoax. They'll be just waiting for you to start exploiting it. Instead, you behave as if the whole thing freaked you out and you don't want to talk about it," Shep said.

"Therefore he becomes more credible," Patrick said. His stomach turned cold as Shep's logic started to make a twisted sort of sense. "He doesn't try to capitalize on it, so people start to wonder if maybe the apparition was genuine."

Shep pointed a finger at Patrick. "Right! So what happens next? The local media gets hungry, the way they always do when someone shuts them out. Their only recourse is to dig up Joey's past and try to put together some sort of story. And what do they discover about this mystery man? Joey Duvaine has recently lost his job. Joey Duvaine has recently lost his entire family. Downtrodden and kicked around harder than Job himself, Joey Duvaine, is a man who has lost his faith. "

Patrick buried his head in his hands. "Oh, God." He tried to imagine Shep's brilliant insanity working alongside Joey's power to influence people. Pepper that with Joey's financial wizardry and Shep's endless supply of cash.... "So what you're telling me," Patrick said to Shep, "is that you're going to exploit the recent misery of your best friend."

Shep grinned. "We're gonna exploit the shit out of him."

Patrick stood. "I'm going home now, boys. Good luck with your miracle."

"Obrien, wait! I need you to be part of this," Shep said.

"You're insane, Shep."

"That's beside the point. I want you to be in on this. If it works out, we could all get rich."

"You're already rich! So is Joey! And if you're so concerned about my financial state, then why don't you just support me?"

"I have enough cash to support one irresponsible life style, and that's my own. Besides. Joey is losing the beach house."

This got Patrick's attention. "Joey? Is that true?"

Joey nodded. "Yeah. I guess old pops made some bad financial decisions while he was on the sauce. I have to sell the Forest Bluffs house just to pay off his debt."

"You are not losing that beach house, Joey!" Shep said. "This plan is going to work, and none of us will have to worry about things like money and taxes."

Patrick looked at him, incredulous. "Why is it so important to you that we all become just like you, Shepherd? That we all adopt your lifestyle? I mean, why is that?"

Shep looked sheepish for a moment, casting his eyes downward, his long blond lashes brushing his cheekbones. "I hate it when you guys go to work," he said. "I get bored."

Patrick stared at his friend. "That is touching, Shep, but I have no intentions of putting my reputation on the line simply because you get bored sometimes. I'm out of here."

Again Patrick started for the door and again Shep jumped in front of him. "Come to my house tomorrow. You don't have to commit, Obrien. Just watch. Russell and Craig are coming over with the equipment."

"Tomorrow? Easter Sunday. Even your timing is inappropriate."

"Come on, Obrien. Just come over to watch. Joey said he won't come unless you do."

Patrick glanced over at Joey, who smiled at him. His impossibly handsome face was completely covered with chocolate.

"Look at him, Obrien. He's pathetic. He needs you," Shep said.

"I am pathetic," Joey added humorously.

Patrick felt the Shep Factor kicking in again. Reluctantly, he agreed to meet them at Shep's house the following morning. He was willing to watch the comedy unfold, as long as the outcome was failure. If at some future date this contrivance of theirs actually succeeded, then he was out. He would have to make the final sacrifice and cut himself off from his friends completely.

He was heading for the door when he paused and turned back to Joey. "Hey Joey? Why can't you just go into politics? You can still use your power to influence people. You can embezzle money, and you can lie your ass off. In politics, people expect that sort of corruption."

Joey frowned at him. "Obrien, be serious. I'd have to wear a suit."

Patrick decided to skip telling Joey about his week at the office. He doubted that Joey would care what Henry Donnelly said about him. Clearly, he had moved on.

Chapter Five

Boston liked to deem itself a modern, booming metropolis, but a space shortage kept it confined in layered clusters, having to raise bridges and dig tunnels rather than expanding outward. Some of the wealthiest neighborhoods sat just a block or two from the poorest. The elite would have had it otherwise if they could, but there was only so much Boston to go around.

Shep lived in one of the older affluent neighborhoods, where eighteenth century brick held stubborn ground. A stone fortress with stained glass windows, Shep's home stood high on a cul-de-sac at the end of a private way. One wouldn't associate the house with someone like Shep, if one were inclined to judge by appearances, as most of Shep's neighbors were.

Shep was a gossip target amongst the residents sharing the posh lane. They were terminally curious as to where this raggedy character got his money. Shep enjoyed letting them wonder. They would stare out their windows as he mowed his lawn, shirtless in a pair of cut off jeans, stopping periodically to swill a beer. Shep would catch them peeking and wave enthusiastically. They'd offer him a curt nod, then run for cover, lest they be forced to converse with this strange inhabitant, who mowed his own lawn instead of hiring a landscaper like the rest of the civilized world.

The neighbors would be at their windows today, Patrick thought as he pulled into the driveway behind Russell and Craig's dingy white box truck. He got out of his car and headed toward the back yard. A spindly man with short black hair appeared from around back and bounded down the driveway with a cable wire in his hand. Black frames supported eyeglass lenses an inch thick. Patrick watched as he cranked open one of the rear doors of the box truck. He rummaged around, then re-emerged with a longer snake of cable. He looked up as Patrick approached the truck. It was one of the Buddy Holly clones, but Patrick wasn't sure which one. The clone smiled. "How ya doing? It's Patrick, right?"

Definitely Russell. Craig would not have said hello. "Hello Russell," he said. Russell nodded, then sprinted off past the garage, disappearing behind the house where the cellar entrance was. No time for chit chat, the great Melvin Eugene Shepherd required his assistance.

Patrick lifted the bulkhead door and made his way down into Shep's gigantic basement. While he was expecting some sort of mayhem, he was overwhelmed by the commotion in the room below. Huge adjustable lights had been set up along the perimeter of the floor, illuminating the barrage of electronic equipment in the center. Patrick saw computer monitors, cameras, metal standing boards covered with impressive looking switches, and something that looked like a laser.

Craig, the nastier twin, was hovering over one of these boards. His hair had grown since Patrick last saw him, the short Buddy Holly style given over to an unruly mess of black waves that stuck out like steel wool. Patrick supposed that Russell was the prettier twin, but that wasn't saying much. Joey sat in the corner of the basement on an electric heater, reading *The Holy Bible*. It was a curious image, Joey in his Brooks Brothers sweater and tiny wire framed reading glasses, trying to absorb a millennium of Christianity in Shep's dusty basement.

Shep stood behind Craig, watching him fuss with the equipment. He spotted Patrick and waved him over. "Obrien! You made it. Good. We're almost ready. Come here for a minute. You have got to see this stuff."

Patrick moved reluctantly toward the cluster of electronics, nearly tripping over Russell, who crawled along the floor in a tangle of wires. Craig looked up as Patrick approached, his usual sour expression pinching his face. "Shepherd, I thought this was a confidential project. How many more people did you invite?"

"He's the last one, Craig. And if you weren't such a rude prick, you'd remember that you've met Obrien, and he's one of my best friends."

Craig made a fake smile on one side of his mouth, then dropped it. "Hello, Obrien."

Patrick nodded at him.

Shep was on to showing Patrick the electronics. His huge green eyes were lit like a child on Christmas morning. "Do you see this stuff, Obrien? This is state of the art! Craig says that nobody in New England has equipment like this. Isn't that right Craig?"

"That's right, Shepherd. Now, could you please ask your large friend not to lean on the beam splitter? It's worth more than his life."

Patrick looked down and realized he had his hand rested on some piece of high tech looking equipment. "Oh. Sorry." He stuffed his hands in his pockets.

"Look at this equipment, Obrien! These guys have quite the operation. Here, watch this." Shep reached for one of the switches but Craig caught his wrist.

"Please don't touch that, Shepherd. It is not a toy."

"Okay, then you show him," Shep snapped, rubbing his wrist. He wasn't used to people saying no to him and it showed.

Craig turned away, giving Shep his back. "I'm trying to work here, Shepherd. Your insistence on playing with everything is wasting time."

Shep stepped forward and grabbed Craig's arm, turning him about. "I am paying you a lot of money for your time, Craig, and if I want to waste it, I will. Do we understand each other?"

Craig tightened his lips. "You're the boss, Shep."

Shep smiled. "Okay then. Now show my friend Patrick the cool little floating thing, before I get pissed off and pull my money from the project."

Craig sighed, then flipped a couple of switches while he played with a black dial on the standing board. A round, three-dimensional object materialized in the corner of the basement. The image stretched from ceiling to floor, and it was saucer shaped. Craig made a few adjustments, and the saucer shrank to the size of a Frisbee. It hovered above the floor, swaying rhythmically from side to side, then it disappeared. "It will only hold for six seconds," Craig said.

Shep jumped up and down, laughing and clapping his hands. "Did you see it, Obrien? Instant U.F.O.! Is that cool or what?"

Patrick was impressed, but reluctant to give Craig the satisfaction of telling him so. "It would never fool anyone," he said with a shrug.

Craig looked down his nose at Patrick. "Oh really? It fooled close to three hundred people in a small town in Kentucky last year." Patrick frowned, and Craig turned away before he could say anything further. Joey mumbled to himself in the corner, his nose still buried in the book. The sight of him, sitting on the electric heater like some misfit theology student was disorienting. Patrick's eyes panned the bizarre swim of images; Joey, the Buddy Holly clones, flying saucers and bibles. Shep and Joey had always been eccentric. It was part of their lure. But now they just seemed nuts, and it was getting less cute with each passing year.

As if in support of this madness, Kelinda appeared at the foot of the stairs. She wore a silky white nightgown that fell to her ankles. Patrick gasped when he saw her. The nightgown was sheer, showing a perfect outline of her slim form. Her chestnut hair tumbled like silk onto her bare arms. "No, Kelinda!" Shep yelled from across the room. "I told you, I need you to be naked! Craig is going to white out your privates."

Kelinda put her hands on her hips. "And I told you, Shepherd, that I'm not going to do this naked. If Craig can white out my privates, then he can white out the nightgown."

Patrick stared at Shep. "What the hell is she doing here?"

Shep pointed his thumb at Craig. "Craig refused to provide the model for the apparition. We had to come up with a Virgin practically over night. Isn't that right, Craig?"

Craig sighed. "As I told Shepherd, this is a confidential project. If I provide the Virgin, and she squawks about it at a later date, then I become liable for ruining the project. This way, Shep is liable if she talks."

Patrick didn't know Kelinda well yet, but had it been his choice, he wouldn't have involved her. He looked at Shep. "Why Kelinda?"

Shep shrugged. "I had to come up with a model for the Virgin overnight. Kelinda looks young, innocent, beautiful, and she has the right hair."

"You said she looks like a cartoon!"

"I never said it was a bad thing, Obrien. She's a very pretty cartoon."

"I think she's amazing," Craig said, staring dreamily across the room at Kelinda.

Russell got up off the floor. "Who, her? She's nothing special."

"How would you know? You're a faggot," Craig said.

Shep let his mouth drop open. "Nice way to talk to your brother, Craig!"

Russell beamed at Shep's defense of him. Craig shrugged. "It's all right, Shepherd. Russell knows he's a faggot. Don't you, Russell?"

"Sure do," Russell said. "Just like you know you're a rude prick."

Joey grumbled in the corner, something about Judas being a butt head. Patrick felt like he was suffocating. "Shep, could I see you outside please?"

Shep seemed to see the desperation in his eyes. "Sure, Obrien. Outside." He turned to the twins. "I'll be back in five minutes. Be ready. We're going to do this."

They passed Kelinda on their way out. She smiled. "Hi, Patrick."

"Hi, Kelinda." His eyes fell to her breasts, vaguely visible under the flimsy silk nightgown. In her hand she held a white veil, presumably to drape over her head.

He and Shep stepped outside and stood on the driveway beside the garage doors. Patrick stared at Shep, realizing now that he didn't know what he wanted to say to him. Shep threw his hands up. "What? What is it, Obrien?"

"Just tell me why you wanted me here, Shep. And don't say Joey needs me. Joey hasn't even noticed that I'm here. Tell the truth this time."

Shep nodded. "Okay, Obrien. The truth is that I need you to stand guard outside while we do the filming. You know, to make sure nobody comes in."

"Oh. I see. I'm the bouncer at this little circus."

Shep threw his hands up. "Well what the hell else are you going to do? You can't be inside because you get all freaked out about the religion thing."

"Why are you doing this, Shep?"

"I'm doing this for Joey. I'm doing this for all of us. You're just too stupid to realize it."

Angry blood stung his cheeks as he glared at Shep's smirking face. Shep had made the 'stupid' comment deliberately to vex Patrick. It bothered him that Joey and Shep were smarter than he was, and Shep knew it. In college, Patrick had to struggle, studying late into the night just to pull off decent grades. Joey and Shep would smoke pot and watch cartoons all morning, then go ace their chemistry tests in the afternoon.

He almost took the bait, but forced himself to calm. Shep was merely trying to enrage him so they could get off the subject. "That's crap," he said. "You're taking advantage of Joey at a bad time. I think maybe your money is running out. You're going to put Joey in the public eye like some puppet on your knee while you suck up the proceeds. You're going to pimp out your best friend."

Shep took a bold step forward and glared up at him. "I would have pimped you out, but you're not as pretty as Joey. Face it, Obrien. I'm the brains, Joey is the beauty, and you're the brawn."

Patrick flushed. "You little prick! You think you're the only one with intelligence around here."

"No, I'm just the only one with balls enough to use it!"

"Balls? You call this balls? I call this cowardice. I call it immaturity. Why don't you get a job, Shep? Are you so bored with your life that you have to invent these elaborate schemes to make yourself feel useful?"

Shep's smirk dropped, and was replaced by something cold. Patrick's instinct was to take a step back, but he held his ground. Shep moved in closer and pointed a finger into his face. "You know nothing about me, Obrien. You know nothing of who I am."

"Oh, really? Well, maybe that's because I had a normal childhood, God forbid. Maybe if I'd been abused, or if my entire family died, I'd be able to feel your pain. Maybe if my daddy had branded me with a horseshoe, I'd have earned the right to act like a fucking lunatic all the time!"

As soon as he said it, he wanted to take it back. The color drained from Shep's face, and Patrick knew he'd pushed him too far. He was about to apologize, but it was too late.

Shep came at Patrick like a streak of tie-dyed lightning and shoved him. Patrick flew backward, slamming down hard onto the tar driveway. He was shocked by the ease with which his one hundred and sixty-pound friend had tossed his own two hundred and twenty-pound body through the air.

Shep jumped on top of him and soon they were rolling around on the driveway, trying to kill each other. The sound of footsteps clomped on the cellar stairs, and then Joey was there, tearing them off of each other, pleading with them to stop. They disengaged, panting and flushed with blood. "I'm sorry, Shep," Patrick said first. "I was way out of line."

Shep looked at him for a long time. Finally he walked over and took Patrick's hand, holding it tight. "Yes, you were. But I was baiting you, and I'm sorry too." Shep backed away and cocked his head, looking serious. "I know what I'm doing here, Obrien. You have to trust me. Okay?"

It was not okay, but Patrick nodded anyway. He was still feeling bad about the horseshoe comment.

Shep gave him a simple set of instructions. Guard the door, and don't let anyone into the basement. Patrick asked if there were any exceptions, like Robin for instance. "Robin is not involved," Shep said. "It's nothing personal. The less people that know about this, the better, that's all. Kelinda has been sworn to secrecy, and I trust the twins. Nobody gets to that cellar door. Okay, Obrien?"

Patrick agreed, and Shep sprinted off to finish his project. When he was gone, Joey turned to Patrick. "Are you okay, Obrien? I don't want to do this if it bothers you that much."

He looked into Joey's wolfen eyes, and wondered how he could possible agree to this madness. Despite a few eccentricities, Joey had always had a fairly rational outlook. Of course Joey had become a bit unhinged lately. "Joey, do you want to be known as the man who tried to con the religious community?"

Joey looked down at his feet. "Quite frankly, what have I got to lose? My reputation? That went out the door at Monty's. I hate my profession, Obrien. But I don't know how to do anything else."

"You can do anything you want, Joey."

Joey looked up at him and smiled. "Yes, so you keep telling me. I only wish I had the same faith in myself that you have."

Patrick stepped forward. "Promise me that you won't go through with it."

Joey blinked. "What do you mean? The twins are already here. And you saw Shep. He's wild."

"I don't mean today, Joey. Finish this fiasco if you must. I mean when the time comes, if the time comes to actually use this apparition thing. Tell Shep you won't do it."

Joey looked down and sighed, stuffing his hands in his pockets. His eyes lifted to meet Patrick's. "I don't like to disappoint Shep. I know how that sounds. But you don't understand. Shep would give his life for me. As twisted as this is, he really thinks he's helping me. If I shoot him down, he'll be crushed."

"Joey, listen to me. I know you've lost a lot. I can't imagine what that's been like. But if you hand over your dignity, then you've truly lost everything." It was a tad dramatic, he knew, but at the moment it seemed the right thing to say. If he had to go a little overboard to sway Joey's logic, then so be it.

It seemed to have the desired effect, as Joey looked conflicted by the statement. He chewed on his lower lip, kicking the ground. Finally he looked up. "Okay. When it comes time to stage the miracle, I won't go through with it.

I'll tell Shep no."

Patrick let out a sigh of relief. He reached out and put a hand on his friend's shoulder. "You're doing the right thing, Joey."

Joey laughed. "Shep's going to be pretty pissed off."

"He'll get over it," Patrick said.

Joey smiled. "Yes, I suppose he will. Now if you'll excuse me, I'm going to watch the making of a miracle."

Patrick relaxed outside, leaning against the garage while the others were doing God knew what in the basement. He hadn't been filled in, but he assumed they were making some sort of holographic image of Kelinda. Where and how Shep planned to use the image, Patrick didn't know. If Joey kept his word, they would not be using it at all. He reminded himself that he'd sworn not to be involved in this latest quagmire. Yet here he was, standing guard like some hired gorilla. He recalled the words he'd spoken to Shep less than two weeks ago, just before the blood-sharing ritual. *This is absolutely the last stupid thing I'll do in the name of friendship.* Or so he kept telling himself. As if in response to his thoughts, the little scar above his wrist tingled.

Chapter Six

The blue and white striped shirt made Patrick look like a sailor on steroids, so he took it off. He stood in front of the mirror trying to decide on an outfit, telling himself that a real man wouldn't fret about what to wear on a date. He snatched up a black ribbed tee shirt from his dresser drawer and pulled it over his head. It accentuated his large shoulders, well-muscled chest, and smaller waist. It made his body look great. Perhaps too much so. He didn't want Kelinda to think he was narcissistically showing off his physique. He frowned at his reflection and tore the black shirt off, tossing it onto the growing pile of clothes on the floor.

He was about to dump the entire drawer onto the floor when the telephone rang. He ran shirtless into the kitchen, his insecurities assuring him that it was Kelinda calling to cancel the date. It was not Kelinda on the phone, however. It was Shep, and he sounded hysterical.

"Patrick, it's Shep. You've got to help me."

Patrick stiffened. Shep and Joey always referred to him as 'Obrien'. Only when something was horribly amiss did they use the name 'Patrick'. For instance, 'Patrick, Joey's mother died,' 'Patrick, Joey's brother died,' 'Patrick, Joey's father died,' and so on. His hand tightened on the phone as he wondered just who the hell could be dead now. There wasn't anyone left. "Shepherd? What's wrong?"

"It's Joey. He took off. I wanted to stage the miracle, and he told me he didn't want to do it anymore. I started screaming at him, Obrien. I said awful things, and now..." Shep paused, taking a long breath.

So Joey had kept his word. Patrick was relieved, and more than a little surprised. He knew how hard it was to say no to Shep. "Calm down, Shep. Just tell me what happened."

"You were right, Obrien. Joey's still too vulnerable for the shit I was laying on him. He flipped out. He said he was going to be with his family and not to bother looking for him."

"Going to be with his family? His family's dead, Shep."

"I know his fucking family's dead! I'm just telling you what he said!"

Patrick had to pull the phone away from his head to avoid an eardrum puncture from Shep's voice. His heart thudded in his chest, prepping for panic. "Shep, you're not saying he's going to do something stupid, are you? You don't think he meant suicide?"

He heard sniffing sounds, like Shep might be crying. "I'm not sure. I went to his apartment but he's not there. I'm freaked, Obrien. I don't know what to do."

Patrick's mind churned, then an idea surfaced. "Wait a minute. Going to see his family? Maybe he meant that he was going down to the cemetery."

Shep sniffed. "I never thought of that. Do you think that's where he went?"

"I'll tell you what," Patrick said. "I'm closer to the Lady of Grace cemetery, so I'll take a ride down there. You don't sound too calm right now, so you stay put. I'll take my phone with me. Call me if you hear from him first."

"Okay. Thanks, Obrien."

After pulling on a dingy gray tee shirt, he called Kelinda and explained the situation to her. He was thankful that Kelinda knew Joey. Any other girl would not have bought the old 'My friend is really upset and I have to go save him' excuse. He promised to call her later with an update on the ongoing saga of Joey losing his mind.

The sun had set, but the sky maintained a dampened twilight. Patrick tugged on the cemetery gates and found them locked. Determining that the semi-darkness was on his side, he glanced about, then hoisted himself up over the gate, landing with a thud on the gravel path inside. There was an instant where he pondered the spookiness of being in a graveyard after dark, but he brushed the thought away. It was corpses he was afraid of, not tombstones. As long as the bodies were covered with six feet of dirt and a big rock, he was okay.

He walked blindly through the rows of stones, letting his eyes adjust to the falling night. He was disoriented and having trouble locating the Duvaine grave, which was pathetic since he'd been to it three times in under a year. Using Saint Mary's church next door as a landmark, he faced the road and got his bearings, then headed down an aisle that felt familiar.

Cursing himself for not bringing a flashlight, he dropped to one knee and used a lighter to read one of the headstones. It was not the Duvaine grave, and the lighter's flame started to burn his thumb. Then something caught his eye in the next row over, a splash of red at the base of a stone. He scrambled over and picked up Joey's red windbreaker, left lying at the head of the Duvaine grave. Decaying flowers littered the grass, and the scent of freshly dug earth lingered in the cool air.

Patrick unzipped the front pocket and found Joey's keys and his wallet. He had been there. He had to still be there somewhere. "Joey!" he called out, but only crickets answered. He replaced the wallet and keys, and ran down the aisle of stones with Joey's red jacket in his hand.

"Joey! This isn't funny. Call out if you hear me!"

He took the red jacket and headed for the gate, intending to search the nearby road for Joey's car. As he swung his body over the top of the gate, he caught sight of something on top of Saint Mary's church next door. It was Joey. He was sitting on the edge of the roof with his legs dangling over. Patrick gasped and landed off balance on the other side of the fence. "Holy shit!" he said.

He broke into a sprint. The new moon cast a soft glow on Joey's silhouette. As he reached the church lawn, he saw a small huddle of spectators. They craned their necks upward at the madman on the roof. "Is he going to jump?" he heard one of them say. The words sent Patrick into an adrenaline-driven frenzy, and he raced for the front doors.

"Don't move, Joey!" he screamed. "I'm coming to get you!"

Joey didn't seem to hear him. His head hung limp on his neck. Only his feet moved, dangling gently in the open air. Patrick tried the front doors and found them locked. He ran to check the other doors, guessing that Joey had gotten up there from somewhere inside the church. The side doors were locked as well, so he moved around to the rear of the building. He tugged on the locked back door, growling in frustration. Behind him was a tiny house connected to the church by an awning, but its windows were dark and lifeless. Patrick ran back and pounded on the little door anyway. "Help me!" he yelled to the darkened door. "I need to get inside the church!"

Getting no response, he ran back around front to make sure Joey hadn't gone plummeting to his death. Joey hadn't moved, but the crowd on the lawn was gaining in size. Patrick examined the front of the building, where statues of angels and saints and olive leaves interrupted the thick gray stones. The decorative architecture stretched upward to the roof, where a band of cherubs blew horns across the front ledge. Patrick grabbed onto an olive branch and began to climb.

He stepped on the cherubs' heads, clung to their horns, pulling himself upward toward the waiting rooftop. He said a silent prayer that the flimsy architecture would be good enough to hold his weight. The voices of the crowd below escalated, thrilled anew by Patrick's daring climb. Patrick was barely aware of them. His only focus was on saving Joey. He felt no fear, which was odd since he was deathly afraid of heights.

Finally reaching the top, he rolled himself onto the roof, thankful that it wasn't a slant. Joey sat on the ledge a few yards away, gazing trance-like at the ground below. "Joey?" he said softly, wary of startling him. Joey didn't move. Patrick hunched down on all fours and began to crawl toward Joey, figuring he could sneak up behind and pull him to safety. He'd worry about Joey's mental state later. It was his physical state that was in danger at the moment.

A flash of white light exploded onto the roof, momentarily blinding him. Patrick's first thought was that it must be a spotlight from a police helicopter. But no sound accompanied the brightness. He shielded his eyes and tried to focus. When his vision cleared, he saw Joey standing safely inside the ledge, with one arm thrown somewhat dramatically over his eyes. The light was concentrated in a beam at the corner of the ledge, and there was something visible within the beam. To his horror, Patrick realized what his eyes were seeing.

There was a woman in that beam of light, three-dimensional yet transparent. Light shot out of her as if she'd swallowed the sun. The flowing gown and veil disappeared into a shimmering haze at her waist. And her face. Her sweet face was Kelinda's. It was Shep's miracle, being projected onto the rooftop somehow. "Son of a bitch!" Patrick said, gaping at the luminous being. Then the apparition was gone, disappeared, as though it had never been. He heard a unified "ooh!" from the crowd below. Joey collapsed onto the rooftop.

⁂

Copie couldn't believe his luck when he saw the guy on the roof. He'd been wandering the streets all day with two cameras sitting dormant in his backpack. His photography teacher had given them the mundane assignment of finding something "real" to take pictures of. Copie already knew what his creatively challenged colleagues would come back with. There would be elderly couples feeding pigeons in the park, mothers pushing strollers, and of course a few shots from 'the hood'.

Being of African decent, Copie found it grievous that some students thought pictures of low-income blacks walking to the market were somehow "gritty". He supposed the shots of old white drunks lying on the sidewalk were no better, but they seemed to like those as well. Copie wanted to find something that would outshine the crap his fellow photography students would come to class with. He looked up as the apparition materialized in a luminous flash. Oh yes. This would outshine them all right. He snapped a picture, and heard the familiar whizzing sound that said he was out of film. "Damn it!"

One picture of this thing was not enough. Snatching the second camera, he fired shot after shot of the glowing woman. Then the vision disappeared. Copie grinned. Including the one he took with the first camera, he'd gotten at least six shots of the thing. This had better get him a top grade, he thought, and picked his backpack up off the ground.

Somebody took hold of his arm with a steel grip. Copie spun about and looked into the cold green eyes of a stranger. He was of medium height with chin length curly hair the color of sand. His face was young, but the wide green eyes that fixed on him looked older. Copie tried to pull away, but the stranger held his arm firm. "Give me that," he said, and yanked Copie's camera from his hand. He let go of Copie's arm and headed off toward the street. Copie ran after him.

"Hey, Asshole! That's my camera!"

The lanky stranger spun about and shoved Copie, sending him back onto his ass. When Copie recovered himself, the thief was gone. "Shit!" He sat on the ground, rubbing his elbow, then climbed to his feet and retrieved his knapsack, feeling the weight of his other camera as he lifted it. Remembering that he'd gotten off that first shot of the apparition, he smiled. One was better than nothing. He only prayed that the picture would come out.

"Excuse me, kid." A squirrelly man with a cheesy moustache appeared at his side. Copie jumped, thinking his assailant was back to take the other camera. "Take it easy, kid! I'm Kevin Wright with the Globe." He flashed Copie a press pass. A reporter. He was a little late. "When I pulled up I saw you snapping pictures. Are you with the press?"

"No," Copie said, brushing himself off. "I'm a student." He turned his back and started to walk away.

"Hey, hold on a minute! I hear there was an apparition. Did you get any shots of it?"

Copie stopped and turned back. The reporter had that hungry look, like he'd happily torture you to death if it got him the story. Copie thought of the one photograph sitting on a slice of film in his knapsack. He was sure this man would buy the picture from him. But then Copie wouldn't get the credit. No, he decided, he would not be selling the picture. It was his, and he would release it when and how he saw fit. "I didn't get any shots of it," he lied. "I ran out of film."

The phony pleasant smile dropped from the reporter's face. Copie had just become useless to him. "Damn it!" he said, slapping his thigh. "Is the jumper still on the roof?"

"You're too late. His buddy climbed up there to get him. It's over."

The reporter looked up at the rooftop, pulling his own camera out of a shoulder pouch. "Maybe I can catch them coming out. Thanks kid." He took off toward the church and Copie gave him the finger behind his back. He didn't like being referred to as "kid". Whistling, he moved off the church lawn and headed toward the bus stop.

☙❧

Joey was slumped on the rooftop a few feet away. Patrick ran to him, grabbing him by the shoulders and shaking him. Joey's head wobbled on his neck, his eyes two slivers of white beneath parted lids. It was an act. Had to be. Enraged, Patrick slapped him hard on the face. Joey didn't react. "Get up you son of a bitch! I know you hear me, Joey. Get up! Sons of bitches. I want to know what the hell is going on!"

Joey's eyes focused for a moment. He looked at Patrick, mumbled something incoherent, then seemingly passed out. Patrick shook him again, but it was like manhandling a rag doll. He supposed he could give Joey the benefit of the doubt. Joey could be a victim, a pawn in Shep's game. But no. Even Shep wouldn't take advantage of Joey while he was suicidal. The whole thing was a premeditated dramatization. And Patrick had played his part well. But those thoughts would have to wait. He had to get them out of there before the police showed up for real.

"Okay, Joey, I'm going to get you out of here. But if it turns out that you're faking, I'm going to drag you back up here and throw you off the roof myself. Do you hear me?" Joey didn't respond. Patrick hoisted him up and swung him over his shoulder like a sack of potatoes. He headed toward a set of cement stairs visible in the corner. "I cancelled a date for this shit, Joey. Do you know how long it's been since I had a date? You damn well better be unconscious."

He had to stop halfway down the stairwell to slide Joey off of his cramping shoulder. After a minute's rest, he picked Joey up like a baby and carried him the rest of the way down. The stairs led to a narrow hallway at the rear of the church, which led to a back exit. Patrick flicked the lock with his thumb and stepped out into the church parking lot. He spotted his car parked next to the gate alongside the graveyard, and he prayed that his throbbing legs could carry Joey that far.

A flash of light hit him. For a moment he expected to see yet another of Russell and Craig's blasphemous apparitions, but it was only a camera flash. A reporter. Patrick supposed he should be thankful there was only one of them. He could see by the crowd out front that Joey had gathered a lot of attention in a short time. "Excuse me, Sir. Could I ask you a couple of questions?" the little man asked.

"No," Patrick said, and shoved past him. He ran for his car, quadriceps screaming as he struggled with Joey's dead weight. He could hear the footfalls of the reporter behind him. He was actually chasing them.

"Hey!" the guy screamed. "Was he trying to kill himself? Did the apparition save him? Just tell me who he is! A name!"

Patrick picked up his pace, finally outrunning the little man even with Joey in tow. Tossing Joey into the back seat, he climbed behind the wheel, started the car and slammed his foot down on the accelerator. His tires sprayed gravel as he tore down the dirt road. He glanced in his rearview mirror just once. The reporter was standing in the center of the road, a sly, satisfied smile curling his lips. In one hand, he held Joey's red windbreaker. In the other, Joey's wallet. Patrick cursed loudly. He couldn't go back now. Anyway, it was too late. The press had Joey's name. It had begun.

Chapter Seven

Flames crackled in Shep's huge stone fireplace and a bottle of champagne sat chilling in a metal bucket. Shep walked into the front room just as Patrick was dumping the falsely unconscious Joey onto the wooden floor. Joey sat up immediately. "Jesus, Obrien!" he said, smirking. "You could be a little gentler. Oh, and thanks for smacking me in the face. That really hurt, you know."

Patrick stood still as stone. "Fuck you, Joey."

Shep tried handing Patrick a glass of champagne. He stood motionless, refusing to accept it.

"He's pissed, Shepherd. I told you he would be," Joey said.

Shep smiled sweetly at Patrick. "Come on, Obrien. Surely you can see why we had to keep you in the dark."

"No, Shepherd. Surely I cannot."

"It had to be believable! It had to look real! Obrien, you were so convincing. The way you climbed up the side of the church like that! It was pure genius."

Joey concurred. "He's right, Obrien. You were incredible. You even got us out of there before the cops came. It was perfect."

Patrick stared at them. "Perfect? Perfect? I could have been killed! I climbed that church because I thought Joey's life was in danger!"

"But Obrien—"

"Shut up, Shepherd! Just shut up!" Patrick took a deep breath, then pointed at his friends. "I have no words to describe the contempt I feel for the two of you right now. You have crossed the line of our friendship. You want to stage a freak show? Do it yourselves. You're on your own. You're on your own from now on." Patrick left, slamming the door on his way out.

Shep sat down on his leather couch and took a sip of champagne. Joey stared at him, concern pinching his brows. "Shep? What are we gonna do?"

"Obrien will come around," he snapped.

Joey looked at the floor, then back up at Shep. "We need him, Shepherd."

"I know that, Joey! I said he'd come around!" Shep stood and paced the room. "Damn it!" he yelled, hurling his glass into the fireplace where it smashed onto the bricks. They were both silent for a moment. Shep walked over to the window and watched Patrick's car back out of the driveway, then tear down the street.

"How can you be sure he'll come around?" Joey asked.

Shep whirled around. "Because he doesn't have a choice! Now does he, Joey?"

Joey ran a finger across the half-moon scar just above his wrist. He shrugged. "No. I guess he doesn't."

Chapter Eight

Somebody smelled really bad. Not that this was a novel occurrence on the public transit system. Patrick had experienced it enough times to turn it into a little game; locate the stinky passenger before the next stop. It passed the time. He was eager to keep his mind occupied this morning so he wouldn't have to entertain unpleasant concepts, like translucent Virgins glowing in the night.

He'd stopped by Kelinda's place after leaving Shep's the night before, still reeling from the incident. It had taken some doing for Kelinda to convince him she hadn't been involved in the night's theatrics. After the scorching betrayal by his two closest friends, he wasn't sure what to believe. He'd also asked Kelinda point blank if she'd ever been in love with Joey. He'd been on a roll and too worked up to hold back. It seemed odd to him that Kelinda would do such an unethical thing as to pose as the Blessed Virgin, and then keep it from Robin, her best friend.

She had assured him that she regretted the decision, and that she had in fact been in love with Joey once. When she was ten years old. The feeling had apparently dissipated when she saw Joey eat worms for money one day in the playground. Patrick told himself that he believed Kelinda on both counts, mainly because she'd kissed him while they were sitting on her couch. But the truth was he didn't know who he trusted anymore.

Damn, somebody really stunk. A tangible layer of dirt mixed in with the standard waft of body odor. Patrick scanned the passengers around him. He studied a freshly scrubbed woman seated across the aisle, then let his eyes drift right to an old man wearing a rumpled, button down sweater. His gray hair was clean and fluffy, his fingernails manicured. Not him. He glanced over at a set of teenagers with multiple body piercings. They looked strange, but they were all drinking Evian. People who drank designer water usually did not forget to bathe.

He turned his head to the left and found the culprit sitting on one of the individual chairs diagonally across the aisle. Oh yes. This was his man. He was young, perhaps in his early twenties, and that was surprising. The stinkers were usually middle aged or older. The guy was visibly covered with dirt. A black greasy substance smeared his face, and his teeth were decorated with what looked like remnants of Oreo cookies. Curly black hair fell to his chin, split in an uneven part down the middle.

The hair looks like Shep's, Patrick thought. In fact, despite the dark hair color and disgusting hygiene, the guy looked a lot like Shep. They could have been brothers. This was unusual, since Shep had a unique look. It was also impossible, since Shep was an only child. The resemblance was uncanny, though. Underneath the grime, Patrick could see the large green eyes, long fringed lashes, and perfect child-like mouth. The stranger looked up at Patrick, his round eyes like emeralds against the greasy camouflage of filth. Patrick sucked his breath in. The facial structure was slightly different than Shep's, but the entire package was strikingly similar.

Having been caught staring, Patrick dropped his eyes to the floor. He opted to dismiss the matter of the vagrant. The guy probably didn't look that much like Shep after all. Patrick was merely preoccupied with thoughts of his friends. Was he going to start seeing Joey and Shep behind every tree now? A therapist would have a field day with this.

Still, he had an overwhelming urge to steal another glance. Keeping his head low, he lifted his eyes to grab a peek. The vagrant wasn't looking at him this time. He was scribbling furiously into an open notebook. Something about the image didn't jibe right. Patrick squinted at the small notebook, with its shiny green cardboard cover. Except for a small scribbling of words in the upper left corner, the cover looked clean and untouched, like something newly purchased. The stranger's dirty fingers curled around a gold pen as he wrote. Patrick did a double take. Gold pen? Why would this filthy vagrant, who looked too poor to pay attention, be carrying a brand new notebook with a gold pen? He promptly reminded himself that it was none of his damned business, forcing his eyes to drop to the floor.

The train began to slow for the next stop and the dirty stranger stood, along with six other passengers. The train's movement ceased with its usual lurch and the vagrant went stumbling forward, body-slamming the man in front of him. The man looked over his shoulder and sneered. The vagrant grabbed the hold bar and found his footing, but did not acknowledge the man glowering at him. Patrick watched the black-haired Shep-alike pass by him. Afraid he would be caught staring again, he dropped his eyes.

He caught sight of something lying on the aisle floor. It was the vagrant's green notebook. It must have fallen out of his jacket when he stumbled. Patrick grabbed it, then reached out and tugged on his dusty, ankle length coat. "Hey, you dropped your notebook."

The stranger turned to Patrick, looking startled. When he saw the notebook in Patrick's hand, his eyes widened. If Patrick had to guess, he'd have said the vagrant looked guilty, like he'd been caught doing something illegal. Patrick held the notebook out and the vagrant reached to take it. As he reached toward the dirty, outstretched hand, Patrick read the two words scribbled on the cover. The words were his name, 'Patrick Obrien'. Patrick gasped. It read 'Patrick Obrien' with the day's date scribbled beneath.

The young man met his eyes and his face paled, visible even with the dirty smears coating his skin. Startling the hell out of everyone on the train, the vagrant jumped over the back of a chair and snatched the notebook from Patrick's hand. He then vaulted up onto the row of booth seats and leapt across the chair backs, cutting the line of departing passengers. A few voices cried out in alarm. When the stranger reached the double doors, he grabbed the hold bar and swung like a monkey out onto the sidewalk.

Patrick ran to the opposite window, scanning the street for the stranger, but he was gone. The other passengers stepped off and the double doors closed as the train moved on. Befuddled, Patrick fell back into his seat. Coincidence. Surely he wasn't the only man with the name Patrick Obrien, especially in Boston. How very odd, though. He gave his head a shake, determined to dismiss the incident. He had enough to be paranoid about lately without worrying that Boston's homeless were conspiring to spy on him.

Patrick was fumed to find his office door open, the light on. He dealt with highly confidential files and nobody was supposed to be in his office when he wasn't there. Except his boss, Henry Donnelly. Patrick stepped in and put his briefcase down. Nothing looked amiss, save for an open newspaper spread out on his desk. He moved in behind his desk and scowled down at the paper. It was spread open to page three. He snatched it up, about to toss it in the trash when he saw the photograph. His coffee cup slipped from his fingers and splattered onto the floor.

On page three of *The Globe* was a picture of Patrick carrying Joey like a sleeping child out of Saint Mary's Church. His strained features grimaced into the camera. Beneath the photo was a caption reading "Prophecy or Prank?" Patrick placed a hand on the desk to steady himself. He tore off the yellow Post-it note that someone had attached. *Patrick, come to my office when you get in.* It was Henry Donnelly's handwriting. "Oh God," he whispered, and eased himself into the chair.

He skimmed the article. It told of an alleged apparition on top of Saint Mary's church the night before. Witnesses interviewed claimed to have been cured of a variety of ailments, from arthritis to migraine headaches. Patrick shook his head, unable to muster the humor to laugh. The article went on to name Joseph Pierre Duvaine of Boston as the man thought to be planning a jump to his death just before the image of the Virgin Mary appeared. Patrick did laugh then as he read the start of the next paragraph. *Joseph Duvaine, the man God would not allow to die, was said to have...*

But it was the last two lines of the article that turned Patrick's blood cold, as they identified Patrick by name, stating that both he and Joey were employees of Parker Investments, a financial organization located in downtown Boston. "Son of a bitch!" he whispered. He looked down at the yellow Post-it in his hand. Donnelly wanted to see him. He didn't have to guess why. All Donnelly had asked was that he not associate Joey's name with Parker Investments. Oops.

"I am so fucking fired," he said, and walked out of his office.

When he reached Donnelly's office, Matthew told him to go right in, that he was expected. The nervous looking assistant chewed his thumbnail, gawking at Patrick like he had a bull's-eye tattooed on his forehead.

Donnelly was at the back wall, staring out the window. "Sit down please," he said. Patrick sat. Donnelly turned away from the window and took his chair across the desk. From a drawer, he drew out another copy of the newspaper and slid it over to Patrick. His own tortured face stared up at him. "Out of sheer, nagging curiosity, I'm going to allow you the luxury of explaining this…incident, Patrick. If you can, that is."

Donnelly's lips were pursed tight. He was clearly furious, but keeping it in check for the time, relishing the moment when he could let the hammer drop. The stress that Patrick had been swallowing over the past week bubbled up. Anger replaced his fear. Anger at Joey. Anger at Shep. Anger at himself for being a gullible fool. Anger at the world. He felt like he could vomit molten lava and burn the last rogue hairs off of Donnelly's round head.

"Are you planning to fire me?" he asked without a hint of emotion.

Donnelly looked taken aback. "Wha-what? I'm offering you the opportunity to explain yourself, Patrick. It ought to prove most entertaining, I suspect."

"I'm not here for your entertainment, Mr. Donnelly. I've been through quite an ordeal, and frankly I'd appreciate it if you'd just get to the point."

Donnelly paused, his face tightening, then he slammed his fist down on the desk. "The point? You want me to get to the point? How about the fact that clients have been calling me all morning to say that they're taking their business elsewhere? How about the fact that the God damned press has been calling, looking for information about Joey? The press! Your little stunt has ruined the reputation of this organization! That is the point, Mr. Obrien!"

"Am I fired, Sir?"

"Of course you're fired you fucking moron!" Donnelly was leaned forward, purple faced.

Patrick stood. "I'll go clean out my office."

He tore through his office in a rage, tossing personal items into a cardboard box. The photographs of his friends went directly into the trashcan. Calvin White stepped in just as he was ceremoniously smashing the picture from the hiking trip. He looked up, surprised to see Calvin. The rest of his co-workers were avoiding him, as though unemployment was a contagious disease.

"Obrien?" Calvin hesitated, like he thought Patrick was going to throw something at him.

"Oh, hey Calvin."

Calvin stepped inside. "I heard what happened. I came to see if you needed any help."

There was genuine concern in the scrawny programmer's eyes, and Patrick was quietly grateful. "I don't have that much stuff, but thanks anyway Cal."

Calvin walked over to the desk. "Is Joey all right?" he asked carefully.

He let out a laugh, and it sounded maniacal, even to him. "Oh, Joey's just fine, Calvin. Joey is always fine. It's the rest of us that are out of step, right?"

Calvin studied Patrick with a furrowed brow. "What about you, Obrien? Are you going to be okay?"

After all he had endured, Calvin's kind words warmed him almost to tears. "I'll be okay, Calvin. Eventually. Thanks for asking."

Calvin grabbed another box and began to help him pack. Patrick found it comforting, simply to have another heartbeat nearby. When the office was cleared, they each took a box and headed toward the stairway that led to the outer parking lot. Patrick had left his car at the Parker building earlier in the week. He was thankful for it now. It would have been humiliating to walk to the train stop with a box full of office supplies. He may as well have worn a big sign that read I JUST GOT CANNED.

Co-workers they passed in the hall pretended that Patrick was invisible. People he'd worked with for five years avoided his eyes. "Is your car here?" Calvin asked as they reached the exit.

"I'm parked out in the back lot. I can take it from here. Thanks, Cal."

"Shut up, Obrien. I'm walking you to your car. I'm not one of those assholes we passed in the hall. I'm a friend."

Tears threatened, and Patrick bit his lip, clinging to his manhood by a thread. "Thanks Cal."

"And stop thanking me. You'd do the same for me. Now let's just get you the hell out of here."

They walked side by side to the back lot, and were halfway to Patrick's car when Calvin held an arm out, stopping him. "Hold on, Obrien."

Patrick looked at Calvin, whose eyes were focused on something in the distance. "What is it?"

Calvin frowned and pointed to Patrick's Honda parked six rows up. News reporters huddled around it like flies swarming a piece of fruit. Patrick thought he actually felt his mind go pop. He thought he would finally cry then, but Calvin grabbed his elbow and tugged him to the side. "Come on. My car's parked over there. I'll give you a ride home."

Patrick climbed into the front seat and looked at the skinny programmer next to him. "I have to say it again. Thank you, Calvin. You didn't have to do that."

Calvin grinned, exposing his extra large teeth. "Actually, I have an ulterior motive. Can I have your autograph, Obrien? Will you sign my newspaper?"

Patrick laughed at the joke and Calvin laughed with him. He found that he couldn't stop laughing, but he didn't care. They laughed for a good five minutes and it was a welcome sound. Then Calvin stopped laughing. "Don't look now, Obrien, but we've got more trouble."

Five or six stragglers from the press were camped out at the end of Patrick's driveway with cameras. "Shit! Calvin, don't stop. Keep driving!" Calvin gunned it and they sped by the apartment house. "Damn it!" Patrick screamed, giving himself over to the tears. "Damn them both! Fucking lunatics have ruined my life."

He dropped his face in his hands and wept. Calvin let him cry without judgment. When he had calmed, Calvin put a hand on his shoulder. "Listen to me, Obrien. I don't know exactly what Joey and Shep did to you, but I do know this. The press gets tired of a story if nobody talks to them. This will blow over. I give it two days at the most. Remember that wood stain on the church door that was supposedly in the shape of the Virgin Mary? The press made a big deal about it. It even slipped into the national news, remember? But it only lasted a couple of days. That's the way with religious stories. It'll die out."

Patrick sniffed, and wiped his eyes. "This wasn't a wood stain, Calvin," he said. "It was a state of the art holographic image, designed by special effects professionals. People are claiming to have been healed by the fucking thing."

"Regardless, it will die out. Nobody wants religion shoved down their throat, and the press knows that. Is there somewhere you can stay until this blows over? And I suggest it not be your parents' house. They've probably got that staked."

Patrick rolled down the window, letting the spring air dry his tears. He thought for a moment, then turned to Calvin. "Can I use your phone?"

⁊⋙

Kelinda readily agreed. What else could she do? Patrick didn't want to seem callous, but she kind of owed him her support. She was part of this whole thing, whether she regretted it or not. Calvin dropped him in front of Kelinda's house, making him promise to call if he needed anything. Patrick thanked him again, grabbed his boxes and sprinted to Kelinda's door. No one was hiding in the shrubs to ambush him. He was safe for the time being.

When he got inside, he used Kelinda's phone to call his house and check messages. There were several calls from local news mediums requesting interviews. Then came his mother's voice, frantic and demanding to know what happened. Great. Just what he needed, another reason for his parents to think him a Godless heathen. They were already on his case for skipping church so much.

There were no calls from Joey or Shep, and this pleased him. As long as they left him alone, he'd work through this mess somehow. Kelinda's doorbell rang and they both jumped. She ran to the window and peered through the blinds. "Is it a reporter?" Patrick asked, panicked.

"No," she said, still peeking out. "It's a florist." She turned and faced him. "You didn't by any chance send me flowers, did you?"

He shook his head. "No."

She glanced out the window again, then turned to him. "Just to be safe, you go hide in the bedroom." The doorbell rang again. "Go on. I'm going to answer the door. If it's a reporter in disguise or something James Bondish like that, I'll get rid of them. Okay?"

Patrick hurried off to her bedroom, feeling silly and paranoid. He stared at the frilly pillows piled high on Kelinda's bed, and listened to her chatting with the delivery man. After hearing the door close, he went back into the living room where Kelinda carried a colossal bouquet of red roses over to the coffee table. She opened the card and read it silently, then looked at him with raised eyebrows. "These are for you," she said.

"For me? How do you know?"

She handed him the card. "Because my name isn't Obrion."

He took the card and read it. *Obrien, sorry about your job. Now you have nothing to lose. Join us.* It was signed, *J & S*. Patrick threw the card down on the table. "They've got to be kidding. After everything that's happened they actually expect me to join them? It doesn't make sense. They've gotten what they wanted. Why don't they just leave me out of it?"

Kelinda sat on the couch and shrugged. "Maybe they don't feel justified without your approval. Robin said you're the responsible one of the group."

Patrick laughed. "Well in this little triangle, that isn't saying much." He paced the room.

"At least they contacted you," Kelinda said.

Patrick stopped pacing and turned to her. "I'm sorry. What?"

"I said, at least they contacted you. I haven't gotten so much as a phone call since I did the filming."

Patrick cocked his head. "Kelinda, they're nuts. Trust me, you're the lucky one."

She shrugged. "I suppose, but it would have been nice to get a thank you after what I did for him."

He moved in close and studied her. "Wait a minute. You said 'after what I did for him'. Who did you mean? Joey?"

She looked up at him and flushed. "I didn't say that. I said what I did for *them*."

Patrick shook his head and pointed. "No. No, I heard you clearly. You said 'him'. What's the deal, Kelinda? Did you do it all for Joey? Tell me the truth."

Kelinda glared, her face flushing. "You already asked me that question once, Patrick, and the answer is still no." She turned and walked into her bedroom, closing the door behind her. Patrick stared at the closed door. Great. He'd been there all of five minutes and she'd locked herself in her room. This was shaping up to be a hell of a day indeed.

He went to the window and tugged open the blinds. The flower delivery truck was pulling away from the curb. As the truck moved on, Patrick caught sight of something that made him suck his breath in. Across the street, scribbling into his green notebook was the dusty stranger he'd seen on the train. The curly haired vagrant looked up and stared directly back at him. In a whirl of billowing coat, he turned and sprinted down the street, leaving Patrick to stare dumbfounded after him.

Chapter Nine

Patrick got his wish, as the press gave up on him within a day. They'd turned all of their focus to Joey, who was being elusive and closed mouthed, just as Shep had instructed. To Patrick's dismay, the tactic was having the desired effect. The story would not die. The local news raced to be the first to locate Joey, who seemed to have dropped off the face of the earth. The level of coverage was ridiculous. Whitey Bulger had received less attention when he disappeared.

Calvin White phoned early that morning to apprise Patrick of the results of his Internet surfing. It seemed that ever since a local station had flashed a stunning, full smiled picture of Joey on the nightly news, thousands of web sites had cropped up in his honor. Patrick cringed at the idea that Shep may have been right about things. He refused to believe that the human element was that naïve. He was forced to re-think this conclusion later that evening when he drove by Saint Mary's church. Groups of religious hopefuls lined the street, leaving bouquets of flowers and kneeling on the ground, hoping for yet another spontaneous apparition.

The Boston talk radio programs had volatile call-in shows regarding the authenticity of the alleged miracle and the integrity of Joey himself, whom they had dubbed "The Yuppie Prophet." The radio hosts would let the callers argue it out over the air, relishing in the controversy and the ratings it provided.

He could not let this charade go on any longer. Unfortunately, he lacked the courage to step forward. His loyalty, however misguided, would not allow him to expose Joey and Shep. So he made a perfectly cowardly decision. He would get someone else to do it.

He couldn't involve Kelinda. She was already overly paranoid about getting caught. He'd clued Calvin in, but he had the same reservations as Patrick, and didn't want the responsibility. That left only Russell and Craig, the Hoax Patrol. He found Craig's name and address on the Internet. He'd been searching for Russell, but he wasn't listed. It seemed that Craig the cantankerous twin was his only choice.

※※

Craig showed not the slightest recognition when he opened the door. "May I help you?" he asked with token impatience.

"Craig, it's me, Patrick." Craig stared at him blankly. "Patrick Obrien. I'm Shep's friend. Don't you remember me? I just saw you a few weeks ago. In Shep's basement?"

Craig looked annoyed. "Oh yes. I remember you now. What do you want?"

"Craig, I was wondering if I could speak to you for a couple of minutes."

Craig looked him up and down, all but sneering at him. "All right. But make it quick. I'm especially busy today."

He followed the mutant Buddy Holly into his apartment, where boxes stacked high on the otherwise empty floor. "Are you moving?" he asked, examining the bare rooms.

"Yes. I'm going out to Los Angeles. I leave in the morning."

Patrick's heart sank. "Is your brother moving too?" he asked, already working on a plan B.

Craig taped up boxes, keeping his back to Patrick.

"No, Russell is staying in Boston. He got a job working nights at one of the local television stations. It seems everyone else is moving though, huh? I'm sure you've heard that Shep and Joey moved out to Forest Bluffs."

Patrick gaped at the back of Craig's head. "Excuse me? They moved out to...what, the beach house?"

Craig chuckled. "Beach house? That's a quaint way of putting it. I've seen pictures of the place. It's enormous. It used to belong to Joey's dad or something. It sits on like a bazillion acres of land."

"Yes, I've been there," Patrick said. "Are you sure they moved out there? Joey said he had to sell that place because he didn't have the money to keep it up."

Craig glanced over his shoulder. "Really? Well he got the money somewhere. He got all new furniture, and even renovated the guest house out in the back field."

Patrick stared at Craig's back, trying to make sense of things. Joey and Shep moved down to Forest Bluffs? Why would they move to the beach house? And why would Joey lie to him about losing the place to his father's debt? But then Joey had lied to him before, quite recently in fact. "Are you here to ask me about the Saint Mary's project?" Craig asked.

Patrick nodded. "Well yes. That's exactly what I came to talk about."

Craig picked up another box and began sealing it with packing tape. "It came out great, don't you think? The apparition? People are really buying it. It's always more of a rush when people believe it. I saw a bunch of them last night kneeling in front of the church." Craig laughed and shook his head. "Priceless."

"Yes, well, that's why I'm here," Patrick said. "People are believing it, and I think it's wrong."

Craig stopped what he was doing and turned around. "You think it's *wrong*?"

"Yes. I think it's wrong. I think you should come clean and admit that it was a hoax. I think you should tell the local press that you created it."

Craig stared at him for a moment, then began to laugh. "You're kidding, right?" Patrick met his eyes, unflinching. Craig's smile dropped. "Oh. You're not kidding. Look, Patrick, take it up with your friend Shep. I'm done with the hoax business. That's why I'm moving to California. I'm going to try to get a legitimate job in the special effects industry. The Saint Mary's job gave me enough money to leave town. I'm not about to tarnish my reputation before I even get to California."

"I'll go to the press myself," Patrick threatened, knowing full well that he didn't have the guts. "I'll tell them about you and your brother. I'll tell them everything."

Craig laughed. "Go to the press if you want to, Patrick. I'll deny it. All of the evidence has been destroyed."

"Maybe your brother will feel differently," Patrick said. "Do you know where I can find him?"

"Who, Russell? Are you kidding? In case you hadn't noticed, Russell is a queer."

"That's a very ugly word to be calling your own brother. Besides, what does Russell's sexual orientation have to do with his willingness to go to the press?"

Craig smirked. "Because, Mr. Politically Correct, Russell is completely in love with your buddy Shep. He'll refuse to turn Shep in just on the off chance that Shep may let him suck his cock one day. He's completely obsessed, has been since college. It's not about Russell being gay. He's just one of those guys that only want what's unattainable. If Russell were a straight man, he'd be going after married women. His crush on Shep has been going strong for close to ten years now. Good luck with that one, pal."

Patrick sat down on the floor and buried his head in his hands. Craig came over and sat down beside him. "Look, buddy, I am sorry about all of this. To be honest with you, I think it's wrong too."

Patrick looked up. "You do?"

"Of course I do. That's one of the reasons I'm getting out. I have my regrets just like you do, but I also honor my agreements. I made a legitimate deal with Shep last year and I don't go back on my word."

Last year? The words fell on Patrick like concrete. "What do you mean you made a deal last year? What kind of deal?"

Craig gave him a strange look. "Well, the apparition, of course. That's when Shepherd first came to me about the project."

Patrick's stomach went cold. "That's impossible. Shep just came up with the idea."

Craig stared at him like he'd lost his faculties. "I'm beginning to understand now. They really left you in the dark, didn't they?"

Patrick shook his head. "What do you mean?"

Craig slid in close and placed a hand on Patrick's shoulder. "Patrick, did you really think that we came up with that sophisticated a concept overnight? Do you know how expensive holographic imaging is? Shep funded the entire project. What did you think? That every bozo in the business had access to that kind of equipment? And the design! That kind of detail takes time and preparation. I'm good, but I'm not that good. I wish I were."

Patrick's head was swimming. "You're telling me that Shep has been planning this for a year?"

Craig looked sympathetic. "Yes, Patrick. He's been planning this for a year. Maybe longer."

Patrick's head whirled with new confusion. He stood up and headed for the door. "I need a drink. Thank you for your time, Craig. Good luck in LA."

Craig followed him out onto the porch. "You seem like a nice guy, Patrick. Can I give you some advice?"

"Sure. Why not."

"Stay away from Shepherd. He's a slimy bastard. He always has been."

Patrick turned away. "Thanks Craig, but that information might have been more useful to me ten years ago."

Chapter Ten

The three brothers sat in awkward positions on the hardwood floor. The expansive room had been a study when Charles Duvaine was alive. It was more of a fancy sitting room now, sparsely furnished with Oriental rugs and soft leather chairs and couches. The fireplace was stone, trimmed with the same shiny dark wood as the floor.

The brothers smiled when Shepherd entered the room, exposing dirty teeth inside their otherwise pretty mouths. They were not men. Not really. Being trapped in human form hadn't exactly been their choice. Shep knew that they quietly resented it, and therefore had no respect for the skin they were in. Bathing, grooming, and otherwise tending to their physical form would imply acceptance, something they weren't ready for. Staying filthy was a sort of rebellion for them, a silent protest. Shep had allowed it for a time, but now he had news for the little imps. Ready or not, it was time for them to become suitable members of society. Or at least a close facsimile thereof.

Shep stood before them, inspecting their grimy faces and dusty clothing. Their curly, chin length hair was matted and oily, their hands and feet blackened with dirt. Their disgraceful condition was his fault. With all the hoax preparations, he'd been crunched for time and had only been able to meet with them sporadically since their arrivals. Their appearance had grossly deteriorated. He found them beautiful of course, despite their current state of degeneracy. Juris had hair so blond that it was nearly white. Allisto's hair was black as coal, when it wasn't covered in dust. Margol was the most different of the three. His curls were the color of fire, a deep flaming orange. They looked up at him with innocent green eyes. The eyes were just like Shep's, though the brothers were not identical to him, or to each other. Each face was slightly different, granting them the gift of individuality.

"All of you listen up," he said. "The time has come for you three to take a more active role in our project. I have assignments for each of you, but there are some ground rules we need to cover if you're going to go unnoticed among the masses. You can start by sitting on the furniture."

They glanced at each other. Juris, the blond, was the sharpest of the three. If anything happened to Shep, Juris would become their leader. It was a frightening thought at the moment. Juris would become stronger with time, but right now he could barely lead himself to the toilet. He had, just yesterday, urinated into the kitchen sink, causing Joey to nearly have a stroke.

Juris lifted himself awkwardly off of the floor and shuffled over to a nearby arm chair, sitting stiffly. He glanced down at Margol and Allisto where they sat on the floor, and motioned to them with his head. Following Juris's lead, the other brothers stood and moved reluctantly to the couch.

"There. That's better," Shep said, smiling. "Now remember. You cannot sit on the floor if you're in public. It draws attention. Get used to sitting on furniture at all times."

"Il oblicheklata chask!" Juris spoke desperately in his native tongue. Shep crossed the room and slapped him hard in the face. He cried out, slinking back in the chair. Shep didn't want to hurt them, but they had to learn and they had to learn fast. Their readjustment period would have to be shortened due to time restrictions.

"Rule number two!" Shep called out, holding up two fingers. "You will speak the languages. You all remember the languages. This is Anglo, or English. This is the language that you will use at all times, especially in public." Shep turned to the blond brother. "Now, Juris. Why don't you repeat your last statement, but this time, say it in English."

Juris glared at him through a forest of white curls. His green eyes were raw with hurt and fear. He rubbed the side of his face where Shep had slapped him. "I said one of us is missing." Juris forced the words out in a strained fashion, sounding a bit like Arnold Schwarzenegger in his early movies.

Shep smiled. "Better, Juris. Much better. To address Juris's concern, I am obviously aware that we are minus one. I couldn't get Klee out on the first try. Not to worry. Nobody gets left behind. When the time is right, we will go back for Klee. Then we will be five again. As it should be."

"We must wait for Klee!" Allisto said, teary eyed. Allisto's English was pretty good, considering. Shep had even sent him out on assignments already. His dark black hair made him less noticeable than Margol and Juris, with their conspicuous red and platinum locks. Though a bit youthful looking, Allisto had been able to pass for just another city vagrant. Shep felt confident sending Allisto into the city, despite his insistence that Obrien had noticed him on the train. Whether or not Obrien had noticed Allisto made no difference. Obrien was too stupid to make any sort of connection.

"No, Allisto. Klee will be with us soon enough, but in the meantime we have work to do. I have no intentions on letting the three of you sit around picking bugs out of each other's hair until Klee gets here." Allisto looked about to cry, but he nodded sheepishly and slumped back onto the couch.

"Alright then," Shep said. "I have assignments for all, but we have to make humans out of you first. We have established that you will use furniture. You will speak English. You will in no way draw attention to the fact that you are different. This means hiding your speed, your strength, and all other extraordinary abilities. You will keep a low profile and try to go unnoticed. And speaking of going unnoticed, there is one more thing…" He'd been dreading this part. He knew it was going to upset them. He stood before them, hands rested on his hips, chin tilted with authority. "You need to clean yourselves up."

They looked up at him, terrified. You'd have thought he'd asked them to castrate themselves. Margol began sputtering his objections in broken English that Shep couldn't help but find humorous. "We don't need care to wash! The flesh keeping unnecessary clean!"

Shep laughed and Margol scowled. "Congratulations, Margol. That was almost a sentence. Don't worry. The language will come to you. In the meantime try not to speak too much in public, okay?" Shep patted his head of orange curls. Allisto jumped off the couch then, backing up frightfully. He

grimaced, revealing teeth decorated with some recently consumed Oreo cookies. Juris looked nervous but he remained seated, watching the others.

"We don't want the shower!" Allisto said. "We are afraid!"

Shep rolled his eyes, breathing an exasperated sigh. "For the last time,
the shower does not hurt. Do you think I would ask you to do something that
would hurt you? You all need to just calm down and listen to me. You will take
a bath. You will wash your hair. You will brush your teeth. I need to send you
all into the city soon and you can't go looking like pigs. It will draw attention
to you. Do you understand?"

They stared at him but nobody moved. Allisto continued to slowly retreat behind the couch. Margol rocked nervously, cradling his own bare foot.
Shep raised his eyebrows at them. "I see. You'd rather I sent you back where
you came from?" Their eyes widened in terror, and Shep felt a stabbing pain
in his heart. He hated using fear tactics. But if he didn't toughen them up,
they could get hurt. They could all get hurt, including Shep himself.

Juris jumped out of the chair. "No! We will not go back. We will be part of
the plan."

"All right then!" Shep said, clapping his hands. "Everyone to the Jacuzzi
room."

Shep trotted enthusiastically toward the door but no one followed. He
turned back expectantly. The brothers skulked by the couch. "What? Oh, no.
Don't tell me you're afraid of the Jacuzzi too." They hung their heads. Shep
decided that it was time for the positive reinforcement. He pulled three chocolate candy bars out of his shirt pocket. Their eyes lit with excitement. Since
their arrival, the brothers had found chocolate to be this world's only redeeming value. They were like men with the souls of children, and like children, they could be coerced. Shep waved the candy bars in front of them.
"Whoever takes a bath gets a chocolate bar." They followed Shep to the Jacuzzi
room with no further arguments.

⚬⚬⚬

Ten minutes later, Joey walked into the little room and was visibly hor-
rified to see the three brothers sitting in the Jacuzzi shampooing their hair.
He looked at Shep, who stood to one side of the tub, supervising. "My father's
Jacuzzi!" he wailed.

Shep laughed. "It's your Jacuzzi now, golden boy."

Joey stared at the tub, his mouth gaped. "My father's Jacuzzi!" he repeated. "They were filthy! And you put them in my father's Jacuzzi!"

"Take it easy, Joey. They're afraid of the shower. I'll clean the tub up
afterward."

Joey shook his head. "What's next, Shep? Are you going to let them use
my toothbrush?"

"I already did."

"What?"

"I'm kidding, Joey. They have their own toothbrushes. Hey, lighten up,
huh?"

Joey pointed to the dirty bubbling of suds that was spilling over the
edges of the tub. "Oh, man! You're not supposed to put soap in there!"

Margol flinched at Joey's angry outburst. Shep glared at Joey. "Keep
your voice down," he said. "You're scaring them."

Joey laughed. "Oh, I'm scaring them, am I? I see. What I sacrificed to get them out of prison wasn't enough. Now I have to walk on eggshells around them?"

Shep took Joey by the arm and led him out of the room. They stood in the hallway out of the brothers' earshot. "Joey, you need to lighten up on them. They're very vulnerable right now."

"I'm sorry, Shepherd, but you have to teach them to clean up after themselves. They're disgusting! One of them pissed all over the wall in the third floor bathroom. And the blond one, Juris? He spilled chocolate milk all over the Persian rug in the library. That's an expensive rug, Shepherd!"

Shep grabbed Joey by the throat and lifted him off of the ground, pinning him to the wall. "You're worried about your rug, Joey? You're worried about your fucking rug?"

Joey choked as he tried to pull loose. Shep slammed him against the wall, making him cry out. Holding Joey's neck tight with one hand, Shep pointed toward the Jacuzzi room. "Do you see those three creatures in there, Joey? They have been locked away in a place that makes your worst nightmares look like Disney Land. They are the superior beings that are going to help us lead the human race into a new age. And furthermore, they are my family. So try and show a little respect. Huh, Joey?"

"Okay," Joey managed to say. Shep dropped him.

Joey rubbed his neck, sucking in gulps of air until he'd caught his breath. When he'd recovered, he straightened up and looked Shep in the eye. "I never meant to insult you. And I never meant to insult them. But you've got to understand. This is all a little strange for me. You've been talking about them for so long, since we were kids. I guess part of me always believed they were fictional."

Shep's anger started to soften. "Well, as you can see, Joey, they are quite real."

Joey nodded, frowning. "Yes. Quite."

Shep grinned sheepishly and ran his fingers through his sandy curls. "Hey, I'm sorry I lost my temper, Joe. It's the pressure, you know? Obrien abandoning us and all."

"Obrien will come around," Joey said, placing a hand on his friend's thin shoulder.

Shep nodded. "Yeah. He'll come around. I'll go make margaritas. You in?"

"Sounds great. I'll be right down," he said, smiling.

Shep trotted down the stairs and Joey's phony grin turned downward into a frown. He peeked back into the Jacuzzi room. The three brothers were taking the dirty water into their mouths and spitting it at each other playfully. Joey shook his head and walked out. "Superior beings my ass," he said, and went down to join Shep.

Chapter Eleven

Patrick supposed Calvin thought it was helpful somehow to keep him apprised of Joey's Internet popularity. Patrick actually found it unsettling, but he didn't say so to Calvin. Calvin was the only friend who still kept in touch with him, after all.

"The Pope got wind of the miracle, and waved it off as a fake," Calvin announced proudly.

Patrick snickered into the phone. "Well. Points for the Pope. What else?"

"Okay, let's see what we've got here. Oh, here we go. Certain Christian groups are outraged at Joey. They feel that if the Virgin Mary saw fit to give Joey a message, then it's his responsibility to share that message with the religious community. There's an angry web site entitled, 'Tell us What She Said, Mr. Duvaine.'"

"Cute. But the coverage is dying out, right? I mean, people are losing interest in this." Calvin was silent.

Patrick felt his nerves start to dance. "Calvin? Did you hear me?"

"Yeah. I heard you. And yes, people are losing interest. But I have a feeling that's all going to change after tonight."

"Why? What's going to happen tonight?"

"You're not going to like this, Obrien."

"I already don't like it. What's up?"

"Spectrum has asked Joey to do an interview."

Patrick laughed. "Spectrum? You're kidding."

Spectrum was one of those programs that floated in journalistic limbo between a legitimate news medium and a gossip show. Although they occasionally uncovered a real breaking story, they weren't taken seriously. How appropriate, Patrick thought, that a tabloid news program would take an interest in Joey. He was still laughing when Calvin said those fateful words.

"Joey agreed to do it."

Patrick stopped laughing. "What?"

"Joey agreed. He's done the interview. It's airing tonight at six thirty. I guess Tara Shane went out to Forest Bluffs and everything."

Patrick went cold. Spectrum was a rag show, but it was national. It was one of those programs people loved to watch, but would never admit it to their friends. The interview would reach a wide audience.

"Patrick? Are you there?"

"Calvin. Are you telling me that Joey is going to go on national television and lie his ass off?"

"I guess. Unless he's planning to come clean."

Patrick doubted that was the case. He was instantly reminded that Joey possessed an eerie power to influence people, but he brushed the thought aside. The public wasn't that stupid. He hoped. As soon as he hung up with Calvin, Kelinda called, all in a tizzy about the interview, and whether or not Joey planned to expose her. She'd grown increasingly paranoid as Joey's popularity escalated, fearful that her father, a Deacon at the local church, would somehow discover her involvement in the hoax. He and Kelinda were officially dating now, and he'd have been thrilled if not for her constant worry about being exposed. He was starting to get irritated with her implications that this was all about her. She seemed to ignore the fact that he was the one who'd gotten his damned picture in the paper.

Regardless, he made plans to meet Kelinda at Monty's to watch the interview. They had tossed around the idea of boycotting it, but in the end they both agreed that they had to see it, regardless of how disturbing it was sure to be.

꩜

They were seated at the bar with a plate of chicken wings in front of them. Patrick had a baseball cap pulled down over his forehead, in case he was recognized. So far this hadn't been a problem. Except for his size, he was pretty much a blender. They ordered beers and Trent the bartender agreed to air the program on the pub's many television sets.

Patrick drank his beer too fast as he watched the silent intro to the program, the words drowned out by the bar noise. The blond reporter stood in front of an iron gate with the late Charles Duvaine's beach house looming in the background. The caption read FOREST BLUFFS, MASSACHUSETTS.

"Trent, this is it," Patrick yelled. "Turn it up!"

Trent hit the volume and Tara Shane's voice vibrated into the room. They had missed most of the introduction, but suddenly, it didn't matter. Joey was on the screen.

"Oh my God!" Kelinda said. "There he is!"

Patrick felt his stomach tighten. Joey looked amazing. Tara Shane had him set up in the cozy dark wood room that had been his father's study. He sat beside the stone fireplace in a burgundy leather chair like he was about to give a presidential address. Megalomaniac, Patrick thought spitefully. He was wearing his wire framed reading glasses. His hair looked to have grown out a bit since Patrick had seen him last, but it was probably because he'd retired his usual jell slicked business man coif. The sleek black locks framed his perfect face, curving under just at his chin. His eyes glowed like pale blue gems against his tanned skin, which was accentuated by the plain white dress shirt he wore with a pair of faded blue jeans. The top two buttons of the shirt were left open, exposing a strand of colorful beads, a la Shepherd.

The look was diversity perfected. Joey was every man. He was the scholar, and he was the hippie. He was mature, and he was young. He was gay, and he was straight. Patrick glanced around the bar, startled to see all eyes focused on at least one of the four big screen televisions. Pool games had stopped. Chatting had ceased. Drinks were frozen in hand midway to the mouth as they stared at the screens in glazed fascination. Joey hadn't even spoken yet.

"Let's get right to the question on everybody's mind, Joseph," the reporter said. "Did the Virgin Mary speak to you?"

Joey wore his blank-faced, zombie expression. "Well, Tara, I'm not really comfortable saying that it was the Virgin Mary. It was the other witnesses who made that particular claim."

Brilliant, Patrick thought. Surely the public expected Joey to try to convince them of something they were highly skeptical of. Instead, he gave the impression that he shared their skepticism. Patrick could almost hear Shep scripting it.

"If not the Virgin Mary, then who was it that appeared to you on that roof-top, Joseph?" The reporter spoke to Joey in slow, even tones, the way one addresses the mentally impaired. The camera closed in to a tight shot of Joey's face. Relaxed and handsome, Joey flashed one of his million dollar smiles.

"I'm afraid I didn't catch her name. I'm sorry, ma'am."

The bar crowd at Monty's chuckled at the comment. "God, he looks good," Kelinda said. Patrick couldn't argue that, for it was an undisputed fact. A blind fool could have sensed Joey's magnetism.

"All right, Joseph," Tara Shane continued, "tell us this then. Were you planning to take your life that night? Were you going to kill yourself before the apparition materialized?"

Joey breathed a long sigh, removed his reading glasses, and rubbed the bridge of his nose. He stared into the distance then, appearing to ponder the question. You could have heard a pin drop in Monty's bar. Patrick did another quick glance around. The patrons stood like statues in front of the television sets. There was something eerie about their stillness. Even through the circuits of television, Joey could command people's attention.

"To be honest with you, Tara," Joey said, "I'm not sure what was going through my head that night. I'd been through a lot of shit. Oh, I'm sorry. Can I say that on TV?"

The bar crowd laughed again. The station bleeped out the word "shit" but the message had gotten through. Joey was a regular guy. He was completely credible. And Patrick felt like he was going to vomit. The program went to commercial, and Patrick ordered another beer, with a shot of tequila this time. Kelinda used the bathroom. When she returned, Joey was back on the monitor.

"What did the vision say, Joseph? Did it speak to you?" The blond reporter was hammering her questions out with force now, giving over her gentle demeanor for a hard ass newswoman approach.

Joey appeared to become uncomfortable with the question. "I don't feel right about discussing that until I've gotten it figured out for myself, Tara," Joey said. "For me to release any message without fully researching its meaning would be irresponsible on my part."

The reporter raised an eyebrow. "When will you reveal the message, Joseph? Certain religious organizations are angered by your silence."

Joey nodded, looking humble and ashamed. What an actor, Patrick thought. "I know that, Tara, and I plan to address this issue in due time. I am seeking a small group of knowledgeable, open-minded people to join me on this quest to uncover the truth behind the apparition's message. The qualifications required for such persons are listed on my web site."

The television flashed a web address on the bottom of the screen. Patrick and Kelinda gaped at each other. "Did he just..." Kelinda started to formulate the question.

Patrick nodded. "Yes. I believe he just invited all of the nuts in America to join his loony bin. Have you seen enough?"

Kelinda nodded. "More than enough. Let's get out of here."

They had gathered themselves up, and were climbing off of their barstools when they heard the reporter say, "Let's talk about Patrick Obrien."

Patrick froze, and looked up at the television. Joey looked directly at the camera and let his eyes fill up with tears. "Patrick Obrien is my best friend. I know the whole thing freaked him out. He won't return my calls. I can't say I blame him. I just want him to know that none of this means anything if I've lost his friendship."

Joey let the tears slip down his cheeks, and Tara Shane handed him a handkerchief, looking pleased with herself. Then the screen flashed the photograph of Patrick carrying Joey out of the church. Patrick felt like he was going to faint. Kelinda looked up at him, and gently grasped his arm. "Come on. You look like you need a scorpion bowl. Let's go get Chinese food."

He nodded. "Yeah. Okay. I need to stop home and change my shirt. I've been sweating since we walked through the door."

"Charming," Kelinda said with a grin, and led him out the door.

Patrick's phone was ringing when they stepped into his apartment. "I'm not getting that," he said. "It's probably my mother calling to tell me what a bad Christian I am."

He went into his bedroom and changed his shirt. When he returned, Kelinda was standing in front of the answering machine, listening. "It's Joey," she said.

Joey's disembodied voice echoed through the living room. "Come on, Obrien. Pick up. I know you're there. You're probably standing in front of the answering machine right now. Just pick up the damn phone."

Patrick picked it up. "That was a lovely interview, Joey."

"Do you think so? I thought I looked kind of fat. I guess the camera adds ten pounds."

"That was the most hypocritical, shameful thing I have ever witnessed. People are calling you a prophet. A prophet, Joey! You're a fucking accountant for Christ sakes!"

He heard Joey sigh, as though Patrick was the ridiculous one. "You're right, Obrien. I should be ashamed of myself. I need guidance. Maybe if you would consider coming out to Forest Bluffs..."

"Forget it, Joey."

"I have your room all set up for you. I know you're not working right now. We could really use a marketing specialist."

"I'm not working because of you, Joey. And it looks to me like you're doing a pretty good job of marketing yourself. Goodbye." He slammed the phone down, and began to circle the room.

"Are you okay?" Kelinda asked.

"Fine. I'm fine," he said. But he wasn't. He was angry and conflicted. Ten years of friendship made it difficult to remain stony, especially when he spoke to Joey directly. He had to keep reminding himself that Joey was completely full of shit. A small part of him wanted to forgive Joey, and go running out to Forest Bluffs just so he could hang out with him again. Seeing him on the television had been almost physically painful. In spite of everything that had happened, he missed Joey terribly. He missed his friends. But his friends had done something appalling. He could not condone it without going against every moral fiber of his being.

"Are you hungry?" Kelinda asked, grabbing her purse off the couch.

Patrick nodded. "I could eat."

"Then I say we go out for Chinese food, get a giant scorpion bowl, and not talk about Joey or Shep for the entire evening."

"That's the best idea I've heard in weeks. Let's go."

❧❧

They were seated in the restaurant with a giant scorpion bowl and a tray of egg rolls between them when Patrick spotted the man at the corner table. He was sitting alone, reading a newspaper. Patrick nearly spit out his egg roll.

"What's wrong?" Kelinda asked.

He leaned in close. "Do you see that sort of grubby looking guy with the black hair sitting diagonally behind me?"

Kelinda glanced over. "Yeah. He kind of reminds me of Shep. Except for the hair color."

"Yes!" Patrick said. "Yes, that's exactly what I thought when I saw him on the train. He's not as dirty now, though." Patrick looked back and watched as a waiter brought the stranger a piece of chocolate cake. He nodded at the waiter, then cast his eyes back down to the newspaper. "I think he's following me!" Patrick whispered to Kelinda.

Kelinda laughed and wrinkled her nose, her cheeks pink from the scorpion bowl. "Following you? Come on, Patrick. Do you know how paranoid that sounds?"

"I'm serious. He was on the train with me, and then I saw him in front of your house. Now he's here."

Kelinda leaned forward. "Patrick, I know you think you live in the hub of the universe, but Boston can be a very small city. He probably lives in the neighborhood."

"He was carrying a notebook with my name on it."

Kelinda spit a spray of scorpion bowl into her napkin as she broke into peals of laughter.

"What are you laughing at? I'm serious."

Kelinda shook her head. She continued to giggle until he had to laugh himself. A notebook with his name on it. It did sound paranoid. "Hey, look!" she said. "Now there are two of them."

"Yeah, very funny."

She shook her head. "No, Patrick. I'm not teasing. There really are two of them now. Look."

Patrick glanced back. Another man had joined the curly haired stranger at the table. He wore the same dusty ankle length coat with jeans. His hair was in chin length curls as well, but his was a pale blond, about three shades lighter than Shep's. The blond looked back at Patrick, saw him staring, and turned to whisper to his companion. The quick glimpse revealed that he had a face very much like the dark haired one. A face very much like Shepherd's. Patrick's head swam. He felt like he was losing his mind.

"Huh. That's weird," Kelinda said, stuffing an egg roll into her mouth. "They must be brothers."

Patrick looked back at the table. The two men were whispering to each other. The dark haired one caught him looking, and went back to his newspaper. Patrick noticed now that the newspaper was upside down.

"You're staring, Patrick," Kelinda said. "Let it go. We're supposed to be having fun."

"It's just so strange, though. It's like Shep is haunting us."

"Shep can't be haunting us, because Shep isn't dead. Here, you need to drink more scorpion bowl."

Patrick looked down at the bulbous ceramic bowl between them. The orange liquid was nearly gone. He looked at Kelinda. "Did you drink all that?"

She giggled. "Oops. I guess we'd better get another one." She was drunk, and did not seem accustomed to being so.

"I don't think we need another one, Kelinda. You're a mess."

She leaned across the table, smiling. "I may be a mess. But you have people following you."

Patrick grinned at her. "How do you know they're following me? They could be following you."

Kelinda appeared to consider this, then stood. Patrick stopped grinning. "What are you doing? Kelinda, sit down."

"I'm gonna ask em. I'm gonna ask em if they're following you, or if they're following me." She giggled and started toward the corner table.

"Kelinda no!" Patrick whispered harshly, but she was gone. She wobbled over to the table where the two men sat huddled over an upside down newspaper and one piece of chocolate cake. They looked panicked when they saw her approaching. She leaned over and spoke to them, but Patrick couldn't hear the words. In one swift action, the two jumped from their chairs and sprinted out the door of the restaurant.

"Hey!" Kelinda called after them. "You didn't answer my question!" She giggled, using the table to steady herself.

Patrick retrieved her and led her back to their table. "Stay here, Kelinda." He bolted out the front door after the two strangers. On the sidewalk, pedestrians strode casually up and down the street, but the bizarre Shep-alikes were nowhere in sight. He turned to a young Asian man who leaned against the building with a cigarette pinched between his fingers. His slanted eyes looked too wide, like something had startled him. "Hey, kid. Did you see two guys with curly hair come running out here?"

The kid nodded, looking spooked. "I saw someone, but they were moving too fast for me to get a good look. Shit! I've never seen anyone move that fast!"

An old Chinese waiter came bounding out of the restaurant looking furious. He pointed to Patrick. "You! Get back inside and pay your bill. Your girlfriend just vomited on my floor! Pay your bill, and then don't come back here. Ever!"

Patrick followed the waiter back inside, shaking his head. This had turned out to be another lovely evening. On the drive home, Kelinda threw up all over his leather upholstery. He dropped her at home, tucked her into bed, then went home to clean out his car. When he finally went inside, he bypassed his bathroom duties and went straight to bed, weary and exhausted.

He'd been having nightmares every night since the apparition. Each nightmare involved saving Joey from some terrible fate. The night before he'd dreamed he was belly down on the top of Saint Mary's church, clinging to Joey, who hung off the ledge by his finger tips. Joey's ice blue eyes had looked up at him. "You were supposed to protect me, Obrien," he'd said, then his hands had slipped free. Patrick had watched helpless as Joey tumbled to the ground, cracking his skull on the cement steps of the church. He'd awoken drenched in sweat, a terrible pain dancing in his temples, the little scar above his wrist throbbing like a newly singed burn.

He dreamed again this night. This time Joey was being attacked by hundreds of poisonous snakes. They were all over him, their jaws wide and suctioned onto his skin. Joey screamed for Patrick to help, but when he tried to move, he found his feet and hands were bound with rope.

He awoke with a start, and a headache that felt like it was splitting his skull in two. The headaches he'd found went hand in hand with the dreams about Joey. He'd gone through a half a bottle of pain reliever in a week. He toddled to the bathroom, hunched over from the pain in his head. He dug the bottle of pills out of the cabinet, tossing back three of them, then he splashed water on his face and studied his pale reflection.

"What's happening to me?" he asked the mirror. "I can't get him out of my head."

Chapter Twelve

The bartender gave Agent Litner a foul look when he ordered a Club Soda, as though his decision to drink a nonalcoholic beverage was a direct insult. Agent Litner did not drink, and wouldn't even be in the bar if not for his boss's insistence. His boss, Agent Michaels, always demanded that they meet at some obscure location, usually a shadowy, rank smelling barroom such as this one.

"Hey, do you want to start a tab?" the bartender asked as he plunked down the Club Soda.

Agent Litner handed him a five dollar bill. "No, thank you. I won't be here long."

Agent Michaels had soundlessly taken the stool next to him as though he'd magically appeared. Michaels was probably the only six foot five black man that could slip into a room unnoticed. He had a military background, and enjoyed showing off his skills. Litner found it unnerving, but never allowed Michaels to see his surprise. He had a few tricks of his own, one of which was being able to maintain a deadpan stare in the face of any situation.

Agent Michaels lit a cigarette. "You called this meeting, Litner. Are you going to talk or are you going to stare at my bald head all day?"

Litner caught himself and dropped his eyes to Michaels' shoulders. Litner was not a vain man, but he was secretly pleased that his own head had a full crop of hair at age forty-four. Granted, it was prematurely white, had been since his twenties. Some suggested that Litner dye his hair, but he couldn't imagine taking vanity to such an extreme. There was something plain wrong about an FBI agent using 'Just For Men'.

"I thought I made clear on the phone what I wanted to discuss, Sir," he said to Michaels. "Did you receive my report? I had it faxed to your office yesterday."

Michaels frowned. "Yes. The report."

"Then you understand why I think an investigation of this Forest Bluffs thing is warranted."

Michaels snuffed his cigarette out. "No, Agent Litner. I do not."

"But Sir, clearly you can see—"

"Agent Litner!" Michaels interrupted. "We have been all through this. Joey Duvaine is clean. Murder was ruled out in all three deaths. He didn't kill his family. You and Agent Rourke need to come to terms with that, and let the investigation go. Let it go, Litner."

Litner turned sideways to face his boss. "This isn't about the deaths of the Duvaine family anymore. And you're the one who asked me to investigate his Forest Bluffs set up."

"I asked you to take a quick look at this Joey Duvaine miracle business. I asked you to look for evidence of tax evasion. As I recall, that is all I asked you to look for."

"But Sir, as you can see in my report, I did find some red flags."

"Did you find tax evasion, Litner? No. You did not. So why are we sitting here?"

Litner's cheeks flamed, and it was a struggle to maintain his deadpan stare. "The report speaks for itself, Agent Michaels. If I'm right about this, and we do nothing..."

"Litner, we have the makings of a religious cult here. We do not fuck with religious cults, unless they are breaking the law."

Litner pulled a manila folder out of his jacket and slid it over to Michaels. "With all due respect, Sir, these are not the Branch Davidians, and Joey Duvaine is not David Koresh."

"Nevertheless. Do you think the Feds would even think of approving an investigation like this with no evidence of a threat?"

"I believe there is evidence, Sir. If you had read my report—"

"I read your report, Litner! You want me to order an investigation because some ninny drew a chart?"

"That ninny is Joey Duvaine's closest friend, Melvin Shepherd, and this was no ordinary chart. We found it in his personal computer files. We had to bypass six electronic booby traps to get at it. That's an excessive bit of software protection for a file that means nothing, Sir."

Michaels shoved the folder back at Litner. "You listen to me, Litner. That beach house is private property, and those people are private citizens. They are private, tax paying citizens, with no criminal history. If this rich little Duvaine bastard wants to sit out there on his dead daddy's land and play God, then he's perfectly entitled to do so. We've got our hands full with terrorist threats, Litner. We do not fuck with religious cults."

"Did you see Joey Duvaine's latest purchase? He bought Arcania foods. And they've begun growing some sort of crop in the fields behind that beach house."

Michaels leaned in close and cracked a wide-mouthed grin. "Maybe they're planting a vegetable garden."

"Must I spell this out for you, Michaels?"

"Watch your tone, Litner. I understand what you're insinuating here, and it's a stretch. A big stretch. Crazy, troubled men do things like this. Men that want. Wealthy young men with above average intelligence just don't do things like this."

Agent Litner slid the folder back defiantly. "Am I the kind of agent who jumps at shadows?"

Michaels shrugged and lit another cigarette. "Come on, Litner. This isn't a personal attack on your work ethics."

"Answer me this, then. Have I ever been wrong?"

Michaels shifted in his seat, avoiding Litner's eyes. "I think you may be losing your objectivity, Litner. It happens. Part of the job. After a while you start seeing terrorist conspiracies behind every tree."

"Answer the question, Michaels. Have I ever been wrong?" He glared at the side of Michaels' head until he was sure he'd bore a hole into it.

Finally Michaels shrugged. "No. You've never been wrong." He whirled to face him. "But there's always a first time! What if this is that first time, Litner? What if you're wrong about this? Do you know what the press, not to mention the courts would do to us? Public sympathy for the Branch Davidians was immense, and everyone knew Koresh was a crackpot. Imagine what would happen if it got out that the FBI was investigating Joey Duvaine, The Yuppie Prophet with the boy next door smile and the pretty blue eyes. Forest Bluffs is like Walton's Mountain. It's fucking Walton's Mountain, and Joey Duvaine is John Boy."

Litner focused his tension and calmed himself. His instincts had never failed him, and he wasn't going to back down now, even if Michaels ordered him off the case. "You say what if I'm wrong, Agent Michaels. But what if I'm right? Did you think about that? What if I'm right?"

Michaels met his eyes, and Litner thought he saw a flicker of doubt in them. Then the brown eyes became stony again. "Okay, Litner. Aside from the evidence in your report, which I see as sheer speculation, why do you smell trouble? And please don't tell me that it's just a feeling."

Litner smiled on the inside. He knew Michaels wouldn't brush his theory off so completely. Litner had stopped countless terrorist plots. He'd earned the right to have his opinion valued.

"Just for a moment, forget about the chart we found in the Shepherd house, and forget about the purchase Duvaine made. Putting that aside, look at the situation they have put themselves in. There is no objective for what they have done."

Michaels frowned. "No objective. Are you referring to Duvaine forming that ridiculous church? And I use the term church lightly."

Litner swiveled in his stool and pointed at Michaels. "Think about it. Have we ever come across one of these groups that didn't ultimately want something? Even that suicide cult that thought the mother ship was coming from outer space had an objective. They all want something, whether it's money, recognition, power, or even death. There is always a goal."

"So what's the difference with this Forest Bluff's crew?"

"Joey Duvaine now has thousands of web sites dedicated to him and his so called miracle. Yet he claims that he wants nothing. He refuses to take donations. He pays his taxes. He isn't asking people to give up their possessions. He's refused to do any more interviews, so beyond his call for 'open minded people to help him find the truth', he doesn't seem to even want recognition. It's all so...quiet. We all know he's not stupid. His IQ is off the charts. The only explanation for his actions is that this guy has been genuinely blessed by God."

Michaels's shiny forehead wrinkled. "You're not suggesting that the Virgin Mary actually appeared to this clown!"

"Of course not. I'm certain it was a hoax. A damn good hoax. But there is a circus quality to the entire thing. It's like...he wants the authorities to think he's a fake. It's almost like he's purposely trying to get us to laugh and turn away. But why?"

Michaels moved his stool in closer. "Maybe to divert our attention from something else. This whole church thing could be a smokescreen."

Litner actually did smile then. "This hoax wasn't done cheaply. It was a lot of money and trouble for someone to go through for personal glory. Don't you think?"

Agent Michaels shook his head, turning away now. "I don't know, Litner.

The rich are different from us. They'll go to great lengths to amuse themselves, and to feed their egos. I respect your opinion, but what you're suggesting that these clowns are up to...it sounds so paranoid."

"The FBI pays me to be paranoid. If I weren't paranoid, that suicide bomber would have succeeded in blowing up the Washington monument last year, just in time for the spring tourist season."

Michaels flipped through the file folder, pursing his lips. "This evidence you collected could all be coincidental. It could mean nothing."

"Yes, sir, it could. But it could be a terrorist plot. Regardless that these are Americans we're talking about. Do you want to take that chance? Let me do the investigation, Michaels. Let me be sure. I'll be perfectly discreet. Nobody even has to know about this."

Michaels studied Litner, as though trying to read a confusing map. "I'll need hard evidence. And I'm not talking about home made charts this time."

Litner breathed a quiet sigh of relief. "I'll get you your evidence. I have a plan."

Michaels scowled. "What is it?"

"Duvaine stated in his television interview that he's planning to take on a group of consultants, or followers more likely. We can try to slip someone in then, but Duvaine might smell it. Also we have no way of guaranteeing that our agent will even be chosen."

Michaels scratched his head. "So if our agent isn't chosen, what then?"

"I have a plan B. His name is Patrick Obrien."

Michaels flipped through the folder again. "Patrick Obrien. The big guy from the roof? You barely mention him in your report. How can he help?"

"He's had a falling out with his friends. We may be able to close in on him and get him to talk."

"And if he doesn't know anything?"

"That's doubtful. He's an old college buddy of Duvaine's, and he was there the night of the apparition. But if he doesn't know anything, he can find out."

"How so?"

"By infiltrating their little beach camp. We can't just go strolling onto Joey Duvaine's property. But an old friend of Duvaine's probably can. I want a sample of whatever they're growing out in those fields. Patrick Obrien is going to get me that sample. If it's nothing but a bunch of vegetables, I leave them alone. If it's something else, then we move forward from there, with solid evidence in hand."

Michaels stared at him, still looking skeptical. "What if this Obrien refuses? What if he gets angry and talks? We can't risk involving the press in this, Litner. It'll be my ass if you're wrong."

"He won't talk. Leave it to me. I'll take care of it."

Michaels stared at him, his dark face conflicted. Litner had never revealed his persuasion tactics, but his record evidenced that they were effective. Litner suspected that Michaels thought him a closet tough guy, making threats against home and hearth to get what he wanted. His tactics were much subtler. For persuasion, he referenced his psychology training, exercising his mind instead of his muscle. Once he got inside of someone's head, he could crack it like a safe. This Obrien character should be a breeze.

"Okay, Litner," Michaels said. "Here's my offer, and it is not up for debate. You use your own team on this, no one else. You keep them muzzled, not a word to anyone. You get the crop samples, and get out. If you fuck this up, I will deny all knowledge of this investigation. I will say that you took this on without my authorization. You will be the fall guy. Is that clear?"

"Yes, sir."

Outside the bar, Litner started his car and Michaels leaned into the driver's side window. "Litner, I know you have a history with that priest down at Saint Mary's church. I hope he hasn't persuaded you into taking this on for personal reasons. I understand he was pretty pissed off about that phony miracle happening at his church. I can't say I blame him. The place is like a damned tourist attraction now."

Litner looked at his boss, his face an emotionless mask. "Father Carbone and I went to high school together, and we are friendly, but I have not spoken to him about this investigation."

It was the truth. He hadn't spoken to Luigi Carbone. Yet. Michaels looked relieved. "But you understand. If this is just some revenge plot for the priest, it would be a conflict of interest."

"I understand. Goodnight, Agent Michaels."

"Where are you off to now, Litner? I thought maybe we could grab a bite to eat."

"I have a meeting with Father Carbone. Take care."

Litner drove off before Michaels could voice his objections, leaving him to glower after the car. Litner looked in his rearview mirror and grinned. He respected his boss's opinions, but ultimately he always did things his own way. His instincts had never failed him, so he had grown to rely on them and them alone. Much of the bizarre evidence in this case was religious in nature, and Father Carbone was a theologian by degree. He was also a personal friend. Litner had never bought into the whole conflict of interest thing. If he had to use his own mother to help solve a case, he would. It wasn't personal. It was just business.

Chapter Thirteen

Cars lined the lush winding road that led up to the beach house. Benign clouds clung to the stretching blue sky, like caps of foam on a calm sea. The sun was still new, casting a dance of early morning shadows around the flowering shrubs and blueberry bushes, like a thousand tiny hands waving. Beyond the locked gates at the end of the driveway, the crowd grew. Perched in clusters at the edge of the road, some of them with portable lawn chairs, they could have been waiting for a parade to come by. But they were not waiting for a parade. They were awaiting their chance to be accepted into the gates and to share in the secrets of Joey Duvaine's miracle. He had, after all, invited them

"Look at them all." From a front bay window, Joey peered through a pair of binoculars. Shep stood at his side, gazing at the crowd with a thoughtful scowl. "How will we choose?" Joey asked, dropping the binoculars and turning to Shep.

"We're going to interview them," Shep said.

Joey uttered a small laugh. "All of them?"

Shep grabbed the binoculars from Joey and peered through. He dropped them after a moment, and scratched his head. "That would take a while."

"Well yeah! Look at all of them. Didn't you think this through, Mr. Plan of The Century?"

Shep scowled at the window. "Not a problem. We let in a hundred and fifty. We choose sixty from that group. That should be enough people to tend to things around here."

"Who has to interview them?" Joey asked, looking uneasy.

"You do, of course."

Joey shook his head and drifted over to a nearby chair, sitting stiffly. "I'm not a good judge of character, Shep."

Shep followed him over. "Don't worry. I'll be right there with you. I've even made up a set list of questions for you to ask. I'll stand by and judge their reactions, read their auras, that sort of thing. The ideal candidate should be mesmerized by your presence, but not so much that they couldn't function. I'll be able to weed out the bad seeds. We don't want any cops or reporters trying to slip in." Joey sat with his hands wedged between his knees, rocking slightly. Shep moved closer, studying him with a tilt of his head. "Are you okay?"

Joey's pale blue eyes lifted. "I'm not sure I'm up for this, Shep. I'm feeling a little unsteady. Not myself, you know?"

Shep stiffened. "Did you have more dreams last night?"

Joey forced a laugh. "I have them every night. They're getting worse,

Shep. I don't know how much more of this I can take. I feel afraid all the time, and I don't even know what I'm afraid of."

Shep sat down beside him. "If the dreams are getting worse for you, then they're getting worse for Obrien too. He can't stay away forever. I'm sorry you have to go through this, but in order to bond Obrien to you, I had to bond you to him as well."

"Well it really sucks, Shepherd, if you don't mind my saying so. You didn't tell me it was going to affect me like this."

"Yes, well I didn't think Obrien was going to be this stubborn."

Joey met his eyes. "You mean you didn't think he was going to be this strong."

Shep's face tightened, his teeth clenched. "He'll be here."

"Shep, what if it didn't take? I mean, what if it didn't work? Maybe we should—"

"Maybe we should what, Joey?" Shep yelled and Joey jumped.

Joey dropped his head and shrugged. "I just think it might not have worked."

"So what are you suggesting, Joey? Huh? Another blood pact? Give me a break! We barely talked him into the first one!"

Shep stormed over to a nearby desk and dug through a drawer. He tossed a plastic cylinder of pills over to Joey, who caught them. "Those are Valium, Joey. They'll keep you calm, and they'll help you sleep. Once Obrien gets here, you won't have to feel any more fear. And he will get here, Joey. I don't want to hear any more crap about the blood pact not working. You saw him climb the side of that church like he had plutonium in his veins. He'll be here."

The interviews went on all day and into the night. Juris would bring each of the candidates in and seat them in a chair across the big oak desk from Joey. Shep stood to the side, a silent observer. Some candidates were discarded immediately, like the women who tried to dive over the desk to get at Joey. Shep even uncovered a would-be spy. Joey was duly impressed, as he'd thought Shep paranoid to even suspect such a thing.

The young man in question had stringy, shoulder length red hair with a face full of boyish freckles, and introduced himself as Ronny Slade. Shep was immediately suspect. The man claimed to be twenty years old, but Shep was sure he was closer to thirty. His strategic dress was a raggedy tie-dyed tee shirt with denim shorts, and a strand of plastic beads around his neck. The beads had the smell and shine of something newly purchased. Apparently they were supposed to look like the beads Joey had worn on his television interview. Shep examined the man's clean, manicured fingernails as he shook the redhead's hand. Relying on his extraordinary senses, Shep discreetly sniffed his own hand after seating him. Ronny Slade's hand had the vague odor lead, with a hint of sulfur. He had handled a gun recently, whether in target practice or in the line of duty.

While Joey questioned him, Ronny Slade acted as if he was overwhelmed at the opportunity to join Joey in his religious quest. His aura, however, remained stable, with just a slight undertone of hostility. Joey's charm did not affect him at all. Only a person trained in discipline could so coldly resist Joey's chemical lure. Shep figured he had to be one of three things; a police officer, a federal agent, or a military man.

When the interview was over, Shep walked him to the door. "Juris will show you off the premises, Mr. Slade. You will not be accepted into our church.

I'm sorry."

Anger flared hot in the man's aura, but he made his face sad. "But I truly think I can help you find the answers. Won't you reconsider?"

Shep laughed loudly. "Go home, detective. Or is it agent? You must be dying to get out of those ridiculous clothes."

The man looked too shocked to come up with a clever protest. He stared open-mouthed at Shep for a moment, then he relaxed and smiled. "How did you know?" he asked, resigned to the fact that he'd been discovered.

Shep shrugged. "It was a combination of things, but I think it was the Wal-Mart beads around your neck that really coined it."

The man nodded. "I told them the beads were over the top. Goodbye Mr. Shepherd."

৵৻

By midnight, they had chosen sixty followers; thirty women and thirty men. There were artists, doctors, executives, students and beach bums. It was a beautiful mix, for now they all held the same goal; to please their leader. Weeding out the rejects had been grueling. The unwanted candidates were led out by the brothers, some quietly, others hysterical, many angry. The new family was set up out in the back fields, in and around the guest house. Tomorrow afternoon, Joey would go out and give his first sermon, then they would be truly his.

Shep sat alone in the sunroom and leisurely smoked a joint. He was pleased with the way things were coming together. There was of course still one soldier out of step. He'd expected Obrien to show up by now. Dear old Patrick was turning out to be more of a challenge than he'd expected. Stupid Mick. No matter. Patrick would join them eventually. If he wanted to wait until he was writhing in pain before he came back to them, so be it. It was his choice. For now.

Chapter Fourteen

The four pain pills Patrick had taken upon waking were finally kicking in, and the searing in his head eased to a dull throb. Last night's dream had been a corker. Joey was strung up and hanged by an angry lynch mob, while Patrick struggled to fight through the crowd to save him. Each time he thought he was getting close to Joey, the crowd would thicken in front of him, preventing his pursuit.

Shuddering at the memory, Patrick adjusted his tie in the bathroom mirror, and smoothed a bit of hair jell across his short red waves. His brother Ryan had just had his second child, and today was the Christening. Patrick had stood Godfather to Ryan's first son, Ryan Jr. who was now three years old. Patrick was looking forward to seeing his little Godson, a quizzical red-haired boy who was more than sure the world revolved around him.

He went into the kitchen and poured himself a cup of coffee, double checking the time on the invitation. He was about to put the invitation down when he did a double take. He hadn't examined it very closely when it arrived, and he'd just assumed that the Christening would take place at the Holy Name parish. That was their family church. It was where Ryan had gotten married, and where little Ryan Jr. had been christened. Patrick studied the invitation, hoping that it would change somehow. Next to *Location:* it clearly stated 'Saint Mary's Parish'. It had to be a mistake.

He picked up the phone and called his brother. Ryan sounded pleased to hear from him. Patrick had been fairly neglectful of family issues lately. "Hey, stranger! I was beginning to think I didn't have a brother anymore. Are we going to see you today?"

"Of course. I wouldn't miss it. Hey, Ryan, if you don't mind my asking, why are you having the Christening at Saint Mary's instead of at Holy Name?"

Ryan was silent for a moment. "Oh. Yeah. Well, mom insisted it be held at St. Mary's."

Patrick felt a knot forming in his stomach. "Why would she do that? We've been going to Holy Name since we were kids."

"I know, Patrick. But apparently mom goes to Saint Mary's now. Ever since your friend Joey had his little miracle."

"Oh, Christ. Are you kidding me?"

"No joke, brother. I take it you weren't as impressed with the miracle as mom was."

Patrick grew silent, not knowing what to say. He hadn't spoken to his brother since the whole thing happened.

"You don't have to tell me about it if you don't want to, Patrick. I imagine it's been a pain in the ass for you."

"You've got that right. I will tell you about it when we have time, Ryan, I promise. All I can tell you right now is that the last thing I want to do is set foot in Saint Mary's church."

Ryan sighed. "Yeah. I was afraid you'd feel that way. It's okay, Patrick. If you want to skip the Christening we understand. Hey, little Ryan wants to say hello."

"Well put him on!"

Patrick could hear the toddler struggling with the phone, and the sound of his breath as he held the receiver too close to his mouth. "Uncle Patrick?" The little voice was high and sweet as honey.

"How you doing buddy?"

Another heavy breath. "We have a new baby. I wanted a puppy but mommy brung Liam home instead. He doesn't do anything. He just sits on the couch and drinks milk. He cries sometimes too."

Patrick laughed. "Well, he'll be old enough to play with you soon enough, Ryan."

"Yeah. I guess. Uncle Patrick? Am I still your favorite boy?"

Patrick felt a hard yank at his heartstrings. "You'll always be my favorite boy, Ryan."

"So you is coming to the church today?" the little voice asked.

Damn. He'd rather gouge his eyes out than go back to Saint Mary's. But he couldn't say no to Ryan, senior or junior. "Of course I'm coming to the church. Tell your daddy I'll see him there."

Walking up the church lawn wasn't as bad as he'd anticipated. It was a bright sunny day, and the church looked different in the morning light. People in colorful outfits poured into the front doors, chatting and laughing. Aside from a few piles of decaying flowers left by hopeful spectators on the lawn, all seemed normal at Saint Mary's. There were no crowds seeking visions of holiness during the day.

Patrick slid into the bench alongside his mother, a thin pale woman with a sharply pointed nose. Her lips were constantly pursed in disapproval, giving her face a birdlike quality. She wore her auburn hair pulled back into a tight bun, and her skin was pale and flawless like Patrick's. She often told Patrick that he should thank her for his lovely skin, and that he hadn't inherited his father's freckles or baldness. His father was only slightly balding, but he harped on it as if he was losing a leg instead of a few strands of hair above the forehead.

The priest trickled water onto the miniature forehead of Patrick's newest nephew. Awakened from a sound sleep, the baby began to squeal. Patrick's brother Ryan and his wife Shay giggled nervously, but the priest was unfazed by the crying. The man didn't look like a priest. He was a handsome, olive-skinned Italian, perhaps in his mid forties, with thick dark hair combed back from his forehead. There was an intensity in the young priest's dark brown eyes that was unlike the usual somber countenance of a clergyman. When he smiled, and he smiled often, his eyes sparkled with warmth and kindness. When he was not smiling, however, he looked a little rough, like he could hold his own in a street fight. It was a strange contrast.

It was time to take communion, and Patrick stood and got in line behind his parents. He was not feeling particularly worthy of receiving the body of Christ, but he had little choice. To sit communion out would be to bear the wrath of his mother, which could be significantly more threatening than God's. So, with hands clasped at his waist, he shuffled forward and hoped the act would not transport him directly to hell.

With just two people ahead of him now, he could hear the priest's deep soothing voice, as he said "The body of Christ" to each approaching parishioner. The priest's tone was heartfelt and comforting. "The body of Christ," he said to Patrick's mother.

"Amen," she said, and the priest placed the small tasteless wafer on her tongue. Blessing herself, she turned and went back to her seat. Patrick stood before the priest now. Up close he could see a tuft of gray at each temple of the priest's black hair. He looked like a handsome hit man in a gangster movie. He raised the wafer.

"The body of..." The priest looked up at Patrick and hesitated. He held the wafer out in mid-reach, his brown eyes wide and startled. "The body of..." he started to say again, and paused. The way the priest was looking at him, Patrick was tempted to check his own head to see if he'd sprouted horns on the way to the altar. Finally the priest's face relaxed and he smiled. The smile was cold, not reaching his eyes. "The body of Christ," he said, and dropped the wafer into Patrick's cupped hands.

"Amen," Patrick said. His legs felt like undercooked noodles as he moved quickly back down the aisle, past his parents, and out the front doors of the church.

On the front steps he sat with his head between his knees. Why had the priest hesitated? The answer came like a dumbbell falling on his head. He did not have horns sprouting from his skull. The priest had simply recognized him. He'd probably seen Patrick's picture in the newspaper. Of course he'd followed the story of the apparition. It happened at his church. Patrick couldn't believe he was fool enough to come here.

Moments later, the crowd came pouring through the front door, and Patrick was able to blend in. His mother wandered over to him, holding the hand of a squirming Ryan Jr., who looked terribly uncomfortable in his little pin-striped suit. "I want to go home!" the child squealed.

"We'll go soon honey," his mother said. "We have to wait for mommy."

Patrick grabbed Ryan Jr. and swung him up onto his shoulders, making him shriek with laughter. "What happened to you, Patrick?" his mother asked. "Why did you walk out like that?"

"I wasn't feeling well. I just needed some air."

She reached up and grabbed Ryan off of Patrick's shoulders. "Well don't hold the children if you're sick!"

"I'm not sick, mom. I just needed some air. The incense eats up the oxygen. It makes me lightheaded."

Patrick spotted the Italian priest up on the stairs, speaking into a cellular phone. It was an odd image, the priest in his black robes, talking into a cell phone like an executive. He flipped the phone closed and slipped it into some unseen pocket beneath his robes, then turned to shake hands with Ryan and Shay as they came out of the church. Patrick was about to sneak away when his mother grabbed his elbow. "Patrick, come meet Father Carbone. He's been just wonderful to Ryan and Shay."

Patrick panicked. He didn't want to go anywhere near that priest. "I think I'm coming down with something after all, Mom. I'd better go home and lie down."

"It will just take a second! Come on, Patrick. I want to introduce you."

She all but dragged him, leading him up the stairs to where his brother stood with the priest. The priest reached out to her as they approached, warmly taking her hand in his.

"Brigid, it's so nice to see you."

"That was just lovely, Father Carbone."

"Thank you Brigid. It's a lovely occasion."

"I'd like you to meet my other son," his mother said, tugging him forward. "Patrick, this is Father Carbone."

The priest extended his hand and Patrick shook it. "Your son?" he said. "No kidding."

"Nice to meet you," Patrick muttered, and tried to slink away.

"Does Uncle Patrick want to hold the baby?" his sister-in-law Shay asked, offering him the frilly-dressed infant.

"No!" his mother snapped. "Patrick is sick. Don't give him the baby." Shay retracted the child as though Patrick had the plague.

"You're sick, Patrick?" Father Carbone asked. "What's wrong?"

"Oh, just a virus or something. I just need to get some rest. If you'll excuse me."

"I have just the thing," Father Carbone called out as Patrick attempted escape. "It's a very special tea. The recipe was passed down from four generations of monks. Come on around back, Patrick. I have some at the house."

Generations of monks? Of course. The great tea-brewing monks. What a crock of shit.

"Thank you, Father, but I don't want to be any trouble."

"It's no trouble at all. I can brew up a pot in five minutes."

His mother looked ecstatic at the idea of Patrick sharing tea with a priest, what with his mortal soul in danger from missing church so much. "Don't be rude, Patrick!" she said. "Father Carbone has offered to make you tea!" Patrick wanted to swat his mother away like a fruit fly.

"That's very kind, really, but I don't think so."

The last thing he wanted to do was be alone with this priest, who looked like a Mafia wise guy. Father Carbone put a firm hand on Patrick's shoulder, his fingers gripping just a bit too tight. "I insist," he said.

Patrick's eyes darted from the face to the white collar. He was a priest, for crying out loud. What was he going to do? Kill him? Poison his tea? Have him whacked in the parish house?

Patrick's brother Ryan gave him a warning glance that said he was protesting too much now.

"All right," Patrick said. "One cup of tea. Thank you, Father."

Father Carbone smiled. "Good. Let's go then. Don't worry, Brigid. I'll fix him right up."

I'll bet you will, Patrick thought. His mind played absurd images of the priest coming at him with a baseball bat as soon as they got inside.

Father Carbone led Patrick around the back of the church to his little apartment, or priest's house, or whatever it was. Patrick had pounded on that very door the night of the apparition, trying to get someone to let him into the church. Where was Father Carbone that night? Things might have been different had Patrick not been forced to scale the damn building.

"Have a seat. I'll go make the tea." The priest gave him a phony smile and disappeared down a hallway. Patrick sat stiffly on a worn-looking chair, examining his surroundings. It was a cozy little space, with paneled walls covered with religious knick-knacks. A set of shelves displayed a variety of books. Along with several bibles, there were some more philosophical books on matters such as immortality and resurrection. Statues of the Virgin Mary graced the end tables, along with a ceramic Jesus or two.

Carbone returned with a large metal tray and set it down on the coffee table. The tray held an elaborate painted tea set that looked like an antique. Patrick was tempted to ask if these mysterious monks had passed that down as well, but decided it was not in his favor to be a wise ass at the moment. "Do you like lemon?" the priest asked, still feigning cordiality.

"No, thank you."

Father Carbone sat on a small couch across from Patrick and poured his tea for him.

"This ought to fix you right up, Patrick."

"Thank you, Father." Patrick decided he could keep up the façade as long as the priest did.

Father Carbone took a sip of his tea and looked up at Patrick, smiling that strange smile. "So Patrick, I didn't realize that you were a Catholic."

"What do you mean, Father? You and I have never met before today."

The priest nodded. "Right. Right. What I meant was I've never seen you in church with your mother."

"Yes, well, we used to go to a different church. I didn't know my mother was coming here now."

The priest took another slow sip of his tea and nodded. "Yes, that's right. Like so many others, your mother started coming here after that business with the apparition." Patrick felt his stomach jump. The priest lifted his eyes. "You heard about that, didn't you, Patrick? The Virgin Mary appeared on the roof of this very church. It was in all the newspapers. I was away on vacation at the time. What luck, huh?"

Patrick pretended to be consumed by his tea cup. He could feel the heat rushing to his cheeks, and he damned his Irish skin. "Yeah," he said finally. "I heard about it." He drained his cup and stood, extending his hand. "Thank you for the tea, Father Carbone, but I really do have to go now."

Father Carbone did not stand. "Why don't you stick around for a while, Patrick. I have some people coming by who want to meet you."

Patrick stared at him, blinking. "I'm sorry?"

"I said stick around. We're just getting started."

"I'm sorry, sir, but I really have to leave."

"I don't think so. Sit down."

Patrick frowned down at the priest. Father Carbone grinned in mock politeness. Patrick laughed, nodding. "Okay, Father Carbone. Enough of this. Why don't you just tell me what your problem is?"

Father Carbone laughed, leaning back and linking his hands behind his head. "What is my problem, he asks. Hmmm. Let's see. What is my problem? Do you mean besides the fact that you turned my church into a fucking circus?"

Patrick was shocked by the profanity. "I had nothing to do with that."

"Oh! You had nothing to do with it. I suppose you just happened to be in the neighborhood that night."

"It's complicated," Patrick said.

"I have time."

"Well I don't. I'm leaving now, Father Carbone. Good bye." Patrick started for the door.

"I wouldn't do that if I were you, Patrick."

He stopped and looked back. "Oh? And why not?"

Father Carbone leaned forward, forming a steeple with his hands and resting his chin on it. "There are three federal agents on their way here now. They want to ask you some questions."

Patrick laughed. "The FBI? You're out of your mind. Goodbye, Father Carbone."

"Go then, Patrick. But I must warn you. This really is the easiest way. If you go to your apartment they will follow you there, and your neighbors will see them escort you out. If you go to the Christening party at your brother Ryan's house they will follow you, and your family will see them escort you out. I don't think your mother would take that well. Do you?"

Patrick's heart thudded. "You're lying. Why the hell would the FBI be interested in me?"

Three hard raps sounded at the door, making Patrick jump. He looked back at Father Carbone, wide-eyed. The priest smiled. "Well. Now you can ask them that question," he said.

The door opened and three men in dark suits walked into the little room. They looked like the kind of FBI agents Patrick had seen in movies, all but one who had long yellow hair to his shoulders. He looked like a professional wrestler, aside from the dark suit and sunglasses. He and another man with a square jaw and crew cut took up guard positions on either side of the door. Their expressions were placid.

The third man moved with a determined stride directly toward Patrick. He had an unmistakable air of authority, the leader. His short hair was so gray it was nearly white. Patrick would have thought him in his sixties until he removed his sunglasses. His face was smooth and unlined, his dark blue eyes wide and clear. He looked far too young to have hair that white, but the lack of warmth in his eyes made it seem appropriate, like his hair had iced over from the coldness within. "Patrick Obrien?" he said, his voice monotone.

Patrick nodded, feeling very small. "Uh-huh."

He held out a badge. "I'm Agent Steven Litner with the FBI. These are Agents Rourke and Ohare. We'd like to ask you some questions."

Patrick's legs threatened to buckle, and he moved over to the chair and sat. "May I see that identification please?" he asked.

The agent handed it to Patrick respectfully. Patrick glanced at it and handed it back. It could have come from a Cracker Jack box for all he knew.

"I haven't done anything wrong."

"No one is accusing you of anything, Mr. Obrien. I just want to ask you some questions."

Patrick glanced at the agents guarding the door. They could have been carved of stone for how still they were. He could see their gun holsters peeking out from under their jackets. Patrick took a deep breath. "What is this about, Agent Litner?"

Seating himself on a chair next to Father Carbone, the agent pulled a notebook from his jacket. "You might want to get comfortable, Mr. Obrien."

Patrick looked down and realized he was sitting literally on the edge of his seat. He moved back in the chair but relaxation was out of the question. Agent Litner did not beat around the bush, but began firing questions at

Patrick as if from a cannon. "Mr. Obrien, what is your association with Joseph Pierre Duvaine?"

"Joey and I went to college together," Patrick said. "We also until recently worked together at Parker Investments."

The agent nodded and scribbled on his pad. "Is that all?" he asked. Patrick was silent. Agent Litner looked up, his navy eyes probing but patient.

"What do you mean?" Patrick asked. "Is what all?"

"Is that the extent of your relationship with this individual?"

"No. Joey's also my friend."

Agent Litner nodded and continued to scribble. Father Carbone made a sound of disgust. Patrick glared over at him. "Does he really have to be here for this?" Patrick asked, pointing to the priest.

Agent Litner gave the priest a quick glance then went back to his scribbling. "Father Carbone is aiding us in this investigation, but he will control himself and remain silent during this inquiry. Won't you, Father Carbone?" The priest shrugged, then nodded.

"What exactly is this inquiry about, Agent Litner?" Patrick asked, although he was pretty sure he knew. Joey and Shep had probably been laundering donation money or something. If that was the case, then they had cooked their own goose. Patrick was not going down with them.

"Please just try and answer the questions, Mr. Obrien. How long have you known Joseph Duvaine?"

"Ten years."

"And during that time, have you ever heard him mention such topics as population control, the destruction of mankind, or acts of terrorism against the United States or any other country?"

Patrick blinked at him. "Say what?"

"Has he ever mentioned or fantasized about creating a national or global catastrophe? Any fascination with genocide?"

Patrick held his hands out in front of him and let out a stifled laugh. "Whoa. Hold on a minute there. Acts of terrorism? Genocide? Agent Litner, I'm afraid you must have gotten some misinformation. Joey is not a terrorist. He's a financial planner."

The priest made another sound of disgust and walked into an adjoining room. Patrick stared after him a moment, then looked across at Agent Litner. "What is this about, really, Agent Litner?"

Agent Litner studied him. "You're telling me that Joseph Duvaine never spoke of formulating biological weapons, or other methods of mass murder?"

Patrick shook his head, incredulous. This had to be a joke. Someone had really led these guys off the track. Patrick laughed, unable to help himself, and Litner's eyes narrowed in annoyance. "I'm sorry, Agent Litner," he said. "I mean no disrespect but you have the wrong guy. Joey Duvaine is a decent person. He's had some emotional problems lately since losing his family, but I assure you he is not dangerous. Joey wouldn't hurt a fly."

Father Carbone stepped quietly back into the room, and he and the agent exchanged a glance. Litner went back to his notebook and flipped a few pages, tapping his pen on the table as he did.

"What about Melvin Eugene Shepherd?" Agent Litner asked.

Patrick shrugged. "What about him?"

"Do you know this individual?"

"Yes, I know Shep. He's a friend."

"Just like Joseph Duvaine is a friend."

Patrick nodded. "Yes. That's right."

"Mr. Obrien, would you say that these two individuals are your good friends?"

Patrick shrugged. "Sure."

"Would you qualify them as your best friends?"

"I suppose."

"Why then do you choose to have no involvement in their newly established church group?"

"I didn't want to be involved in that. We have conflicting views."

Agent Litner almost smiled, but it was hard to tell. His facial expressions didn't change much. "Now we're getting somewhere," he said. "These conflicting views that you have, what do they involve?"

Patrick shrugged. "Just the whole idea. I think it's ridiculous."

Litner slid forward in his chair. "What are they planning, Mr. Obrien? You must tell us. No matter what it is."

Patrick frowned. "What are you talking about? They're not *planning* anything. They're the least organized people I know. The biggest plan I've ever seen them make is deciding what time to meet at the bar for happy hour. Half the time they can't even get that right."

Agent Litner looked at him like he was daft. "Mr. Obrien, I think we have a misunderstanding here. For what reason did your friends orchestrate a hoax that might put Joseph Duvaine into a position of prominence within the religious community?"

Patrick shook his head and placed his hands on his temples. "Wait a minute. You knew it was a hoax?"

"Of course we knew it was a hoax."

"Then what is this investigation about?"

Agent Litner began tapping his pen on his temple furiously. He looked about to pop a vein. "Mr. Obrien. We don't care that they created the damn hoax. We merely want to know the reasoning behind it."

Patrick snickered. "Come on. You're the FBI. You can't figure it out? It was a money scam! Donations. Tax free dollars! Surely you looked into all of this. Joey was about to lose his father's beach house. He had a lot of debt to pay off. Are you guys for real? Because so far I'm not impressed."

Father Carbone cocked his head to one side, studying Patrick. "My God, son. Either you are one cool cucumber, or you really don't know jack shit."

Patrick turned to Agent Litner, who wore the same expression as the priest, eyeing Patrick like he was some sort of enigma. "What?" Patrick said. "What is it exactly that I'm supposed to know?"

Agent Litner frowned at him, twirling his pen like a baton. "Mr. Obrien, how well do you know your friends?"

Patrick thought about it. "Well, I'd have to say that I know them as well as one person can know another person. They've been like brothers to me for years. I know everything about them. Why?"

Agent Litner looked him in the eye. "May I call you Patrick?"

"Please do."

"Patrick, listen to me. Charles Duvaine was not having any financial problems, and your friend Joey was never in any danger of losing that beach house. The mortgage on the Forest Bluffs house was paid off, as were all the taxes for the next year. Charles Duvaine had millions in the bank and Joey received an enormous inheritance along with a life insurance policy when Charles died. Joey Duvaine is a rich young man. He is keeping up the taxes and other expenses on that beach house and he hasn't accepted a dime from so called church donations, or any other outside sources. We've had him under surveillance for some time now."

Patrick felt faint. "What are you saying?"

"I'm saying that whatever reason your friends had for starting a church group, it wasn't for money."

Patrick shook his head. "No, you're wrong," he said. "That doesn't make sense. Of course it was for money. Shep said so himself. Why else would they do something like this?"

Litner raised his eyebrows. "That, Mr. Obrien, is the question I've been trying to ask you."

Patrick looked at Agent Litner, then at Father Carbone. "If it wasn't for the money, then I don't know why they did it. Unless…"

"Unless what?" Agent Litner asked.

"Well, Shep has been known to pull scams just to see if he could."

Litner scowled. "That is irrational."

"Yeah, well you'd have to know Shep. He's not the most rational person I've ever met. But whatever the reason, I can assure you that there is no conspiracy, Agent Litner. I'm sorry to disappoint you but my friends are not terrorists. They're too stupid."

Again, Litner and the priest exchanged one of those knowing glances. The FBI agent looked back at Patrick. "Did you just call Joey Duvaine stupid?" he asked.

Patrick shrugged. "I did. Why?"

"Patrick, I have to ask you again. How well do you know your friends?"

"I told you, they're like brothers to me!"

"Why then did you break off all contact with them? Why have you cut all ties with the two people that you deem to be 'close as brothers'?"

Patrick threw his hands up, exasperated. "I told you! Because of what they did!"

"What did they do?" Litner asked.

Now it was Patrick's turn to look confused. "The apparition! The phony miracle of course!"

Agent Litner studied him now, like he was trying to decide his next move in a challenging chess game. He thwacked the pen on the side of his temple repeatedly. Patrick wondered if the self abuse with the pen was a nervous tick, a concentration tool, or an offshoot of some deeply submersed mental disorder. Either way, it was unnerving. "Are you telling me Patrick, that the only reason you ended a ten year friendship is because they staged this phony apparition?"

Patrick nodded. "Yes."

Litner shook his head. "There must be more to it than that. If they're planning something, however horrible, you have to tell us."

"I already told you. I ended the friendship because of the apparition."

Father Carbone sat next to him now. "Patrick, why would this offend you so much that you would disconnect yourself from them so completely?"

"Because it's wrong. What they did is wrong."

"It's *wrong*?" Agent Litner said, sneering.

Patrick nodded. "That's right. You know, fooling people like that. Pretending to be something they're not. Shit. Joey doesn't even believe in God."

"So you broke from your friends due to some sort of virtue?" Litner asked.

Patrick shrugged. "Yes. Is that a crime?"

Agent Litner flipped through his little notebook. Patrick fell back into his chair, sighing. He felt like he was suffocating, the little walls of the priest's house closing in on him. "Just a few more questions, Mr. Obrien. Where is Melvin Eugene Shepherd from?"

"Shep is from Texas. Why do you ask?"

"Because he doesn't exist."

"What? Of course he exists. His father was abusive, so Shep was put into foster homes when he was little. He got shuffled around a lot."

"Yes, I have heard the sad tale," Litner said with a heavy note of sarcasm. "But the fact remains that all records verifying his existence stop showing up when traced back more than thirteen years, just before he moved in with the Duvaine family. Even the social worker that placed him with the Duvaine's can't be traced. It's like your friend Shep just popped up out of thin air."

Patrick shook his head. "That's impossible. I know Shep. He talks about his past. Have you checked court documents? Social security numbers and such?"

Agent Litner gave him a look. "Thank you for that valuable advice, Mr. Obrien, but I work for the Federal Bureau of Investigation. I know how to trace a name."

"Oh, right. Sorry."

Litner continued. "Regarding Mr. Shepherd. Has he ever expressed any interest in genocide, production of biological weapons, acts of terrorism against—"

"No!" Patrick said, cutting him off. "For the last time Agent Litner, I am telling you that you have the wrong guys."

"How can you be so sure?"

"Because they're my best friends!" Patrick felt hot tears streaming down his cheeks. He dropped his head and wiped his eyes, feeling foolish and out of control. "I've been under a lot of pressure lately," he said softly. "I've just been under a lot of pressure."

Agent Litner sighed. "I do not enjoy having to upset you. You say that your friends are not criminals. I hope you're right. I want you to be right. In fact, I'm going to give you the opportunity to prove you're right."

Patrick didn't like the sound of that. He looked up at the white-haired agent. "What do you mean?"

"Your friends have started growing a field of crops on Joey's property in Forest Bluffs. Do you know what they plan to use this crop for?"

"How the hell should I know?"

Litner was unfazed by the nasty retort. "You received a phone call from Joey Duvaine the night of his television interview. It seems that your friends would like very much for you to join them."

"You've tapped my phone?"

"We need a sample of that crop, Mr. Obrien. Judging from your friends' desire to have you with them, I'd say you could easily obtain that sample for us."

Patrick's jaw dropped. "You want me to go to Forest Bluffs? Spy on my friends? Steal crops? Why can't you do it yourselves?"

Agent Litner's blue eyes dropped. "We tried to infiltrate the group when they were recruiting members. Mr. Shepherd figured out that our decoy was an agent."

Patrick laughed. "You shouldn't underestimate Shep."

"Yes, we are beginning to realize that. The fact remains that the Duvaine residence is private property. We need probable cause. Now will you help us, or not?"

Patrick glanced at the statuesque agents guarding the door. His eyes found their gun holsters and he looked back at Agent Litner. "I don't want Joey and Shep to get hurt," he said. "I don't care what they've done. I don't want them hurt."

"They will not be harmed, Mr. Obrien. If this crop proves questionable then we will make inquiries according to the law. You've been watching too many movies. We are not the bad guys."

"Yeah, that's not what I hear. Are you responsible for those curly-haired freaks following me around? Because they're starting to piss me off."

Agent Litner frowned. "We are not having you followed, Patrick. We've been keeping surveillance of your home, nothing more."

"Yeah. I wonder."

"You seem to believe in your friends' integrity, Patrick. You have a chance to prove me wrong here. Please, Patrick. Prove me wrong."

Litner stared blankly at Patrick. The room grew very still. "Can I think about it?" Patrick asked finally.

"You have forty-eight hours."

"Two days. I'll give you my answer. May I go now? It smells like feet in here."

Agent Litner glanced at the agents by the door. He made a quick gesture with his hand and they stepped aside, allowing Patrick to pass. "We'll be in touch, Mr. Obrien," Litner called after him.

"I'm sure you will," Patrick said.

He was about to step out the door when Father Carbone called after him. "Patrick, wait. Can I ask you just one question before you leave?"

Patrick turned back. "What is it, Father?"

The priest was thumbing through a worn-looking book. He stopped at one of the pages and frowned at it. "You never did any sort of blood ceremony with your friends, did you?"

Patrick felt the breath leave his body. He fingered the little scar above his wrist. Father Carbone looked up at him expectantly. "A what?" Patrick asked, his voice barely above a whisper.

"A blood ceremony," the priest said. "Mixing your blood with theirs? A ritual of some sort?" Patrick stared at the priest, unable to speak. Father Carbone interpreted his shocked silence as anger. "I'm sorry, Patrick. Of course you didn't. Never mind, then. Go on home."

Chapter Fifteen

Kelinda pushed open the heavy wooden door and hesitated, waiting for the lightning bolt to come down from above and cremate her. When it did not, she moved inside and let the door swing shut behind her. She could see the statue of the Virgin up by the altar and turned away, avoiding its eyes.

Patrick's words repeated in her mind. She had gone against her beliefs, lied to her best friend, and risked her reputation. But for what? That answer was easy. Because Joey Duvaine had asked her to. What else would she have agreed to that night Joey came to her house, hypnotizing her with those blue eyes, asking her to grant an old friend a favor? Conspiracy? Murder perhaps?

Joey had no idea of the influence he had on her. This was no accident. She'd observed him closely over the years. Women who mooned over him too much were immediately discarded. Joey needed to feel like you didn't want anything from him, or he'd run. He always behaved as if he was already spoken for somehow. So Kelinda had played the game, never lingering her gaze on him too long, never flirting. And now Joey was comfortable around her. Yet he was no more interested in her than he'd ever been. After they'd completed the filming at Shep's house he'd slung an arm platonically over her shoulders and told her that she was a good friend. A good friend.

She knew the obsession was childish, and she'd tried to deal with it as such. She'd even moved out of state for two years, thinking that would get him out of her system. But she'd wanted Joey for too long. She'd wanted him while she was still too young to know what that wanting meant. She was poisoned with him. And as with any addiction, the only cure was abstinence. Or perhaps substitution?

Patrick was the first man who'd sparked her interest in years, made her turn her head away from her unrequited obsession. So she had found a nice Irish Catholic boy that her parents would love, and she was actually attracted to him. She only hoped now that the Joey fixation wouldn't screw it up.

She had a grip on the truth now, and the truth was that Joey had used her. He'd used her as a prop to raise him up on a golden cloud of recognition and fame. And he'd left her in the dust without so much as a word since. Without ever considering that she carried the keys to his destruction. Had he forgotten how easily she could thwart his plan? With a single phone call to the press she could pop Joey Duvaine's heavenly bubble and watch laughing as he dropped painfully to the ground. But first...confession.

She walked toward the back of the church, determined to emotionally purge herself of Joey once and for all by confessing to God what she had done. Each step she took required determined force. She'd promised Joey she'd say nothing to anyone about the hoax. She'd given her word. Did confessing to a priest count as squealing? To hell with Joey, she thought, and stepped behind the curtain. "Bless me father for I have sinned."

"Kelinda?" a smooth deep voice behind the curtain said. It was a voice she knew. Damn it. Father Bello was a friend of the family. He played golf with her father. She was hoping to get Father McShawn, who didn't know her personally. Under normal circumstances she would have been thrilled to hear Father Bello's voice behind that curtain. He was a chipper old priest with a trusting smile and a white Santa Claus beard. But she didn't want to speak to a friend today. She wanted to speak to a stranger, a tranquil, faceless voice from behind a dark curtain.

"I thought Father McShawn was taking confessions today," she said.

"Father McShawn is down with the flu. Do you have a problem giving your confession to me, my child?"

"No, Father."

"Good. What is it that weighs so heavy on your soul?"

"I have blasphemed, Father."

"Have you taken the Lord's name in vain?" the voice asked. She nearly laughed. Taken the Lord's name in vain? Oh, if that were all she had done. No taking the Lord's name here. That sort of blasphemy is for sissies. Now holography....that's different.

"No, Father. I have not."

"Kelinda, how have you blasphemed?"

"It was the Blessed Virgin," she said.

"So you have taken Mary's name in vain then?"

"No Father. I have not."

"Help me to understand, then. How is it that you have blasphemed the Blessed Virgin?"

She was beginning to sweat, hearing Joey's words in her mind now. *I must first have your promise that you'll never speak about this project. I need you to swear on it, Kelinda.* The walls of the tiny cubical seemed to close in around her. She wanted to tell Father Bello everything. It would feel wonderful to let it all pour forth from her, the whole sordid tale. But her throat was constricting. "Father Bello, why don't you just give me the worst penance you have."

"Why Kelinda! I cannot give you penance if I do not know what it is you have done. You must confess your sins to God. These are God's laws. I cannot bend them at will."

"I know, Father. I'm sorry." She tried to say the words. *I was the miracle apparition on Saint Mary's church.* But the words would not pass through her lips. Instead, she said, "What's the worst sin you've ever heard, Father Bello?"

"I suppose murder."

"What sort of penance would you give for that?"

"My child! Have you committed murder?"

"No! Of course not."

She heard Father Bello sigh. He was losing patience with her and the walls of the cubicle were shrinking. "Kelinda, whatever is this great sin, you must give it to God. You must let Him be your judge. To hold onto this sin, is to destroy your spirit."

Her breathing had become shallow and she felt about to pass out. A bead of sweat trickled down the back of her dress. "I'm sorry, Father. I can't."

She ran out of the back door of the church, sandals slapping on the stone path. She was about to turn up the driveway toward the street when she bumped head first into someone and nearly fell over. The stranger grasped her arm to steady her.

"I'm sorry," she said. "I wasn't watching where..." The words caught in her throat as she looked into the large green eyes of the man she'd run into. It was the dark-haired stranger she'd seen at the Chinese restaurant, the one Patrick claimed had been following him. She gasped. He smiled at her, still holding her elbow. He looked different now, clean and well-dressed in a pair of tan pants with a crisp white tee shirt. He was not wearing any shoes. His black hair was neat and shiny, falling in ringlets to his chin. His skin was slightly sunburned. The reddish-brown tint fell across his nose and cheekbones, exactly the way Shep tanned in the summer. And she realized now that he was attractive in that same odd way Shep was attractive. The resemblance was startling. Robin had always said Shep had no family. But still...those eyes. They could have been plucked right out of Shep's head save for the black lashes that framed them.

Kelinda took a step back and pulled her arm away. "Who are you? What are you doing here?"

"Did you confess your sins to God, Kelinda?" the stranger asked.

She went cold. "How do you know my name?"

"The chosen one would like to speak with you, Kelinda." The stranger spoke with a strange accent, like each word was an effort.

Kelinda made a face at him. "The chosen one? Who is the chosen one?"

"Joey Duvaine is the chosen one."

Kelinda flinched. She remembered Patrick's words at the restaurant. *How do you know they're following me? They could be following you.* "How do you know Joey Duvaine?" she demanded.

The stranger gave her a quizzical look. "Joey Duvaine is the chosen one," he said, as if this should explain everything.

Kelinda uttered a short laugh and stepped backward. "Well you tell him I said hello, but this is not a good time. I've got to go now."

She turned and sprinted off through the side yard, determined to get away from the stranger as quickly as possible. She thought she was moving pretty fast until he caught her arm, whirling her about. She glared at him. "What the hell do you think you're doing? Let go of me, you freak!"

The stranger frowned, looking slightly hurt. "I told you before. The chosen one wishes to speak with you. You must come with me."

"I am going nowhere with you. I don't even know you!"

"But you must. I have orders."

Kelinda laughed. "You have orders? What does that mean?"

The stranger shrugged. "It means that I have no choice. And neither do you."

Chapter Sixteen

Kelinda sat in silence as Allisto pulled the white van through the front gates and down the long, shrub-lined driveway. She was saving her anger for Joey. To release it on this stranger beside her would be a waste of rage. Of course she was afraid to speak to the stranger now, after what she'd seen him do.

When he initially took hold of her in back of the church, she'd jammed her heel into his kneecap and sprinted toward the street. He'd cried out in pain, but amazingly he caught up with her again as she neared the side of the road. This time he gripped her arm and wouldn't let go.

She'd thought about screaming for help, but before she could execute that plan he'd clapped a hand over her mouth and dragged her back behind the neighboring post office. The windows of the building were dark, the business closed for the evening.

"Please do not fight me," he'd said. "I do not wish to hurt you."

She'd looked into his wide green eyes. He seemed distraught, even a little frightened which was odd since he was the one attacking her. "If you don't want to hurt me then let go of my arm!" she'd said, tugging her elbow back.

The stranger held firm. Her feet shuffled and kicked as he dragged her toward a white van. "I told you, I have orders!" he said, sounding frustrated as he struggled with her. "If you'd just stop fighting..."

It was then that Kelinda whirled about and kneed him in the crotch with every ounce of strength she could muster. She saw his green eyes widen and his jaw drop as he grunted in agony. She'd expected his grip on her arm to loosen, but he held firm as she tried to twist away. Still holding her elbow, he doubled over, taking deep breaths. When he was able to straighten up again his eyes gleamed with rage, and she felt real fear for the first time.

The stranger extended his arm outward, pushing Kelinda as far away from his body as he could without letting her go. She stumbled with the action, which was like a poorly executed dance move. Once he'd forced her away from him, he turned his eyes toward a nearby mailbox. Sucking in a deep breath, the stranger let out a shriek that was like the death cry of some giant bird. With her free hand, she covered her right ear.

The mailbox shattered. Scraps of blue metal propelled through the air. Shredded streamers of white paper fluttered like confetti all around them. Shielding her head with her free arm, Kelinda stared in disbelief at what was left of the mailbox. What hadn't shattered into the air appeared to be melting, bending like wax as it collapsed into itself. A flat slate of blue metal teeter-tottered over and landed with a metallic clang at her feet.

He'd turned to her then, looking embarrassed as tiny shreds of paper mail fell onto his black curls like snowflakes. "Please, Kelinda," he said. "Please do not make me angry again. I am having trouble...controlling myself. I need more practice. Do you understand?" Kelinda had nodded, though she did not understand, not at all. Regardless, she'd gone peaceably with the stranger after that. "My name is Allisto," he'd said cheerily when they got into the van, as if they were going to be old friends now.

⁓⁓

The Forest Bluffs house loomed before them like a polished mountain as they glided down the driveway. She thought the acre of manicured lawn in the front was impressive until they pulled up alongside the garage and she caught sight of the rolling green fields out back. She spotted a barrage of figures moving around out there, tending to some sort of crop.

Allisto led her into the house through an entrance inside the garage, and she found herself walking through the biggest kitchen she'd ever seen. It had a high ceiling and a large tile island in the center. A set of glass sliding doors revealed a giant, wraparound deck. The deck looked out onto the back yard, which extended on to a sprawl of woods on one side, and a stretch of fields on the other. Another smaller house sat midway out alongside the rows of wheat, or whatever it was. Despite her fear and agitation, Kelinda couldn't help but be impressed with the property. Joey's parents certainly hadn't been lacking in cash.

"This is the kitchen," Allisto said, as if it was no big deal. "If you will follow me please if I could take you up steps, I am to bring you to the chosen one please."

Kelinda frowned at the back of Allisto's head as she followed him up a spiral staircase. He formed his sentences with great effort, and he walked like he was being held up by strings. Strange duck, whoever he was. Or whatever he was, she thought, remembering the exploding mailbox trick. She'd ordered her rational mind to believe a letter bomb had destroyed that mailbox, but part of her knew that was bull. She supposed she should be grateful that it was the mailbox that got it and not her, as she had been the true target of his anger.

On the second floor they came to a closed door. Allisto knocked once and opened the door, gesturing for her to step inside. "Wait in here please. He will be with you short."

Kelinda turned into the room. It looked like a hotel suite, with a stylish sitting area, a vanity table and another small table with a set of chairs. The smaller table was all decked out with candles, cloth napkins and silverware. A bottle of wine sat in the center with two wine glasses. Across the room under a large glass window was a king-sized bed with a canopy and a sheer flowing curtain draped over the sides. It looked like something a medieval queen would sleep on.

"This is my room," a voice behind her said. She whirled about and sucked her breath in when she saw Joey standing in the doorway. She'd forgotten how painfully stunning he was, and she forgave herself for being such a weakling all these years. "I thought we could talk in here if you don't mind. This is the only place I can get any privacy," he said.

He stepped inside and closed the door. She stared at him, unable to move. Her original plan was to promptly clock him in the face as soon as he presented, but as he moved toward her in a shifting of blue jeans and tanned flesh, she found that the fight had gone out of her. He was literally glowing. His skin, his eyes, his teeth, all gleamed as if lit from some inner candle. His hair had grown an inch or so since she'd seen him last, and it fell soft and sleek, curling in just above his chin.

Something was very different and it wasn't just the hair. She could feel his energy from across the room, his chemistry mingling with her own like electric fingers caressing her soul. She could almost taste him. Ashamed at her weakness, she struggled to cling to the anger that had fueled her on the ride over. "Well well well," she said. "If it isn't the chosen one. I'm looking forward to hearing your excuse for sending that freak of nature to manhandle me."

Joey stopped, eyeing her thoughtfully, then he moved over to the little table and sat down. "I needed to speak with you," he said.

"Ever hear of a telephone?"

"Why don't you have a seat?" he said, pushing the other chair out from the table with his foot.

"Why don't you kiss my ass," she said.

She allowed her anger to reign freely now, as it was the only thing combating the lust that threatened to melt her into a puddle of swoon. Joey stood then and walked toward her, frowning. He stopped just before reaching her. "You're upset," he said.

"What gave you that idea?"

He took another step forward and she instinctively stepped back. She could smell his spicy scent and it was making her dizzy. He reached out and stroked a strand of her hair. "I'm really sorry about bringing you here against your will. Shep was afraid that if I made direct contact with you, someone might see us and figure out that you were the apparition of the Virgin. I wanted to contact you sooner, I swear, but I couldn't take the chance. I've been having you followed, and I'm sorry. I just had to know you were all right."

Joey made his face look pained, like he was about to cry. She remembered that face from his television interview. He'd used it to express remorse over losing Patrick's friendship. This display was just as calculated.

"Don't you mean that you wanted to make sure I wouldn't spill the beans about your phony miracle? Isn't that why you had me followed, Joey? Isn't that why you're having Patrick followed too?"

Joey shook his head. "No. No, you're wrong. It was only because I care for you." He closed the gap between them and took her hand in his. "You believe me, don't you?" he asked, staring into her eyes. His thumb caressed the palm of her hand.

The closest Joey had ever come to touching her was a brotherly pat on the back, or a high five. Now he'd touched her twice in under a minute, intimately as though it was something he'd always done. She struggled to concentrate on the anger. "You care for me? Is that why you scared the shit out of me by having that freak abduct me? Is that why you've been torturing Patrick? Because you care so much for him? Give me a break, Joey. You wanted to make sure we didn't rat you out."

Joey dropped her hand and cocked his head. "Do you think Patrick will come looking for you? When he finds out you're here?" he asked. His tone was hopeful.

"What are you talking about?" she asked.

"Obrien," he said. "He's grown fond of you. He'd come out here if we had you, wouldn't he?"

She took a step backward. "*Had* me? You don't have me, Joey. You'll never have me. I'd like to get a cab home, please."

Joey crossed his arms in front of his chest. "Kelinda, listen to me for a minute." He took a step toward her and she automatically took a step backward. He noticed. He looked down at her feet, then slowly lifted his eyes to meet hers. In mockery, he took another slow step forward. She took a step back. "Why are you doing that?" he asked.

"Doing what?"

"Backing up every time I come near you?"

She didn't answer. He looked confidently amused as he took another step toward her. She held her ground, refusing to let him see her discomfort. He took a final step and she could feel his breath on her face. For years she'd dreamed of being this close to him, and while her body reacted with excitement, her mind told her to run for the door and keep running. "What kind of game are you playing, Joey?"

He smiled. "What do you mean?"

"That guy Allisto called you the chosen one. Are you starting to believe the crap people are saying about you? That you're a prophet? Let me refresh your memory, oh great one. The miracle was a fake. You are a fake, Joey."

"Messiahs are made, not born, Kelinda."

"I beg to differ."

"What did you say to Father Bello? That is the priest you confessed to, isn't it?"

"So that's what this is about. You're afraid I told the priest about you."

"Did you?"

"Of course not." She struggled to sound indifferent, but her heart raced in her chest, urging her to take flight. It was silly to feel threatened, she told herself. This was still Joey after all. It was Joey that she used to play kick ball and steal street signs with. It was Joey that used to eat worms. But she did feel threatened. What would Joey and Shep do if they thought she'd betrayed them?

"I believe you," Joey said after a long silence. "I believe you said nothing to the priest."

Relief washed through her, but she tried not to show it. "I don't care what you believe. I'm going home now."

"No you're not," he said.

She laughed, but a wave of panic coursed through her. "Excuse me?"

"You're not going home. You're going to stay here. With me. With us."

She started to respond when he gripped her around the waist and pulled her into him. When he pressed his mouth against hers she was overcome with a dizzying euphoria. Tiny specs of light danced across her closed eyelids. With the taste of his tongue came a drug-like rush. He disengaged, and she felt like he was ripping her soul out by breaking the contact. She looked into his pale blue eyes, felt his breath tickle her lips, and her legs started to give out. "I feel funny," she said.

"I know," he said. "Don't worry. You get used to it." He kissed her again, catching her under her rear before she fell.

Chapter Seventeen

The priest's words repeated in Patrick's mind like a taunting mantra. *You never did a blood ceremony, did you?* He examined the fading scar above his wrist. *A ritual of some sort?* It meant nothing. The priest was crazy. The FBI agent was crazy. Joey and Shep were crazy. But he knew everyone could not be crazy. Something was going on and it was high time to stop ducking his head in the sand and figure it out.

He was certain that his friends were not anti-government terrorists. Joey and Shep didn't care about the government enough to terrorize it. And he refused to entertain the idea that they meant to harm anyone. He had to admit that doing Agent Litner's bidding would one way or another give closure to the situation. He wanted to prove Agent Litner wrong, but that was just the persuasion tactic that the agent was using, and Patrick hated to be manipulated. He was trapped.

He'd wanted to discuss the situation with Kelinda but she hadn't returned his calls in days. At first he'd thought she was trying to ditch him, but ignoring his calls just wasn't her style. He was reasonably sure that if Kelinda wanted him to take a hike, she would promptly tell him to do so. Now her phone had been disconnected and he was starting to get worried.

He finally decided to call Robin. He wasn't looking forward to the call. He and Robin Duvaine had butted heads since the day they'd met, but at the moment he had nowhere else to turn. Robin answered after three rings. "Hello?"

"Robin, hi. It's Patrick."

"Who?"

"Patrick. Patrick Obrien. Christ, am I that forgettable?"

"Oh. Hi, Obrien. What's up?" Her usual spitfire tone was missing. She sounded forlorn and defeated.

"Robin, this is going to sound odd, but have you seen Kelinda? I've been trying to get in touch with her for days, and now her phone's been disconnected. Frankly, I'm a little concerned." There was silence on the other end of the line. "Robin, are you still there?"

He heard her sigh. "Yeah. Oh man, I'm sorry Obrien. She didn't tell you, did she? Unbelievable."

"She didn't tell me what? Is she in some kind of trouble?"

"No, she's not in trouble. She moved out to Forest Bluffs. She's living there now. She's part of Joey's church."

Patrick felt like he'd been punched in the testicles. His mind swam, trying to make sense of the words. "She, um, she what? Is she...is she okay?" He was struggling to keep his cool but he knew Robin could hear his voice shaking.

"She's okay I guess. I really wouldn't know, though. They don't let me talk to her when I call."

"Oh. I see. Well, um, are you okay Robin? You don't sound like yourself."

She sighed. "I don't know, Obrien. Shep's been a real prick since this miracle thing. He's finally agreed to let me visit this weekend. I'm supposed to go out there tomorrow and stay over, but he's kicking me out the next morning. He says he has work to do. Can you believe that? Work to do. The guy hasn't had a job since I've known him. But I'm going. I want to see what's going on out there and why they won't let me talk to Kelinda. When I call, they always tell me she's at the store or in the shower or something. If it's any consolation, Obrien, she didn't tell me she was going either. I had to find out from her parents that she'd moved to Forest Bluffs. The idiots think it's a real church. Can you imagine?"

Patrick felt nauseous and lowered himself into a kitchen chair. Why would Kelinda move to Forest Bluffs? She of all people knew what a scam it was. Hell, she *was* the scam.

"Robin, can I ask you something?"

"Sure, but if you want me to tell you why she did this, I don't have the answer. I think she's a fool to leave you."

The compliment warmed him. Robin had never spoken kindly to him before. Perhaps he'd never given her the chance. "No, it's not that, but thanks, I was wondering if Shep ever talked to you about his past. His childhood."

"Of course. I know all about the abuse, the branding with the horseshoe, foster homes and all that."

Patrick wasn't sure what he was trying to say. The thoughts formulated in his mind as he spoke them. "Is that all he ever told you? I mean, is that the only story?"

"Well, yeah. Why, isn't that enough?"

"I guess. I just think it's strange that we all heard the exact same story, probably word for word. But he never mentioned anything else about his past. I mean, he must have other memories."

"Oh, Jesus, Obrien. You're starting to sound like my Aunt Betsy."

The comment took him by surprise, and he remembered the dirty look Betsy had given Shep after Charles's funeral. "Robin, why doesn't Betsy like Shep?"

"Well, Aunt Betsy has been suspicious of Shep since he and Joey were in high school. She and Uncle Charles got in a big fight over Shep years ago. They didn't speak for months. You never heard about that?"

"No, but it seems there are many things I've never heard about."

"Yeah, well, don't give it too much thought. I love Aunt Betsy, but she's a kook. Trust me, Obrien. Shep is not that complicated."

That's what I used to think. "Hey, Robin? Will you give me a call when you get back from Forest Bluffs? I just want to know if Kelinda is okay."

"Sure, I'll call you."

"Do you promise?"

"If I say I'll call then I'll fucking call!"

Patrick grinned, finding the familiar crassness comforting. "Okay, Robin. Take care."

He was not reassured by Robin's assessment of Shep. Shep was a lot of things, but uncomplicated was not one of them. He hated to admit that the

FBI had prompted suspicions about his friend. They'd said Shep didn't exist on paper. He supposed the FBI might fabricate something like that in order to achieve their goals, namely getting Patrick to go undercover for them. But he had his own suspicions about Shep now, and they had nothing to do with the FBI. His desire for answers was beginning to outweigh his desire to distance himself.

They had Kelinda. And for some reason they wanted him too. But for what? Where did he fit in? He made a snap decision. He was going to pay Aunt Betsy a visit. It was time to get some answers, and Betsy was as good a place as any to start.

The front windows of Betsy's house glowed with the dampened amber of candlelight. The house seemed oddly still without funeral guests milling about. As Patrick was getting out of his car, an attractive blond man stepped out of the side door and started down the steps. Betsy came out onto the porch behind him. "Goodbye Seth!" she called out. "I'll see you next time."

The young man waved and skipped toward his car. Patrick startled him, and he jumped. "Oh, hello," he said. "Are you here for Betsy?"

"Well yes, I—"

"Oh, man. You won't regret it!" he said. "She was right on the spot for me. Have fun."

The man moved toward his car, whistling. Patrick stared after him with a befuddled frown. "Hey, tough guy!" Betsy called down to him. "To what do I owe this honor?"

Patrick smiled and walked to the door where Betsy caught him in a bear hug. Her crew cut had grown in a bit, and she now had an inch and a half of yellow hair that stuck straight up. "I'm not interrupting anything, am I?"

"No, not at all. I just finished up with a customer."

Patrick raised his eyebrows. "A customer?"

"Yes. I'm doing psychic readings now. It's going really well."

Patrick nodded. "Oh. That kind of customer."

Betsy opened the door and led him inside. "Well what did you think? That I'd become a hooker?"

Patrick laughed. "No, of course not."

"Liar. I should send you away right now, but I'm just too damned nice." She led him into her familiar living room where candles burned on every shelf and end table. "Let me turn some lights on," she said. She blew out the candles, flicked on a lamp and curled up on a chair next to the couch where Patrick had seated himself. She wore a long burgundy velvet dress with black beads across the bodice and matching black beaded slippers. Her face was pretty and delicate, similar to Robin's. She'd probably be considered very attractive if she'd grow some damned hair.

"Nice outfit," Patrick said, smirking.

She laughed. "Yeah, well, I have to look the part, you know. If you come out looking like a housewife the customers don't take you seriously, no matter how gifted you are. It's the same with the candles and incense. They don't really do anything except help the customer relax. I love my work. I get paid to be a freak." Patrick laughed and Betsy laughed with him. Still grinning, she asked "Why are you here, Patrick?"

"I need to talk to you about Shep."

Her smile dropped. "Oh, shit," she said. "I was hoping you were having girl trouble or something. Shit. I'd better get some brandy."

Patrick looked on, confused as she darted off into the kitchen and disappeared. She returned with a bottle of brandy and two snifters, placing the items on the small table between them. She filled the glasses halfway and handed one to Patrick. Tossing hers back, she immediately poured herself another. "Wow," Patrick said. "I've never seen you drink before, Betsy."

She took a swallow and breathed a long sigh. "Yes, well, you've never asked me about Shep before."

Patrick was silent for a moment, watching her. She had grown instantly agitated. "I'm sorry, Betsy. I didn't realize this would upset you. I've heard that you're not too fond of Shep. I'd like to know why. Will you tell me?"

She pointed at him. "Before I say anything, I need to know why you're asking. It's not that I don't trust you. You're honest, I can see that in your aura." Patrick glanced around himself, half-expecting to see a colorful hue emanating from his body. Betsy continued. "You see, the last time I spoke up about Shep, it nearly started a family feud. Joey and Robin are all I have left now. Oh, beside my sister, but she's a pain in the ass."

Patrick moved closer, looking directly into her eyes. "Betsy, I swear that whatever we say here tonight stays between us. But I'm confused. How did speaking about Shep cause a family feud?"

Betsy poured herself a brandy, avoiding his eyes. "Are you sure you want to open up this can of worms, honey?"

He nodded. "Yes. I need some insight into Shep's past. It's important, Betsy."

Betsy gazed into the distance, as if seeing something long forgotten. "The last time I spoke up, nobody believed me. Damned fools, God rest their souls. They defended him as if he was their own son. Well, they're not around to defend him anymore, now are they? Cheers."

She tossed back another shot while Patrick watched in amazement. She couldn't weigh more than a hundred pounds.

"Betsy, why don't you ease up on the brandy and tell me the whole story."

She turned to him. "You first, tough guy. I'd like to know why after all these years you've come to question the authenticity of your dear friend, Shepherd." She said the name with venom.

❧❧

Patrick started talking, and the tale spilled from him like water through a broken dam. He let fly a stream of babble without pause, telling her about the incident with Joey at Monty's, the phony miracle, losing his job, and finally losing Kelinda. He left out the part about the FBI and the odd Shep-alikes he'd seen following him around the city. Betsy didn't interrupt. She nodded, or frowned, or shook her head while he talked. When he described the blood pact, her face went chalk white.

"So that's about it," he said. "That's everything that's happened until I showed up here tonight, barring a few minor details."

Betsy patted his hand. "Oh, believe me, honey. That's enough." She turned away, shaking her head. "I knew that little shit would ruin Joey eventually. He's dangerous, Patrick. But it's too late for Joey now. It's too late. I can feel it in my bones."

"Please, Betsy. You've got to tell me something, anything. I feel like I'm losing my mind here."

Betsy studied him for a moment. "Okay Patrick. I'll tell you my story.

Under one condition. You let me do a psychic reading on you."

Patrick leaned back and crossed his arms, cocking an eyebrow. "A reading? Oh, I don't know, Betsy. I'm not really comfortable with that psychic stuff."

She grinned. "You don't believe in it. Do you?"

"Sure I do," he lied.

Betsy's smile widened. "Don't lie, Patrick. When you lie your aura gets little green spots."

Patrick laughed. "That's just the Irish in me. Those are leprechauns."

Betsy grew somber then and took his hand. "It's important that you believe in my ability before I tell you this story. Otherwise, you'll just think I'm a kook, like everyone else does."

"I don't think you're a kook, Betsy."

"Then let me do the reading."

Something went "CLANK" outside and Betsy jumped. "What was that?" she asked, wide-eyed. Patrick went to the window and looked out, but saw nothing. He went out the front door and stepped onto the lawn, scanning the darkness. The air was fragrant with spring smells, including that of a very powerful skunk. He went back inside and bolted the door.

"I think it was a skunk. Are you okay?"

"I'm fine," she said, but she looked a little jumpy. "So, what about the reading?"

Patrick wasn't comfortable with Betsy giving him a psychic reading, but she had always been so kind to him, he couldn't refuse her anything. "Will it hurt?" he asked, grinning. Betsy looked pleased that he'd agreed, and went and fetched a candle. She brought it over to the little table next to the couch. She lit the candle and softened the lights in the room.

"Come back and sit down," she said.

"I thought you said the ambience was bullshit."

"It is, but you non-believers need all the help you can get. Now come sit down."

Patrick sat as Betsy lit several incense sticks. "I'm getting the full treatment, huh?" He felt the need to make nervous chatter. Betsy smiled, but said nothing as she prepared the room.

Finally, she came back and sat across from him. She closed her eyes and took several deep breaths. "Give me your hand."

"What, no foreplay?" Patrick joked.

Betsy took his hand in hers. "I want you to think of a blank sheet of paper. Clear your mind."

Patrick tried to comply, but it wasn't easy. His mind had become fairly overcrowded as of late. He closed his eyes. The orange candlelight illuminated through his lids. He concentrated on that light, and the softness of Betsy's tiny hand on his. She brought her other hand over and squeezed his palm. "Your mother is a redhead too," she said.

Patrick opened his eyes a slit. "Yes," he said. He was surprised but far from amazed. It could have been a good guess.

"Her name is Brigid. She makes you tense."

Patrick opened his eyes and studied Betsy. She sat very still with her eyes squeezed tightly shut. Her tiny fingers dug into his palm. "You're afraid of boxes," she said, and he scowled at her.

"Boxes?" he asked.

She shook her head, her brows knit. "No. No that's wrong. Not boxes. Caskets. You're afraid of caskets. Coffins. Corpses."

"Isn't everyone?" Patrick snapped defensively.

"I'm just telling you what I see, Patrick."

"I know. I'm sorry."

Betsy's face smoothed and she breathed deeply. He watched as the smooth countenance tightened into a frown once more. She opened her eyes and looked at him. "Someone has been following you. Did you know that?"

Patrick nodded, feeling the hairs on his arms stand erect. Betsy closed her eyes again. "Yes. Yes, I definitely see a dark shadow behind you. It's a man. Are you aware of this person, Patrick?"

"Yes," he whispered.

"Could you picture his face for me? Picture him in your mind if you can."

Patrick imagined the dusty stranger he'd spotted so many times. He pictured him sitting with the blond look-alike at the Chinese restaurant. A shiver of fear passed through him. Betsy's eyelids fluttered. "Yes," she said. "Yes, I see. Two men, one dark, the other light. I see a train. The dark man, on the train. The train is green."

"Yes," Patrick said. "I saw him on the train. He was on the green line with me."

Had he known Betsy was legit, he would have fessed up about the strangers following him. He hoped she wouldn't be angry that he hadn't mentioned it. Betsy was gripping his hand too tightly and Patrick wanted her to stop. He wanted this over. It was starting to frighten him.

"I see the other one," she said, digging her nails into his flesh. "Blond hair. Blond curls. Lovely. Different. He's not like us. Not like us. He is...he is...he is..."

Betsy gasped and pulled her hand back, her eyes springing open. She shook her hand out as if she'd touched something hot.

"What? Betsy what is it?"

She shook her head, then got up and turned on the lamp. She stared at him, rubbing her arms. Patrick stood. "Damn it, Betsy! You said, 'he is'. He is what? What did you mean?"

"He is here," she said.

"What do you mean? Who is here?"

"The man with the blond hair. The one that's been following you. He's here."

Patrick shook his head. "That's impossible. I'm sure nobody followed me here. Are you sure?"

Betsy nodded. "It wasn't a random impression. It was too close. He's here, Patrick. I saw him in my mind, sitting out back in the shrubs next to the bulkhead."

He stared at her, telling himself he didn't believe her even as goosebumps broke out on the back of his neck. "You're sure about this, Betsy?"

She nodded adamantly, hugging herself. Patrick grabbed a cast iron poker from the fireplace set and made his way quietly out the side door. A sweat formed on his forehead, though the night was cool and breezy. He crept around the side of the house and headed toward the back yard. Skunk odor lingered in the air, mingling with the sweet scent of new blossoms. Treading softly, he moved in a half crouch until he rounded the back of the house.

As he came upon the bulkhead, he heard a vague crackling sound coming from the shrubs. He stopped and squatted low to the ground. There it was again, a crackle, then a tearing of paper followed by a crunching sound. It certainly sounded like an animal. There was something in the shrubs, but it was more likely a skunk than his mysterious follower. Afraid now that a skunk might spray him, he held his breath and proceeded silently. His heart pumped wildly in his chest, sounding in his ears loud enough to wake the neighbors. Paper crinkled. The skunk had most likely gotten into a bag of trash. He knew he had to take the last step around the corner to see with his own eyes. With the fireplace poker raised over his head, he rounded the corner and used his right foot to part the shrubs next to the bulkhead.

It was not a skunk. The blond man sat curled up with his knees pulled against his chest. He was surrounded by Hershey's candy bar wrappers, and his face was smeared with chocolate. He was so engrossed in gnawing on a half-eaten candy bar that he didn't notice Patrick. Until Patrick gasped.

The stranger's head whipped up. Seeing Patrick, his eyes widened and he uttered something in a foreign language. Patrick didn't understand the words, but he was pretty sure it was the equivalent of "Oh Shit".

The stranger shot up and dove over the shrub, achieving an impossible height before he hit the ground, rolled a summersault and broke into a sprint. Stunned, Patrick stood frozen, watching the stranger dart into the small patch of woods that separated Betsy's neighborhood from the one beyond. Betsy ran up beside him. "Who was that? It looked like Shep!"

"I know. But it wasn't Shep. Stay here, Betsy." Patrick took off after the stranger, struggling to match his speed, which was uncanny. He strained his eyes to keep sight of the halo of bouncing platinum curls as the stranger leapt through the trees like a deer. The gap between them widened, and Patrick had all but resigned that he wasn't going to catch him. Then the stranger tripped on a tree root. He rolled a couple of times, then got up and kept running. The stumble allowed Patrick to nearly close the gap between them. They ran; the stranger swift and agile, Patrick awkward and heavy footed. He was close enough to reach out and grab a handful of blond hair when Patrick tripped and went down. In a last desperate attempt, he swung the fireplace poker outward on his way to the ground. The little hook caught the other man around the ankle and they both hit the ground with a thud.

Patrick scrambled to his feet and stood over the man. The stranger rolled onto his back, holding his ribs and wincing. Patrick brought the iron poker down, holding it threateningly over the blond man's face. "Don't move asshole." It was a tad too Dirty Harry, but in a pinch it would do. The blond smiled up at him, but said nothing.

"What's the matter?" Patrick asked. "First day with your new feet?"

In strange broken English, he responded, "Actually, it has been a few months with my new feet." He turned onto this side, laughing heartily at his own comment until tears rolled down his cheeks. If it was a joke, Patrick didn't get it.

"Why are you following me?" he demanded.

The man looked up at him, grinning. "It seems that you are the one who was just following me. Yes?"

"Cut the crap wise ass. Are you working for the FBI?"

This sent the stranger laughing again, holding his stomach and rolling to one side. Patrick had a momentary chill as the cackle took on a trace of familiarity. It was damn close to Shep's laugh.

"What are you laughing at?" he asked.

The stranger looked up at him. "I laugh because I am so happy you ask me this question." Patrick couldn't decipher the accent. It was like a cross between an Austrian and a three-year old.

"What does that mean?" Patrick asked. "Why are you so happy I asked you that question?"

The blond man's smile dropped. "Because now I know that you know nothing." He was on his feet in a flash with Patrick's makeshift weapon in his hand. Patrick stared dumbfounded at his own empty hand, then at the fireplace poker the blond held. He'd never seen anyone move so fast. The stranger looked at Patrick with wide green eyes. Like Shep's, they were a bit too large for his face. He threw the poker into the woods, grabbed Patrick by the shoulders, and shoved him backwards, sending him hurling through the air. Patrick slammed back-first onto the ground, knocking the wind out of him.

For several seconds he couldn't move, and he was sure his enemy would come to finish him off. But when he was able to sit up, the stranger was gone. He glanced around and realized that he was nearly back to Betsy's lawn again. The wiry blond man had thrown him almost twenty yards.

When Betsy returned from checking the doors and windows, she had a glass of water and two pain-killers for Patrick. "Take these. You're going to be sore tomorrow after that fall you took."

Patrick lay on the couch, feeling like a giant bruise. "It wasn't a fall. I was thrown."

Betsy frowned at him. "Patrick, who was that man? What haven't you told me?"

So he told her about the sightings of the curly-haired strangers. He also told her about his visit with Father Carbone and the FBI, with all of their crazy suggestions and propositions. Betsy stared at him for several seconds "Jesus Christ, Patrick."

Patrick nodded. Betsy poured herself another brandy and studied him with pursed lips. "Maybe I ought to tell you my story," she said. "Then you can decide if you want to go out to Forest Bluffs and bunk down with your old buddy Shepherd."

Betsy talked, and Patrick listened, hoping that she was about to tell him Shep had banged up the family Volvo or some minor crime like that. No such luck. "As you know, at age fifteen Shep came to live with my brother Charlie and his wife Marie, Joey's parents. He started out as a foster child. Joey's mom had a big heart. Kids would come and kids would go, but this was different. It became apparent after a very short time that Shep would become a permanent part of the Duvaine family. Marie called him "a keeper". He and Joey were both freshmen in high school, and they hit it off from the get go. Joey's brother Jeffrey was still in grammar school, so it was nice that Joey had someone his own age to spend time with."

Betsy paused and sipped at her brandy glass. She held it up to the light, as if seeing the past in the golden liquid. "Everyone fell in love with Shep, with his upbeat personality and his crazy sense of humor. Everyone thought it was the best thing for Joey. I did too, at first."

"What changed your mind?" Patrick asked.

She smiled. "I loved Charlie. He was my big brother. I was out of work at the time, so Charlie hired me to baby sit Jeffrey after school everyday. Joey was too old for a baby sitter, but not quite responsible enough to watch Jeffrey himself." She shook her head, looking sad. "Poor Jeffrey. He was such a sweet kid." She wiped a tear and got her composure.

"At any rate, I was at the house a lot. Joey started going through changes. It was subtle, but I noticed. He cut himself off from all of his old friends, until it was just Shep in his life. Friends he'd had since early childhood were discarded for no apparent reason. Joey wouldn't even return their calls. Everyone else in his life was whittled away, until it was just Joey and Shep, in their own private little world. Until you came along, Patrick, I was afraid Joey would never have another good friend. I mentioned the changes to Marie, but she just laughed at me. She said that Joey was happier than he'd ever been, his grades were fine, so why worry?"

Patrick nodded. "So he cut himself off from his friends. What other changes did you see?"

"He stopped acting," she said.

Patrick sat up, grateful for the pain-killers. "Did you say 'acting'?"

Betsy nodded. "You knew Joey was a child actor, didn't you?"

"No, but I'm starting to guess there are a lot of things I don't know about him. What kind of acting? Plays and stuff?"

"More than that. He was in commercials and a couple of television specials. His acting coach said he was a natural. He loved it. We all thought it was his calling. Then he met Shep, and he just stopped. He told his parents he wasn't interested in it anymore."

Patrick considered the way Joey had been able to sit in front of a camera and spew bullshit on national television. "Betsy, I have to be honest. Lots of kids go through weird changes at that age. So far you haven't told me anything that can't be explained as teen angst or rebellion."

Betsy smiled sourly. "Yes. So far. Until that afternoon. It's burned into my memory." She rubbed her arms nervously.

Patrick leaned forward. "What happened?"

Her frightened eyes met his. "I didn't blame Shep for the changes in Joey. Not until that day. Shep and I actually got along well. But that week, Joey's aura started to change. I know everyone thinks I'm a nut, but I really can see auras. Joey's became clouded with something I couldn't quite place." She shuddered, then continued.

"I was set to baby-sit over the weekend so Charlie and Marie could go down to the beach house for their anniversary. I got there a little early on Friday afternoon so I could do some studying for a class I was taking. The house was supposed to be empty, because all the kids were supposed to be in school." She paused again, rubbing her arms. Patrick found himself wanting to turn more lights on.

"I was settled in at the kitchen table when I heard a noise coming from below me. Joey's bedroom was down in the finished basement. He kind of had his own little pad down there. I went to the top of the stairs and listened. It sounded like Shep's voice, but he seemed to be speaking in another language."

Patrick's blood chilled, remembering the odd words the blond stranger had spoken before bolting over the shrubs. Was there a connection? Was Betsy completely full of shit? He just didn't know. "What did you do?" he asked.

"I went down there," she said.

"Were they home? Were Joey and Shep down there?"

"They were down there all right, and I surprised the hell out of them. I went down into the outer room and saw that Joey's bedroom door was closed, but the light was on. I crept up to the door and listened. Then I heard it again, like...chanting. I'd hear Shep's voice, then Joey's voice repeating the strange words. Something made me push that door open. To this day, I don't know why. Normally I would have knocked. But I didn't. I pushed the door open, and Joey looked up and yelled my name. He said, "Betsy! Get the hell out of here!"

She fell silent, looking off into the distance. "He was shocked as hell to see me. And I was shocked as hell at what I saw. They were sitting Indian style on the floor, both of them shirtless. There was a plastic tarp underneath them, presumably to save the rug. A dagger lay between them on the floor, and Shep had several bleeding wounds sliced into one of his arms. I told you that Joey yelled my name when I opened the door and startled him. He also spit out the blood he was drinking from one of his mother's crystal wine glasses."

Patrick gaped at her. "Blood? He was drinking blood? Are you sure?"

Betsy nodded. "Quite sure. I snatched the glass from him and sniffed it. It was blood. I think it was Shep's blood. Joey stared up at me, half-naked with blood dripping down his chin, clearly horrified that I'd walked in on whatever they were doing. 'What are you doing here?' he asked me. I looked at the glass of blood in my hand, and said, 'Maybe you should tell me what exactly *you* are doing here, Joey.'"

Betsy's face flushed pink at the memory. She shook her head, looking down at her lap. "The part that really killed me happened next. Joey turned away from me. My Joey, my nephew whose diapers I used to change, he looked away from me. He turned to Shep, like Shep was the all-fucking-mighty, and he said, 'What do we do?' He asks Shep this! Like I wasn't even in the room. So Shep stands up and snatches the glass of blood back from me. He says 'Mind your own business,' and he shoves me out the door and slams it in my face."

Patrick shook his head. "What did you do?"

"I was stunned. I just stared at the closed door, listening to Joey have a panic attack. He kept screaming at Shep, asking him what they were going to do now. Shep kept telling him to calm down, that he would handle it. So I pounded on the door, demanding that Joey come out and talk to me. But it was Shep who finally stepped outside the door. I asked him what the hell was going on in there. He told me that nothing was going on. 'You didn't see anything,' he said to me. Of course I told him to kiss my ass, that I did see something, and that Joey's parents were going to hear about it. Shep said, 'Do what you have to do, and I'll do what I have to do.' He started to turn back toward the bedroom, when I grabbed his arm. I grabbed the arm with the bleeding cuts. Then something...happened."

Her shoulders trembled, and Patrick took her hand. "It's okay, Betsy. Tell me what happened."

"I saw something when I grabbed him. It was like, a vision in my mind. I can't even describe how terrifying it was."

"But I thought you didn't get random psychic impressions. I thought you had to sit down and concentrate the way you did with me," Patrick said.

She nodded. "Normally that's true. I don't know why it happened like this. I assume it was because the arm I grabbed had the wounds. I got Shep's blood all over my hand when I grabbed him."

"So what did you see?"

"It was like nothing I've ever experienced. Everything flashed white, then I got this image, like I was transported to another place. I saw blackness so dark that it blotted out all light, consuming all that lived. I lost my breath, overwhelmed with the feeling of being trapped, imprisoned, hopeless. I pulled my hand back and the vision ended, but I was left with a feeling of such deep, deep sorrow and desperation, that I almost collapsed. I stared at Shep and he stared back at me. Then he said something I'll never forget. He waved his finger at me as you would to a naughty child, and he said, 'You peeked.'" She shook her head, her eyes distant. 'You peeked,'" she repeated.

"So it was like he knew what you had seen?" Patrick asked.

She nodded. "I think he definitely knew. I said, 'I don't know what kind of sick crap you're into, but if you bring any harm to Joey, I'll see that you pay.'"

"Did he say anything to that?"

Betsy chuckled. "Oh he said something all right. He smiled. The little bastard actually smiled at me, and he said, 'Joey doesn't belong to you anymore. He belongs to me now.'"

Patrick was torn between two emotions. One was the almost irresistible desire to write Betsy off as a nut case. The other was the cold fear that he did not really know the friends he'd lived side by side with for the past ten years. *How well do you know your friends?* The FBI agent's words tried to surface but Patrick forced them away. After a few sips of brandy, Betsy completed her tale.

"When Charlie and Marie got home from the beach house on Sunday, I told them all about it. But Shep had gotten to them first, conniving little bastard. He'd called them down at Forest Bluffs and told them this bullshit story about how he and Joey had gone hiking in the woods and gotten scraped up. He said that when he and Joey got home from their hike, the house was all smoky and it smelled funny like marijuana. He told them that I was acting all paranoid and accused him and Joey of devil worship. Of course I denied it, but Joey had confirmed the bogus story. Two days later, Marie was cleaning the bedroom I had stayed in. She found a bag of marijuana and a bag of cocaine in the dresser drawer. Shep had obviously planted the drugs there, but Charlie and Marie told me I could no longer baby-sit the children. There was nothing more I could say. I was afraid I'd never see the kids again, but eventually it blew over. From that point on, Shep and I never spoke of the incident. We both just pretend it never happened."

The room fell silent as Patrick tried to choke down the story. The clock on the mantle chimed. Finally, he stood. "Jesus, Betsy. What did you have to tell me that for?"

She frowned. "You asked me to."

Patrick ran a hand across his forehead and circled the room. "Jesus, Betsy," he said again. "I mean, this is too much."

Betsy shrugged. "It's the God's honest truth. I swear it."

Patrick shook his head. "Impossible. I practically lived with those guys in college. I've seen at least one of them every day for the past ten years. If they were into any weird ritualistic shit, I would have known. I would have known!"

"Maybe you don't know your friends as well as you think you do," Betsy said.

Patrick looked at her and smirked. "Yeah. I've been hearing that a lot lately."

Betsy stood and went to Patrick, placing a hand on his large shoulder. "I'm sure you have nothing to worry about at any rate, tough guy. The little psycho seems to actually like you."

"Nothing to worry about?" Patrick said, and rolled up his sleeve, showing Betsy his newly formed scar. "I let that little psycho do this to me."

Betsy examined the tiny half moon scar and ran a finger over it. The scar tingled. She looked up at him. "You have to go see that priest again. You have to ask him what he meant when he asked you about a blood ceremony."

Patrick nodded. "I'll go see him tomorrow."

Betsy looked serious then. "Patrick, if you can get Joey back, I mean...get him away from Shep..."

"I'll do what I can, Betsy."

"Then you'll do it? You'll go out to Forest Bluffs?"

She looked hopeful. Patrick wanted to do what Betsy asked of him, but the thought of going out to Forest Bluffs still made him want to go hide under a rock. Even more so now that he'd heard Betsy's macabre tale of Joey and Shep's happy blood play.

"I'll do what I can," he said again, and wished her goodnight. It was the best answer he could give her.

Chapter Eighteen

Copie double-checked the door to the photo lab to make sure it was locked, though the chances of someone coming around this late at night were slim. Most of the other students were home sleeping or out partying, but he took precautions anyway. He'd grown increasingly paranoid since the erupting coverage of the apparition. Given the obvious value of the photo he now possessed, he had chosen not to include it in his portfolio for his final grade. He'd received a B minus instead of the A he'd wanted, but it was of no concern to him now. He had his future career sitting on a piece of film.

After locking the door, he went back and sat before the image on the computer screen. When he'd first developed the film, the apparition appeared as just a big white blob of light. Copie had nearly cried. He'd been determined though, and had done his best to clean the image up, sharpening it and removing much of the light. He played with the shadows until he finally conjured a semblance he was happy with. It wasn't perfect, but it was there. Or rather, *she* was there.

It was a woman, her hands clasped just below her chest, her head covered with a glowing drape of veil. The body was indecipherable from the waist down, where it became translucent. A garment was visible, a vague line of fabric just above the chest. Her face was sweet and serene, her lips curved at the corners in a maternal smile. It was perfect.

But it was wrong. He made himself dizzy staring at the photograph, trying to determine what it was that screamed out 'fake' to his subconscious mind. Copie liked to think he had a good eye, and he trusted his instincts. Something about the picture told him that the apparition was bogus. He examined the photo until his eyes burned. Finally, he had to walk away and clear his head.

Unlocking the door, he went down the hall and poured himself a cup of coffee. He returned with his mug and locked himself in again. After several minutes of musing he decided that staring at the photo for another hour would make him crazy, and probably blind as well. He resigned to give it one more perusal, then put it away for the night. Tomorrow he would call the local news station and let them make of it what they wanted, as long as they gave him the credit. He grinned, imagining the blind envy of his colleagues.

He seated himself in front of the computer screen once more and gazed at the image of the glowing woman. "What are you hiding?" he whispered to the photograph. As if in answer to his question, his eyes were drawn to something on the apparition's body, something he hadn't noticed before. At the top of her breasts, where the scoop of fabric met the flesh, was a tiny, X-shaped blur, right in the center of her chest. "Wait a minute. What the hell is that?"

He closed in on the object and magnified it. The image became clearer. He boxed it off and magnified it again. "Holy Mother of God," he whispered. "Or perhaps not." He printed out a copy of the image. With a pencil he traced the line of the object on the garment. There was no question. It was a decorative bow, the kind one might see on a modern woman's bra or nightgown.

Copie stood up, smiling at the photo in his hand. "A bow!" he said. "That's a pretty fancy nighty for such an ancient being," he said to the picture. He smiled. "I've got you," he said. "Whoever you are, I've got you."

He picked up the phone and dialed the news station he had chosen. He was thrilled. This definitely upped the stakes. Not only did he have the only photograph taken of Joey Duvaine's miracle, but he now had proof, more or less, that it was a fake. "I'm going to be famous at the tender age of nineteen," he said to the empty room.

A male voice answered. "News desk, how may I help you?"

Copie explained his situation to the man on the phone. He described the nature of the photo he possessed, along with his suspicions about the Virgin Mary showing up wearing the latest in fashion sleepwear. The melodious young voice was cooperative and chatty. He asked Copie for his name, address and personal information, and Copie stated his wishes that he be given full credit for the photograph.

"Not a problem," the voice said. "In fact, we'd like to do a personal interview, if that's all right with you."

"Of course," Copie agreed, beaming. "Shall I come down to the station tomorrow then?"

"Actually, it would be better if we could send someone over tonight."

Copie frowned. "Tonight? Isn't it too late?"

The voice laughed. "We work around the clock here and we don't want to take the chance of you having a change of heart, or deciding to give the story to someone else."

"Oh. I see. Okay."

"Are you at home right now?"

"No, I'm at the university film lab. It will take me a while to shut everything down."

"Just give me the address to the film lab. Do you have all of the photos with you?"

A simple question, but Copie felt a cold warning tug at his senses. He dismissed it as excitement. "Yes, all of the photos are with me. I guess I'll just wait here then."

After giving the address, he hung up and went into the little bathroom, locking himself in. Locking the bathroom door had become a habit. It was the last door along a wall of darkrooms, and when the place was full of students, someone was always barging into the bathroom, thinking it was another dark room. Copie had been caught with his dick in his hand once because of this, and had never forgotten to lock the door since.

He rinsed his face and wished for a toothbrush. He hadn't intended on speaking to the six O'clock news with nasty coffee breath. His reflection stared back at him from the dusty mirror over the sink. His tiny braids had gone askew from nervously running his fingers across his head. His brown eyes were too wide, and his usual coffee brown skin looked pale and ashen. He supposed he was just tired.

Still, something in his mind screamed out danger. His instincts had always been strong and he'd relied on them. But why were his instincts telling him to run now? Run from what? From success? No way. Not this time. He deserved this success. His instincts could kiss his ass.

⁂

Now this is the real miracle, Russell thought as he hung up the phone. He'd been covering the news desk nights ever since Craig moved out to Los Angeles. Russell would have been perfectly happy working on the small hoaxes they'd been doing. But Craig had dissolved their business and left Russell with no direction. Now he had to work the graveyard shift, earning a dog shit salary until he figured out what he wanted to do with his life.

But that wasn't entirely true. He knew what he wanted to do. Russell had told Shep in no uncertain terms that he would like to be involved with the Forest Bluffs church. He'd promised to be helpful with whatever Shep asked of him and to stay out of the way when he wasn't needed. Shep had told him that once things settled down, he'd see if he could find something for Russell to do. And God knew Russell would do anything for Shep. Shep had everything he wanted, including a seemingly endless supply of cash.

Now it was time to prove his loyalty. Russell was about to save the day. Odd that he would be manning the news desk when the call came in from that photographer. It was like...fate. Shep would be grateful.

One of the odd-speaking brothers answered the phone and Russell ordered him to fetch Shepherd, that it was an emergency. The brother tried to argue that Shep was very busy, and had asked not to be disturbed. After some foul language and abusive threats on Russell's part, Shep was finally summoned to the phone.

"Hey Russell. How's TV land?"

"We've got problems, Shep. You'd better listen to this." Russell told him about the call from the photographer, claiming to have pictures of the apparition. He'd even boasted proof that it was a hoax, Russell told him. Something about a bow on a nightgown. When Russell finished talking, he was met with silence. "Shep? Are you still there?"

"Yeah. Listen, Russell. Does he have all of the pictures with him?"

"He says he does. I got his home address just in case. He's expecting a reporter to go down there tonight. I called you right away, Shep."

"You did the right thing. You're really saving our asses here. Thanks, man."

Russell beamed with gratification. "You're welcome, Shepherd. I'd do anything for you. You know that."

"Russell, do you have a press pass?"

"I can get one. Are you asking me to go with you?"

"You were the first one he spoke to. You can go in ahead of us, feel the situation out, see exactly what he's got. We'll wait outside. Are you in?"

"Of course," Russell said with enthusiasm. "I'd love to help."

"Russell, do you know what you're agreeing to?"

Russell paused, uneasy. "What do you mean?"

"We can't have people going around calling Joey a fake. We just can't have that. Do you understand?"

Russell shifted in his seat. "Well, um, you're just going to steal the pictures, right? I mean..." Russell laughed nervously. "I mean, you don't intend to hurt the photographer."

Shep was silent for a moment. "Russell, are you happy working at the television station? Is that your dream life?"

"No! I hate it here. You know I hate it. Why?"

"Because I think it's time you joined us at Forest Bluffs. You'd like that. Wouldn't you?"

Russell was ecstatic. Whatever uneasiness he'd felt melted away at the prospect of spending every day with Shep. "Oh, I'd like that very much, Shepherd. Very much."

"Then you'll help us?"

Russell paused. "Whatever you need, Shep."

Shepherd slammed the phone down hard and Kelinda jumped. She was sitting at the kitchen table, picking at a plate of food and trying desperately to get Joey's attention. Joey was drunk, slumped in his chair with a bottle of brandy. Shep stormed across the floor and snatched Kelinda's plate from the table, smashing it to the floor. Kelinda shrieked as he wound up and kicked the table over.

"What the hell is wrong with you?" she demanded.

"I told you," he said, pointing. "I told you not to wear that fucking nightgown!"

He went downstairs to the den where the brothers were attempting to play pool. Margol had the stick backwards as he shot randomly at the balls. "Let's go!" he yelled. "We've got a situation to take care of." They brightened. They loved a mission. "I need both vans loaded. Allisto, do you still have the key to the work shed?"

Allisto nodded. "Yes, Shepherd."

"Good. We're going to need some explosives."

❧❦

The loud knock startled Copie, who had amazingly dozed off. "Be right there!" he yelled, jamming a stick of wintergreen gum into his mouth. He opened the door to a young man with thick black glasses and short wavy black hair. He held up a press pass. "Copeland Smith? I'm Russell from the station. We spoke on the phone."

"Yeah, come on in." Copie led him into the film lab. "Would you like some coffee or something?"

"Coffee would be nice," he said. A throat cleared out in the hallway, and Copie turned to look at the open door. Russell glanced back as well. "On second thought, no coffee. I'm fine," he said.

Cope shrugged. "Okay. Suit yourself."

Russell leaned in and studied Copie now, his brows furrowed. "Jesus. You're just a kid. How old are you?"

Copie puffed himself up. "I'm old enough," he said. Russell continued to stare at him, an awkward hesitance in his eyes. Copie frowned. "Are you okay?"

"I'm just fine," Russell said, forcing a smile. "Why?"

"Because you're looking at me like I have a terminal disease or something." Russell laughed. A throat cleared outside the door again and Copie glanced back. "Is somebody out there?"

"Oh, that's just my cameraman. He'll be in when he's ready. Let's see these photos of yours, shall we?" Russell asked, rubbing his hands in a gesture of excitement.

"Sure. Come on over here." Copie led Russell to the computer station where the image of the apparition glowed on the screen. Russell gazed at it, a dreamy smile edging his lips. Copie picked up a manila envelope and dumped out the hard copies he'd made. "As you can see here," Copie said, leaning in to show Russell, "the decorative bow is clearly visible on the neckline of the garment. In this picture, I've outlined it with a pencil."

Still smiling, Russell took the picture and glanced at it, then his attention was diverted back to the glowing monitor. "May I?" he asked, pointing to the keyboard.

Copie nodded. "Sure. Go nuts."

Russell sat down and commenced a furious tapping of keys. Copie watched in amazement as the image gained clarity. Russell played around with the lighting and managed to tweak the apparition into a far cleaner image than Copie had been able to achieve. Copie gasped in amazement. Russell gave the keyboard a final tap, then leaned back in his chair, smiling. "I've got to admit, I was hoping someone would get a picture of this," he said.

Copie leaned in, grinning at the image, which had un-obscured detail now. "Wow! You're really good at that," he said. "Are you a photographer too?"

"Something like that," Russell said, examining the paper photos now. "It looked real, don't you think, Copeland? From the ground?"

Copie shrugged. "I suppose it looked as real as any supernatural vision. Bear in mind that I have nothing to compare it to."

Russell nodded as he spread the pictures out on the desk. "Oh, it looked real all right. I'm a fucking genius. Did you know that, Copeland?"

Copie cocked his head to one side. "Excuse me?"

A medium sized man with curly hair the color of sand stepped through the doorway. "Stop feeding your ego, Russell. We have business to attend to."

A cold sensation grabbed Copie as he looked at the other man's wide green eyes. He'd seen that face before, but he couldn't place it. Russell held up the pictures. "Hey, Shep! I don't suppose you'd let me keep one of these as a souvenir. This is some of my best work!"

The other man smiled. "I don't think so, Russell."

Copie looked back and forth between them. Something was terribly wrong here. Three more men stepped through the door then, lanky, curly-haired youths that looked like they could have been brothers to the first. None of them had film cameras. Copie's eyes shifted back to the other man. He remembered where he knew him from. He was the stranger from the church, the one that had pushed him and stolen his camera.

"Is there another computer file of this image? Or is this the only one?" Russell asked.

Copie backed away from him, pointing to the four new arrivals. "Wait a minute. Who the hell are they?"

Russell was tipped back in his chair with his feet on the computer table. "These are my associates. The handsome guy right there is Shepherd, and the others are, um, oh shit! I can never remember their names."

The one called Shepherd came forward while the others stood at the door like guards. "All right," he said. "Let's stop fucking around, kid." He grabbed Copie by the throat and forced him into a chair. "Where do you store the computer image, and where are the rest of the pictures?"

Copie couldn't find his voice, bewitched by the cold green eyes that stared down at him. "You don't want to talk?" Shepherd said. "Let's make a deal then." He grabbed a pen and pressed it hard against the soft flesh beneath Copie's eye. Copie whimpered. "How about, you tell me where the image is stored, and I don't gouge out your eye. What do you say?"

"It's on a disk!" Copie called out. "The disk is in there. I swear to God, it's only on the disk. These aren't even my computers! I'm just a student!"

Still holding the pen to Copie's eye, Shep gestured to Russell, who popped the disk out of the computer and examined it. He pecked at the computer keyboard, scanning the files on the hard drive. Finally, he turned to Shep. "He's telling the truth. It was on the disk, that's all."

"We can't take any chances," Shep said, releasing Copie. "We have to destroy everything here. Margol?"

"Yes, Shepherd," the redhead answered.

"Check out his apartment just in case. Juris? Bring that other stuff in now. Allisto, help Juris set the charges."

The blond and brunette left the room and returned with canisters. Copie saw a break as they cleared away from the exit. He bolted for the door, thinking he was moving pretty fast until Shepherd grabbed him by the hair and yanked him back. Copie fought, but Shep and Russell ultimately subdued him and tied him to a chair with something that looked like dental floss. "This string will disintegrate in the blast," Shep told Copie as he wound it around his legs. His tone was casual, as if they were discussing the weather, not the manner in which Copie would be murdered. "You know, I don't want you to die, kid. I am sorry about all of this, but what can I say? You were literally in the wrong place at the wrong time."

"Then let me go!" he pleaded. "Just destroy the pictures! I won't say anything, I swear. And even if I did, I'd have no proof! Nobody would believe me. Please, you don't have to do this."

Shep shook his head. "Sorry, kid. This project is too important to leave loose ends."

Russell had joined the others in their preparations. They had set up some type of charges and now the curly haired ones were joyfully dousing the place with gasoline. Shepherd looked over at them and scowled. "Hey! Take it easy on the gas! We need it for the trip to Pearl Chasm next week. Or have you forgotten that your beloved brother is still in prison?"

The others re-capped the canisters, looking guilty. They gathered their equipment and moved out, leaving Copie tied to a small metal chair. Shep smoothed a strip of duct tape over Copie's mouth. "Good luck, kid. Happy trails."

They left him alone. Copie wheeled his chair to the locked door, but he had no thumbs available to flick the lock. Panic assaulted him as he heard vehicle engines start up from outside somewhere. He was going to fry. He was going to fry for being in the wrong place at the wrong time. *No! Not like this!* He swallowed his fear and forced himself to think, a reckless jumble of survival-driven thoughts. Then his eyes spotted the bathroom door, left open a crack from his last visit. The bathroom had a small window just above the toilet. He shuffled like a mad sand crab over to the door and thrust himself head first into the tiny room, using too much momentum, and nearly toppling over.

He put pressure against the string binding his lower legs, urging it to loosen just a bit. He was able to manage a crouching stand, with the chair strapped on his back like a tortoise shell. His arms still wouldn't budge. He used his chin to drop the toilet seat cover. Resting his knees on the edge of the toilet, he shuffled himself to the back of the bowl, positioning his head against the wall as he struggled to get up onto his toes. He wobbled unsteadily, becoming too aware that he had nothing to break his fall. One shoe-tip reached the toilet cover, and he groaned, using every bit of strength his foot had to hoist his weight to a standing position. The arch of his foot cramped and he thought he'd pass out from the pain. Then he was there, standing on top of the toilet, with the window in front of him.

He spotted two white vans in the far lot, parking lights on. They were waiting to see if the blast was a success, no doubt. With this thought, Copie slammed his head into the glass. It didn't break. A strangled scream came up from his throat and he slammed his head again. This time a jagged crack spider-webbed across the glass. Four more desperate thrusts and he was through the window. But he was stuck.

The chair did not quite fit, so he was lodged half in and half out, like Winnie the Pooh stuck in Rabbit's hole after eating too much honey. He cursed against the duct tape and tried wiggling himself forward, but the chair was wedged. From his waist up he was out in the open air, looking down at the grass a foot below. From the waist down, he was still in the bathroom.

An ear shattering explosion tore through the lab as one of the charges ignited. Copie began to pray silently as tears streamed from his eyes. Another explosion came in a rush of heat. This one blew the bathroom door in off its hinges. The corner of the door struck Copie just below the knees, sending him ripping forth in a rupture of splintered wood and spraying glass. He landed with a thud on the grass outside, his face and legs stinging with blood. He squinted up at the window and saw thick flames licking into the bathroom.

With his last bit of strength, he forced himself and the chair into a painful roll, turning end over end until he was several yards from the building and could move no more. The final blast came with a belch of scorching heat, and Copie buried his face into the earth. Fragments of flaming debris landed daintily on his skin, burning him. The last thing he heard before he passed out was the sound of the two vans driving away

Chapter Nineteen

The train stopped at the end of the line and Patrick got off. The red-haired Shep-alike got off the train too, but he proceeded quickly in the opposite direction. Patrick watched him walk off down the street. His stride was awkward, yet fluid at the same time. He seemed to be walking almost solely on the balls of his feet, as if both ankles were sprained. The other stalkers had moved that same way, like they had two wooden legs.

The redhead looked back over his shoulder, and Patrick froze. He had the large green eyes, straight, sculpted nose, and rosebud mouth. Baby face. Patrick swooned, a surreal disorientation seizing him as he stared at this new stranger. He seemed surprised to see Patrick staring back at him, and he quickly turned away, flipping the collar up on his jacket and quickening his pace. Patrick resisted the urge to chase him down and question him under the threat of death. His sanity was all he had left. He refused to lose it. Turning his attention away from the departing stranger, he began walking home.

Robin sat on his front porch, waiting. She wore a baby blue tee shirt, white shorts, with a ball cap and sunglasses hiding her face. A few strands of blond hair escaped from under the cap. He'd nearly forgotten her promise to contact him when she returned from Forest Bluffs. He trotted up the steps toward her. "Robin! How did it go? Did they try to poison your Kool-Aid?"

She looked up, and even with the dark sunglasses hiding her eyes, he could see that she was not in a joking mood. "Can we go inside, Obrien? We need to talk."

"Yeah, of course," he said, "Come on in."

He led Robin to the sofa, where she sat, removing her hat and glasses. Her crystal blue eyes looked strained and weary. Wavy blond locks fell soft and loose around her shoulders. The baby blue tee shirt matched her eyes. She looked soft and inviting, and Patrick quickly reminded himself that Robin was Shep's girlfriend. Not his. "So I take it you didn't have a very good time," he said, offering her a glass of wine, which she gratefully accepted.

She took a long swallow of the wine, then looked up at him. "It was weird, Obrien. It was really, really weird."

"Did you see Kelinda?" he asked, unable to restrain his curiosity.

"No. She wasn't there. They claimed that she went away for the weekend to visit friends. That's bullshit. I know all her friends."

Patrick was stunned to see her hands shaking as she brought the wine glass to her lips. It was unsettling to see her so rattled. She was usually such a hard ass. "They don't want me to see Kelinda. I don't know why. But she's living there all right. I saw her stuff. I saw her cat too."

"Did you see Shep? And Joey? How were they acting? Are there followers? Do they—"

"Hold on, Obrien," she said, holding a hand up. "I'll get to all of that. But there's something I need to tell you first. It's about Kelinda." She looked into his eyes, her face serious.

"But you said you didn't see Kelinda."

"I didn't. I saw her stuff."

"Her stuff? You mean her clothes and personal items?"

"Yes," she said.

She took a breath and let it out slowly, as if preparing for something. Patrick's patience was wearing thin. If she was going to drop a bomb, he'd rather she's just let it fly. "Robin, I don't know where this is headed, so whatever it is that you want to tell me, just spit it out."

"She's fucking Joey."

Patrick blinked twice. "Excuse me?"

"I said, she's fucking Joey. Kelinda, I mean."

Patrick looked off into space, showing no reaction as he struggled to absorb the statement. Robin waved a hand in front of his face. "Obrien? Are you okay? Don't bug out on me, man. I haven't even told you the really weird parts yet."

Patrick looked at Robin. "Kelinda and Joey? Are you sure?"

"Pretty damn sure, yeah. I told Shep I wanted to leave her a note. He said she was staying in the back bedroom on the third floor. So I go up there, and the room is completely empty. Nothing in the closets, nothing in the drawers, nothing that belongs to Kelinda."

Patrick moved closer to Robin on the sofa, intrigued now despite his shock. "So what did you do?"

"Well, by this time I'm getting suspicious, but I'm also a little freaked out because Shep comes up and starts watching me like a hawk. I write a quick note and leave it on the pillow. Later that night, after Shep fell asleep, I went exploring. I went into Joey's room. Her clothes were in his closets. Her birth control pills on the lamp table next to the bed. Suitcases, her cosmetics, even her tampons for Christ sakes."

Patrick leaned back on the couch, thinking. He didn't want to believe it of course, but somehow he wasn't as shocked as he should have been. Somehow, he knew. Somehow, he had always known. He turned to Robin. "That's pretty compelling evidence, but are you sure she's actually sleeping with him, and not just storing her stuff in there?"

Robin gave Patrick a look. "Listen to me Obrien, and trust me. A woman does not leave a box of tampons in a man's room unless she's been intimate with him."

Patrick nodded. "Yeah. I suppose you're right."

Robin placed a hand on his shoulder. "I'm sorry, Obrien. But I thought you should know."

Patrick waited for the hurt to come, but it didn't. Perhaps rejection and betrayal were becoming commonplace. Had he finally gone numb? Or were his feelings for Kelinda not what he'd thought they were? Whatever the reason, he felt nothing, except a befuddled curiosity. The last time he'd seen Kelinda, she was still riddled with guilt, and fearful that someone would associate her with Joey. Now she was sleeping in his bed.

"So what's this other weird stuff you have to tell me?" he asked.

Robin wrung her small hands. "Okay. There are a group of followers that work in the fields by day and tent out around the guest house by night. They build campfires, play music, and dance like a bunch of gypsies. All in all they seem to be having a pretty good time."

Patrick smirked. "Sounds like your average cult. Does Joey make them bow down and kiss his feet?"

Robin smiled. "No. None of that. He does go out and give speeches to them. I wasn't allowed to watch. The followers seem mesmerized by him, but they also seem comfortable around him. Shep said that they even have them all up to the big house for barbecues sometimes."

Patrick frowned, resting his elbows on his knees. "I'm sorry. The big house?"

"That's what the followers call the beach house. They live in the guest house, but Joey lives in 'The Big House'."

"How quaint. What else?"

Robin's face took on that strained look again, and Patrick caught veiled fear in her eyes. She leaned in close to him. "There are these three guys that live in the big house with Joey and Shep. I heard Shep refer to them as 'the brothers'. They do errands for Shep, and they supervise the gardening out in the fields. They hang on Shep's every word like he's the answer to some prayer. He screams and yells at them, bosses them around, but at the same time he seems quite fond of them. He even pets and kisses them sometimes."

Patrick's jaw dropped. "What?"

Robin nodded. "Yeah, I know. I told you, Obrien. It is really weird out there."

"So who the hell are these guys? Why do they get to live in the big house? Oh God, now I'm saying it. I mean the beach house."

Robin shrugged. "I was introduced to them, but no explanation was given as to who they were, or what was their function. Shep avoided the subject when I brought it up, and I think he was going out of his way to keep me away from them. But I couldn't help but be curious about them, especially since they look so much like Shep. It's creepy. It's like they could really be his brothers."

Patrick felt the hair on his arms stand at attention. "Did you...did you say they look like Shep?"

"Yeah. What's wrong?"

Patrick buried his face in his hands, then looked up at her through a mask of fingers. "Oh, God. Was one of them blond, one a redhead, and one a brunette?"

Robin scowled. "Yes," she whispered. "How did you know that?"

Patrick shook his head. "I can't believe this. I think those are the guys that have been following me."

"Following you?"

"Yeah. It's been going on for a while now. I've seen all three of them. They're on the train, they're in the restaurants I go to...I even chased one of them through the woods at Betsy's house. God, I've been so stupid! All this time it's been Shep having me followed. I thought it was the FBI."

Robin uttered a small laugh, and studied Patrick. "You went to Betsy's? My Aunt Betsy's? And did you say FBI?"

"Yes, but that's a whole other story. Did they talk funny? The three guys I mean. Did they have a weird accent?"

"Well yes, but—"

"Damn it!" he yelled, slapping his thigh. "It's got to be the same guys. I can't believe Shep is having me followed."

Robin put her hand on his. "Patrick, shut up and listen to me. It gets worse."

"Worse? How could it get worse?"

"They have the scar."

Patrick frowned. "Huh?"

"The scar. They have the scar. The three guys that live in the house, the ones that look like Shep. They all have the scar." Her eyes looked haunted.

Patrick shook his head. "I'm not following you. What scar?"

"*The* scar. The one on Shep's back. The upside down horseshoe. They all have it."

"That's impossible. Why would they have the scar? Shep's father gave him that scar when he was little. He branded him with the horseshoe because—"

"I know," Robin said, cutting him off. "Because he was unlucky. I've heard the story too, Obrien. But I'm telling you, these guys all have the identical scar."

"That's crazy! How do you know this?"

Robin raised her eyebrows. "I saw it with my own eyes. I told you I went exploring when Shep fell asleep. I sneaked downstairs and spied on them. They were with Joey. I don't know what the hell is wrong with Joey, but he was drunk as a skunk the whole time I was out there. Anyway, they were all in the Jacuzzi room. Joey was tossing bars of soap at them, and telling them to take a bath because they were getting their filth all over his new furniture. So the three brothers stripped out of their clothes and got into the tub. I saw them all naked. I saw their backs, Obrien. They had the scar. I saw it."

Patrick frowned at Robin. "But why? Why would they have the scar?" He hadn't meant to yell, but it came out that way.

Robin's china doll face scrunched in annoyance. "I don't know why they have the damned scar!" she yelled. "I'm just telling you what I saw, Obrien!"

Patrick stood, holding his arms up in surrender. "Okay, we both need to calm down. There has to be a rational explanation for all of this. What did Shep tell you about the brothers?"

She shrugged. "Not much. When I asked him about the resemblance, he said that they liked to imitate his style, but that he was not related to them. He's completely full of shit, don't you think? You've seen them. There is no way that those guys aren't related to him."

Patrick walked to the window and stared out, hands on his hips. "Why would Shep lie? He always told me he was an only child."

"Yeah, same here," Robin said. "No brothers, no sisters, no cousins even." Patrick turned back to face her. She stood and walked over to join him. "Hey, Obrien, I've told you an awful lot here. I think it's time you answered one of my questions."

He glanced at her uneasily, knowing what she was about to ask. "Sure. What do you want to know?"

"Was the miracle a fake?"

He silently cursed Joey and Shep. How was it that he ended up being the one to tell Robin that her boyfriend and her cousin were a couple of sleazy con men? She watched him expectantly. He smiled sadly at her. "Of course it was a fake, Robin."

She let her breath out as if she'd been holding it. Calmly, she nodded. "I figured as much. I mean, I love Joey, but he's no saint. Or prophet for that matter. Were you involved? Or maybe I don't want to know."

"I knew about it, yes, but I opposed the idea. I begged Joey not to go through with it. He promised me he wouldn't. They tricked me into going to the church that night. Shep told me that Joey was contemplating suicide, and that he went to be with his family. They knew I'd deduct that he'd gone to the cemetery. I did. That's when I spotted Joey on the roof of the church. I thought he was really in trouble. I didn't realize it was a set up until I got to the roof and that...*thing* appeared."

Robin frowned at Patrick. "They really did that to you? Joey and Shep?"

Patrick smirked coldly. "They claimed that my ignorance made the whole thing more real. That was their excuse for betraying me and risking my life. Good theatre."

Robin dropped her head. "Now I understand why you're not out at the Bluffs with them. I mean, I thought it was strange, you know? You three have always been so inseparable. Shit. They've really gone off the deep end."

"Yeah," Patrick said. "Now you see why I'm so shocked that Kelinda would move out there. I mean, she of all people..."

He trailed off, seeing the stunned look on Robin's face. "Are you telling me that Kelinda was involved in this too?"

Patrick felt a stab of guilt for betraying Kelinda's trust. He imagined her in bed with Joey, and the guilt dissipated. "Kelinda was the model for the apparition. Kelinda was the Virgin Mary."

Robin turned away from him. Surprisingly, she laughed. "Was it Russell and Craig? The Hoax Patrol?"

"Yes," he said.

Robin laughed and leaned against the couch. "I can't believe I didn't figure it out sooner. But Kelinda! I can't believe Kelinda would do this. Her dad's a deacon for crying out loud. Why would she agree to be involved in something like that?"

She and Patrick looked at each other as the realization hit them. "Joey," they said in unison.

Robin moved in and took Patrick's hand. "Do you think you could talk to Joey? Do you think you could get him out of there? He'll listen to you, Obrien. He looks up to you."

Patrick doubted that Joey looked up to him in anything other than height. But he did want to try and get Joey out of Forest Bluffs, at least before the Feds got hold of him. Along with Betsy, this was now the second woman from the Duvaine family that had asked him in no uncertain terms to save Joey's crazy ass. The problem was, he wasn't sure Joey wanted to be saved. He wasn't sure about anything anymore. And the priest's comment was still echoing in his mind, demanding an explanation he wasn't sure he wanted to hear. *You never did a blood ceremony, did you?*

He looked at Robin's pleading face. "I think there's something you need to hear. But you have to promise not to freak out."

She shrugged. "Okay. No freak-outs. What is it?"

Patrick told her about the FBI and his visit with Father Carbone. "They want me to infiltrate the group out at Forest Bluffs. For some reason, they're interested in what they have growing in the fields out behind the house."

"The fields? Really? It just looked like a bunch of wheat and grain to me.

Shep said it was some sort of investment project. What does the FBI think it is? Drugs?"

"I'm not sure, but they want to know desperately enough to trust in me. They want me to go out there and pretend to be all cozy with Joey and Shep again. My time is about up. I have to give them my answer."

Robin gave him somber blue eyes. "You're going to do it."

"I don't think I have a choice."

"I don't want Joey to get in any trouble," she said.

"Neither do I. I want to prove to the FBI that Joey and Shep aren't doing anything illegal. All I have to do is get a sample of the crop, and I'm out of there. If it's nothing but a bunch of wheat as you say, then they leave it alone."

"And if it's not?"

Patrick sighed. "If it's not, then I don't know what they're going to do."

Robin looked thoughtful, tapping her chin with her index finger. "You know, if you wanted to re-infiltrate, it would be really easy for you. They talk about you all the time out there."

"Who talks about me?"

"Joey, Shep, hell I even heard some of the followers talking. Joey seems particularly upset that you're not out there."

Patrick frowned. This was the part he didn't get. "What sort of things did you hear them say?"

"Just little comments like 'Obrien will come around' or 'things will be better when Obrien gets here'. I even heard Shep tell one of the brothers that Joey would stop drinking so much when you got there."

Patrick shook his head, scowling. "That is fucking unsettling. I've made it clear that I have no intentions on joining them. Why would they think differently? And why does it matter to them if I go out there or not?"

"I can't answer those questions, Patrick. I'm just saying that if you did want to go out there and spy on them or whatever, it would be a breeze. They'd welcome you with open arms."

"I don't know," he said, doubtful. "I think they'd be suspicious. They know me too well. They know I wouldn't just suddenly have a change of heart like that."

Robin shrugged. "From what you've told me, they're trying to break you down, leave you so frustrated with your life that joining them is the only option. They obviously expect you to crack eventually."

Patrick stood. "I have to go see somebody before I make my final decision. I need to ask that Father Carbone about something he said to me."

"I'm going with you," she declared.

Patrick shook his head. "No. You're not."

"Why? If this is going to help Joey then I want to be involved!"

"Sorry, Robin, but no way. You're too close to the situation. You can't be objective."

She put her hands on her hips, "You're close to the situation yourself. You've been Shep's bitch longer than I have."

Patrick narrowed his eyes. "I'm gonna pretend I didn't hear that. You can't go. I know you, Robin. You get defensive when it comes to Joey. The priest will say one thing about him and you'll go valving off at the mouth. If anyone talks about Joey, you rough them up."

She laughed. "Rough them up? I do not make a habit of manhandling clergymen. You make me sound like a lunatic."

Patrick smirked at her and raised an eyebrow.

"Fuck you, Obrien."

He held his hands in front of him. "I'm only saying that you may hear some unsettling things about Joey and Shep. I'm not saying that I'm going to sit there and listen to lies about them, but I do want to hear what the priest has to say. And I want to know why the FBI is doing this investigation in the first place. If they're going to accuse my friends of terrorism, or whatever the hell this is about, then they'd better have some damn good reasons."

Robin hung her head. Much to his dismay, she started to sob. It completely disarmed him. "Oh, no. Come on, Robin. Don't cry!" She continued to weep tiny muffled sounds into her hands. Patrick went to her and pulled her in to his chest. He expected her to pull away but she let him hold her. He lifted her chin and wiped her eyes. She allowed him to do so. He looked into her crystalline blue eyes, just a shade darker than Joey's but similar in shape. "Your eyes are like Joey's," he said, uncomfortable suddenly. He'd never been this close to her.

She nodded. "So I've been told."

He felt strange and warm with his arms around her. He could smell her soapy scent and feel the bones in her shoulders, and the way her back curved into her tiny waist. He was afraid to hold on to her, but he was afraid that if he let her go too abruptly she would sense his discomfort.

"Let me go see the priest with you," she said. "I might be able to help. I know Joey and Shep as well as you do."

"That's true, you do. But how do I know you won't rough up the priest?" he said, grinning.

"You're going to have to trust me," she said.

"Oh? Everyone I've trusted lately has turned on me like a snake. Why should I put my faith in you? I've already got one Duvaine on my shit list."

She rested her head on his chest. He never imagined there would be any heat between him and Robin, but he felt his heart flutter with the movement. He forced the thoughts out of his mind. Things were complicated enough. Robin unwrapped herself from him. He was relieved, and a little disappointed. "We both got left out in the cold, Obrien. That means they don't trust either one of us. Isn't that reason enough to bring me into the fold? I mean, who else have you got?"

Patrick laughed. "Nobody, I suppose."

"So can I go?"

He looked into her blue eyes and felt something tug at his heart. Maybe it was the eyes. He could never say no to those eyes while Joey was wearing them, and being a heterosexual, Patrick found Robin far more appealing. "Okay, you can go. But I'm warning you, you have to stay calm. I don't know this priest very well and he kind of gives me the creeps."

Robin raised her eyebrows. "The *priest* gives you the creeps?"

Patrick nodded, grinning slightly as he thought of Father Carbone, with his explosive rants and shocking profanity. "This is not your average priest." He grabbed his keys off of the coffee table. "Let's go. You can judge for yourself."

Chapter Twenty

Father Carbone came to the door in his pajamas, haphazardly pulling on a bathrobe. He squinted through the screen at Patrick and Robin.

"Hello Father Carbone. Do you remember me?" Patrick asked.

To his surprise, the priest offered him one of his warm smiles. "Mr. Obrien. You're a little hard to forget. I wasn't expecting you."

"I know, I'm sorry. I need to speak with you. This is my friend Robin Duvaine. May we come in?"

The priest opened the door and waved them inside. Carbone shuffled into the living room, indicating that they follow. He was far less intimidating in his blue and green checkered bathrobe. His black hair was pushed up on one side where he'd been laying on it. "Are you going to help Agent Litner?" he called back. "Because he'll tell you everything if you are. You really shouldn't be coming to me first."

"I'm here to speak with you right now, Father. Not Litner. It concerns what you said to me as I was leaving yesterday. About..." Patrick grew uneasy as he looked at Robin's eyes, watching him expectantly. He had not told her about the blood ceremony. "You asked me about a ritual," he said.

Father Carbone stopped in his tracks. He turned around and stared at Patrick, then turned his sleepy gaze to Robin. "Duvaine, huh? Any relation?" Robin had been silent, as Patrick requested. Now she nodded politely.

"Yes. Joey is my cousin."

Carbone raised an eyebrow at Patrick. "I really can't tell you anything without Litner's authority, and even if I could, I'm not so sure this young lady should be here for this," he said. "You've probably put the investigation in jeopardy by even speaking to her."

Robin walked over to Father Carbone and put her face within an inch of his, looking hostile. "I thought you said this guy could help us. It looks to me like he's pretty useless. Let's get the hell out of here."

Patrick sighed. "Damn it Robin! What did we talk about?"

Carbone held his hands up. "All right, just calm down a minute, people. Take a seat on the couch, would you?" Robin and Patrick remained standing. Carbone widened his eyes. "I said take a seat on the couch." They both sat. Father Carbone's thug-like demeanor was back. "I can fill you in a bit regarding the religious issues that were thrown into my lap, but you're going to have to talk to Litner if you want the other facts. That's my final offer, so don't bother to ask me anything that I can't answer, because my lips are sealed. Got it?" Patrick nodded, happy to be getting any information at all.

Carbone continued. "I have to ask you Patrick, first, do you trust this girl, and second, do you want her to hear what I'm going to say, regardless of the consequences?"

"What consequences?"

Carbone looked solemn. "If you involve her in this, then she too will be under the watchful eye of the FBI. This isn't a game."

Patrick looked at Robin, and wondered if he should be involving her. She met his eyes, and her thoughts were clear. She didn't give a shit about being monitored by the FBI. She only wanted to help Joey. "Robin knows Joey and Shep as well, if not better than I do. We're on the same side of the fence."

Father Carbone ran his fingers through his hair. Shaking his head, he said, "I don't feel right about this."

"What if I said I was going to help Litner?"

Carbone looked at Patrick and his expression changed. "If you can swear to that, then I would be more willing to share what I know with you. If you're just blowing smoke up my ass to get me to talk, then you and I are going to have a serious confrontation at a later date." The priest puffed himself up, looking like a street punk suddenly.

"On the level, Father Carbone. I intend to help the FBI. I want to cooperate, but I still haven't got a clue what's going on here. I'm the one going out on a limb here, so cut me some slack! After all, I'm agreeing to help without any solid information." Patrick leaned over and looked at Carbone seriously. "I am more confused than I have ever been in my entire life. I'm asking you, Father Carbone, as a priest, to please help me. Help me to understand. Please." His emotions were on the surface lately, and for once, he allowed them to show. Hey, if he had to live with being an emotional basket case, he might as well start using it to his advantage. He let his eyes mist up with the tears that came so easily lately, stopping them just before they erupted.

Carbone looked compassionate. "Okay Patrick. We'll talk, but under certain conditions."

"Name them."

"I call Litner first thing in the morning and set up a meeting."

Patrick stiffened. The spooky white-haired FBI Agent made him uneasy. "Fine. We talk to Agent Litner tomorrow. What else?"

Father Carbone pointed a finger at Patrick and Robin. "I want no hostile interruptions from either of you until I'm finished talking." He pointed directly at Robin. "I mean it. I don't care how much bullshit you decide this all sounds like. I want no yelling, and no storming out. You are not the only ones feeling a little volatile lately if you catch my drift. Now do we have a deal?"

"Agreed," Patrick said.

Carbone shifted his gaze to Robin. "How about you, Super Girl?"

Robin nodded. "Agreed." She leaned back on the couch. Carbone looked satisfied.

"Good. Now keep in mind, I can only show you the small aspect of this investigation that concerns me. I'm aiding the with the theological portion of their findings. What Agent Litner has to show you, well, you'll have to wait and hear that from him. Fair enough?"

Patrick nodded. "At this point, I'll settle for any information you can give me."

"Good then. Stay here. I'll go get the stuff. Does anyone want tea?"

"Sure," Robin said. Carbone left the room and Robin leaned in to Patrick.

"What stuff?" she whispered. Patrick shrugged. Five minutes later, the priest returned with the tea set. He set it down and left the room again. He returned right away with a cardboard box, which he placed on the coffee table.

"Gather round kiddies, it's show and tell time." Carbone pulled out a leather notebook, two manila envelopes, and placed them on the table. They were clasped tight, something bulky inside. He left the room again, and returned with a velvet sack. With a clinking of metal, the priest pulled out a series of elaborate daggers. Robin reached for one of the envelopes but Carbone snatched it back. "Don't touch anything until I say! Believe me, you don't want it all at once."

"What are you talking about? What is all this stuff and what's in the envelopes?" Robin demanded.

Patrick was studying the daggers. "Cool knives," he said. "Where did you get them?"

"They belong to your friend, Melvin Eugene Shepherd. Or at least they did until the FBI confiscated them."

Patrick looked up at the priest with dismay. "These were Shep's? I've never seen them before."

The priest nodded. "The knives and the journal, along with the contents of these envelopes, were found in hidden in Shepherd's home in Boston." The priest took a deep breath. "The FBI enlisted my help for several reasons. One is that the apparition appeared on my church. Lucky me. The second reason has to do with my having a PHD in Theology. I'm an expert on religious history. And thirdly, I went to high school with Agent Litner. He's a friend of mine, although I hadn't seen him in some time before this happened."

"You have a P.H.D. in Theology?" Patrick asked. "Couldn't you be making more money if you were teaching somewhere?" Patrick knew it was the wrong question as soon as he saw Father Carbone's malignant stare.

"The priesthood is a calling, not a career choice."

"Oh. Of course. Forgive me. Go on, please," Patrick urged.

"Fine. Agent Litner came to me with this box of goodies to see what I could make of it all. The notebook seems to be a sort of hand written scripture, and I use the word scripture loosely. "

Father Carbone pulled open the leather notebook with the handwritten pages. "We believe this little journal here is done in the handwriting of your friend Shepherd." Carbone looked up for a reaction.

"Let me see that!" Robin demanded, harshly. Father Carbone gave her a warning look. "I'm sorry. It's just that, I know Shep's writing. I'm only trying to help." Reluctantly, Father Carbone handed her the leather book. She opened it up and made a disgruntled face. "What the hell is this? It's not even in English."

"Indeed. Some of it, if you look further in, actually is in English, but the language shifts in and out. At certain points it becomes German, then Spanish, and see here? This is Latin. Some of the language I don't recognize at all, neither does the FBI, so I'm assuming it's written in some sort of code. But the parts that are written in recognizable languages are what boggled my mind the most. It's as though the author had such a fluent use of all the languages, that he just flowed in and out of them haphazardly."

"It has pictures!" Patrick exclaimed.

"Yes. The pictures were actually most helpful in interpreting the pages that had indecipherable language. This book is referred to in several places as a "testament". See here at the top of each page? It's called 'The Book of Zirub'. I did some research in my theology books and tried to find references to that name because it sounded vaguely familiar to me, but I came up with nothing."

"I can't believe Shep did any of this." Patrick said, skeptical.

Father Carbone flipped to the back page of the hand written-notebook. He pointed to a few words scribbled haphazardly along the corner of the page, as if in a mindless doodle. "Do you recognize the handwriting, Patrick?"

Patrick looked at it. It did look like Shep's writing. He looked at Robin, who nodded. Carbone went back to the beginning of the notebook. "Fading genius that I am, I had to get some help from some of my former colleagues. We stayed up and studied this book for two nights, trying to come up with some semblance of the story it told so we could let the FBI know what it meant. Like I said before, the drawings really helped, but bear in mind that this is only one interpretation, and we took liberties in filling in the blanks." Father Carbone had a 3" by 5" card inserted into each page of the book.

"Each card describes what is written on the page, as well as what we think is illustrated." Father Carbone looked at Patrick and Robin, his eyes serious. "Are you kids sure you're ready to hear this?"

Patrick took Robin's hand in his. "The notebook tells a story?" Robin asked, her voice quivering a bit.

Carbone nodded. "That's what a testament is, after all. Should I go on?"

"Tell us what it means," Patrick said.

The priest turned to the first page, where an amateur drawing showed a man in a black hooded cape, coming out of a hole or a tunnel. "I love a picture book," Carbone said, "This clearly shows a figure coming through some sort of tunnel. It speaks of beings coming through, or crossing over from another place. The closest translation my colleagues and I could come up with for the caption beneath is, "Those who were trapped."

"Who are 'Those who were trapped'?" Patrick asked.

"I have no idea," the priest said. "We're not even sure those are the right words. You'll have to bear with me. Even the modern language is very vague."

"Please, continue," Robin said.

Father Carbone turned the page, where another little white note card was wedged between the pages, a tiny cheat sheet. The illustration was of a boy, standing in front of a sunset. "This says something about a child being chosen," Carbone said. "Then something about the one who crossed over finding the child. See this word here?" Carbone pointed to the scribble. "We think it means either 'to cross over' or 'to come through from another place'. It's referring to the figure in the black cloak."

Patrick stared at the drawing of the little boy and a shiver went down his spine. Why would Shep write all this stuff? And when did he learn all these other languages? Father Carbone looked at Patrick, seeming to sense his unease. "Things get weirder from here, Patrick. Should I go on?"

Patrick shrugged, trying to look nonchalant for Robin's sake. "Of course. It's just a bunch of crazy crap that Shep wrote down. He was probably stoned."

Carbone looked at him. "Next page. There is no picture here, but we found this to be rather interesting. It speaks of removing the child from his earthbound family. This along with the calming of the soul will allow the child to begin to follow his chosen path."

"The calming of the soul? What the hell is that?" Robin said.

"This one I know." Carbone said, looking pleased. "The calming of the soul. It's been used by primitive tribes over the years, and even by Native American's as a sort of focusing tool. Some people believed that if the soul was put to sleep, or calmed, that the mind could focus without hindrance, without distraction."

"Without feelings?" Patrick said suddenly. "Without a conscience?"

Robin looked at him. "Patrick, you're not suggesting..."

"I just think it's a bit of a coincidence, don't you Robin? Did Joey cry even once when his family died? And what about that? Being removed from his earthbound family?"

"No way, Patrick!" she said. "You're just looking for things now. We can't help Joey if you start getting as crazy as Shep."

Father Carbone closed the book. "I've clearly said too much."

Patrick and Robin both turned. "No," Robin said. "I'm sorry for the outburst. I want to see the rest of the book. Please."

"I don't believe you can stay calm."

"We will. We promise. Don't we Patrick?" Robin gave him a look.

Father Carbone eyed them both suspiciously, but finally he opened the book again and turned to the next page. He held the book out for them both to see. It was another illustration. It depicted the boy, now drawn as a teenager, kneeling before the cloaked figure, who was pouring blood from a wound in his arm into the boy's open mouth. Patrick recalled his conversation with Aunt Betsy.

"Gross! What are they doing?" Robin exclaimed.

Carbone picked up the little index card. "This page speaks of a gift of power, power that is transferred from the one who was trapped, to the chosen boy. Now see here on the next page..." Father Carbone turned the page to show a more elaborate illustration of the boy, standing before a crowd of people with light shooting out of him. The people in the crowd smiled up at the boy with adoration. "It claims that the boy will now have the power to enchant. At least we think that word means to enchant. It's either enchant or hypnotize."

Patrick and Robin had both grown quiet. "There are only a few more pages, but I think they are most interesting. As you can see here, the boy is shown carrying a sword. As I turn the page here, it shows the boy standing with a new figure, someone different than the previously seen hooded figure. See here?"

The new picture showed the boy standing next to a tall, shirtless muscular man. He had broad shoulders and a strong square chin. He was holding a large shield. A caption was printed beneath the picture in an undecipherable language.

"What does that say?" Patrick asked, pointing to the picture.

"It says 'The Sword and The Shield'. Patrick, do you remember when I asked you if you ever did a blood ritual?"

"Yes, I certainly remember that."

"Well, this is why," he said, and flipped the page. Patrick sucked his breath in as he gazed upon the picture. Three figures, the cloaked man, the boy, and the new muscular figure all stood in a circle. The chosen boy had his arm joined at a wound on the wrist with the muscular man. Little droplets of blood were drawn leaking from the two men's wrists. The cloaked figure stood by watching, a bloody dagger in his hand.

"Holy shit!" Patrick said. "Holy shit!"

"Yes, you said that already. This looks familiar to you, yes?"

"Holy shit! Those words right there. What do those words mean?" The caption underneath the picture had printed, 'Esk ul kalde ich hlada ich dar'. Shep had spoken those strange words that night out on Joey's balcony, when they had performed the childish blood ritual.

Father Carbone picked up his little index card. "I don't know what those mean, but there's a caption just beneath it in Spanish, so I'm assuming it means the same thing."

Patrick swallowed hard. "That doesn't say 'unity and brotherhood', does it?"

Father Carbone's brown eyes looked sharply over the card. "I'm afraid not. It means, 'The Shield Protects the Sword.'"

Robin looked at Patrick. "Patrick? I don't understand."

Patrick reluctantly explained the blood pact that the three of them had performed the night of Joey's madness at Monty's bar. He told them how Shep had said it would be good for Joey's morale, and about the dagger with the jewels on it.

"Did you stand in a circle?" Father Carbone asked.

Patrick nodded and pointed to the picture. "That's how we stood, out on Joey's balcony. Exactly like that. This is nuts. That would mean that they staged the whole thing. The argument, the fight, everything. Why? How long? How long had they been planning this? It's crazy!"

"Shepherd is a lunatic," Robin said softly. "I've been sleeping with a lunatic."

Patrick shook his head and held up a hand. "Wait a minute here. Father Carbone, as sick as this all may sound, does it really make Shep dangerous? I mean, don't get me wrong, I'm not pleased to discover that my friends could win an academy award for their acting, but nobody has been hurt by this. Not really."

"Well, this isn't the document that disturbed the FBI. Litner has that one. There are a couple of more pages of text." Carbone looked up at Patrick seriously. "It speaks about the Shield being bound by blood to protect the chosen child, or 'The Sword', at all costs. It goes on like that for a while, about the Shield being the protector, then the text just stops. "

Father Carbone pointed to a tiny, erratic scribbling on the lower left corner of the page. "See here, is a scribble along the side that looks like it was written in anger. See how the pen digs into the paper?"

Patrick looked. It was not written in English, but it had six exclamation points after it, and the letters were large and angry-looking. There was a tear in the paper where the pen had been thrust right through the page. "What does that say?"

"It says, 'Eli, Eli, lama sabachthani'. They are the words spoken by Jesus Christ after hours of suffering on the cross. It means, 'My God, My God, why have you forsaken me?'"

"Oh," Patrick said. "I learned that in Sunday school years ago. Bad memory." Patrick looked down at his arm and found that he had been rubbing the tiny scar made from the dagger. He looked up at Father Carbone, his Irish face white and haunted. "What did they do to me, Father Carbone?"

The priest took his hand. "In my opinion, they didn't do a damn thing to you. Joey and Shep are quite simply deranged. As far as this so-called blood pact is concerned, I'd get a tetanus shot if I were you, then I'd stop worrying about it."

Patrick shrugged. "I guess you're right. It's just that I've been dreaming about Joey every night. In each dream I'm trying to save his life. The dreams are monstrous. They wake me up with headaches."

Father Carbone leaned forward and looked him in the eye. "They're dreams, Patrick. That's all. It's your subconscious trying to sort through everything that's been happening to you. The fact that you're having bad dreams has nothing to do with yours or anybody else's blood. The only power anyone has over you is that which you give them."

Patrick nodded, but he was remembering the strange shock that had passed through his arm when Shep said those odd words. He remembered the pressure as Shep sandwiched Joey's arm to his.

Robin shook her head. "How can you be so sure that these characters in this testament are supposed to be Patrick and Joey, Father? I mean, this could all be a coincidence."

"I was skeptical too, Robin," the priest said. "Until I saw these." Father Carbone handed Patrick one of the envelopes. "Here. Look at this one first. These two envelopes were well hidden in Shepherd's house." On the outside of the envelope, were the words "The Sword" written in ball point pen. It was Shep's handwriting.

Patrick pulled the contents out and spread it onto the table. They were photographs, dozens of them, and they were all of Joey. They went in order it seemed, starting with pictures of a six year old Joey running on the beach. More childhood snapshots followed, all taken from a distance. Some were in the park, some in Joey's back yard. They advanced to Joey in Junior high school, a bevy of different photographs of Joey performing in school plays; Joey as Macbeth, Joey as Dracula, Joey as the Captain of the H.M.S. Pinafore.

Robin thumbed through the pictures. "Where did he get these? I've never seen any of these pictures before."

Patrick flipped through the rest of the photos. There were a few more of Joey at about fourteen playing street hockey, and then there were no more. "Robin, how old was Joey when Shep moved in?" Patrick asked.

"He was fifteen. Why?'

"I don't know. This is just too weird."

Father Carbone replaced the pictures and handed Patrick the second packet. "If you think that's weird, you ought to love this." The second envelope had the words, "The Shield", written in the same blue pen on the outside. Patrick hesitated. "Go on, take it," Father Carbone said.

Patrick's heart sped as he reached into the envelope to pull out the contents. It was more pictures, only this time they were all of Patrick. They started with Patrick in junior high school. A twelve-year-old Patrick threw a baseball in the school field. Then there was a slightly older Patrick leaping over hurdles in a track meet. There was Patrick at the school gym with a crowd of friends, Patrick lifting weights, Patrick playing soccer. "Jesus, that was back in high school! Shep didn't even meet me until we were in college. It doesn't make any sense!"

"Yes," Carbone said, "he did not meet you until college, but it appears he may have *chosen* you long before that."

Patrick stared at the priest. "That's crazy. No way."

"Are you sure?" Father Carbone reached into the pile and handed him the last picture. It was Patrick arriving at college on his first day. He knew it was his first day because his parents were with him in the picture, and he was carrying his stereo into the dorm.

Patrick stared at the picture, gaping. "Why?" he asked Father Carbone. "Why me?"

"If I had to guess, I would say it was because of your size and perhaps your athletic ability. Did you do anything extraordinary when you were younger? Something that might have drawn attention to you?"

"Not really. I was a typical jock. You know, high school sports hero, that sort of thing."

"Were you ever in the newspaper?"

Patrick shrugged. "Yeah, I was in the paper all the time. So were a lot of other athletes."

"Hmm," Carbone said. "Would you say you are a loyal person Patrick?"

"I'm the most loyal guy you could ever meet. What are you getting at Father Carbone?"

"It sounds like you'd make someone a fine body guard."

"Body guard?"

"Yes. You're big, exceptionally athletic, and loyal. Sounds like a winning combination to me."

Robin shook her head. "I don't believe Shep did any of this. It's just not logical."

Father Carbone raised his brows at her. "Is it logical for a self proclaimed atheist to decide overnight that he wants to form his own church, using his grief stricken best friend as the front man?"

Robin shrugged. "Anything's possible with Shep. If you only knew him."

Something slammed loudly against the screen door. The three of them jumped. Father Carbone ran to the door. Patrick was sure that he was going to see one of the curly-topped Shep-alikes creeping around outside. Instead, a very young black man stood swaying on the porch. His face was bleeding along his forehead, and the dripping blood had caked onto the tiny braids that adorned his head. Patches of skin on his arms looked burned and his clothes were nearly shredded. Carbone opened the door.

"Please," the boy said weakly. "They're trying to kill me." He took one step and collapsed on the floor.

Chapter Twenty-One

"He's hurt bad. Let's get him to the couch," Father Carbone said. He and Patrick each grabbed an arm and carried the wounded young stranger over to the couch and lay him down.

"We need to call an ambulance," Father Carbone said.

The kid twitched and his eyes fluttered open. He grabbed the priest's arm. "No ambulance! You can't call anyone. I'm begging you, just let me stay here for a while."

"But son, you have burns on your arms and your face is badly cut. You need medical attention."

"Please. It looks worse than it is. Please, no ambulance." The kid's voice was pleading and raspy. His brown skin was ashen. "They can't know I'm alive! Don't you see? They'll try to kill me again!"

"He's delirious," Robin said.

He looked at her for a moment then fell back on the couch, silently crying. "I'm not delirious. I wish I were," he said between tears.

Father Carbone knelt next to the couch and took the boy's hand. "You're safe here. I want to help you, but I need to know what happened to you."

"They blew up the photography lab," the kid said. "They blew it up with me in it. I got out. I got out just in time. When I got home, my apartment was torn apart. I couldn't stay there. I didn't know where to go. I figured this was a good enough place. This is where it all started."

Patrick, who had been standing behind Father Carbone, stepped forward now. He walked toward the couch where the young man lay. "Who did this to you? Who blew up a lab? Where did this happen?" he asked.

The kid looked up, focused on Patrick, and his eyes widened with new terror. He sprang off of the couch and crawled backward on the floor, pointing a shaking finger up at Patrick. "I know you! I've seen you! You're one of them!"

Patrick took a step back. "Hey, I don't know what you're talking about, pal."

The kid looked up at Father Carbone, still pointing at Patrick. "He's one of them. I saw him that night! He's with them!"

Patrick stared at the dark-skinned teen, where he squatted on the floor, crawling slowly backward, crab style. He couldn't be much more than eighteen years old. Even through the scrapes and bruises, his brown skin had the taut glow of youth. His nose was long and delicate, his eyes more gold than brown. He was wearing Khakis and what was left of a pale pink button down shirt that screamed of The Gap. His tiny braids, aside from being currently smeared with blood, were neat and silky. He looked like College. He may have gotten himself into some trouble, but it was clearly something he was not accustomed to.

Father Carbone got down on the floor and crawled slowly toward the kid. "Nobody here is going to hurt you, son. This man here is an acquaintance of mine. Why would you think he would hurt you?"

The kid was shaking. "I saw him the night he climbed the church. He knows that Shepherd guy, the one who tried to kill me."

The room fell into shocked silence. Robin stepped cautiously toward the kid, who crouched on the floor like a cornered animal. "I'm sorry. Did you say Shepherd?"

The kid looked up at her suspiciously. "I thought this church would be safe," he whispered. "I thought I'd be safe here!"

Robin grabbed him by the collar. "What did you say about Shepherd?" she screamed. "You said something about Shepherd!"

"Robin, stop it!" Patrick tore her off of the boy.

Father Carbone knelt on the floor next to him. "Listen to me. This man Patrick is not going to hurt you. Whatever was done to you, I can assure you that nobody in this room was part of it. Now why don't we get your wounds cleaned up, then we can all sit down and discuss this rationally."

The kid looked around the room, his gaze lingering on Patrick. "Okay, but none of you better try anything. I escaped death once tonight, and I'll do it again if I have to."

"What's your name, son?" Father Carbone asked gently.

He rose up on shaky legs, and moved gingerly back to the couch, wincing and clinging to his ribs. He stuck his hand out to the priest. "The name is Copie."

Chapter Twenty-Two

The day was a dream of sunshine and spring breezes. Now that the nasty business with the photography student was taken care of, they were all in high spirits. Joey and Shep sipped margaritas on the deck and watched the crowd of followers dancing all over the yard. Some of them congregated on the huge deck, playing hackey sack or making blender drinks at the bar. It was quite a spectacle. Joey adjusted his lawn chair and leaned back sighing. The music was festive, and the followers were clearly ecstatic to be there.

"It looks like a Grateful Dead concert, doesn't it?" Shep said.

Joey scowled. "Yeah, but instead of LSD, they're juiced on tequila. Hey where's Allisto with those burgers? Didn't you tell him to make the paddies?"

"Yeah, he's in the house making them now. The poor thing. I thought he was going to faint when I handed him the ground beef. Allisto is not a big fan of cow flesh."

Joey laughed. "Allisto is not a big fan of any flesh. Even his own."

Shep's lips tightened. "I know, but he's come a long way. He'll get used to it in time. Hey, speaking of flesh, how are things going with Kelinda?"

Joey frowned. "She's weird. How long do I have to keep being her boyfriend?"

"Indefinitely, unless you want me to kill her. Why? What's the problem?"

Joey shrugged. "She makes me uncomfortable."

Shep laughed loudly. "Oh please. Your biggest problem is that you have to have sex with a beautiful woman."

"It's not that. I like the sex, it's just that it's gotten...weird."

Shep raised an eyebrow and sat up in his chair. "Weird? Oh do tell. Does she want to call you Daddy or something?"

"Don't be gross. It's nothing like that."

"What then? Why are you being so tight-lipped? This is me you're talking to."

Joey shifted uncomfortably in his lounge chair. He looked around, then leaned in close to Shep. "All right. I don't think she even likes me any more. You know what I mean? I feel like she's going through the motions just so she can get...it."

Shep looked confused. "It?" He moved his chair closer to Joey, interested now.

"Yeah. You know. It."

"So she's using you for sex. Big deal. You're using her too."

Joey shook his head. "I'm not talking about straight sex. We hardly ever do that any more. She seems to be addicted to...well...it."

Shep grimaced. "What the hell are you talking about? She's addicted to what? What it? Sex?"

"No. I mean, she's addicted to IT!" Joey said in a loud whisper.

Shep frowned, then nodded as the realization hit him. "Oh. You mean, it it."

"Yes. It it."

"You are talking about your semen, right?"

"Shhh! Yes!"

Shep struggled unsuccessfully to suppress his crooked grin. "Why didn't you just say so?"

Joey's eyes shifted around the deck to make sure no one was listening. "It's embarrassing!" he hissed in Shep's ear. "Just forget I told you anything."

Shep took a long haul off a joint and let the smoke drift out of his nostrils. "Hmm. I don't know about her being addicted to it. I've never heard of such a thing. Why do you think that?"

Joey laughed, a sharp breathy sound. "It's like she's getting high off of my bodily fluids. When I kiss her, she sucks the saliva out of my mouth. I feel like I'm at the dentist every time we make out. The other day, she and I went for a jog around the property. I spit on the ground once, and she gave me a look like I was wasting precious gold. Oh, and after she, you know..."

"Sucks you off?" Shep asked seriously. He was leaning forward now with hands clasped between his knees like a patient psychiatrist.

Joey's lip curled. "How quaintly put. Yes, after she does that, she lies there with this bizarre expression on her face, like a heroin addict that just got a fix or something. This lasts for about five minutes, then she gets up and leaps around the room, dancing like she's on an adrenaline rush. When the little dance thing is over, she just takes off, and I don't see her again until she wants more. Sometimes I don't see her for a whole day, and then she's just there suddenly, climbing all over me. I'm telling you Shep, it's creepy, man."

Shep stubbed out the joint on the arm of the lounge chair. "Huh. I always wondered what an unsupervised contamination might do. I never wanted to risk it with Robin. We always used condoms."

"See, this is what I'm worried about, Shep. You gave me your blood for years. Nothing like this ever happened to me."

Shep laughed. "No, Joey. You never danced merrily about after a blood ritual. Our situation was completely different though. My blood was given to you with the proper ceremony, in a controlled environment. I drew a specific power out in you."

Joey nodded. "Yeah, the enchantment thing. I know."

Shep nodded. "Right. You see, it's the mix of my blood, and your human blood that draws people to you. Human instinct is so deeply buried that they don't realize they're sensing your blood. They only know there's something special about you. They think they've made a connection. That's why these zombies here listen to everything you say. They can't sense my power, because it's completely foreign. But when my essence is mixed with your human essence, watch out. It flows in you. They don't know what they're seeing, but they see it, something more, something beyond this dismal world. And you're not even fucking any of them."

Joey's lip curled up again. "So what you're saying is, I may have overloaded Kelinda."

"Precisely. Think about it, Joey. If one speech from you can mesmerize sixty people, what do you think a load of your jizz, directly ingested, is going to do to Kelinda?"

Joey wrinkled his nose. "I preferred it when you were calling it my essence."

"Your essence then. It transfers elements as well as blood does. However you slice it, it's going to change her somehow. She's got something more than human running through her veins now, and part of her probably knows it." Shep looked concerned then. "She hasn't exhibited any special abilities, has she?"

Joey squinted as a beam of sunlight fell across his eyes. "Special abilities? What do you mean?"

Shep shrugged. "Well, technically it is possible for her to take on some of our attributes, even though I haven't specifically drawn anything out in her. She has after all been directly infected."

Joey rubbed his forehead, looking worried. "You know, the followers seem to have become quite fond of Kelinda lately. Do you think there's a connection?"

Shep squinted at the sunlight. "Could be. She may be radiating her own essence now. To play it safe, I'll tell her to stay away from the fields. Let's keep these house parties to a minimum too. I don't want anyone controlling these people but you."

"So what do I do in the meantime?"

"Just keep an eye on her."

Joey shrugged. "Well it's not that easy. Granted, she follows me around until she gets what she wants, but then she just disappears. Then she's just done with me, you know?"

"Oh you poor baby. Do you feel used?"

"Yes I do. I feel like a piece of meat."

"Speaking of meat, I'm going to go see what's keeping Allisto with those burgers. If these zombies keep drinking on an empty stomach it's going to get ugly."

Shep stood and headed toward the house. He was almost to the sliding door when he heard a loud pop like a firecracker, then an explosion. The party guests screamed, and scrambled in all directions. Shep turned back just in time to see Joey fall off of his chair. Someone had shot him. Blood gushed from his left shoulder, forming a red stain on the pale wood of the deck. Juris and Margol came running out of the house. "Get him inside!" Shep screamed. "Get him inside now!"

Chaos. The bullet hit Joey's shoulder and then ricocheted off the gas grill, exploding one of the propane tanks. Luckily nobody was standing near the grill, but the sound of the explosion sent the followers scrambling for cover wherever they could find it. Only the brothers remained unruffled. Juris and Margol followed Shep's instructions and got Joey inside the house. They scooped him off the deck and carried him quickly through the back slider as blood gushed from his shoulder onto their clothes. Shep followed them in. They sat Joey down at a kitchen chair. Allisto came running out of the pantry wearing rubber gloves. He had scraps of raw hamburger all over his shirt. Shep wiped away Joey's blood with a towel and examined the shoulder.

"Bullet didn't go in. It looks like you just got grazed."

Joey winced as Shep pressed his finger around the puffy wound. "Okay, grazed," he said, "but was I the target?"

Shep ignored Joey's question and tossed Juris the key to the medical supply cabinet. "Clean and dress it, Juris. Use the homemade balm to stop the bleeding. I'll be back."

"Shepherd!" Joey demanded. "Was I the fucking target?"

Shep looked at him. "Stay inside."

❧

He ran down to the basement and got a pistol out of the locked cabinet. He quickly loaded it and holstered it inside his pants, concealing it with the long tee shirt he wore over his jeans. This was bullshit, he thought. Obrien should be handling this. He ran back up the stairs and straight out the back door. "Where are you going?" Allisto called after him.

"Watch Joey!" he screamed back.

He stepped out onto the deck and stopped short as a few dozen pairs of eyes stared fearfully up at him. He'd forgotten about the followers. It had been Joey's idea to invite them all up to the big house for a barbecue. Joey wanted them to feel like part of the family. Well, they'd been shot at now. He wondered how they liked the indoctrination. They sat hunched in fearful poses all around the deck and the lawn. Some were still curled up under tables and chairs, but they came out when they saw Shep.

Brin-Marie, a twenty-five-year-old former nurse with a particularly obsessive love of Joey, came running toward Shep. Her brown hair was cut short, boyish, but she was tiny and had a pretty face so she could pull it off. Big fat tears streamed down her cheeks. "Is Joey dead? He's dead isn't he!" she wailed.

"Joey is fine. Everyone come. Listen up." They came crawling slowly out of their hiding places. "I'm going to find out who fired that shot. I need you to go back to your camps for your own safety," he said. They stared at Shep blankly, a montage of newly made gypsies who had given up their lives to live in service of Joey Duvaine, the prophet. None of them moved. "Didn't you hear me? I said go back to your camps where you'll be safe!"

Their eyes glazed with the intangible spell Joey had cast over them. They knew that Shep was more or less running things at The Bluffs, but it was not Shep who kept them there. It was Joey. The poor dears thought they were still in control of their own thoughts.

"We want to see Joey!" one of the young men yelled.

"Yes!" another chimed in. "We want to know if Joey is okay. Have him come out and show us that he's all right! Then we will leave. Not before."

Shep was losing his patience. Mindless drones, exercising what they thought was their right to question him. They were all too far-gone to realize that they had no rights. They were simply addicts, concerned that their drug of choice had been taken away from them. He couldn't control the contempt in his voice when he spoke. "People, let me explain this to you mindless fucks as simply as possible. Joey can not come outside, because somebody might take another SHOT at him!" He slammed his fist down on the patio table for emphasis. "Now would you morons please do as I say before the shooter gets even further away than I suspect he already is?"

The crowd's gaze suddenly shifted to look behind Shep. Their faces lit up with smiles. Shep turned around to see that Kelinda had appeared outside of the door. The bright pink hair still surprised him. Shep had told Joey to change Kelinda's appearance if she was going to be seen with him. With the long dark hair, she'd looked too much like the apparition. It was Joey who had insisted on the pink hair dye. Kelinda's new chin length, layered hairdo glowed magenta neon under the sun. Joey had a sadistic sense of humor at times. It was a control thing, Shep supposed. Joey seemed disappointed that Kelinda had maintained a certain level of control and self respect since she'd arrived. As enamored as Kelinda was with him, she still found the audacity to disagree with Joey, even yell at him occasionally. As odd as she had become since her arrival, she still carried herself with a sort of maniacal dignity. She spent most of her time with the followers, and they adored, her, treating her like a queen.

Kelinda walked forward, and the crowd visibly softened at the sight of her. Much to Shep's dismay, the pink hair was actually flattering on Kelinda, accentuating her delicate features. She was dressed in a long black gauze dress, with multiple strands of pink beads around her neck and her wrists. The hot pink beads matched her hair exactly. The carefully matching outfits were no doubt a way of showing Joey that he had not rattled her by making her dye her hair such an outlandish color.

She walked to where Shep was standing, and smiled, calming the crowd as she approached. "Now Shepherd, you're just upset," she said. "You didn't mean to call our wonderful friends morons, did you?"

She gave Shep a warning look. Shep shrugged. "No. I didn't mean it," he said, through clenched teeth.

"Kelinda! Is Joey all right?" Brin-Marie yelled.

"A bullet grazed Joey's shoulder," she said in a soothing tone. "He'll just need a few stitches. He sends you all his love, but he is concerned for your safety. He wishes for you all to return to your camps for the time being."

Without further question, they all filed off the deck and headed back through the fields toward their camps. As soon as they disappeared into the fields, Kelinda's sugary smile dropped. She looked at Shep. Lately she looked at him with hatred, not fear as she originally had. He wasn't worried about it. If she ever went against him, he'd simply put her down like a sick dog.

"You can't talk to them like that!" she said. "They're very sensitive."

"Why don't you go paint your toe nails or something. Let me worry about business."

"Find who did this," she said sharply, then turned and walked quickly back into the house.

"Yeah, try to refrain from sucking the blood out of Joey's wound, Vampira!" he yelled after her. She either didn't hear him, or completely ignored him.

∼≈

Another house sat up on a hill directly to the left of where Shep stood. The big brown house was the only one visible from Joey's back yard. Shep squinted up at it. It wasn't quite as large as the Duvaine house, but it was set high and probably had an extraordinary view of the distant water. And of the Duvaine house. Shep looked over at the melted gas grill, estimating the direction in which the bullet had come. He looked back up at the neighboring house. The bullet had come from that direction. Whoever had fired that shot, if they were still there, would be expecting police. They would not be expecting Shep.

After a ten minute trek through a wooded back trail, Shep stood at the edge of a rusty old gate surrounding an overgrown garden that led to the back of the big brown house. The place was still, yet he thought he heard music echoing from somewhere inside. Shep placed his hand on his pistol. If the shooter was lucky, the gun would be the only killing tool Shep would use. If they pissed him off, well, there were more creative ways to administer punishment, though he wasn't privy to wasting his energy on such trivial matters.

He proceeded into the garden, tearing his way through the dead scrub. As he got closer to the house, the music became clearer, Credence Clearwater Revival. Shep pushed open the back door and found himself in a simple yet outrageously orderly kitchen. Cups and canisters were lined up with precision along the counters. The place was dark and lifeless. An American flag hung from one of the windowpanes like a shade. With the gun out in front of him, Shep moved carefully into an adjoining room where a glass cabinet displayed shotguns, rifles, and hunting knives, all polished to perfection. On the wall opposite the weapons cabinet hung a mounted moose head, its dead eyes keeping watch on the guns. Next to that was a banner with gold lettering that read, VETERANS OF WAR. "Great," Shep whispered. "It's the fucking Deer Hunter."

Music traveled down from a narrow carpeted stairwell that Shep found off of the next room. He crept up the stairs with his back to the wall, accidentally knocking down a rack of military medals. "Shit!" he muttered. The music was extremely loud, so he doubted the occupant heard the medals fall. The muffled tune became clearer as he rounded the top of the stairs. The twangy guitar sounds were overlaid with a raspy voice singing, 'I put a spell on you, because you're mine...'

With the gun in front of him, Shep turned the corner to find himself in a narrow hallway. More military paraphernalia hung along the walls. The man was so still that Shep didn't even notice him at first. He was seated in front of a window in the small room at the end of the hallway. His back was to Shep as he looked out. On the floor to the man's left was the boom box responsible for the screeching music. Shep moved slowly down the hall toward the tiny room where the stranger sat in a high back chair looking out at the world. He had gray hair down to his shoulders. Shep would have thought it was a woman if not for the hairy arm that hung over one side of the chair, holding a stereo remote control. A grayish blue tattoo decorated the man's lower arm, along with a jagged scar across the elbow.

Shep entered the room, moving in closer so he could see over the man's head to the window. The window looked directly down onto the back yard of the Duvaine residence. Shep could see the deck, the field of crops, and even the tiny dottings of the follower's campsites. He watched as Margol and Allisto stepped out onto the deck and sprayed the melted grill with a powdery fire extinguisher.

The volume of the music dropped. Shep looked down and saw that the man's thumb was on the little volume button on the remote. Shep grew still as death as the room fell silent. He held the gun steady, pointing it at the back of the stranger's head, then took a silent step backward. He didn't want to get blood and brains all over himself. He was wearing new jeans.

"Are you that much of a pussy that you'd shoot an old man in the back?"

Shep flinched, surprised to hear the man speak. He was sure he'd been undetected. "Turn around then. Let me see your face."

The man didn't budge. Shep hated veterans. Many of them had lost their minds and their souls on some grassy battlefield long ago. Men without souls were very difficult to scare. It was distressing. "I said turn around, or I will indeed shoot you in the back."

The man still didn't budge. Shep wasn't about to walk around to face him. He might be holding a gun in his lap. "You must be quite a hero, judging from all those medals I saw on the walls. It would be a shame after all that bravery and valor to be shot in the back by a pussy like me. Don't you think?"

"That would be a damn shame, wouldn't it boy?" The man swiveled his chair around to face Shep. His face was tanned dark with leathery lines around the eyes. He was not as old as Shep would have thought. He didn't look more than fifty, but they were fifty hard years. His upper body was well muscled. His legs looked strong as well under the desert print camouflage pants he wore. His eyes were cold and black with the sharpness of life experience. There was humor in those eyes too, but it was a contemptuous humor. A green bandana swept his long gray hair off his forehead, and a black tee shirt clung to his well-developed chest. White chest hairs stuck out of the top of the shirt near his neck. The man grinned, and Shep took a step back. Damn it. He hated when they weren't scared.

"Did you take a shot at my friend?" Shep demanded. "Did you fire a bullet into a crowd of people, you fucking psycho?"

The man continued to smile. "Son, do you see a gun in my hands?"

"No but I see a damned arsenal downstairs. I'm going to ask you again. Did you fire a gun at my friend?"

The man shook his head. "No sir, I did not."

With the weapon still pointed, Shep took a step closer to the window and glanced out. "Someone fired a shot from this direction. I come over here, and I find you sitting at your window with a direct view of the patio where the bullet made contact. You've got a house full of guns and a bad attitude. Would you say that's a big coincidence?"

The man shrugged. "I just came up here a few minutes ago. I didn't fire a weapon, and I didn't see any one else fire one. When I sat down, all I saw was those Moonies of yours walking through the field."

Shep lowered the gun slowly, deciding he wasn't in the mood to clean up a messy corpse. "This better not happen again. If it does, I'm coming after you." Shep turned and walked out of the room into the hallway.

"Maybe one of those Moonies tried to kill him. Did you ever think of that?" the man called after him.

Shep stopped and turned around. "They are not 'Moonies' you fucking cracker jack. Those people worship Joey. None of them want him dead."

The man chuckled. "The rabbits know when there is a snake hiding among them. He can camouflage himself in the tall grass, hidden from their innocent eyes, but they can still sense him there. They can smell him."

"Yeah, blah blah blah. You've been warned, soldier." Shep trotted back down the stairs and headed out the back door. He tore through the scrubby dead garden to the rusty gate. As he shut the gate behind him, he heard the volume on the stereo in the house crank up again. The man was singing along, quite badly to the lyrics of the song. *I put a spell on you, because you're mine*.

Shep cursed as he made his way back through the woods. He should have killed the bastard. Now he would have to keep Joey inside during the day. What was he thinking? Oh well. He could always kill him later. He shouldn't have to deal with these distractions. This was supposed to be Obrien's job. Obrien's little rebellion was becoming less and less cute as the days went by. Shep had had enough. It was time to get Obrien out here so he could start doing his job.

Shep decided he would have to turn the heat up a little. He had seen to it that Patrick lost his job, and his girlfriend, but that hadn't seemed to faze him. Shep would just have to find something that did faze him. He was fuming when he got back to the house. Having focused all of his anger on Obrien, he went for the phone. He was done coddling the stupid Mick. He'd been doing that for ten years, and it was about enough. Allisto followed him into the library, but said nothing. Allisto followed Shep around a lot, like a toddler, wanting to be with Shep all of the time. He sat down on the floor and watched Shep dial the phone. Shep got Obrien's answering machine, and seethed while he listened to the message. *'Hi, this is Patrick. I can't get to the phone right now. Please leave a message, and I'll call you right back.'*

Shep let his rage spew into the phone. "Obrien, you bone headed piece of shit! I think I've been more than patient with you, you potato-eating, self-righteous moron. Do you know what I'm offering you? I'm offering you freedom. Not the kind of freedom you get when you're old enough to be on Medicare, which is the only freedom you'll get in your pathetic life unless you come out here and join with us now! You think you're making a choice by staying put? Well let me tell you something. You're choosing death. You've got nothing without me. How have you been sleeping, Obrien? I certainly hope your dreams have been pleasant. Make the choice, Patrick. Stop the pain. Or it will only get worse."

Shep hung up the phone and felt better. Obrien's answering machine was a far better listener than Obrien himself. Allisto shifted positions on the floor and Shep jumped, having forgotten that he was in the room. Allisto was a mess, looking skunk-like with his black hair frosted in fire extinguisher dust. "Well," Allisto said smirking, "that'll get him out here for sure."

Shep grinned at him. "Sarcasm, Allisto? Did you learn that in the city?"

"No Shepherd. I learned that from you."

Shep sat down on the floor with him. He took Allisto's face gently in his hands. "Allisto," he said, his tone serious and soft, "I want to ask you something, and I want you to tell me the truth."

"Of course, Shepherd."

"Do you blame me? Do you blame me for all that has befallen us? I need to know how you feel. I need to know how all of you feel."

Allisto reciprocated Shep's action by reaching out and touching his face. "We follow you willingly as we always have, as we always will." He cupped Shep's cheeks as he pressed their foreheads together. "You ask if we blame you? Only to blame you for saving us, for tending us, and for keeping every promise you've ever made to us. Your hand did not trap us, Shepherd. Your hand freed us."

Shep held Allisto's head and nodded, as his eyes gave way to tears. "Thank you, Allisto," he whispered. "Thank you."

A throat cleared at the doorway and they both looked up to see Joey standing there. "If you two are done making out, I need someone to go to the store for me. We're out of brandy."

"Feeling better Joey?" Shep asked as he stood, pulling Allisto to his feet.

"Yeah. Just fucking peachy. I love getting shot. Brandy?"

"I'll send Russell."

"Fine." Joey left the room.

Shep looked back at Allisto, who hung his head sadly. "What is it, Allisto?"

He shook his head. "It's nothing. Nothing."

"Allisto, if you have something to say..."

"It's just, well, I'm worried about next week's mission. I miss Klee. I'm worried that..."

Shep pointed at him. "Don't say it. Don't."

Allisto cast his eyes down. "I'm sorry."

"We will get Klee out, Allisto. No one gets left behind. I keep my promises, you said so yourself. We will get Klee out! Understand?"

Allisto nodded. "Ylchnec hlaf bis, Zirub."

Shep smiled sadly. "We're supposed to be speaking English, Allisto. Remember?"

Allisto shrugged.

"I'm going to let it go just this once. And incidentally, I love you too."

Chapter Twenty-Three

For the second time in twenty-four hours, Patrick and Robin climbed the set of stone steps that led to the tiny house behind the church. They had not succeeded in interrogating young Copie the night before. Robin had begun to clean and tend to Copie's burns. The process brought out the pain, and Copie had started to scream. Father Carbone, clearly not a physician, decided to remedy the problem by giving Copie Tylenol with Codeine that he'd had in his medicine cabinet from an old knee injury. Contrary to Patrick's objections, Father Carbone administered the drugs to the suffering boy with a chaser of whiskey. Copie passed out cold, leaving the three of them to stare at the unconscious teen and wonder what his involvement in this madness was.

They'd stopped for breakfast on the way over and discovered much to Patrick's dismay that all of his credit cards had been cancelled. Neither he nor Robin voiced what they were thinking, that Shep was responsible somehow. It was far too early for paranoia. Copie himself answered the door, looking well-rested. He was wearing a pair of black pants and a black sweater that presumably belonged to Father Carbone. "Come on in. The priest is making tea," he said.

Patrick wondered if Father Carbone had a giant crate somewhere filled with nothing but tea. The man pulled the damned tea pot out for everything. Attempted murder? Tea. Terrorist conspiracies? Tea. Armageddon? Tea. Copie whistled as he made his way back to the kitchen table. His wounds were nasty but they appeared to be healing. It didn't look like there would be any permanent scarring. "You must have gotten out of that lab just in time," Patrick said, examining Copie's face.

Copie snickered. "You have no idea."

Father Carbone came into the room and set the infamous tea set down on the kitchen table. His pajamas from the previous night had been replaced with a traditional black shirt and white priest's collar, black pants and shoes. Copie looked Father Carbone up and down. "Well. I guess you really are a priest," he said.

Father Carbone laughed. Copie grabbed a cinnamon roll from the plate of pastries. "You look better than you did last night," Robin said to Copie.

Copie nodded. "Yeah, well, nobody's trying to kill me today. That tends to take it out of you."

Patrick smiled. The kid was certainly high spirited. He did look better. The color had returned to his skin, which was the color of coffee with milk. His skin had a smooth youthful glow, and his golden brown eyes were clear and sharp. "How old are you, Copie?" Patrick asked.

"I'm nineteen. How old are you?"

"Older than that. What kind of name is Copie?"

"Is this an interrogation?" Copie said as he chewed his cinnamon bun.

Patrick's smile dropped. "Perhaps you have not been made aware of the gravity of the situation we are in here," Patrick said. "This is serious, kid."

Copie widened his eyes in exaggerated surprise. "Oh, is it serious? You don't say! You'd think I would have figured that out when I was almost BURNED ALIVE!"

"Relax Copie," Father Carbone said. "Does anyone have a picture of Shepherd?"

Patrick frowned. "What for?"

Carbone rolled his eyes. "Am I the only one thinking here? We need to know if the Shepherd that tried to kill Copie last night is the same Shepherd that we know. Or at least you two know."

He looked at Patrick, then Robin. She grabbed her purse and pulled out a wallet-sized photo of her and Shepherd at the ocean. He had his arm around her. They both looked tan and happy and, well, in love. For some reason it was painful for Patrick to look at. Robin handed the picture to Father Carbone. He held it up and stared at it. "So," he said. "That's him."

"That's him," Robin said softly. Father Carbone handed the picture over to Copie. Copie took it, glancing at Robin uncomfortably as he did. He looked at the picture. Robin sat nervously twirling a lock of her blond hair. Copie looked at her but said nothing.

"Well?" she demanded. "Don't spare my feelings! Is it him or isn't it?"

Copie handed the picture back. "Yes. I'm sorry. It is the same guy."

Robin took the picture and stuffed it back into her purse. Tears streamed down her face. Patrick put a hand on her shoulder. "Copie, why would Shep want you dead?"

"Because of the photograph. I told him I'd destroy them all, but he wouldn't let me go. He kept talking about loose ends and how his project was more important than my life. He said some really bizarre things to me."

Patrick shuddered. He could deal with the fact that Shep was morally void, but murder? His mind refused to accept it. "What photograph? What are you talking about?"

"Copie why don't you just start at the beginning," Father Carbone said.

Copie nodded. "All right. The beginning. Let's see. My name is Copeland Smith, and I'm a recently-graduated photography student. I was on a school assignment the night Patrick played Hercules and scaled the wall of St. Mary's church. The night the Virgin Mary appeared on the roof. I was down on the street. I had two cameras with me, one in my knapsack and one in my hand. By the time the apparition appeared, I only had one shot left, so I took it and I ran out of film. I chucked that camera in my knapsack and pulled out the second one. I got about four more pictures of the thing before it faded and disappeared. That's when that Shepherd guy came along and ripped the camera out of my hands. I went after him but he pushed me, hard, and I fell. He's a strong little bastard."

Patrick and Robin both nodded knowingly.

"Lucky for me, or so I thought at the time, he didn't know about the other camera. I ended up with one single shot of the apparition. It was destroyed last night. I was nearly destroyed along with it."

Father Carbone looked thoughtful. "How did Shep come to find out that you had this other photograph in your possession?"

Copie explained about the enlargements he made of the photograph, and finding the bow on the nightgown. "I called the local television station. Here I was, thinking that I was going to be this big news hero. The guy at the news desk said he wanted to come down and interview me right away. The next thing I know I'm being ambushed by these thugs. That Shepherd guy is a cold motherfucker." Copie looked at the priest. "Oh, sorry Father."

Carbone waved him off. "Continue, please."

Copie touched one of the cuts below his eye, wincing. "I knew they meant to kill me because they were discussing their business right in front of me. I guess they figured that there was no need to keep their mouths shut, being that I would soon be dead."

"They?" Carbone asked. "Were there others with him?"

"Yes. Three of them were foreigners, I could tell by the way they talked. They all had that same bad Shirley Temple hair. They came with that guy from the television station. His name was Randy. No, wait a minute. It wasn't Randy. It was Russell."

"Russell?" Robin said, sounding shocked.

"Yes. It was Russell. I'm sure of it."

Patrick looked at Robin. "Craig said Russell was working at the television station. He said he was working nights, to be exact."

Father Carbone shrugged. "I'm trying to keep up here guys, but who the hell is Russell?"

Patrick explained. "Russell, along with his twin brother Craig, was the technical creator of the translucent Virgin that appeared on your church, Father Carbone. Man, I knew Russell had a thing for Shep, but I never thought he'd take it so far as to kill for him. What did he look like Copie?"

"He had short dark hair and black glasses. Kind of a dweeb. He looked a little like Elvis Costello."

"Shit!" Robin said.

Father Carbone looked at her. "Same Russell?"

Robin nodded, looking defeated. "I can't believe this," she said.

Father Carbone got up and paced the room, rubbing his chin. The rest of them sat silently, waiting for him to speak. Patrick wasn't sure how it had happened, but it seemed Father Carbone had been made the ringleader. In a very short time, Patrick had gone from despising the priest to feeling somewhat comforted by his presence. The priest finally stopped pacing and came back to the table. "Okay, listen up. Patrick, Robin and I will meet with Agent Litner today. A secret, secure location has been arranged. I'm sure he can arrange for protective custody for Copie until this thing is resolved. You can stay here for now Copie, just don't go outside."

Copie looked from the priest to Patrick, then back again. "Whoa, wait a minute here," he said. "Agent Litner? What is Agent Litner an agent of exactly?"

"The Federal Bureau of Investigation," Patrick answered. "We are knee deep in shit here, Copie. Aren't you glad you dropped by?"

Copie put his hands on his head. "Hold on a minute. The FBI is involved in this, and you guys want to stick me in a closet while you go talk to them? These people tried to kill me! I want to be involved!"

"Son, there is a lot more going on here than you know about. We can't risk involving you," Carbone said, putting a fatherly hand on Copie's shoulder.

"What do you mean, we can't risk involving you? So you're a federal agent now? You're a priest! And Patrick, why are you suddenly so important?"

"The FBI asked me to become involved in this investigation, Copie, not that I have to justify myself to you," Patrick said.

"Yeah?" Copie said. "Well the FBI is going to ask me to become involved once they know what I know. I heard those freaks talking while they were rigging the lab. They're planning something. Something big, and I know where and when it's going to take place."

"They're planning something? Like what?" Patrick asked.

Copie crossed his arms stubbornly in front of his chest. "That's between me and the FBI," he said. "I can't risk involving you."

Patrick stood up. "You little creep! You have no idea what I've been through!"

"Oh, what you've been through? Raise your hand if you almost got blown up last night." Copie raised his hand and looked around the room.

Patrick smiled in spite of himself. Even Robin chuckled. They'd been under so much stress it was good to have someone around with a sense of humor. That had always been Shep's contribution to the group, and now that it was gone, it was missed.

"All right, Copie," the priest said. "But you'd better have something valuable to say. Agent Litner can smell a lie better than anyone I know."

"Hey, I wasn't bullshitting you," Copie insisted. "I really did hear Shepherd say something about an outing next week."

"Fine," Father Carbone said, "but it's ultimately up to Agent Litner whether he wants to involve you or not. Patrick, you said these guys had been following you, so the FBI has arranged...Patrick? Are you all right?"

Patrick was gripping his shoulder wincing in pain and he'd started to sweat. Robin touched his arm. "Patrick? What the hell is wrong with you?"

"Ahhh!" Patrick screamed, still gripping his shoulder as he dropped off of his chair onto the floor.

Father Carbone ran to him. "Patrick! What is it? What's wrong with you?"

"I don't know! I'm getting these shooting pains in my shoulder. It's like someone's sticking a hot poker into me!"

The priest reached down and touched the spot Patrick had been holding. He flinched and went white. "My shoulder! Oh God!" He writhed on the floor.

Robin and Copie ran to Patrick. "What the hell is the matter with you?" Robin yelled.

Patrick stiffened, his head thrust back as the images flooded his mind. He saw people running and screaming. He saw blood on Joey's deck. He felt fear. He was vaguely aware of Father Carbone's voice saying, "He's having a seizure!" Then it all stopped. The pain was suddenly gone, and Patrick was alert and trying to sit up.

"Jesus Christ, Obrien!" Robin helped him to sit up. "What the hell was that about?"

Patrick rubbed his shoulder. The pain was gone but he was left with a dull throbbing. "It's Joey. I saw his face in my mind so clearly. Something must have happened."

They looked at him as though his marbles were falling out of his ears. "Excuse me?" Father Carbone said.

"Joey. I'm not sure, but I think he's been hurt."

Robin scrunched her face up. "Joey's been hurt? How the hell would you know that?"

"I don't know!" he yelled. "I don't know what's happening to me!" Patrick sat on the floor rocking as the pain gradually dissipated. He tried explaining to them about the dreams he'd been having. Lately, when the nightmares woke him, he was left with a throbbing pain in his head that took large doses of Ibuprofen to dull. Father Carbone and Robin looked concerned, and Copie looked at him like he was a mental patient. "You got some weird shit going on here!" Copie stated bluntly. "I'm not sure who's nuttier, you or those freaks that tried to kill me."

"We could do without the commentary Copie," Father Carbone said, as he tried to help Patrick into a chair. Patrick shrugged him off and stood on his own.

"I have to go outside for a minute," he said.

"What for?" Robin demanded. "Obrien, tell us what just happened! You scared the shit out of me!"

"I have to make a call," he said, pulling his new cell phone out and heading for the door.

Robin caught up with him. "You're going to call Forest Bluffs, aren't you? After everything we just heard, you're going to call Shepherd!"

"Robin, I have to make sure Joey's all right."

"You're losing it Obrien," she said desperately.

"Robin, just give me five minutes, okay?" She finally let go of his arm. Patrick stepped out onto the little stoop with his phone, leaving the others with bewildered looks on their faces.

He dialed the number and Shep answered. "Forest Bluffs Ministry," said the familiar voice.

"Shepherd. It's me."

"Obrien! Well, this is certainly a surprise. Have you called to tell me you've come to your senses?"

"No. I'm calling to see about Joey. Is he all right? Did something...happen to him?"

"What the fuck do you care?"

"I care! Now just tell me, Shepherd! Is he all right?"

"Why don't you come on out here and see for yourself?"

"Damn it Shep! Don't do this. Just tell me if he's all right. Please."

There was silence on the other end of the line. Patrick thought Shep was going to hang up on him, then he heard him sigh. "Some sniper took a shot at Joey. The bullet grazed his shoulder, but he's all right."

Patrick let his breath out. "Thank God. Thank you for telling me."

"You know, this wouldn't have happened if you were here looking out for him. Can't you just come down for a day or two, just so we can talk about things?"

"If you want to talk about things Shepherd, why don't you come down to my apartment? Come back to the city. Then we can talk."

There was a hesitation. Patrick knew Shep would not agree. For whatever reason, the plan was to get Patrick to Forest Bluffs. "I'd love to, Obrien, but this is a bad week for me. I'm going out of town on Wednesday, and—"

"Good bye Shepherd."

"Obrien Wait!"

Patrick hung up. He walked back into the little kitchen. "Well it appears Copie was right," he said. "Shep just told me that he's going out of town on Wednesday."

"What about the pain in your shoulder?" Robin said. "Nothing's wrong, right?"

Patrick grew still. "Joey was shot in the shoulder. He's fine. The bullet just grazed him." They all stared. Patrick grew uncomfortable under the weight of their eyes.

"Shot? Who the hell shot him?" Robin asked.

"I don't know."

"How could you have known that?" Copie asked.

"I told you, I don't know. Joey and I seem to have a link, ever since..."

He did not finish the thought. Father Carbone finished it for him. "Ever since the blood pact. That is what you were going to say, isn't it?"

Patrick shook his head. "I don't know."

"Well did you ever have psychic impressions before?" The priest kept his voice calm but he looked rattled.

"No. Never."

Copie began to pace. "Oh man. This is some creepy shit."

"Amen," Father Carbone. "Maybe this will make more sense after we talk to Agent Litner."

"Maybe it won't," Robin said.

⇜❧

They rode in near silence for an hour, until finally the car slinked up alongside the darkened double doors of a nightclub called "The Caboose". The stiff-looking agent put the car in park and got out. He opened their door and stuck his head in. "Follow me, and do exactly as I say," he said.

They followed the agent through the double doors into a lobby area where a woman stood behind a podium with a cash register. The agent spoke to the woman briefly. He turned back to them and said, "Stay here." He followed the woman into the club and was gone. The four of them stood around the lobby awkwardly. The club looked empty aside from the bartenders and wait staff, who eyeballed them suspiciously from inside the darkened room.

"This is a joke," Copie said.

"Don't be so cynical, Copie. You wanted to come, remember?" Father Carbone reminded him.

Copie shook his head. "No! That's not what I mean. I mean, this is literally a joke! Think about it. A blond, an Irishman, a black man and a priest walk into a bar. The four of us are a bad punch line waiting to happen."

They all laughed heartily, enjoying the temporary stress release. They were still snickering when Patrick turned and saw Agent Litner standing at the entrance of the adjoining room, watching them. His white hair looked blue under the filtered club lights. "If I'm not interrupting your fun, you can all follow me," he said.

Father Carbone took the lead and the rest of them followed behind. "So, Luigi," Agent Litner said, glancing back at Copie and Robin, "you have indeed collected quite an entourage since we last spoke."

"As I told you on the phone Steven—"

"Save it, Carbone." Litner did not sound pleased. Patrick felt responsible for the additions to their little group. He was like Dorothy from the

Wizard of Oz, picking up stray characters to aid him on his quest. Litner led them to a small private room where a muscular man with long blonde hair and a short yellow beard sat waiting at a table. Patrick recognized him from the other day at Father Carbone's. He was one of the door guards. The man stood when they entered the room, and Patrick felt small for the first time in his life. The man was a mountain.

"This is Agent Rourke," Litner said. They all shook hands and joined him at the table. Agent Litner pulled out a folder and got right to business. "Father Carbone has briefed me on the events that have transpired since we last spoke, Mr. Obrien. Am I to assume that you have a good reason for betraying the confidence of the FBI and bringing these other people with you?"

Patrick was speechless for a moment. This was not getting off to a good start. "Robin and Copie can both help. Robin knows Shep and Joey better than anybody does. Copie has information that he acquired in a life threatening altercation with Shep."

Agent Litner stared at Copie and narrowed his eyes. "Yes, Copie. Father Carbone informed me of your little mishap. What is this information that is so valuable?"

Copie opened his mouth to speak, but Patrick cut in. "Hold on a minute, Agent Litner. You can start by telling me why the hell you're investigating Forest Bluffs in the first place. I've seen Father Carbone's little collection of Shepherd paraphernalia. I doubt the FBI became involved because Shep had some strange photographs and a hand-crafted journal. Carbone said you had something worse."

Litner glared at Father Carbone, and Patrick was thankful he wasn't on the receiving end of that cold stare. "Oh he did, did he?" Litner said. "Well, Father Carbone, what else did you tell him? Perhaps I should just log him into the FBI computer, give him my password and let him go!"

The priest shook his head. "You don't understand, Steven. I told Patrick that I couldn't give him all of the details. That he would have to ask you what prompted the initial investigation of Forest Bluffs."

Agent Litner stared at Patrick, his face unchanged. "Are you agreeing to the terms that we discussed, Patrick?"

Patrick nodded. "Yes. I'll go to Forest Bluffs. But I want some answers first."

Litner studied him. "Very well." He pulled a sheet of paper out of his folder and gave it to Patrick. Patrick examined it. It was a computer graphic design of a world population chart, the statistics ranging from the present day to fifty years in the future. The numbers correlating to the number of human beings on the planet decreased at a steady rate as the years went by, with a jagged line drawn to illustrate the digression. The chart showed the world's population take a drastic plunge over the next thirty years, then begin to level out again.

Patrick shrugged and put the sheet aside. "Is this supposed to mean something to me?"

"Read the caption in the top left corner," Litner ordered.

Patrick sighed and picked up the chart. It had a caption printed along the top of the page which read, 'Population Predictions/After Arcania.' He looked up at Agent Litner. "After Arcania? What the hell is Arcania? I don't understand. Where did you get this chart?"

"It was in the possession of Melvin Shepherd," Litner said. "It was in his computer files. I assume he created it."

Patrick shook his head, still lost. "What does this chart have to do with anything?"

Litner looked around the table. "Have any of you heard of Arcania?"

Robin shook her head. Patrick shrugged. "Arcania Foods?"

"Yes, exactly." Litner said.

"I've heard of them, but I don't know anything about them. Is that the Arcania that's referred to on this chart?' Patrick asked.

"We think so." Litner said.

He did not offer further explanation. Litner's brief answers were getting tiresome. It seemed he had to coax every last word out of the man. "Agent Litner, you obviously have a theory here. It might help if you actually speak to us about it," Patrick said with annoyance.

It was Agent Rourke who answered. "Arcania Foods. Their chief product is wheat and grain. They make mostly bread and cereal products. You know, crackers, cookies, breakfast cereals and whatnot. They own a lot of smaller brand names that you've probably heard of. They're not the best selling brands, but they are the most widely distributed grain food products in the world, perhaps because they are moderately inexpensive. Arcania's products are exported to almost every country in the world." Rourke stroked his little beard. He looked like a Viking that someone forced into a suit as a cruel form of torture.

Patrick nodded. "Okay, so what does Arcania foods have to do with this chart?"

Agent Rourke leaned across the table and pointed a big finger on the paper. "As you can see here, the predicted world population begins a steady drop starting at the end of this year. The page is marked 'After Arcania'." Agent Rourke looked at Patrick as though this explained it all.

"Yes, I can see the word Arcania, Agent Rourke. If there is a point here, I'm not getting it. What does any of this have to do with my friends?" Patrick asked.

Agent Rourke looked to Litner, who nodded for him to continue. "Charles Duvaine, your friend Joey's late father, owned quite a bit of stock in Arcania Foods. He had stock in other companies as well, being a successful business-man. When he died, all of this stock went to his only living son, Joseph. Joseph has recently sold every bit of stock his father left him. He sold every bit, except for the Arcania Food stock. Not only did he not sell his shares of Arcania Foods, he used the money he got from selling other stocks and bought more shares of Arcania. A lot more shares."

"How many more shares?" Patrick asked.

"Joey Duvaine now owns Arcania Foods," Agent Litner said. "This is not a crime. He can buy whatever the hell he wants. What we would like to know is why his sudden purchase of Arcania Foods would cause a potential drop in human population, starting at the end of this year. That is if we are to take this chart of Shepherd's seriously. "

Patrick cocked his head. "Are you sure? Joey never mentioned buying a cereal company."

"Maybe the Virgin Mary told him to do it," Agent Rourke said, smirking.

Patrick made a disgusted face at him. "You have no idea how not funny that is."

Agent Litner cut in. "We hope against hope that this chart is a joke. I admit that this is all speculation, but we still have to follow protocol. Point A, Joey buys up Arcania Foods. Point B, we find a chart in Shepherd's computer that predicts a drastic drop in the world population, and I'm quoting, 'After Arcania'. Point C, Joey and Shepherd have cleared land in the back of his late father's house and are now growing some sort of crop. Do you understand our concern now, Mr. Obrien?"

Now that the picture was clear, Patrick could not find his voice, so he simply nodded.

"It's a matter that can be resolved simply," Litner said. "We need to know what Joey is growing out in those fields, and what he intends to do with the crop."

Patrick shook his head. "But Arcania Foods is huge. I'm sure they have their own agricultural farms. Why would Joey grow his own grain for distribution? It doesn't make sense."

"Indeed it doesn't," Litner agreed. "But along the same lines, why would your friend Shepherd create a computerized chart that shows the world population decreasing over the next fifty years? All statistics indicate that the world population will continue to steadily increase. Only some sort of drastic intervention would cause it to go the other way."

Robin gasped. "You're not suggesting that my cousin Joey is going to poison people!"

Agent Litner looked slightly pained for a moment, and then he made his face blank again. "We simply have to investigate all of the possibilities. We've already inspected the product at Arcania's distribution plants, and that product is clean. Now all we need to do is make sure that this crop they're growing out at Forest Bluffs is biologically sound."

Robin looked close to tears. "You people are wrong about this. I've known Joey all my life. You're trying to tell me now that he's cultivating some sort of contaminated food substance? You're wrong. You're wrong."

Agent Litner put a hand on Robin's arm, the first human gesture Patrick had ever seen him make. "I hope we are, Robin. I am asking Patrick to help us to disprove this theory. In order to do that, we need to get samples of those crops."

"What about the brothers?" Patrick asked, looking at Robin. "You said they had the scar. How do you explain that?"

Agent Litner perked up. "Wait a minute. What brothers? What scar?"

"Shep was branded with a horseshoe when he was a boy," Patrick explained. "Robin recently went out to Forest Bluffs to visit Shep. She claims that three of Shep's house guests have the exact same scar on their backs, and that he calls them 'the brothers'. They're the same crew that has been following me around. Also, they were with Shep when he allegedly tried to kill Copie."

Copie glared at Patrick. "Allegedly? Allegedly? You think I made this all up? I just burned myself?"

"I'm sorry Copie!" Patrick snapped. "It's just difficult for me to accept that Shep is capable of something like that!"

Copie stood up, furious. "Well I hate to burst your bubble Patrick, but your friend is a homicidal maniac!"

"Sit down please." Litner's voice was calm but it held enough weight to force Copie to comply. Litner looked at Robin. "What else do you know about these 'brothers'?"

"Well," Robin said, "they all look similar to Shep, as though they could actually be his brothers. They speak with an accent and they walk funny, like they're being held up by strings or something."

Copie raised his hand. "I know something about the brothers."

"Oh yes," Agent Litner said, "You have some information for us, Copie?"

Copie looked around the room as though he wanted to make sure no one was hiding in the shadows. He leaned across the table, closer to Litner, and whispered, "Another one is coming!"

Litner gave his head a tilt. "Another what?"

"Another brother! They said so when they were getting ready to roast me."

"What did they say exactly? Can you remember?"

Copie looked nervous, but he proceeded. "They were dousing the place with gasoline, and Shepherd said something like, 'Hey, don't waste that, we need it for the trip to Pearl Chasm next week.'"

Litner stopped tapping his pen. "Pearl Chasm? That place isn't even open to the public anymore. Did they say anything else?"

Copie swallowed hard. "He said something like, 'don't forget that your brother is still in prison.'"

Litner stared at Copie so hard that Patrick was afraid Copie's head would explode. Copie began to run his hands nervously over his head, sending his tiny braids sticking out in all directions. Finally Litner spoke. "Are you sure he said prison?"

Copie nodded. "Yes. He said that their brother was in prison."

Litner tapped his pen on the table as he thought. "There are certainly no prisons out at Pearl Chasm. It's just a bunch of old caves. It used to be a tourist attraction years ago but the state shut it down after a wall collapsed on a couple exploring the caves. They were both killed. That place has been off limits to hikers for nearly fifty years. Prison, huh?"

Copie nodded again. "That's what he said."

Agent Litner actually smiled. "Thank you Copie. You have been most helpful."

Father Carbone looked genuinely surprised. "That was helpful?" the priest asked. "How so?"

"The FBI has a source out near Forest Bluffs, an agent on my team," Litner said. "He feeds us information about the goings on out there."

"Is he on the inside?" Robin asked.

"No. Nobody can get inside. They have border guards, if you can believe that. I'm assuming they're part of Joey's following. That's why we need Patrick. The information that our source gathers is limited because of these location restrictions. He did, however, recently inform us that some activity is going on indicating that Shep is planning some sort of trip, packing up a couple of vans. One of the supplies that he saw being loaded was canisters of gasoline."

Copie brightened up. "Gasoline! You see? I told you I wasn't bullshitting!"

"Moving on," Agent Litner interjected, "we now know where they are going, more or less. What we need to know now is when."

"Wednesday," Patrick said. "Shep told me he was going out of town Wednesday."

Agent Litner turned to Patrick. "Well then. Wednesday it is. Perhaps we shall see what mysteries lurk in the life of Melvin Shepherd after all." Patrick drummed his fingers on the table. Litner's blue eyes shifted toward him.

"What is it, Patrick?"

Patrick shrugged. "I was just wondering who is going to tail Shep out to Pearl Chasm."

"You need not be concerned with that. It will be assigned to agents on my team. They have the appropriate surveillance experience," Litner said. Patrick drummed his fingers again, shaking his head. Litner scowled. "What is it now?"

"Well, these agents of yours, are they going to be carrying guns?"

"They will be armed. If you have an objection to our plan, either state it or shut your mouth."

Patrick struggled to come up with a diplomatic way to say that he didn't trust the FBI.

"I know that the FBI can be a little trigger-happy. I wouldn't want anyone to get hurt. I mean, as far as we know, Joey hasn't done anything wrong."

"Mr. Obrien, the God damned FBI is not trigger happy!" Litner shouted.

"No, I think Patrick has a point," Robin interjected. "Joey and Shep tend to be a little bit eccentric. What if your agents misinterpret something they see? I think that someone who knows Joey and Shep should go."

Agent Litner shook his head. "Like who? Patrick? Absolutely not. He has no surveillance experience, and he is a civilian. It's too dangerous."

"Why is it dangerous?" Patrick asked. "I'm just going to spy on them! If I get caught, I'll just say that I wanted to talk to Shep, but I was afraid to go to the house, so I followed him."

"What if you see something he doesn't want you to see?" Agent Litner asked. "Take a good look at our friend Copie over here. He saw something Shepherd didn't want him to see, and he almost lost his life."

"We won't get caught," Robin said.

Agent Litner raised an eyebrow at her. "We?"

"Yes, Patrick and I will go."

"Oh you've got to be kidding me. I'm not about to start sending civilians to do the work of experienced professionals."

Patrick leaned forward and met Litner's stare. "If not for we civilians, you would have nothing. As I recall, you couldn't even slip an agent past Shep. You asked for our help, so accept our help."

"It's out of the question. I am sending my team, and that's the end of it."

"Then we'll follow your team and make sure they don't fuck up."

Litner glared at Patrick.

Patrick's stare didn't falter. "If you don't let us go, I won't cooperate with this investigation. I won't go undercover, and I won't get you your crop sample."

"You little shit!" Agent Litner said, slamming a fist on the table. His deadpan face momentarily twisted in frustration. "You gave me your word!"

"I take it back."

Litner tossed his pen onto the table. "I've met sociopathic terrorists that were easier to negotiate with than you! This is out of the question. My team will refuse to work with civilians."

"Then we'll have to go by ourselves," Patrick said.

"Can you tell me why you have to be such a pain in the ass about this, Obrien?"

Patrick grew quiet. Then softly, in almost a whisper, he said, "My best friends are trying to destroy my life, Agent Litner. I would like very much to know why."

Agent Litner's face went from angry to placid again. "Yes," he said. "Yes, I would like to know why too."

"Good. Then we agree on something."

Litner simply glared at him.

❧

Darkness had fallen when they stepped into the refreshing night air. Two black cars with tinted windows were waiting just outside the door of the Caboose. Agent Litner instructed Patrick and Robin to get into the first car, where the driver would to take them on a scouting mission up to Pearl Chasm. Patrick assumed that this meant they would be allowed to do the surveillance mission, but he didn't push the issue. He had a feeling he'd pushed Litner as far as he could for one day.

As the car carrying Patrick and Robin drove away, Father Carbone leaned in to Agent Litner. "You agreed a bit too easily to let those two kids go out on a surveillance mission, Steven. That doesn't sound very official to me," he said.

"It's complicated," Litner said without making eye contact.

Father Carbone leaned in again. "Tell me the truth, Steven. Are you off the clock on this investigation?"

Litner looked at him. "Not exactly, Luigi. If my investigation proves to be justified, then I am on the clock. If it proves to be a waste of time, or worse, a disaster, then my superiors will deny all knowledge of it. So I have a little extra slack on this one. I can pretty much get the job done however I see fit."

"But what if they get hurt? What if something happens to them?" the priest looked conflicted. Agent Litner glanced over at the vehicle as it turned out of the parking lot. He walked toward the curb, leaving the priest's question hanging there. Father Carbone knew better than to ask again. If Agent Litner had wanted to answer, he would have.

Agent Rourke started to open the door to the second car when he froze suddenly. The huge agent was staring off into the club parking lot. Father Carbone and Copie followed his gaze. In the corner of the lot was a large blue trash dumpster. In the darkness, the culprit's platinum blond curls were his downfall. They shone like a halo as he peeked out from behind the dumpster.

"Patrick was right," Father Carbone whispered. "These brothers aren't very good at being discreet."

"Nobody move," Agent Rourke said, slowly drawing his gun. "Do you see him Litner?"

"Yes," Litner said, drawing his own gun. "Copie, is that one of them?"

"Yes. It's not Shepherd, but it's definitely one of the brothers," he whispered.

"If he gets away he'll warn Shepherd, then it's over," Agent Rourke whispered.

Litner turned only his eyes toward Copie and the priest. "Stay put," he said.

The curly-topped stranger must have realized he'd been discovered, because he sprang out from behind the dumpster and ran across the parking lot at an uncanny speed.

"Let's go!" Agent Rourke yelled, and he and Litner took off after him, guns drawn. Copie and Father Carbone watched in a panic as the two agents caught up with the man at the perimeter of the parking lot. They probably wouldn't have caught the man at all, but the blond stranger seemed unsteady on his feet and nearly tripped twice. This slowed him just enough for the agents to tackle him around the ankles.

He did not stay down for long, however. Soon he was on his feet again, fighting like a wild animal, and screeching like one as well. The curly-headed blond was not a large man by any means, but it soon became apparent that he was outlandishly strong. He tossed the brawny Agent Rourke off of his back with a quick thrust of his shoulders. Agent Rourke's eyes sprang open in shock as his enormous body went tumbling end over end onto the pavement.

This left Agent Litner, clinging with all his might to one of the man's arms. The man tossed Agent Litner about erratically, back and forth like a rodeo rider as he struggled desperately to free himself. Agent Rourke got back on his feet and ran to help Litner by grabbing the man's other arm. With an agent on each arm now, the blond brother went into a spin. The scene became almost comical as the FBI agents became part of a human windmill, spinning uncontrollably as they struggled to take the man down.

Father Carbone looked desperately at Copie. "If he gets away, he'll tell Shepherd that Patrick met with the FBI. He'll also tell Shepherd that you are alive, Copie. Nobody will be safe."

Copie nodded. "Then hike your skirt up, Father. The FBI needs our help."

Copie and the priest ran across the parking lot. Father Carbone dove forward and grabbed the man around the knees. The man stumbled a bit but still did not go down. Copie jumped on his neck and got him into a weak headlock. With the four of them hanging off of him, the blond man finally fell to the ground, writhing and screeching as he continued to attempt escape.

With considerable effort, and four pairs of hands holding him down, Agent Litner was able to cuff the man's wrists behind his back. To everyone's amazement he snapped the chain on the handcuffs and was suddenly free again. Agent Rourke was quick though, and soon had the culprit's hands behind his back again. Ignoring for the moment the bizarre fact that the stranger had broken through a set of heavy-linked handcuffs, Litner reapplied another pair, and then doubled them up with a second set of cuffs. The double set of cuffs seemed to hold the stranger's hands this time, and Litner let go of him and stepped back.

No sooner had he done so, than the capture spun about and kicked Agent Rourke in the chest, sending him flying across the pavement for a second time. "Sit on his legs!" Agent Litner screamed. They threw their combined weight on his legs and Litner was able to double cuff his ankles. Once he was restrained, they all stepped back, breathing heavily and staring with amazement at the sneering stranger with his shining white curls. Emerald eyes glared up at them with pure hellish rage.

Someone's cellular phone rang, a tiny muffled sound. Litner and Rourke checked their own phones, but they were not the source. Litner searched the blond captive and found the ringing phone inside his jacket. With a knee planted firmly on his captive's chest, Litner flipped open the little phone. As soon as he pushed the answer button, the blond man screamed, "Shepherd!"

Agent Litner's hand came down, landing a vise grip over the man's delicate mouth. Then, with the tiny black phone to his ear, Agent Litner heard Melvin Eugene Shepherd's voice for the first time.

"Juris? Hello? Juris what the hell is going on? You were supposed to check in twenty minutes ago!" He paused. Litner said nothing. Juris struggled to free his mouth from his grip. "Juris?" the voice said. Abruptly, the line went dead. Agent Litner closed the phone and tossed it in his pocket, removing his hand from his capture's mouth.

"So, your name is Juris," he said.

The stranger spit at Agent Litner. "How do you know my name?"

"Well, my polite friend," Litner said, wiping the spittle off his jacket with a handkerchief, "I believe that was your buddy Shepherd on the phone. It seems you were late checking in. It seems that you are going to be very, very late checking in. Now, what do you say we go somewhere and talk?"

Juris spit at him again. Agent Litner wiped the spit off of his jacket a second time. He looked up at Agent Rourke, who was glaring at Juris. Agent Rourke was not used to being tossed around by a man less than half his size. "Put him in the trunk," Agent Litner said. Agent Rourke happily complied, lifting the shrieking Juris up and hoisting him over his shoulder. Copie, looking terrified, backed away as Rourke carried the hysterical handcuffed man past him.

Agent Litner looked at the priest. "Thanks Luigi. If you and the boy hadn't helped out, we would have lost him."

Father Carbone nodded graciously. Copie looked at the priest. "Luigi? Your name is Luigi Carbone? Christ! Did you just fall off the garlic truck?"

The priest put an arm around Copie. "Get used to it kid. You're staying with me, remember? If you don't like garlic, I'm afraid you're going to starve in my house."

"Great," Copie said. "Patrick and Robin get to go off on government missions, while I have to hang out with Father Canolli over here."

"At least you'll be safe," Agent Litner said. "Now let's get in the car before another one of those freaks comes crawling out of a trash heap."

Chapter Twenty-Four

Father Carbone's apartment had a basement beneath it that stretched underground where it connected to the church through a locked door. It was a long open space, full of dust and old furniture, with a few tiny windows set just above eye level. Old pews sat stacked up along one side wall. Broken down statues of the Virgin and the infant Christ were scattered here and there like wax phantoms in the shadows. Copie and Father Carbone had covered the little windows with black construction paper as Agent Litner had instructed, adding to the ominous darkness of the place, which was lit by one measly overhead bulb.

The capture, which they now knew was called Juris, still hadn't uttered a word. Agent Litner had interrogated him for hours, but Juris simply stared at him with feral hatred in his otherwise lovely green eyes. Juris did not speak, but he did make noise. He hissed, he shrieked, and he spat. He refused all food that was presented to him. He sat in the dimly lit basement, cuffed and tied to a high back velvet chair that Father Carbone had dragged out of the corner. Whenever Juris caught Carbone staring at him, he would laugh at him. It was a disturbing cackle, a maniacal sound.

Agent Litner stopped by again the following afternoon and tried to make Juris speak. Copie had stayed upstairs and made tea while Carbone and Litner dealt with things in the basement.

Litner came stomping up the stairs and into the kitchen, with the priest right behind him. "He's as tight-lipped as a snapping turtle," Father Carbone said.

"And equally pleasant," Litner added. The agent looked angry and flushed. One side of his white hair was pushed up from running his hands through it, and he had a red blotch on one temple from slapping his pen against it.

"What are you going to do with him?" Copie asked, hoping against all hope that Agent Litner planned to move Juris out of the church basement. Just knowing that he was down there made Copie uneasy.

"He's going to have to stay here for the time being. Patrick and Robin are following Shep out to Pearl Chasm tomorrow night. I'm hoping they come up with some clue. After that, Patrick will be sent out to Forest Bluffs to get the crop samples, and we can wrap this up one way or another."

"So why can't you hold Juris at FBI headquarters or something?" Copie asked.

Litner looked at him coldly. "That's my business, Copie. Please don't ask me any more questions." Agent Litner threw on his jacket. "I have to go prep Patrick and Robin for their trip. Try to get Juris to eat something. Unfortunately, he's no good to us dead."

Father Carbone stepped up. "Are you going to tell Patrick and Robin about our new house guest?"

"No. They don't need distractions right now. We'll tell them about Juris when they get back." Father Carbone wrung his hands. Litner looked up from buttoning his jacket. "Is something bothering you Luigi?"

"Well, they've surely realized that Juris is missing out at Forest Bluffs. What is the Shepherd going to do when he discovers that he's lost one of his little sheep? Will he come looking for him?"

The question made Copie's eyes widen with new fear. Agent Litner headed for the door. "They won't look here. They have no reason to. Both of you stop being so afraid. He's just a man."

"So why did it take four of us to take him down?" Copie asked. "And how did he break through that first set of handcuffs?"

"Adrenaline!" Agent Litner snapped, and walked out the door, letting it slam behind him.

Copie turned to Father Carbone. "Well. Your FBI pal is a tad more agitated than usual."

Carbone shrugged. "He doesn't like it when he can't figure things out. That's what Litner does. He figures things out."

Copie looked spooked. "Man. If Litner is getting scared, then I might as well hang it up."

"I didn't say he was scared. He's just frustrated. This case is turning out to be...unusual."

The priest looked thoughtful for a moment, staring into his teacup. "I'm tired of tea. What do you say we get rip-roaring drunk? I for one think we've earned it."

Copie smiled widely. "That is the most enlightening thing I've ever heard you say, Father. Let's turn some holy water into wine!"

"That's a little out of my league, but I do have some brandy in the cabinet under the sink."

Chapter Twenty-Five

Shep stared at the phone, struggling to retain his mind lock on Juris. He caught the hazy image of a priest's collar, then nothing. Juris's energy was silent. "Fuck!" he yelled, tossing the phone across the room. It smashed on the wall. Allisto and Russell came running into the room. They looked at Shep, then at the shattered phone.

"What's wrong?" Russell asked.

Shep ignored him. He walked to the bottom of the spiral staircase. "Margol! Get your ass down here." The red-haired brother came stomping pell mell down the stairs and joined them in the kitchen. They all looked at Shep hesitantly. "Juris is missing," he said angrily.

Allisto's face fell. "What has happened to Juris?"

Shep shook his head, pacing. "I'm not sure. I called his phone. He called my name once, but then there was nothing. I tried to hone in on his mind. The only image I got was a priest's collar. Wherever Juris is, there is a priest involved." He turned to Kelinda, who had stepped cautiously into the room, looking curiously at the broken telephone. "I find it coincidental that the last thing Kelinda did before she joined us was to visit a priest and go to confession. Now, oddly, there was a priest involved in my brother's abduction!"

"I never told Father Bello anything!" Kelinda screamed. "If there is a priest involved, it's not Father Bello! He's just an old man. You leave him alone!"

Shep smirked. "You protest too much, princess. Oh Margol?"

"Yes, Shepherd."

"Do you remember that matter we discussed the other day? About the loose ends?"

"Yes, Shepherd."

"Now is the time. Take care of it."

"Yes, Shepherd, but what about Pearl Chasm?"

"You'll be back in time to go. It should only take you a few hours to take care of Father Bello."

Kelinda ran from the room and tore up the stairs, crying. Shep watched her go, then turned back to Margol. "Now get going. Find Juris and bring him back. And make sure Father Bello's holy voice is silenced. Permanently."

☙❧

Father Bello hummed a hymn to himself while he cleaned up the altar from mass. There had been more children in church lately, and this pleased him. He wasn't fooling himself. He knew the children came to mass because he looked like Santa Claus, in his red robe with his long white beard. That was fine. Whatever brought the people in was good. They had no miracle apparitions to draw people in like Father Carbone down at Saint Mary's. All of the local churches had taken a bit of a hit after the image of the Virgin appeared down there.

He placed no blame on Father Carbone, as some of the more gossipy priests had been doing. Some of them were saying that Father Carbone staged the miracle himself to draw more people and money to his parish. Father Bello did not share this opinion. He knew the little Italian priest, and found him to be an honest God-fearing man. Besides, he had heard through the grapevine that Luigi himself thought the apparition to be a hoax, and was addled by all of the attention his previously quiet church was receiving.

Father Bello's deep singing voice echoed acoustically throughout the empty church as he gathered what was left of the holy gifts on a tray and got ready to transport them. *"We gather together to share The Lords blessing..."* He stopped singing as he got the sense that someone was watching him. He spun about face, but the church was empty. Only painted angels and saints stared back at him. He gave his head a shake, then began to hum again.

He stopped as he saw a dark form move quickly past the window outside. He stood motionless with the tray in his arms as he stared at the stained glass, his voice caught in his throat. Had he seen someone pass by? Perhaps it was someone looking for confession. He put down the tray and walked to the back door, peering through the rectangular windows. He saw no one. He shrugged, and then headed back to the altar, retrieving the tray he'd left there.

The tray slipped from his hands and smashed to the floor as Father Bello turned to walk off of the podium. He hadn't heard the front doors open, but there was a man standing in front of the altar, a mere ten feet away. Father Bello gasped. "Oh heavens! My dear young man! I didn't hear you come in. You gave me quite a startle! Look, I've dropped everything."

The beautiful young man stared up at him with no expression. He was so still that it was hard to tell if he was even breathing. His hair was parted down the middle and came to his chin in a wreath of fiery red curls. His eyes were like enormous shining emeralds against his slightly sunburned skin. His nose was straight and strong, but his mouth was a tiny red kiss of child-like pout. He was like an oversized doll, perfect in every way except for the stare. The look in those eyes made Father Bello's hair stand on end. "May I help you son? Would you like to give confession?"

The child thing spoke. "You mean the way Kelinda Wade gave you confession?"

Only the stranger's lips moved. He stood with his arms by his sides, slightly bent. His head was bowed, so his eyes had to look upward to glare at the priest.

"Kelinda Wade? Do you know Kelinda?" Father Bello remembered his last meeting with Kelinda, when she had run out of the confessional refusing to tell her sins to him. "How do you know Kelinda? What is this about?"

"Where is my brother?" the red-haired stranger asked.

"I'm sorry? Do I know your brother? Young man, if we've met before, I apologize, but I just don't remember you."

"Answer the question, priest. Where are you keeping Juris?"

Father Bello felt the first shiver of fear run through him. He took two steps backward. "I assure you, I don't know anyone by that name. What is your name, son?" Father Bello could see his own cell phone, sitting with his wallet a mere five feet away on the front pew bench. He took a slow, careful step to the side.

"That is not important, but if you must know, my name is Margol."

"Well, it's nice to meet you, Margol. That's an unusual name."

Margol tilted his head slightly, keeping the priest in his line of sight as he eased his way toward the phone. "I wouldn't touch that phone, Father Bello. That would upset me. Now tell me where my brother is."

Father Bello paused. A bead of sweat ran down his temple. "I swear I don't know your brother! Now please, Margol, I'm going to have to ask you to leave."

The red haired stranger laughed. "You can ask."

Father Bello's heart was pounding in his chest. He made a conscious effort to stay calm. He had dealt with disturbed parishioners before. It was almost always a cry for help. If he could only get through to this young man... "What is it you want Margol? Why have you come here?"

"I've come to find my brother. And to kill you."

So much for chit chat. Father Bello sprinted for the phone. Margol turned only his head, and it flew off of the bench and smashed onto the floor, as though an invisible hand had swatted it. Father Bello stopped in mid sprint, and stared in disbelief at the shattered pieces of plastic on the church floor. He lifted his gaze to Margol, who stared back at him with the same non-expression. "How did you do that?" Father Bello quickly blessed himself. "What are you?"

"I am the Elite Guard."

Father Bello proceeded carefully. This man was definitely insane. Sure, the trick with the phone was impressive, but what this man claimed to be was just not possible. He was mentally ill. Father Bello's thought it safe to humor him. "Elite Guard, huh? Then you are tasked with protecting the byways between the realms."

Margol smiled. "Not anymore," he said, and dove through the air in a flying somersault.

The priest ducked out of the way and ran for the back door. The stranger chased him and caught his robe, pulling him to the ground. Father Bello cried out. "Help! Somebody help me!" Margol turned him over and placed his hands around the priest's neck. He applied a bit of pressure and Father Bello let out a whimper.

"I'll ask you one more time, priest. Where is my brother?"

"I swear! I don't know your brother!" Father Bello squealed.

With his hands still around the priest's neck, Margol leaned back and appeared to be looking at the air around Father Bello's head. His pretty features furrowed into a frown. "You are telling the truth. You really do not know where Juris is," he said with an air of disappointment.

"Yes! I am telling the truth! Please, let me go."

"I apologize for calling you a liar. I still have to kill you though. I have orders."

On a desperate whim, Father Bello reached behind him and pulled on the tiny podium next to the door. The metal bowl of holy water clattered to the floor. Father Bello turned his head, gasping as Margol began to apply pressure to his neck. He grasped the metal bowl, which had about an inch of the holy water left in it, and smashed it into his assailant's face. Margol laughed.

Then he stopped laughing.

He let go of Father Bello's neck and rubbed frantically at the side of his face where the water had hit. An ear piercing howl shrieked from his parted lips, an inhuman sound. Father Bello felt his calm completely let go. "I baptize you!" he screamed at his attacker. "I baptize you, in the name of the Father, and of the Son, and of the Holy Spirit! HA! I baptize thee, Margol!"

To his amazement and horror, the assailant's left cheek began to break out in large reddish hives, then he lurched backward on unsteady feet, trying to wipe the water off with his tee shirt. Still pawing at his face, the red head ran stumbling out of the church. The big wooden doors shut with an echoing slam.

Father Bello collapsed onto the floor. Stricken and disheveled, he crawled toward the altar. He picked up the plastic fragments from the shattered phone, and stared at them. "Never should we meet our idols, as they are bound to disappoint us," he said. He turned his eyes upward to the portrait of the risen Christ. "Give me strength, Lord. I know I'm not supposed to be frightened, but I am, Lord. I am." Still clinging to the shards of plastic, he fell to the floor and wept.

Chapter Twenty-Six

Patrick studied Litner uneasily. The agent sat on Patrick's couch, tapping his pen furiously against his temple. "So Robin and I scouted out the location. Everything's set to go," he said. The Agent looked up, nodded distractedly and went back to his temple thwacking. "Agent Litner, is something bothering you?"

Litner stopped whacking his head. He looked up. "Why don't you come sit down, Patrick. There are some things I need to tell you before you take this trip."

Patrick sat on the other end of the couch. "What's up?"

"Patrick, the mission I am sending you on has not been approved by my superiors. In fact, they know nothing about it."

"Oh. Um, okay. Why?"

"I am on a very short leash with this investigation. I'm authorized to get the crop samples but beyond that, I'm on my own. Things have gotten far more complex than I'd anticipated."

"I'm a little confused, Litner. Are you telling me that the FBI isn't really all that interested in Forest Bluffs?"

"Not as interested as they should be in my opinion, and the opinion of a few of my colleagues. I'm risking my career for this. That's how strongly I feel that I'm right. There is something dangerous in the works out there at Forest Bluffs. I can feel it. It's like a pebble in my shoe, but I just can't get it out."

Patrick shook his head. "So why doesn't the FBI just trust your professional opinion and back you up?"

Litner stood up and walked over to stare out the window. "Patrick, you said once that you thought the FBI was trigger-happy. Well, when it comes to situations like this, regarding church groups, one could say that the FBI is actually gun shy. They exercise great restraint."

"But you don't share that point of view?" Patrick asked.

"Absolutely not. The religious terrorist has proven to be the most dangerous type of terrorist ever encountered. For the religious terrorist, violence is a sacrament."

Patrick raised his finger. "That may be true Agent Litner, but Joey and Shep are not hijacking planes. They're growing plants."

"View it as you like, but know this. You will not be under FBI protection. If you insist on surveying Shepherd yourself, you are on your own. I'm giving you one more chance to back out and let my team handle this."

Patrick shook his head. "No way. I need to go, but not for your obsessive curiosity, or to prove something to the FBI. I need to go for my own peace of mind. You say that you need answers? You don't even know Joey and Shep. If anyone needs answers, it's me."

Litner nodded. "Fair enough. I need to give you something. Here." Litner handed him a piece of paper with a word scribbled on it. "Don't say it out loud. Just read it and remember it."

Patrick looked at the paper. The words 'Little Buttercup' were written in pencil. "Cute. What does it mean?"

"It's for when you join your friends at Forest Bluffs. I told you I have an agent on stake-out near Joey's house. I'll have him contact you if need be. That's his code name."

Patrick looked at the paper again. A Federal Agent with the code name Little Buttercup? "Okay. Whatever."

"Will you remember the code name?" Litner asked harshly.

"Of course. It's kind of hard to forget."

"Good. Now give me that back." Litner snatched the paper from Patrick's hands. He walked over to the sink and set the paper on fire, letting it burn to a crumpled black ball of ash, then washed it away with the running water.

"Wow. I feel so top secret."

"This is no joke, Patrick."

Patrick laughed. "Oh, I forgot. There's no room for humor in the FBI. You know, you need to relax, Litner. You're going to snap one of these days. Hey, do you want a beer or something?"

"I don't drink."

"Of course not. What do you do to relax?"

"Games. Electronic Chess. I solve puzzles."

"Puzzles? But that's not a break! That's too much like what you do for a living!"

"I enjoy it."

"Well all right then. It's your life."

"I've been to see Robin already. I've told her none of this. I'll leave it up to you if you want to fill her in," Litner said.

"I don't think it will matter to Robin that the trip is unauthorized. All she cares about is getting Joey back before Shep drags him into any real trouble."

Agent Litner looked uneasy. Patrick saw something in his eyes. "Agent Litner, why do you get that look whenever I talk about Joey? There's something you're not telling me."

"It's not important. We have no proof of anything. Let's just get some and get you out of there."

Patrick moved in closer to Litner, eyeing him suspiciously. "I want to know why you don't believe that Joey is innocent. You don't believe it, do you?"

"My personal opinion is not important. One should never speak about matters that have not been proven."

Patrick crossed his arms. "All right. I'm asking you as a friend then. I'd like your opinion."

"We are not friends."

"Fine then, I'm asking you as an interested acquaintance, okay? Litner come on! It's a little late to be getting tight-lipped. Tell me. Tell me!"

Litner glared at Patrick. "You are annoyingly persistent and enragingly intuitive. Are you sure you don't want to work for the FBI?"

Patrick smirked. "Talk to me Litner."

"You're only going to start ranting and raving again about what a wonderfully decent person Joey Duvaine is."

"So be it. Just talk."

The stoic agent walked across the room and leaned against Patrick's recliner. His gold pen came out and he twirled it like a baton as he spoke. "The investigation of Joey Duvaine did not start with Forest Bluffs. He had been investigated before, but the case was dropped due to lack of evidence."

"You're not going to tell me he killed his family."

"Let's just say that the matter of the untimely deaths in Joey's family was looked into. Of course we already had a file on Joey, and the evidence—"

"Wait a minute," Patrick interrupted. "You already had a file on Joey? Why?"

Litner looked quizzically at him. "From when he was a child, of course." Patrick stared at him blankly, not understanding. Litner shook his head. "Patrick, you really don't know who he is, do you?"

Patrick shrugged. "What do you mean?"

Litner shook his head. "I honestly thought you knew this. Patrick, Joey has the highest I.Q. ever recorded. And that was back when he was six years old."

Patrick frowned momentarily, then grinned. "Uh-uh. That's impossible. I mean, Joey's smart, but he's an idiot too, you know what I mean?" Litner stared back at him, his face blank. Patrick's grin disappeared. "You're serious?" he asked. Litner nodded. Patrick blew a puff of air out of his mouth. "I've got to sit down." He lowered himself onto the couch then looked up at Litner. "The highest I.Q. ever recorded?" he asked.

Litner nodded.

"Joey?"

"Joey."

Patrick shook his head. "I can't believe it. Does he know?"

"Yes, I believe he does. The FBI began testing on him when he was a child, but his mother put a stop to it. She wanted him to be raised like any other child. She was afraid all the attention and testing would hurt him psychologically. So the government was forbidden from having any contact with the family. I of course wasn't in the bureau then, but knowing how they work, I'm sure they were aggressive in their inquiries. This child was, after all, the most intelligent human on the planet. I'm sure Marie Duvaine had good reasons as a mother to shut Joey away from it all."

Patrick chewed his lip for a moment, then looked up. "What about Albert Einstein? What about his I.Q.?"

"Joey's is higher."

"What about—"

"Higher. We could do this all night, Patrick."

"Why didn't he ever tell me? It doesn't make any sense."

"Nothing about Joey makes sense, which is one of the reasons I've had my eye on him for so long. That kind of intelligence can be dangerous when channeled in the wrong direction. And from what I know of your friend Shepherd, well, need I say more?"

Patrick nodded. "Joey's handed himself completely over to Shep."

"Right. And since he's obviously got no interest in using his mind productively, we can only surmise that he is using it counterproductively."

"Did you ever think, Agent Litner, that genius or not, maybe Joey is just plain lazy? Did you ever think that maybe he lacks the drive to do anything productive?"

"Within the past two months, Joey Duvaine has bought an international food distribution company, started a sizeable church group, and become a nationally recognized religious figure. There are over three thousand websites on the Internet dedicated to him and his so called vision. I would say something like that takes a bit of drive, wouldn't you? You still seem to have the naïve opinion that this was all some sort of accident, a whim of Joey and Shep's. I believe it is blatantly clear now that all of this has been a carefully premeditated plan. A plan you knew nothing about, yet still are somehow a part of."

Patrick rubbed his temples, trying to absorb that Joey was the world's smartest human. It would not sink in. He could only picture Joey sitting in front of the television in his underwear, smoking a joint and scratching his balls. He gave his head a quick shake. "Tell me this then. If Joey is this great genius, why didn't he go to a better college? I mean, my college wasn't bad but it wasn't Harvard either. And why did he work for Parker Investments for that matter?"

Agent Litner raised an eyebrow. "Perhaps to keep an eye on you."

Patrick felt goose-bumps erupt on his arms. "A guy named Craig, one of the twins that designed the Virgin Mary Hoax told me that Shep had been devising plans for the apparition nearly a year before. Do you think..." Patrick stopped talking. He needed to take a breath before he voiced the unsettling thought. "Do you think Shepherd was planning to do this before Joey's family died?"

Litner sat down in the adjoining chair and leaned over with his elbows on his thighs. "I don't know for sure, Patrick. I can tell you this, though. They began tilling those fields out at Forest Bluffs the day after Charles Duvaine's funeral. It was as though they were on a tight schedule."

Patrick hung his head. "They. You keep saying 'they'. I still can't believe Joey could be involved." He lifted his head and met Litner's eyes. "Tell me about the investigation into his family's deaths."

Litner stared back at him. "Are you sure?"

"Yes. I want to know. Tell me."

Litner's pen tapping went into full swing as he spoke. "Well, they were all ruled accidents. However, Joey's mother Marie was not killed by the impact of the car crash. She died of blood loss after a shard of glass from her windshield penetrated the carotid artery in her neck."

"So?"

"Jeffrey Duvaine was killed on a hunting trip. His friends claim that he got separated from them when he insisted he saw a deer that none of them could see. They went their own way, vowing to catch up with him. A supposedly rogue arrow from some other hunter killed Jeffrey. The other hunter was never found. The problem I have with his being mistaken for a deer is the bow and arrow set found in the woods, the one that matched the weapon that killed him, had a scope on it. Whoever shot that arrow would have been able to see exactly what he or she was shooting at. The arrow was a direct hit to Jeffrey's carotid artery in his neck. Again, he died of blood loss."

"You can't prove that someone meant to hit him. It could have been an unlucky accident. Or the culprit could have been drunk. What are you going to tell me next? That someone forced a heart attack on Charles Duvaine? Did

Joey walk up to his father and say "boo" really loud so he would have heart failure?"

"No. The heart attack Charles Duvaine suffered was legitimate. He also suffered severe blood loss however."

"Because he fell through the glass table," Patrick insisted.

"Yes, fell." Litner said warily. "A shard of glass from the coffee table miraculously ended up slicing his carotid artery when he...fell. His blood alcohol was so low it was almost unreadable. The alcohol in his stomach had not absorbed into his blood stream yet, indicating that he had consumed it only moments before he died. He also had bruising on the back of his throat, indicating that something, possibly a bottle neck, was violently forced down there."

"Bullshit," Patrick said. "I saw the condition of that house after he died. Charles Duvaine didn't need any help putting a bottle in his mouth."

"He had called a cleaning service that morning and scheduled them to come out that afternoon. He had also stopped all deliveries from the liquor store nearly two weeks before."

Patrick scratched his head. "Do you really think he was murdered?"

"I think that three family members dying from the exact same neck wound in the same year is suspicious. That is all I'm saying."

Patrick felt like screaming at Litner, but that was just what Litner had said he would do, so he restrained himself. "It can't be murder," he said.

"Well, I'll give you this. It is highly unlikely that someone would go to such lengths to make these deaths look like an accident. There are much easier ways."

"Yes! That's true." Patrick said, relieved. "Finally, you're making sense."

"Unless they needed something from the death scene."

Patrick looked irritated again. "Like what?"

"Blood."

"Blood?"

Litner nodded. "In each death, a major artery was severed. Have you ever seen how much blood can come out of a human body?"

Patrick grimaced. "I'm happy to say, no, I have not."

"Well it's a lot. You'd be amazed."

"What is your point about the blood exactly?"

"There wasn't enough of it."

"Excuse me?"

"There wasn't enough blood left at the scene of each death. There should have been more. There should have been more blood in Marie Duvaine's car. There should have been more blood on the ground around Jeffrey Duvaine's neck, and there should have been more blood soaked into that rug where they found Charles Duvaine out at Forest Bluffs."

Patrick unconsciously fingered the little scar above his wrist. "What happened to the blood? Or let me rephrase that, Agent Litner. What do you think happened to the blood?"

"I think they took it with them."

"They?"

"The killer. Whoever committed those murders took a sizeable amount of blood from each victim before leaving the scene."

Patrick made a sour face. "Why? Why would they take the blood?"

"Damned if I know. You asked my opinion, so there it is. I trust you find this information comforting in some way?"

"No sir, I do not." Patrick was silent for a time. Why would someone want to steal blood? Why not go to a blood bank and steal it, if that were the case?

"I see that look in your eyes Patrick, and I regret telling you any of this. I don't want you distracted on this mission. Please, bear in mind that these are only opinions and unproven theories. I ask you to please put it out of your mind."

"But you believe it, don't you Agent Litner? You believe Joey is connected to the deaths somehow."

"I'm one man, Patrick. There is always the possibility that I am completely full of shit."

Patrick smiled at the comment. "I thought you were never wrong?"

"Yes, well there's always a first time."

Patrick knew that the agent did not believe himself to be wrong. Somehow, Patrick didn't think Agent Litner was wrong very often. However, he did not believe that Joey was capable of the atrocities Agent Litner had mentioned. Joey's family was killed by a series of accidents. Patrick resigned himself to this, but when he went to sleep that night, his mind kept hearing Shep's voice as he'd stood with a dagger in his hand on Joey's balcony that night.

'Blood is family, and family is blood.' The memory of the words made Patrick shudder.

As he slept, the thoughts transformed themselves into a dream, an image of Joey being nailed to a cross by hooded figures somewhere in a dense, dark forest. In the dream, Joey hung there limp on the cross as gallons of blood spilled out of the wounds on his hands and feet. As Patrick approached, Joey lifted his head and smiled. Blood poured out of his mouth like a waterfall. "Blood is family, Obrien," he gurgled as the red liquid gushed through his teeth.

Patrick awoke screaming in his bed. The headache was worse than it ever had been. After popping three pain pills, he padded into his darkened living room and replayed Shep's most recent telephone message. Shep's voice was like a screwdriver through his brain. *How have you been sleeping, Obrien? I certainly hope your dreams have been pleasant. Make the choice, Patrick. Stop the pain, or it will only get worse.*

Patrick ripped the answering machine out of the wall and tossed it across the room. Make the choice, Shep had said. Patrick decided right then and there that he would make a choice. As his head hummed with pain, he became startlingly aware of one thing. The blood pact they made was not simply an act of deranged immaturity as Father Carbone had suggested. Joey and Shep had done something to him that night on the balcony. They had done something to him, and they were damn well going to un-do it.

Chapter Twenty-Seven

Agent Litner sensed that something was askew as soon as he opened Father Carbone's screen door and stepped inside. Two empty brandy bottles lay on top of the rubber recycle bin, and the floor was littered with tiny aluminum candy wrappers. Muffled voices emanated from the basement. Litner froze and instinctively drew his gun, proceeding silently to the basement door. As he crept down the wooden steps, he heard Copie laugh, then a sound like dice spilling onto a table.

The air in the stairwell hung with a rank, misty smoke. Litner rounded the bottom step, and could not believe his eyes. Juris was still tied to the chair, but now he had a small fold-out table pulled up in front of him. Copie and the priest were huddled in chairs around the table with Juris. A bottle of brandy sat on the edge, and a stubby cigar dangled from the corner of Juris's mouth. They had a board game spread out in front of them, and Copie was shaking a pair of dice. Someone had tied Juris's curls back from his face with a bandana.

"Excuse me? What the hell is going on in here?" Litner replaced his gun as he stepped into the room. Juris saw him first.

"The FBI is here to knock me around some more!" he cried out, then threw his head back and laughed drunkenly.

"You got him to talk," Litner said.

Father Carbone and Copie both turned around. "Agent Litner!" the priest called out jovially. "Come join us! We're playing Trivia!"

"No thank you. What the hell has been happening here since I left?"

Copie tossed something to Litner, which he caught. It was a Hershey's candy kiss. "Juris likes chocolate," Copie said. "Juris really, really likes chocolate. Oh, and brandy."

Juris bent his head down and placed his mouth on the spout of the brandy bottle. Holding it with his teeth, he tipped the bottle back, taking a long swill, then masterfully placed it back on the table without spilling a drop.

"You guys got him drunk? We're supposed to be getting information from him, not making him incoherent!"

Copie stood up and weaved toward Agent Litner, pointing defiantly. "Now wait just a minute Agent! Since you've been gone, we have discovered that Juris loves chocolate, hates churches, and knows everything there is to know about science and nature. Correct me if I'm wrong, but that's exactly three more things than you learned from him."

Litner tightened his frown. He looked at the priest. "Luigi?"

The priest nodded. "Copie's right. Juris claims to hate churches. He insists that he can't stay here. He wants to be moved to another location. Says he doesn't care if we lock him in a wooden shed somewhere, as long as it's not in the church."

"Why can't he stay here?" Litner asked.

Father Carbone looked up, raising his eyebrows. "If he stays here, *they* will find him." Father Carbone turned his head so Juris couldn't see, and twirled a finger next to his ear.

"They will find him? Who are *they*?"

Carbone shrugged. "That much, he won't tell us. He merely claims that it is not safe for him here."

Juris looked up. "Not safe!" he concurred.

Litner walked over and took Copie's abandoned seat next to Juris. "Juris, why isn't it safe for you to stay in the church? What are you afraid of?"

Juris spat in Agent Litner's face. A stream of brandy colored spittle dripped down his cheek. The stoic agent calmly pulled out his handkerchief and wiped it off. He turned back to Copie and the priest. "Well. It seems your new friend has yet to learn manners."

"He doesn't like you," Copie said.

"Yes, thank you Copie."

Father Carbone picked a playing card out of a rectangular box. "Agent Litner, you've got to see this." The priest turned toward the prisoner and read from the card. "Juris, what does the term 'Scientific Notation' mean?"

Juris took a small breath, and said, "A system in which numbers are expressed as products consisting of a number between one and ten multiplied by an appropriate power of ten. Now when are you going to get me out of this church?"

Ignoring his question, Father Carbone picked up a calculator that rested on the table. He turned back to Juris as he punched the keys. "Juris, what is eight thousand, six hundred and fifty-two divided by seven?"

Juris yawned. "One thousand two hundred and thirty-six. Now when are you moving me from this church?"

"That's impressive." Litner said. "Why don't you ask Rainman over here something useful, like why his compatriots are on their way out to Pearl Chasm?"

Juris's head snapped up. His pale face flushed red and his mouth tightened. Litner smiled. "Well, well. It looks like I struck a nerve. Tell me, Juris. What do your friends plan to do out at Pearl Chasm, and why do they need all those supplies they packed?"

Juris began to screech like an animal, struggling against the ropes that bound him. He spun his head to look directly at Litner. "You cannot interfere!" he screamed. "You stay away from that cave, FBI! You stay away from that cave! I will snap your neck! Let me out of here! I will snap your neck!"

Litner stared placidly at Juris, unfazed by the emotional display. "Cave, did you say? I was not aware that they were actually going into a cave. Thank you Juris, you have been most helpful. Copie, get Patrick and Robin on the phone. I have some last minute information for them." He knew he would not really be calling Patrick and Robin. He'd made the statement to vex Juris. It did not have the desired effect.

Juris stopped struggling. He looked at Litner with an odd expression, and then he began to laugh. The cackle sent a chill down Litner's spine. "I laugh because you are a fool! Shepherd will smell Robin instantly. He will discover them, and he will kill them."

Copie wrinkled his nose. "Did you say he would *smell* her?"

Juris looked at Copie. "He knows her scent." He looked back at Litner. "You should not underestimate Shepherd!" he hissed.

Litner flinched. Hadn't Patrick spoken those exact words to him at their first meeting? *You should not underestimate Shepherd.* Agent Litner had an almost self-destructive desire to meet Melvin Eugene Shepherd face to face. This Shepherd character was as slippery as an eel and his movements as difficult to predict. Litner had to admit something to himself. For the first time in his career, he was significantly challenged.

As mysterious and adept as Shepherd seemed to be, Litner still did not buy the bit about him being able to smell Robin. But, just in case, Litner would tell her to go easy on the perfume.

"What's the matter FBI?" Juris taunted, "Are you worry now that you fuck it all up?" Litner was brought out of his mental tangent by Juris's grammatically challenged question. He had the strangest speech inflection. Whatever it was, it was clear that the hostile blond did not grow up speaking English. Litner crossed his arms in front of his chest.

"Where are you from?" he asked.

Juris grinned. "Texas."

Agent Litner laughed, as did Copie and Father Carbone. "That's funny," Litner said. "I have a lot of colleagues from Texas. They don't sound anything like you. What is your last name, Juris?"

"Kiss my ass."

"Lovely. Is that Swedish?"

Juris refused to speak again, sitting with his quiet glare as Litner tried again to extract any meaningful information from him. Eventually he gave up. The three of them went back upstairs, and Father Carbone made tea to counter the effects of the brandy.

A nagging concern plagued Litner's mind when he thought about Patrick and Robin going on this mission. He'd grown fond of them. Perhaps it was because they spoke straight to him. In the bureau, everyone was so guarded. Including himself. As jaded as he was, his new acquaintances seemed to see through all of that. Somehow, they looked beneath his hardened exterior. They saw the real him, and they called him on it, without hesitation. Had he called them acquaintances? They were merely people involved in a case, he reminded himself. Yet he had to admit that he liked being around them. He wasn't used to people treating him like a person, which was clearly what these kids saw him as. Not a federal agent, but a person. He said a silent prayer for their safety.

Chapter Twenty-Eight

Patrick studied Robin as she peered through the long black binoculars at the highway below. They were stationed high on an overpass that looked down over the freeway. Litner had issued them an enormous, beat up gray pick-up truck. They wore moderate disguises, hats and sunglasses. "Is Litner sure they're going to take this road? We should have seen them pass by now," she said.

Patrick took the binoculars from her. "Maybe they're running late. I'm sure Litner knows what he's doing. He's very efficient."

Robin examined Patrick with a twisted smirk. "It sounds to me like Patrick has a new best friend."

Robin seemed determined to taunt him. Patrick didn't mind. He had gotten to know her a little better these past few days. Teasing him was something she did when she was nervous. Since he seemed to have developed a terrible crush on Robin, he was happy to oblige, and let her verbally abuse him whenever she felt the need. "Admit it Patrick. He's your hero. You want to be Agent Litner when you grow up."

"I'm trying to keep watch for the vans, so could you shut up please? Oh shit! There they go!"

Patrick spotted the two white vans traveling at a high speed down the center lane of the highway. He threw the truck in gear and headed down the private road toward the highway as Litner had instructed. Robin grabbed the binoculars and leaned into the windshield. "Oh yeah. That's them. Don't get too close, Patrick."

⁓⁓

The ride to Pearl Chasm from Forest Bluffs took an hour and a half. The beach scrub towns gave way to more suburban settlements as they headed west, past the city, where Massachusetts still harbored some unscathed forests and farmland. Patrick did ninety miles an hour down the highway until he spotted the white vans off in the distance, then he let off the gas a little.

"What's in the bag?" Robin asked.

Patrick grinned, handing her the paper bag at his side. "I got you a Coke. Oh, and a present."

Robin smiled. "A present? What kind of present?"

"It's jewelry," Patrick said. "I hope it's your style."

Robin opened the brown bag and grinned widely as she pulled the colorful candy necklace out. "My God! I haven't seen one of these since I was a kid!" She stretched the elastic and pulled it over her head. The pastel chain of tiny circular candies hung decoratively around her neck.

"Do you like it?" Patrick asked, smiling at the way it clashed with her striped tank top.

"It's the nicest jewelry I've ever received," she said.

Patrick laughed, but he felt awkward suddenly. Robin looked sincerely touched by the silly gesture. He admonished himself for the excitement he felt being alone with her. She could not possibly share his growing affection for her. "I've seen some of the jewelry Shep's gotten you," he said. "I don't think the candy necklace can compare."

Robin frowned. "Shep bought me some expensive things, yes. But only because he's incapable of showing his love in other ways." She shifted in her seat. Patrick glanced her way.

"You don't still love him, do you?"

"No," she said. "I'm not sure. Part of me will always belong to Shep I guess."

Patrick slammed his hand down on the dashboard, surprising the hell out of Robin, and himself. "Well that's just great Robin! Just great."

"What is your problem, Patrick?"

"Robin wake up! Shep is not the person you thought he was. You told Litner you didn't have any reservations about this mission, and I backed you up. Now you're telling me you still have feelings for that psycho?"

"Enough with the mission there, James Bond. I'm as capable as you are. You were practically Shep's girlfriend too."

Patrick knew he was being childish and cruel, but his jealousy would not stay his words, "He doesn't love you, Robin, and you're an idiot if you think so."

He saw the anger swim through her and knew he was rubbing salt in an age old wound, verifying all of the doubts she'd held within since falling head over heels with Shep at age twelve. He felt like a shit. What the hell was he doing? But he knew. He was falling in love with another woman who wanted someone besides Patrick. He felt the perpetual fool.

"I know he doesn't love me, Patrick! And I'll tell you who's an idiot. You are, O'Brien. I told you that your supposed girlfriend, Kelinda, was sleeping with Joey. And what did you say? You said 'oh, my gosh, oh me oh my. I hope Kelinda is all right! We have to go saaave her'!"

Patrick gave her a dark stare, and his face flushed. Robin grinned at him. "You are the sap, Obrien. Not me."

Now she was salting his wounds. Patrick wouldn't look at her. He stared at the road ahead, a scowl on his face. Finally, he spoke. "You know now that Shep is twisted, Robin. You know that everything you ever thought he was is a lie. Yet somehow you still care for him. How pathetic is that?"

She turned to face him. "I'd say less pathetic than you knowing that Kelinda is up there at Forest Bluffs humping Joey night after night, yet somehow, you still care for her."

Patrick cut the wheel hard and pulled the truck over to the side of the road. He threw it in park and turned to Robin, whose face was frozen in shock. "I don't care about Kelinda! Damn it, Robin! I care about you! Jesus! You drive me up a wall, but you're the only woman I think about now."

Patrick immediately turned away and laid his head on the steering wheel. The words had come out in the heat of argument, and now he wished he could take them back. The silence weighed a ton. "What did you say, Patrick?" she asked softly.

"You heard me," he said without looking up.

"I think I need to hear it again."

He looked at her then. "I'm sorry," he said. "I shouldn't be making this trip any more awkward. You don't have to say anything. I realize that you probably don't share my feelings, and that's okay. We don't ever have to talk about it again, but please, please, stop bringing up Kelinda. I don't love Kelinda. I never did."

Robin nodded, looking shocked by his honest confession. He took her silence as rejection, and he turned to put the car in gear. Before he could drive off, Robin reached over, grabbed him around the neck and pulled his face to hers, kissing him. He stiffened a little, surprised, then returned the kiss feverishly. When they finally disengaged, he was dizzy with emotion and desire. "Okay," Robin said.

"Okay what?" he whispered.

"Okay, I won't mention Kelinda again."

Patrick smiled. "We have to catch up with the vans. Could we perhaps, continue this at another time? Or was it merely a moment of weakness?"

Robin leaned in again. They locked onto each other and kissed, insistently, until finally Robin pulled back. "We can continue this another time. Next time, it won't be in a beat up old pickup truck though. Right?"

"I promise," Patrick said. "Just promise me that it's over between you and Shep."

She promised him, and seemed to mean it. For the most part. He knew however that what she said had some truth to it. Part of her would always belong to Shep.

୨୭

Patrick almost missed the exit to Pearl Chasm. It had certainly been an interesting ride, and he was flying with the knowledge that Robin reciprocated his interest in her. He knew he had to shake the warm fuzzy feeling if he was going to concentrate on the task ahead. The truck crawled up a narrow gravel road, around the back side of the entrance to the caves, where barbed wire edged the property. 'No Trespassing' signs stood firm every ten yards, a stark warning in black and white. They found their hiding spot, huddled in the woods up along a ridge that overlooked the caves and climbing trails. Patrick parked the truck behind the trees. They spotted the two white vans parked down near the bottom of a cliff at the mouth of a narrow opening in the rock.

"How did they get down there?" Robin asked, peering through the binoculars as she stepped out of the truck. Patrick got out and quietly closed the door, rounding the front of the vehicle to join her.

"I guess the Feds aren't the only ones that know a secret road in," he said.

A company of people came out of the opening in the rock below and meandered toward the vans. "Get down!" Patrick whispered. They ducked behind a boulder. They were set up above the caves, buried in a tangle of woods and rocks, but it was best to be safe. Although they had no idea what was to ensue down there, they both knew that getting caught would be a very, very bad thing. Patrick didn't want to admit that he was beginning to fear Shep, but it was so nonetheless.

Patrick grabbed the binoculars from Robin and raised them to his eyes. He saw two of the brothers. One was the red-head that he had only glimpsed once on the train. The other was the more familiar black-haired rogue who had been tailing him in the city. With them was a petite young woman with very short dark hair. They were pulling boxes out of one of the vans. The young woman pulled out what looked like a first aid kit, and followed the two brothers back into the cave.

Robin looked at the surrounding woods, then down over the chasms. "Patrick? Have I got my bearing straight here? Because I seem to remember that FBI agent pointing to that cave down there where the vans are parked. I think that's the one. You know. The cave that collapsed? Where those people were killed years back?"

Patrick looked around, then shrugged. "I don't know. Maybe. It all looks the same to me."

The two brothers emerged from the cave again, and grabbed a couple more boxes out of the van. "They are definitely setting up for something," Robin said.

"Oh shit! There he is!" Patrick said, attaching himself to the binoculars. "Who?"

"Shepherd. He's with that shorthaired woman."

Robin grabbed the binoculars. "Let me see." Patrick let her have them. "Oh yes. I've seen her before. She lives out at Forest Bluffs. She's one of the field people." From some unseen road below, another car pulled up and parked alongside the vans. "Now who the hell is this?" Robin asked. It looked like an older model Cadillac. An old man with white hair and a slightly crooked back climbed gingerly out of the car.

Shep walked over to meet him. They spoke briefly, then the old man walked back and opened his trunk. He pulled out a wide, flat case and placed it on the ground. He shut the trunk and picked up the case, carrying it awkwardly toward the opening of the cave. The man looked extremely frail, and was clearly having trouble carrying the large case. Shep did not offer to assist. He simply locked up the vans, and strode past the old man into the cave. The old man quickened his pace, shuffling with tiny struggling steps into the cave until he was out of their sight. Patrick and Robin waited for several minutes, but no one else came out of the cave.

"I guess they have everything they need. Hey, who was that old man?" Patrick asked.

Robin squinted down at the area below. "I have no idea. There's something else weird though. One of them is missing."

"One of who?"

"The brothers. One of them isn't here, unless he's inside the cave. It's Juris, the blond."

Patrick didn't care about Juris. He was merely relieved that there were only five people down there to contend with. He was beginning to relax a bit, thinking that this would be a breeze, when Robin spoke those fateful words. "We have to get closer. We can't see anything from here, and its getting dark."

"Closer?"

"Yes. Closer, Patrick. How are we supposed to see what they're doing if we don't go down there?"

"Litner said we're not supposed to go inside the caves," he responded nervously.

Robin's bravery clearly outweighed his. Ignoring his protests, she climbed over the boulder and began to shimmy down the rock face. Reluctantly, Patrick followed, struggling to maneuver the jagged black rocks that stuck up out of the earth like miniature hardened volcanoes. As the sun fell, shadows enhanced the blackness of the terrain. It was a hazy night and the moon was covered with a solid sheet of clouds. Their eyes adjusted accordingly, but the darkness was menacing. Patrick almost lost his footing twice as rock fragments congealed like marbles under his feet. The terrain was unstable. Pearl Chasm was a network of cliffs and natural caves formed into a cluster of mountainous rock. The entire cluster made up nearly a square mile of the black rock. Some of the terrain was flat, but boulder peaks jutted violently out of the earth throughout.

Finally reaching level ground, they stepped behind a rock wall mere feet from the narrow mouth of the cave. The vans and the old man's Cadillac were just to the left of them. They were silent for a time, afraid of being surprised by the brothers on another trip out to the vans. They stood motionless as the sky grew blacker. "I don't hear anything," Patrick whispered.

Robin leaned in to speak directly into his ear. "They must have gone down deeper into this cave. We're going to have to go inside."

Patrick tried to make his voice hushed. "No! We don't know where they are. What if someone sees us? If we go walking around in that cave we could run right into them."

Robin held up a finger, signaling for him to be quiet. "Shhh. Listen. Do you hear that?"

Patrick strained his ears, and he did hear a sound, a vague mumbling coming from somewhere inside the cave. The sound seemed to have a rhythm to it. "Are they chanting?" he whispered, his eyes wide. Robin looked at him, their faces almost touching. The chant grew louder for a time, then it abruptly stopped. Robin stepped out from behind the rock and peered into the entrance of the cave. "Robin! Get back here!"

"I just want to have a look."

"They might have guards posted," he insisted.

She looked back at him, hands on her hips. "Then who's doing the chanting?"

"Good point." He stepped around the rock wall and joined her. The mouth of the cave was dark, but an orange hue emanated from somewhere deeper in.

"I think they have lanterns or something," Robin said.

"I don't want to find out," Patrick said.

Robin turned to face him. "If we don't go inside and see what they're doing then this trip was a waste of time!"

Patrick took a deep breath and blew it out slowly. "They're just a bunch of people with delusions of grandeur, right?" he asked, trying more to convince himself than Robin.

"That's right," she said. "There's nothing to be afraid of. They're probably in there reading poetry and drinking wine."

Patrick took Robin's hand. "Don't let go of my hand. We'll feel the walls for guidance until we find the lighted parts," he said, trying to sound brave.

"Okay," she said. "Let's go."

With hands linked, they slid through the moist darkness of the cave. Patrick tried not to think of bats as he felt his way along the cold wall. The cave branched off into a series of narrow corridors that made a gradual descent into the earth. At one point the tunnel opened up where a tiny underground waterfall bubbled soothingly into a little pool. The place was amazing. If not for the unpredictable jutting out and turning of the rock walls, one would have thought the tunnels were man-made. The water had beautifully sculpted the strange underground labyrinth. The orange glow grew brighter, and soon they could hear voices in the distance.

They slid with their backs against the wall, stopping just before the corridor gave way to a large open cavern. The tunnel ended here. Patrick and Robin tucked themselves tightly against the darkest part of the corridor. They could see the others in the dimly lit cave just ahead. The place was aglow with candles along the surrounding walls. Another little arc of candles was set up on the ground beneath the rear wall, where a circle the size of giant beach ball was drawn onto the stone with a thick dark substance.

Shep stood in front of this painted circle, touching parts of it with his fingertips, pulling back his hand, then repeating the act on a different part of the circle. Allisto and Margol stood behind him looking on. The old man knelt on the ground off to the side with the big case open before him. He was checking the contents, instruments of some sort. The boxes and canisters that they had loaded in were stacked neatly in a corner on the other side of the cave. The tiny woman with the short hair was methodically setting up medical supplies on top of one of the boxes.

Patrick spotted a jagged rocky ledge to the right of the cave. It jutted up ten feet out of the earth, leaving about two feet of clearance from its ledge to the cave ceiling. It looked like it had once been part of the wall itself, most likely the effect of the collapse, if indeed this was the same cave. Aside from all that, it looked like a great place to hide and view the goings on down below. Patrick tugged on Robin's shirt, and pointed to the high ledge of rock. "Look," he said, "balcony seats."

She shook her head. "No way," she whispered.

"Why? It's dark along that side wall. They won't see us crawl up there."

"But they'll hear us!" she whispered. She was right. These rocks were unpredictable, and all it would take was a pebble falling while they climbed to draw Shep's attention. As if in answer to their prayers, the old man started up some sort of power saw. The sound whirred loudly into the darkness, cutting through the calm. What they needed a power saw for was a mystery Patrick was not ready to confront. Robin tugged at him. "Let's go!" she said.

With the buzzing of the saw to mask their advance, the two of them scuttled up the ledge and put themselves onto their stomachs. Once on top of the ledge, they had a perfect view of the goings on below, but they were also shielded by the darkness in the corner of the cave. The power saw abruptly cut to silence, and the silence was replaced by Shep's voice, already into the latter half of a sentence. "...until I tell you to turn on the saw! What the hell are you trying to do, Dr. Lichtenstein? Ruin my concentration? I'm working here!" Shep railed at the old man, who stood shakily with the big saw in his frail, bony hands.

"I-I'm sorry, Shepherd. I just wanted to make sure it was working all right. It's been a while since I've used it."

Shep walked over to the old man. "Don't worry, Doctor. This is the last time you will ever have to use the saw."

The shaky gray haired man looked petrified of Shep, but he stuck his chin out defiantly. In a quivering voice he said, "You're damn right this is the last time! I can't go through this again! I'm an old man! I don't care what you do to me anymore, or how much you threaten me. My reputation means nothing now. This is the last time. I need to give my conscience some peace before I die!"

Shep sighed impatiently. "This is the last time because Klee is the final member of my family, not because you refuse, you arrogant old bag of guts. Give me that saw."

The doctor looked uneasy. "What do you want it for?"

Shep circled the doctor. Margol watched with vague interest as Allisto walked over to the pile of supplies where the young woman was setting up bandages and syringes. She handed Allisto several plastic containers with lids on them. Whatever was about to happen had been pre-arranged. Allisto took the containers and walked over to stand patiently behind Shep, who was circling the doctor like a hunter closing in on its prey. The doctor looked at Allisto now, and at the plastic containers he held.

"Wait a minute," the old man said. "Why are the containers empty? Where is the sacrifice? Who had to die today so that your foul kind can live?" The doctor glanced over at the little dark-haired woman in the corner. "Is it the woman?"

Shep shook his head. "No, Dr. Lichtenstein. Brin-Marie is one of our people. It is your blood we will be using today. You are the sacrifice. Surprise!"

The man began to shake. "No!" he whispered. "You can't kill me! You need me! I'm the only one that can do the amputation! You don't know how to operate the saw!" The old man held the power saw to his chest protectively. His wrinkled chin quivered.

Shep laughed. "Come on old man. I've seen you do it enough times. Did you think I wasn't paying attention? I can do the amputation myself."

"No!" the old man cried, sounding more frustrated than frightened. "No! I've lived in fear for years because of you! At least let me die in peace! I cannot die here, not by your hand. I will not be part of this abomination!"

Shep snatched the saw from the old man with one swift action. The old man took a shaky step backward and stumbled onto the ground. He looked up at Shep. "Foul creature! You will burn for all you've done."

"You should be thanking me. All of your sins will be forgiven. I'm giving you a gift. You haven't exactly been a model citizen, remember? There was a time when you were a very naughty boy. Now, you know the drill. You have two choices. You can take it in the neck, or you can take it in the wrist."

The old man made a desperate, futile attempt at escape, but Shep caught him by the collar. "Fine, have it your way, doctor. If you won't take your medicine like a big boy, I'll have to force it on you."

Patrick looked down at Shep, and it was like looking at a stranger that had taken over Shep's body. But of course, that wasn't the case at all. This was the real Shep. It was the other Shep, the Shep that Patrick had known for ten years that was the imposter.

Margol held the man while Shep took his hand, pulling his feeble arm out straight. The man whimpered. Using the tip of the saw, Shep made a deep slice in the old man's wrist. Blood seeped in a steady flow from the papery skin. Patrick felt Robin begin to shake next to him, and he put an arm on her back. Inside him the knowledge grew that he was seeing something he was never meant to see, something that went beyond the attack on this old man. He was seeing Shep in his true form.

They meant to kill that old man, and Patrick knew that all moral law dictated that he try and stop this from happening. But if he exposed himself now, he was more than a little sure that Shep would kill him and Robin as well. As horrified and sad as he was for this poor old doctor, he was not willing to risk his and Robin's lives for the stranger. So, disgusted, he watched, as Allisto came over and caught the man's blood in the plastic containers, filling each one systematically.

When that task was complete, Margol let go of the old man, who fell to the floor. Shep looked down at his unconscious, of perhaps dead body. "Now he's in the way," Shep said with annoyance. He picked the man's limp form up and tossed him across the cave, where he landed on his back at the bottom of the ledge where Patrick and Robin lay. Patrick looked down at the man, who lay face up, with his eyes slightly parted. He was breathing.

Robin was leaning over, staring down at the discarded body of the old man. The doctor's expression changed then. Patrick couldn't imagine that he was seeing them. He shouldn't even be awake after losing that much blood, and he was still bleeding. But he was definitely conscious. He clung to his wrist in a feeble attempt to stop the bleeding. Patrick glanced over at the rest of the company. Shep was back to touching and poking the painted circle on the wall, as though he expected it to change somehow.

Looking back down at the old man, Patrick saw a weak smile edge his pale lips. Robin was waving her fingers. Patrick grabbed her wrist. "What are you doing?" he mouthed. She pointed to the old man on the ground below. With a tiny crooked finger, the doctor waved up at them. A weak smile played at the corner of his lips. He had seen them. He then took that crooked finger and placed it to his pale lips, a silencing gesture. The man dropped his hand, turned slowly to his side, and began to write something in the dirt. It seemed an incredible effort to perform the paltry task. When he'd finished, he looked up at them, and pointed to the message, which they could not read from where they lay. He pointed again, then his hand dropped, and he let out a long sigh as his eyes glazed over.

The old man was dead. Robin looked like she was going to cry. Patrick put his hand over her mouth and shook his head. She nodded, but she was shaking again. She dropped her head and buried it in her arms. Patrick hoped Shep's little ceremony was almost over. Poetry and wine indeed. This was a horror show. His eyes drifted back to the stony room below, where Shep was running his hands along the wall within the enormous painted circle. Shep looked over his shoulder to where Allisto squatted on the floor with the plastic containers. "Bring me the blood," he said. Allisto stood up but did not move. He looked uneasy. Shep turned to him. "Allisto! Did you hear me?"

"Are you sure it is time, Shepherd? I don't think the circle is ready yet."

Shep stormed over. "Do you doubt me, Allisto? Huh?"

The black-haired brother flinched. "I just think maybe it is too soon."

Shep glared at him. "I got you out, didn't I, you little shit?"

Allisto nodded. "I know, Shepherd, it's just that when Margol came through, the circle was—"

"It is never easy, Allisto, and it is never exactly the same. I got Margol through, didn't I? I got you through, and Juris too!"

"Yes. I'm sorry."

Shep looked over at Margol, who stood stoically with his hands clasped in front of him. "How about you, carrot top? Is your confidence in me as weak as your brother's?"

Margol shook his head. "No, Shepherd. You know what is best. Allisto, give Shepherd the blood."

Allisto moved hesitantly forward and handed the containers to Shep. Shep took them carefully. "Brin-Marie?"

The little woman with the pixie haircut looked up from her first aid supplies. "What is it, Shepherd?"

"Could you check on the doctor for me? Just make sure he's dead."

"Yes Shepherd." Brin-Marie walked over to where the old man's body lay and placed a finger on his neck. She leaned in and listened to his chest. Patrick pulled his head back into the shadows as she stood. "He's dead, Shepherd."

"Good. The blood of the newly departed doesn't exactly work unless the bloke is actually departed, now does it?" Shep looked around grinning as if this was supposed to evoke a laugh. When no one laughed, he shrugged.

Walking back over to the wall, he placed the blood containers on the ground. He opened one container at a time, smearing blood along the rim of the painted circle. It dawned on Patrick then that the big circle on the wall had never been painted at all. It was merely stained with blood, presumably from other such ceremonies performed in the past. When all six containers had been emptied, Shep ran his hands through the blood on the wall in a circular motion. He began to chant softly, the language foreign.

Allisto and Margol came up behind him and joined him in whispering the strange words.

The circle began to steam. Steam? Patrick leaned in closer and squinted. A steam was rising off of the wall, as though the blood Shep had smeared on it was cooking. A stagnant, metallic odor filled the air. Shep took a step back then placed his hands directly into the center of the circle. He pushed against the wall until his forearms were shaking. Finally, he stepped backward, exasperated. "Damn it!" he screamed.

Allisto and Margol looked terrified. Shep turned, examining their faces. "It's okay," he said. "We'll just try again." He laughed nervously. "Don't worry! Margol, it took three tries to get you out! Remember, Allisto?"

"Maybe we need more blood," Allisto said.

Shep's face became angry. "You want more blood, Allisto? Fine." Shep stormed over to where the dead doctor lay. Patrick shuddered at how close Shep was. He could have reached down and touched his sandy curls. Shep picked the body up, threw it over his shoulders and moved back to where the others stood. He smiled coldly at Allisto. "Let's give it some more blood then, shall we?" Shep reached in his pocket and pulled out a knife. Swinging the doctor's body off of his shoulders, he made a deep cut across the dead man's neck. He grabbed the old man by the hair and pulled his head back until the wound gaped open, then he panned the body back and forth the in front of the wall, trickling the sluggish stream of blood across the painted circle. When the charade was over, he once again tossed the body across the cave. Patrick was thankful that Shep had thrown the corpse in the other direction this time. He didn't think he could handle the dead man staring up at him with a gaping neck wound.

"There! Happy now, Allisto?"

Allisto looked like he was going to cry. "Please Shepherd. Please. Just try again." Allisto's shoulders began to tremble.

Shep walked over to Allisto and kissed him on the mouth. Holding Allisto's head in his hands, he said, "Don't be scared. I love you Allisto, my brother. Don't worry. It's going to work this time. You're going to help me. Both of you."

Shep's hands were shaking, and he had tears streaming down his cheeks. Whatever endeavor they were attempting, it had them all in an emotional uproar. Allisto nodded and took Shep's own head in his hands. Margol came over and embraced the two of them. They all began to chant, as tears streamed down their cheeks. Robin lifted her head at this, and looked on with amazement at the emotional display. The three of them disengaged suddenly.

"Let's do it," Shep said, and rubbed his hands together. The three brothers stood before the bloody circle on the wall and began to chant. Side by side, they pressed their palms against the wall, each making a series of circular motions, feeling the wall, as though searching for an opening. There was a tangible anticipation in the little cave that Patrick could feel with each shallow breath he took. The steam began to rise from the circle again, and soon the air became rank with the smell of blood. Patrick had to cover his nose to keep from gagging.

More smoke filled the cave now as the wall within the bloody circle seemed to be heating up with some unseen fire. The brothers' chanting became louder and more insistent. The chanting abruptly ceased as Shep called out "I'm in!"

The statement was followed by a whirl of activity. Patrick was having trouble seeing through the haze of smoke, but it looked like Shep's hands were submerged in the wall, from his forearms down, as though the stone in the center of the circle had melted. Brin-Marie came rushing forward to watch. The brothers stood on either side of Shep, each holding on to one of his shoulders to brace him. Patrick and Robin leaned forward, struggling to see what was happening through the smoke. "Easy. Easy." Shep yelled out. "Okay! PULL!"

The brothers began pulling Shep backward, but his arms appeared to be stuck in the wall. This did not deter them. They pulled on him with all of their might. "I have contact! PULL!" Shep yelled again.

They pulled. The haze of smoke grew thicker before Patrick's eyes, and he was thankful for it, because what happened next defied explanation. Something, or someone, came through the wall and landed with a splat on the cave floor, taking Shep down with it. Patrick rubbed his eyes and stared at the smoking circle, which once again looked like nothing more than a solid mass of rock. But something had just shot out of that circle in the wall, like an over sized infant from a stony womb. With the crowd of people that now scurried around the thing, Patrick could not see what it was. What he could see was another pair of hands still clasped to Shep's, who had fallen to the ground when the thing came through. Shep released the hands and stood, shouting instructions. "Is he breathing? Get him up! Get him up!"

A loud screech echoed like a giant bird's call through the cave. After the screech came a sobbing, like an infant's cry, only much deeper. The sound was heart breaking, full of pain and anguish. Shep, the two brothers, and Brin-Marie were now huddled around the crying thing on the ground. Patrick glanced at Robin, who at some point had buried her head in her forearm again. He wondered how much she had missed.

"Bring me the saw. It's best to do this right away," Shep said to Brin-Marie, who scurried to get the saw. The power saw sprang into life, and the loud whirring was second only to the tortured screams that could be heard over it. The saw whirred for a good ten minutes, then fell silent. A mind-piercing series of anguished screams followed, cutting through the silence like a razor blade. The thing on the cave floor was repeatedly taking in long labored breaths, followed by a piercing, high pitched howl. After five or six of these horrifying screams, they tapered off to a quiet whimpering, and the cave was still once more.

Patrick was suddenly aware of how close he was to Shep and the others when they began to speak. They had dragged the thing toward the center of the cave, and now stood directly below where Patrick and Robin hid. "I'll get the gauze," the woman said. "We need to stitch that up."

"NO!" Shep's voice called out. "Do not stitch the wound. Put that cream I gave you on it. It will disinfect it and restrict the capillaries."

"But we have to stop the bleeding!" Brin-Marie said, raising her voice for the first time.

"This is no ordinary balm, Brin-Marie. It will stop the bleeding. Trust me on this. Now do as I say."

Patrick was frozen, afraid to peek over the ledge and view the scene he was hearing. They were so damned close. Robin was like a statue beside him. At least she had stopped shaking. Patrick had been afraid that Shep would hear her bones rattling.

"Is that blanket ready?" Shep's voice again.

"Ready," said one of the brothers.

"Bring it here."

The whimpering started again, and Patrick could no longer resist the urge to look. He lifted his head just enough to view the scene below. He almost wet himself when he saw exactly how close they were. He could have spit on their heads. The woman, Brin-Marie, walked over to the pile of supplies and returned with a large needle and syringe. A wet, naked man lay on a blanket, on his side, curled up into a ball and shaking. He was glistening with a slick wet substance and he was covered with blood. The tiny wet ringlets of his hair were platinum, streaked with dark red blood. The rest of the group knelt around him. Margol, the red-haired brother, blotted the naked man with a towel, cleaning the blood gently of his shoulders and neck.

Shep looked up at Brin-Marie, whose gloved hands held the syringe. "No. Take that away. No drugs. Not yet."

Brin-Marie looked upset. "But he's in such pain!"

"I need to make sure he has his mind before you go drugging him up. Wait."

The naked man wept. His hands covered his face as he lay on his side crying. Although his face was covered, Patrick could clearly see one thing. He was one of them. He was a brother. Even wet, his hair hung in the chin-length ringlets they all shared. But who the hell was he? How had he gotten into the cave? Robin lifted her head, and was looking down at the naked man as well. Patrick leaned in to her. "Is that Juris?" he whispered.

Shep lifted the naked man's chin. Blood streaked his pale face like war paint. The man had his eyes shut tight. The eyelids were swollen, as an infant just come through the womb. "Open your eyes," Shep said, in a soft, loving tone. The swollen eyelids fluttered, then opened as tears streamed. The eyes were large and crystal green. Though his face was covered with blood, Patrick could see before Robin told him that this was a completely new individual.

"That's not Juris," she whispered. "Different features."

His nose was smaller than the rest of them. This man, even wet and bloody, was clearly the fairest of them all. His beauty was striking, even with the messy gore that covered him. His hair was white like Juris's, but his face was much softer. He was less masculine than the rest, with rounded, doll-like cheeks. He could have been carved of porcelain for how perfect his skin was. His nude body was thin and wiry, yet sculpted with muscular tone, just as Shep's was. The man blinked, looking at Shep with confusion and fear.

Robin looked at Patrick. "Where did he come from?" she mouthed. Patrick looked at her and shrugged. She had not been watching. It was just as well. They looked down, mesmerized. Shep knelt on the floor with the bleeding man.

"Can you hear me?" he asked softly. The man pushed himself up onto his shaking arms. He blinked through the blood on his forehead and focused on Shep. Then he looked intensely at his own hand, which he held out before him. He grimaced at it, as though it was not a hand, but a tumor that had just sprouted from his wrist. He opened it and closed it into a fist. He wiggled his fingers, then let out a sob. Shep took his hand and gently lowered it.

"Klee, can you hear me? Do you recognize me? It's me. It's Zirub." Robin and Patrick exchanged a confused glance at the strange name.

Allisto stroked the man's wet hair. He spoke to him in soothing tones, but it was not English. The young man turned to Allisto, seeming to respond to the words. He held his hand up to Allisto, showing it to him. "Plefarr!" he whispered to Allisto. "Plefarr!"

Allisto nodded, looking sad. "I know."

The man screamed then, holding his hand over his head for all to see. "Plefarr!" he yelled in horror.

Shep turned the man's head back to face him. "Listen to me, Klee. Focus. Look in my eyes, Klee. It has been a long time, but you must try to remember, Klee. You chose this. You chose this."

The blond stared back at Shep, still grimacing. "Plefarr!" he sobbed.

"I know, Klee," Shep said soothingly. "Do you remember the languages? This is English. Plefarr. Say it in English, Klee. Plefarr. What does it mean?"

The bloody man looked at Shep now with something like recognition. His eyes showed a flicker of understanding. "Say it?" he asked uncertainly. His speech was even choppier than the other brothers, but hell, it was English. Shep looked delighted.

"Yes! Say it, Klee! Scream it out!"

The bloody stranger straightened up and tried to stand, but he fell to the ground as though his legs were made of rubber. Shep caught him, and helped him into a kneel. "Don't try to use your legs yet. Speak, Klee. Say it aloud. Say it in English."

The blond man held both hands out in front of him, like a surgeon ready for gloves. He looked down at the rest of his body with obvious horror. "Plefarr!" he said softly. He looked at Shep and began to whimper again.

"Say it in English, Klee," Shep urged.

"Give him a break. He doesn't remember," Margol said.

Shep reached out and smacked Margol sharply across the face. "You went through this too, Margol! Try to have a little patience!" Shep turned his attention back to the one called Klee. "He remembers. Don't you Klee?" Shep smiled at him.

The bloody stranger looked around the cave, seeming to become aware. He focused on the other people, as if noticing them for the first time. New blood had run down his back and over his arms. Klee let out another sob, and held his hands out in front of him. Again he looked down at his own body, then up at Shep. "Flesh," he said.

Shep nodded slowly, smiling. "Yes Klee. Flesh. Pleffar is flesh."

Klee looked horrified. "No!" he shook his head. "No! Flesh! Flesh! Fleeeeessshhh!" Klee turned his head and caught sight of Margol standing next to him. He held his hands out to Margol, showing them to him. "Flesh! Margol, flesh!" he sobbed.

Margol and Allisto both beamed. They looked at Shep who mirrored their grin. "He said my name," Margol said, his voice choked with emotion. "He remembers. He said my name!"

Shep, still beaming, looked over at Brin-Marie, who stood to the side with a shocked expression. "You can give him that shot now, Brin."

"Huh?" she said, stunned.

"The shot, Brin-Marie. Give Klee the shot. Now I know he's all right. I don't want him in pain."

Brin-Marie seemed to come out of her trance. "Oh. Right. The shot." Brin-Marie gave Klee a shot in the buttocks while Margol wiped his back with a cloth again. She then rubbed ointment across the section of the back that Margol had cleaned. Shep ordered Allisto to begin packing up the vans. There was a flood of commotion while they all struggled to do their jobs, and to keep from pissing off Shep.

Shep struggled to get Klee to his feet. "Come on," he said, slinging one of Klee's arms over his shoulder. "Come on up. You're okay."

As Shep turned Klee around, Patrick and Robin got a clear view of the naked man's back. Between his shoulders was a shockingly deep wound, clearly visible now that the blood had been cleaned away. It was red with fresh blood, and shaped like an upside down horseshoe.

Robin sucked her breath in at the sight of the grizzly horseshoe-shaped wound. Patrick reached out to cover her mouth, but it was too late. Shep froze. "Everybody shut up!" he ordered. "I just heard something." Margol and Brin-Marie stopped moving.

Allisto came strolling back into the cave from being outside loading up the van. He stopped short when he looked at Shep and the others. "What is wrong?" he whispered.

Shep looked around the room. "I'm not sure. I thought I heard something." Patrick felt Robin begin to shake violently next to him. The movement caused tiny flecks of rock to scatter, making small sounds. Patrick rolled on top of her, suppressing her tremors with his weight. It had the desired effect, and the cave fell silent once more. Shep was still on alert. "Nobody move a muscle. I smell something in here."

He walked around the cave, stopping to sniff the air every few feet like a dog. He came back around and stopped directly beneath the ledge where Patrick lay on top of Robin. Patrick tried desperately not to breathe. He could still feel Robin shaking against his body. Shep sniffed loudly. "I definitely smell something. It's familiar."

Patrick held tight to Robin, wrapping both his arms around hers to help control the shaking.

"It's definitely a sugar substance." He sniffed the air again. *Fee Fi Fo Fum*, Patrick thought as he struggled to remain motionless. His own arms were beginning to tremble. It was so damned quiet in the cave with all of them standing still! If someone didn't move soon, he was sure he'd give them away. To make matters worse, he had a terrible itch building above his left eyebrow, and he thought he might sneeze from all of the residual smoke in the air.

"It's candy," Shep announced suddenly. "I smell candy."

Patrick looked down at Robin. She glanced up at him wide-eyed, and nervously fingered the candy necklace she still wore. Oh Shit, Patrick thought. He looked down at Shep, and wondered if he'd be able to harm him if forced into an altercation. Whether or not it had been deception, he had thought of Shep as his friend for ten years. Those feelings did not just disappear. As with a jilted lover, pain and anger replace the affection, but only time can truly dissolve the love.

Shep turned to the brothers. "Which one of you cheese heads brought candy into this sacred place?" he asked angrily. "Both of you come here. Empty your pockets!" *Please God*, Patrick thought, *let one of those curly-headed scrubs have a piece of candy in his pocket!*

"I don't have any candy," Margol said choppily, with assurance.

"Me neither," Allisto said, coming forward. "You can check my pockets."

Patrick watched Shep rummaging through the pockets of his two look-alike cronies. Neither one of them had any candy.

"Is this what you're smelling?" Brin-Marie asked.

Shep walked over to her and took something from her hand. "What is this? Bubble Gum?"

"Yes. I'm sorry. It was in my pocket. I didn't know it was forbidden. I meant no disrespect."

Shep examined the gum and took a long whiff of it. "All right. That must be it. Let's get the hell out of here."

Patrick let out a quiet sigh of relief as the activity ensued below and the noise level in the cave elevated once more. Robin was still shaking. They watched as the rest of the boxes were hauled out of the cave. Shep and Brin-Marie brought the bloody naked blond man to his feet again. They wrapped a blanket around him and began walking him out of the cave, each with an arm slung over their shoulder. His weak legs bent in all directions.

"Candles?" Brin-Marie inquired.

"Leave them," Shep said. "They'll burn themselves out."

After several trips in and out, Patrick and Robin were finally left alone in the cave. They lay silently, staring at the candles down below, not daring to move. The walls and the floor of the cave were covered in blood and the air stunk with that rank metallic odor. Dr. Lichtenstein's mutilated body had been rolled in a sheet and taken out with the boxes like an inanimate piece of cargo. Now the only sounds were of their own breathing, and the distant bubbling of the tiny waterfall in the exterior corridor.

After a patient fifteen-minute wait, they agreed to climb down from their hiding spot. When they got to the ground, Patrick hugged Robin to him. "Are you all right?"

"Let's not talk about it until we get out of here, okay? I just want to get the fuck out of here."

Patrick agreed. He wanted to run screaming from the cave as well, but not before he looked at what the good doctor had written in the dirt. He led Robin over, and the two of them hunched over the faint scribbling, straining their eyes. "It's a name," Robin gasped.

"Yes, I can see that," Patrick said. "The question is, who the hell is Wesley J. Shepherd?"

Robin shrugged. "Well that last name is certainly familiar. Do you think it's a relative of Shep's?"

Patrick shook his head. "Who knows. We'll talk to Litner about it. Maybe he can trace the name."

"Can we go now Patrick? This place is making me sick. All I can smell is blood and I need fresh air." Patrick happily agreed.

They headed toward the cavern opening, dodging the blood stains where they could. Two of the candles had already burned out and it was getting harder to see. Robin grabbed Patrick's hand as they crossed the cave, heading toward the exit tunnel. She tripped suddenly and tumbled to the ground, nearly pulling Patrick's arm out of the socket on her way down. He was jerked to the ground as well, landing hard on his elbow. "Oh shit!" he said rubbing his elbow. "Are you okay?"

Robin sat up. "I'm fine. I tripped over something." She lifted her legs and sprung backward. "Oh Gross! What is that?"

Patrick leaned over and examined the object. It was an animal carcass of some sort. There were long white feathers stained with fresh blood. "It looks like a bird."

Robin wrinkled her nose. "Why would they kill a bird?" She got up on her knees and leaned in more closely, poking the large white object with her finger. "It looks a little big to be a bird, Patrick. Maybe a swan. A big swan."

"Pick it up," Patrick said."

"No way! It's dead. You pick it up."

Patrick lifted the bloody thing off the ground and spread it out. Its wing span was longer than his body. "Big fucking bird!" he said. "What do you think it was?" Patrick looked over the fanned-out wings at her. "Robin?" Robin's eyes were wide with shock. "What's the matter?" he asked. "Oh. I see. The body is missing. Maybe they ate it like Ozzy Osborne."

"Patrick," she said, her voice shaking. "There was no bird."

"What?"

"Turn it around, Patrick."

Patrick turned it over and lifted it up again, spanning the wings outward. There was no bird in the center of those wings. There was only a thick piece of cartilage and a few broken fragments of bone connecting them. From that connecting bone hung scraps of red meaty flesh and gore. Robin stepped forward and took Patrick's arms. She guided them, pushing the wings closer together until he could see what she wanted him to see.

It hit him then, and he gasped. The cartilage connecting the wings had a distinct shape, like an upside down horseshoe. Patrick dropped the wings and took a step back. He looked up at Robin, wide eyed. "What the fuck!"

"Look!" Robin said, pointing to the ground a few feet away. The power saw lay abandoned or forgotten in the dirt. The blade was red with blood, and a few gruesome chunks of flesh and cartilage clung to its circular blade. Patrick opened his mouth to speak, then closed it again. He shook his head.

He didn't have time to formulate the thought because they both heard Shep's voice suddenly. He was coming up the tunnel, screaming at somebody. Robin grabbed Patrick's arm. "They're back! Come on we have to hide!"

They scrambled quickly back up on to the ledge and ducked themselves down just before Shep and Margol entered the cave. Shep was angrily ranting at Margol, who was carrying canisters of gasoline. "I give you one simple task, Margol. One simple job to do and you fuck it up. Do I have to do everything myself?"

"You distracted me!" Margol protested. "You were checking me for candy and you were rushing me!"

"Yeah, yeah. Excuses. Just do it and let's get out of here," Shep snapped. "Oh, and look! You left the saw here too. Very nice, Margol. Real swift work." Shep picked the saw up and shook it off. Margol opened the canisters of gasoline and doused the bloody white wings that lay on the ground. He emptied several canisters, completely saturating the wings, then he lit a match and dropped it. The wings made a 'woof' sound as they burst into flames. Shep and Margol stood by, watching the wings burn for several minutes. Their eyes were blank, looking strangely sad as they concentrated on the flames.

"That's good," Shep said finally. "Let's go."

Margol put the cap back on the canisters, and the two of them walked quickly out of the cave.

Chapter Twenty-Nine

Nobody spoke. Nobody even moved. The three of them stared over the coffee table at Robin and Patrick where they sat on the love seat. "Well? Isn't anyone going to say anything?" Patrick asked. The three of them continued to stare. They looked literally dumbfounded. Except for Agent Litner of course. His face was always a blank slate. Patrick squirmed as the silence continued.

It had taken twenty minutes to fully report everything that had happened down at Pearl Chasm the night before. And they had reported all of it, holding nothing back. Now, as Patrick looked at those three faces, staring back at him with identical expressions of disbelief, he wondered if they shouldn't have edited the recalling of the story. Clearly, the little group was not swallowing it.

"Wings, did you say?" Father Carbone asked, wincing.

"Yes, that's right. Wings," Patrick answered.

The priest said nothing further. None of them did. The clock ticked on the wall. Patrick had never heard Father Carbone's kitchen so quiet. Finally, Copie stood up and did a quick pace of the room. He returned and sat back down, looking quizzically at Patrick with one finger resting on his chin.

Patrick held his hands out expectantly. "Okay Copie. You obviously have something to say, so let's have it."

Copie nodded. "All right. Did you take any hallucinogenic drugs before you went into that cave?"

"Hey fuck you Copie! You weren't there!"

"Angels, Patrick? Are we talking about angels here?"

"I never said anything about angels, Copie!" he snapped. "I'm merely reporting what we saw."

"But that's what you're implying, right? That we have blood-crazed angels running around?"

Patrick clenched his teeth. "I don't know what they are, Copie. I'm just telling you what happened."

"Take is easy, Patrick," Father Carbone said. "Let's all calm down here. Now I have to say, Copie had a good point. If not angels, then what are you two suggesting here?"

Patrick shifted uncomfortably. "Well, Robin and I were discussing it, and we think maybe it's some sort of...genetic mutation."

Father Carbone raised his eyebrows. "A genetic mutation? This isn't like a sixth toe, Patrick. You're talking about wings here."

"I'm aware!" he yelled.

Father Carbone sighed. "I'm not trying to patronize you Patrick, but you said yourself that neither one of you actually saw these wings attached to a person. I mean, this naked person, this Klee…he wasn't actually, how shall I say, *wearing* them?"

Patrick gave the priest a sarcastic sneer. "No, Father Carbone. Nobody was wearing them when we saw them. And I never suggested that anyone was. I've merely given you the facts of what happened. So tell me, what would be your explanation of this, oh holy one?"

Father Carbone drummed his fingers on his face. "Well, the two of you witnessed something horrible. Under the stress of seeing someone killed, and the strangeness of the ritual, perhaps you let your imaginations run away with you."

"I agree," Copie said. "I mean, you find a pair of wings on the ground, and you just assume that they were on this bloody guy's back?"

"How do you explain the power saw and the wound?" Patrick asked him.

"They're crazy man! They obviously marked this guy with that saw as part of some sick ritual they have. And as far as people spitting out of rock walls like a fetus through some giant womb, well, I think the priest is right. You were under stress. The cave was full of smoke. Your mind started playing tricks on you."

Agent Litner got up and walked out of the room. Robin had been sitting silently next to Patrick, but now she too spoke up. "You weren't there, Copie! You didn't risk your life. All you've done is sit on your ass and whine."

Copie let out a laugh. "Yeah. That, and almost getting burned alive by your wingless boyfriend."

"It's getting old, Copie." Patrick said.

Robin went back to her silent maniacal rocking. She was in rough shape and Patrick was getting concerned. She hadn't been quite right since they left the cave. At times she was nearly catatonic, as if she'd disappeared into some private world inside her head where things made sense. That was just his luck. He had found the girl of his dreams, and now he was going to have to visit her in a loony bin.

Father Carbone buried his face in his hands and sighed. Patrick looked at him expectantly, but the priest remained silent. Copie continued to taunt. "So in a nut shell, Obrien, no pun intended, this thing comes through the wall from God knows where, no pun intended again. They take a hack saw—"

"Power saw," Patrick corrected him.

"Excuse me, they take a *power saw*, cut off its wings, give it a Band-Aid and they're ready to go?"

Patrick ignored Copie now. His focus was on Father Carbone whose face was still buried in his hands. "You believe me. Don't you, Father Carbone?"

Father Carbone lifted his head and peered at Patrick through a mask of fingers. "I don't believe in angels, Patrick."

Patrick breathed a dismayed gasp. "But you're a priest! How can you not believe in angels?"

"I'm sorry, Patrick. I just don't. I had to study them in school, but they just didn't seem credible to me."

"Great. That's just great, Father Carbone. You just re-wrote half of the Bible. So who told the Virgin Mary that she was pregnant with the Son of God? Elvis?"

"I agree with Father Carbone," Copie said. "Angels have become way too trendy. My mother collects little angel figurines. They're all over the house. The things are definitely over-exposed. They're on mugs, bumper stickers, stupid TV shows. They're just tacky."

Patrick stood up. "Is anybody listening to me? I don't give a shit if there are too many angels on fucking coffee mugs! Besides, how do we even know where all those myths came from? These winged beings might have been aliens all along, and primitive cultures just worked them into their religion. Trust me, there is nothing Godly about these creatures!"

Agent Litner came back into the room, executing his usual habit of tapping his temple with a pen. He'd been so quiet that Patrick had nearly forgotten he was there. "So Patrick, it's time to go over your next step," he said. "We need to discuss our plans regarding your infiltration of Forest Bluffs."

Patrick studied Litner. "What?"

"We have to hatch out our plan. We need to send you out there as soon as possible."

"Are you nuts, Agent Litner? You still want me to go out there and live in that house with those...people? Have you heard a word I've said? Those house guests of Joey's, Shep included, are not exactly *normal*."

"I don't care," Agent Litner said.

"You don't care?"

"No. I don't care. I don't care if they're little green men from outer space. It's still a matter of national security, and I still need those crop samples. We had a deal, Obrien, and I expect you to uphold your end of the bargain."

Patrick could not believe his ears. At this point, he'd rather gnaw his own arm off than go anywhere near Shepherd, never mind live in the same house with him. "Are you truly a heartless robot, Litner? You weren't there! You didn't see it. It was carnage! It was the stuff of nightmares! Just look what it's doing to Robin."

Robin rocked back and forth, her eyes distant. Agent Litner leaned against the doorway twirling his pen like a baton. "What's wrong with her?" he asked casually.

Patrick sneered. "What's wrong with her? Do you mean beside the fact that she's been sleeping with a non-human for the past six years?"

Copie gave him a confused scowl. "A non-human?"

"Shepherd," Patrick said. "Or should I say Zirub." He rolled his eyes, remembering the name Shep had called himself. "At any rate, she's entitled to have a little melt down after what we witnessed last night."

Father Carbone narrowed his eyes. "What was that name you used?"

"Zirub? That's the name Shep used to refer to himself in the cave when he was speaking to Klee."

"That name is in that crazy little journal he wrote. It still rings a bell with me. It did when I first read it. I know I've heard that name in the past."

"Are you sure?" Patrick asked hopefully.

Carbone nodded. "I'm sure I know that name from somewhere. I need to make a phone call. I have a colleague over at Saint Christopher's who studies the celestial hierarchy. He may be able to sort some of this out."

"Hey, I have an idea!" Copie said, bright eyed. "Let's ask him!" Copie pointed to the floor.

Now Agent Litner looked uneasy. He cleared his throat. "I don't think that's a good idea, Copie. Let's all relax and have some tea, shall we?"

Patrick looked suspiciously at Litner, then at Copie, who looked suddenly guilty. "Let's ask who?" Patrick said. "Who did you mean, Copie?" Copie avoided Patrick's eyes. "Copie, I asked you a question. You said, 'let's ask him'. Who did you mean?"

Copie cringed, glancing uneasily at Agent Litner. "Well, um, you know those guys we've been calling the brothers? The ones with the curly hair?"

"I spent the entire night in a cave watching them play with blood. What is your point?"

"Well..." he glanced at Agent Litner, then at Father Carbone.

Carbone nodded. "You might as well tell him, Copie. He's going to find out sooner or later."

"Tell me what?" Patrick demanded.

Copie shrugged. "Well, we sort of caught one of them."

Patrick frowned at him. "You *caught* one of them?"

"Yes. We caught one."

"What are you talking about?"

"You have Juris. Don't you?" It was Robin's voice. They all turned. "It's Juris. Isn't it?"

Father Carbone walked toward her. "Yes. How did you know his name?"

"I spent a weekend at Forest Bluffs. I met him. I noticed that he wasn't in the cave with the others last night."

"Would someone please tell me what is going on?" Patrick demanded.

Agent Litner came and stood before him. "It was a necessary precaution, Patrick. We found Juris spying on us outside the club the night of our meeting. He must have been following you. Had we let him go, he would have warned Shepherd and the others about our collaboration. So we had to...detain him."

"So where is he?" Patrick asked. "I want to see him. Are you keeping him downtown somewhere?"

"Patrick I want you to stay calm," Litner said.

"Where is he?" Patrick demanded.

"He's in the basement," Father Carbone said softly.

Patrick looked at the priest. "I'm sorry. Could you repeat that? I thought you said he was in the basement."

The priest nodded. "He is."

"What? Here?"

"He's tied to a chair," Copie said.

Patrick and Robin looked at each other, then they both headed for the basement door. The other three followed. "Please, Patrick wait!" Father Carbone called after him. "Try not to upset him. He has a hangover!"

Patrick flipped the cellar light on and trampled down the wooden stairs with the others in tow. He could not believe his eyes when he stepped onto the cement floor and entered the long spacious basement. It was the light blond man who even with his head hung down to his chest looked strikingly like a brother to Shep. It was the one he'd caught eating chocolate bars in the shrubs at Aunt Betsy's. His hands were cuffed behind his back, and his body was wrapped with wire. It was a sad sight, sort of like viewing a lovely but dangerous animal cruelly caged up. Robin stepped up alongside Patrick. Juris did not look up when they entered the room. He appeared to be sleeping. The only sign of life was when his long hair moved up and down slightly with each breath he took.

Robin looked over her shoulder at the others. "Has he been tied to that chair since the meeting?"

Litner nodded. "We can't risk untying him, Robin. He's extremely strong, and prone to violent behavior."

"Have you been feeding him?" Robin asked.

"Of course," Father Carbone said. "But he won't eat anything but chocolate and he won't drink anything but water and brandy."

"It appears that he has unusual body chemistry. He seems able to slow down his own metabolism, as though he is literally saving his strength. He has exhibited precious few normal bodily functions since the second day he was here," Litner said.

Patrick furrowed his brow. "Has he said anything?"

"Och fee!" Juris exclaimed, and they all jumped. He had lifted his head and was glaring at Patrick. "Och fee!" he repeated, a look of disgust in his narrowed green eyes. His white curls were unkempt and stood out like so many springs atop his head.

Patrick matched his stare. "Well well. Look who's up. What is that you're speaking? Klingon?"

Juris's face tightened. "Betrayer!" he hissed. "You are a filthy betrayer!"

Patrick laughed, a high-pitched guffaw that edged on madness. "I'm the betrayer? That's certainly an interesting perspective, Juris. Do you even know what your precious Shepherd has done to betray *me*?"

Juris spit at him, just missing Patrick's face as he ducked to the right. Patrick grimaced and took a step backward.

"He does that a lot," Father Carbone said.

Patrick looked at Father Carbone. "I want to see his back," he said. "Robin said they all have the scar. I need to see it with my own eyes."

Juris turned his head and grinned at Robin. "It's lovely to see you again, Robin. You smell even better than chocolate."

"Do not speak to her!" Patrick growled. This only made Juris smile more.

"She does not belong to you, Obrien. She belongs to Shepherd. I have more right to speak to her than you."

Now Robin's face flushed with anger, and she approached Juris. "You listen to me, Goldy Locks. I don't belong to anyone! And if I were going to belong to someone, it sure as shit wouldn't be that murdering freak you call your brother! You can tell him that!"

Juris glanced over at Agent Litner. "I'd love to, Robin. But I don't think I will be telling Shepherd anything anytime soon. In case you hadn't noticed, I've gotten myself into a bit of a bind."

"I need to see his back!" Patrick repeated.

"We can't risk untying him. I'll get you a pair of scissors. You can cut his shirt if you want."

The priest clomped up the wooden stairs and returned momentarily with a pair of kitchen shears, which he handed to Patrick. Juris simply stared. Patrick rounded the back of the chair and held Juris's shoulders forward while Robin cut down the back of his shirt, skillfully avoiding the steel ropes. She dropped the scissors and tore the shirt open, exposing his naked back. Patrick gasped. The scar was there. It was nearly identical to Shep's, if not a bit fresher looking.

"My God," Patrick said.

"I told you," Robin said. "They all have them."

Patrick moved around the chair. "Where did you get the scar, Juris?"

"Fuck you, Obrien."

Patrick turned away, giving his back to Juris. "Fine," he said, cracking his knuckles and stretching his back. "Then I guess you don't want to hear about what happened to Klee."

Juris looked like he'd been punched. He straightened up, his face serious, almost childlike. The arrogant smirk was gone. "You-you have seen my brother Klee?"

"Maybe," Patrick taunted.

Rage flashed in his green eyes and Juris shook. "You tell me! Damn you! If you saw Klee you must tell me. Is he alive?"

"Where did you get the scar, Juris? And don't tell me that your daddy branded you. That one's been used."

"Fuck you! Dirty betrayer!"

Patrick moved in closer and leaned over so he was face to face. "Have it your way. If you won't tell me anything, then I won't tell you anything."

Agent Litner leaned in to Copie's ear. "He's good. He should have been an interrogator."

"Yes," Copie agreed. "He's much better than you were." Agent Litner gave Copie a scowl.

Father Carbone walked over and strung a crucifix around the prisoner's neck. Juris flinched a little, then he grinned. "What is that for, Priest? Do you think I am a vampire?"

"I don't know what you are, Juris. Why don't you tell me?"

"Why don't you bite me?"

Robin grabbed a handful of Juris's hair and tugged his head back. "What the hell are you?" she demanded.

Juris smiled up at her sweetly. "Oh, just a regular guy." Robin looked into his eyes for a moment longer, then let him go.

"Who is Wesley J. Shepherd?" Patrick asked, remembering the name the old doctor had written in the dirt. Juris whipped his head around and stared at Patrick with open shock.

"What did you say?"

"I said who is Wesley J. Shepherd?"

Juris looked at Patrick as though he had performed a magic trick. "Where did you hear that name?"

"From a dead man. Do you know the name?"

Juris shook his head. "No. He does not exist."

"If you don't know the name, then how do you know he doesn't exist?"

"Do not play mind games with me, Obrien. You will lose. Tell me where you heard that name. I know it was not from Shepherd."

"Oh? And how do you know that?"

"Because Shepherd will not speak that name aloud. Shepherd will never speak that name again."

"Why? Who is Wesley and what is his connection to Shep?"

Juris sat tight-lipped. Patrick had filled Agent Litner in about the name the old doctor had written in the dirt just before his death. Litner had assured him that if Wesley J. Shepherd existed, either now or anytime in the past, Litner would find him. Patrick was beyond curiosity about the name now, especially in light of Juris's reaction. What did the name mean? It was clearly something of great consequence if Shep himself refused to utter it aloud.

"I'd like some chocolate please," Juris said.

"No. You get no chocolate until you answer one of our questions." Father

Carbone crouched down on one knee in front of Juris. His brown eyes were focused and intense. "You're quite beautiful, Juris. That worries me."

"Why is that, priest? Are you afraid I'm going to steal one of your little boyfriends?"

Robin and Patrick exchanged a smirk. Juris shared Shep's ruthlessly keen ability to vex and taunt. He was, in fact, so like Shepherd, that Patrick was finding it increasingly difficult to despise him. He feared him much more than he hated him. His speech seemed to have improved tremendously. When Patrick had encountered him at Aunt Betsy's, he spoke with a much slower and more broken inflection. It was as though his total verbal capacity had accelerated over the short time since he'd seen him.

Father Carbone continued. "The Bible says that a demon is never more dangerous than when disguised as an angel of light."

Juris chuckled. "The Bible was written by men who would sell their daughters for a herd of goats."

Father Carbone rested his chin on his fist. "Have you fallen, Juris?"

Juris spit at him. Litner casually strolled over and handed the priest a handkerchief, which he used to wipe the spittle off of his cheek. "You are a stupid priest. There is no such thing as a fallen one," Juris said with contempt.

"Where did you get the scar?" The priest pressed on.

"Give me some chocolate and I will tell you."

"Tell me and I will give you some chocolate."

Juris remained silent. Father Carbone stood up and crossed his arms. "You mock my beliefs, yet you say it is not safe for you in this church. Why is that?" Juris looked uneasy, but said nothing. "Answer me!" the priest yelled.

Juris cringed and his eyes darted around the room. He was getting agitated suddenly. "Keep your voice down!"

"Why should I keep my voice down? Who are you afraid is going to hear me?" Father Carbone yelled up into the ceiling. "Hey! Everyone! There is a fallen one in my basement!"

Juris struggled against the ropes that bound him. "You must be silent! It is not safe!" he whispered.

"Hey!" Father Carbone screamed again. "If there is anyone listening, I have Juris, the fallen one in my basement!" he screamed into the air.

Juris threw his head back and let out a sound that left them all covering their ears. It was a wild, inhuman screech, like the echoing death cry of a long-extinct bird. Patrick and Robin had heard a similar screech come from Klee in the cave at Pearl Chasm. Juris's wail finally ceased and the windows in the basement rattled until one of them cracked. The room fell silent. They all uncovered their ears. Juris glared at Father Carbone, panting and out of breath.

Carbone walked over to the window and peeled back the paper that covered it. The glass had a jagged crack down the center, like a fine spider web. He turned and looked at Juris with amazement. Juris, still panting, tilted his head back, focusing on Father Carbone through narrowed eyes. "Have I fallen, you ask me? You would fall too, priest, if someone cut your fucking wings off."

No one spoke. They were all stunned. Juris turned to Patrick. "You asked me where I got the scar. I answered you. Tell me about Klee," he said with desperation.

Patrick glanced at Robin. She nodded. No one wanted to hear that scream again. Patrick looked back at Juris. "Your brother Klee is very much alive. The last time I saw him, he was wrapped in a blanket and being helped out of the cave by Shep."

Juris's face lost a bit of its anguish, but he still looked suspicious. "Describe Klee to me. Tell me what he looks like."

Patrick moved forward and sat on his feet in front of Juris. "I didn't get a very close look, but from what I could see he looks like the rest of you freaks."

Juris sneered. "You could have speculated that through deductive reasoning. Give me details."

"He was wet and bloody, but I'm pretty sure his hair was your color. He looks more like you than he does the others, but his features are more child-like."

Juris appeared to be considering this, but he still did not look completely at ease. Robin spoke up then. "He was yelling something. He was yelling something in another language. Shep made him say it in English, then they gave him a pain killer."

Juris's eyes opened a little wider. "What was the word? What was he yelling?"

"Flesh," Robin answered. "He was screaming the word 'flesh'."

Juris let out a sigh of relief, and nodded. "Plefarr."

"Yes. That's it." Robin agreed. "Plefarr. Flesh."

Juris looked at Robin softly. "Thank you," he said quietly as fat tears streamed down his face. "Thank you, Robin."

Robin's face softened as Juris began to weep, and it made Patrick want to scream. He got off of the floor and approached her. "Don't be fooled by the sentiment, Robin. It does not redeem him. The only thing these freaks care about is each other. Everyone else, including the lot of us, they would kill in an instant without remorse."

Robin shrugged. "At least they care about something."

"I want to be moved out of this church," Juris demanded, his tone vile again.

"Sorry. No can do," Litner said.

Juris stared at them all for a long time. His gaze lingered on Copie. "Fine. May I at least have some chocolate now, young one?"

Copie looked at Father Carbone, who nodded his approval. Copie grabbed the bag of Kisses and approached Juris unabashedly. He had spent a good deal of time with the prisoner now, and he was no longer afraid. He unwrapped two kisses and held them out in front of Juris's face. "Open up," he said.

In one fluid motion, Juris hunched his body down then pressed his knees out, snapping the steel ropes that held him below the waist. His upper body was still secured to the chair, but he was able to thrust his legs upward and catch Copie around the neck, holding him in a scissor lock between his knees. Patrick went diving forward to help Copie. Juris twisted his knees a little and Copie whimpered. "I wouldn't, Obrien. Come any closer and I snap his neck." Copie groaned as Juris squeezed his legs tighter.

Agent Litner had drawn his gun and was pointing it at Juris. "Let him go, Juris."

"You can shoot me, FBI, but not before I can snap his neck. Untie me and take the cuffs off."

"I can't do that, Juris. Just let him go."

"Not until you make a concession. I want to be moved out of this church. I want to be held elsewhere."

Litner nodded. "Fine. I can have you moved to a new location within twenty four hours."

"You have twelve hours. And I want more chocolate and brandy."

"Well," Litner said, stony as ever, "that's a bit out of my job description, but I'm sure the priest can accommodate you. Now let Copie go."

"Just one more thing. Father Carbone? Would you mind removing this atrocious piece of jewelry from around my neck?"

Father Carbone moved carefully forward, pulled the crucifix over Juris's head, and backed away. Juris took a deep breath. "Thank you." He unlocked his knees and Copie dropped to the floor.

Robin ran to Copie, who was shaken but not harmed. Litner quickly retied Juris's legs, doubling up the steel ropes. Juris did not fight him. "Copie are you all right?" Litner asked.

"He is alive, FBI," Juris said. "I kept my part of the bargain. Do you keep your promises?"

Litner finished securing the ropes and stepped back. "All right, Juris. I can't say you've been a treat, but you've been more cooperative than usual today. I'll have you moved to a new location as soon as possible. Father Carbone will get you your chocolate and brandy."

Father Carbone crossed his arms stubbornly. "I didn't agree to that."

"Get the man, or whatever he is, his brandy, Father Carbone. Patrick, you need to come with me. We have a mission to prepare you for." Litner headed for the stairs. The rest of the company followed closely behind him. They had all had enough of the basement, and of Juris.

"Let's go, Patrick," Litner demanded when they got up to the kitchen.

Patrick looked at Robin. He wanted to say so much to her, but he wasn't sure where they stood. So much had happened, and he was afraid that she might be regretting the kiss they had shared on the way down to Pearl Chasm. Much to his delight, she ran to him and they fell into a deep passionate kiss. They disentangled and he held her to his chest. "Be careful out there," she said. "You owe me a real date, remember?"

"I'll come back in one piece. I promise," he said, clinging to her, not wanting to let go.

The rest of them looked on sheepishly. Father Carbone grinned. Even Litner raised a quizzical eyebrow. "When did you two start sucking face?" Copie asked bluntly.

"Just so you know, Robin," Agent Litner said, "I'm going to have Patrick tell Shep that he has to come back to Boston once a week for a consulting job. This may not be necessary if he can get the crop sample the first week, but we just can't be sure. We will use that time for briefings, since we can't risk contacting him by telephone once he's moved out there. Patrick, let's get moving. I want to get this damn thing figured out and have it over with."

Father Carbone walked Agent Litner and Patrick outside to the car, gazing at the passing traffic for several minutes after they'd gone. He was not anxious to go back inside, where something inhuman sat quietly hostile in his basement.

Chapter Thirty

"I want to go out! Are you listening to me?" Joey threw another hunk of cheese. Shep continued to tap away at the computer as the cheese bounced off of his shoulder and joined the other pieces on the floor around his chair. Joey's tirade had been going on for nearly an hour now, and Shep's patience was wearing thin.

"For the last time Joey, you cannot leave the house. It's too risky. Oh, and please stop pelting me with cheese. You're being immature."

"I am going to lose my shit if I don't get out of this house, Shepherd."

Shep sighed and turned to Joey, who sat sideways in a leather recliner. He picked up another piece of cheese from the tray and tossed it across the room where it bounced off of Shep's temple. "I want to go out!"

Shep struggled to stay calm. "Did you or did you not get shot last week? Have you forgotten so soon? Do you know what I've been doing for the last two hours?"

"No, but I'm sure you're going to tell me, and I'm sure it's going to be very boring."

"Let me enlighten you," Shep said. "I have been scouring the hundreds of web sites that have cropped up on the Internet in your honor. Aside from the ones calling for your death, you also have cyber stalkers now, most of them women who are intent on finding you so that they may bear your children. If we go out in public you could cause a riot, or get killed, or both."

Joey pouted and kicked the tray of hors d'oeuvres off of the end table with a loud clang, making a catastrophic mess on the floor. Shep could scarcely blame him for going stir crazy. He'd kept him completely under guard since the shooting. He'd even had the followers come inside the house to hear Joey's sermons in the library. He knew his measures were extreme, but these were extreme times, and if something happened to Joey, Shep's entire purpose would be defeated. He would not let that happen.

"I can't stay in this house forever, Shep. Why can't we go out and have a couple of drinks? God, what I wouldn't give for a night at Monty's."

"Do you want to ruin all that we've worked for so you can have a couple of tequila slammers?"

Joey crossed his arms in defiance. "I don't care about the booze. I can drink here if I want. I need to see people. Real People! Not these zombies we've got living out in the fields. I need socialization, and live music. And women! I need to see lots of women!"

Shep logged out of the computer and stood up. "Listen, boy wonder, you have to be patient. This is a very critical time. Once the crop is harvested and the product is dispersed, we can all relax. Eventually Obrien will be here, and you'll be able to roam around as you please. And if it's women you want, Kelinda is naked in the Jacuzzi as we speak."

Joey made a face. "I don't want her. She's changed. She's just another zombie now."

"She's a zombie because of you, you idiot. May I remind you that we could have avoided all of this if you had just let me kill her?"

"You can kill her now if you want. I don't care anymore."

"Well it's too late now! Her parents know she's out here!" Shep shook his head. "This is all irrelevant." Fifteen years of planning, and Joey chose now to fall apart on him. It was bad enough that Obrien hadn't come through yet. He could not lose control of Joey too. Part of Joey's behavior was due to the fact that Shep had kept him drunk nearly twenty-four hours a day, but that could not be helped. Alcohol was the only thing that calmed the fear in his blood. Except for Obrien of course, but the stupid Mick was still holding out on them.

As though reading his thoughts, Joey said, "I miss Obrien." His face was sad and wistful.

Shep stormed over. "Oh stop that! You do not miss Obrien. Your blood misses him, that's all."

Joey shook his head sadly. "It's not just that, I think I actually miss him, Shep. Obrien listened to me, you know? He laughed at my jokes. He didn't treat me like a hand puppet, the way you do."

"Oh boo hoo. Your ego misses Obrien. Are you forgetting that I put your soul to sleep? You don't have any feelings therefore you cannot possibly miss Obrien. He will be here, mark my words. He will come because the blood running through his veins instructs him to."

Joey stood now. "Oh really? Then why isn't he here? Huh? Why isn't it working, Mr. Plan-of-the-Century?"

"Obrien will come around! It's just taking a little longer than I anticipated. He will be here soon, and he will be behaving like a trained dog!"

Joey yawned deliberately.

"Joseph Pierre Duvaine, are you listening to me?"

"I want to go out, Shepherd."

"Oh, mother of mercy," Shep said, and threw his hands in the air, walking away.

"I'll wear a disguise. Please Shepherd? You can get the brothers to protect me. And Russell."

Shep shook his head.

"Why not?" Joey pushed, whining like a toddler.

"Because Juris is missing, Klee is too weak yet, and Margol has welts all over one side of his face. He looks like he won third place in an acid fight."

"What? Why?"

"Long story."

"And what about geek boy?"

"Russell is staying in and cleaning the basement with a toothbrush tonight. He's being punished for trying to peek at me while I was in the shower."

A grin spread across Joey's face, and he bit his lower lip to stifle his laughter.

"Yes, yes. Very funny indeed," Shep said. "I'm sure Russell will find the rats I planted in the basement equally amusing."

Joey shook his head. "Man, you are so mean to that guy. You should really back off. I've seen the look in his eye lately. The guy is going to snap."

"And why is this relevant?"

Joey shrugged. "He's the only one who will play video games with me. Besides, we have enough problems without having to deal with a psychotic nerd."

"Don't worry about Russell. The torture is good for him. It builds character."

Joey got up and circled the room, rubbing his hands thoughtfully. Suddenly he brightened, and turned to Shep. "Hey! What about the followers? We can get some of the followers in the field to come with us! God knows they'll do whatever we say, and some of those guys are huge! We can take Devin and Carlos. Come on Shep. Cut me some slack. I'm dying here."

Shep was too exasperated to stay angry. He supposed he would have to agree to this, if only to maintain Joey's sanity, and his own if Joey kept riding him. Joey was right about Devin and Carlos. They were big guys. They had both been high school football players before they joined the church. And they were ominous-looking. They had recently shaved their hair into Mohawks, and died them bright pink seemingly as a tribute to Kelinda, who they viewed as some sort of Goddess. Regardless of their reasons, the result was two large, fairly scary looking men. They would make formidable bodyguards.

"Fine," Shep said finally.

Joey did a double take. "Really? Do you mean it?'

"We can go out for a little while Joey, but I make the arrangements. I say where, I say how, and when I say it's time to go home, I don't want to hear any arguing."

Joey squealed with delight and danced about. "I'm going out! I'm going out! I'm going out!"

"Call out to the guest house and get Devin and Carlos over here. I'll round up Margol and Allisto. We'll need their strength if things get out of hand. By the way, you're looking a little ripe, boy wonder. I'd hit the shower if I were you. I know you're out of touch, but I'm fairly sure women still prefer men who bathe."

Joey ran his fingers through his chin length black hair, which had gotten stringy and unkempt. "I was going for that Jesus of Nazareth look. I hear Jesus only bathed once a month, baptisms aside."

Shep shook his head, wincing. "Oh, you're a fucking riot, Joey."

Joey took off down the hall. Shep went to find the brothers, shaking his head and muttering to himself. "The things you have to put up with when you're trying to take over the world."

Shepherd gathered Allisto and Margol in the downstairs den. They were quickly joined by Joey and the two followers Carlos and Devin, who immediately professed to Shep what a great honor it was to be chosen as Joey's protection. Their hot pink Mohawks stuck up like frightened feather dusters atop their otherwise bald heads. Shep wondered if they might ironically serve to draw more attention to the group instead of deterring it. But he supposed as long as people were gawking at them and not Joey, it was all right.

Shep called ahead to a bar called the Island Hut and spoke with the owner, who was most cooperative. He had promised Shep security and crowd control, and Shep had promised him a 'contribution' for his efforts. Joey smiled when he saw Allisto and Margol, who had actually cleaned themselves up. Their heads were a tangled mass of rebel curls, but they were clean and well dressed. "Hey! You guys look great!" he exclaimed. Joey's smile dropped when Margol tuned his head to face him. At Shep's instruction, Margol had put flesh colored ointment on the bulbous hives that covered one side of his face, but the ointment did not serve well to hide the angry-looking welts he'd received in his altercation with Father Bello.

"Holy shit!" Joey exclaimed, staring at Margol without a bit of candor. "What the hell happened to you?"

"I got baptized," Margol answered sheepishly.

Joey shook his head. "Bummer, man."

Shep clapped his hands to get the small crowd's attention. "Okay, listen up people. We're going out tonight, and I need you to act as bodyguards. I realize that this is not what you signed on for, but due to circumstances beyond my control, this is the way it has to be."

"We don't mind at all, Shepherd!" Devin exclaimed. Carlos was quick to add his agreement. Shep thanked them. He was secretly repulsed by their incessant zombie ass kissing, but if their ass kissing would help keep Joey safe, so be it.

"Margol and Allisto, the same rules apply tonight as whenever you go out in public. Do not do anything to draw attention. Try to be as human as possible, okay?"

"Where are we going?" Allisto asked.

"We are going to a beach club to see a band."

Margol raised his hand, but Shep immediately cut him off. "Please don't ask me why, just do as I say." Margol put his hand down. Shep continued. "The bar is within walking distance from the house. I want Devin to walk on Joey's right, and Carlos and Allisto to walk on Joey's left. I'll take up the front, and Margol will cover the rear. We'll cut through the back woods to avoid the main center of town. This should bring us out by the gazebo, leaving thirty feet or so to actually walk along the sidewalk. We should be fine. But that doesn't mean we can relax. I want you all on full alert. No one gets near Joey. Understood?"

They all nodded.

"Here, put this on." Shep tossed Joey a long black cape with a hood.

Joey caught it and held it up, sneering. "I'm not wearing this. I thought we were supposed to be laying low tonight."

"The hood will mask your face. Just put it on, Joey."

Joey took a long swig off the rum bottle he'd been carrying around. "Okay. Whatever." He threw the black cape over his shoulders. It looked stunning on him. He was freshly showered and his black hair fell soft and sleek around his chin. The cape emphasized the stark whiteness of his silk shirt, which he wore with dark jeans and black boots. Joey's wolf blue eyes darted around the room when he realized that everyone was staring at him. "What? What's everyone looking at? Do I have spinach in my teeth or something?"

Joey's magnetism was emphasized by the unnatural blood, but his beauty was all his own. Even Shep had to stop and stare. The brothers, who rarely noticed anything, particularly fashion, gazed at Joey with open awe. "May we wear capes also?" Allisto asked.

Shep shrugged. "Sure. But you're not going to look like that in them."

Shep worried as he studied Joey in all his enchanting splendor. He had the distinct feeling this was not going to be an uneventful night. "Okay. Let's get this over with," he ordered.

Patrick peered through the binoculars, squinting to see in the foggy darkness. He squatted behind a rock, intent on spying until he formulated a plan. He couldn't exactly walk up to the door, ring the bell and say, "Hi honey, I'm home." He had a perfect view of the back deck but could see nothing of the goings on inside the house. Shep and his matching creatures were nowhere in sight. Then suddenly his luck changed.

The back slider opened and five figures stepped out onto the deck. Patrick adjusted his binoculars. He immediately saw Margol and Allisto. They were wearing long black capes. He panned the binoculars, his sight falling on two men. They wore Mohawks, bright pink. He panned a little to the right and his sight landed on Shep, who was pushing the others into a line. To his dismay, Patrick felt a stab of affection at the sight of his former friend. Of course, he wasn't trapped in a cave now watching Shep slaughter seemingly innocent old men.

The slider opened again and another figure stepped out, swaying and carrying a bottle. He stood taller than the rest. It took Patrick a moment to realize this was Joey. As the others, he was wearing a black cape, with the hood drawn casually back around his shoulders. He looked like some sparkling knight from the days of Camelot. Patrick's binoculars fogged up and he had to wipe them with his shirt. He refocused, only to see that the deck was now empty.

"What the..." He scanned the surrounding area, finally locating the company of six making their way through the back yard into the woods. They had put on their hoods and Patrick could only identify Joey because he stood taller than the rest. They had him wedged between them as they proceeded on like a band of Grim Reapers.

Patrick dropped the binoculars as he realized they were headed straight for him. He pressed behind his concealing rock. Shep's voice could be picked out as the company moved closer. It was an eerie sight, the six of them moving up the hill through the fog. Patrick's temples began to throb violently then and he had to drop the binoculars and rub them. The company passed within ten feet by the boulder where Patrick hid. His head swam with dizziness and he had to cling to the rock for support. A cool sweat broke out on his forehead. He peered over the top of the boulder, just in time to see Joey stop short. Whoever it was that was walking behind him slammed right into Joey's back, uttering an "ugh!"

Shep turned around at the sound. "Joey!" he hissed. "What the hell is wrong with you?"

Joey pulled his hood back and shook his head. He stood there swaying. "I don't know. I feel funny. I'm kind of dizzy all of a sudden." Joey placed his hands on his head, just as Patrick's temples began to throb furiously. He held his breath and struggled to make himself invisible. He could hear Shep's frustrated sigh.

"You feel funny because you drank half a bottle of rum, you hamster brain. You wanted to go out, and you nagged me for an hour! Don't tell me you want to turn back now!"

"No, no. I guess I'll be all right. Let's just keep moving."

Patrick heard the six pairs of feet continue on, snapping twigs along the way. The further on they moved, the more his dizziness subsided. When he was sure they were out of range, he lifted his head and looked on after them. He pondered Joey's reaction to coming within close range of him. With all of the strange dreams and psychic impressions he'd been getting of Joey, it had never occurred to him that Joey may be experiencing the same things. The thought made Patrick's hair stand up on the back of his neck. What the hell had Shep done to him? What had he done to all of them?

Perhaps Joey could still be saved from whatever unsavory fate Shep had cut out for him. Then there was the matter of the crops, and his promise to Agent Litner. Get the crop sample, and get the hell out. How hard could that be? He could fake a friendship for a couple of days. After all, Shep had done it for ten years. He took a deep breath and made his way quietly on through the woods.

The night air came off the water in gentle gusts, transforming the sticky heat to a slightly cooler temperature. The dense fog moved in like a herd of scattered ghosts. Forest Bluffs had its wealth like other coastal towns, but closer to the end of the peninsula the atmosphere began to change. The scrubbed landscape and churches gave way to a honky-tonk section of town, dawning amusement parks, water slides, clam shacks and video arcades. Pedestrians were freer with their dress, and their attitude. Homosexuals walked hand in hand without fears of vexing, and teens with pierced bodies skated up and down the boardwalk, while older tourists mixed frozen drinks and laughed merrily aboard their docked boats. Live music spilled out onto the street from the bevy of clubs and restaurants.

Perhaps it was this liberal décor, or perhaps it was the fog that allowed six figures clad in black hooded cloaks to drift virtually unnoticed up the crowded street. Unnoticed that is, until they were within three feet of reaching the Island Hut's front door. A random gust of wind blew Joey's hood back, exposing his face to a young couple passing along the sidewalk. The woman recognized him. Much to her male companion's fury, she flung herself at Joey. "Joey! Joey, touch me!" she screamed. "Put your hands on me!"

"Michelle! Stop it! What are you doing?" her confused boyfriend pleaded with her. The brothers stepped in and blocked her path to Joey as best they could. Carlos and Devin seemed too stunned to move. It took Allisto and Margol's action to snap them into shape, and they followed by pulling the woman back away from Joey. Drunk and awkward, Joey fumbled to replace his hood.

The woman broke free of Devin's grip and managed to de-cloak Joey once again, taking a few strands of hair off his head this time. "Joey!" she screeched. Her screaming drew attention from the street and the word spread in seconds. Joey Duvaine, the Yuppie Prophet, was on the street. They came running from all sides. Some came out of curiosity to see this new celebrity. Others were simply drawn in by the sight of him. A dozen voices shouted, and Shep felt the swell of panic oozing its way up his tightened throat.

"Joey, what did The Virgin say?" someone yelled.

"Joey, when will the world end?"

"Joey, let me touch you!"

"Touch my baby!"

Not all of the shouts were of a friendly nature. He also heard a male voice scream out, "You bunch of fucking freaks!" and another female voice screech, "Burn in hell you Godless phony!" Oh well, Shep thought amidst his brewing panic. Can't win em all. Didn't need em all. Sixty percent would do.

The wind kicked up off the water bringing the first peltings of rain, making it difficult for them to hear each other. Shep raised his voice over the crowd and the wind, directing his cohorts and waving his arms. "Inside!" he yelled. "Get him inside, damn it!" They struggled to do just that but every time they attempted to shove Joey toward the front doors of the Island Hut, another three people would jump in front of him, asking to be touched, enlightened, or in a couple of cases, fucked.

Suddenly the doors to the Island Hut swung outward and two muscular men broke through the crowd. One of them looked directly at Shep. "You Shepherd?"

"Yes." He had to raise his voice to be heard over the rain.

"I'm Sully. We spoke on the phone. You need some help here?"

"Yes! Yes! Help us get him inside!"

The two burly men ran to the aid of the others. They boxed Joey in and pushed him through the crowd like a tank. Once they were all inside, they shoved out the arms and legs that threatened to break through from the street crowd, and slammed the doors closed. The one called Sully threw the dead bolt. Shep removed his hood and gave Joey a toxic stare.

"Should I say 'I told you so' now or later?" he asked.

Joey shrugged. "It wasn't that bad. It could have been worse."

"Oh, yes. It could have been worse if one of them popped a couple of slugs into you, Joey. I ought to—" Shep had forgotten that Sully and the other brawny man were still standing there, staring at them. Shep smiled at them. "How you doing? My name's Shepherd."

Sully stuck his hand out and Shep shook it. "Yes Mr. Shepherd, we spoke on the phone. I own this place. This is Stu," he said, pointing to the other man, who was a pile of swollen muscles with a head. "Come in. Please," Sully said. "Make yourself at home. It's mostly locals here tonight. And don't worry. We won't let anyone hurt him in here. We're honored that you all wanted to come down and hear the band."

Shep thanked Sully, but he was a bit put off by his comments. *Won't let anyone hurt him?* Shep was aware that his own methods were overly cautious, but he didn't truly believe that any significant number of people were out to get Joey. Most of the web sites he'd scanned spoke his praises.

The place was in full swing but nobody inside seemed to have noticed them yet. Stu strongly suggested that they leave their 'coats' in the coatroom. They all handed him their capes, which he examined with raised eyebrows, then disappeared to hang them. Unlike Sully who was all open arms and friendly smiles, the muscle-bound Stu seemed uneasy. He stole sideways glances at Joey, who was narcissistically smoothing out the sleeves of his silk shirt.

The band was playing a jumpy dance number as they proceeded into the main section of the nightclub. It was a large open space with a stage to the front and a circular bar set up in the center. The high wood ceiling was strung with tiny white lights and lobster traps. The room was dimly lit, the tiny white lights giving the bar a warm cozy glow. A crowd of people danced merrily in front of the stage. They found stools at the bar, and soon Shep saw the familiar looks of awe and fascination on the faces of the patrons as they saw Joey.

They seemed to catch a whiff of Joey first, pausing before their eyes followed the scent and finally fell upon him. Humans could still smell blood, they just weren't aware of it. The smell of blood in humans changed as often as it did in other beasts, creating a different odor for anger, lust, fear, and a host of other emotions. When they did react to it, they called it a sense. They weren't aware of how literal the translation of that word was.

So, they stared. To Shep's surprise and relief none of the patrons approached them. When he mentioned this to Joey, a young man sitting next to them overheard. He explained to Shep that Sully had made an announcement at the bar earlier that Joey Duvaine was coming down. He warned the patrons that anyone who bothered Joey or his companions would be tossed head first out of the bar, regardless of age or gender. Shep was beginning to like Sully.

Shep watched the patrons huddle at the bar to stare at Joey, as though they were gazing upon God Himself. *Oh come let us adore him,* Shep thought, and smiled. He was pleased with the results of his creation. Joey was Shep's own personal Frankenstein's monster. A tad prettier, and a whole lot smarter, but Shep enjoyed the analogy nonetheless.

He was still on alert, but soon even he began to feel at ease. The conversations did not cease because Joey was there, nor did the music and the dancing stop. People kept a respectable distance. The brothers were sitting at the bar, laughing and joking with Devin and Carlos, all of them drinking chocolate liqueur like it was water. Shep warned them to slow down, but they didn't listen. He was worried about their ability to protect Joey, should the need arise. Margol and Allisto had the strength of ten men, but a strong drunk was a drunk nonetheless.

Joey took Shep's arm suddenly. "Hey, look at that guy over there," he said. Shep followed Joey's pointed finger and gasped when he saw the man sitting alone at the tiny table five feet from the bar. "Isn't that the hermit that lives in the house up on the hill next door to us?" Joey asked.

Shep glared toward the table. It was the veteran with the flowing gray hair and the cold leathery face. The man slid his glance their way. He was dressed in desert print fatigues with a white tank top and brown bandana tying back his long, salt and pepper hair. Deep lines surrounded the coldest eyes Shep had ever seen on a human. The man's eyes tightened when he looked at Joey, and Shep saw a seething hatred behind them.

"Holy crap," Joey whispered. "I think he hates me!"

"Don't go near that guy. Don't even look at him," Shep warned. "I think he's the one who shot you."

"He's looking at me like I'm the plague or something."

"Just stay away from him. He's dangerous."

Joey continued to stare at the man. "It's fascinating," he said. "He's completely unaffected by me."

"I know," Shep said.

Joey looked quizzically at Shep. "Why doesn't the blood work on him?"

"He's a veteran of war," Shep said, taking a long sip of his beer. "War changes people. It rips their souls out."

Shep glanced over at the empty stools where the brothers had been sitting with Carlos and Devin. They were gone. Great. Just when he might need them, they disappear. He caught sight of the bright pink Mohawks bouncing around up on the dance floor, along with Margol and Allisto's jostling curls. "Useless!" Shep hissed. He was about to go drag them off the dance floor and reprimand them, but when he turned to tell Joey, Joey wasn't there. Shep was horrified to see that Joey had taken a seat across the table from their gray-haired neighbor. Shep darted to the table and grabbed Joey by the shoulder. "Joey! What are you doing? Come back to the bar. Now."

Joey pushed Shep's hand off his shoulder. "So as I was saying, I think we're neighbors. I'm from the Forest Bluffs Church, right down the hill from you."

"Joey, let's go," Shep warned. "I mean it, leave it alone."

"I know who you are," the man said with a gravelly snarl.

"Sir, your eyes speak a thousand curses when you look at me," Joey said, using his practiced sermon voice. "May I ask why?"

The man chuckled coldly. Shep tried to make eye contact with the brothers, but they were fully engrossed in their simulated dance thrashings. He looked around for Sully and Stu, but Stu was busy behind the bar and Sully was nowhere in sight. His only choice was to disarm the situation himself. He grabbed Joey by the arm. "We were just leaving," Shep said to the Vet.

"I don't mind telling him what I think of him," the veteran said, his black eyes pinned to Joey's pale ones. "As long as you asked, you make me sick."

Joey shook Shep's arm off. He was obsessed with wooing this man, who he seemed to view as some sort of personal challenge. Shep was ready to kill Joey himself. He leaned in close. "Joseph, I am not going to fight this gorilla for you. Back off, and let's go back up to the bar."

Joey defiantly ignored him. "So I make you sick," he said to the man across the table. "Fair enough. But tell me this, my brother. Why, exactly, do I make you sick?"

The man leaned in, placing his elbows on the table. "I am not your brother."

"Still," Joey pressed on, tapping a finger thoughtfully on the side of his chin, "that doesn't explain your ill feelings toward me. Is it because I've been chosen by God?"

The man laughed loudly, throwing his head back and slamming a fist on the table. He returned his gaze to Joey. "I fought for my country, boy. I put my very life on the line. I have seen horrors that your stunted little mind can't even imagine."

"That doesn't explain why you hate me," Joey said, with a coldness of his own. They looked across the table at each other, and Shep felt the calm before the storm. "I'm just another American citizen," Joey said, "trying to spread spiritual awareness. I'm trying to contribute some good to society."

Shep almost laughed at the prophetic bullshit Joey was spewing. The veteran remained still. "Son, you have about as much spiritual awareness as Adolph Hitler, with only half the balls."

"So you think I'm a madman?" Joey asked, twitching his eyebrows in an effort to look maniacal.

The veteran leaned forward. "No, I think you're a pretentious little prep school faggot, sitting out there on your dead daddy's land, planting seeds and playing with your little faggot friends. You concocted this church so you could drop out of productive society, not so you could contribute to it. You are a cowardly, deceitful, unproductive waste of air that needs a few dozen mindless morons stroking your dick every day just so you can feel good about yourself. When I was in the wars, I saw men so afraid that they would freeze up and shit themselves right there on the battle field. But in my entire life, I have never seen a man as scared and pathetic as you."

No one spoke for several seconds. Joey pursed his lips, and nodded. He looked up at Shep. "That probably would have hurt my feelings if I had any. Huh Shep?"

Shep stifled a grin. "Yes, Joey. If indeed you had feelings, that definitely would have hurt them."

Joey looked back at the man, and began to snicker. Shep saw blind rage pass across the man's weathered countenance. The veteran grabbed Joey's wrist, pinning it to the table. With his other hand he pulled a large dagger from out of his boot and held it up in front of Joey's chest. "You want to feel something, pretty boy? I'll help you feel something!"

Shep grabbed the hand that held Joey's wrist. "Let him go soldier. I don't want to have to hurt you." Shep glanced around, but no one seemed to be paying attention. He didn't want to draw attention to himself by throwing this knife wielding redneck across the room. He gave the man's wrist another squeeze, letting him feel a fragment of his unnatural strength. The old man winced, but continued to hold fast to Joey's wrist. "Let go of him!" Shep hissed. "What the hell do you think you're doing?"

The veteran held the knife over his head in a striking pose. "I'm doing the world a great service. Die! False Prophet!" he screamed and brought the knife down swiftly to Joey's chest.

Shep was about to stop the blade with his hand when a large arm shot out and grabbed the veteran's wrist, stopping the knife just three inches above Joey's heart. The arm came out of nowhere, it seemed. Shep looked up at its owner, and a grin spread across his face. The hulking redhead pulled the veteran up out of his seat and twisted his wrist until the knife came loose and clattered on the floor. The man struggled as Patrick Obrien easily forced him into an iron headlock. "Are you okay?" Patrick asked, looking down at Joey. Joey was too stunned to speak, rubbing the place on his chest where the knife would have gone in. Sully and Stu, now seeing the commotion, came running over.

"What happened?" Sully asked.

"This piece of shit tried to stab Joey," Patrick answered.

"I'll call the police," Stu said.

"No!" Shepherd stood. "No police. Please. We'll just leave."

Stu looked confused, but he nodded. "All right. If you're sure."

"I'm sure. No police."

Patrick gave the veteran to Sully and Stu, who ceremoniously tossed him head first out the back door. Patrick turned to Shep. "Are you crazy bringing Joey here? What were you thinking, Shepherd? Come on. We have to get him out of here."

A sly, satisfied grin spread slowly across Shepherd's mouth. "Nice to see you, Obrien."

Chapter Thirty-One

Another hairline scratch appeared on Juris's cheek and began to bleed. He shrieked wildly, ducking his head to dodge his unseen attacker. Father Carbone looked on helplessly, shifting from one foot to the other in a nervous jig. "Please, Juris! Whatever you're doing to yourself, stop this!"

Juris persisted with the illusion that he was under attack from some invisible force. Carbone stared with fear at the razor thin cuts that now decorated Juris's fair skin. It looked as though a cat had scratched his cheeks, yet the priest saw nothing strike him. The cuts appeared like magic. He knew that it was not unheard of for wounds to mysteriously appear on untouched skin. There were of course the cases of the stigmata, where bodily abrasions would erupt, resembling the wounds of Christ. This was different, though. Suddenly, the priest felt a gust of air pass by him as though from a fan. The strange breeze swept Juris's hair up and he screeched as a new mark appeared. Carbone could sense an energy in the dusty basement. Something was down there with them, and it was hell bent on hurting Juris. Luigi Carbone was more frightened than he'd ever been.

"Juris, tell me how to stop it!" he screamed. Juris writhed and struggled against the steel ropes that held him.

"You can stop it by getting me the hell out of this church!"

Father Carbone grimaced as he gazed at Juris's face, which looked like he'd been whipped with tree branches. Moving to the bottom of the stairs, he yelled up to Copie. "Did you get a hold of him yet?"

"I'm trying!" Copie yelled back. Upstairs, a shaken Copie was frantically trying to get Agent Litner on the phone. A nasal-sounding woman answered his private line. "FBI, Special Agent Steven Litner's office."

"Yeah. This is Copeland Smith. I need to speak with Agent Litner right away."

"Agent Litner is out in the field, sir," the woman said politely. "Is there something I can help you with?"

Copie was bordering on hysterics, his voice elevated to a fanatic squeak. "This is an emergency! I need to speak with Agent Litner now! There must be some way you can get a hold of him!"

"All right, Mr. Smith, calm down. I will contact Agent Litner for you, but I need to know the nature of the emergency."

"Just tell him it's Copie and that there's a problem with the house guest."

"The house guest, sir?"

"Yes! Damn it! Just get him on the phone!"

"Please hold."

Copie listened to hold music while Juris continued to screech down below. It was a high pitched echoing cry, the likes of which Copie wished he'd never heard. He'd hear that sound in his nightmares. There was a clicking sound and Agent Litner was on the line. "Copie, it's Litner. What's going on?"

"Agent Litner! You've got to come out here and move Juris, man! There's some creepy shit going on and I for one am ready to bolt for the door!"

"Copie, calm down. Take a breath, and tell me exactly what's been happening."

Copie was nearly hyperventilating. From below he could hear Father Carbone's voice as he struggled in vain to calm Juris. "It started about an hour ago," Copie explained. "Father Carbone was over at the church giving mass, so I was all alone in the apartment when I heard Juris screaming. I ran down to the cellar and he was completely freaking out. He had two bleeding scratches on his face, and he kept saying that 'they' had found him."

"Scratches? Are his hands still cuffed?"

"He's still restrained. Then right before my eyes another scratch appeared. I felt the air move. I felt it, Litner. It was like something passed by me really fast, but there was nothing there! I'm scared! You have to come right now! Juris is losing his mind down there!"

As if in support of this, Juris screamed loudly. "I can hear him," Litner said calmly.

"He's been calling for you, and he's begging to be moved!"

"All right Copie, stay calm. I'm about an hour away, but I'll leave right now. I have the new location ready and we can move him as soon as I get there."

"An hour? A fucking hour? That's not good enough! He's got scratches all over his face. He'll look like shredded beef by the time you get here!"

"I'm sorry, Copie. That's the best I can do. Try wrapping his face in gauze bandages. I'll be there as quickly as I can."

Copie forced himself to take another breath. "Okay Litner. Okay. But if his head starts spinning around, I'm out of here. I don't care how many people want me dead."

Copie hung up and ran down the stairs to join Father Carbone. "Litner will be here in an hour to move him."

"An hour?" the priest cried in disbelief. Copie relayed his conversation with Litner. The priest found a first aid kit and the two of them wrapped Juris's head with white gauze bandages, leaving only his eyes, mouth and nostrils exposed. He looked like something from an old mummy movie. Soon, tiny spots of blood began to seep through the bandages. Father Carbone looked at Copie. "Are you sure he said an hour?"

"It's the best he can do. How's he doing?" Copie asked, pointing a thumb toward Juris.

"Whatever it was seems to have stopped for the time being," Carbone said.

Those green eyes looked directly at Father Carbone. "It's still here, priest. Can't you see it?" Juris hissed. "I told you it wasn't safe! You should have listened to me!"

Carbone knelt down in front of Juris. "Juris, we see nothing. You must explain this to me so I can help you."

Juris chuckled through his bandages. "Forgive me, Father. I had forgotten about your limited human perception. You are a priest. Are you not supposed to believe in things you cannot see?"

"Yes, I suppose. I cannot physically see God but I have faith that He is there."

Juris rolled his eyes. "I do not mean God. My enemy hovers in that corner over there by the window." Juris nodded his head toward the upper corner of the basement ceiling, where the tiny window met the wall.

Copie pointed. In a shaky whisper, he said, "Up there?"

"Yes, young one. Do you see that the curtain moves though there is no source of breeze in this stagnant space?"

Copie and the priest both looked up at the small window at the top of the basement wall. A dusty, floral-patterned valance hung above it. It moved up and down as though a gentle breeze was blowing it. Copie gaped at the curtain but Father Carbone was skeptical. "I'm sorry Juris," Carbone said. "I don't see anything. You'll just have to wait until Agent Litner gets here. I can't move you without his authorization."

Juris began to writhe, gasping in air as though he was in the presence of a noxious gas. After several seconds of this he calmed and turned his bandaged head toward Father Carbone. His eyes shone out of the white cotton mask like reflective marbles. "I'll make a deal with you, priest. If I can prove to you that there is something in here, something you can see with your own eyes, will you move me outside? Will you take me off the property?"

The priest frowned. "Just how exactly would you do that?"

"There is a way to make your puny mind see the unseen. I will tell you how, but you must promise to move me off of church property. I'm not asking you to untie me. You can put me in the graveyard next door until your FBI friend comes."

Father Carbone looked at the blowing curtain, then at Copie, whose eyes were big as saucers. "Father Carbone," Copie said, "It wouldn't hurt to move him next door. I know I'd like to get him out of here, and I suspect you feel the same."

The priest paced the room. "Okay Juris. You say we are in the presence of this entity that scratched up your face. Show me."

Juris breathed a quick sigh of relief, then began to give instructions. He told Carbone to get a spray bottle, the kind used to mist plants, and mix a multitude of ingredients together; holy water, vinegar, mint leaves, talcum powder and salt. He told him that once he had these items together, to bring the spray bottle downstairs to him, and he would add one last ingredient.

Father Carbone went upstairs and did what Juris asked. He had a moment of panic when he thought he was out of vinegar, but then he found an old bottle in the rear of his spice cabinet. He walked over to the church and slid quietly through the side door. Jimmy the altar boy gave him an odd look as he poured a bowl of holy water into the yellow, plastic spray bottle. Father Carbone smiled and nodded at Jimmy as though this was perfectly normal.

Once he had the holy water, he hurried back across the lawn and into his house, taking the steps down to the basement two by two. "I've got it," he announced and accidentally bumped into Copie at the bottom of the stairs.

"Bring it here," Juris commanded. Father Carbone approached him. "The final ingredient is my blood," Juris said. "You have to cut me."

Father Carbone stopped short. "I am not cutting you, Juris."

"You must. You need only make a small slice in my thumb. You can do it priest. Just don't get any of my blood on your skin. You, young one, go and fetch the priest a knife."

Copie looked uncertain but he bounded up the stairs and returned with a steak knife. Reluctantly, Father Carbone took it. "Hold the bottle underneath my hand. Make a small cut in my thumb and squeeze at least five drops into the mixture," Juris said.

Father Carbone hesitated, grimacing.

"Do it!" Juris snapped. Father Carbone walked around behind him and knelt down, holding the bottle just below where Juris's cuffed hands were. He made a thin slice along the prisoner's thumb and the blood began to seep. He squeezed six drops of the dark red liquid into the squeeze bottle, then replaced the lid pump.

"Okay Juris. It's done, but this is starting to feel like bullshit," Carbone said.

"Give it a shake," Juris said. Father Carbone gave the bottle a few hard shakes, then looked to Juris expectantly. "Good. Now go over to the corner and mist the air just under that curtain."

Father Carbone looked to Copie for reassurance. "Go ahead!" Copie urged. "What are you waiting for?"

"Oh, very brave you are Copie," the priest snapped. "Would you prefer to do the honors?"

Copie backed away. "No sir. You're the witch doctor. You do it."

"Stop bickering! Do it now!" Juris screamed.

Father Carbone walked cautiously over to the corner near the window, and sprayed a pink mist into the air. Nothing happened. "Spray it again," Juris ordered.

The priest did. A pink mist came out, hung in the air, and dissipated. Carbone looked over his shoulder at Juris. "Nothing happened."

"Again!" Juris yelled. "Keep spraying! Don't be shy with it!"

Father Carbone sighed and began to saturate the air in front of him with repeated sprays of the strange concoction. Nothing happened. He turned around to yell at Juris when Copie saw the thing start to materialize. "I told you, there's nothing—"

"Look!" Copie screamed.

Carbone turned around, and stumbled backward, tripping over a mop bucket as the translucent image took partial form in front of him. "What?" he said, gaping up from the floor. He struggled to his feet. "What is that?" he whispered.

There were three feet of what looked like a feathered wing, the translucent image of a body, and half of a face. The form was not solid. It was more like seeing a film projection.

"Spray it again!" Juris yelled. Carbone stepped forward and pumped the bottle directly at the fading image, and the form became whole. The silky white wings moved softly and rhythmically like waves on a calm sea. The body was now materialized enough to see detail. Its hair was like pure light, curling softly around a smooth, placid face. Only the huge round eyes seemed to have life, and they were set in a concentrated stare on Juris. Father Carbone let out sigh of awe. It was the most beautiful thing he had ever seen. He sprayed another quick mist at the thing, then it turned on him and he dropped the bottle.

Its lovely face distorted in rage, lip curled up, bearing a menacing set of sharpened teeth. It made a guttural sound like a wild dog about to strike. Father Carbone stumbled backward to where Copie stood. "Shit!" he squeaked. "It growled at me!"

The creature spread its glorious wings behind it and dove like a fighter jet across the room at Juris. Juris screamed as the thing circled over him, hovering and hissing. The ghostly image ran a glowing hand across Juris's face and clawed off one of the bandages, which hung in a strip, leaving a portion of skin beside Juris's nose exposed. Juris screamed.

Copie bolted up the stairs and was gone. The priest screamed up after him. "Copie! Damn you! Get back down here. I need your help!"

The noises coming out of the disembodied creature were a muffled sound, as though they were being transported into the room from some far away place. It sounded like the distant voices sometimes heard as background noise when talking on a cellular phone with a bad connection. It circled Juris, speaking choppy, vaguely syllabic sounds. Juris ducked and squirmed as the thing circled over his head.

Father Carbone heard a metallic clank come from behind him. It was Copie. He had gone outside and was opening the bulkhead door. Father Carbone ran to the bulkhead and helped him push it open from the inside. A flood of warm air blasted his face as the door opened. "Copie! I thought you'd run home to mommy."

"Tempting, but no. Drag Juris over here and I'll help you get him outside."

Father Carbone nodded. "Got ya." He walked cautiously back to where Juris sat. The creature's image was beginning to fade. Suddenly, the thought of not being able to see the thing and knowing it was there was more frightening than actually seeing it. He grabbed the yellow spray bottle off the floor, gave it a good shake, and pumped a couple of rounds of the mixture at the back of the circling enigma. He immediately regretted doing so.

The translucent creature turned with a lightening fast swoosh and came right at Father Carbone. It stopped within an inch of his face, its large glowing eyes matched up directly with his. It bared its teeth, which were more like fangs, and roared like a tiger, setting the windows to rumble. To see something so beautiful instantly become something so terrifying was almost unbearable. Father Carbone felt his bodily functions turn tail, and warmth spread over his legs as he wet his trousers. The thing quickly retreated and turned its attention back to Juris, leaving the priest to stand shaking and paralyzed with fear.

"Don't worry!" Juris yelled. "It cannot hurt you. It thinks it's protecting you."

Father Carbone still couldn't move. Then Copie was there, shaking him. "Carbone! Carbone! I realize that this is probably the highlight of your religious career, but can we please grab Juris and get the fuck out of here?"

Father Carbone shook himself. "Right. Let's do it." They each took hold of one side of the velvet armchair, tipped it, and began dragging Juris across the basement floor toward the waiting bulkhead. The translucent creature gazed at them for a moment, placid and beautiful once more, then faded completely.

They were both sweating by the time they got Juris and his chair out of the basement and over to the front gates of the graveyard. They were not far from the church but they were off the property, and this was as far as Juris was going until Agent Litner got there. They sat down with their backs against the fence, both of them panting, waiting for their nerves to calm. When Copie got his breath back he looked at the priest and wrinkled his nose. Looking down he said, "Did you..."

"Yes, Copie, I wet myself. You can tease me about it at a later date. Right now, I just don't care."

Copie nodded. "How's our boy?" He stood and walked over to Juris, who gazed up at him through a half tattered, bloody bandage. Copie unraveled the bandage and examined Juris's face. It was a map of red, razor-thin gashes. "Wow. Are you going to be all right?"

"Such concern," Juris said coldly. "I will heal."

Copie looked spooked. "So Juris, you probably know what I'm going to ask you next."

Juris smirked. "Knowing your colorful vocabulary, young one, it will probably be something like, 'what the fuck was that thing'."

Father Carbone stood and joined Copie. "You must be damned indeed. I've never heard of an angel growling and bearing fangs like that."

Juris looked up at him. "That was not an angel, priest."

"It had wings!" Father Carbone said.

"So do birds, bats, houseflies and certain tropical fish. Not everything with wings is an angel. That was a Schlarr."

Carbone frowned. "A Schlarr?"

"Yes, priest. A Schlarr, or what your religion calls a Principality. Look it up in your little books if you like. And incidentally, it is not unusual for an angel to hiss and growl."

"Well I've never heard of such a thing!"

"That shows how much your stupid race knows. Angels are despicable creatures."

"So what are you then?" the priest asked.

Juris grinned, then the grin faded to a cold stare. "I am something else. The FBI is coming. I'll be leaving you now."

Father Carbone and Copie looked up at the empty road. Thirty seconds later, Agent Litner's black car rolled down the street and pulled up in front of the church. Copie called out, and waved Litner over.

"Good bye priest," Juris said. "We shall meet again."

"Only in my nightmares," Carbone said.

Agent Litner had brought Agent Rourke with him, and they loaded Juris into the car. Agent Rourke seemed to take particular pleasure in roughly tossing Juris into the back seat. He had clearly not forgotten about being thrown across a parking lot at the nightclub. Father Carbone gave Litner a compact version of what had happened. Before he got into the car, Agent Litner turned back to Father Carbone, his face unsettled. "Didn't you say you had a friend that was well versed in these matters?"

Carbone nodded. "I called Father Bello yesterday, but I got his answering machine."

Litner met his eyes. "Call him again. I'll be back." Agent Litner got in the car as Father Carbone pulled his cellular phone out of his pocket. As the car pulled away he saw Juris's head of curls in the back window. Juris gave him a sly smile, and mouthed the words, *see you soon*. He looked entirely too pleased with himself for someone who was on his way to yet another prison. The priest furrowed his brow suspiciously.

The little phone in Father Carbone's hand popped free and shattered, exploding in a shower of plastic and electronic components all over the church lawn. Father Carbone yelped and shook his hand as he stared in disbelief at what was left of his phone. He looked up and caught sight of Juris laughing as the car turned the corner out of sight.

Chapter Thirty-Two

It took Patrick several seconds of disorientation before he remembered why he was not in his own bed. He stared up at the unfamiliar ceiling beams, watching the tree shadows dancing in the morning sunlight. Birds formed a chorus and somewhere a dog barked. All seemed peaceful. Normal. He sat up and glanced at the clock on the unfamiliar dresser. It was 6:00 a.m., and the enormous house was still and quiet. My God, he thought. I'm here. I'm actually here.

He could feel Joey's presence like an extra heartbeat in his chest, and knew that he was asleep in his bedroom down the hall. Patrick's own room was a small, clean guestroom at the end of the third floor. Shep had not questioned why Patrick was suddenly there. He'd simply shown him to his room. In fact, they'd said very little each other after leaving the bar. Joey's only comment had been, "Hey Obrien, I got shot, you know," as though it was some sort of honor.

The re-infiltration had been so easy. All Shep had asked was if he planned to stay. Patrick had told him yes, and explained that he had to return to the city once a week for his consulting job, to which he replied, "Whatever you want, Obrien. You're a guest here, not a prisoner."

He got out of the twin bed and padded over to the dresser with its gorgeous antique mirror. It must have cost Joey a fortune to refurnish this house. A fortune he claimed not to have only last month. Last month? It seemed like years ago. He had a moment of panic as he looked in the mirror at his own friendly, innocent face. He would never pull it off. He couldn't fool these people. They knew him better than he knew himself. "No," he whispered.

He stopped the thought from taking hold, stifled the panic as it threatened to rise and overtake him like an army of fears. He would have to fool them. He would have to. This time, he was the actor. This time, he was the spy. He thought of Robin and the way she'd kissed him before he left. He wanted to get back to her. He wanted his life back. At least what was left of it.

He made his way down the first set of steps, then padded down the spiral staircase to the first floor. The house looked a far sight different than the last time he'd been there. Sun streamed through the enormous windows, spotlighting the gorgeous furniture and shiny wood floors. The place was clean and tastefully decorated. Patrick wasn't sure what he'd expected to find at Forest Bluffs, but this wasn't it. He'd imagined a fraternity house hovel, complete with beer lights and girly posters, not a photo set for *Better Homes and Gardens*. Whatever the boys were up to out here, they were living well while they were at it. Extremely well, he thought as he padded across the genuine Persian rugs.

Patrick seemed to be the only one up. He was glad. This would give him time to look around, and perhaps even go for a walk outside. The sooner he got those crop samples, the sooner he could go back to the city, and to Robin. He stopped short upon entering the giant kitchen. Platinum blond curls adorned a head bent over a bowl of cereal at the breakfast nook. At first Patrick thought it was Juris, and he gasped. The stranger turned his head at the sound. Much to Patrick's relief, it was not Juris.

It was Klee, the new arrival he'd seen naked and sobbing in the cave that dreaded night. He was significantly fresher looking, and quite attractive without blood and soot all over him. Bright green eyes gazed at Patrick with innocent trust. He had a dainty, sculpted nose and a tiny pink mouth, which he held his spoon in, frozen in mid-bite. His skin was like porcelain with a healthy dust of rose across each cheek. Of all of the brothers, Patrick thought this creature looked the most inhuman, only because he was so impossibly perfect. But then again, perhaps they all started out this way, fresh, innocent and childlike. *Like something newly born*, he thought.

The pause had gone on far too long, each of them frozen, staring at the other. Finally Patrick stepped into the kitchen and approached the breakfast nook. "Hello there. I don't think we've met. My name is Patrick."

The blond man popped the spoon out of his mouth and struggled to form his words. "I know. They have been waiting. Waiting for Patrick. My name is Klee." His voice was clear as a bell and his vocabulary was fairly good, but he formed his words with a robotic strain. He sounded very much like a toddler just learning to speak. "Do you want some Cocoa Puffs, Patrick?" Klee held the spoon out expectantly, his wide eyes open and trusting. Patrick smiled.

"No, thank you." He pulled out a stool and sat down across from Klee at the breakfast nook. There was something different about this one, Patrick thought. He was missing that behind the eye glare the other three brothers had. They always looked like they were quietly planning someone's demise. Patrick sensed an overwhelming innocence in this creature that sat before him crunching his cereal. Milk dripped down his chin and he wiped it with his arm. He wore a tee shirt and a pair of sweat pants, both of which Patrick recognized as Shep's.

"Klee, I didn't see you out last night. Were you at the bar with the others?"

Klee shook his head of spring curls. "No. I could not go. I hurt my back." Patrick shuddered, remembering the gaping wound he'd seen on Klee's naked back at the cave. He looked up at Patrick over his spoon. His eyes were even larger than Shep's, his nearly translucent lashes reaching above his white eyebrows when they were fully open. "You are to stay with us here from now on. Yes?" He sounded sincere and hopeful.

"Yes Klee. I'll be staying here."

Klee went back to his Cocoa Puffs. "Good. You will like it here."

Patrick smiled at the friendly blond creature, who shoveled cereal into his tiny mouth with great enthusiasm. "Do you like it here, Klee?" Patrick asked. He found himself speaking to him in soft careful tones, as though Klee was a small child. He was not. His body was that of a man aged somewhere between eighteen and twenty-five.

"Oh yes!" he answered. "I like it very much. So much better here," he said.

"Oh? Where were you before?" Patrick asked, sensing that he was about to get some information of value.

"I was nowhere," Klee said casually.

"Nowhere? Oh, I'm sorry," Patrick said. "I didn't mean to pry. You don't have to tell me where you're from if you don't want to."

Klee looked at him, his eyebrows knitted in honest confusion. "But I just did," he said.

⁓⁓

"Okay, Klee." Patrick jumped at the sound of Shep's voice. "Breakfast is over. Go on upstairs and get in the tub." Klee dropped his spoon and picked the cereal bowl up to his mouth, drinking the chocolate milk residue until the bowl was drained. He scooted off his stool and obediently placed his bowl in the sink, then ran heavy-footed like a toddler out of the kitchen. As Patrick watched him round the corner, he caught sight of the back of Klee's tee shirt, which was stained with flecks of dried blood. Patrick immediately cast his eyes downward.

"You're up early," Shep said, and sat himself down in Klee's spot across from Patrick.

"Yeah," was all Patrick could think to say. He looked across the counter at Shep, who kept his eyes downward as he spun a quarter on the nook. He was fidgeting. He's as nervous as I am, Patrick decided. This was an awkward moment for both. He took the opportunity to study Shep. His curly chin length locks that Patrick used to think of as blond, now seemed darker after looking at Klee and Juris. Patrick took in all of the details of Shep, examining him as he never had before. He wasn't sure what he was looking for. He'd gazed upon Shep a thousand times before. Perhaps he was looking for a sign, something that he'd missed back in college, and all of these years since. Something to signify that he wasn't human.

Shep continued to spin the coin with his eyes cast down, his long eyelashes brushing gently along his cheekbone. Patrick studied the sun-tanned youthful skin, the fleshy softness of his eyelids, the way his bottom lip curved over his chin a little too far, giving him a permanent pout. He looked at the bones of his hands, the curve of his wrist, and the veins that ran through the indent at the bend of his inner arm. There was nothing unusual that he could see. It was still just Shep.

A flood of emotions overcame him. Patrick had the urge to grab Shep and shake him, shake him until he broke apart. In the next instance he wanted to hug Shep and beg him to confess the truth, no matter how horrible. What he wanted more than anything was to ask him why. Why had he, Patrick Obrien, been left in the dark, while others like Joey were brought into the fold? Why was he lied to, betrayed, used. But he said none of these things. He sat there in the early morning light, sharing an awkward silence with Shep, who seemed too uncomfortable to even look at him.

"So," Patrick said, desperate to break the silence. "The house looks nice."

Shep looked up at him with a sheepish smirk. His green eyes danced with humor. "You think so?"

"Yeah. I like what Joey's done with the place. Who would have guessed there were hardwood floors under that old rug, huh? And those antique end tables must have cost a fortune."

Shep snickered. Looking down at his fingers, he said, "You know, Obrien, I imagined this a million times. You and I sitting across the table from each other, face to face at last. I thought of a thousand things you might ask me, a thousand possible ways the conversation would go. But never in my wildest imaginings, did I think that our first conversation would be about decorating."

Patrick had to laugh, and it felt good. He did not let the laughter linger as he was afraid it would turn to tears. He didn't want this to feel good. Sitting here sharing a laugh with Shep like this felt all too familiar, and it was breaking his heart. "So are you saying that you will answer my questions now?" Patrick asked carefully.

Shep looked him in the eye. "I'll tell you anything you want to know, Obrien. I want to start things out on the right foot this time. I know you think I treated you badly. If I had to do things over, I'd do them differently, but I can't change that now."

Patrick met his eyes. "Who are they, Shep?"

Shep held his stare for several seconds, then looked down and began spinning his coin again. "They are my brothers," he said, and looked at Patrick for a reaction.

"Your brothers?" Patrick struggled to appear shocked.

"Yes, Obrien. I lied to you when I said I was an only child."

"Well, that explains the resemblance. But why, Shep? If you had brothers, why did you lie about it?"

Shep began to spin an elaborate combination of lies and half-truths, peppered with some genuine emotion. "My father abused us all. When social services took us out of the house, we got separated. I only just recently found them. I always said I was an only child because it was too painful to talk about them." Shep pulled on a lock of his hair, a familiar gesture that told Patrick he was fabricating. Then, his face changed and became sincere, more sincere than Patrick had ever seen him. "I have them all back now, and I'm never going to lose them again." Patrick could see in Shep's eyes that the last statement was no lie.

Shep seemed to catch himself then, and he made his face pleasant again. "Anyway Obrien, you know by now that I was having you followed."

"Of course. No offense Shep, but your brothers aren't exactly discreet."

Shep nodded humbly. "I am sorry about that. But we needed to keep tabs on you. You understand, don't you?"

"You should have known that I'd never turn you in, no matter how pissed I was at you." Again Shep nodded. He seemed to be winning Shep's trust back. He struggled to make his face as dumb and innocent as possible.

Shep sighed and ran a hand across his sandy curls. "I was hoping you might be able to help me with something."

Patrick shrugged. "What is it?"

Shep's face became conflicted. He clasped his hands together and leaned forward. "I have another brother, Patrick. You've seen him, I know you have. His name is Juris. I believe you chased him in the woods out at Betsy's house?"

Patrick flinched at the mention of Juris, but managed to hold a poker face. "Yes, I remember him. He wasn't at the bar last night, was he?"

Shep stared at him hard and Patrick could feel his suspicion. "No Obrien. He wasn't at the bar last night. He's missing. He disappeared on your watch. I sent him to Boston to follow you, and I haven't seen him since. You wouldn't know anything about that, would you?"

Shep's docile demeanor had in an instant changed to hard and accusing. Patrick felt his heart quicken, and struggled to calm his body. He pretended to think. "He's the other blond one, right?"

"Yes." Shep stared at his eyes intently as if trying to read a message printed on them.

"Actually," Patrick said, "the last time I saw him was at Betsy's. Now that you mention it, I haven't seen him since." Patrick made his face blank as he looked back at Shep, careful not to avoid his eyes or make any shifty movements that might give away that he was lying. Shep kept staring at him, and Patrick was afraid he would start to sweat like a criminal under a hot light. Finally Shep sighed and leaned back in the stool, linking his hands behind his head. The disappointment was obvious as he closed his eyes and shook his head.

"I don't know what to do. I'm worried sick. If anything happens to Juris it will be my fault."

"I'm sorry Shep. I wish I could help."

Shep shrugged mournfully. "Well, if you didn't see him, you didn't see him."

Patrick actually felt sorry for Shep for a moment. Then he forced himself to think of Copie when he'd first come to Saint Mary's with his cuts and burns, a look of terror in his eyes. His sympathy faded. Another image flashed in his mind; Shep slicing the wrist of the old doctor in the cave, despite his pleads and protests. He had to keep summoning these images, because it was so hard to look at Shep and not think of him with affection as he always had. He must keep reminding himself that this thing that sat in front of him was not his friend, but some murdering, scheming, otherworldly being.

But as he watched Shep rub sleep out of his eyes, he felt conflict. This was the Shep who had taught him to guzzle a full beer in one swallow. It was the Shep who had helped him get through chemistry class by showing him simple ways to look at the formulas. It was the Shep who used to lounge around in his underwear and watch The Three Stooges with him every Sunday morning. *It was the Shep who smeared a dead man's blood all over a cave wall after slicing his throat with a saw blade.* Oh yeah. There was that too. It was only seven o'clock in the morning, and already this visit was turning out to be harder than he expected. Part of him longed to just tell Litner to go fuck himself, and then grab a straight jacket dive into the lunatic soup with the rest of them. That tiny, gutless part of him wanted to give himself over to the horror, and beg Shep to put his soul to sleep, as he had done to Joey. After all, life would certainly be easier without remorse. Of all the conflicts he felt, he defied this one with the most vehemence.

A sleep rumpled Russell came bounding into the kitchen. He stopped short so suddenly that Patrick could almost hear the skid marks being laid. His thick black glasses flew off of his face and landed, unbroken, on the floor. Russell quickly retrieved them and placed them back on his nose, blinking through them at Patrick. "Obrien?"

"Hello, Russell," Patrick said contemptuously. He wanted to dive over the breakfast nook and throttle Russell to a pulp for trying to kill Copie. It appeared he did not have the same reservations about hating Russell as he did toward Shep.

"Obrien! Wow. I guess I really did miss something by staying in last night."

"Russell, could you give Obrien and I some privacy please?" Shep said. "We have some things we need to discuss."

Russell looked mortally wounded. "You're not going to be staying here permanently, are you Obrien?" Russell's face was full of hate as he cast his dark eyes on Patrick.

"Russell!" Shep shouted, making even Patrick jump. "Your jealousy is getting tedious. I'm trying to be patient with you, but you just keep pushing me. Now could you please fuck off before I get angry?" Russell stormed out of the kitchen in a huff. Shep looked back at Patrick. "Do you see what I have to put up with?"

Patrick forced a half smile. Man, this place was nuttier than he thought. Shep jumped off the stool. "I'm going to grab a shower. Joey has to speak in the fields at eleven, but you and I can take a walk first so I can show you everything. Why don't you get cleaned up and meet me in the sunroom for coffee and pastry in, say an hour?"

"Sure," Patrick agreed, and watched Shep bounce out of the room. Coffee and pastry in the sunroom? This was certainly a well-funded cult. Wasn't it just like Joey and Shep. They wanted to play David Koresh, but they didn't want to be uncomfortable at all while doing it.

Patrick heard Joey's voice muttering on the staircase as Shep met him half-way up. "Don't you have a hangover?" he heard Shep ask him,

"Yeah, but it's my last one. I won't need the booze now."

"How do you feel?" Shep asked him. They had lowered their voices now and Patrick had to strain to hear the answer.

"Safe," Joey whispered.

Moments later Joey came shuffling into the kitchen. After downing two full glasses of water, he came and sat down. Patrick smiled at Joey, unable to help himself. He was glad to see him. Joey looked great with his new longer hair and stunning wolf eyes. He frowned at Patrick, looking wary. "Wow. I forgot how big you were," he said.

Patrick tilted his head. "Huh?"

"Your muscles, Obrien. I had forgotten what great shape you were in."

"Your point, Joey?"

Joey grew very still, biting his lip nervously. "Do you want to beat me up a little?" he asked.

Patrick shook his head. "Joey, what the hell are you talking about?"

"Because if you want to knock me around a little, I'd rather get it over with now. Just don't mark up my face, okay?"

"Joey enough of this. Why would I want to beat you up?"

Joey cast his eyes downward then looked up at Patrick shyly. "You know about me and Kelinda. Right?"

Ah. So that was it. Joey was afraid Patrick was still pining over losing the queen of the manor. Patrick had scarcely thought about the fact that Kelinda was with Joey now. Sure, he was rather not looking forward to seeing her, but in the larger scheme of things, it didn't matter at all. "Yes, Joey. I know about you and Kelinda."

"And you're not mad?"

Patrick sighed and pretended to mull it over, enjoying that Joey was experiencing some discomfort over it. Finally he shrugged. "No."

Joey looked relieved. "No?"

"No. I'm not mad. Not at all."

Joey collapsed with a sigh. "Oh thank God." Patrick couldn't hold in his` laughter. Joey looked serious again. "Obrien," he said, putting a firm hand on Patrick's shoulder, "I'm really glad you're here."

"Me too Joey," he lied.

~&~

Kelinda came flowing into the kitchen wearing a black Lycra jumpsuit with hot pink butterflies on it. She went right to the refrigerator and didn't seem to even notice Patrick. She stood with her back to them, fumbling around with a carton of yogurt. Her once long silken hair was a chin length festival of hot pink spikes. Patrick couldn't believe the change in her. She'd gone from Cleopatra to Marilyn Manson. It was like invasion of the beauty snatchers. Joey glanced back over his shoulder, watching Kelinda struggle with the lid of her yogurt.

"Kelinda?" Joey said.

"What the fuck do you want?" she said without turning around.

Joey smiled. "Oh Kelinda, pumpkin? Look who's here, sweetie."

Kelinda turned to him with a tired sneer. Her face dropped when she saw Patrick, as well as the yogurt she was holding. It fell to the floor with a splat, thick gobs of blueberry goop shooting out in sticky streaks all over the tile. Patrick offered her a mechanical wave. She gaped at him, looked fleetingly down at the fallen yogurt, then back up at Patrick again. She opened her mouth to say something, then closed it again. Then, abruptly, she turned and left the room. Patrick heard the front door slam as she went outside.

Joey grinned at Patrick. "She's overcome with emotion," he said.

Patrick smirked. "Yes, I can see that."

Chapter Thirty-Three

Shep took Patrick out through the back yard and into the fields with the purpose of familiarizing him with operations. They hadn't gotten twenty yards and Patrick was already awestruck. Everything was different. He'd spent time on this property years ago while Joey's parents were still alive. Charles and Marie Duvaine had allowed Joey to spend weekends in the guesthouse with his friends. Now that same guesthouse was surrounded by a herd of tents and a flurry of activity as people went in and out, hauling supplies.

They busied themselves like ants, crawling here and there across what was once a vast stretch of rolling green fields. Patrick remembered looking out onto those same fields when he was still a student, and thinking how lucky Joey's family was to have such an abundance of untouched land and natural forest. The rolling fields were no longer vacant. Stalks of tall plants the color of red clay swayed gracefully in the breeze, bending rows of bushy heads as far as the eye could see. He gazed ahead at the sea of plants, trying to see something ominous in them.

He walked alongside Shep past the weird red plants, taking in the spring air, which held an unusual scent. It was the plants. They smelled vaguely like burning rubber. Shep's curls blew wildly in the wind, whipping against his sun-tanned skin as he led Patrick over to the guesthouse. Patrick wanted to ask him about the plants and a thousand other things, but he was on sensory overload. His head twisted in all directions as he took in the sights around him.

There were strangers everywhere. They greeted Shep enthusiastically as he came upon each little section. Shep exchanged witty repartee, or gave instructions as he went. Patrick couldn't count how many people there were. Shep had said there were under a hundred, but they were so spread out it seemed like more. Looking off into the distant expanse of crop fields, Patrick saw silhouettes of bodies moving amongst the rows systematically.

They stopped in at the guesthouse, which looked nothing like the cozy cottage style flop that Patrick remembered from his early twenties. All of the furniture had been cleared out, replaced with rows of bunk beds. Aside from the fleet of beds, there didn't seem to be much of anything but boxes of food supplies and farming equipment. And a well stocked gun rack. Patrick glanced uneasily at the guns. Shepherd either didn't care to explain the guns, or didn't see it as an issue worth mentioning. Instead he talked about the bunk beds, explaining that most of the followers tented outside by the fields, but that this was the main shelter for when the weather got bad. They left the guesthouse and continued their stroll, making their way further back into the fields.

A stretch of open land past the guesthouse was being utilized as a make-shift parking lot, where a fleet of large white box trucks sat in rows. They each had the words "Arcania Quality" printed along the side in dark green letter-ing, with a little drawing of a sprout as a logo. Patrick felt his stomach tighten, remembering his conversations with Agent Litner.

The crops were divided into sections that were manned by a group of six followers. Of this group, four people scurried around within the rows of the crop, prodding the earth or examining the bushy heads of the plants with gloved hands. The other two of the company stood guard, one on either side of the field. These people were armed, wearing menacing looking guns in shoulder holsters over their light clothing. Patrick could hold his tongue no longer. He turned to Shep, who was busy pulling his windblown curls back into a red bandana. "Shepherd, what the hell is this stuff, and why are you growing so much of it?"

"It's grain, part of an investment project Joey's entered."

"What kind of investment?" Patrick asked.

"Have you heard of a company called Arcania Foods? They distribute wheat and grain products to food manufacturers."

"I've heard of them," Patrick said cautiously.

"Well, Joey owns the company now. It had proven extremely lucrative for Charles, so Joey thought it would be a good investment. They used to be a fairly small distributor, but their client list has grown considerably in the past five years. They have clients all around the world now."

Patrick looked back over his shoulder at the fleet of white trucks grow-ing smaller the further out they trekked. What did not make sense, was why Joey would go to the trouble to actually grow crops on his own land for this company. "But, Arcania has been around for a while, Shepherd. Don't they have their own grain farms?"

Shep nodded. "Oh, sure they do. All of this product is supplemental."

"Supplemental for what?" Patrick asked.

"The crop you see here is going to provide a surplus for Arcania. This is all for charity."

Patrick did a double take at Shep, who was smiling and waving at the field workers as they passed. "Charity? You? Oh you've got to be kidding me."

"I kid you not, Obrien. It was Joey's idea. Hell, combined, we've got more money than God now. We wanted to do some good. Is that so hard to believe?"

"Well, yes, actually," Patrick said.

Shep stopped dead and stared at Patrick. He looked genuinely hurt. "We're not the monsters you think we are, Obrien."

Patrick glanced over at one of the young men who wore a gun strapped to his body. The security measures seemed awfully tight for a crop of grain that was not even going to fetch a price, and he said so to Shepherd.

"The guns aren't to protect the plants!" Shep explained. "They're to pro-tect Joey! Someone tried to shoot him recently, Obrien. If you were a sniper and you wanted to sneak onto the property, what would be the best way to hide yourself?"

Patrick saw what he was getting at. "Through the crop fields?"

"Exactly. We need to protect Joey and ourselves from any and all poten-tial threats. There are a lot of weirdoes out there, Obrien. You can't be too careful." Yes, Patrick thought. There are also a lot of weirdoes in here. Patrick's fingers reached out to brush the head of one of the plants. Shep grabbed his hand roughly before he made contact. "Don't touch that please. The oils in your hand could contaminate it."

Patrick pulled his hand back and glanced again at the gun-toting follower who stood guard. The man gazed at Patrick suspiciously, then saw that he was with Shep and turned away. Getting a sample of this stuff wasn't going to be as easy as he'd thought.

Shep periodically stopped along their surveillance walk to chat with followers and introduce them to Patrick. After each encounter, Shep would give Patrick a short profile of the person he'd just met, including what they had done for a career before joining Forest Bluffs. To Patrick's amazement, there were doctors, artists, scientists, and a wide variety of other intelligent, seemingly normal folk. They did not appear to be missing their former lives. They had all given themselves over to a gypsy style, wearing mostly loose cotton clothing with a lot of tie-dye and canvas. It was like living in Shepville.

A little pixie of a brunette with a head of short boyish brown hair came leaping forward to greet Shep. "Shepherd! I solved the water problem in the third sector, and I found that box of supplies you were looking for last week."

"Thank you, love. Patrick, this is Brin-Marie. Brin has been quite an asset to our little group out here." The girl beamed proudly at the compliment. She looked like she was waiting for a puppy treat. Patrick went cold. It was the girl from the cave, the one who had been administering the painkillers to the wounded Klee. "Brin-Marie is also a nurse," Shep added. Well, that made sense. Shep was using her medical skills to his own advantage. Patrick wondered if Brin-Marie ever imagined while she was back in nursing school that she'd be treating a wing amputation one day. Judging by her behavior that night in the cave, she didn't seem to mind.

"Pleased to meet you," Patrick said, and offered her his hand. As though noticing him for the first time, she turned to him, pulled the rubber glove off of her right hand and gave Patrick a quick, indifferent shake.

"Brin, did you hear me? This is Patrick," Shep said to the girl. When she didn't react, Shep gave her a knowing look. "Patrick Obrien," he added.

Realization flashed across her obedient face, and she quickly turned to Patrick. "Oh! Oh my. Welcome Patrick! We're so happy to have you here!" She beamed with delight.

"As you can see," Shep said to her, "I've solved a few problems of my own."

"I guess you have," she said, smiling at Patrick as though he was the answer to some prayer.

⁂

His unease spread as they walked and other people made his acquaintance in the same enthusiastic fashion, as though they had all been waiting for him. Strange behavior aside, the followers were conscientious workers, and none of them seemed to question for a moment what their purpose was in the little camp. Each section of fields was run in an almost military fashion, with each member of the group carrying out a specific task without question. Shep was in control of these people. He could see it in their eyes. They agreed with every statement he made, laughed too loudly at his jokes, and followed his orders to the letter.

Efficient as they seemed, the image of normalcy shattered later that morning when Joey came out to give his sermon. At the first sight of Joey,

they morphed into something weird and mindless. The followers had organized themselves into a crowd at the center of the open field, waiting. The
collection stood watching as Joey approached with his entourage, Russell,
Kelinda, Allisto, Margol and Klee. Joey was wearing a long white priest's robe.
He beckoned Patrick to join his little fiefdom. Patrick felt like he should be
playing a flute or waving a banner. In his mind he heard drums beating, and
baroque music announcing the arrival of the king.

The three brothers immediately took up posts along the sides of the
fields, relieving the guards so that all of the followers could attend the sermon. There was an eerie silence among the crowd. They stared at Joey, their
faces dazed and dreamlike. It was almost a sexual gaze, mixed with a blank-
ness that looked drug induced. Patrick felt embarrassed for the followers,
and for himself. He tried to slink back a little, but Shep immediately noticed
and pulled him forward. "Stay right with Joey," he said softly.

Patrick gave Shep an odd look, which he ignored. Apparently the fact
that Patrick was Joey's official protector was now out in the open. Patrick
stepped up alongside Joey, feeling like the biggest ass in the world. Kelinda
stood on the other side of him like a delicate pink queen. Shep stood off to
one side with Russell, both of them silent with heads bowed. They stood there
like that for what seemed like ten minutes, the crowd of five facing the crowd
of sixty.

The followers waited patiently, eyes focused on Joey with a combination
of awe and something like hunger. Finally, Joey lifted his arms in the air, and
Patrick saw a visible change come over him. He made his face blank and
serious, his eyes scanning the crowd purposefully, as though he would look
each one of them in the eye. "Let us pray," he said finally, and bowed his head.
The followers bowed theirs in response.

Patrick stared at Joey. *He's acting*. He had never seen him execute such
a presence as this. Joey began to speak, and Patrick could not take his eyes
off of him. He droned on and on in the same majestic tone as the googily eyed
onlookers gazed. What he was talking about, Patrick hadn't the slightest clue,
and he doubted sincerely if Joey did either. Patrick was no scholar, but he
knew gibberish when he heard it.

"We come together once again to thank the fate that brought us here, to
the minds that ask the questions, and to the hope that seeks the answers."
Say what? His voice was deep and commanding. The young men and women
smiled up at him as though he was showering them with pearls of wisdom.
He was saying absolutely nothing of substance, but they didn't seem to notice.
"And now that we are charged with the tasks that lead us into the searching,
we shall be assured that all debts will be paid, and the faithful will be born
unto the sanctity of the land!"

The crowd broke into cheers and a chorus of amens and hallelujahs.
Patrick had a moment when he was so afraid that he was going to laugh that
he bit down on his tongue hard enough to draw blood. To distract himself he
looked off into the distance where Allisto, Margol and Klee were supposedly
guarding the perimeters of the fields. They were engrossed in a friendly com-
petition of who could spin their gun into the air and catch it with the most
accuracy.

Klee was amusing to watch, as his walk was the most awkward. He
moved with kind of a half skip, as though he was walking across hot coals. He
was definitely a favorite, a baby sibling. The other brothers seemed overjoyed

to be with Klee, tousling his white curls playfully and laughing loudly as they watched him try to catch his own gun after tossing it too high in the air.

Patrick was startled out of his observations of the brothers by sudden applause from the crowd. He looked up and found that the entire crowd was focused on him. Joey was looking at him too. Patrick panicked, confused. Joey leaned in and whispered, "Obrien! I just introduced you, you space shot! Wave or something!"

Patrick forced a smile and waved uncomfortably at the crowd. After Patrick's introduction, the followers formed a single file line and came forward, one by one. Joey placed a hand on each one of their heads, after which they went on to resume their work in the fields.

The brothers came back across the field to join them as King Joey and his court walked back up to the main house. Russell trailed behind Shep like a puppy. When they got out of range of the crops, Joey let out a loud hoot. "Man I feel good today!" he yelled, and tossed himself into a summersault. Joey came back and wrapped an arm around Patrick's shoulder. "Obrien, I feel so much better now that you're back with us. So much better. I'm not even drunk!" Upon saying this, Joey took off in a sprint up to the house. All the better. Patrick had no idea what to say back to him aside from 'Hey buddy, nice cult you've got here'.

What a bunch of fruitcakes. He wanted desperately to voice this opinion, but he reminded himself that he was supposed to be faking enthusiasm. He thought about the strange red field of swaying plants, and wondered how the Christ he was going to get his hands on them.

"Party tonight, Obrien," Shep said. "In your honor. What are you drinking these days?"

"Oh, no. Don't have a party on my account," Patrick said. He'd been hoping he could lock himself in his room until the rest of them went to sleep, then sneak out and grab a sprig of that crop. Shep would hear none of it.

"We are having a party tonight, Obrien, and you will be there. You're the guest of honor. Don't be a wimp. It's good for morale."

"Oh yeah? Whose morale?"

"Everyone's!" Shep said, and darted off after Joey.

Patrick sighed and made his way reluctantly up to the big house. He moved slowly, letting them all get up ahead of him. "This was a bad idea," he muttered.

"What was a bad idea?" a voice behind him asked. Patrick spun around. It was Klee. He had trailed behind the others, unable to keep up with their quicker pace. Patrick looked into his questioning, innocent eyes.

"Oh, um, these pants. It was a bad idea to wear these pants. They're all dirty now," Patrick lied, brushing the imaginary dirt off his cream colored Dockers. Klee frowned, his tiny mouth forming a perfect pout. Patrick swallowed hard. Klee wasn't buying it. Perhaps he was not so innocent after all. "What's the matter, Klee?"

"Your aura is angry, Patrick."

Patrick was so stunned by the comment that he couldn't respond. Apparently Klee had some special abilities, and if Klee had them, Shep had them too. Patrick would have to watch his emotional levels from now on. "Don't you like us, Patrick?" the curly-topped blond asked with a heartbreaking sincerity.

"Oh, Klee. I like you very much. Really." He wasn't lying. He did like Klee.

He was telling the truth, and he let Klee see it in his eyes.

Klee frowned at him a moment longer, then the frown became a smile. Patrick smiled too, and patted him on the back. Klee jumped and cried out. "Ahh! Please, don't touch the back! Painful."

Patrick yanked his hand back, realizing what he'd done. "Oh, sorry Klee. I'd forgotten that you...hurt your back."

Klee ran pell mell up to the house. His tee shirt was dotted with blood from the oozing back wound. A chill went down Patrick's spine, and he looked warily down at the hand that he'd patted Klee with. "I've got to get the fuck out of here," he said, and made his way up to the house.

Chapter Thirty-Four

Father Carbone set the tray down on the table a little too hard. It was hot in the kitchen, despite his attempts to cool the place down with portable fans. The priest was irritable. Robin and Copie had been bickering since her arrival a half-hour before. Now that Copie had his own unbelievable tale of supernatural proportions, Robin could not resist the urge to challenge him with doubts and sarcasm as he had done to her and Patrick. Agent Litner was there as well. On the outside he appeared to be resting casually in one of the kitchen chairs, leaning back with one arm on the table. He was, however, going to town on his temple with his pen, a clear sign that the bickering was starting to get to him as well.

"I can't believe that you of all people doubt our story, Robin! We didn't laugh at you when you came back from Pearl Chasm with tales of discarded wings!" Copie said.

Robin leaned over the table, meeting Copie's eyes with a smirk. "You said it was my imagination running away with me. And as for the discarded wings, at least they were solid. I was able to pick them up and touch them with my own two little hands. You're talking about transparent beings that fly through the air and scratch people! Who's the nutty now, Copie?"

Father Carbone slammed the teapot down on top of the silver tray. "Enough! I didn't call you all over here so we could argue about whose story is bullshit and whose story is true. We need to stick together on this! Now everyone listen up. I finally got a hold of my colleague, Father Bello last night. We had a rather interesting discussion. The reason I've called you all here is because Father Bello is on his way over to speak with us. He has some things to share about his long time studies of the celestial hierarchy. Hopefully, he can shed some light on all of this...craziness."

Agent Litner finally put his pen away and scooted his chair in closer. "Is this Father Bello truly an expert on these matters?" he asked.

"Yes, Steven. He's been doing research on the subject for thirty years. It's a bit of a hobby. But most importantly, he has some limited information regarding a mythical being by the name of 'Zirub'."

Robin stiffened. She recalled Klee, the bloody blond creature blinking his swollen eyes as he gazed up at Shep in the cave. She could hear Shep's words clearly in her mind. *It's me. It's Zirub.* "What has he found out?" she asked.

"That's all he told me over the phone. He'd rather tell us the rest in person. There was something else however, something you should all know."

Now it was Litner's turn to stiffen. He did not like having new information sprung on him. "What is it?" he demanded.

"Father Bello had a visitor. A visitor who tried in vain to strangle him. He described him as a young, green-eyed man, slight of build with flaming red curls that reached down to his chin. He confessed his name to be Margol."

Copie and Robin both gasped. "Where does Father Bello preach?" Copie asked.

"Saint Christopher's, in the North end."

"Why did Margol visit him? What's the connection?" Robin asked.

Father Carbone looked at her, and she saw fear on his face. "He told Father Bello that he was looking for his brother. He was looking for Juris." The room fell silent. Father Carbone continued. "Somehow he had gotten the idea that Juris was being held by a priest. He simply had the wrong parish. A series of coincidences and misinformation led him to Father Bello, but I'd say that's a little too close for comfort. I for one am glad Juris has been moved out of my basement."

"What do they want?" Litner demanded suddenly, cutting into the pondering silence.

Father Carbone looked at him. "Pardon?"

Agent Litner repeated the question, placing emphasis on each word. "What-do-they-want? Damn it!"

"Who?"

Litner sighed. "These angels. There, I said it. Tell me what they want!"

"They are not angels," a voice outside the front door said. They all turned to see a chubby face adorned with a snow white beard, peering in through the screen. Father Carbone leapt from his chair to open the door.

"Father Bello! Please, come in. It's good to see you."

"Likewise, Luigi." The man stepped through the door, exuding a presence of kindness and warmth as he glanced around the little table. He wore the classic black pants, black shirt stretched a little too tight around his belly, and a white priest's collar. He seemed uncomfortable in the evening heat. His face was flushed pink, though it looked like a color his cheeks always wore. He smiled at the group, giving a courteous little nod. "Hello. I'm Father Bello."

They made introductions, and Father Bello was given a seat as Carbone poured him a cup of tea. Litner looked impatient with the pleasantries. "Father Bello, what can you tell us about these oddities we've been encountering? Something of value I hope. I have a civilian planted in their nest out at Forest Bluffs, so I'd like to know exactly what we're dealing with, for his safety's sake," Litner said. The bearded priest ignored him. "Father Bello? Did you hear what I asked?"

Father Bello took a long sip of his tea, clearly not intimidated by Litner's pushy demeanor. He placed the teacup down, then reached down to the floor to retrieve the canvas bag he'd brought with him. Slowly, he pulled books out of the bag, and placed them in a careful order on the table in front of him. Agent Litner sighed once, but kept his mouth shut.

When Father Bello had finished, six books lay in front of him. Some were old, with weakened bindings and tattered covers. Two of them were bright and colorful children's books, with a decorative collection of fairies, elves and apron-wearing kittens dancing across the cover.

He made minor adjustments, moving a book a quarter inch to the right, smoothing their covers. He seemed deeply enthralled in the organization of it all, when he looked up suddenly, taking in the impatient eyes that surrounded him at the table. He nodded. "Right. Let's get to it then, shall we?"

Agent Litner jumped in at the prompt. "You said when you arrived that they are not angels. What are they? What did you mean?"

"That is correct. They are not angels. They are Powers."

"Powers? What the hell are Powers?"

Father Bello leaned back in his chair and clasped his hands over his round belly. "There are nine orders of rank in the celestial hierarchy. From lowest to highest, they are Angels, Archangels, Principalities, Powers, Virtues, Dominations, Thrones, Cherubim and Seraphim. Seraphim are the highest on the totem pole, and angels are actually the lowest. That is if you can call a celestial being low! They're still a far sight higher on the food chain than we are!" Father Bello laughed heartily. The others did not. Catching their seriousness, he stopped laughing and cleared his throat. "So, anyway, calling these Powers 'angels' is actually an insult to them. They are three levels further up in rank."

"In rank?" Robin asked.

"Yes. Think of it as the armed forces. They each have designated ranks, and with each rank, comes specific tasks and duties. For instance, actual angels are the closest to the material world, serving as holy messengers for humans, while the higher ranked bodies, like Dominations and Thrones rarely if ever see the material world. Are you following me?"

"Barely," Litner said. "How can you be sure that Shep and the brothers are Powers, and not something else?"

"Well for starters, Margol told me he was the 'elite guard', code for a Power. I assume he felt it safe to reveal this, thinking that I would soon be dead by his hand."

Copie nodded. "Yes, they tend to spill their guts when they're about to kill you."

Father Bello leaned over and took Copie's hand. "I heard of your close call son. Your strength of spirit and will is impressive." Copie smiled, pleased.

"Could we get back to business please?" Agent Litner said.

Father Bello turned his warm smile to Litner. "Ah, yes. Agent Steven Litner. You have strength of will as well. Yours, however, is born of restraining your own happiness."

Agent Litner gave him a sarcastic smile. "Well, Santa, maybe you could bring me a pony for Christmas this year. Now, tell me about the Powers. What is their designation and what the hell are they doing here?"

Father Bello resigned himself to the fact that he was not going to warm Litner's cold heart. He sat up straight and placed his hands on the table. "Fine." He opened one of the older looking books but did not read from it as he spoke. Instead, he looked around the table at all of them. "The Powers hold one of the most dangerous jobs in the hierarchy. They are responsible for maintaining the borders between the realms. They are the first line of guard between the material and the immaterial worlds. What does this mean? Well on a lighter note, they are responsible for ensuring that souls that leave the mortal world get to heaven safely. Sounds like a fairly cushy job, right? But guarding the celestial byways between the realms is not always so easy. They are constantly guarding against demonic attack, and serve as a major battle line against unwanted entities. They are a most valuable order."

Robin drummed her fingers thoughtfully on her teacup. Father Bello looked at her, giving her time to formulate her thought. "So, they're like the border patrol," she said.

He nodded. "Exactly. A most responsible job. Unfortunately, more angels from the rank of 'Power' are listed as fallen from grace than any other member of the celestial hierarchy. Some consider this to be due to their close proximity to the nether regions."

"So, they have a tendency to get too involved with their work?" Carbone asked.

Father Bello smiled then, but the sparkle had gone out of his eyes. "The temptation to travel to other realms must be overwhelming. They are constantly at watch of creatures who are spiritually lesser than they are. They guide angels on their way out of the region, and help chart their course to the material world. Powers themselves, however, are forbidden to travel to the nether regions, including earth."

"Why?" Father Carbone asked.

"They are far too powerful to become material," Father Bello answered. "The lower beings, such as angels, archangels, and principalities can slip through and remain masked by human eyes, appearing only when they deem it necessary, to pass a message along or whatnot."

"So the lower angels have a cloaking device," Copie said.

Father Bello laughed. "Something like that. For the Powers to go to earth however, they would have to be made flesh, and this is unacceptable."

"Why is it unacceptable?" Litner asked.

Father Bello scowled. "You see, it was feared that the Powers would not be able to conceal whatever heavenly gifts they brought with them."

"Heavenly gifts?" Copie asked.

"Gifts, supernatural power, magic, call it whatever you like. If the Powers entered a lower realm, bringing their exceptional abilities into a place that possessed none, it could create a dangerous shift in the balance of things. They would possess knowledge and abilities not yet discovered by the lower beings."

"In other words," Carbone said angrily, "someone might get hurt."

"So, God doesn't allow these Powers to go to earth," Robin said. "Why would any of them defy God? If God is supposedly so all-encompassing and wonderful, why would any being go against his wishes?"

"That's a good question, Robin, and I think I can answer it. You've got to understand something," Father Bello said. "Only the highest of the celestial ranks take orders directly from God. These creatures we are dealing with, these Powers, take orders from their superiors, other members of the hierarchy. Most of them have never laid eyes on God, so to speak. These Powers are required to stay in the borders, just outside the kingdom. They can feel the warmth of the paradise they guard, but they rarely if ever are invited in, because of the duties they hold. You see, lower creatures in the hierarchy are not so different from you and me. They are required to have faith that their commands are coming from on high. Most people assume that all celestial beings just hang out with God all day. This is not so. Many of them question his existence just as we humans do."

They were all silent for several minutes, absorbing the information. Robin broke the silence, airing the question on everyone's mind. "What does this have to do with Shepherd and his brothers? You believe them to have once been Powers, I got that much. But what are they doing here? What's their deal?"

"Ah yes," Father Bello said. "This brings us to the story of Zirub." He closed the book in front of him, and picked up one of the colorful picture books.

"What is that?" Agent Litner sneered. "A children's book?"

The ruddy priest nodded. "There are very few legitimate writings about celestial beings that have any basis in fact. Even the bible refers to them with some rarity. When Father Carbone called me with the name Zirub, I too found it familiar. I knew I had encountered it briefly in the past, probably from readings I had done in school, but for the life of me I couldn't find it. I couldn't find it in any legitimate literary venue, that is. I searched scriptures, essays, all manner of writings, but nothing turned up the name Zirub. When I finally found it, it was in the oddest of categories. Folklore."

"You mean it's a fairy tale?" Copie asked.

Father Bello chuckled. "Ancient folklore was written for the entertainment of adults. They had no television, you know. Some of it is quite crass and not meant for children. You should read the early German version of Cinderella."

Agent Litner cleared his throat loudly. "The book, Father Bello?" he said impatiently.

"Oh, yes. This is a collection of stories that were printed about a hundred years ago, but their origins are impossible to date. The one I found is simply called 'The Story of Zirub'. It reads like a bedtime story, but I wouldn't read it to children unless I wanted to give them nightmares. I'll give you the condensed version, as some of it can get rather wordy." He opened the book.

"Basically, it talks about a band of five angels. They refer to them as angels here, most likely because that's what people understand, but I still hold fast to my theory that they are actually Powers. Anyway, most people think of a band as a musical reference, being that angels are often depicted carrying trumpets and harps and such. But in this case, it seems to refer to a small group or a collective."

"Like a street gang?" Copie asked.

"More like a pack of wolves. Or a family. There's a definite familial element to it. So this band is led by a celestial named Zirub, who wanted very much to be allowed to go to earth."

"Does it say why?" Agent Litner asked.

Father Carbone rolled his eyes. "Litner needs his 'why' at all costs, Father Bello."

"Actually," Father Bello said, "Agent Litner has a very good point. I too was bothered by the fact that this story did not explain the motive behind this Zirub's urgency to reach the mortal world. And there had to be a damn good reason. According to my research, the process for a Power to break through as flesh is not a simple matter at all, or a pleasant one. It is a violent, dangerous transition that could result in his destruction. He must have had a good reason, it just doesn't list it here. The only clue we have is that Zirub made the decision to go to earth immediately after the death of Christ. There may be a connection, or it may just be coincidence. They don't mention it here, so we just don't know."

Agent Litner nodded. He seemed satisfied, and pleased that Father Bello had taken his question seriously. "Please Father Bello, continue."

"Yes. So shortly after the death of Christ, this Zirub put in an urgent request to go to earth. He was denied of course, being a Power, a being forbidden to enter the mortal world."

"Let me guess," Robin said. "He went anyway."

"Of course. Otherwise, I doubt we'd be having this conversation." Father Bello pulled out a tiny pair of wire-framed reading glasses and placed them on his nose, adding to the Santa Claus image. Looking down at the colorful book, he continued. "Against the better judgment of his superiors, Zirub talked the rest of his band into joining him, and made the journey. It says here that he found a back door. I don't know if that means he went behind God's back, or if it is a literal translation. It makes sense however, knowing that Powers chart the material journeys of the lower beings. They know all the back roads, so to speak. At any rate, the band was discovered gone before they reached their final destination. Earth."

Father Bello paused. Copie stared at him, wide eyed. "Then the shit hit the fan, am I right?"

Father Carbone gave Copie a little nudge, but Father Bello ignored the profanity. "It hit the fan all right, Copie. Zirub's band abandoned their guard to go seek earth, leaving their posts wide open. A demonic tribe entered the kingdom of heaven. A battle ensued, and luckily the tribe was driven out by Powers from another sector. His superiors, angered by the lapse in security, shut both Zirub's entrance to earth, as well as his entrance back to the heavenly realms, leaving him unable to proceed, and unable to retreat. They could not go forward to earth, and they could not come back to where they had come from. They were stuck, trapped in the void for all time."

"What is this 'void' exactly?" Agent Litner asked.

Father Bello took a deep breath, and looked at the page in front of him. "The void is described as the vast nothingness. It is the darkness and the nowhere that was before God created the Heavens and the Earth."

Father Carbone shivered. He glanced around the table and saw that Robin and Copie were both rubbing their arms. It was as if on some primitive level, they all knew what the void was, and feared it above all things. The idea of nothingness was a concept the human mind could not quite wrap itself around. "How does it end?' Copie asked, his voice lowered to a whisper. Father Bello turned a couple of pages. He spoke slowly now, his jovial demeanor given over to a solemn countenance.

"In the nothingness, the other members of the band began to go insane. All except for Zirub, their leader, for he was stronger than the rest. He felt responsible for their fate, having talked them into taking the journey with him. Rather than watch his beloved band lose their minds in the darkness, he put them all to sleep, where they would remain in a sort of stasis until he woke them. He would spend eternity in the void, searching the darkness for a Cripulet."

"A Cripulet?" Agent Litner perked up, his impatient gaze given over to a look of intrigue.

Father Bello nodded. "A Cripulet is a thing of myth and legend. Some believe that there are areas of the fiber between the realms that have worn thin in places, leaving a soft spot. These soft spots are called Cripulets. It is believed that beings from other realms have occasionally passed through these Cripulets and into our world, either by accident or otherwise. Cripulets are said to be found mainly in deep ocean or mountainous caverns, places that have done a lot of geological shifting. Some believe that the myths of such creatures as the mountain Sasquatch and the Loch Ness monster are actually creatures from another realm, which inadvertently slipped into our world via a Cripulet. It's like an inter-dimensional doorway. Just as there are Cripulets to other worlds, there are supposedly Cripulets that lead to the void, and from the void, back into our world."

Father Carbone looked at Agent Litner, who seemed rattled by this latest information. "Steven, you look like you know something. Have you heard of these Cripulets before?"

Agent Litner paused then shook his head. "No. No, I've never heard of a Cripulet. It's just intriguing, that's all." Father Carbone nodded, but his gaze lingered on his friend. Litner seemed to be lying. Carbone let it go, knowing that secrets were part of being a government agent. It was probably the old *If I told you, I'd have to kill you* scenario. If Litner knew something about Cripulets, it was something he was not willing to share.

Robin mentioned the way Shep had that one section of rock marked off with a circle of blood on the cave wall. "Could that have been one of these Cripulets you're referring to?" she asked.

Father Bello did not appear surprised by the question. "Yes, Robin, Father Carbone told me about what you witnessed in the cave. Pearl Chasm is thought to have formed near the end of the last ice age, approximately 14,000 years ago. The chasm may have been formed by the sudden release of dammed up glacial melt water. It is a prime location for a Cripulet, assuming that such things actually exist."

"Pretty creepy bedtime story," Copie said. "Is that the end of it?"

Father Bello flipped through the pages. "Just about. There's a bunch of malarkey at the end about thunder being caused by Zirub trying to break his way through to earth, and so on. Things to scare kids. Oh, and there's a scripture quotation at the very end, from The Epistle of Jude. Would you like me to read it?"

Agent Litner shrugged. "You might as well."

Father Bello cleared his throat and looked down his nose through his wire-framed glasses.

"And the angels who did not keep their proper domain, but left their own abode, He has reserved in ever-lasting chains under darkness for the judgment of the great day."

Copie snickered. "Well, I guess 'He' had better get some stronger chains, because the suckers got out early."

"Can I ask a practical question?" Robin interjected. "If we are going to assume that this story has some basis in truth, and that these things did happen, then who wrote it all down? How did we come to know about it in the first place?"

"I thought of that as well," Father Bello said. "Throughout history, there have been accounts of actual messenger angels appearing before humans and telling them tales. It's all through the Bible, as if this happened regularly. Perhaps this tale was passed on in such a manner. Why they would feel the need to tell the tale of Zirub, I do not know. Perhaps they wanted to let us know that even they are not above God's law. Or, maybe they just like to gossip. Either way, we have a decision to make before we go any further with this discussion."

"What is that?' Father Carbone asked.

Father Bello stroked his white beard nervously. "We need to determine, here and now, if we are going to proceed on the assumption that the one you know as Melvin Eugene Shepherd is actually this mythical character, Zirub."

Robin blew out a long slow breath. It was hard enough to accept that Shep was a closet maniac. To believe that he was some sort of mythical character was nearly impossible. Although this Zirub did sound like kind of an idiot, regardless of his celestial origins. She met Father Bello's eyes. "What are our other options?" she asked.

He shrugged. "Well, the way I see it, there is only one other feasible explanation. That would be that Shepherd is a scholar of ancient folklore. In so thinking, for whatever reason, he has read the story of Zirub, and has gone to great lengths to parallel it to his own life. Personally, I'm not buying that. Everyone in this room, including myself, has witnessed things as of late that go far beyond a natural explanation. Oh, except for Agent Litner. Am I right?"

All eyes turned toward Agent Litner, who held his usual blank expression. He nodded. "That is correct. Aside from witnessing a rather unsavory scream from Juris that caused several windows to crack, I have not personally witnessed any of these unexplainable events. I have only the testimony of the others to judge by."

Robin looked hopeful for a moment. "If you have a more logical explanation, I'd be thrilled to hear it, Agent Litner."

"I believe it," Litner said. "I think Shepherd is Zirub."

"What?" Robin said.

Father Carbone looked especially surprised. "You Steven? You believe it?"

Agent Litner looked at him, his face unreadable. "Yes. I do."

Carbone shook his head. "But you're the rational one! Furthermore, you haven't even seen any of the really weird shit!" Father Bello grinned. He seemed highly amused that Agent Litner should be the first one to profess his belief in the boogie man.

"You can all stop staring at me like I just had a sex change right before your eyes," Litner said. "It's a simple matter of logic and reasoning."

Father Carbone narrowed his eyes to slits. "Wait a minute. I know you, Steven. You're playing some sort of head game with yourself."

Litner nodded. "The worst mistake I've seen agents make is underestimating their opponent. Sometimes, the truth about someone is so horrifying, that we just can't believe it. This leaves us at a disadvantage if the opponent truly is the horror we suspect. For instance, a terrorist has a baby in his arms. You must always assume that he will indeed kill that baby if you don't stop him. I have learned that it is wise to go into a situation under the assumption that the worst case scenario is true. If we imagine the worst, then there are no surprises. Therefore, in this case, the worst possible scenario is that Melvin Eugene Shepherd is not of this world. Nor are his brothers."

Father Carbone looked at Litner sideways. "And you're okay with that?"

Agent Litner shook his head. "Hell no. I'm not convinced that any of this supernatural business is legitimate. But I have to go under the assumption that it is. Don't you see? I've been underestimating this Shepherd character all along. If I tell myself that he is some sort of crazed other worldly being, then I can't possibly underestimate him again."

When they had all quieted down, Father Bello had them take a vote. They reluctantly agreed that they would proceed under the assumption that Shepherd was Zirub, and that the story, however tainted by the retelling of it over time, had to have some merit of truth. Agent Litner still wanted his 'why', and

Robin wanted to take a bath in holy water after coming to terms with the fact that she had been sleeping with a non-human for the past six years. Father Carbone came up with some 'why' questions of his own, which he directed at Father Bello.

"I can understand that celestial beings are not perfect, but these brothers, how did they get so...evil?"

"They are not evil," Father Bello answered.

Carbone was not pleased. "With all due respect Father Bello, I had one living in my basement until recently. They tried to kill Copie, and evidence points to the fact that they've killed others. Christ, one of them tried to kill you! If not evil, then what?"

"They were following orders, Luigi. It's what they do. They don't know from morality. They come from a place where all commands are divine."

"Do you mean that they truly don't know the difference between right and wrong?"

"Where they come from, there is no wrong. They don't question the commands that their leader gives them. Right and wrong are not concepts they understand. Don't you see? This is one of the reasons they are forbidden to cross the realms! They are not prepared to live in this world." Father Bello lowered his voice to a whisper then. "They're not supposed to be here!"

"What about Shep?" Robin interjected. "Does the leader know the difference between right and wrong?"

"Ah, yes," Father Bello said, leaning back. "Shep is clearly of a higher intelligence than the others."

Father Carbone whistled. "Well, considering how smart we found Juris to be, that's rather frightening."

Father Bello eyed him, looking serious. "If the dating of this story is even close to being correct, we're talking about a being that stayed awake for over two thousand years looking for a way out of his confinement. Persistent little bugger to say the least."

Father Carbone shook his head. "So we're dealing with a creature who outsmarted God somehow. Oh yeah. I think we can take him."

"Man!" Copie said, shaking his head. "How do you stop someone like that?"

Father Bello shrugged. "Maybe we shouldn't."

This got Agent Litner's attention, and he turned to Father Bello. "Excuse me?"

Father Bello held up his hands as if to ward off the heat of Litner's gaze. "I'm just saying, hypothetically speaking, we can't be sure that this isn't all part of God's plan."

"Oh come on!" Litner snapped. "I find it hard to believe that God would put any portion of his so called plan into the hands of a lunatic like Shepherd."

"I'm just speculating," Father Bello said. "I mean, who says it's our place to interfere?"

"The United States Government says it's my place to interfere," Agent Litner said. "No offense to the clergymen in the room, but I don't answer to God. I answer to a six foot four black man by the name of Agent Michaels, and he is awaiting my interference as we speak."

Father Bello looked solemn but not deterred. "I know that, Agent Litner. I just want you to be careful. You need to be ready for anything. I don't know what a couple of thousand years of nothing can do to one of these creatures, but I'm betting he's not just a little insane."

"Shep has to have a weakness. He must," Litner said determinedly. "Everyone and everything has a weakness. Even the waves of the ocean will die without the moon. Shepherd has a weakness. We just need to find it."

"What about the brothers?" Robin said. "He clearly loves them."

Agent Litner shook his head. "We took one of his brothers away and he's still functioning quite nicely. I'm talking about something that gets to him. Something that could throw him off guard at just the right moment."

"Wesley J. Shepherd," Robin said. "The name that Dr. Lichtenstein wrote in the dirt. Juris recognized it as soon as we said it, remember? He said Shep refuses to speak that name aloud."

Litner studied Robin. "You're right. I haven't had a chance to profile the name yet. I'll get to that later tonight."

Robin smiled at him. "You must be losing your edge, Agent Litner."

"Yes, well, I've had a lot on my mind," he said. Robin's smile dropped to a concerned frown as she watched him begin beating his temple with his pen once again.

Father Carbone perked up suddenly. "Hey, speaking of Juris, what about the other thing in the basement? The apparition that made me wet my pants. What the hell was that?"

Father Bello began consulting his books. "You said Juris called it a Principality?"

"Well, yes and no. He called it a 'Schlarr.' He said that our religion calls it a Principality."

Father Bello scanned the page. "Ah, here it is. Principalities are just below Powers on the list of ranks. One of their main duties is given to the protection of religion."

"That makes sense," Father Carbone said. "While the thing was…growling at me, Juris made a comment. He said something like, 'It can't hurt you, it thinks it's protecting you'."

Father Bello frowned. "These Principalities must be able to sense if there is a threat to the church. Clearly, this being saw Juris as a threat."

"Huh." Copie said. "I'm listening to all of this talk about these beings having great powers and such, but we really didn't see any evidence of that with Juris. I mean, aside from the fact that he's outlandishly strong."

"And telekinesis," Father Bello said. "Both Father Carbone and I had our cellular phones shatter, seemingly by magical forces."

Robin shrugged. "Humans have been known to exhibit telekinesis. That's still no big deal in the larger scope of things."

Father Carbone stood up. "Juris did seem to shatter my phone, but not until he was leaving the church grounds." They all stared at him, not understanding. He looked around the table. "Did it ever occur to any of you that the church made Juris weak, in more ways than one? Perhaps that's why he wanted to leave so badly. That and to avoid a confrontation with the Schlarr."

"Perhaps being in the church deadened his power, drained his strength," Robin said.

Father Bello looked at Agent Litner. "Would that imply that being away from the church would make Juris stronger?"

Agent Litner straightened up. He pulled out his cell phone and left the room. He returned after five minutes and put his phone away.

"Well?" Robin asked anxiously.

"Juris is still detained," he said.

Copie blew out a lung full of air. "Thank God."

"I've upgraded him to a twenty-four hour watch. I've warned the guards to be on alert for anything unusual. I also had them reinforce his restraints. I'm not sure I buy the bit about the church making him weak, but I don't want to take any chances. As Father Bello said, we need to be ready for anything." Agent Litner pulled a small black tape recorder out from under the table then. He pushed a button and it made a whirring sound.

"You taped all of this?" Father Bello asked.

"Patrick will be in the city mid-week for a briefing. He needs to be informed of this new information."

"I'm not a betting man," Copie said, "but I predict that this information won't make Patrick feel any safer out there at Camp Crazy."

Agent Litner finished rewinding the tape and popped it in his briefcase. He was picking up and preparing to leave. He looked at Copie. "The information might not be settling, but I know Patrick will want to have it. He's had enough deception for one lifetime."

"Which brings up another point," Robin said. "What about the hoax? How does my cousin Joey fit into the whole Zirub scenario?"

"We definitely don't have all the pieces to this puzzle," Father Carbone said, "but we know that whatever Shep is planning to do here, he can't do it alone. You saw those scriptures he wrote. Joey is the Sword, and Patrick is the Shield. He had to get Joey into a position of prominence somehow, like a false prophet. He's going to use him for something. He has a plan in the works, and he's had to use his earthly resources to bring it about."

"So what we have here," Father Bello said, "is a genuine celestial being, using false prophecy and false miracles, to create a real catastrophe."

"What about Joey?" Robin asked again. "Am I the only one concerned with getting him out of Shep's claws?" She looked around the room, but no on answered. Her face tightened. "Fine." She said, and began to pack her things up as well.

Copie looked at her, frowning. "Where are you going?"

She looked briefly at the two priests. "To see a witch," she answered, and walked out of the house.

Chapter Thirty-Five

Kelinda rocked slowly and sensuously on top of him. The room was filled with the watery golden half-light of candles. The golden hue flickered outside the sheer drapery that hung like a tent from the canopy of Joey's enormous bed. She had the whole scene set before he walked through the door. She had been waiting, ready. She had wasted no time.

Her breathing became quicker as she slid her naked body up and down his, their hot skin gliding like velvet against each other. She was so beautiful, he thought. But he did not love her, and he knew that she did not love him. At least not anymore. She feigned affection for him now, while once it was genuine. It didn't bother him. It was merely an unexpected change. He also got the sense that she was hiding something from him, something dark and sinister behind the sweetness of her rich, full lipped smile.

Her sexual desire was real enough. Of this, he was sure. She truly could not get enough of him. But it wasn't about him anymore. It wasn't about Joey Duvaine, boy wonder. It was his fluids she wanted. This had bothered him once, but now he didn't care. Shep was the one behind all of the mystical crap, and Shep could be the one to worry about it.

Kelinda delved her tongue into his mouth as though she would eat him alive. At the same time she expertly moved her hips against his, careful not to go too fast lest he waste his precious explosion before she was ready. His arousal, combined with the scent of the candles made his head spin wildly. His orgasm started with a shudder in his abdomen, causing him to suck in his breath. This was the signal she'd been waiting for. In one fluid motion, she dismounted and dropped down, sliding her lips onto him a mere second before ejaculation. It was precise timing. He arched his back, ecstasy pulsing in waves as he surrendered his fluids to her welcoming mouth. His stomach tightened and he collapsed as the last electric current of pleasure passed through his body, leaving him limp. As always, she didn't want to let go, coaxing every drop from him with a suctioning force.

"Enough!" he said. She did not retreat. He grabbed her head and painfully pulled her from him. "I said enough!"

She stretched her back and took a deep breath, her cheeks flushed pink. She closed her eyes and fell back onto the bed, smiling, running her hands through her hair, down her neck, over her breasts and ribs. He had seen the ritual before. She was like a junky after a fix. Finally, she got up and slinked over to her closet, slipping into a sheer black dress that came to her mid calf. She spun delicately and the bottom of the dress flared out like a bell. She crossed the floor, dancing merrily like some macabre ballerina.

Joey watched her from the bed. "Why do you always wear black now?" he mumbled. He was spent and could barely lift his head to look at her. She went over to the vanity mirror and picked up a brush.

"Because black is the only color that looks good with this outrageous hair color you picked out for me. Besides, I look good in black, don't you think?"

Joey lay like a dead man in the bed. "You'd look good in anything," he said without a hint of emotion.

"My my, Joey," she said. "Was that a compliment from the man without a heart?"

"I have a heart. It's just different than yours."

"Not so different anymore," she said, as she applied a hot pink lipstick, then a sheer gloss over her full lips.

"Where are you going?" he asked.

"Just out to the fields," she answered curtly.

"You know Shep doesn't want you going out to the fields, Kelinda. Not without one of us."

She turned away from the mirror, peering at Joey's lump form beneath the sheet. "Shep doesn't let me do anything. Those people are the only friends I have now."

"They're a bunch of zombies," he said, his voice muffled through the side of his pillow.

"Perhaps, but you really shouldn't talk like that. After all, they are your followers. They worship you." Joey remained silent. "So? Are you going to tell?" she asked.

He was on the cusp of sleep. "Am I going to tell who, what?"

"Are you going to tell Shep if I go out to the fields?"

Joey turned over and pulled the covers over his head. "I don't care what you do."

Patrick sat in the dark outside on the deck, his back leaning against the house. He was hiding from the brothers, who couldn't seem to give him a moment's peace. His 'party' ended up being a small affair, consisting only of himself, the brothers, Joey and Shep, Kelinda, Russell, and one or two of the followers. Apparently Shep stopped having full-scale parties after the last one, where Joey was nearly taken out by sniper fire. Go figure.

It was a mad house, this place. The Forest Bluffs Home for Wandering Lunatics. To make matters worse, the brothers, who had spent weeks stalking him from darkened corners of the city, now viewed him as their buddy. It was so strange. Due to the simple fact that Shep said so, Patrick was now a member of their family. They had transformed him from prey into pal overnight, because that was what they were instructed to do. Had they no opinions of their own?

Patrick supposed he should have been relieved that his undercover performance was going so well, but it was a bit of overkill. The brothers smothered him, treating him like an interesting new toy.

He heard the blender whirring from inside and he smiled. He had finally managed to pry the brothers off of him by introducing them to the wonderful world of frozen chocolate mudslides. He'd shown them how to mix the ingredients together, using the blender to whip the creamy concoction. When they tasted the frozen chocolate drink, you'd have thought Patrick had invented the wheel.

On the first try, Margol had forgotten to put the cover on the blender, and frozen mudslide had sprayed in an explosion all over the room and everyone in it. The brothers thought this was hysterical, and tried to repeat the performance, until Patrick convinced them that the results were much more practical if they blended the drinks with the cover on. They'd been at it ever since, giving Patrick the golden opportunity to sneak out for a breath of fresh air.

The music was still too loud inside, but he could hardly complain about that. He was the one who had turned it up in order to drown out the sounds of Kelinda and Joey having sex one floor up. He had come to terms with the fact that Kelinda and Joey had a sexual relationship, but hell, he didn't need to listen to it.

The blender whirred again, and he heard the raucous giggling of the brothers as they mixed up yet another batch. Strange creatures. He had taken his chances and asked Shep earlier in the evening why the brothers acted in the strange manner in which they did. "Something happened to them," was all Shep would say.

The screen door slid open to his left suddenly, and Patrick pressed his back up against the house into the shadow, fearing that it was Allisto or Margol coming to retrieve him. It was Kelinda, and she did not see him sitting there. She was radiant in a sheer black dress with a long strand of black pearls hanging around her neck. He watched her step off the deck and walk into the night, the strange dress flowing behind her like a dark ghost. She did a little dance move, then a spin, before she quickened her stride and headed out toward the fields.

He watched her drift off into the moonlight, this woman who he had once viewed as the epitome of the sweet, wholesome, All-American girl, with her dreamy eyes and long chestnut hair. He thought about the extent to which he had been wrong about people, and decided that this was not the time or the place to be exploring that particular failure.

A beam of moonlight shone through Kelinda's dress as she leapt like a dancer into the woods. Patrick suddenly found himself extremely curious. He stood up and looked around, then moved off the deck and followed Kelinda into the woods. He stayed a close distance behind, but not so close that she would hear his footfalls. The moon was so full and bright that it almost appeared to be daylight. White birch trees glowed bright amidst their darker cousins. Patrick caught a glimpse of Kelinda's pink head as she sprinted forward through the woods toward the open fields.

He found that he was panting, struggling to keep up with her as she leapt gracefully through the thick woods like an exotic deer. Patrick wondered if Kelinda had always had such stamina, or if he himself was getting out of shape. The woods began to give way to the clearing, and she skipped across the grass, waving her hands in the air as she hummed some indecipherable tune.

As the woods broke into the open field, Patrick noticed the dark red heads of the crops swaying gently in the night air. There were no armed guards at watch now. His nose caught the plants strange burned rubber scent and his spirits lifted as he thought about snatching one of them, here in the cover of the night. The follower's campfires formed orange dots in the distance, and the moon cast an exhilarating glow on the fields. Kelinda spun and leapt, laughing to herself as she made her way toward the campfires.

They had come upon the first section of crop, and Patrick immediately dropped to his knees and crawled toward them. He reached his fingers out, meaning to snap one of the plants off at the stalk, when a pain shot through his arm, sending him reeling back onto the earth. He stifled a cry and rubbed his tingling arm until the pain let go to a numbing throb. He looked back at the crops and saw a series of small metallic boxes thrust into the earth every few yards. An electric fence of some kind. Sure, Patrick thought, just growing a few extra fields of grain for charity's sake. No big deal at all. Yeah, right. No big deal, they just needed armed guards and electric fences to protect it. He lifted himself off the ground and took off after Kelinda.

Kelinda's pink head led him closer to the camps, and he heard the first tinklings of music. It was rhythmic, insistent, almost tribal sounding. The beat was heavy and the music was wild and exotic. It made him think of gypsies. He saw the followers then, gathered in the center of the open field just to the right of the crops. The followers were dispersed here and there around a large fire. The music was coming from a band of six set up in front of a cluster of tents. The crowd danced to the hypnotic beat, moving like phantoms around the glow of the giant bonfire. They were having a party of their own. Full carafes of red wine sat out on makeshift tables and benches.

Patrick crouched down behind a tractor where he could watch the scene undetected. Kelinda glided into the crowd, turning and swaying seductively in the firelight, her lithe, naked form clearly apparent under the flimsy black dress. The followers became aware of Kelinda's presence gradually, and hands began reaching out to touch her as she passed through them. They did not cling, but simply brushed her arm, or stroked her hair, then went back to their dancing.

It seemed they were accustomed to Kelinda joining their parties. A man took her by the waist and they began to dance together. They moved erotically, rhythmically, their bodies almost touching, but not quite. Kelinda threw her arms over her head and the man took her hand, twirling her off to the waiting arms of another man, who danced with her briefly, then passed her along to a woman, who in turn passed her to another man. This went on for a time, Kelinda taking turns dancing with the different followers, until finally she broke off and made her way to the perimeter, where a dozen or so people were chatting pleasantly with each other. They seemed in awe of Kelinda as she approached. She chatted with them in a familiar fashion.

Patrick crawled across the ground like a soldier and settled in behind another tractor, five feet from where Kelinda and the others stood. One of the women she was talking to was Brin-Marie, Shep's little foot soldier with the boyish haircut. Gone was the dutiful soldier routine. She seemed relaxed, and smiled openly, smoking a cigarette.

"Is he really better, Kelinda?" a young man asked her eagerly.

Kelinda turned from Brin-Marie and smiled at him. "Oh, he's better all right," she said, and smiled ruefully. Two women crowded around her, giggling.

"You're killing us," Brin-Marie said, as she ran a finger along Kelinda's cheek. "Your face is hot. Did you get it or not?"

"You tell me," Kelinda said, and pulled Brin-Marie's face to hers, kissing her long and deep on the mouth. Patrick was surprised to discover that he could still be shocked by something. Kelinda let her loose and Brin-Marie reeled back as though she would faint. One of the young men caught her. She opened her eyes and smiled at the man, who looked at her expectantly.

"Well?" he asked.

"Oh yes," she said. "She has it."

Brin-Marie's statement seemed to make the little company happy, as they began to cheer and hoot. Kelinda laughed heartily, then skipped over to an empty bench, climbing up onto it. The wind whipped her sheer black gown, and her pink hair glowed in the firelight as she raised her arms and looked down over the crowd. The music stopped and the followers shuffled over, forming a crowd around her. Patrick felt his heart rate escalate. What the hell was this all about?

"Come!" she shouted. "And let me share his essence!" The statement caused a series of tasks to be performed. A portion of the crowd went back to the tables and began picking up the carafes of wine. They then formed a line in front of Kelinda. Another woman stayed behind at one of the long wooden tables, and began spreading out dozens of tiny plastic cups.

A red haired boy, who looked no older than sixteen, walked up to the chair and handed Kelinda a small blade. She took the little knife and made a cut along the tip of her thumb, then held the thumb up for all of them to see. "A drop for each bottle!" she yelled, and the crowd broke into cheers. The wine carriers came forward then, one at a time, as Kelinda squeezed a drop of her blood into each carafe. Once the blood had been added, they systematically brought each bottle of wine over to the long table. The woman who stood behind it stirred each carafe with a straw, then poured a shot sized amount of the red liquid into the little white cups.

This went on until all of the wine cups were filled. Kelinda licked her thumb, then jumped down off of the bench to join the crowd. They all pushed forward and took a cup of the wine, immediately tossing it back into their mouths. Patrick watched in amazement as they ran their tongues along the inside of the little cups to sop up every last sticky drop. The woman who had been setting up the cups finished her own shot, then sucked the remaining wine eagerly out of the stirring straw.

Out of the eerie silence, the music kicked up again and the insistent drumbeat echoed out into the night, vibrating through Patrick's body with each rhythmic pulse. The crowd began to dance again, spinning and leaping around the fire as though they were made of air. They thrashed about in seeming ecstasy, turning and flickering as though they were part of the fire. Patrick risked one last glance at Kelinda, who danced alone under the moon, her hands raised up to the sky. Then he crawled like a frightened spider across the ground until he reached the edge of the woods.

In the shield of the forest he broke into a sprint, desperate to get as far away from the fields as he could. He tripped over a root once, and smacked his head hard on the ground. He did not stop. The pain could wait. He kept running until the woods gave way to Joey's back yard, then he slowed, making his way carefully back up to the deck. He found the house pretty much the way he had left it. No one seemed to have missed him. Shep was tapping away on the computer upstairs, and Joey slept like the dead. The brothers, having discovered the agony of an ice-cream headache, had given up their mudslides and were now warming themselves in the Jacuzzi.

Patrick crept off to his assigned bedroom and locked the door. He lay staring at the ceiling, unable to sleep as he tried to make sense of what he had just witnessed. Why was Kelinda feeding the followers her blood for God sakes? What was it with these people and blood? Between Joey, Shep and now Kelinda, Patrick would never look at a damned paper-cut the same again.

Chapter Thirty-Six

"Hello Aunt Betsy."

Betsy peered through the door at Robin, alarm settling on her face. "Oh no. Who's dead? Is it your mother? It can't be your mother. I spoke with her this morning."

Robin laughed. "Relax, Betsy. Nobody's dead this time. I just want to talk to you."

Betsy's shoulders dropped. "Oh, thank God. I don't think I could do another funeral. No offense to your mom."

"None taken."

Betsy held the door open. "Come on in, honey. Can I get you something? I was about to have some tea."

Robin almost gagged after all of the tea she'd had at Father Carbone's over the past week. "No thanks. I'm fine." She followed Betsy into her spacious kitchen and took one of the stools that surrounded the island, watching her young aunt as she prepared her tea by the stove. Her baldness was growing in, and now her yellow hair had become a short pixie. Betsy carried her tea over to the island and smiled at Robin. She put her tea down, then reached out and touched Robin's temple.

"Well, someone's life has been busy lately. Your aura is all lit up like a Christmas tree."

Robin shrugged away. "Come on, Betsy. You know I hate it when you do that creepy psychic shit."

Betsy smiled. "All right Robin. Why don't you tell me why you're here."

Robin grinned. "I need your help with some of that creepy psychic shit."

Betsy laughed. "Hypocrite!"

"Yes, that I am. I want to show you something." Robin reached into her bag and pulled out the tattered journal, Shep's hand-written supplement, 'The Book of Zirub'. She slid it across the counter. Betsy ran her finger slowly across the cover.

"My word. This looks interesting. Where did you get it?"

"I stole it from a priest. He's going to kill me if I don't get it back before he notices it missing."

"You stole it from a priest?" Betsy looked shocked.

"Relax, Aunt Betsy. He's a friend of mine."

Betsy raised an eyebrow. "Well, as long as you only steal from your friends. What is this?"

Betsy opened the book and scanned a few of the pages. "They're drawings. Very strange. This isn't even written in English. At least most of it isn't."

"I think this book might have something to do with Joey," Robin said. "Oh, and, um, Shepherd."

Betsy flinched at the mention of Shep's name. She looked down at the book like it was a filthy thing, then back up at Robin.

"I need your help, Betsy. I think Joey is in trouble."

Betsy looked at her long and hard. "Yes," she said, "I'm certain that he is."

"You knew?" Robin asked.

"I don't know all of the details, but I know Joey isn't Joey anymore."

"Then you have to help me. I want you to look at this book. I think Shep did something to Joey, something involving his blood. You know about this stuff, Betsy. You can figure out a way to reverse it."

Betsy stood. "How much do you know, Robin?" she asked.

"What I know is mostly speculation. I do know one thing for sure though. Shep is dangerous. You were right about him, Betsy. We need to get Joey away from him."

Betsy walked abruptly toward her, stopping just in front of her stool. "What is he?" she asked. Robin was shocked. The very question indicated that Betsy knew somehow that Shep might not be human. Betsy had always been mistrusting of Shep, but until now, Robin just thought it was a vague impression she got from him. She stared back at Betsy, and lied.

"I don't know," she said.

Betsy narrowed her eyes. "You're lying. You know what he is, don't you? Tell me. I've been waiting a long time to have confirmation of this. Tell me what he is, Robin."

"I'm not sure, Betsy. That's the truth." Robin's face grew solemn. "I can't give up on Joey."

Betsy shook her head. "Joey's gone, Robin."

"How can you say that?"

"Because it's true! And if you had eyes in your head you'd see it too. Joey is gone. Shep took him from us. He's been gone for a long time."

She walked away, into the next room. Robin yelled after her. "Damn it Betsy! I know you know about stuff like this! If it's a spell then it can probably be reversed." She had trailed Betsy into the living room. Betsy turned to face her.

"Robin, I give psychic readings. I'm not a witch, or a fucking magician for that matter. Even if this blood spell could be broken, what makes you think I could even begin to know how to do that?"

Robin walked past her on to the large oak bookshelf that ran along the wall. She began pulling books from the shelf, and reading their titles as she tossed each one of them on the floor. "*Modern Witchcraft, Ancient Rituals, Vaudan Blood Rites, The Power Within...*" Robin kept tossing the books onto the floor until they formed a messy pile in the center of the room. Betsy watched her warily. Finally, Robin turned and looked over the books at Betsy. "Oh, no. You know nothing about stuff like this. That's why you have at least two dozen books on the subject."

"Those are books I read out of personal interest, and for entertainment."

Robin frowned at one of books on the floor, a book about Native American spirituality. She looked up at Betsy. "Have you ever heard of something called 'the calming of the soul'?"

Betsy shook her head and turned away. "I told you, Robin, I don't know anything about..."

Betsy stopped speaking and wheeled about. "The calming of the...what did you just say?"

"The calming of the soul," Robin repeated. "I have reason to believe Shep used this ritual on Joey. It's supposed to be a Native American thing."

A flicker of recognition passed across Betsy's face, and she darted toward the bookshelf. She found another book and began flipping though it. "I know I've seen that somewhere," she said. Robin felt a flicker of hope. Betsy stopped at a page, and scanned it. Then she smiled. "Oh, yes. I remember reading about this. The calming of the soul." She looked up at Robin. "Son of a bitch. Is that what Shep did to Joey? All this time I figured it was some sophisticated ritual that was beyond my understanding."

"So you can reverse it?" Robin asked hopefully.

Betsy looked at her seriously. "I'll make you a deal, Robin, and this is not up for debate. You tell me everything you know about Shep, and I do mean everything, and I'll try to find a way to get Joey back."

Reluctantly, Robin agreed. "I don't know where to start," she said.

Betsy took a seat on the couch. "Start at the beginning," she said.

Robin joined her on the couch. She wasn't sure what the beginning was as far as Shep was concerned. She thought back to the words spoken by Father Bello, shortly before she left Carbone's kitchen. She leaned in close to Betsy and whispered, "He's not supposed to be here!"

Betsy nodded. "Yeah. That much I figured out on my own."

Hours later, Robin was in her car heading back home. She wondered what would happen if she were to be pulled over by the police and searched. She could only imagine their reaction to find her carrying a little bottle of blood in her purse. *No officer, no biological weapons here, just a bottle of ceremonial blood. It's a family thing.* She felt better about things, but still had her doubts. It didn't help her faith when Betsy kept saying, 'this probably won't work' as they were concocting the potion. Betsy kept insisting that she didn't know what she was doing. She had eventually come up with something, however. Now they would just have to wait and see how things panned out.

The blood had to be administered all at once, and words had to be spoken, so slipping it into Joey's coffee was out of the question. It also had to be administered by a blood relative, puns aside, so giving the blood to Patrick to administer would be futile. As far as Robin going back out to Forest Bluffs, she'd rather chew on broken glass. She'd have to think on it.

Chapter Thirty-Seven

Agent Litner listened intently as Robin described the phone call she'd received from Shep the night before, after returning from Aunt Betsy's. She was shocked that he'd called. He claimed that he could sense that something had changed, and he wanted to know why she'd suddenly stopped pursuing him. His tone was suspicious, and she'd had trouble hiding the fear in her tone when she spoke to him. Shep ended the conversation by saying that he no longer trusted her, and that he wanted her to move to Forest Bluffs where he could 'keep an eye on her.'

The conversation had left her sleepless, in a state of panic. "He wants me to move out to Forest Bluffs. Can you believe it? This is completely out of character for him. Do you think he really suspects something?"

"I doubt it. Don't worry, we'll figure this out." Just hearing Litner say the words made her feel better. He had that deep authoritative tone. She felt safe when Litner was around, as though everything would ultimately be all right. It was probably a comfortable illusion, but after hearing Shep's angry voice, she'd take it. Litner tapped his pen on Robin's glass coffee table. She was tempted to ask him to stop, but he had that distant look he got when he was in deep thought.

He slipped the pen behind his ear then and leaned forward. "You said it was out of character for Shep to demand to see you. Is it also out of character for you to refuse to see him?"

Robin looked at him carefully. Her brow creased. "Perhaps it is a bit out of character, but a lot of things have changed."

"Would you have gone out there if you knew nothing of this investigation?" he asked. Robin tried to imagine what she would be thinking if she hadn't made these new discoveries.

"Yes, I suppose I would have."

Litner gave her a look. "Have you ever refused him before, Robin? Ever?"

"No, Agent Litner. I have never refused Shep before." She straightened up, pointing at him. "I hope you're not about to suggest that I go out there! I won't do it."

"Patrick will be getting those samples this week, if all goes well. If he doesn't get them, we may have to contend with Shep a while longer. I don't want to rouse any of his suspicions before we get what we need."

Robin shook her head. "I can't go out there. Absolutely not."

"Is this about Patrick?" he asked.

"This is about me! Do you know what it would mean if I went out there? Shep would expect me to sleep with him. Aside from the fact that I'm with

Patrick now, I don't want Shep touching me! I know what he is now. I'd give that fact away. He can read me, Litner. He'd know. I'm better off at a safe distance, limiting my contact to the telephone. Trust me."

Litner rubbed his temples. "You've never rejected him before. Correct?" Robin nodded. "Then we have no way of knowing how he will react to your rejection of him."

"Well we're just going to have to wait and find out. I watched Shep kill somebody last week. You can't ask this of me, Litner. It's too much."

Litner looked at her, and she thought she saw a flicker of compassion. Finally he nodded. "You're right. I have no right to ask that of you. But speaking of watching Shep kill somebody, I found Dr. Lichtenstein, the old doctor from the cave. The one you said served as a human sacrifice."

Robin perked up. "You did? Tell me everything."

Agent Litner pulled a folder out of his briefcase and opened it up. "A Dr. Simon Lichtenstein was reported missing by his wife last week. His age and photograph match the description of the old man you saw killed in the cave. He was a retired orthopedic surgeon. His specialty had been amputations."

He let Robin absorb the information. "Why would he ever have agreed to become involved with Shep?" she asked.

Litner remained placid, but she could see by the subtle tilt in his head that he had it all figured out. "I don't believe the doctor's involvement was voluntary. There is a record of disciplinary action against him, which somehow never panned out. There were allegations that he had inappropriate contact with his patients. He was charged, but then suddenly the charges were dropped."

"Inappropriate how?" Robin asked.

"They were unconscious."

Robin made a face. "Yeesh. That is disgusting." Robin got a disturbing mental image of the old doctor pawing at some poor unconscious lump of flesh on a sterile table. "Why wasn't he ever convicted?"

"All allegations were dismissed due to lack of evidence, according to police files. The evidence they had obtained mysteriously disappeared. There was a video tape, you see. A camera had been set up in one of the operating rooms by a class of medical students for educational purposes. Dr. Lichtenstein was apparently unaware of the camera, and was caught on tape doing whatever it was he did to his unconscious patients. Then, the video tape simply disappeared out of the police evidence room. Eventually, Dr. Lichtenstein's license was reinstated and all charges had to be dropped. This happened decades ago, mind you."

Robin looked into Litner's eyes, trying to discern the message behind them. "So what happened to the evidence?" she asked.

"After what you heard from the doctor's mouth out at Pearl Chasm, I'd say someone was blackmailing him."

"Shepherd," she said with conviction. "But how many years ago was this? Shep would have been a child at the time."

Litner shrugged. "Assuming that Shep ever was a child."

Robin waved her hands in front of her face. "Let's not go there, okay?" Timelines aside, it did make sense. She tried to remember the old man's pleas. He'd said something about being an old man, and not caring what they did to his reputation anymore. Shep probably had in his possession the video tape that could have convicted the not so good doctor. It would have destroyed

Lichtenstein. Litner said he had a wife. It would have destroyed her as well. Robin wasn't sure if the knowledge that Dr. Lichtenstein was a criminal pervert made her feel better about his death or not.

"What was Shep blackmailing him for?" she asked.

"Isn't it obvious? He needed someone who knew how to do amputations," Litner stated bluntly, still holding the demeanor that this was a perfectly normal case. "Clearly he chose someone who had a great deal to lose. I'm sure the amputation was a grizzly task, even for a professional. Not to mention what it would do to a sane person's mind."

Robin nodded. "I suppose it would take such a desperate person. After all, if some freak wanted to hire you to cut wings off of...oh Christ. It all sounds so crazy."

"It's actually sounding less and less crazy to me," Litner said. Robin studied him with interest. He was an odd duck, Litner. He was clearly thrilled that the pieces of this little puzzle were beginning to fit together, yet he paid no heed to the fact that there were otherworldly elements at work. She didn't want to test her imagination and guess about the things Litner had seen in his line of work. If he viewed beings with wings as small potatoes, then she probably didn't want to know

Another thought came to her then, and she perked up. "Hey, what about Wesley J. Shepherd? Did you find him yet?"

Litner frowned, looking disappointed. "Ah. The elusive name in the dirt. I've been doing a search. The problem isn't finding a match to the name Wesley J. Shepherd. Unfortunately, there are hundreds of them. I'm still in the process of narrowing it down. I'm cross-referencing the name with anything and everything that might have a connection to this investigation. I hope to turn up something by this evening."

Robin nodded. "So what do we do about Shep?" she asked, hoping to make it Litner's problem and not her own.

"We have to come up with a damn good reason as to why you are suddenly so disenchanted with him," he said.

She shrugged. "Why not tell him the truth?"

Litner looked surprised. "The truth?"

"I don't mean to tell him that I've discovered he used to resemble a seagull. I'll tell him the partial truth, that I'm sick of his shit. He doesn't call me for months at a time. I'm tired of the games. I'll tell him that I'm finally ready to move on. I've grown. I'm not about to go running back to him just so he can break my heart again. How does that sound?"

Litner smiled. "Very convincing."

"Yeah, well I've wanted to say those things to him for a long time. I was just too much of a pansy to do it before."

Agent Litner lifted the telephone off its cradle and handed it to her. "Do it."

She grimaced at the phone. "What? Now? But he gave me three days."

"I don't want to wait three days to see what Shepherd's reaction is going to be. If this is going to cause us a problem, I want to know about it now."

Robin hesitated, but finally took the phone from him. She swallowed hard, and dialed the number to Forest Bluffs.

⁂

Morning light streamed in through the enormous sky light, casting an ethereal glow on Shepherd where he stood cradling the phone to his ear. He was a vision of sweetness in the sunlight, a phenomenon marred only by the stream of raging obscenities that spewed from his perfect mouth like a prayer. "God damned stupid bitch! What do you mean no? You can't tell me no, you fucking bitch, whore mother-fucking..."

Russell stood beside Shep, seething as he listened to the one sided conversation. It was the skanky blond Duvaine bitch again. She had called Shep this time. From the sounds of it, she was telling Shep that she no longer wanted to see him. She was, in effect, dumping him. Shep was shouting at her one moment, and emphatically begging the next. He was actually begging her to come out to the Bluffs! It was pathetic, a trait Russell had never seen Shep exhibit before. Shep was supposed to be the one in control all of the time. It was one of the things that made him Shep. Russell felt his anger and jealousy rise to new heights as he listened to the words Shep spoke.

"Robin, please. Just come out for a week and give me a chance to change your mind." He paused, listening to the response, then his face tightened again. "What the fuck is your problem, Robin? I swear to God, you'd better reconsider this!"

Russell shook his head. The stupid bitch was actually rejecting Shep. Didn't she know how lucky she was that Shep wanted her? Russell would have given anything to hear Shep speak to him like that. On a whim, Russell reached out and touched Shep's shoulder. "Hey, just hang up the phone, man. If she doesn't want to come out, then the hell with her."

Shep turned to Russell with fury in his eyes, noticing for the first time that he was standing there. He put the receiver to his chest. With eyes like cold green steel, he glared at Russell and said, "Get away from me you fucking faggot!" Shep turned his back to him and brought the phone to his ear. "Sorry Robin. I just had to pull Russell out of my ass. Now what were you saying?"

Rejection swam through Russell's veins, turning to a cold hatred that sucked the very breath out of him. For a moment he couldn't move. He simply stared at the back of Shep's head, at his lovely sand-colored curls, and wanted to rip them out one by one. He wanted to strangle him with the phone cord he twirled playfully around his fingers. He wanted to kill him. He stormed out of the room before Shep could see the tears of fury that stung his eyes. Shep would only take pleasure in seeing him cry, and Russell did not want to give him any today.

His body shook as he trailed up the spiral staircase to the second floor. He needed to calm down. If he flared off at Shep now, Shep might send him away. As much as he wanted to hurt Shep, he didn't want to be sent away. He stormed down the hallway toward his room, determined to lock himself in and play a few hours of Doom. The violent video game was a quiet therapy. He would pretend that every well-armed monster that jumped out was Shepherd, and he would blow its animated brains out accordingly.

Something caught his eye as he passed the Jacuzzi room, something that made him stop in his tracks. He turned his head slowly, and his eyes fell upon a vision of such loveliness that he had to adjust his glasses to make sure it was real. Klee stood before the Jacuzzi wearing nothing but a pair of clean white underpants. His back was to the door, so he didn't see Russell watching him. Russell gazed at the young blond brother who had only recently arrived. He was built so similar to Shep, right down to the brutal scar that marred his perfect back. Like Shep, his body was thin, yet perfectly sculpted, narrowing at the waist with rounded buttocks.

Klee's scar was a darker color than Shep's. If Russell didn't know better, he'd have thought it was fresh. Shep offered little explanations about the brothers, and Russell didn't ask. He pretended to accept Shep's explanation that a Norwegian family had adopted them all, though he knew that this was probably bullshit. He had heard Shep tell four different versions of that same story to other people.

Russell watched Klee test the bubbling water with his fingers. He told himself to move on, to go to his room and commence his video murder rampage. Then Klee stepped out of his underwear, and Russell was grounded where he stood. The skylight lit his pale blond curls as the amazingly naked boy stepped delicately into the tub, lowering himself into the steaming water, his magnificent body disappearing into the bubbles. Klee sighed and leaned his head back, with an arm resting on either side of the tub.

Russell walked into the room and crept quietly about, gazing at Klee's child-like face. His eyes were closed, making him nonetheless beautiful with his long lashes. A light mist of water was forming above his pink lips, and Russell felt a stirring deep within him. Klee was like a sweet, golden version of Shep, only he was pure and untouched by Shep's cynicism. His mouth was even more sensual than Shep's. Russell had seen Klee's eyes, and they were as wide and green. He wondered what it would be like to press his mouth against those lips, to look into those green eyes, as he'd always wanted to do to Shep. Of course this was not Shep, it was Klee.

Russell realized that Shep's cynicism and nastiness was part of what attracted him, but Klee had an innocence that he found almost equally appealing.

Like a man in a trance, Russell moved toward the tub. Klee's green eyes opened suddenly, and he smiled. "Russell!" he said cheerily with his choppy accent. "Won't you join me?"

Russell swallowed hard. He looked back at the open door, knowing that he should go walk through it, and move on down the hall. Instead, he walked quickly over and shut it.

"Yes. I believe I will join you," he said. To hell with Shep. He had consistently treated Russell like so much dog shit. Now, to make matters worse, he was trying to get that whore to come out here and live with them. Well, two could play at that game. Russell placed his glasses on one of the little plant tables, and stripped out of his own clothes.

He stepped into the tub and felt the gooseflesh rise as he lowered himself into the steaming bubbles. Klee had his arms resting back behind his head, his eyes closed again. Russell stared at the beautiful boy, and thought for the first time that Klee was perhaps more beautiful than Shep. He was, quite possibly, the most beautiful creature Russell had ever seen. He was not surprised to find himself fully erect. What he was going to do about it was another story. He studied Klee. Russell wondered how old he was. He certainly looked legal. Could he be a virgin? Doubtful. No one with an ass like that could go untouched for this long.

Russell moved over next to Klee. Klee glanced at him. He did not look at all uneasy by Russell's movement. "Klee, if you don't mind my asking, how old are you?"

"I am older than recorded time," Klee answered quite seriously. Russell broke into laughter at the comment, and Klee laughed in response. His smile was so open and friendly, so unlike Shep's.

"Good answer Klee. How about another question." Russell moved in closer until he was right beside him. Klee did not move away. Either he didn't mind, or was completely unaware of the come-on. "Klee, have you ever been with a woman?" First thing's first. If the kid wasn't gay, well, he'd learned from Shep that conversion was futile.

Klee looked at him, his perfect brow furrowed in confusion. Then he relaxed and nodded. "Yes," he said. "I ate cereal with Kelinda this morning."

Russell smiled. This kid was really naïve. "No, Klee. I'm not talking about eating cereal. What I meant was, have you ever had sex with a woman?"

A flicker of understanding passed over Klee's green eyes, and he nodded. "Oh. The sex. No. I don't do the sex. Margol said that chocolate was better. Shep does the sex. Shep is more human than we are."

Russell slid his hand onto Klee's thigh. "Oh, I don't know, Klee. You can be as human as you want to be."

Klee seemed unfazed by the hand on his thigh. He looked innocently at Russell, and lowered his voice to a whisper. "Shep wants me to become more human," he said, as though it was some big secret. He leaned in close to Russell's ear. "He says I have to learn, but I don't think I know how to yet."

Russell slid closer to Klee, and placed a gentle kiss on his lips. "I can teach you to be more human," he said. He expected Klee to pull away. Klee did not, but he did not seem at all impassioned by the kiss either. Instead he looked quizzically at Russell.

"That was a kiss. Kelinda kisses Joey."

Russell laughed. "Kelinda does a lot more than that to Joey," he said.

"What else does she do?" Klee asked.

Oh, this is too easy, Russell thought. He almost got up and left, but then he thought of Shep's comment. *Get away from me you fucking faggot!* Russell moved his hand up Klee's thigh and slid his fingers onto the soft flesh of his uncircumcised penis. He began to fondle him gently. To his surprise and delight, Klee immediately began to stiffen under his touch. He didn't seem accustomed to the sensation. He gasped and a look of panic fell over his face. Was it possible that Klee had never been touched? It was beginning to look that way. "What is this?" Klee said, panting. "What do you do to me?"

"I'm showing you how to be more human," Russell said. He ran his free hand through Klee's platinum curls, a gesture he had so longed to do to Shep. On one hand, Russell felt that he was doing something wrong. Klee seemed so genuinely innocent. But this was no child, after all. They were two consenting adults. Even if this was a sexual awakening, it was Klee's choice.

"Do you like it?" Russell asked, as he made his movements more rhythmic.

Klee gasped again. "No. Yes. I do not know. Is this human?"

"Yes," Russell whispered in his ear, taking in the fragrant aroma of his hair. "I can do something for you Klee. Something that's even better than this. But you have to come to my room, and you can't tell Shep about it."

Klee pushed Russell's hand away then. "That is not possible," Klee said. "I have to tell Shep everything."

Russell felt a panic arise in his gut. Would Klee tell Shep about this? "Klee, you can't tell Shepherd. Don't you see? Shep will be angry if he knows that I'm the one who taught you. Do you understand?"

Klee stared at Russell in confusion. He shook his head. "No, Russell.

You must never lie to Shepherd."

"We're not lying, Klee. We're just not volunteering the information. Do you see the difference?"

Before Klee could answer, the door swung inward and Patrick Obrien came storming into the room. Russell quickly moved away from Klee. Patrick glared at Russell. Russell had thought that perhaps he didn't like Patrick, but now he was sure of it. The big Irish thug had but two expressions. He either looked pissed off, or confused. Right now he looked pissed off. Russell looked up at his angry blue eyes, and wished that Patrick were not so big. He walked over to the tub and grabbed Russell by the arm, pulling him out of the tub and tossing him onto the floor. "Get the fuck away from him, Russell!" he said.

Russell struggled to pull on his discarded underwear. "Obrien, it's not what you think."

Patrick loomed over him like a big red ball of fury. The veins in his well-formed biceps bulged. "It's not what I think, Russell? I'll tell you what I think. I think it's time you got a boyfriend, and stopped wasting your time making passes at people who don't want you."

"How do you know who wants me and who doesn't?" Russell said.

"Stay the fuck away from him!" Patrick said, pointing one muscular arm toward Klee, who sat huddled in the tub looking frightened and slightly ashamed.

"Why?" Russell demanded, his anger taking over his fear. "Because I'm gay? Is that it? Are you a homophobic, Obrien?"

"Oh please. Don't pull that shit on me. This isn't about sexual orientation and you know it. If it were Kelinda in that tub groping him, I'd have done the same thing to her. He doesn't understand this!" Patrick said, pointing to Russell's scantily clad body. "A moron could see that he's innocent, and you're no moron, Russell!"

Russell was about to argue, then thought better of it. Klee's innocence was startlingly obvious, he realized now, and he'd been wrong to pursue him. However, Obrien was still all red and scary looking, so Russell went another route. "I never touched him! Klee, tell him. I never touched you, right?"

Patrick went and knelt down next to Klee. Klee looked terrified. "It's all right Klee. No one is mad at you. Just tell me. Did Russell touch you?"

Klee glanced over at Russell, who had taken the opportunity to replace his glasses and begin pulling on his pants. Patrick gave Russell a warning stare and he turned away. "Don't look at Russell, Klee. Look at me. Did he touch you or not?"

Klee glanced once more at Russell, then back at Patrick. "No Patrick. He did not touch me."

"Well it's a good thing." Patrick glared back at Russell. "Stay away from him Russell, or you'll have to answer to me." Russell grabbed his shirt and sprinted out of the room.

After Russell and Patrick had gone, Klee sat alone in the tub. He was afraid to get up. His penis was swollen and filled with a most unusual aching. It hurt, but it felt good. He wanted it to stop, but he wanted it to continue. There was a slight dizziness in his head. He waited several minutes and finally the swelling went down. He hurried and got dressed. He had to join the others out in the field. He hoped that Shep would not try to read his thoughts today.

It was midnight. Russell sat in front of the glowing computer screen playing a Star Trek simulation game. He'd been in his room for hours, not wanting to come across Shep, for fear that he would see in his eyes what he had done and surely torture him to death. He had helped out in the fields all day, and was relieved as hell to discover that Patrick had opted not to tell Shep about finding him in the tub with Klee. He was so grateful, that after dinner he had approached Obrien, and thanked him for his candor. Patrick had responded by threatening to remove Russell's kneecaps if he ever went near Klee again. Having grown rather attached to his kneecaps, Russell agreed.

There was a soft tap at his door. Russell's stomach dropped. The knock came again. Who would be knocking on his door at midnight? He was sure that Obrien had changed his mind and ratted him out. It was probably Shepherd at the door, come to kill him in many intricate fashions.

Russell opened the door a crack. Klee stood there, wide-eyed in a pair of faded blue jeans with no shirt or shoes. His fair skin had acquired a golden color from the day's field work. Russell's breath caught in his throat as he stared at this perfect creature in front of him. God was surely tempting him. And it was unfair. He really liked his kneecaps. "Klee, what are you doing here? Go on. Take off. You have to get out of here!" Russell waved his hand to shoo him away.

Klee glared at him, his eyes set in emerald rage. He was shaking.

"Klee, what is it? What's wrong?"

Klee shoved him and Russell stumbled backward. Klee shut the door behind him and pointed a shaky finger at him. "You did this to me!" he hissed.

Russell shook his head, frightened by the desperate look in the usually placid boyish face. "Klee, what are you talking about?"

Klee reached down and unzipped his soft faded jeans. He was not wearing any underwear, and his erection was enormous. Russell stared, unable to speak. "You did this to me!" Klee said again. "Now it keeps happening!"

Russell didn't know what to say. "I'm sorry Klee."

"Fix it!" Klee demanded.

"Huh?"

"Fix it Russell. You put it there, now you make it go away!"

Russell looked at the ceiling and raised his hands up as if to God. "Give me a break here Lord! This is not a fair test!"

Klee gave him an odd look. "The vessel is not listening to you," he said. Russell thought it was an odd thing to say, but he forgot it as soon as his eyes fell upon Klee again, with his beautiful tan body. Even the small brush of pubic hair was blond. He stood before Russell with his jeans undone, a creature of such sensual beauty that it hurt to look at him. And he was asking Russell to help him remove his erection.

Then he thought about Obrien, and Shep. He thought about his kneecaps. "Are you going to tell Shep if I help you?"

Klee shook his head. "No. I won't tell anyone. Just do it." His voice sounded older suddenly, more mature, or perhaps it was just what Russell wanted to hear.

He locked the door and threw Klee down on the bed, covering his mouth with his own. He went to work on his body, trailing down his chest, his stomach, his ribs, lingering on his hips, circling the sharp bone with his tongue. Klee began to make sounds, and they grew louder until Russell had to cover Klee's mouth with his hand. Klee ejaculated almost immediately after Russell slid him into his mouth. He bit down on Russell's hand hard enough to leave marks, but Russell didn't mind. The pain was delicious. He normally did not swallow, but this was different. He wanted every minute part of this amazing creature. He let the hot liquid slide down his throat. Klee bit down on his hand even harder. Without even touching himself, Russell ejaculated into the shorts he wore, releasing his own ecstasy as he swallowed Klee's.

Moments later, Russell sat on the edge of the bed trying to shake a dizzy spell. His glasses had fallen to the floor in the throes of passion. He picked them up and walked across the room to place them on his dresser. On his way back, another dizzy spell hit him and he had to grab the bed for support. He lowered himself into a sitting position, and looked at Klee, who lay with his eye's closed, breathing more slowly now. Russell glanced at the tooth marks on the side of his hand and smiled. "So, was that better than chocolate?"

Before Klee could answer, Russell heard a sound from somewhere down the hall. He panicked. "Get up Klee. Get dressed. You have to get out of here." Klee didn't argue. He seemed barely aware of Russell as he pulled his jeans on and zipped them up. Without even a glance back, he was out the door and gone. Russell stared at the closed door, frowning. "Well, I know I'm not the love of his life, but he could have at least said good bye."

He lay back on the bed, woozy and disoriented. "I feel funny," he said to the empty room. He closed his eyes and fell asleep.

Russell was surprised when he awoke to see the next day's light coming in through the blinds, accompanied by a chirping chorus of birds. He had slept right through the night. He looked down at himself. He was still in his shorts from the previous night. He must have been out cold the moment Klee left the room. He wondered for a moment if he'd dreamed the whole thing, then he felt the sticky residue beneath his shorts. "Christ!" he said, pulling his shorts back, disgusted with himself. "I've never been too tired to change before bed."

He sat up and looked around the room. His heart pounded as uneasiness brewed inside him. Something was different here. He rubbed his eyes and gave his head a quick shake. He couldn't quite place it. Everything in the room looked strange. He stared at the lamp in the corner of the room, then at the chair, and the objects on the desk. Everything looked smaller somehow, more defined. What the hell was going on?

He glanced over at the dresser where his glasses sat. Something dawned on him as he looked to the left of the discarded glasses at the box of nasal spray he'd left out. He stared. He could read every tiny word printed on that box. He gasped. The things in the room weren't smaller; he was just seeing them clearly. Without his glasses. But that was impossible. He was nearly legally blind without his glasses. But here he was, reading the tiny letters on the small green and white box on the other side of the room. It couldn't be.

He closed his eyes tightly for several seconds, and then looked across the room at the dresser again. He saw his glasses. Fearfully, he let his gaze slide toward the tiny box of nasal spray and tried to read the words printed on it. *Do not operate heavy machinery while taking this product. Consult a physician if symptoms persist beyond five days.* Russell gasped. "Holy shit," he said. "I can see."

Chapter Thirty-Eight

Patrick took the boat over to Boston, relishing in the freedom of the surrounding ocean and open sky. It felt like heaven. He'd never imagined how claustrophobic he could feel in a place as big as the Forest Bluffs property. Regardless of its spaciousness, the subtle madness imminent within Joey's little coven was suffocating. The rusty old ferry was a welcome change.

He was not surprised when he saw the wisps of curly black hair peeking out from behind a newspaper on the other side of the boat. It was Allisto, using the ever so handy 'hide behind the paper' tactic. Patrick grinned. Shep obviously did not trust him yet, despite his show of indifference regarding Patrick's "job" in the city once a week. Patrick studied the figure behind the newspaper. He was wearing a pair of Shep's baggy jeans, and the long gray cotton jacket that Patrick had seen him in that first time on the train. Patrick decided it was time to have a little fun with Shep's incompetent surveillance team.

He bought two coffees at the snack counter and went and sat down right next to his would-be spy. Allisto dropped the paper slowly, and turned to see Patrick sitting directly beside him. Allisto's eyes were a darker color than the other brothers', or perhaps it was the contrast of his black hair that made them appear a deeper emerald green. They were pretty, the way dangerous toxic waste floating atop a calm river can be pretty. "I got you a coffee Allisto. It's chocolate mocha, your favorite." He offered the Styrofoam cup to Allisto, who reluctantly took it, looking like a trapped rat.

"Thank you," he said, his eyes darting around the moving boat as though looking for a means of escape.

"So, Allisto, do you have business in the city today?" Patrick asked pleasantly.

Allisto shifted on his bench seat. Patrick could almost hear his inhuman brain straining to formulate a lie. "Yes. Yes. I um, yes. I need to collect some supplies for Shepherd."

"Great!" Patrick said. "You could come down to my office this afternoon. We can have lunch together!" Patrick patted Allisto's shoulder affectionately. Allisto looked panicked. He shook his head.

"No. I am sorry, Obrien. That is not possible. I need to go right home after I get the...supplies."

Patrick nodded. "Oh. I see. You're a busy man, Allisto. I'll leave you to your newspaper."

"Thank you," Allisto said, sounding a little too relieved.

Patrick stood and made as if to leave, then turned around again. "Oh,

Allisto, just one more thing. You can tell Shepherd that if he has me followed again, I will leave Forest Bluffs and I will never come back. Enjoy your day." He walked off whistling, leaving Allisto to stare dumbly after him.

The glass doors read 'Baytown Financial Consulting'. Patrick walked through them and said hello to his phony receptionist, as Agent Litner had instructed. He walked down a narrow hallway and stepped into his phony office, closing the door behind him. Once inside, he found the lever that moved the file cabinet, revealing the hidden elevator. The double doors opened, and he stepped inside. He felt silly. Patrick Obrien, secret agent man. Oh well. Who was he to question Litner's tactics? The man was a professional paranoid.

The elevator stopped and the doors opened to a room where Agent Litner sat at a desk with Robin perched in a chair across from him. Robin ran to Patrick. She was wearing a short black sundress that accentuated her lovely blond hair. He held her as she clung to him. "We weren't sure if you'd be here," she said. He gave Robin a passionate kiss. He wanted to send Litner out of the room and throw her down on the desk. Instead, he withdrew from the kiss and took the other chair in front of the desk.

Litner looked at him impatiently. "Tell me you have samples for me," he said.

Patrick shook his head. "I couldn't get near the crops alone. They have the entire field under armed guard during the day. I even tried to get in at night, but they have electric fences set up, and God knows what other precautions that I haven't discovered yet."

Agent Litner looked worried. He tapped his pen on his temple. "Damn. We have to get our hands on that stuff. Do you think you can work something out?"

Patrick shrugged. "I'll find a way. I don't want to stay out there any longer than I have to. Oh, and by the way, I'm fine. Thanks for asking."

Litner's lips curled into a very slight smile. "I'm sorry Patrick. There's been a lot going on."

"Fill me in," Patrick said.

Litner did. He told him about the meeting with Father Bello, and let him listen to the tape. Patrick's ruddy cheeks went pale at the references to Zirub and the Cripulet. Litner also told him about his discoveries regarding Dr. Lichtenstein, and his suspicions that Shepherd was blackmailing the old man in order to get him to perform surgical tasks for him. Litner never once said the word wings. He kept it rational, like it was any other investigation. Patrick was silently grateful for that. Litner had a way of making things feel just a bit less nightmarish, as though the bizarre facts of this case were just so much triviality for the United States government.

Litner also told Patrick about Shep's phone calls to Robin, which sent a deep cold rage through him. It was an unfamiliar emotion. He was used to being jealous of Joey, not Shep. When all was said and done, Litner looked Patrick in the eye and said, "So, that's what's been happening here. How are you doing out there, really Patrick?"

Patrick grabbed Robin's hand. "So far I'm safe, and they've been treating me like part of the crew, though they still seem slightly suspicious of me. I plan to get those crop samples this week Litner, and I'm not saying that to please you. I want out of that God-forsaken funny farm."

"Do you really think you'll be able to pull it off?" Litner asked hopefully.

Patrick thought about it for a moment then nodded. "The crops are guarded, but they're not impenetrable. Shep and Joey may be a tad suspicious of me, but the followers aren't. They think I'm terribly important. After all, I live in the big house."

Litner scowled. "The big house?"

Patrick tried to explain the hierarchical madness that was the Forest Bluffs church. "You see, Joey is treated as a god, and the other occupants of the house are demi-gods. This includes Shepherd, Russell, Kelinda and of course the brothers. And now apparently I've been included in this little court. I was introduced to the crowd during a sermon last week. I guess it was my coming out party."

"Kelinda is one of these revered people as well?" Robin asked, looking surprised.

Patrick laughed a humorless sound. "Oh yeah. She's like the fucking Queen of Sheba out there."

Robin shook her head. "She used to be so practical. I still can't believe she's involved with this madness. It's like she's completely changed."

"Oh, you have no idea," Patrick said, thinking of the little blood and wine party he'd witnessed.

Litner's pen tapping had moved from his temple to the top of his desk. The speed of the tapping seemed to increase with his anxiety level. "Who is in charge out there? Is it Joey Duvaine?"

"No. Joey is just the front man, Shep is the one running things. Joey is the great and powerful Wizard of Oz, but Shep is definitely the man behind the curtain."

"I knew it!" Robin said.

Patrick looked at her. "I didn't say Joey was innocent, Robin. He may not be running the show, but he is the star player."

Robin looked disappointed. "So, did you see the new guy? The one from the cave?" she asked, changing the subject.

Patrick rolled his eyes. "Oh, yes. I saw the new guy all right. His name is Klee and he's very sweet. The kid's back was still bleeding. I could see it oozing through his shirt for Christ sakes."

Litner actually shuddered. "Is there anything else I should know before we move on to new information?" he asked.

Patrick thought. So much had happened in the past week. "Oh, as you know, they do realize that Juris is missing, and Shep's not happy about it. He told me that Juris was on my watch when he disappeared. I played dumb, but they're not going to stop looking for him. It's one of the things they are most adamant about. All five brothers need to be together. Nobody gets left behind. They talk like that all the time. It's kind of touching, in a creepy dysfunctional family sort of way."

"Juris has been moved to a classified location. It was part of the deal we made with him for not snapping Copie's neck." Litner paused, shaking his head. "I swear that kid Copie has nine lives. Anyway, the odds of them finding Juris is unlikely, but we still have to move fast. Get me those samples, Obrien. I don't care if you have to dance an Irish jig and sing Praise the Lord. Just get the samples, and get out of there."

"I'll have them by next week's meeting. I assure you. So what's this new information you have?"

Agent Litner's dark blue eyes flickered with a smile as he pulled an orange folder out of his desk drawer and placed it in front of him. "I have a surprise for the two of you." Litner paused, and leaned across the desk. "I found Wesley J. Shepherd," he said.

"What?" Robin and Patrick said the word simultaneously. Patrick had nearly forgotten about the name the old doctor wrote on the dirt floor of the cave before the life drained out of him. Litner looked extremely pleased with himself, like the only kid in class who had the answer to a complicated math problem.

"Who is he?" Patrick demanded. "Is he connected to Shep somehow? Is he connected to the doctor? Is he..."

Agent Litner held a hand up for patience. "Slow down. For starters, Wesley Jackson Shepherd is a man who does not want to be found. I consider myself damn good at finding people, and I had a bitch of a time tracking him. I came up with a lot of Wesley Shepherds that just weren't the right one. Our Wesley has changed his name seven times in the past thirty years. He now goes by the name Jonathan Jones."

"How inventive," Patrick said. "So how did you determine that this particular Wesley is the one we're looking for?"

Litner stared at Patrick and Robin. "Because this particular Wesley Jackson Shepherd is the surviving son of a couple that was killed in a cave collapse at Pearl Chasm fifty-two years ago."

He let them absorb the information. "Wow," Patrick said softly. "You are good, Litner."

Litner remained stone-faced, but his pen tapping had stopped and his lip had stopped twitching. He was back in control.

"So there's our connection to Pearl Chasm," Robin said, "But what do we have besides the last name that connects him to Shep, or the dead doctor for that matter?"

The agent grinned confidently. "Well, I'm not sure about the doctor, but I believe I know where our old buddy Zirub got his fake name from. It was Wesley's parents, the ones that died in the cave." Litner pulled a photocopy of a newspaper article from the orange folder and handed it to them. "Here is an article about the accident. Look at the first names of the deceased."

Patrick and Robin scanned the article.

A young Massachusetts couple died on Saturday after a cave collapsed at the popular Pearl Chasm Park in Western Massachusetts, leaving orphaned their only child, ten-year-old Wesley. The recreational park has been closed indefinitely pending an evaluation of the caves and hiking trails. Services for Melvin and Eugenia Shepherd will be held on Wednesday.

Robin gasped. Patrick looked up at Agent Litner. "Do those names sound familiar?" Litner asked.

Patrick nodded. "Melvin and Eugenia Shepherd. Melvin Eugene Shepherd. I don't suppose this is a coincidence."

"There are too many coincidences," Litner said. "This is our man. Our Shep knows this Wesley character somehow."

Robin shook her head. "Why would Zirub take this couple's names as his own? What's the connection, Agent Litner?"

Litner drummed his hands on the desk. "I don't know. Why don't we ask

Wesley J. Shepherd?"

Robin and Patrick stared across the desk. "You mean you actually know where he is?" Patrick asked.

"That's the best part," Litner said. "Wesley J. Shepherd, also known as Jonathan Jones is alive and well, and living in Layton, New Hampshire."

"Are you shitting me? That's only—"

"An hour away," Litner said. "Wesley was ten years old when his parents died, and that was fifty two years ago. That would make him sixty-two years old now. I say we pay the man a visit."

Patrick looked at Robin and then back at Litner. "Today?"

"Yes, today. You don't have to catch the boat back to Forest Bluffs until five o'clock. We have plenty of time to make the drive, ask the man some questions, and have you back in time to catch the boat. What do you say?"

Patrick smiled. "I say you're a genius, Agent Litner."

"Well, I do what I can. Did anyone follow you today?"

Patrick remembered Allisto then, and his heart sank. "Yes. Allisto followed me. I'm sure he's lurking right outside the building somewhere."

Agent Litner grinned. "I figured as much." He picked up the receiver of the black phone on his desk. "Yeah, it's me. Could you send Frankie in now? Thanks." Litner hung up the phone and leaned back in his chair, linking his hands behind his head.

Patrick raised an eyebrow. "Frankie? Who the hell is Frankie?"

"You'll see."

The door opened and a large man walked through it. He was about six foot three, muscular with short wavy reddish blond hair. His physical appearance was nearly identical to Patrick's. Robin laughed. "Holy cow! Patrick it's you!"

Patrick stared in disbelief at this man who looked more like him than his own brother. Frankie smiled at him. "You must be Patrick."

Patrick stood up and shook the man's hand. "Frankie, I presume?"

The big man looked to Litner for instructions. Agent Litner stood and walked out from behind his desk. "Robin and I will step out for a moment. I want the two of you to change clothes. We're going to send Frankie out the front doors in the hopes that Allisto will take the bait and follow him. Make it quick. Time is a luxury we don't have today."

"I'd stay and watch the two of you change, but it would just be too weird," Robin joked.

Robin and Litner left the room. Once they were gone, Patrick and Frankie changed clothes wordlessly. Patrick wondered if Frankie worked for the FBI. He was in far better shape than Patrick was. Frankie's stomach was a flat rippling mass of toned abdominal muscles. Patrick's own gut needed some work. He hadn't exactly had time to get to the gym lately.

Minutes later, Patrick, Robin and Agent Litner watched a television monitor that showed a surveillance camera's view of the front steps of the building and the surrounding street. They watched as Frankie, dressed now in Patrick's Boston Celtics tee shirt and jeans, trotted casually down the front steps and walked off down the city sidewalk. Thirty seconds later, Allisto's head of black curls appeared from behind a magazine stand, and he shuffled down the street after Frankie. Litner nodded his satisfaction as he watched Allisto trail the phony Patrick. "These brothers may be shrouded in the mysteries of another world, but in this world, they're predictable as hell."

They were getting close to something. Patrick felt it like maniacal butter-flies doing a frenzied ballet in his stomach. His temples tingled. He was no longer in denial about his perceptions. He knew that his senses had been heightened somehow with the transmission of Joey's blood. He accepted it. It was amazing the things he'd been willing to accept since seeing a man pulled through a solid rock wall. Extra sensory perception was trivial by compari-son.

Agent Litner sat in the driver's seat, with Patrick beside him and Robin in the back. Litner appeared to be sensing something as well. The gold pen was out, and the temple beating was in full swing, growing more rapid as they passed each sign that read "Layton". Robin leaned forward between the two front seats of the car and stared at Litner. Litner glanced at her quickly then returned his eyes to the road. "What is it Robin?" he asked impatiently.

"Would you stop that pen tapping please? Christ, Litner! You're going to give yourself a brain hemorrhage."

Litner gave her a befuddled glance. "What do you mean?"

"What do I mean? You're constantly beating yourself on the side of the head with that pen. It's making me nuts!"

Litner stopped tapping and examined the pen curiously. "Huh. I never noticed."

Patrick turned to Litner. "You never noticed that you were maiming your-self with your pen every time you got anxious?"

"I was not aware." He looked at Patrick out of the side of his eyes. "I really do that?"

Patrick pointed to Litner's temple where a red splotch was already form-ing. "It's right here, and it's all the time."

Litner glanced in the rearview mirror. He rubbed the spot on his temple. "Well. That explains why I'm always sore there."

Patrick looked back at Robin who sat smirking in the rear of the car. "He's a genius, you know," Patrick said.

Robin nodded. "I'm aware."

The landscape became more rural and the trees crowded around them until there was only a narrow winding road surrounded by plush forest. They passed a metal sign that read ENTERING LAYTON. The last semblance of the civilized world disappeared when the asphalt of the road they were driving on gave way to gravel that kicked up under the tires, making pinging sounds as it hit the metal. The day darkened around them as the forest shrouded the land from the sunlight. "Are we still going the right way?" Patrick asked, peer-ing out his window at the nothing.

"This leads to the road that Jonathan Jones lives on," Litner answered.

Robin rolled down her window and a pine-scented breeze filled the ve-hicle. "Wow," she said, taking in a deep breath. "This is amazing. It's hard to believe we're only an hour from Boston."

Litner turned the big black car left onto an even narrower gravel road that went into a steep climb. The car's engine hummed up an octave as it climbed the darkened road. They passed at least six signs that told them they were on a private way, and that trespassers would be prosecuted. The trees overhead were so tall that they bowed over, forming a canopy above the road. At the top of the hill, the road leveled out, then it just stopped, becoming a small clearing that led to a driveway.

At the end of the driveway was a picturesque log cabin, sized more like a permanent home. Litner eased the car up the driveway and killed the engine. The sounds of birds and other woodland creatures bombarded them, mingling with a soothing trickling sound made by a quietly running stream that separated the side yard from the woods.

A large golden retriever came bounding toward the car to greet them with teeth bared and an alarmed, incessant bark. Robin rolled her window up quickly. Patrick was still looking at the surrounding landscape. "Wow. This guy is a real loner. There is absolutely nothing up here."

"Nothing but this dog that looks like it's going to eat us," Robin said. The dog had jumped up onto the side of the car and was barking directly at Robin through her closed window.

"What is he hiding from up here?" Patrick asked.

Agent Litner looked at him pointedly. "You should never go into a situation with pre-conceived notions. It alters your judgment. If you assume that this man we're about to meet is hiding something, then you're going to look for things that may not be there. For all we know, this guy knows absolutely nothing about Shep."

"Hey, is anyone else worried about this dog?" Robin asked, leaning back from the window. "Old Yeller here doesn't seem happy to see us."

Agent Litner looked back at the dog with vague interest. He got out of the car and shut the door. Robin and Patrick stayed in their seats, watching. The dog immediately ran around the car and went at Litner, barking furiously at him with its snout wrinkled. Litner looked down at the dog. "Stop it," he said with authority. The dog's nose smoothed and the barking ceased. It whimpered once then turned and slinked away toward the side yard.

Patrick and Robin exchanged an astonished stare. Robin shook her head. "Government freak," she whispered.

Agent Litner peered through the car windows at them. "Are you guys coming?"

They made their way up a flagstone walkway that led to the front door of the log home. Somewhere a woodpecker hammered away. Squirrels made daring jumps across the endless treetops that surrounded the solitary house. Litner led the way with Patrick and Robin trailing nervously behind, both holding back their steps just a bit. No one knew what they would find here. If it had something to do with Shep's past, Patrick was betting it would be something weird.

Agent Litner gave three hard raps on the wooden door. The golden retriever watched them from the side of a small tool shed several yards away. The dog's ears perked up when Litner knocked, but he stayed where he was. The door swung inward slowly. A cautious-looking man of about twenty-one eyed them warily. He had short yellow hair with fringy bangs, pale blue eyes and flawless skin. His eyes were accentuated by the baby blue short-sleeved button down he wore with a pair of neat tan shorts. The first thing Patrick thought was that the kid had eyes like Joey's, so light blue that they were almost white.

"May I help you?" he asked. His voice was cordial, cultured sounding.

"We're sorry to intrude on you like this," Litner said with a smile. "We're looking for a Jonathan Jones. Does he live here?"

Patrick noticed for the first time that Litner was not wearing his usual black suit. He had given it over for a pair of brown dress slacks and a white polo shirt. Litner was acting. Now he'd seen everything.

"Jonathan Jones is my father," the kid said politely. "He is here, but I'm afraid he's quite ill. May I ask what this is about?"

"I am terribly sorry," Litner said. "Nobody told us your father was ill. My name is Morgan, Roger Morgan. These are my associates, Patrick and Robin. We're from the Massachusetts Historical Society. We just wanted to ask your father a few questions for a research project we're doing. May we come in for a moment? We've driven quite a long way, and I'm afraid the lady has to use the bathroom."

The yellow haired boy looked over Litner's shoulder at Robin and Patrick. He smiled sheepishly, but Patrick saw something in his placid eyes. He had the look of a cornered animal. He was terrified of something. Of them? "Sure. Sure, come on in. You'll have to forgive me if I seemed a bit rude. You see we don't get many visitors up here, and the knock on the door took me by surprise."

"Not at all," Litner said. Patrick wanted to laugh at all the cordiality going on, none of it genuine.

They followed the young man inside onto a wide stone foyer. The house was deceivingly small looking on the outside. Inside, it was enormous. There was no second floor, and the ceilings were high, cathedral style. The place had a huge stone fireplace and wooded beams that ran midway along every wall. Plastic duck decoys decorated the mantle of the fireplace, with lots of pictures of hunting dogs and deer sipping at streams. There was only one thing that didn't match the country motif, and Patrick noticed it immediately. There were multiple crucifixes of all shapes and sizes strung along the walls in various spots. Patrick saw Robin do a double take at them. Many people have a few religious items on their walls, but this was like a shrine. Patrick did a quick count. There were eight crucifixes on one wall.

"It's just down the hall to the left," the kid said to Robin.

"Excuse me?" Robin said.

"Didn't you have to use the rest room?"

"Oh, yeah. Thanks."

As Robin passed, the kid offered her his hand. "I'm Jon Jr. by the way. Nice to meet you." Robin shook it, then proceeded down the hallway. Patrick mused again about the cordiality with which the kid spoke. It was like meeting Richey Rich in the flesh. Jon Jr. offered his hand to Agent Litner, and then to Patrick. His handshake was firm and his smile was warm, but he still looked spooked. Robin returned and Jon led them into a large open sitting room with another fireplace. A genuine bear skin rug lay on the floor like a giant piece of road kill.

Jon urged them all to sit down. There were more crucifixes on the wall in this room. This time Patrick saw Litner noticing them in his own quiet way. "I'm afraid my father has cancer of the pancreas," Jon announced suddenly.

"I'm so sorry," Litner said humbly.

Jon nodded. "Thank you. He is dying. I've been up here caring for him for months now. Once the doctors told him that there was no hope for recovery, he wanted to leave the hospital immediately. I knew he'd want to die up here. He loves this place."

"It's a beautiful place," Robin said.

"Thank you."

No one spoke for several seconds. Jon looked awkwardly at them as he sat with one buttock leaned on the arm of a chair, drumming his fingers on his thigh. "So, Mr. uh, Morgan is it?"

"Roger Morgan," Litner said, and flashed another happy guy smile.

"Perhaps you should tell me what this is about. My father may be too weak to speak with you. He has good days and bad days. I would be happy to answer whatever questions I can for you. Why is the historical society interested in my father?"

Patrick's eyes were drawn to a closed door just outside the room they were in. Was Wesley J. Shepherd, a.k.a. Jonathan Jones in there, withering away like an autumn flower? He pictured a sixty-two year old man lying in a bed, shrunken by the cancer that conquered his body.

"I know this must be a terrible time for you, Jon, and I appreciate your cooperation," Litner said. "I'll get right to the point. We're doing a historical piece for a New England news program about natural caves in the area, and Pearl Chasm in particular."

The young man nodded casually, but his face turned the color of chalk. "I see," he said in a whisper.

Litner pretended not to notice the kid's sudden discomfort. "Tell me, Jon. Is your father's birth name not in fact Wesley Jackson Shepherd?"

Jon flinched. He took a breath, trying to make it casual. After another awkward silence, Jon forced a strained smile. "Well. You are a resourceful bunch, now aren't you? The answer to your question is yes. My father was indeed born Wesley Jackson Shepherd. How did you know that?"

Litner pressed on, ignoring the question. "Is your father also the same Wesley J. Shepherd, only child of Melvin and Eugenia Shepherd, who lost their lives in a caving accident at Pearl Chasm fifty-two years ago this fall?"

Jon's face went stiff. He wrung his hands and let out a nervous laugh as he hopped of the chair. "Well. I'll be damned. You *are* a resourceful bunch. Your talents are wasted on the historical society, Mr. Morgan."

"Thank you," Litner said.

"You see, the thing is Roger, that what you are referring to is a deeply personal account," the boy said. "I'll have to check with my father to see if he is feeling well enough to speak with you himself. You see, I'm not sure that he would be comfortable with my discussing this particular topic with you."

"We don't want to be any trouble," Agent Litner said with a look of compassion.

"Oh don't worry, Mr. Morgan. My father is a very spirited man, even now. If he doesn't want to talk with you, he will plainly tell me so. But, after all, it doesn't hurt to ask. You did drive all the way from...where are you from?"

"Boston," Litner said.

"Ah, yes. Boston. If you'll all just wait here, I'll go in and check on dad. Excuse me."

Jon left the room. Patrick watched him walk through the closed door just outside the sitting room and shut the door behind him.

"He's weird!" Robin whispered.

"What do you mean?" Patrick asked. "He's very handsome. Not that that's your type."

She gave him a look. "I don't mean his face. Did you see what he was wearing? Who wears clothes that fussy just to hang around the house? Not to mention those shorts are so out of style. Nobody wears pleats anymore."

"Well, we can't all be as stylish as you Robin." Patrick smiled as he looked down at her short black sundress. She looked lovely, but she did not look like she worked for the Massachusetts Historical Society.

"Yeah, well maybe if Mr. Mysterious over here had told us what our mission for the day was, I would have dressed the part," she said, pointing a thumb toward Agent Litner. "Which reminds me. How come Patrick and I didn't get fake names, ROGER?"

Agent Litner was staring at the closed bedroom door. He cocked an eyebrow at Patrick. "How long has he been in there?" He walked toward the closed bedroom door, then stopped, listening. Robin and Patrick turned toward the door as well as a sharp scraping sound, like a window being opened echoed from somewhere inside the room.

"Do you think the old man will talk to us?" Patrick asked. Agent Litner didn't answer. He was scowling at the closed door. His gold pen was out and he was tapping it against his temple with his head cocked to one side.

Robin looked at Patrick. "Oh-oh. Litner's thinking again. What's wrong Litner?"

He continued to stare at the closed door, frowning. "I don't know. Maybe nothing." He walked up to the door and tapped on it. "Jon?" he called out. He was answered with silence. He tapped his knuckles on the door again, a little harder this time. "Jon, it's Roger. Is everything all right?"

No response. Litner looked back at Patrick and Robin. Patrick shrugged. Litner knocked a third time, with his full fist this time. "Jon, do you need some help in there?" Again, there was no answer. Agent Litner turned the knob, finding it locked. He jiggled it a few times, then pushed his weight against it in a quick, solid motion, and the door swung inward. Litner disappeared into the room. Patrick and Robin stood by the couch, watching with matching expressions of confusion. Then Agent Litner's voice called out from the room. "Son of a Bitch!"

Patrick and Robin sprinted to the room. It was a quaint, country style bedroom. The bed was made up with multi-patchwork quilts and ruffled pillow shams. But the bed was empty, as was the room. Litner stood in front of an open window looking out into the stretch of yard in the back of the house, which led into the thick woods. "He took off," Litner said. "He went through the window."

"Who?" Patrick asked. "The old man?"

Litner lifted his leg, hoisting himself over the window ledge. "There is no old man," he said, and dropped out of the window onto the grass.

Patrick and Robin went to the window in time to see Litner sprinting off into the woods. "What the hell is going on?" Robin asked.

Patrick shook his head. "You've got me."

They both leaned over the windowsill, straining their eyes to see into the woods where Agent Litner had disappeared. A moment later someone screamed. It was a cry of pain, and it sounded like the young man Jon's voice. Robin and Patrick looked at each other. "Should I go help Litner?" Patrick asked.

"No! We don't know who this Jon guy is. He could be a serial killer!"

"A serial killer wearing Ralph Lauren?"

"They don't all look like Manson, Patrick. Besides, Litner knows what he's doing. Need I remind you that you are an accountant, not a Federal Agent?"

"Sure. Rub it in. Hey! I see them!"

Agent Litner's snow white hair and Jon's wispy yellow head were easy to spot coming out from a clearing in the woods. Jon had one arm slung over

Litner's shoulder, favoring his right leg. Patrick ran out of the bedroom in search of a back door. Robin followed. They found a back door and sprinted to where Litner was half-carrying the young man across the lawn. Jon was grimacing, his handsome young face twisted in pain. "What did you do to him?" Robin asked Agent Litner.

"I didn't do anything to him. He tripped over a log while trying to outrun me."

The blond man grunted. "I think I sprained my ankle," he said in a breathy voice.

"Let's get you inside," Litner said. "Patrick, help me out here."

Patrick grabbed Jon's other arm and they carried him back into the house. They set him down on his leather couch. Litner propped his leg up onto a pillow and began examining the ankle, which was already swollen and beginning to turn colors. "This is going to need some ice. Robin, could you get some ice?" Litner said.

"No, Robin. Do not get me any ice," Jon said sharply. He glared at the three of them now, all pretense of pleasantry gone from his face. "Who are you people?" His face showed more fear than anger. His pale blue eyes darted from Litner, to Patrick, to Robin, then back again.

"Why did you run like that?" Patrick asked.

Jon hoisted himself up into a sitting position. "I don't have to answer that. I don't have to answer anything! This is my house! You're not from the historical society. Who are you people, and what do you really want?"

Patrick felt nervousness rise inside of him. Litner remained calm. "Where is your father?" he asked.

"My father is dead," he said with hostility.

Litner shook his head, taking the pen out from behind his ear. "He is not dead," Litner said calmly. "No death certificate has been registered for Wesley Jackson Shepherd, or any of his other chosen names."

Jon slid backward a bit, wincing as his foot fell off of the pillow. "How the hell would you know? If I say my father is dead, then he is dead. I'd like you all to leave now."

"If he is dead, then why did you say he was in the other room?" Litner asked. The agent had a knack for ignoring the statements he didn't choose to address, like Jon's ordering them out.

Jon was on the very edge of the couch now, leaning back as though Litner would be poisonous to the touch.

"Look," he said, "tell me what you people want, or get the hell out of my house. I am a private citizen. You are trespassing. I'm going to call the police."

"You don't have a telephone," Litner said. Jon's eyes widened, and there was no mistaking the fear in them.

"Okay. That's it. Get out."

Patrick's panic escalated as Jon stood up and hobbled backward away from them. Things were getting out of hand, though you couldn't tell by looking at Litner. He sat calmly on the couch, tapping his pen on his thigh. Patrick stepped forward. "Agent Litner, maybe we should go," he said in a panicked whisper. It wasn't until Litner turned to Patrick with a death stare that he realized he had used Litner's real name. And his title. Oops.

Jon's face fell, and he paled further. "So. It's agent, is it? Who sent you?"

"Where is Wesley J. Shepherd?" Litner pressed.

"Why do you want to know?" Jon screamed, wild eyed.

"Now take it easy, Jon. We just want to ask him some questions," Litner said, standing. The young blond man hobbled backward until he was leaning against a cherry wooden table with drawers. His hands were behind him, holding the desk for support. Even Agent Litner didn't expect to see the gun until Jon pulled it out from behind him and aimed it at them.

"Don't move. If you come near me, I will shoot you!" Jon shouted.

Litner held his hands over his head in a gesture of surrender. "Take it easy Jon. Nobody is here to hurt you."

Jon was shaking as he held the black handgun in front of him menacingly. "Let me leave," he said. "I know you were sent to kill me. I'll kill you first if you try."

"We mean you no harm, Jon," Litner said. "You misunderstand our motives. If you would just let us explain..."

"You don't need to explain. I know who sent you. I'll kill myself before I give him the satisfaction!" Jon turned the gun then and pressed it against his temple.

"No!" Patrick screamed and took two steps toward Jon. Jon turned to him, keeping the gun pointed at his own head.

"Don't come any further Patrick, if that's your real name."

"Patrick, please step back and let me handle this," Litner said calmly.

Patrick looked at Litner. "No. No I won't. You are not handling this well, Agent Litner."

Litner's face stiffened. "Excuse me?"

"He has a gun to his head! I wouldn't say it's going well. Would you?"

"Patrick," Litner said the name with an unspoken warning. Patrick stared back at him, his face desperate. He did not want to see anymore blood this month. If this kid blew his brains out, that would be it. Patrick's mind would snap like the worn out twig that it was.

"Please, Litner. Just tell him the truth!" he begged.

Jon's face was still fearful, but he looked at Patrick curiously now. "You!" he said to Patrick. "You tell me why you're here." Jon pointed the gun at Patrick's forehead.

Patrick looked at Litner, who waved his arm at him in a resigning gesture. "Go ahead, Patrick. You've already messed up my strategy. You may as well start running your mouth."

Patrick took a careful step backward. "An old man was murdered recently," he said to the boy. "A doctor. He was killed in a cave out at Pearl Chasm."

Jon flinched and brought the gun down a couple of inches. "What did you say?" he whispered.

Patrick held his hands up in front of him as he took a slow step forward. "Before this old man died, he wrote the name Wesley J. Shepherd in the dirt. Agent Litner traced the name to this address. So you see we don't want to hurt anybody. We just need to ask your father some questions."

Jon looked distant for a moment. He still held the gun but it was lowered mainly to the floor now. He looked at Patrick and shook his head, a flood of emotions struggling to form on his handsome face. "Was it...Dr. Lichtenstein?" he asked in a whisper.

Patrick nodded with new enthusiasm. "Yes. Yes! Dr. Lichtenstein. Did you know him?"

Jon took a step toward him. Patrick felt Robin jump where she stood.

Patrick signaled a hand behind his back, urging her to stay calm. Jon cocked his head to one side and stared at Patrick.

"Are you a cop?" he asked.

Patrick shook his head. "No. I'm not a cop."

Jon took another step, gazing at Patrick like he suddenly held some amazement. "If you aren't a cop, then how are you involved in this...murder case?"

Patrick swallowed hard. Jon's presence was making him feel funny the closer he got.

"Personal reasons," Patrick said.

Jon took the last two steps, closing the gap between Patrick and himself until they stood eye to eye. Patrick looked into Jon's pale blue eyes and felt something tug at his subconscious. Jon carefully reached his fingers out and touched the side of Patrick's neck. Patrick flinched but didn't move. Jon then raised his hand up and trailed a finger along Patrick's temple, just to the left of his eye, as if he was testing something. He moved even closer now and stared into Patrick's eyes. The room fell still. Patrick's heart was beating furiously in his chest as he waited to see what Jon was going to do next.

A look of stunned realization fell over Jon's face then and he gasped, taking a step back.

"My God!" he said, his eyes still locked on Patrick's. "You're The Shield, aren't you?"

The words made Patrick's head reel. "What did you say?" he asked, his voice turned to a whisper.

"You are The Shield. He is The Sword, and you are The Shield. Do you know what I speak of?" Jon's eyes were pleading, terrified.

"Yes," Patrick said in a cautious whisper. "Yes, I know what you speak of."

Jon licked his lips, his eyes still frozen on Patrick's. "Then it has begun again," he said.

Patrick felt his body go cold. He forced himself to breathe so that he could form the words and speak. "How do you know about that? How can you possibly know about that?"

Jon swallowed hard. "How do I know? By the shattered look in your eyes, and the smell of his blood in your veins," he said.

The two men stared into each other's eyes as if trying to read a secret printed on the other's soul. Patrick shook his head, his face pulled in a grimace of confusion. "Who are you?" he asked the blond stranger.

"I am Wesley Jackson Shepherd. I am the one you are looking for," the yellow haired youth answered.

Patrick shook his head. "You? But...But you're—"

"I'm sixty-two years old."

Chapter Thirty-Nine

Wesley J. Shepherd put his gun back in the desk drawer. They'd agreed to exchange information, but mistrust and tension still ran high in the room. Wesley opened a bottle of wine and sat across from them in his puffy leather chair. Patrick and Robin were on the couch, and Agent Litner remained standing near the adjoining love seat. Wesley took a delicate swallow of his wine and swirled the red liquid with an air of sophistication that did not match his youth. "So," he said, "who wants to start?"

"Why don't you start, Jon? Or is it Wesley now?" Patrick asked.

"Wesley is fine. I've been hiding behind other names for years. It's refreshing to use my real name for once. But you're the guest, Patrick. Why don't you speak first?" Patrick stared back at him and said nothing. Wesley laughed. "I see how difficult this is going to be. You want information from me, but you don't trust me enough to give me information in return. I, in turn, am willing to give you information, but I do not completely trust you."

"Do you really claim to be sixty-two years old?" Robin asked him.

He swirled his wine, watching the streams of red lines form along the edges of the crystal. "I don't just claim it. I am it."

Patrick could hold his tongue no longer. "How do you know Shep? You do know him, don't you?"

Wesley jumped at the mention of Shep, and nearly spit out his wine. His lips tightened and he lifted his eyes to Patrick. "Shep," he said. "He's still calling himself that, is he?"

Patrick frowned. "Yes. He is...still calling himself that."

Wesley looked at Patrick, a question formed on his puzzled brow. "How is it that you can leave your sword?"

The question caught Patrick by surprise. "My sword?"

"Yes. You are the Shield, am I right?"

"I suppose."

"Then you must have a sword. How is it that you can be away from your sword?"

Patrick scratched his head. "Do you mean Joey?"

Wesley looked off into the distance. "Joey." He whispered the name. "Joey," he said again, forming the word carefully with his lips. He turned back to Patrick. "How were you able to leave your...Joey?"

Patrick shrugged. "I just did."

"Do you live with him?"

"Yes. But I've only been living with him for a short time. Why?"

Wesley looked at him with open fascination. "You must be very strong."

"What do you mean?"

"Don't you get headaches? If you're away from him, I mean."

Robin looked befuddled as her head turned back and forth between them as if watching a tennis match. Patrick pondered the question. Did he get headaches? That was an understatement. "Yes, I get headaches."

"How long have you been living with him?"

Patrick stood up. "Look, I don't understand these questions. You seem to know what's been happening to me better than I do. You know all about this, don't you Wesley?"

Wesley looked at Patrick sadly. "Yes," he said. "I do. He chose to keep you rather less informed this time. At least he's learned something."

Patrick went forward and stooped down in front of the young looking stranger. "This time? What do you mean this time? Are you saying this has happened before?"

The wistful blond poured himself another glass of wine. "You are most definitely tainted with Zirub's blood. This can only mean one thing. It has started again." Wesley's hand shook as he brought the wine to his lips.

"What do you mean?" Patrick asked. "What has started again?" Wesley did not answer.

"Who are you Wesley?" Robin asked softly.

Wesley smiled sourly. He stood up and took a bow. "Who am I? I am the chosen one. The original."

"What do you mean, 'the chosen one'?" Patrick asked.

Wesley flopped back down in the chair. "Do you see the life that your friend Joey is living? Well, that was supposed to be me. I was the first. I'm the one your pal Shepherd made all of his mistakes on. I, my good people, am Zirub's self-proclaimed, fuck up. Cheers." He tossed back the remainder of the wine in his glass.

Patrick took his seat on the couch again. Now they were finally getting somewhere. Robin gazed at Wesley. "You obviously know Shepherd. How did that come to be?" she asked.

Wesley chuckled. "Do I know Shepherd? Oh yes. Better than I care to. I swore I'd never speak of this. In fact, I swore on my own head. Under threat of death. And other unsavory things."

"Please," Patrick urged. "We think Shep may be planning something. Something horrible."

Wesley laughed. "Oh you can bet on it."

This got Litner's attention. "Do you know what he is planning?"

Wesley shook his head. "Not exactly. We never got that far ahead in his plans to discuss actual details. Surprising really, considering the time spent planning. I was only ten years old when I first encountered him."

"What?" Robin said. "Are you trying to say that Shep is at least sixty-two years old as well?"

Wesley shook his head. "Fifty-two actually. Fifty-two earth years anyway."

Robin shook her head. "This is difficult for me to accept. Shep and I were...intimate."

Wesley looked at her, alarmed. "Did you use condoms?" he asked.

"I beg your pardon?"

"I said, did you use condoms?"

After a moment of shifting in her seat uncomfortably, she looked back at him. "Yes," she said. "We used condoms."

"Always?"

"Yes, always. Why? Does he have aids or something?"

"No. He doesn't have aids. He does have...something, however."

"You're losing me," Litner said suddenly. "Please, Jon, Wesley, whoever you are. Start at the beginning."

Wesley nodded. "The beginning. Okay. Have you heard of a mythical being known as Zirub?"

"A priest showed us the story," Litner said.

The yellow-haired boy stood and limped up in front of the fireplace, staring at the crucifixes as he spoke. "This band of five Powers went against the wishes of their superiors and crossed the byways, with all intentions of making it to earth. Their entrance was blocked as their plan was discovered before they reached their destination. When they tried to retreat back to where they came from, that entrance was blocked as well. They were trapped in the shapeless void. And so on. And so on." Wesley spoke the words with a heavy dose of cynicism, as if he'd heard the story so many times that it sickened him. "I know this tale well," he said bitterly. "Zirub himself taught it to me. He made me memorize it."

"So the story is true then? Zirub and his band were trapped for two thousand years in the darkness?" Patrick asked, still unwilling to believe that his long-time pot-head friend Shep was some sort of mythical character.

"Two thousand, four hundred and sixty one years, to be exact. If you've read the folklore, you know the rest. The others in the band began to go mad in the void. Zirub felt responsible for their plight. He put them to sleep, vowing to find a way out, or in, whichever came first. He spent all of those years alone, testing the space around him for one of the soft spots that exist between the fabric of the realms."

They watched Wesley, waiting for him to continue. "Zirub found his soft spot. The ironic thing was he wasn't really looking for it at the time. Zirub's emergence into this world was...an accident. The day my parents died, that was the day he came through." Wesley paused, looking off into the distance. "Even he didn't know how it had happened. One moment he was trapped, the next he was free, flesh and blood, lying on the floor of a collapsed cave in Massachusetts. There was a low-grade tremor that day. Pearl Chasm sits on a fault line because of the way it was formed. That place never should have been made into a State Reservation to begin with. At any rate, the wall did collapse, and my parents, Melvin and Eugenia, were killed."

Wesley took a moment. "I had to go live with my Aunt Roberta. I was only ten years old, but I was the smartest kid in school, and equally advanced in other ways. I was independent to the point of being considered strange. My aunt, however, saw only a vulnerable little boy who had just suffered a terrible tragedy. She wouldn't even let me go to the funeral for fear that it would traumatize me. That ate away at me. They told me that my parents were dead and I believed them, but I had no closure. I needed to go to the place where they died. I needed to see where it happened. So one day I skipped school and took a taxi to Pearl Chasm."

Patrick thought about Joey and his supposed genius. The similarities between Wesley and Joey became more apparent by the minute. "You say you were the first chosen one," Patrick interjected. "Why were you discarded?"

Wesley dropped his eyes to the floor as if in shame. "I did something to Zirub, something to make him hate me above all others. But we jump ahead.

I must first tell you how it started."

Patrick nodded. "Please, go on," he said, overjoyed to be finally getting some sort of explanation, however bizarre.

"I found the cave right away," Wesley continued. "It was still surrounded by yellow caution tape. The cave had been bulldozed out and cleared of rubble. So, I went inside." Wesley's eyes were distant as he relived the events of a ten-year-old boy's most painful experience.

"The cave had been cleared. The blood had sunk into the earth and stained the stone parts of the floor. My mom and dad. Nothing but a rust colored stain on a sheet of rock and dirt. I fell to my knees and I cried, wanting to sink into the ground and die with them. I don't know how long I stayed in that cave, kneeling in my own tears and my dead parents' blood." A tear fell down Wesley's cheek but he made no move to wipe it. He was elsewhere.

Wesley glanced at them. "When I finally left the cave, the light outside was fading. I remember how frightening the Chasm looked as I stood there alone in that eerie evening light, amidst the black rocks and tunnels. I started to follow the trail out through the woods. That's when I saw him." Wesley paused and took a breath.

"He was standing up on a cliff, watching me. I'll never forget the sight of him looking down on me like that. He was like another jutting rock, a phantom, still as stone, and watching me with those enormous eyes. If not for his curls and the way they blew in the wind, I'd have thought he was a statue. I ran. The stranger on the cliff did not follow me. Not that day, anyway."

"And this was fifty two years ago," Litner said with a tone of disbelief.

"Yes, Agent Litner. This was fifty two years ago."

"And you're sure this was the same man that Patrick and Robin know."

"If it is Zirub, I have something that may help convince you." Wesley went over to a small box that sat on a corner table. He pulled on the bottom and slid something out. He handed it to Patrick. "This is the only one I kept. I don't know why I even kept this. I must be out of my mind."

Patrick stared at the photograph. "Mother of God," Robin said, taking it from him. They both studied the faded black and white photograph. It was Shep, no question about it. He stood in front of a basketball hoop, spinning a ball on his finger. He was not looking at the camera. His sandy curls were tied back in a ponytail, his face quite visible. The picture was faded and worn, but Shep looked unchanged. Patrick examined the photo. It had a date on the corner of the white border. According to the date, the picture was taken forty-five years before.

Patrick stared dazed at the photograph, thinking of Shep and how he stayed looking so young despite his lack of exercise. Sure, he was a vegetarian, but only because meat disgusted him. He was no health nut. He drank like a fish and smoked pot like a fiend. Was it possible? Clearly the answer was yes. Shep did not age normally. Patrick's head was spinning.

"Okay Wesley. I guess I'll have to believe you. But what is it all about? What is all this about the chosen one and the plan and the church?"

"I know nothing about a church, Patrick. I've been shut away here for many years. I have no phone and I have no television. I can only tell you my own experiences with Zirub."

"Fair enough. What does Shep want?" Patrick asked.

Wesley's expression darkened. "Everything. He wants everything."

"Everything? Explain."

Wesley looked terrified, his eyes darting around like he expected Shep to burst into the house at any moment. "Zirub approached me as I was leaving school two weeks later. I immediately recognized him from Pearl Chasm. He was so striking. I couldn't have forgotten him, though I had only seen him fleetingly. He asked me to come with him. He said he had things to show me. Now as I said, I was not a stupid child. I knew about perverts, and there was no way I was taking off with some hippie looking stalker who wanted to show me things. Besides, he talked funny and he walked like he had a rod up his ass. Pardon my language."

Patrick and Robin exchanged a glance. "Like the brothers!" she said.

"It's hard to believe Shep was ever…like them," Patrick said.

They turned back to Wesley when they heard his wine glass shatter onto the brick fireplace. He was gaping at them. "I'm sorry. Did you say…the brothers?" he asked.

Robin and Patrick looked at each other, then back at Wesley. They nodded. Agent Litner walked over and began to clean up the shards of glass. Wesley put a hand to his forehead. "Then he…he's gotten them out? The brothers?"

It was Litner who spoke. "Yes, Wesley. He's gotten them out. All four of them."

Wesley held on to the mantle as if he'd collapse otherwise. "Hey, are you all right?" Robin said, and went to his side. He held a hand up and seemed to gather himself.

"I apologize, I just wasn't expecting to hear that. Never mind that for now, you can fill me in when it is your turn to speak." It appeared Wesley was going to let the matter of the brothers drop, but then he turned to them, his face pained. "What are they like?" he asked.

"The brothers?" Patrick asked. Wesley nodded. Litner led him back to the chair and made him sit down and put his foot up. "Well," Patrick said, "they look like Shep. Not exactly like him, but similar. They're a bit odd. Clearly intelligent, but no common sense, you know? They are inhumanly strong. They speak with an accent, as if they've just learned the language."

Wesley frowned. "Bright eyes, baby talk, seemingly harmless, right? Walk like they're breaking in a new set of legs?"

"Yes," Robin said.

"Well they don't stay that way!" Wesley said sharply. "Make no mistake. They are extremely dangerous. They only appear innocent because they are still adjusting to life in the flesh. Shep was the same way once, all stumbling and stuttering and seemingly naïve. Trust me, it doesn't last. In time they will be as clever and diabolical as he is."

Patrick though of Klee crunching on a bowl of cocoa puffs, and he couldn't imagine he had a diabolical bone in his body. Yet he believed Wesley. Wesley stood again and began to hobble toward the crucifixes. Patrick gazed at the back of his blond head, waiting for him to speak again. He seemed lost in thought. "Wesley, how did Shep…I mean Zirub get you to go with him?"

Wesley laughed bitterly. "At first he told me he was an angel sent by my parents to take care of me. I laughed at him. I told him that only a moron would tell such a tale and expect anyone to believe it. He didn't like being spoken to that way. So he melted my shoes." Wesley looked at them. "While they were still on my feet."

"He melted your shoes?" Robin said. "How?"

Wesley looked at Robin. "By looking at them." The three of them must have looked flabbergasted because Wesley laughed. "That's right folks. It was the beginning of a long relationship of physical coercion. Look here." Wesley removed one of his boat shoes and showed them his foot. It was covered with puffy white burn scars.

Patrick stared at the scars. He couldn't believe that Shep had physically harmed a ten year old boy. "That's awful," Patrick said. "All that for calling him a moron?"

"Yes, that was Zirub, sadistic from the start. He tended to my wounded feet by making some sort of herb mixture, but it didn't take care of all the damage."

"He melted your feet and then kissed the boo-boo," Patrick said. "That's the Shepherd I know. He'll verbally degrade you until you're nearly in tears, then pat you on the back and offer to buy you beers all night."

Wesley smiled at him. "Then you know him well, Patrick."

"Not that well. I thought he was human. Silly me."

"Well, he practically is human now," Wesley said. "He's had fifty-two years of practice. Anyhow, he brought me back to the cave and we dug up his wings. He showed me the wound on his back. I must say I was overwhelmed. I was a clever kid, but I was not beyond my childhood longings. I had just lost my parents. I was looking for answers, guidance, magic. Zirub gave me those things. He told me the truth. He said that somehow my parent's accident in the cave had set him free. He said that I need not worry about my life any longer. He would watch over me. I was the chosen one."

"Why you?" Robin said.

"My parents' death brought about his life into this world. It was meant to be, he told me. That's why he took their names. Melvin Eugene Shepherd, after my parents, and his, he said. He said he knew when he saw me walk out of that cave, that I was the one he had come to find."

"That's all very prophetic, but what the hell did he want you for?" Litner asked.

Wesley smirked. "Are you a religious bunch at all?"

Patrick shrugged. He was a Catholic, but admitted to himself that he had never really taken it all too seriously. "Not really, to be honest with you," he said.

Wesley nodded. "Neither was I, before, that is." He glanced up at the multitude of crucifixes on the wall, then looked back at his guests. "Do you know why Zirub made that fateful trek to the material world?"

"No!" Litner said a bit too loud. He looked around as if someone else had said it. "No," he repeated more softly. "That's the one thing that wasn't in the book Father Bello had. Why did he decide to leave his post and go to earth? What was the urgency?"

Wesley hobbled over and sat down on the floor in front of them, filling his wine glass. "Let me start by telling you, Shepherd is insane."

"Duh," Robin said.

Wesley held up a hand for patience. "Let me also tell you that Zirub, who is one and the same person, is also insane. I think perhaps he always was, even in his previous life. You see he insists that it was all his idea."

"What was all his idea?" Patrick asked.

Wesley raised his eyebrows. "The big 'it'. The Messiah. The Son of God. The Light of the World. Zirub thinks he came up with the idea."

"But if Shep-I mean Zirub..." Patrick was stumbling over the names. Wesley stopped him with a wave of his hand.

"It's okay, Patrick. You can call him Shep. It doesn't bother me. He's been using my last name for a long time."

"Okay. Why did Shep think he invented Jesus?" Patrick asked. "We are talking about Jesus here, correct?"

"Well, yes, but Shep claims that 'Jesus' wasn't his name when he lived. He refers to him as 'The Vessel'. But you misunderstand," Wesley said. "He doesn't think he invented Jesus. He thinks he invented the concept."

"Shep says that according to God's law, human beings are supposed to discover the mysteries of the world around them until they ultimately have everything they need to live in paradise. On this earth, there are cures to every disease, answers to every question, and fulfillment for every angst. We simply have to learn how to use it. Shep calls it the Science of Worlds."

"The Science of Worlds. Carbone said that's a term Juris used," Litner said.

Wesley turned to Litner, his face crumbling with emotion again. "Juris? You've met him? Juris?" Wesley looked sad. He seemed envious that they had all met the brothers.

"Yes, I've met Juris," Litner said. "He is a most unsavory fellow. You're not missing a thing, kid."

Wesley smiled shyly. "Thank you Agent Litner. But don't call me kid. I am quite a bit older than you."

Robin clapped her hands. "Back to the messiah thing."

"Very well," Wesley said. "Shep told me humanity was supposed to naturally progress to this higher level of enlightenment. The problem was they weren't progressing at all. They had trouble living together without killing each other. Their souls were coming through the byways poisoned. Being that the Powers are the first line at the border of the realms, they were always the first to see these darkened souls. They had to usher them in before they were cleansed. According to Shep, it was disgusting to behold. They were turning away from the light and their spirits were becoming dark."

"That's just human nature," Patrick said.

"Precisely Shep's point, Patrick. In his mind, it was clear that humanity was not going to reach enlightenment by way of free will. They needed a push in the right direction. So Shep decided they needed a higher being to become flesh, and reveal the secrets of God to the lost sheep of humanity. Now he absolutely insists that this was his idea, and that he brought it to his superiors. Apparently it was a good one, because it was determined that a messiah would be born unto the world of men. Bravo. Zirub got what he wanted, right? Wrong. He claims that the celestials fucked up."

Patrick raised a finger. "Celestials fucked up?"

"Those are his words, not mine. You see Zirub wanted to send a celestial being down to earth. According to him, his superiors stole his idea and never gave him credit for it. He also claims that they twisted his original concept to their own liking, turning it into a grossly ineffective plan. You see, ultimately, it was not a celestial being that was chosen to go to earth." Wesley paused, and looked around the room.

"Jesus," Robin said softly.

Wesley nodded. "Yes, the Vessel. A mortal child was chosen and infused with the Holy Spirit. We all know that part of the tale. Shep's complaint was that The Vessel was far too human, and that he was not allowed enough power to persuade the masses toward the truth. Shep believes that free will is a flaw, and that humanity needs to be strong-armed toward the truth, not led to it gently. He simply didn't like the way the whole project, *his project*, was being handled."

Robin laughed. "Oh, man. Patrick, isn't that just like Shep's ego? Even after Jesus was walking the earth, Shep still insisted that it was his 'project'."

"That's right," Wesley said. "So you see when The Vessel was crucified, Zirub went absolutely nuts. According to him, the crucifixion was not supposed to happen. Completely uncalled for, and preventable at that. He was furious that The Vessel was allowed to die because of bad management decisions. So what did he do? He gathered his posse and high-tailed it down there to show em how it was done. He was going to prove a point. He was going to do it himself, and do it right this time."

Patrick snickered. "He was going to prove a point huh? All he ended up proving was that he could get his ass thrown into the realm of darkness for over two thousand years."

Wesley turned to Patrick, his face serious. "Yes. But he's out now. Isn't he?"

Patrick's smirk dropped. "Is that what he's doing? After all this time, he's still going to try to do things his way? Is this supposed to be some sort of Second Coming?"

Wesley nodded. "So he thinks. He started giving me his blood when I was fifteen. Just as God had put part of himself into The Vessel, so Zirub would put part of himself into me. He would create his own messiah. Closely monitored, carefully controlled, and one hundred percent guaranteed."

Wesley frowned. "Shep carried part of what he used to be, into his mortal body when he crossed over. He is flesh and blood, but he is not like us. His mind has power. His blood has power. His bodily fluids, when transferred into a human with the right rituals, can create the power to enchant."

"Why didn't he just become the messiah himself?" Robin asked.

"He can't," Wesley answered. "He has extraordinary abilities, but he does not possess the power to enchant, not by himself anyway. Only when his essence is mixed with a human's will it be recognized by other humans. Only then will the enchantment be effective."

"So you were supposed to be this new messiah. Wesley, what happened?" Litner asked. "Rumor has it that Shep won't even speak your name aloud."

Wesley looked deeply hurt by the comment. "Still?" he said. "He still won't speak my name?"

"Apparently not," Litner said. Patrick frowned at Wesley. It was almost as if he still cared what Shep thought of him.

Wesley seemed to shake off the melancholy. "He performed a series of rituals on me. I drank his blood. I said the strange words he told me to say. By the time I was twenty years old, the power in me was already apparent. I could hold a room full of people captive for hours just by telling them about my trip to the dry cleaners. They would stare at me, and compete for my attention. Everyone wanted to be near me. I had been given the power to enchant. I must admit, at first, I liked it. I liked it a lot. And I liked him. Shep had been with me since I was ten years old, teaching me, molding me, caring for me. He was my family. I loved him. I worshipped him. He was mine. Or so I thought. What I didn't realize then was that he was not mine at all. I, in fact, was his."

Wesley paused and chuckled bitterly. "I was such and easy target. By the time I should have been old enough to come to my senses, it was too late. When I reached adulthood, we posed as friends, as we now appeared to be the same age. Finally, he could begin showing up at my Aunt Roberta's house for visits. It was wonderful. It was like having an invisible friend that had suddenly come to life and everyone else could see him too."

Wesley took a sip of wine from the new glass Litner had brought him. His hands were still shaking. "I was ready to become the messiah he wanted me to be. He said he had a plan to put me into the limelight and make others see me as a man chosen by God. He said I needed to be in a position of power when the awakening came."

Litner flinched. "The awakening?"

"Yes. The awakening is the event he claimed would take place to make the people fear for their salvation. An event that he himself would bring about. But first, he had to get the brothers out. This had always been an obsession with him, getting the brothers out of captivity. He claimed that he wanted to have the messiah plan in effect before he brought them through, so that they would know that his actions had not been in vain. He was afraid they would be angry with him for getting them all imprisoned, and he wanted them to see that he did indeed have a plan. He spoke of them for so long that quite frankly I began to wonder if they even existed at all. But then one day, he told me that the time had come to get the brothers out."

Wesley's eyes darkened. "We began going to the cave night after night. It was grueling. He struggled to re-create the circumstances that existed when he was brought through the Cripulet the day my parents were killed. We set charges in an attempt to simulate the tremor. Nothing happened. We set off explosion after explosion, but the Cripulet simply would not open."

Wesley looked up at all of them, his blue eyes rimmed with tears. "Then he discovered the horrible, wonderful truth; that it must have been the presence of blood that opened the Cripulet. We tried everything. We used my blood. We used his blood. We even stole blood from blood banks. He came up with special formulas and ritual blood chants, but nothing worked. He marked the spot where the Cripulet was with a circle of blood, so that he wouldn't forget, but each time he tried to reproduce the effects of the accident that brought him through, he was met with defeat."

Patrick chilled, recalling his own visit to the cave. "What about the old doctor?" Patrick asked. "What about Dr. Lichtenstein?"

Wesley nodded. "Yes, it was this time period that I met Dr. Lichtenstein. Shep was so calculatingly clever that when he first came into this world, he had mind enough to find a surgeon to help him remove his wings. He found Doctor Lichtenstein. The doctor was about to be arrested for molesting his patients. He was caught on tape fondling an incapacitated young boy. Shep got hold of the tape and paid a visit to the good doctor. Shep wanted his services, and his silence, or he would release the tape to the press, the authorities, and to his wife. I can't imagine what Dr. Lichtenstein's first reaction to seeing a man with wings was. But he did perform the procedure and was there every time after, with us in the cave, waiting with his saw in case one of the brothers made it through."

"What caused you to part ways with Shep?" Patrick asked.

"Yes. The parting of the ways." Wesley hung his head of fringy blond bangs over his eyes. Patrick found it so difficult to look at this stunning young man and see him as a sixty-two year old, trapped in that lithe young body. "For the first time since I'd known him, I started to doubt. He claimed that something catastrophic was to occur in the future, after I had been established as a religious figure."

"What is this catastrophic event?" Litner asked.

Wesley looked at him sadly. "I just don't know. He spoke of leveling the playing field, if that means anything."

"Leveling the playing field?" Litner asked.

"Yes. Making things even. He said that he should have the same chances that The Vessel had. That way no one could say that he cheated." Agent Litner was going to town on his temple with his pen. Wesley gave him an odd look. "Agent, are you all right?"

Litner looked up. "Leveling the playing field. Could he have been talking about the population of the world when Jesus lived?"

Wesley shrugged. "I never thought of that. But yes. That would make sense."

Litner looked up at Patrick.

"I know," Patrick said. "I'll get the samples." Wesley looked confused. Patrick urged him to keep talking.

"So all this talk of catastrophic events started to get to me. But that's not what did it. I remember the day he came to my house. I was sitting in my apartment with Rollie, and Shep came in."

Patrick raised an eyebrow. "Rollie? Who is Rollie?"

Wesley looked uncomfortable. "Rollie? He was my...friend. Anyway, Rollie and I were sitting there and Shep comes in. He was off the wall! I'd never seen him so excited. He said that he'd finally figured it all out. He sent Rollie out of the room so he could speak to me alone. So Shep tells me that the missing ingredient was what my parents had provided. The blood had to be from the newly departed. In other words, someone who had just died. He said we needed a human sacrifice. He told me he wanted to use my Aunt Roberta."

Robin let out a long breath. "You've got to be kidding me, Wesley. What did you do?"

"I told him no, of course. I said that he had gone too far, and that he could not kill my aunt, the woman who had raised me. Well he got very angry. He told me that I should be willing to make this sacrifice for the brothers, and that Roberta would be better off in the next world. I refused. We argued. We came to blows. That's when Rollie came in." He hesitated again, looking uneasily at Patrick.

"Wesley, who is Rollie?" Patrick asked again. Wesley ignored him.

"I continued to tell Shep no. He performed another ritual on me. He called it 'calming the soul'. It was supposed to put my soul to sleep, in effect, sedate my conscience. Without my conscience I wouldn't care who he killed. It didn't work. He would have had to perform the ritual before he made all of the changes in me. It was something he'd overlooked, apparently. He grew more frustrated. Then one day he called and asked me to meet him at the cave."

Wesley hung his head and tears began to stream down his face. Robin went to him and placed a comforting hand on his shoulder. "When I got to the cave, he'd already killed Aunt Roberta," Wesley said between heartbreaking sobs. "She lay dead in the corner. He'd cut her throat and filled jars full of her blood. Dr. Lichtenstein was waiting with the saw, looking horrified. I was so upset I started thrashing him with my fists. He told me I was a disappointment, and that I would just have to learn to deal with unpleasantness if I wanted to be his messiah. I sat by sobbing as he rubbed Aunt Roberta's blood along the rim of the Cripulet."

His face was twisted in pain as he relived the events. "I looked up, and the Cripulet was smoking. I stopped crying and walked over because I was so amazed. It was finally happening. The Cripulet was opening. As much as I hated Shep at that moment, I couldn't help but gaze at him, and marvel at his unparalleled genius. Shep stood before the smoking circle, elated, as the very stone began to melt and soften before my eyes. Shep must have taken my presence there as cooperation, because he turned to me and said, 'Be ready to help me when I say.' He placed his hands on the center of the Cripulet, and the most amazing thing happened. His hands sank into the stone wall. When he was nearly up to his elbows, he jerked back. 'I have something!' he yelled. 'Grab on to me and pull!'"

Wesley looked around the room. "Grab on to me and pull," he repeated, more softly. "I don't know what made me do what I did next. It could have been the madness of it all finally setting in, or it could have been my Aunt Roberta's dead body lying in the corner. I came in behind Shep, and grabbed onto his shoulders. Instead of pulling him back as he'd asked me to do, I pushed him forward. I pushed him as hard as I could. I tried to push him right through the wall, right back where he came from. He started to slip into the wall."

Wesley looked at them. "This is why he will not speak my name. I did the worst possible thing anyone could have done. I tried to push him back into the void."

Patrick and Robin wore identical looks of fascination. Agent Litner was blank-faced. With his pen tapping his temple, he said, "I take it you did not succeed."

Wesley looked pained. "I've never seen such a look of horror as the one on his face that moment, when he realized what I was trying to do. But he was stronger than I was. He broke his contact with the Cripulet. He pulled himself out, and the circle stopped smoking. The stone hardened almost immediately. He turned on me then, and I'll never forget that expression. It was beyond anger. It was beyond hatred. Tears ran down his cheeks, and then he screamed. 'How could you?' How could you?' And at that moment, even with my aunt's corpse lying a few yards away, I was sorry. I was sorry for having hurt him so deeply. And I repeated those words to myself. How could I? How could I?" Wesley wiped the tears from his eyes, lost in his memories.

They sat silently, taking in the emotional weight of the story. So Wesley had tried to send Shep back into the realm of darkness. Yes, Patrick thought, that would explain why Shep was significantly pissed off at his original golden boy.

Litner stood. He started to tap his pen on his head, then stopped, as if realizing. He looked at the pen and put it in his pocket. He paced the room, then stopped in front of Wesley. "How did you ultimately get away from him?"

Wesley looked embarrassed. "I begged for his forgiveness. Can you believe that? He beat me to a bloody pulp. I didn't even fight back. Dr. Lichtenstein tried to stop him, to no avail. All the while he was beating me, I kept telling him that I was sorry. I must have been truly pathetic in my apologies, because by the end of the day he had forgiven me. But the truce did not last. The last straw for me came the next day. You heard me speak about Rollie before. Rollie was my Shield." He looked at Patrick for a reaction.

"Your Shield? So Rollie was like me?" Patrick asked.

"Yes. Rollie was the Shield to me, just as you are the Shield to this Joey person."

Patrick shook his head. "See, this is the part I don't get. Why the big emphasis on the protection?"

"Protecting the chosen is one of the most crucial elements to Zirub's plan. Zirub's entire motivation, his entire argument for leaving his post and risking it all, was that Jesus was not meant to die like that. According to Shep, the Vessel was simply not provided with the proper protection. He had all those followers, but they were all just humans. When the time came, there was not a single man that was willing to sacrifice himself to save the Messiah. It was beyond human capability to sacrifice one's own life, Shep said. The survival instinct was too strong. So if Shep's new improved messiah was hurt or killed, it would defeat his whole purpose. It would show that his plan was just as flawed as the original. So he made sure that that was never going to happen. He created a human shield. A man bonded by blood to protect the chosen one at all times, at all costs. That was Rollie. And now, Patrick, that is you."

Patrick shrugged. "So I'm the body guard. I get it."

Wesley gazed at Patrick for a long time. "No, Patrick. I don't believe that you do get it. You are bound by blood to protect him. Do you know what that means?"

Patrick shrugged. "I can feel it if he gets hurt."

Wesley shook his head. "That is only part if it. Whether you realize it or not, Patrick, you are no longer in control. Protecting Joey is not a choice for you now. Your body will react if he is in danger. Your body will protect him, with or without your consent. You will throw yourself into oncoming traffic if that's what it takes."

Patrick recalled the night he'd stopped the man in the bar from stabbing Joey. He had seen the knife and feared that he probably wouldn't get to Joey in time. Then somehow, he had. He remembered the rush of adrenaline, and how strong he'd felt as he wrestled the man into a head lock. His reaction had been automatic. But did that mean he was not in control? He didn't think so. It did get him to thinking about his blood, however. He stared at Wesley's youthful face.

"What about my blood, Wesley? What about the Shield? Am I going to have abnormal aging? What are the side effects of being the Shield?"

"I wish I could answer that Patrick, but I just don't know. You see, my Shield is dead."

Patrick's body went cold. "How did he die?"

Wesley hung his head. "You've probably been wondering why you were left out of the loop. You want to know why they didn't just tell you about the project. Am I right?"

Patrick nodded. "They kept everything from me."

"There is a reason for that," he said. "Shep made his mistakes on Rollie as well. We had spent years getting to know him, drawing him into our circle. He was strong and agile, and fiercely loyal to those he cared about. I used my enchantment and Shep used his guile and humor. Probably much the way your friends courted you, Patrick. The difference was, once Rollie was part of our little group, Shep came clean and told him everything. Rollie didn't really believe any of it, but he was used to Shep and I getting weird at times. He went along with the blood pact, but only because he didn't really think it would do anything. When he found out that it was all true, well, it was just too much for Rollie. He couldn't handle it."

"How did he find out that it was real?" Patrick asked in whisper.

"It was the day Shep came and told me he wanted to use a human sacrifice. I told you he sent Rollie out of the room. When Shep and I came to blows, Rollie came back in. Shep was about to throw a heavy iron lamp at me. He had such a temper."

Patrick nodded knowingly.

"Rollie saw what Shep was about to do, but he was all the way on the other side of the room. Shep let the lamp fly, and at the same time, Rollie let himself fly. He dove through the air, went about twenty feet and deflected the lamp with his body. He didn't get hurt. Not physically anyway. I remember when it was over, Rollie stood up and just looked at us. Then he looked down at himself, as though his body did not belong to him. The move he made, diving across the room to protect me, it wasn't voluntary. He knew it. He'd felt it. I'll never forget the way he looked at us that day. Like we were monsters."

He glanced at Patrick and something passed between them. Patrick couldn't bring himself to speak, so Robin asked the next question.

"What did Rollie do?" she said softly. Wesley avoided Patrick's stare, as though the very sight of him was somehow painful.

"I found out what he did after the night in the cave. Rollie took a ride down to the Cape. It must have been dreadfully painful for him to drive that far away from me. He got terrible headaches if we were too far apart. But he took the drive nonetheless, probably loaded up with painkillers. He pulled his car over, got out, and threw himself off the Bourne Bridge."

There was a long silence, and then finally Patrick stood up. A cold sweat had broken out on his forehead. "So this is it? He fucked up on you and this Rollie character so he just starts over? He starts over with Joey? And me?"

Wesley nodded. "Basically, yes. He keeps changing the rules. I left him no choice. I did not have the luxury of having my conscience removed. I cared for Rollie. He was my best friend. When Rollie killed himself, I had had enough. I told Shep I was leaving him, leaving him for real this time. He did everything in his power to persuade me to change my mind. But I stood firm. I told him he would have to kill me. I was actually quite sure that he would kill me. He said I didn't deserve death. I had betrayed him like no other. From that day forward, he refused to even speak my name aloud. But he let me go, on the condition that I retreat from society and never speak of him to anyone. He said that if I chose not to live with him, then I would be forced to live the rest of my days alone."

"And you agreed to this?" Litner asked.

"I had no choice," Wesley said. "He can find me no matter where I go, because of the blood. He ordered that I change my name every ten years, just to be safe, and he set me up here. He wanted me in purgatory, alone forever. I've been living here ever since."

"He set you up here? In this house?" Patrick asked.

Wesley nodded. "Now you know why I'm so nervous about having you all here. Who do you think owns this house? I certainly don't have any money. Shep pays for everything. I have no contact with the outside world. No television, no radio, no newspapers. That dog you see outside was a stray I found in the woods. When it dies, I'll be alone again."

"When did you last you hear from Shep?" Litner asked.

"It was about twenty years ago. He just showed up at my door one day. I nearly fell over, I was so surprised. He had come to show off, to gloat. He had found a replacement for me. A boy genius with eyes as blue as the spring sky. He said he had seen him on the television, and of course, it was fate."

"Oh God," Robin said. "He's talking about Joey."

Wesley shrugged. "Shep never told me his name. This is your friend? Joey?"

"Yes," Patrick said. "Joey Duvaine. Haven't you heard of him?"

Wesley laughed. "Patrick, I don't even know who the president of the United States is. I'm completely cut off. It was part of my punishment."

Patrick scowled. "So he just finds another extraordinary kid, and boom? Instant messiah?"

Wesley shrugged. "Pretty much. He swore he would not make the same mistakes that he had with me. He would calm the boy's soul first, so he'd have no subordination problems. Then, when the time was right, they would find a Shield, free the brothers, and resume the execution of his plan."

"Why did he bother to tell you any of this?" Patrick asked.

"He wanted me to know that I had not stopped him. He wanted me to hurt. The look in his eyes...it was as if I'd just betrayed him the day before. He was still wounded by what I'd done to him. I guess he always will be. That's the last time I saw him. That was twenty years ago."

Wesley looked expectantly at them. "So," he said after a long silence, "May I presume that my dear, dear Zirub has been busy these past twenty years?"

It was now their turn to talk. With the help of Robin, and occasionally Agent Litner, Patrick gave Wesley a condensed version of all that had befallen him, starting with the apparition of the Virgin Mary, and ending with Patrick's undercover quest to steal the crop samples. Wesley absorbed the information as a starving dog would a feast of scraps. When it was finished, he reclined back on the chair, and set his sprained ankle up high on a pillow.

Agent Litner checked his watch. "We have to go now Wesley," Litner said. "I'd like to come back and speak with you again. I think you may be helpful to this investigation."

"No," Wesley said. "This has been most enlightening, but I'm afraid this is our last meeting."

Litner looked shocked. "You won't help us? You said yourself that Shep is planning something catastrophic. Have you no regard for human lives that may be lost?"

"I can't take the chance. He'll know." The fear was back in Wesley's eyes now.

"Can you offer no suggestions? Nothing that will help us gauge his reactions?" Litner looked furious.

Wesley pointed at Agent Litner. "You have no idea what kind of a creature you're up against! He is like a dangerously insane child. And you want to walk in there and take his candy away. How do you think he's going to react when he discovers that he's been betrayed for a second time? First by his Sword. And now by his Shield." Wesley looked at Patrick, who swallowed hard.

"Thanks for your help," Litner said sarcastically.

The company of three headed for the front door. "Patrick?" Wesley called after him.

Patrick stopped and turned around. "What is it?"

"Don't let him see your fear," he said. "He can read your thoughts." Patrick went cold. Litner took his arm and led him out the door. They were running late and he had a boat to catch.

Chapter Forty

Patrick tried for three days to get near the plants, to no avail. It wasn't as though the followers weren't willing to let him in. They flocked around him like he was Sir Galahad every time he went out to the fields. They offered him wine and food when they saw him. Strangers whose faces he didn't even know walked alongside him, chatting him up as though they were old friends. Some of them even offered to sleep with him. Aside from an occasional sandwich, he declined all of their offers.

So he had access to the inner sanctum of the crops. The problem was, he was never alone. One of the brothers was always at his side. On this particular morning, it was Allisto. The brothers tried to play it off like they really wanted to hang out with Patrick, but he wasn't buying it. It didn't take a genius to figure out that Shep still didn't trust him to wander the property on his own. Poor Klee was the worst of the lot. His lying skills were not yet up to par. It was obvious Klee had been warned not to reveal too much information to Patrick. Just the day before, Klee had 'volunteered' to accompany Patrick on his walk out back. When they were out of anyone's earshot, Patrick tried asking him again where he was from. Klee had looked at him, panic-stricken, and said "Texas."

Later that night, Patrick had strolled into one of the sitting rooms where Klee was playing a video game. Before Patrick uttered a word, he stood up and yelled "Texas!" then ran out of the room, heavy-footed, like a toddler.

When Klee would leave, then Margol would appear. They were so obviously on shifts, taking turns keeping watch over his actions. It was insultingly obvious. Shep either thought Patrick was a total idiot, or he didn't care that he knew he was being surveyed. As the week drew closer to his second meeting with Litner, Patrick grew frustrated and began to panic, thinking that he might not be able to get the crop sample in time. But he had to get it. That sample was his ticket out of Forest Bluffs. And he did so want to be out of Forest Bluffs. The more time he spent there, the more strange things he saw.

Earlier that day he'd encountered Margol sitting on the back deck with a dead bird in his lap. He was picking it apart, either out of curiosity or for amusement. Shep had given Margol permission to dissect woodland creatures after he'd caught him in the fruit cellar cutting up a corpse stolen from the City Hospital morgue. While Allisto the dark haired brother despised the human body, Margol was apparently fascinated with it. So now Margol's fetish was restricted to animals. Points for Shep.

When Patrick walked out onto the deck, Margol had a wing ripped off, one clawed foot in his hand, and was using his other hand to pry off the beak.

He'd looked up briefly when Patrick came through the sliding glass door, then gave his attention back to dismembering the tiny feathered corpse. Patrick had nodded, smiled, then turned right back around and gone inside.

He finally came up with and idea as he passed Kelinda on the way in. He had seen her coming and going as she pleased around the Bluffs, and not even thought twice about it. Until now. Kelinda did not know it, but she was about to do Patrick a very big favor.

He found her around dinner time. She was in the bedroom she shared with Joey, sitting at her vanity mirror. Patrick watched her silently as she applied pink lipstick with a tiny brush. She was dressed in a long black gauze jumpsuit, and bejeweled as though she was about to attend some grand affair. Patrick had a feeling he knew where she was off to. Another little wine tasting seminar, perhaps?

She looked up as he entered the room. Her eyes scanned him with vague interest, then she turned back to the mirror and began applying blush. "What do you want?" she snapped. Patrick came into the room and closed the door behind him.

"That's a fine greeting for an old friend," he said.

"Cut the crap, Patrick. I know how you feel about me, so why don't you just tell me what you want."

Patrick moved to stand behind her in front of the large oval mirror. She stopped with the make-up and looked up at his reflection. Her blue eyes glimmered with confusion. He knew they would not be interrupted. Joey and Shep were still out in the fields, and he had distracted the brothers by whipping up a big batch of chocolate mudslides. "I need a favor, Kelinda."

"You don't say."

"I need to get a sample of that crop out there. The problem is I can't seem to get a moment alone with the brothers up my ass all day. I've watched you go in and out of there like you own the place. I want you to take this baggy, and fill it up for me. Make sure no one sees you."

Patrick held the little zip-lock bag out in front of her. She turned away from the mirror to face him. "Are you crazy? No way, Patrick. I'm not risking my neck for you. I've seen what Shep does to his own flesh and blood when he's angry. Sorry sweetie, but you're not worth it."

She turned back to the mirror and began running a brush through her wild pink hair. Patrick laughed. She looked up and met his eyes in the mirror. He held the baggy out to her again. "You will do this for me Kelinda."

She stood up defiantly and came around from behind the chair. "Fuck off," she said. She tried to push past him, but he blocked her way. She glared up at him. "Get the hell out of my way, Patrick. I will not help you betray Joey."

Patrick grabbed her wrists and spun her around to face him again. "Hey!" she cried as he pinned her up against the wall. He didn't want to hurt her. He just wanted to scare her. By the look on her face, it was working. He leaned in close.

"You dare talk to me about betrayal?" he hissed.

"Let go of me! You can intimidate me all you want. I won't do it. Do you know what Shep will do to me if he finds out?"

"Now you listen to me, Kelinda. If you refuse to do this, I might just have to tell Shep what you've been doing out in those fields at night." Her eyes widened and her cheeks flushed. "That's right," he said, smiling. "I think he'd find your taste in wine rather interesting."

"You bastard! You followed me! What are you, some kind of stalker?"

"That's right Kelinda. I'm a stalker. I'm a mad stalker, and I've been following you. But that's not what's important. What's important is that I know that you've been sharing more than smiles with those zombies out there."

She tried to look defiant, but fear was evident in her eyes. He felt badly about it. This wasn't his style. But it was the only way, so he kept up the tough guy stance.

"You have no proof," she said. "I'll deny it. Give it up, Patrick. You can't win here. You are much too weak!" She said the last word with emphasis, smiling as if she'd gotten the better of him. He smiled back at her.

"Okay Kelinda. Let's go." He opened the door and began dragging her out into the hallway.

She fought against him. "What are you doing?"

"We're going to see Shep. We're going to see right now who he believes, me or you."

"You're crazy! I'll expose you! I'll tell him you want the crop!" He pulled on her, dragging her slowly down the hallway as she fought against him.

"Guess what, Kelinda? I am crazy. I don't fucking care anymore. You can tell Shep whatever you want. But if I go down, you're going down with me!"

He pulled on her harder then, dragging her toward the stairs. "Okay! Stop!" she screamed.

He paused, looking down at her. "Okay, what?" he asked.

"Okay, I'll help you. Now let go of my arm you fucking orangutan."

He let her go and they walked calmly back to Joey's room. She straightened her jumpsuit and smoothed her hair, and sat back down at the vanity. "How much do you need?" she asked with venom. Patrick gave her the sterile zip-lock bag.

"Clip off about five sprigs and put them in here." he said.

She looked up at him and snatched the bag. "I guess you haven't been outside in a while," she said.

"What do you mean?"

"There are no more sprigs. They've been chopping it down all afternoon. It's harvest time. They start grinding it down to powder and loading it into drums tonight."

Patrick ran to the window. Sure enough, the plants were being cut to the ground and hauled over to the guesthouse. He looked back at her. "Then you'll just have to do it tonight."

"Fine," she said, and tucked the baggy into her pocket.

"Kelinda, what is it for? The crop?"

She held her hands up. "How should I know?"

"Oh I think you know a lot of what goes on around here."

"True, but I don't know what the crops are for. They're grinding it up and putting it in storage drums in the guest house. They've got trucks out here that they're eventually going to load the stuff on. I don't know where it's going after that. I swear that's all I know, so manhandling me won't do you any good. Fucking bully."

Patrick couldn't help but smile. She smiled back at him, though she was clearly trying not to. He felt a terrible pain stab his soul. He had cared about Kelinda. He still did, even if the romance was gone. Somehow he still felt that none of this had been her choice. She tried to act as though she was perfectly fine with her current situation, but he saw the pain and fear in her eyes.

"Kelinda, I'm getting out of here soon. Why don't you come along? You don't belong out here. You must miss your family. Don't you want to get away from all of this craziness?"

She turned away, her face pained. "My family is here now, Patrick."

"I don't believe that. I think you're scared, and I can understand that. But this is not the only way. There are people that can protect you."

She stood then and faced him. Tears brimmed in her eyes. "You don't get it, Patrick. I can run from here, but I can't run from what I've become. They're monsters. They're monsters, and now, I'm a monster too."

"You don't have to be."

"Look at me! Can't you see it? Can't you see what he's done to me?"

"Who?"

She met his eyes, looking sad. "Joey. I loved him, you know. You were right about that. I'm sorry Patrick, but I did. I loved him since I was twelve. I loved him while I was with you. But not anymore. Not anymore. He used it against me. He thinks he's smarter than I am." She pointed a finger to her temple and giggled. "But I'm going to get the last laugh. You see, I don't care what happens to him anymore. Isn't that strange?" Her eyes looked distant, trance-like. "In fact, I don't care about much of anything anymore. So you see I'm not so different from him now, Patrick. Stop trying to save me. Start worrying about yourself."

"Come on Kelinda. You're not a monster. You haven't changed so much."

She came toward him. "Oh, really?" she said. She walked over to the fireplace and picked up one of the iron pokers. She tossed it to Patrick. He caught the heavy rod, and shrugged.

"What?"

She took it back from him and held it in front of her. She stared at it for a moment, concentrating. Then with one swift movement, her tiny white hands bent the iron poker, and tied into a knot like a pretzel. She held out the twisted poker to Patrick, who took it. She looked at him sadly. "Still think I haven't changed so much?"

He stared at her with open shock, then looked down at the iron knot he held in his hand. "How did you..."

"It's Joey's fluids. I've inherited Shep's strength from Joey's blood. I'm infected with him." Patrick stared at her, not knowing how to respond.

"It all comes from Shep, you know," she said. "I heard them talking about it when they thought no one was around. It alters everyone differently, they said. They don't know just how much it's affected me. I don't want them to. I hate it, Patrick. The only thing that helps is when I give it away. Those people living out in the field are like drug addicts. They get a little bit high every time Joey talks to them, but he doesn't talk to them nearly enough. He doesn't visit them like I do. He leaves them hungry, longing, craving for more. So I give it to them. I share with them the little piece of Joey that I have inside me now."

"Kelinda, this is insane. We've got to get you some help."

"Help?" she laughed. "You still don't get it, do you? I need him too. I'm an addict, Patrick. But at least now I'm not the only one. Every one of those followers is just a little bit more special now than they were when they got here."

"Don't you see? Joey took my control away from me. I'm not even in charge of my own body anymore. But now I have control over his followers. At least I can take that from him. Call it poetic justice."

"My God, Kelinda."

"I'll get you your crop samples, Patrick, but don't fuck with me. And don't you ever tell Shepherd what I've been doing, or I'll break you in half." She left the room, leaving Patrick to stare at the floor in shock.

Later that night, Patrick answered a light tapping on his door. Kelinda thrust the baggy at him. It was filled with a grainy reddish substance. "Thank you," he said. She left without speaking. She was probably a lost cause after all, he decided. But when he looked at the sample in his hand, he was too elated to care. Tomorrow was his day to go to Boston. This time, he would not be coming back. He was going home.

Kelinda started when she walked into the bedroom and saw Joey standing there, waiting for her. "Joey! I thought you were downstairs."

He was holding the fireplace poker that she had tied into a knot. He held it up for her to see. "Did you do this, Kelinda?"

She looked into his pale eyes and saw the horror there. She enjoyed that look in Joey's eyes. She wanted to see more of it. He deserved to be horrified. "Yes," she said. "I did that."

Joey looked at the twisted piece of metal in his hand, then back at Kelinda. "I don't think you should sleep in here anymore," he said. "I've moved your things to one of the guest rooms down the hall."

At first she was shocked, then furious. Who was he to put her out after all he'd done to her? She wouldn't let him see the upset. She forced a cold grin to spread across her lips. "Whatever you say, Joey. You're the messiah."

Chapter Forty-One

It started out as a good day for Patrick, if there was such a thing at the Forest Bluffs house of horrors. Shep physically abused those closest to him, Margol dissected tiny animal corpses, and Joey played God with the blood-crazed zombies in the field. All families have their issues.

Patrick dressed quickly, eager to get to the city and deliver the samples to Agent Litner. He was even more eager to see Robin. He put on a pair of light blue jeans and a navy blue tee shirt. Reaching under the mattress, he pulled out the baggy full of the grainy red substance and stuffed it deep into his front pocket.

He took the few possessions that he could not live without out of his bag and put them into his brief case, then went off in search of Shep. The house had so many damn rooms. He expected to find Shep in the library, but he wasn't in there. Instead he found Margol and Allisto seated at the computers. Their fingers tapped furiously at the keys. They had certainly come a long way from the dirty stumbling stalkers he'd first encountered.

He moved out of the library and continued his search for Shep. Finally finding him in a rarely used sunroom on the first floor, just off the huge kitchen. Patrick paused at the doorway without entering. Shep and Klee sat Indian style across from each other on the big Persian rug. They were both in boxer shorts, shirtless and barefoot. There was about three feet of space between them.

"Okay Klee. Try it again," Shep said softly. They seemed unaware of Patrick standing in the doorway. A foot-high, painted vase sat on the rug directly between them. Beautiful shades of red and deep blue formed elaborate designs along the circumference of the vase. Klee stared at it intently. He closed his eyes and brought his fingers to his temples. What happened next left Patrick baffled. He held his breath as he watched. Liquid began to drip down the sides of the vase and onto the rug. Patrick wanted to get a closer look but he stayed frozen in the doorway. Something told him he was not supposed to be seeing this. The liquid ran in thicker streams now. First it was the color of blood, but then darker colors swirled into the little waterfall until it was a rainbow of streams oozing down the vase.

The beautiful designs dripped off the glass, forming a mottled pool at the bottom of the vase. The long neck and spout shriveled then and made a slow sideways bend as the vase melted and collapsed like it was made of Playdoh. Klee opened his eyes and threw his hands over his head in a 'tah-dah' pose. He smiled at Shep. "I destroy it. Yes?"

Shepherd shook his head, frowning. "No. You melted it, Klee. You were supposed to shatter it."

Klee looked at the remains of the vase and his face fell. "I melt it?"

"Yes, Klee."

Klee looked about to cry. Shep crawled around the melted vase and stroked his hair lovingly. Patrick was always floored by these displays of affection. Shep soothed Klee softly as Klee gave in to the tears. "Don't cry Klee. It's all right. Even Juris had trouble with this at first."

"I lose my concentration," Klee said, his voice wet with tears.

Shep rubbed his shoulders. "Okay, that's a start. Now try and think, Klee. What was it exactly that made you lose your concentration?"

Klee wiped his nose with his wrist and pointed to the doorway where Patrick stood. "I smelled Patrick," he said.

Shep's head spun like a boomerang, his eyes wild when he saw Patrick standing in the doorway. "How long have you been standing there?" he demanded. His voice was harsh, without the friendly pretense he'd been using on Patrick since his arrival.

"Not long," Patrick said. Fear gripped his gut. Shep stood up and grabbed a small shovel from the fireplace. He shoveled the damaged remains of the vase into a paper bag.

"That's enough for now, Klee."

Klee got up and trotted out of the room like he hadn't a care in the world. Shep finished cleaning the mess then glanced up. "What do you want?" he said sharply. Patrick didn't like his tone. He reminded himself not to show his fear, as Wesley had advised him.

"I just wanted to let you know that I'm heading out. I'll see you later on tonight."

"Heading out where?"

Patrick scowled at him. "Well, to my consulting job of course. To Boston. I go once a week. Remember?"

"No," Shep said, shaking his head firmly.

"No, you can't remember? Shepherd, I just went last week."

Shep shook his head again, fussing with the rug and avoiding Patrick's eyes. "I don't mean, no, I can't remember. I mean no, you can't go," he said.

Great. Patrick didn't need this now. The bulge of the plastic baggy felt hard and heavy in his pocket. He was too close to rapping this bogus assignment up to have things stopped on a whim because Shep was in a bad mood. "What do you mean I can't go?"

"You can't go, Obrien. Joey will freak out. He gets scared when you're not around, and I can't coddle him all day. I'm having problems with Robin and I have a lot on my mind."

Patrick stiffened. Problems with Robin? Robin was not Shep's to have problems with. She was Patrick's Robin. Damn it. "What kind of problems?" he asked, a bit to sharply.

Shep looked up at him. "That's none of your business, Obrien."

Oh, you have no idea how much of my business it is, Patrick thought. Shep did seem overly agitated. The young man that Patrick used to think of as the most laid back person in the world was wound so tight he looked like he was about to snap. Since Patrick's arrival at Forest Bluffs, Shep had been going out of his way to give Patrick the impression that he was still the same old happy-go-lucky Shepherd. Now it seemed he hadn't the energy to keep up the facade. Something was really bothering him. Could it really be Robin's rejection? If that was the case, Shepherd had just better get over it. Robin was not coming back to him. Not now. Not ever.

"I didn't realize you were still seeing Robin," Patrick said. "I've noticed that she hasn't been around."

Shep straightened up. He looked at Patrick then looked at the floor, as if pondering the statement. He shook his head. "No. You don't understand, Obrien. It doesn't matter if Robin and I don't speak for weeks at a time. We'll always be together. She loves me. She's just being stubborn. She'll come crawling back. You'll see."

"Maybe she's just finished with you," Patrick said. This got Shep's attention.

"Finished with me?" He took a few steps closer to Patrick. "Is that what she told you? That she was finished with me?"

Patrick shrugged. "Well, she said something to that effect." Patrick was being spiteful, and he knew that Agent Litner would kill him if he heard him taunting Shep on this matter. But he just couldn't help himself.

Shep looked furious. "Finished with me." He repeated the words to himself, looking enraged.

"Why don't you just let it go Shep? The relationship is over. No big deal."

Shep glared at him. "Never. I will never let it go. While there is a breath in my body, that girl will belong to me."

Okay, drama queen. Patrick wanted to strangle him, but he forced himself to let the matter drop. He couldn't let his feelings for Robin lead him into an emotional confrontation. He had another matter to contend with now, and that was that Shep was telling him he could not leave the property. "I have to go to Boston now, Shep. The consulting firm is expecting me. I can't just blow it off."

He was sure that Shep would just wave him off at that point. Instead, he turned and stared at Patrick, hands on his hips. "I said no."

Patrick felt a strange heat pass through the room. Shep's eyes sparkled against his tanned face. They were not the placid kind eyes he'd been showing Patrick the last two weeks. The shields were down, and there was something else in those eyes. There was power. Patrick sucked his breath in as he thought he saw Shep's green eyes gleam like a cat's. He struggled to hide the flinch. "Shep, you can't tell me that I can't go to work."

"Obrien, listen to me. You don't need that consulting job."

"I have to keep my skills sharp," Patrick said, using Litner's words now. His own voice sounded small to him.

"For what? Your future? I give you everything you need right here. I cannot risk losing you, Obrien. Joey can't handle it. You'll stay here."

Patrick's heart beat like a drum in his chest. He was sure that Shep would smell his fear, so he tried to turn it into anger. He forced himself to take a defiant step forward, though the last thing he wanted to do was get closer to Shep. His skin prickled with an unseen energy. It seemed to be coming off of Shep in waves.

"I am not one of your lackeys, Shepherd. You don't tell me what to do. You can't make me stay here."

Shep chuckled, an animal sound deep in his throat. "You see, that's where you're wrong. I can make you stay here. I'd rather it didn't come to that. I'd like you to stay voluntarily."

Shep moved forward now. They stood face to face, mere inches between them. Patrick looked down at his smaller friend. Their size differential was no comfort. It never had been. But now there was real fear. It was easy to whisper about blood rites and wings while seated at the cozy table in Carbone's kitchen. To confront such matters with Shep himself was something he wasn't mentally prepared for. "You don't control me," Patrick said. His voice wasn't as firm as he'd intended it to be.

Shep laughed. "I control everything in this house and on this land, Obrien. Haven't you figured that out yet?"

"You're getting delusional Shep. I'm worried about you."

"Call me whatever names you want. You're still not leaving this property."

"Really? We'll see about that."

Patrick turned to leave the room. The door slammed shut in front of him. Stunned, he looked over his shoulder at Shep. "It must have been the wind," he said. Patrick shuddered. This was not good. He did not want this confrontation. He just wanted to get out of this nut house and to the safety of Agent Litner's office. He was so close. He shouldn't have bothered to say good bye to Shep at all. Now it seemed it was too late.

Patrick went for the door when Shep grabbed him by the back of his tee shirt. Before he knew what happened, Shep had flipped him. He was flat on his back with Shep's wiry body standing over him. His curls hung in his face as he loomed over Patrick. "I don't want you to get hurt, Obrien. Please trust me. This is for your own good."

Patrick glared up at him. Shep actually looked concerned, which was confusing. "You don't want me to get hurt? Then why did you just throw me onto the floor, you crazy fuck?"

Shep's eyes looked pained again, an expression that Patrick did not understand. "Please, Obrien. The pain will be much worse for you if you try to leave now. You've got to believe me."

"Why? Because you've always been so trustworthy?" Patrick lunged up at him, grabbing one arm and tossing Shep to the right. Shep scrambled to his feet with lightning speed and blocked his path to the door. Patrick went at him, meaning to toss him out of the way. Then Shep did something terrifying. He held his hand up in front of him as if to ward Patrick off. Shep's hand never made contact, yet Patrick's body was hurled to the side of the room with a force that knocked the wind out of him. Shep came over and looked down at him as he gasped for breath.

"Please don't continue this, Obrien. You don't understand. I don't want to hurt you. I just can't let you go."

Patrick stared up with open shock. He was afraid of Shep's power of course, but he was more frightened that Shep was no longer hiding it.

"Don't fight me, Obrien. I don't want things to be like this. I want us to work together."

"Yes, work together. I want that too!" Patrick lied, hoping to sweet talk his way out of the room. "We can discuss that when I get back. After I go to the city, we can sit down and talk about working together more."

"You lie, Obrien. I can always tell. Your aura gets little green spots."

"Yes, so I've been told." He struggled to his feet. He felt a nasty bruise starting at his hip. "I'm leaving, Shep. You're going to have to kill me to keep me here."

Shep frowned at him. "The truth is Obrien, you really can't leave. The blood won't let you."

Patrick snickered. "That's funny, I could have sworn it was you who wouldn't let me."

"I'm trying to save you some pain, Obrien. I figured if you thought it was me keeping you here, you wouldn't go. You've spent too much time with Joey now. The bond has solidified. The blood will stop you. Please don't try it, Patrick. I care about you. I really don't want to see you in pain." Shep's eyes were sincere and pleading. He had used Patrick's first name, which meant he was very serious.

"You're crazy," Patrick said.

"That's beside the point. You don't have to be afraid. You're part of it now. Can't you feel it? Didn't you feel it when you threw me? It went through you!"

"What went through me?"

"Power. Energy. Blood."

"Crazy," Patrick said, pointing at Shep, moving past him to the door.

"Have it your way, Patrick. I won't try and stop you. And I do care about you, regardless of what you think. But you can't hide from it. It's inside of you. We're all tied together now. You, Joey, and me. Bonded forever."

"Lucky me," he said and went for the door. Sweating profusely, he grabbed the door handle and was happy to find that it opened.

Margol was outside waiting for him. Hadn't he been in the library? Damn they were fast. "Where are you going, Patrick?" he asked.

"Anywhere but here, Margol," he said. Margol looked over Patrick's shoulder at Shep, waiting for instructions.

"Let him go," Shep said. Margol stepped aside and Patrick went out the door. He walked past Joey and Kelinda who gave him an odd look. He kept walking right out the front door and proceeded down the driveway. The front gates opened for him as he approached, and he stepped out onto the street. He felt better already.

Nobody came after him, and nobody tried to stop him. He made his way up Ocean Way, letting the sea breeze lick his face. He was going home. He was going home if he had to walk, swim, or fly all the way. He had nearly made it to the stop sign at the bottom of the hill when the first pain ripped through his head.

He fell to the left into one of the scrubby blueberry bushes that ran along the side of the road. It felt like someone had stuck a hot poker into his ear and through his brain. He hung his head for a moment and the pain dulled to a light throbbing. He was all right again. No big deal, he told himself. People get headaches, right? He began to walk forward when the second pain hit him and he stopped in his tracks, gasping. He forced his feet to keep moving. The pain intensified, becoming a flash of white light across his eyes.

He collapsed onto the road. A montage of images flashed in his mind with the pain. The images of Joey spilled into his vision so sharp and clear that he thought he was dreaming. He saw Joey falling from the church roof, Joey getting stabbed repeatedly in the chest by the crazy veteran at the bar, Joey getting shot. With each new image, another shudder of white-hot pain shot through Patrick's skull and down his spine. He crawled backwards a few feet, crab-style and the images faded slightly, dulling the pain. Still sliding on his rear end, he went backwards up the hill, back toward the house, sweating and panting. A few more feet and the images stopped altogether. The pain had subsided, but his body was shocked.

He found himself lying on the side of the road shivering. A chipmunk ran out of the bushes then retreated back. A motorcycle rumbled by. Its driver gave Patrick a double glance before he sped off down the road. Patrick stood up slowly, his head still throbbing. He took a cautious step forward and the searing pain started to return. Defeated, he turned and headed back toward Joey's house. It was only when the salty wetness leaked onto his lips that he realized he was crying. This was bad. This was beyond bad. He couldn't leave Forest Bluffs. He was in a world of trouble.

The front gates at the driveway opened when he returned, like a giant pair of jaws welcoming him back into the belly of the beast. He walked through them and up the front lawn, but did not go back into the house. He was too upset and frightened to face anyone. Instead, he walked around the side of the house and meandered through the back yard and into the woods. Nobody stopped him. Clearly they knew now that he could not leave, so there was no need to watch over him anymore. Joey's blood had taken over the watch now.

He walked off into the thick woods until he was a good distance from the house. He sat down on a large flat boulder and looked around himself. He was flanked on all sides by trees. Tiny chirping sounds of the forest engulfed him. He lay back on the rock, watching the beams of sunlight cut through the trees above him. He sobbed. What was he going to do? This changed everything. If he couldn't leave Joey, then he couldn't leave Forest Bluffs. He couldn't go home. He couldn't get the sample to Litner. He couldn't go back to Robin. Looking up above him at the tree tops, he prayed. He couldn't remember the last time he had prayed. He asked God to please help him out of this mess. He added that God was, after all, indirectly responsible for this. Had he kept a better watch over his minions, Shepherd would not be walking the earth in the first place. He wasn't sure if blaming God was a good idea, but he finished the prayer with an Amen, and closed his eyes.

A strong hand pressed down on his mouth, stifling his scream. Patrick tried to jump up but the firm hand held his head down on the stone. He hadn't heard anyone approach.

Patrick tried a second time to sit up when the cold butt of a gun pressed against his temple. The stranger removed his hand from Patrick's mouth, but kept the gun to his head. His unseen assailant stood silently behind Patrick where he lay on the rock. Patrick raised his hands slowly over his head and said, "I'm not moving. You don't need the gun."

His assailant removed the gun from his temple. Patrick sat up and turned around, expecting to see Shep or one of his grunts. He sucked his breath in at the sight of his assailant. It was the crazy long-haired man that had tried to knife Joey in the bar. His gray hair hung in a scraggly mess down past his shoulders. A map of lines surrounded his dark eyes. He was dressed in camouflage pants with a black tank top. His arms were tattooed, well-muscled and powerful-looking. He kept the gun pointed on Patrick, but made no move.

"You!" Patrick gasped. His eyes dropped to the gun. Much to Patrick's relief, he holstered it.

"Keep your voice down," he said.

"Please," Patrick said, "I don't want any trouble. Just walk away. I won't tell them I saw you."

"Why were you crying?" he asked. Patrick didn't answer. He took a step closer. Patrick shimmied backward on the rock. The weathered-looking man stopped and held his hands up, showing them to Patrick. "Whoa. Take it easy there, Little Buttercup. I'm not going to hurt you."

Patrick blinked at him. "What did you say?"

"I said relax, Little Buttercup." The man's voice was steady and authoritative. It was not the voice of a lunatic. An alarm went off in Patrick's subconscious. Little Buttercup, the man had called him. The code name Agent Litner had given him. This man was not a deranged veteran at all. He was Agent Litner's scout.

"You're a Federal Agent!" Patrick said excitedly, moving forward on the rock.

The old man's hand went over Patrick's mouth again and he froze. Leaning in close, he said, "It kind of defeats the purpose of using a code name if you're going to be yelling things like that out. Now doesn't it?"

He removed his hand. Patrick sighed. "Sorry. I'm just...surprised."

"Save it, Obrien. We don't have much time. Why were you crying?" the man asked again.

"I can't leave!" Patrick whispered, and the tears came again. He looked up at man. He had that FBI scowl that Agent Litner got when he was thinking too hard. It was odd to see that expression on this scraggly-looking character. The long hair and the Rambo get-up seemed even more ridiculous now that Patrick knew he was a federal agent.

"I saw you go out the front gates. You came back. Why?"

"They've done something to me. Physically. I can't leave." Patrick explained the pain he experienced as he'd tried to move away from the property. The agent scowled as he listened.

"Do you have the samples?" he asked.

"Yes."

"Give them to me. I'll get them to Litner."

Patrick pulled the baggy out of his jeans and handed it over. The man examined the bag, then quickly stuffed it into a side pocket in his pants. "What about me?" Patrick asked, his tears threatening to come again.

"Take it easy, Obrien. We'll figure something out. We're going to get you out of here."

Patrick hung his head in despair. The agent leaned over. "Hey! Look at me." Patrick did. The man's dark eyes stared at him intensely. "We will get you out of here, Obrien. Do you understand me?" Patrick shrugged. "Hey!" the agent said again. "My name is Agent Walsh. I'm a member of Agent Litner's team, and I keep my promises. We all do. If we have to strap Joey Duvaine to your back like a fucking papoose, we'll get you out. Okay?"

Patrick smiled in spite of himself. The words were strangely comforting. "Okay," he said.

Agent Walsh scanned the woods around them with a paranoia that matched Agent Litner's, then he looked back at Patrick. "I'll get this to Litner, and I'll tell him what's happened. Sit tight and don't make waves. Don't do anything until I contact you."

"How will you contact me?"

"I'll leave you a sign on the back deck. When you find it, come out to this rock again. You've done your part. We'll take it from here."

Patrick certainly hoped so. The FBI was his only hope now. The knowledge of that was far from comforting.

Chapter Forty-Two

Robin had the most unsettling feeling that Litner was losing control of this investigation. Patrick was stuck at Forest Bluffs, yet another 'unexpected hindrance'. The stony agent had damn well better come up with a solid plan soon, because she was losing faith rapidly, and losing her mind at the thought of Patrick stuck out there at Camp Blood. She pulled into her driveway and turned the car off. She slung the heavy gym bag over her right shoulder, and kept it to the side to avoid bumping the long stairwell.

She saw him as soon as she opened the door and stepped into her apartment, seated in her favorite living room chair. His arms rested patiently on the sides, his feet on the floor, his eyes staring blankly at her. She gave a little yelp, not a blood curdling scream, but more like the abrupt involuntary hoot you give out upon finding a spider on your pillow. "Hello Robin."

Her first instinct was to run. If she'd had time to think about it, she would not have done so. To run meant that she feared him, and she did not want him to know that she did. Unfortunately, her instincts were not in the mood to reason things out. She turned and darted back out the door. Margol and Allisto came out of nowhere. They must have been hiding somewhere in the outer hallway. They each grabbed an arm and shoved her back into her apartment, closing the door behind her. Margol used extreme force, either accidentally or on purpose as he thrust her into her living room. She stumbled and landed on the floor, still clinging to her gym bag. Shep remained seated during the whole ordeal, watching calmly. A pain shot through Robin's knee as she hit the floor.

Pain always angered her, and for the moment, the anger made her forget her fear. She glared up at the one who was responsible for her pain, Margol, with his red curls and face full of welts. "Well," she said. "Don't you look pretty."

The comment seemed to upset him. Allisto gently touched the marks along Margol's cheek, scowling. "I will heal!" Margol said to her, slapping Allisto's hand away.

She climbed up off of the floor and brushed herself off, then turned slowly to face Shep. "What did you do to him, Shep? Mark up his face so he wouldn't look prettier than you?"

Shep met her gaze with his round green eyes, a hint of humor giving the corners a tilt. His skin was suntanned, and his dark blond hair had that streaky look it always got with the approaching summer. She felt something stir inside her, and it wasn't anger or fear. She was still physically attracted to him, and it made her want to kick her own ass. Oh well, she thought. Just because she still wanted him didn't mean she wouldn't kill him if she had to.

Margol and Allisto stood guard in front of the door preventing her escape. She was trapped in her own home. "What the fuck do you think you're doing, Shepherd?" She struggled to keep the fear out of her voice, but she heard a slight quiver anyway.

"You seem upset, Robin. Have I been neglecting you again?"

"I prefer it if you neglect me."

"Since when?"

"How many times do I have to go through this with you, Shepherd? We discussed this on the phone." She stood before him where he sat like a judge, and she the defendant thrown before the court.

"I've stopped calling you for up to three months before. You always came back to me."

"I was a lot younger then," she said firmly.

"It was last year, Robin."

"Yeah, well I was a lot younger last year. What makes you think you can just come into my apartment whenever you please?"

Shep drummed his fingers on his knees and looked around the apartment smugly. "Well, for one thing, you gave me a key." Oh, right. She'd forgotten about the key. "You never took it back. You never said I wasn't welcome."

"Oh really? How about the part when I told you I didn't want to see you anymore? Didn't that maybe give you the slight impression that you were no longer welcome to just stroll into my home at will?"

Shep stood and walked around the coffee table. Putting a finger to his chin, he said, "Yeah, about that not wanting to see me anymore thing. I'd like to discuss that."

"There is nothing to discuss."

He looked at her. He was too close and she could smell his familiar scent. "Oh I think there is. In fact, I think there's a lot to discuss. For instance, there is the matter of your behavioral changes as of late. Your attitude toward me has been out of character to say the least. That got me thinking."

He'd been standing in a relaxed pose with his hands in the pockets of his jeans. He pulled something out of his pocket, and began to twirl it playfully as he circled her. "I got to thinking that maybe there's more to your sudden change of heart than saving your self-respect from my less than adequate dating practices. I'm not buying that, you see. I know you too well."

"People change," she said.

He raised his eyebrows. "Oh do they? Do people change, Robin?" He twirled the thing in front of her face and she finally recognized it. It was the candy necklace Patrick had given her the day they rode out to the caves. It had been hanging ceremoniously on her bedroom mirror. Shep thrust his hand out, hanging the candy necklace in front of Robin's face. "What is this...thing?" he asked through gritted teeth.

Robin felt a swell of fear. "That is a candy necklace. Haven't you ever seen one? Oh that's right. You had a deprived childhood." She realized after she said it that cracks about Shep's childhood no longer held any weight. Shep had, after all, fabricated his childhood. The whole abusive father story had been an elaborate fiction designed to ward off questions about his true past, and the real reason that his back was so brutally scarred.

"I know it's a candy necklace you wise-ass bitch. Where did you get it?"

She ordered herself to stay calm. Even Shep was not that intuitive. If he had sensed anything at all, it was vague. He could not possibly know where the necklace had come from, or he wouldn't be asking. She decided to stall, to find out how much he knew. This was an old familiar practice between them. He'd always known how to read her, but she had always excelled at annoying him into saying more than he'd intended to. This gave her a better idea of where she stood, and exactly how much trouble she was in.

"What difference does it make where I got it?" she said snottily. She could see his lips tighten. His round eyes narrowed just a bit as he fixed his gaze on her. He looked at the necklace.

"It makes a difference to me."

"Why? It's just a candy necklace. What is the problem?"

"The problem is, ROBIN, that you had it hanging on your bedroom mirror."

"Is that a crime?"

He began to circle her again. She stayed where she was, even though the feel of him coming around behind where she couldn't see him was unnerving. "I know you, Robin. You forget that, I think. You don't hang things on your mirror unless they mean something to you. Now, seeing that this is a cheap dirty piece of shit necklace made of confectionery sugar, what value could it possibly hold? What could make this necklace so important that it would earn a coveted spot on your mirror? Hmmm?"

He had come around to face her again. He took the colorful strand of candy loops and pulled it over his own head. It hung festively around his neck. She wanted to rip it off. Apparently it showed on her face. "What's wrong? Does it make you angry to see me wearing this? Why would you care? It's just a piece of costume jewelry. It's made of fucking candy!"

His anger flared and she took a step back. "What is your point, Shepherd? Enough with the candy necklace already! Christ on a crutch!"

"Who gave this to you, Robin?"

"I bought it for myself."

"Bullshit. You've always been a bad liar. Who is he?"

"Who is who?"

"You know who. The guy who gave you this necklace."

"What guy?"

He pointed a warning finger at her. "Don't do it, Robin. Don't drag me into one of these Abbott and Costello circuitous arguments. Just answer the damn question."

She remained stoically silent. Keeping his eyes on her, he removed the necklace and held it before his face. He breathed in deeply, smelling it. "Did I ever mention that I have an extraordinarily keen sense of smell?" he asked.

"No."

"Well I do. Do you know what I smell when I bring this necklace to my face?"

"Sugar?" she said snidely.

"I smell you. Not your perfume, not your soap or your shampoo, but you. I smell your sweat. And it smells like passion. It smells like desire. You see, these are the subtle changes in your scent that only I can define."

"You're crazy. No one can smell desire."

"Oh really? Animals can."

"Well that makes sense. You are an animal."

"So are you! So are we all!"

She began to walk toward her bedroom. "Don't start, Shepherd. I'm not in the mood for one of your nature of the beast lectures."

He grabbed her arm and tugged her back hard. She gasped. He had never hurt her before. She looked into his eyes and was frightened by what she saw. She couldn't place it, but his eyes looked different. It was as though the shields were down. Rage swirled in the reflective green around his pupils. "Who gave you the candy necklace?" he growled. "I'll find out who he is. You know I can. It would be a lot easier if you just tell me." She said nothing. "Fine," he said. "You don't have to tell me who he is. It makes no difference now. You won't be seeing him anymore. You're coming with me."

"The hell I am." She stood defiantly. She was only five foot four, so she had to look up at Shep, who was five foot ten. They had been so perfect for each other physically. Their bodies had fit together like pieces of a puzzle. She forced those thoughts out of her head, reminding herself that he had just announced he was going to kidnap her.

He looked over her head at Margol and Allisto. He didn't say a word, but they came over and stood behind her. She glanced back at them nervously. "I want you all to leave now. If you don't leave now, I'm calling the police."

"That's going to be a bit difficult with no telephone," Shep said, casually examining his fingernails.

She glanced over at the end table where her phone usually sat. It was gone. Her eyes darted to the wall where the kitchen began. The wall phone had been removed as well. Real fear gripped her now and she turned to run for the door, pushing through Margol and Allisto. At least she thought she had pushed through them, until she felt herself being lifted off her feet. Margol held her in a bear hug, with one hand clasped over her mouth.

Shepherd shook his head at her. "You'll thank me for this. It's what you really want. You'll see." She struggled against Margol, trying with all her might to bite his hand so she could tell Shep to fuck off one more time, but he held her with an iron grip. "Get her things together as we planned. Meet me in the van. Don't take too long."

Robin's eyes darted to the window. The light had faded into darkness during this altercation. He must have planned it this way. It was far easier to kidnap someone in the dark. Shep strolled casually out of the apartment, closing the door behind him. Margol half-pushed and half-dragged her into the bedroom, with Allisto following behind. Once they got her inside, Margol tossed her aside. Allisto stood in front of the closed bedroom door with his arms crossed in front of him like a guard. "Pack," he said, pointing to her bed where someone had left her suitcase open. She looked at the two of them. Angels, demons, whatever they were didn't matter. They were hired muscle. They were servants, and they had but one master. They looked so like Shep with their chin-length curls and wide green eyes. Those child faces that masked what they were.

She picked up the suitcase and threw it onto the floor. "Fuck you!" she said. Margol and Allisto exchanged a glance, and then Allisto came forward and grabbed her. She thrashed and fought against his iron grip as he pulled something down over her head, some sort of sack or hood. Claustrophobia engulfed her, and she started to scream. She sucked the soft cloth of the sack into her mouth with every inward breath and panic set in. She fought like a wild animal, but was no match for the strength of the hands that held her. Then the sack was removed.

Margol moved in on her immediately, pushing her up against the wall, continuing her sense of being closed in. "Listen to me Robin," he whispered in her ear. "You have choices here. You can come with us carrying none of your possessions, with a bag tied over your head, or you can pack up your personal belongings, and walk out that door with us in a civilized fashion. Either way you're coming with us."

She glared at him, but said nothing. He must have interpreted her silence as submission, because he loosened his grip on her shoulders and stepped back a bit. She tilted her head back and brought it forward, head-butting Margol square above the eyes. He staggered, bringing his hands to his head, then he grunted as she jammed the heel of her foot into his knee. She dove for the door. Allisto was quick, and his arm shot out and grabbed her elbow just as he reached the door knob. He squeezed her elbow just hard enough to show his unnatural strength. She looked into his cold green eyes and saw the truth in them. He'd hurt her for Shep. He'd do anything for Shep.

He let her go, then stared silently as she threw some clothes into the suitcase. She spotted the little vial of blood she'd concocted with Aunt Betsy. It sat in the corner of her underwear drawer. She stuffed it into a pair of socks and packed that too. After grabbing a few pairs of shoes from her closet, she zipped up the suitcase and glared at her captors. Allisto held his hand out toward the door in an "after you" gesture. She moved out the door, comforted that she may have the weapon to their destruction tucked neatly in a pair of socks in her suitcase.

Chapter Forty-Three

Dr. Juliet Wang was the only woman Agent Litner had ever been in love with. At least it was the closest thing to love he'd experienced. The affair had been short but intense. He had honestly thought that things would work out between them. She seemed so much like him. She was brilliant, serious, and regimented. She had a self-discipline that matched his. She, in response, appreciated these traits in him. Unfortunately, like most women, she soon discovered that there was not much else to Agent Litner. He did not let the regimentation go at the end of the day, as she did. With him it was a personality trait, not a work ethic. His stony coldness was not easily melted, and when it came down to it, he could not change who he was. Much to his disappointment, even Juliet Wang, the most serious of women, desired a certain amount of intimacy from him.

The closest interaction he had with civilian life was when he profiled some monster on a terrorist scheme. Of course all of those monsters had been human. Father Carbone had been right to suspect he had prior knowledge of Cripulets. A team of scientists had accidentally opened one in India years before. A two-legged reptilian figure had come through, looking startled. They'd reported that it looked vaguely humanoid, with sharp intelligent eyes. Seemingly aware of its mistake, it had darted back through the portal, which closed immediately after. The Feds had been researching Cripulets ever since.

He liked to think he'd changed since his mind had been opened by such things, softened somewhat, but it would do him no good with Dr. Juliet Wang. She had married someone else. They remained friends and colleagues, as Juliet still did a fair share of work for the Bureau. Their relationship was purely professional now. Agent Litner, however, still felt the flutter of anxiety as he stepped into Juliet's laboratory. He thought the butterflies would have quieted by now, but as he came through the double doors and saw her standing in front of a microscope, they were as active as ever.

She glanced up at him through a pair of safety goggles, her eyes smiling as they fell upon him. "Hello Dr. Wang," he said stoically.

"Hello Agent Litner," she said, emphasizing the 'Agent' to mock his formality. He felt uncomfortable calling her by her first name. It conjured up too many intimate memories. She removed the safety goggles and walked around the long table to greet him. "Have a seat." She signaled to a chair alongside the desk.

He slid stiffly into it. "What have you got for me?"

Juliet slid in behind the desk and opened a folder. She placed a pair of wire frame glasses onto her nose. He tried not to stare at her big dark eyes, with their enchanting almond shape and slight slant at the corners. Instead he looked at her lip as she chewed the end of her pen. He forced his eyes to fall on the folder she had in her hands. "Well, it's not poison," she said with a shrug.

Litner startled in his seat. It was not the answer he was expecting. "It's not poison? Are you sure?"

She raised her eyebrows and nodded. "At least it's not showing up as a toxin on the test chart. We also tested it on some of the lab animals. Aside from a little digestive discomfort in the rats, it seems to be a harmless substance. It's very unusual, but harmless."

Litner felt his world falling around him. He had been so sure the crop was toxic. This ruined his entire theory. Without the crop, he had nothing. "Okay, so it's not poison. What do you mean it's unusual? Unusual how?"

She searched her desk and pulled another folder out of a stack of paper work. "I have Donald's agricultural report here. Have you ever heard of Triticale?"

"Sure. It's genetically engineered grain. Am I close?"

She smiled. "Fairly close. It is a manmade cross-breed. It's like the love child of hexaploid wheat and diploid rye. The two are crossbred to make the seed hardier, among other things. This stuff can grow in the oddest of climates. It can even grow in the winter."

"So this is Triticale?" Litner asked.

She shook her head. "No. It's like Triticale in the sense that it's a manmade cross-breed, but it's not Triticale. Seeing a genetically modified seed is not the unusual part. Hell, most crops out there have some genetic alterations."

"So exactly what is this stuff?"

"That's the unusual part. Donald says he's never seen anything quite like it. There seems to be some of your average wheat in there, and a generic form of grain, but there's another substance that we just can't identify. There's a strand running throughout the mix that doesn't come up on any known charts. It's whatever gives it that reddish brown color. See this?"

She held up a diagram, a bunch of letters connected by straight lines. It looked like a puzzle. "What is that?" he asked.

"This is the chemical structure for the unknown substance. We can break it down to its base elements. We simply can't identify it. As far as our agricultural expert is concerned, it's an unknown. Who's growing this stuff anyway?"

"I'm sorry. That's classified, Dr. Wang."

She smiled. "Of course. But please Steven, call me Juliet. We are friends, aren't we?"

He shifted uncomfortably. "Of course we're friends Dr...Juliet. These tests you conducted on the lab animals...are the results indicative of the effect the substance would have on humans?"

She shook her head. "Not necessarily. I would say that it is more than likely that if the substance does not harm animals, then it won't harm humans. As far as being one hundred percent sure, I can't say. There are differences in our chemical make-ups. There are, after all, diseases that we contract that animals cannot, and visa versa. But still, a toxin would have shown up on the machine in the original reading."

"Then we need to test it on humans," Litner said with resolve.

She looked at him, her face blank for a moment, then she sighed and took the glasses off. She rubbed her eyes. "You know I can't do that, Steven."

"It's important," he said. "You've done human testing before."

"Steven, this is an unknown substance. I personally don't believe it to be harmful, but it's still an unknown. I can't test it on humans now. I won't. Even if we could get approval, which we won't, I wouldn't feel comfortable putting people at risk."

"I'll volunteer," he said, his face stony.

"No."

"Why not?"

"We'd never get approval for it and you know it."

"Fuck the approval!" he said.

Juliet looked up at him with open shock. He hadn't realized how loose his emotions and his dialect had become since he'd been working on this investigation. The personalities of Patrick and the others were rubbing off on him. He was immediately embarrassed by the uncharacteristic outburst.

"I don't think I've ever heard you curse before, Steven," Juliet said with a smirk.

"No one needs to know about this test, Juliet. Just you and I."

"Steven, that's crazy. You don't know what this crop is! I'm not going to be responsible for harming you. I just can't live with that."

"If you get caught, you can just say that I stole the substance. Say I administered it to myself."

"It's not my career I'm concerned about, Steven. It's you. You've never taken risks like this before. Why now?"

"Please Juliet. Please." He looked at her and tried very hard to let her see his sincerity. It was difficult, since his normal expression was deadpan. He'd spent years perfecting the vacant stare. He'd almost lost the ability to show emotion. Juliet stared back at him and he saw her soften.

"Is this really that important, Steven?"

"It could be," he said honestly. "I have to be sure, Juliet. This is one of those times that I need that hundred percent."

She sighed and shook her head. "All right. I'll give you the absolute smallest dose of the substance possible. You're going to have to undergo a complete physical exam, before, during and after you ingest the substance. I do mean complete, Steven. It is not going to be pleasant. They will extract every fluid you have, as well as some you didn't know you had. You're going to feel like a human pin cushion. And that's only the safe part. Still want to do this?"

He smiled at her then. "You're not actually trying to frighten me, are you?"

Her smile matched his. "Oh, I forgot. The big bad agent isn't going to be afraid of a few needles."

"Will you hold my hand?" he asked.

Juliet shook her head. "Wow. A sense of humor. When did you develop that?" She'd meant the statement as a joke, but saw in his eyes that it had cut him to the quick. His rigid personality had been the major cause of their break up. "I'm sorry, Steven. I didn't mean that. It was cruel."

"No," he said, "it was pretty funny actually." He grabbed his briefcase and gave her a quick kiss on the cheek. She looked surprised and a little bit sad. "I do appreciate this, Juliet," he said. "Now, where do I go to register as a lab rat?"

Chapter Forty-Four

Patrick sat alone on the deck. Shielding his eyes with his hand, he peered out at the fields and at the falling pink sun that lit them. He could see the shadowy figures of the followers loading barrels of the red grain into the guest house and into the backs of the Arcania trucks. It made him nervous. Something was going to happen very soon. Patrick tried not to let his doubts consume him. Agent Buttercup, or Walsh, or whatever his real name was had promised to get him out safely. He prayed that he could trust the old coot.

Robin still had not arrived. When Klee let slip that Shep had gone to the city to collect her, Patrick wasn't sure whether to believe him or not. Now all he could do was wait, beside himself with worry for her safety. He heard noises in the kitchen and turned to look through the closed glass door, but it was only Joey and Russell. The sliding door opened and Joey pushed Russell out onto the deck. "Go get some air!"

Russell walked slowly onto the deck and weaved over to a nearby lounge chair, falling into it. He looked dazed, and he wasn't wearing his glasses. His short wavy black hair was pushed flat in the back as though it hadn't been brushed in days. He sat sideways on the lounge chair and began to rock back and forth, humming softly to himself. Patrick glanced up at Joey who stood just outside the door, gazing thoughtfully at Russell. "Obrien, could you keep an eye on Russell for a while?"

Joey wore an old tee shirt with a baseball cap pulled over his newly lengthened hair. He looked like the old Joey. He looked like the Joey that worked in a financial office and played pool on the weekends, not the enchanting false prophet of Forest Bluffs. Patrick felt a twinge of affection at the sight of him. He still held the stinging memory of what their friendship had been, however calculated and false on Joey's part. "Did you say you want me to watch Russell?" Patrick asked, confused.

Joey nodded. "Please. I think he dropped acid or something. He's all fucked up and I can't watch him. I have to make dinner for Klee."

Patrick glanced at Russell, puzzled. He shrugged. "Sure. I'll watch him. I guess."

"Thanks, Obrien." Klee peered out from behind Joey's shoulder and stole a glance over at Russell. He looked concerned and a little bit guilty. He saw Patrick looking at him and he turned and ran back into the house. Joey went in after him and shut the door.

Patrick dragged his chair over to sit near Russell, who seemed to be watching things that weren't there. "Hey Russell. Why aren't you wearing your glasses?"

Russell looked at him suspiciously. "They broke," he said.

The sliding door opened then and Joey stepped outside carrying Russell's thick black glasses. "Russell, I found your glasses behind the computer desk." The glasses were intact and unbroken. Russell took them from Joey and put them in his shirt pocket. Klee peered out from the doorway like a frightened deer. Joey walked back to the house, pushing Klee inside a bit roughly. Klee allowed himself to be led back inside the house, but his haunted eyes never left Russell.

Once they were alone again, Patrick looked at Russell, who stared straight ahead, humming softly. Patrick doubted that Russell's condition had anything to do with drugs. Forest Bluffs had a way of driving people bughouse. Perhaps Russell had seen or heard something that his mind wasn't ready to digest. As far as Patrick knew, Russell was unaware of the truth about Shep and the others. "Russell, Joey just gave you your glasses. They're not broken. Why don't you put them on?" Russell ignored him. Russell's black glasses had some of the thickest lenses Patrick had ever seen. Theoretically, he should be damn close to blind as a bat without them. "Russell? Are you all right?"

Russell turned his head slowly until his eyes focused on Patrick. A flicker of awareness passed over his face. "Obrien."

"Yes, Russell, that's my name."

Russell grinned. "Did you know that you look like a Viking? I mean, if you grew your hair long. You'd make a great Viking, Obrien."

"Russell, did you take something? Are you on something right now?"

Russell's face went blank. "Sort of," he said.

"What did you take? Was it acid?"

"No."

"Mushrooms? Mescaline?"

"No."

Patrick leaned in closer to Russell, who was back to staring at the air in front of him. His pupils did seem a bit dilated. "Russell, tell me what you're on."

Russell looked at him with fear now. "I can't tell you. You won't believe me. And if you do believe me, you'll hurt me."

"Why would I hurt you, Russell? I'm trying to help you."

"Yeah, right. You despise me."

"Look Russell, I know we haven't exactly gotten along lately, but I'm trying to help you now. Just tell me what you ingested."

Russell's face twisted into a grimace. He leaned in close and lowered his voice to a frightened whisper. "There's something going on, Obrien. It's the brothers. There's something weird about them! Do you see the weirdness? They're not normal!"

Patrick sighed. "The brothers' weirdness is not in question, Russell. Tell me what's got you so spooked."

Russell winced. "You said you'd break my knee caps if I ever went near him again."

"Break your knee caps. Are you talking about Klee?" Russell sat tight-lipped. "Russell, tell me! Does this have something to do with Klee?"

Russell's haunted eyes met Patrick's. He looked different without his glasses on. In fact, he looked different period. Despite his obvious terror, his face had a healthy glow, contrary to his usual ghostly pallor. "Russell? Are you listening to me?"

"He came to me. It wasn't my fault. He came to me."

"Who came to you? Klee?"

Russell began to shake so violently that Patrick was afraid he was going into some sort of fit. He knelt down and held Russell's arms. "Russell, my God! What's the matter with you?"

"I'm scared, Obrien. I'm so fucking scared. I thought I was scared of you, but I'm more scared of whatever's happening to me. Maybe you should just kick my ass. Maybe that will make it go away. Kick my ass Obrien! Just kick my ass!"

Patrick shook him hard. "Stop it! Russell just calm down! I'm not going to touch you, but you have to tell me what's going on!" Russell jerked his head up and looked into the night sky. His eyes darted around at the air as though watching things move. Patrick looked up but saw nothing. "What are you seeing, Russell?"

Russell brought his attention back to the deck. "I see too much!" he whispered.

"But your glasses—"

"I don't need them anymore!"

Patrick stood up and walked to the other side of the deck. "How many fingers am I holding up?" he called over to Russell as he held up four fingers.

"Four," Russell said without hesitation.

Patrick adjusted his hand so that only his index finger stood up. "Now how many..."

"One," Russell interrupted.

Patrick walked slowly forward. "You really can see. My God, Russell. How did this happen?"

Russell looked at Patrick. The new moonlight shone on his messy black hair, making him look even more crazed. "It wasn't a miracle of God. I can tell you that."

"What then?"

"Klee. It was Klee. He did something to me. I know it sounds crazy, but I'm sure he did this to me. He did something to me! Well, that's not entirely accurate. I did something to him. But he asked me to. He asked me to!"

Patrick rubbed his chin and took the seat next to Russell. He did not want to ask the question, but he knew he had to. "Are you talking about sex?"

Russell flinched and slid his chair back, away from Patrick. "Not exactly."

"Oral sex then?"

"Are you going to hit me?"

"Just answer the question, Russell. Did you...?"

"Yes. I did." Russell flinched as if expecting a blow. Patrick just looked at him. The guy had to be damned scared if he was risking a beating. Patrick would have thought him mad, but he knew to some degree what it meant to get fluids from one of the brothers. He doubted that Shep had a clue just how much of this precious celestial essence was being haphazardly shared all around him. The stuff was flowing like water and Shep had no idea. He thought he was in control.

Patrick was uncomfortable enough discussing heterosexual sex. This was almost painfully embarrassing. But he had to know how much of the old angel cocktail Russell had been exposed to. "Russell, when you were with Klee, did he...um..."

"Yes, Obrien. He came."

"And did you...uh..."

"Swallow?"

"Yeah. That."

"Yes, Obrien. I took it all. Every drop."

Patrick sat back and stared at Russell as he pondered the situation. Russell grew uncomfortable under his gaze. "What is it, Obrien? Why are you asking me all these questions?"

Patrick hung his head but couldn't think of a response that wouldn't make Russell more of a basket case than he already was.

"Obrien, tell me! You know something about this, don't you? What's happening to me? Tell me what's happening to me!" he screamed.

Patrick grabbed his shoulders and pushed him back on the lawn chair. "Don't yell, Russell. I do know one thing. Whatever this is that's happening to you, you have to keep it quiet. Do you understand me? You have to hide it!"

"Why?"

"Because you dipped your hand in the wrong cookie jar, that's why. You shouldn't have done it, Russell. Not with Klee. Not with any of the brothers."

Russell hung his head and cried. "I know. I only did it to get back at Shep. He was on the phone, begging Robin to come back to him. I just got so jealous! I..." He began to sob then, and Patrick actually felt sorry for him. After a moment he stopped crying and looked quickly behind him, as though he'd felt something.

"What are you seeing Russell? Tell me about it."

Russell looked at the sky again. "I'm not sure. Maybe they're demons come to take me to hell, where I belong."

"Why do you think you belong in hell?"

Russell hung his head in his hands. "You wouldn't understand. You've probably never done one wrong thing in your whole life. I'm not that strong. I did something terrible. I did something unthinkable. A young man is dead. He's dead because I couldn't say no to Shep. And now I'm going to pay. Now the demons have come to take me off to hell."

Patrick realized then that it was Copie that Russell was referring to. He'd almost forgotten that they all still thought Copie had been killed in the lab explosion. He watched as Russell began to tremble again. At least the son of a bitch had the decency to feel bad about it. He wanted at that moment to tell Russell that Copie was alive and that Russell had no murder on his conscience. But of course he couldn't do that. He wasn't about to blow his cover just because Russell was having a bad cum trip.

"Russell, listen to me. You're not dying, and you're not going to hell. At least not right now. You've just been exposed to something...foreign."

Russell looked up and blinked twice. "Foreign?"

"Yes."

Russell shook his head. "I can see colors. Colors that glow around everything. They're around you right now, Obrien."

"Do you mean auras?"

"I don't know what the hell they are. I see flashes of light pass by me. I can smell things more strongly, and I can hear things. If I try, I can listen to conversations going on down the street. I can even hear things that people think sometimes. You've got to help me, Obrien! If you know what this is, you have to tell me!"

"My telling you what I know won't do you any good! I can tell you this though. If you keep acting like this, Shep is going to figure out what you did. Do you hear me? He'll know. And he'll kill you, Russell. You have to get a grip on yourself. Am I getting through to you?"

Russell looked at him seriously. "I'm scared. I mean really scared."

Patrick gave him a meaningful look. "We're all scared, Russell."

Something made a loud crash inside the kitchen and they both looked up. Patrick could see Shep's sandy curls through the slider, and his heart leapt. This meant they were back, and more than likely Robin was in the house somewhere. Then he saw Joey push Shep. Shep went right back at him and then the two of them stood chest to chest, screaming at each other. They looked like two puffed up roosters about to start pecking at each other. Patrick could see their mouths moving and strained facial expressions, but could not hear the words through the closed glass door. "Christ, what now?" Patrick said.

Russell looked through the slider at Joey and Shep's display. He cocked his head to one side. "Shep and the others just got home," Russell explained. "Robin is with them. Joey didn't know she was coming. He knew nothing about Shep's plan to bring her out here. He's upset."

Patrick stared at Russell. "You heard that through the closed sliding door?"

Russell nodded. "Yeah. I told you I wasn't right." He leaned forward in his chair again, listening. "Joey says that Shep made a promise to him and that now he's broken it." Russell turned to Patrick. "What kind of promise do you suppose Shep made to Joey?"

Patrick stood up, his eyes locked on Shep's image through the glass. "He promised never to involve Robin."

Russell shrugged. "Involve her in what?"

Patrick gave Russell a quick sideways glance, then headed for the doors. "Obrien! Involve her in what? I don't understand what's going on!"

Patrick turned around. "Believe me, Russell. It's better that way."

Russell frowned. "You know, Obrien, they think you're the stupid one."

Patrick smiled. "I know."

"They've underestimated you, haven't they?"

"I certainly hope so, Russell."

⁓⁓

Shep and Joey ceased their argument as soon as Patrick stepped inside. They both turned and immediately put on their innocent eyes. "What's going on guys?" Patrick asked.

Joey smiled like a movie star. "Nothing. Just talking."

"Nothing. Everything's fine," Shep added.

"Oh cut the bullshit, guys." They looked surprised, their fake smiles wilted a bit. "Why is Robin here?" Patrick asked.

Shepherd flinched. "How did you know?"

Patrick shook his head, rolling his eyes as if Joey and Shep were just so ridiculous. "I could hear you screaming at each other from out on the deck."

Shep glanced at the closed glass door, scowling thoughtfully. He looked back at Patrick, making his face pleasant and docile. "Robin is out for a visit."

"Is she all right?" The question left his lips before he could stop it. It made Shep angry.

"Well of course she's all right! What kind of a question is that?"

Margol and Allisto rounded the bottom of the staircase and strode into the kitchen with their new, less robotic swaggers. "She is all settled in," Allisto said.

"Thank you Allisto. See that she gets whatever she needs."

The fury returned to Joey's eyes and he whirled on Shep, ignoring for the moment that Patrick was standing there. "Why won't she come downstairs, Shepherd? What the hell did you do to her?"

Shep grabbed Joey's collar and pulled him in so that they were eye to eye. "She's tired, Joey. Nothing more. If you want to go talk to her yourself, go ahead, but get the fuck out of my face!" With that, he shoved Joey backwards hard. Joey stumbled but caught himself. Klee began whimpering in the corner, hiding his face. Shep pointed toward the cowering blond. "Now you made Klee cry. Come here Klee."

Shep went to Klee and stroked his hair soothingly. Joey sneered at the display and headed toward the stairs. "I'm going to talk to my cousin."

"I'd like to go see her first, if you don't mind," Patrick piped up. Joey stopped in his tracks. Shep looked up at him as well. Even Klee gave him an odd frown.

"You, Obrien?" Joey said. "You don't even like my cousin. Why the hell do you want to talk to her?"

"Yeah," Shep added. "Why do you want to talk to Robin?"

Patrick thought fast. Why did he want to talk to Robin? "Because, I've been looking at nothing but your ugly faces for the past two weeks. I'm unable to leave here, and it would be nice to have a conversation with someone else for a change." They stared at him as though he had said something preposterous. He threw his hands in the air dramatically. "What? Okay, fine. I'll just go talk to myself, or shoot myself. Christ! Do you know how fucking boring it is around here?"

Shep stared at him for a moment more, then waved his hand. "Okay, okay. Go talk to Robin, Obrien, if it will make you shut up and stop whining. She's in the room across from yours. I am so sick of playing nursemaid to everyone around here. And what the hell is wrong with Russell?" Shep signaled toward the deck, where Russell sat alone on a lounge chair, staring at his own hand as though it held some fascination. Klee's face turned a deep shade of crimson.

⁓⁓

Patrick had to restrain himself from taking the stairs two by two. Instead he walked calmly up the two flights and proceeded down the hall toward the back bedrooms. He was relieved that Robin would be staying across the hall from him. At least he knew Shep had no suspicions as far as that was concerned. He stood before the room at the end of the hall and tapped lightly on the door.

"Fuck off you fucking freaks!" It was Robin's voice.

"Robin, it's Patrick."

The door swung open. He stared at her, drinking in every tiny aspect of her appearance. She'd been crying. Patrick felt his fists clench. "Did they hurt you? I'll kill them."

She pulled him inside and shut the door. He wrapped his arms around her and she melted into him. "We have to stay cool, Patrick. I'm really scared.

I think Shep suspects something."

They sat together on the small single bed and exchanged brief accounts of what had befallen each of them since they last spoke. When Robin told Patrick about her abduction, the veins popped out in his neck. "Don't do anything, Patrick. These guys are truly nuts, and they're incredibly strong."

"Yeah, I'm aware. I think their strength grows over time. Even Klee seems to be getting stronger."

Robin looked disturbed. "If their strength grows, does that mean Juris is getting stronger too? He's locked tight in a warehouse somewhere in South Boston, and Litner said he's guarded, but..."

"Oh shit. I forgot about Juris. If he gets out, we're screwed. I mean, more so than we already are."

Her face fell. "We have to get a message to Litner to beef up security on Juris."

"Leave that to me. Why does Shep want you out here so bad? You know he didn't even tell Joey about this. Joey's pissed."

"Well good for Joey then. I don't know exactly why this is suddenly so important to Shep. He doesn't believe that I just happened to stop loving him. He thinks he can change my mind."

"Change your mind? How so?" Patrick asked, a jealous edge to his voice.

"I'm not sure. He claims he can make me love him again."

Patrick shuddered. "Normally that would just sound like the desperate ramblings of a jilted lover. But in Shep's case, it makes me a little wary."

"You're not suggesting that he can bespell me somehow? I'm not one of his zombies, Patrick."

"Have you seen Kelinda yet?"

"No. Why?"

He shook his head. "I'll let you form your own opinion about that one. Just remember, when you see her, that she's been infected."

Robin wrinkled her nose. "Infected?"

"Yeah. Things are weirder than you think around here. Let's just say that the stock has sailed on bodily fluids."

Suddenly they both heard Kelinda's voice, screaming angrily from down the hall. "Margol get your ass back here!" she wailed. "I'm talking to you! Stop trying to lure my cat out onto the deck! She doesn't have any claws!"

Patrick looked at Robin and grinned. "Oh, yes. Stock has sailed on bodily fluids, as well as animal corpses."

Robin shook her head. "I don't want to know. But that reminds me." She dug something out of her bag and held it up to Patrick. "It's blood."

"Oh Christ, Robin. The last thing I want to see right now is more blood. What the hell is this?"

"It's the vial we made at Betsy's. It's supposed to restore Joey's conscience. I figured it might break his bond with you as well." She shrugged. "That is if it works."

Patrick shook his head. "I just can't take it if you start playing with blood too."

She tossed it back into her bag. "Hey, might as well fight fire with fire. Or blood with blood as the case may be. You never know. It's worth a try."

"I just find it hard to believe that one little vial of blood will counteract whatever Shep did to Joey. It sounds too easy. We're talking about some strong stuff here. Everyone has a different reaction to being infected with Shep's blood. Kelinda, Russell..."

"Russell? What happened to Russell?"

Patrick waved his hand in dismissal. "Never mind that for now. The point is everyone who's gotten infected without Shep's knowledge is losing their mind. For real."

"Of course they are!" Robin said. "It's like Father Bello said. This was never meant for humans of this time period. Shep and the brothers are not supposed to be here in the first place. They're certainly not supposed to be sharing their bodily essence with we lowly homosapiens."

Patrick sighed and rubbed his temples. "I'm beginning to understand now how these crops could be dangerous. I kept thinking that Agent Litner was overreacting. After all, it's not like Shep has his finger on the button of some warhead. But if he has this much knowledge about the earth and the things that grow on it, then these crops could be anything. They could do anything. We just don't know."

"Yeah, well, hopefully we'll know soon. Say a prayer for our modern archaic science that the lab will be able to figure it out."

The sound of approaching footsteps startled them. "Someone's coming." Robin looked fearfully at Patrick. "Kiss me."

He gave her a deep kiss that wanted to linger. The knock on the door stopped it. Patrick leaned his lips into her earlobe. "I won't let anything happen to you," he whispered.

She smirked. "My hero."

"I'm serious. I'm right across the hall if you need me."

The door swung open just as Patrick moved off of the bed. Shep stepped inside. Robin retracted like a threatened cat at the sight of him. He spoke to Patrick, but his eyes were fixed on Robin with a longing that made Patrick's stomach lurch. "Obrien, Joey would like to see Robin now. That is if you're all through chatting."

"Sure," Patrick said. "He could have come up himself," he said, getting increasingly annoyed by the way Shep was staring at Robin. Shep turned his green eyes to Patrick then.

"Yes, I told him the same. It seems he didn't like the way you looked in the kitchen. He was afraid you might hit him."

Patrick laughed. "Hit him? I couldn't hit Joey if I tried. Literally."

Shep grinned a little. "That's true." Shep left the room. Patrick gave Robin's hand a quick squeeze and retreated to his own room across the hall.

Chapter Forty-Five

Patrick's eyes sprang open in the dark. He lay there unmoving, knowing that something had awoken him, but unsure as to what it was. His heart thudded, making swishing sounds in the drums of his ears. He listened intently to the silence. Then came the familiar tingling sensation and the dull throbbing at his temples. Joey was in trouble.

Whatever it was, it was not life threatening, he was almost sure of it. There were varying degrees to the physical reactions he experienced when Joey's well being was threatened. The current reaction wasn't as strong as when Joey was shot, for instance. That experience had been like a severe blow to the head. This was more a slight tugging at his senses. Joey had probably just stubbed his toe or something. This blood bond was swiftly becoming a pain in the ass. The mental tugging pulled him up and out of the bed before he made the conviction to do so. He stood in the dark, looking down at his body disparagingly. He was aggravated by whatever substance was forcing his body to do things without his consent. He would have gotten up to check things out anyway. He didn't need to be pushed. Then he heard Joey scream.

The cry held more anger than fear or pain. Nonetheless, Patrick's body leapt for the door before his mind told it to do so. He leaned out, peering down the long darkened hallway. A dim light from the top of the stairs brightened the hall enough so that Patrick saw two shadowy figures. He reached out and flipped a switch and the hallway lit up. Kelinda was curled up on the floor, inching backwards away from Joey. She was wearing a short black lace negligee. Her lower lip and chin were wet with fresh blood. At first Patrick thought that Joey must have hit her. Then he saw the small gold dagger still gripped in her delicate hand. Joey stood over her, his face twisted in rage.

"You crazy bitch!" he screamed. "Aaagh!" he cried out as he gripped a small wound at his wrist. Blood seeped slowly through his fingers. He removed his hand from the cut and examined it. "You crazy bitch!" he said again. He seemed at a loss for any other words.

Patrick heard a crash from across the hall and Robin's door opened. She peered out at him, holding a shard of glass in her hand. "Are you okay?" he whispered.

"Yes, I'm fine. I just broke my own booby trap." She discarded the glass. "What's going on?"

They both peered down at the bizarre scene taking place in the center of the long hallway. Kelinda slunk back against the wall in a defensive posture. She had the look of a child who'd been caught doing something wrong and was about to get a spanking. Another light went on in the lower hallway and Shep came bounding up from the second floor. Allisto and Klee followed shortly after. Shep stopped short, taking in the scene. "What the fuck is going on, Joey?" he demanded.

"I was sleeping and she came into my room and cut me! She cut me with that knife. She was trying to drink my blood! Crazy bitch!" With his good hand Joey made a fist and pounded the wall behind him. It was clear that he was showing restraint by hitting the wall, and not hitting Kelinda. A framed picture dropped onto the floor and shattered as Joey pounded the wall repeatedly. With each blow he shouted the words "Crazy bitch, crazy bitch, crazy bitch!"

Margol came leaping down the hall looking like a ghoul in a long black robe, his sleep-ruffled curls sprouting like orange horns about his head. Shepherd, dressed only in a pair of boxers, walked determinedly over to Kelinda, where she hunched in near fetal position on the floor. She looked up at him, her eyes full of hate. Shep put a hand on his hip and wagged his finger at her. "Kelinda, what did you do?"

A sly smile formed on her lips as she wiped the blood off her chin with the back of her hand. Robin looked at Patrick, horrified. Patrick just shrugged and continued to watch the show. Shep grabbed the knife from Kelinda's hand and wiped it on his shorts. "This dagger is mine," he said.

"I'm done, Shep," Joey ranted, holding his hands up. "I'm all done with her. This is the last straw. Keep her away from me!" Joey stormed off down the stairs. "Crazy bitch!" he called back over his shoulder.

Shep gave the brothers a serious look. They seemed to read his mind because Margol and Allisto immediately went to Kelinda, each grabbing one of her arms and hoisting her to her feet. She shrieked and began to kick and fight like an animal. "Lock her in the den downstairs," Shep said, yawning as if this were all routine. Allisto and Margol carried her down the hallway toward the stairs and she continued to scream and kick like a deranged mental patient.

Robin leaned in to Patrick. "Does this sort of thing happen often?"

He grinned at her. "To quote Alice Cooper, welcome to my nightmare."

With Kelinda gone, this left only Shep and Klee standing in the hallway. Shep turned his attention to Klee, who was staring, wide-eyed down the hall at Patrick and Robin. "Klee, go back to bed," he ordered. Klee continued to stare. It took Patrick a moment to realize that it was not they he was staring at. It was she. Klee gazed at Robin with what could only be described as a dopey grin. If he were a cartoon, he would have had little hearts floating around his head. Shep followed Klee's gaze. He frowned at Robin, then turned back to Klee. "Klee!" he yelled. Klee jumped and looked at Shep. "Go to bed!"

"Is that her?" Klee asked him softly.

Shep glanced back down the hall at Robin. "Yeah, that's her."

"She is so beautiful," Klee said dreamily.

"Enough, Klee. Go back to bed, now."

Klee turned then and ran back down the hall, disappearing at the stairs. Shep walked toward Patrick and Robin where they stood just outside their bedroom doors. His jaw was set stiff. He stopped just before he got to them, his curls framing his face like a halo, his huge green eyes darting back and forth between them. "Is there a problem here?" he asked. Patrick almost laughed but he held it in. Robin did not. She laughed openly.

"Yes, actually," she said. "There is a problem, Shep. Nobody told me that it was crazy bitch night. I would have brought my propeller hat."

Shep's eyes narrowed. Patrick could stifle his laugh no longer. As if in response to Robin's comment, Joey could be heard down in the kitchen yelling "Crazy bitch!" and then something crashed to the floor.

Robin looked at Patrick. "Patrick? Did you know it was crazy bitch night? Because I wasn't told."

"There was a memo," Patrick said, in mock seriousness. "It clearly stated that tonight was crazy bitch night. You didn't get it?"

She looked back at Shep. "No, but then again, I'm new here. Nice little sleep-away camp you've got here, Shepherd. Top notch." She gave him a double thumbs up. Shep stood there for a moment longer, glaring at them, then he walked briskly away, disappearing around the corner. When he was gone, Patrick and Robin grinned at each other.

"That was fun," Patrick said.

"Yeah," she agreed. "Good night Patrick."

Patrick felt better about things as he went back to sleep. It had been so long since he'd been able to look at Shep without fear. Robin had enabled him to do so, if only for a moment. He knew that he was still knee deep in shit, but at least he wasn't standing in it alone anymore. Now he just prayed that Agent Litner would find a way to get them the hell out of there before it got any deeper. He could feel a tension building out at Forest Bluffs, as though some force was gaining speed, building up pressure, and it was only a matter of time until it blew and all hell broke loose. Or perhaps that was a bad choice of words. They had enough problems with things breaking loose into their world. At any rate, something was coming to a head soon. It was a tangible anticipation that Patrick could feel all around the property now. A shit storm was coming. Be it Shep's own storm or one triggered by the FBI, Patrick wanted to be out of there before it hit.

Chapter Forty-Six

Agent Steven Litner sat in the small, clean waiting room, perusing the files in his briefcase, making phone calls, doing whatever he could to look like he wasn't as nervous as he felt. Dr. Wang...Juliet, had called him in that morning to discuss the results of the grueling tests he'd been undergoing since the ingestion of what they now termed 'substance X'. Actually, she hadn't called him at all. She'd had an associate call for her, the first indication that something was wrong. Whatever she had to tell him, she wanted to do it in person. He took a deep breath and tried to force his eyes to concentrate on the case file in his hands.

He hadn't had any adverse physical reactions to the substance, at least none that he knew of. He felt as healthy as ever. Besides, she had only given him a pinch of the stuff. What harm could it possibly do him? It hadn't even given the monkeys a stomach ache. He fingered through Melvin Eugene Shepherd's file. Shep to his friends. Shep to his enemies. Zirub to his family. Even with the newly acquired knowledge regarding Shep's supposed origins, he still baffled Litner. He had managed to literally pop up out of thin air, producing legal documents verifying his existence, and legal documents verifying his lack of existence in the past. His past records had been officially lost, including those of his supposed family, leaving a perfectly untraceable, yet legally unquestionable trail. He had covered all of his bases with a thoroughness that Litner had seen only in the keenest of professional spies.

Computer technology was clearly child's play to this man, or whatever he was. If he was capable of this, then logic would dictate that Shep could easily hack into any system he pleased, secure or not. So why hadn't he? If his goal was indeed to destroy life, then why hadn't he just tapped into a nuclear arsenal somewhere? Litner was of course glad that Shep had not chosen this route. The problem was he couldn't understand why. Why, why, why?

Litner shut the folder abruptly. Trying to figure Shep out always gave him a headache. This is what he got, he supposed, for complaining that nothing challenged him. We get what we ask for, and Litner had silently wished for an opponent who could challenge his skills. No one had ever been able to stay a step ahead of Litner, not even the most diabolical of terrorists. So finally, he'd been sent his coveted opponent. He supposed he should be flattered that the search had to be stretched beyond this world to find such a foe, but he was not. No, Steven Litner was not flattered at all. Steven Litner was scared. He was scared for maybe the first time in his life.

Juliet came through the double doors and Litner jumped, spilling the contents of the file onto the bench beside him. So much for looking calm. He finished shuffling the papers back into his briefcase before he dared meet her eyes. Finally, he looked up at her. Her shoulder length hair was so black it had a blue sheen. She kept her almond-shaped eyes cast downward. She held a folder in one hand and a pen in the other, nervously clicking the end with her thumb. He forced a smile. She smiled back but he didn't like the look on her face. Her lips were pursed too tightly together.

Clapping his hands, he leaned forward. "So Doctor, what's the damage? Am I going to make it?"

She stepped into the room and sat down beside him, placing the folder on her lap with her hands resting on top of it. "Well Steven, as they say, I have good news and bad news. Which would you like first?"

His heart galloped at the threat of the bad news. "Let's hear the good news," he said, struggling to make his face blank.

"All right," she said, speaking softly as people did when they were about to drop a bomb on your head. "As I suspected, this substance is not poisonous. Blood and urine came back normal. There are no visible toxins in your readings. So as far as I can tell, whatever this substance is, it won't kill you or make you sick."

"So I'll live," he said, unable to mask the relief he felt.

She nodded, smiling slightly. "You'll live."

He let out a brief sigh of relief. "Okay Juliet. Let's have the bad news."

She looked down at her lap. She appeared to be gathering her courage. Finally, she looked up at him, and her eyes were strained and sad. "The test results did show one fluctuation. I'm baffled by the result, since we only gave you a milligram of the unknown substance. I still can't figure it out, but we've re-tested three times and the results are accurate."

"What is it Juliet? Please, just tell me."

She paused. "There was an abrupt drop in your sperm count." She let the statement hang there.

He shrugged. "My sperm count?"

"Yes. There was an abrupt drop after the second set of tests. I've never seen anything like it."

"Abrupt drop?" He shrugged. "What did it drop to?"

"Zero. You're sterile, Steven."

Chapter Forty-Seven

The kitchen at the Duvaine's Forest Bluffs summer home had always been a point of awe for Patrick. It was enormously spacious, with a plethora of pane glass windows running along the upper wall facing the back yard. The early morning light streamed into the kitchen in soft beams of gold, eliciting a sense of well being and comfort. He and Robin were prisoners, but even knowing this, it was a hard pill to swallow. Their confines hardly looked like a prison, with its hardwood floors, expensive rugs and private bedrooms. They were free to live like royalty in this glorious place, having everything they could possibly desire at their beck and call. Everything but freedom.

The two of them sat at the tile breakfast nook and sipped gourmet coffee. Robin turned toward the sound of shattering glass that echoed repeatedly from behind the closed sunroom door. It was the room Patrick had stumbled upon Shep and Klee's "training" session. By the sounds of it, Klee was no longer melting things all over the floor. He had progressed to breakage. "Now what the hell is that sound?" Robin asked, grimacing as she strained to hear.

"I believe that is Klee, learning to shatter things with his mind."

"Charming," Robin said.

"Yes. They grow up so fast, don't they?"

Russell came drifting zombie-like into the kitchen wearing an inside out bathrobe and two different shoes. Robin stared at him, but he didn't seem to notice her. He dug through the refrigerator, pulled out a gallon of chocolate milk, and retreated back up to his room with it. Robin leaned across the nook and pointed in the direction Russell had gone.

"Don't even ask," Patrick said.

She shrugged. "Okay."

The nut parade continued as Joey came trouncing heavy-footed into the kitchen wearing one of his ridiculous ceremonial robes. This time it was a flowing purple number with a black satin trim. Robin's eyes widened when she saw him. She claimed that she and Joey had shared a nice chat the night before. She'd told Patrick that she was convinced that Joey could be redeemed from the wrath of Shep. Patrick wondered if she'd feel the same way after hearing one of Joey's so-called sermons.

"Nice outfit, Joey," she said, biting her lower lip to stifle a laugh.

Joey stumbled for the coffee. "Yeah, yeah. I know. I have to go out and have a little chat with my so-called followers. Kelinda is missing."

"Missing? I thought you guys locked her in the den," Robin said. "Listen to me. I've been here one night and already I sound as loony as the rest of you."

Joey gave Robin a sideways glance that said he didn't appreciate the comment. "Someone busted through the window last night," Joey explained. "It was broken from the outside. Shep thinks the followers are hiding her somewhere."

"Would they do that without consulting you?" Patrick asked, seriously. "You must be losing your edge."

Joey nodded. "That's what I'm afraid of, Obrien." He disappeared out of the back sliding door. He was a strange sight indeed; a startlingly handsome man of twenty-eight dressed in a purple priest's robe with a backwards baseball cap and high-top sneakers. The white coffee mug he carried was decorated with pink roses that spelled out the word 'mother'.

"Hey, can we go outside? I never thought I could feel so restricted in a house this size," Robin said.

"I hear you. Let's go out on the deck."

The spring air was fragrant and warm, but as always, it had an odd underlying scent. It was the smell of the crop. The strange burning rubber odor filled the air, even more now that the plants had been cut. Robin pulled the end of a lounge chair around, then stopped as a flurry of petals fell off of the seat. "What the..." They both stared. The chair was completely covered with tiny yellow flowers, at least a hundred of them, fresh, as though they'd been just picked. "What's this all about?" Robin asked as the pile of flowers spilled off of the lounge chair on to the deck.

"It looks like Margol's handy work," Patrick said.

"Margol likes flowers?" Robin asked, surprised.

"No. Margol likes dead things. He dissects things and then leaves them on the deck to decay. We're usually talking about woodland creatures. I'd be thrilled if he's turned his attention to flowers."

Robin shrugged. "I just can't imagine the red-haired freak out picking buttercups."

Patrick startled. "What did you say?"

"I said Margol is a freak."

Patrick shook his head. "No, not that. What kind of flowers did you say these were?"

Robin picked one up and twirled it between her index finger and her thumb. "Why they're buttercups of course!" She held it under Patrick's chin. "Do you like butter?"

He grabbed her arm and tugged her. "Come on. We have to go for a walk in the woods."

Robin let him drag her off the deck. "What's wrong?"

"Margol didn't leave those flowers. It's a message. Litner's scout has a code name. It's 'Little Buttercup'. Something must be up."

Robin followed Patrick into the trees. "Well. It's a good thing I was here, then. You'd have never gotten your message. You really didn't know those were buttercups?"

Patrick glanced back at her. "No, Robin, I don't know my flowers. Does this mean it's over between us?"

"I'll let it slide if you get us the hell out of here soon."

"I'm working on it. Come on. Follow me."

Robin stepped carefully over the scrubby path, trying to keep from tripping on the tree roots.

Agent Walsh stepped out from behind a tree, and Patrick had to cover Robin's mouth to keep her from screaming. He'd forgotten to warn her about

Walsh's appearance. Agent Walsh had on his token camouflage pants with a black tank top. Tattoos colored his muscled forearms, and his hair was tied back into a long gray braid. Agent Walsh smiled at Robin's reaction.

"It's all right Miss Duvaine," he said. "I'm one of the good guys."

Patrick let go of Robin's mouth and she breathed a long sigh, placing her hand to her chest. "Robin, this is Agent Walsh. He's a member of Litner's team."

"Litner wants me to deliver this message in person. Come with me, both of you," Walsh said.

Neither questioned him, they simply followed along a semi-beaten path. The mention of Agent Litner's name had left them stoically silent. They all knew what this was about. The results of the crop tests were in.

Agent Walsh stopped alongside a pile of brush and sticks. He kicked at the twigs and leaves on the ground, spreading them out to reveal a metal lever attached to a flattened wooden door, level with the earth. Agent Walsh pulled up on the lever and a beam of dusty daylight shone down, revealing a set of wooden steps leading into the earth. "Wow. What the hell is this?" Patrick asked.

"I think it used to be a bomb shelter," Agent Walsh said. "Now those Moonies use it for storage. I just discovered it was here early this morning. Two of those curly-headed clowns went down here to check it out. They were looking for that girl with the pink hair. She ain't down there though."

Robin looked at Agent Walsh. "Do you know where Kelinda is?"

"I saw them last night," Walsh said, scratching the back of his head as his eyes darted at the trees around them. "They came out of the fields, five of em. They broke a window downstairs and pulled the girl out. They've got her hidden somewhere beyond the property line."

"Do you ever sleep?" Patrick asked.

"Don't have time to sleep. Come on. Follow me." Agent Walsh stepped down into the hole in the earth and they followed. Patrick lowered the door down on top of him and it was pitch black. Agent Walsh pulled a flimsy string attached to an overhead bulb and the place flooded with a dull light. They came down to the bottom of the dusty wooden steps into a storage area. The floor was earthen.

"It stinks down here!" Robin said, holding her nose.

"Yes, I know," Walsh said. "Someone had a body down here. Most likely within the last two months. The dampness tends to trap the smell."

Patrick grimaced. "A body? You mean a dead body?"

"Yes. I don't know when, and I don't know why, but somebody had a corpse down here."

"How do you know?" Robin asked.

"Because I know what rotting human flesh smells like."

Robin and Patrick held identical faces of disgust. "I don't suppose it could have been a really big possum," Patrick said, knowing all too well that it must have been Margol's little science experiment with the stolen corpse.

Walsh turned and faced them. The lines around his eyes looked softer in the dim light.

"I heard from Litner. He's gotten the results of the crop analysis. We're pulling you out. It's going to happen fast. Before the end of the week."

Patrick let out a sigh of relief, then the apprehension returned to his face. "What did they find in the crop, Agent Walsh?"

"Let's just say that if that crop reaches its destination, the global population is going to drop dramatically in the very near future."

"Are you saying that the crop can kill people?" Robin asked softly.

"No," Walsh said. "It can't kill people. It can prevent them from ever being born."

Patrick gasped. "Sterilization?"

Walsh nodded. "If we don't stop its distribution. Litner's organized a team and a plan is laid. Theoretically, confiscating the drums should be a piece of cake."

"He won't let you," Robin said. Patrick and Walsh both looked at her. "Shep will know. He'll smell it coming. He'll try to stop you, and he definitely won't let you take Joey."

Walsh nodded. "I know. That's where you two come in. I'm going to send a signal to you on the night of the siege. Be ready."

"What kind of signal?" Patrick asked.

"Gun shots. You will hear gunshots coming from the direction of that old brown house next door. Shep will think it's me, his old buddy the veteran come back to cause trouble. With any luck, he'll go over to check it out. He wants me dead something awful and his anger will win out over his caution. I'm aware of his unusual strength, so don't think I'm going to try wrestling him. I'll get him restrained into a steel trap. That's when we get you two out. You've got to find a way to get Joey Duvaine out to the guest house with you. As soon as you hear the shots, that's where you head, to the guest house. Litner will be there waiting for you. Do you understand?"

"How are we going to get Joey to come with us?" Robin asked.

"I'm afraid that's up to you. You all know him better than I do. Can you do it?"

"Well find a way. We'll figure something out," Patrick said. He'd drag Joey by the hair if he had to. "What happens next?" Patrick asked.

"If all goes as planned, our team takes control of the fields, confiscates the trucks, and gets the hell out before Shep knows what hit him."

"What's going to happen to Shep and the brothers?" Robin asked. "Are the Feds going after them?"

Walsh shook his head. "Litner doesn't want to risk it until the crop is safely away. He doesn't want his team going up against Shep and the others. The plan is to take Joey Duvaine only, avoiding a direct confrontation with Shepherd until we get what we want."

"Did you shoot Joey?" Patrick asked suddenly.

Walsh met his eyes. "Pardon?"

"Joey got shot in the shoulder at a barbecue. Shep said the crazy vet did it. Is it true? Did you take a sniper shot at him?"

"Yes."

"Why?"

"To keep him on the property. They had him going out to the store and the beach and whatnot before that happened. I needed to scare the sons of bitches so they would keep Joey on the land where I could watch him. It worked. He only left the property once after that to go to that nightclub, and I was there, as you recall."

"But you shot him!" Patrick said. "You could have missed and hit his head, or a vital organ!"

"No, I couldn't have," he said.

"You're telling me that there's no chance whatsoever that you could have accidentally aimed just an inch to the left and killed him?"

"No chance."

"You're that good a shot, are you?"

"Yes sir, I am."

Patrick was out of comebacks. "Well...don't do it again. I feel everything that happens to Joey, and that really hurt." Walsh just nodded. Patrick breathed deeply and gagged. "Okay Walsh, what's the bottom line? I need to get out of this cellar. I have claustrophobia and the smell is making me sick."

"The siege will happen some evening this week. I wish I could be more specific but I just can't. There are still a few details to be worked out, and I have to do some sneaking around tonight to set up for Litner's plan B."

"His plan B? You mean if the shit hits the fan while you all try to take the crops?"

"Exactly. Litner is aware that a thousand things could go wrong. The prime directive is to make sure those crops don't leave the property unless it's under FBI control. We hope to take the product with us, but if that's not possible then the crop must be destroyed, right then and there."

Robin winced. "Destroyed? You're going to blow shit up, aren't you?"

"We are going to destroy the product, yes, but only if there is no other choice."

"So you might have to blow shit up," Patrick added.

Agent Walsh shrugged. "If that's the way you want to put it. Yes. We may end up...blowing shit up."

Patrick was wary. It didn't sound solid. Aside from Shep and the brothers, they also had sixty Joey-loving zombies whose sole purpose, aside from worshiping Joey, was to guard those crops. No, this was not going to be easy at all.

Later that night, Patrick tossed and turned in his bed. Part of his sleeplessness was caused by his subconscious waiting for the sound of gunshots, but part of it was a nagging question that hadn't occurred to him before. How would his own conscience handle deceiving Shep on a larger scale, i.e. a raid on Forest Bluffs by the FBI? It was so hard to stay focused around Shep, and it was so easy to forget that Shep was going to get what was coming to him. He'd brought this on himself. Patrick had simply helped the process along by agreeing to work with the FBI. He was doing the right thing. So why did he feel like a shit? He wished his feelings of affection for Shep would just hurry up and disappear. It would be nice to have them gone before he betrayed him.

Giving in to the insomnia, Patrick left his bed and made his way down to the kitchen for water. He was about to round the bottom of the darkened stairs when someone grabbed his arm and tugged him back. "Obrien."

He spun about, stumbling, and looked into Margol's cold green eyes. "Margol?" As far as he could remember, Margol had never initiated a conversation with him. Hell, the creepy redhead rarely spoke at all. Now he looked at Patrick directly, and Patrick saw that rare yet unmistakable shine in those eyes. It was the same shine he'd seen in Juris's eyes as he sat tied to a velvet chair in Carbone's basement. It was intelligence. A quality they all had, yet masked so well that it was easy to overlook. He felt a chill. It was like finding out that a pet could talk.

"What is it Margol?"

Margol pushed him gently and Patrick had to walk backwards. Before he knew it they were standing in the dining room to the right of the front door, away from prying eyes. "You may have Shepherd fooled Obrien, but you can't fool me."

"Margol what is this? What are you talking about?"

"Shep doesn't see it because he doesn't want to see it. But I see it. And I smell it. You stink, Obrien."

"I stink?" He'd showered twice to remove the stench of the fruit cellar.

Margol's eyes were fierce and angry, his voice a deep throaty whisper. "You stink, Obrien, and it's not just from that fruit cellar. You stink of deception!"

Patrick went cold, as the redhead seemed to have read his thoughts. "Look, whatever Margol. I don't know what you're talking about. Can I go now please?"

Margol circled him like a cat. Patrick didn't dare move. "I see you, Obrien. I see the lies. I see the fear. It all radiates from you like a vapor. It hangs over your head like a neon sign."

Patrick was suddenly very afraid. It was not just hearing Margol speak. It was hearing Margol speak to him with such tact, and with nearly perfect English. "Margol, I'm not in the mood for metaphors."

"I'm watching you, Obrien. And the girl too. If you think she's going to leave Shepherd and be with you, you're fooling yourself."

Patrick struggled to mask his shock. It wasn't easy. He forced out a phony, high pitched laugh. "Don't be ridiculous, Margol. Robin and I are friends. Why would I want her to leave Shep?"

Margol grinned like a mad doll. He took a step forward, forcing Patrick further into the darkened dining room. "Poor Obrien. You just can't seem to hold on to a woman. They'd all rather be with your friends. They'd all rather be with somebody better, somebody smarter, somebody more interesting than you. Face it Obrien. You bore the women you love. You bore your friends. You even bore me."

Patrick felt a bead of sweat drip down his back. "Get away from me, Margol." His voice sounded small and breathy with fear.

Margol grinned. "Or what? I am half your size, yet I frighten you. Why is that?" Patrick remained silent. Margol's grin dropped. "Tell me, Obrien. Do you know what we are?"

Patrick stared at him, saying nothing.

"Ah," Margol hissed venomously. "You do know. Then it is as I thought. What a burden that knowledge must be. How frightened you must feel." Margol reached a hand out and stroked Patrick's cheek. Patrick jumped back as if he'd been stung.

"Don't touch me!" he hissed.

Margol laughed. "Oh, don't worry. It is not a contagious condition."

Patrick wiped the sweat off of his brow. "If you're so convinced that I'm this traitor, then why wouldn't you tell Shep and just get rid of me?"

"Because I love my brother. For whatever unfathomable reason, he wants you to be part of our family. Shepherd is all that matters to me, and I will do my best to shield him from such unpleasantness as this. I'd rather take care of this problem myself, so that he can concentrate on more important things. So let me warn you, OBRIEN!" Margol grabbed him by the shirt and pulled him in close, so close that he had to crane his neck up to meet Patrick's eyes. "If either one of you, you or the girl do anything to hurt my brother, I'm going to tear you open and pull your intestines out. And I'm going to enjoy it."

He let go of Patrick, giving him a shove. Patrick spilled backward and landed on his back underneath the shiny oak table. By the time he'd crawled out and gotten to his feet, Margol was gone.

Chapter Forty-Eight

The two stout guards sat playing cards at a small fold-out table in the dank little room. Juris stared at them from his place in the corner. He'd have thought the FBI underestimated him, leaving him under the guard of these two clowns, if not for the multiple layers of thick shackles that had been added to his wrists and ankles. Of course he had other talents that they did not know about, talents that no chains could restrict. He was still tied to the same high-backed chair from Father Carbone's place. The FBI had been afraid to risk untying him. He wondered what Litner had told them. The two rejects guarding him now clearly had no idea who he even was. The FBI had hired them to baby-sit, and they were not taking the job seriously.

He glared at them from his corner of the room. His gaze was unnerving and he knew it. The little one kept stealing wary glances at him. He had thick black hair with a bushy unkempt moustache beneath a stumpy little nose. His eyes were beady and brown and seemed to suck back into his face. Juris found him repulsive. He could tell by the smell of the man that he ate mostly meat. He wrinkled his nose in disgust when the little man's beady eyes fell upon him.

"Hey, what are you looking at, freak?" the little man said, mustering a tough guy tone.

"A dead man," Juris answered, smiling.

The two guards laughed and continued their card game. The second man was a tall, thick blond of about thirty-five with a gut that hung like a pendulum over his belt. He was clearly one of those men that referred to himself as 'big' even though most of his bulk came from double cheeseburgers instead of the weight room. But his eyes were kind and soft, unlike his little cohort, who looked like he wanted to punish the world for making him short. Juris could not believe the FBI had left these two incompetents to guard him. But they relied on the power of their iron chains and steel wire to keep him subdued.

Everything was physical to humans. It was all about the body. Little did they know that their bodies were the weakest part of them, an afterthought to house their true essence, an essence they ignored. They'd rather chomp on dismembered cows and pull on their own sexual organs than explore the power of their mind and spirit.

Juris's strength was returning since he'd been taken out of that dreadful church, but he hadn't been able to test it. He wasn't sure that he could break through the thick linked chains before the idiot guards could get to him. It would be another couple of days before he could be confident that he had recovered from his time spent at the church. But he didn't have a couple of days. He had heard the whispers of the agents who had come to reinforce his restraints. They were planning a siege on Forest Bluffs. He needed to get out of there now so he could warn Shepherd. And he would get out. Tonight. All he needed was to get close enough to incapacitate one of them. The other he could deal with alone.

Since he was himself incapacitated, he would need one of the guards to come to him. All he had to do was get one of them to stand up and walk across the room, within ten feet. He chose the little one. He was obviously a loose cannon with an inferiority complex. Juris was sure he could taunt him to the point of fury. He stared hard at the side of the man's head, sending out tiny electric pulses, just enough to make him uneasy and feel Juris's stare. It worked. He turned to look at Juris again. "I asked you stop staring at me you freak!"

"Why don't you come and make me," Juris answered calmly.

The little man looked at his partner and pointed a thumb in Juris's direction. "Get a load of this guy. Hey, you talk pretty tough for a guy wearing iron shackles."

"And you talk pretty tough for a short, impotent faggot," Juris responded. He had heard that particular insult on a television program that Shep made him watch during his training. Shep had wanted them to get used to the language and phraseology of the Americans. If it had the desired effect, the little man should be significantly insulted.

It seemed to have worked. The stout man with the moustache stood from the card table and started toward Juris. "Let it go, Stanley. It ain't worth it," The big blond one said. The little man stopped, then returned to his seat grumbling. Juris was disappointed. As he sat down, the guard pointed at Juris.

"You'd better keep your mouth shut freak! I don't know why the FBI thinks you're so dangerous, but I'll tell you what. I'm not scared of you, so watch your mouth!"

Stanley the guard went back to his card game, thinking he'd gotten the better of Juris. Juris racked his brain for an insult potent enough to force the guard to approach him. He was not as practiced at this sort of thing as Shep was. He thought about things he'd heard Shep say that had set off people's anger. It needed to be something offensive enough to warrant a beating. Finally, he thought he had it.

"Hey Stanley, what is that thing on your face?" Juris asked.

The short mustached guard sneered at him, then looked at his big blond partner. "Hey Chuck, the freak sounds a little like Schwarzenegger, don't he?"

The blond agreed and they both laughed. Juris repeated the question. "Hey, guard. What is that thing on your face?"

The little man threw his cards angrily down on the table and turned to Juris. "It's a moustache, you idiot! Haven't you ever seen a moustache before?"

"Yes," Juris said. "I saw one of those on your mother the other night, but she was putting pants over it."

The big blond guard spit his coffee out as he broke into peals of laughter. Stanley looked at his friend furiously. "Yeah, real funny Chuck. Real funny. Encourage the freak why don't you!"

Chuck continued to laugh. "I'm sorry Stanley. It was funny!"

Stanley stood again and pointed a stubby finger at Juris. "You'd better shut your mouth!"

"Sit down Stanley," Chuck said, still laughing. "The guy's just baiting you."

"Yes, Stanley," Juris said, "Listen to your boyfriend over there. I'm just baiting you."

Chuck's smile dropped at the boyfriend comment. Nothing like an assault on the masculinity to get a reaction. "Gag him," the big blond said coldly.

"My pleasure!" Stanley said, grabbing a roll of duct tape from a shelf near the wall. Bingo. Come to me, Juris thought. Come to me.

Stanley walked his stocky form slowly across the room toward Juris. Juris quieted his mind and felt the tingling as he summoned his energy. He focused all of this energy on a tiny point in the center of the little man's forehead, trying to remember everything Shep had taught him in their training sessions. Stanley was grinning as he strode forward, twirling a roll of duct tape around his index finger. Juris waited, silently urging him to come closer. The guard was about nine feet away when Juris released his mind and sent a wave of pure energy crashing forward at Stanley's forehead.

Stanley stopped and dropped the duct tape. His eyes widened and he placed both hands on his head. "Ah!" was all he managed to get out of his mouth before it happened. He was still standing when his skull exploded, sending tiny splatters of blood, brain and shattered bone fragments across the floor and on to the walls. With nothing but a few strands of gore and a piece of spine sticking out of his neck, Stanley's body dropped to the floor.

The blond guard was still seated at the little fold out table. A fan of playing cards fell elegantly from his hand onto the floor as his mouth opened to a perfect circle. A tiny whimpering sound was coming from somewhere deep within him, like a scream trapped in a darkened closet. He appeared too shocked to move. His hand was still clasped in the card-holding position.

"Chuck? I would like you to stand up and come unlock these chains," Juris ordered. Chuck did not move, his eyes glued to what was left of Stanley's ruptured head. "Oh, Chucky? Did you not hear me?"

The big man looked at Juris with blind terror. He blessed himself and scrambled out of the chair with all intentions of bolting for the door. Juris felt his inner power awakened now, pulsing beneath his skin, waiting for another outlet. He waited until Chuck had his hand on the door knob, then mentally threw himself against it. The knob slipped out of Chuck's hand as the door slammed shut in front of him. The big guard wiggled the knob desperately, making high pitched sounds. Finally accepting that the door was not going to open, he went still. Slowly, he turned around and looked at Juris. His face was pulled back in a grimace of fear and tears streamed. His hand started to trail to his hip, toward his gun.

"I wouldn't touch that gun if I were you, Chuck. That would upset me." Juris's tone was commanding, and Chuck drew his hand back away from his gun.

"Please," he said in a soft, shaking voice. "Please don't kill me. I have a child."

"I have no desire to kill you, Chuck. I simply desire to be free of these restraints. So come on over here and unlock these shackles, or I'll be forced to do to you what I did to Stanley here."

Chuck's eyes flicked to Stanley's decapitated form. The seepage of blood spread out like butterfly wings opening. It had nearly covered the entire floor. Chuck came forward slowly, trying to step around the blood, which was nearly impossible. He tiptoed daintily along the edge of the wall where the blood had not yet reached. In a squeaky high-pitched whisper, he prayed as he approached, *"Blessed art though amongst women and blessed is the fruit of thy womb, Jesus. Holy Mary, Mother of God, pray for us sinners now and at the hour of our death, Amen."*

He got within a foot of Juris and stopped. He was trembling, his round pink face a sheen of sweat. "The handcuffs first," Juris said. Chuck pulled a ring of keys off his belt and began fumbling through them with shaking hands. He dropped them once, but finally found what he was looking for. He moved back behind Juris and unlocked the shackles that bound his wrists, then unwound the connecting chain. It dropped to the floor with a loud clank. Juris flexed his wrists. He looked down. "The ankles now."

Chuck did not hesitate. He came quickly around front and unlocked Juris's ankles, removing that chain as well. He looked at the steel ropes that still bound him. "I'll need to go get the wire cutters for these," he said.

Juris smiled. "That won't be necessary." He flattened his arms to his sides, took a deep breath and snapped the wires. He did the same with his legs, and the wires broke with a *ping* and fell to the floor. He was free. He stood from the chair and stretched his back. Chuck gaped at him.

"What the hell are you?"

Juris smiled at him. "If I told you that, I'd have to kill you."

Chuck nodded carefully. "Does this mean that you...you...won't kill me?"

Juris thought about this as he bent his neck and cracked his knuckles. "No, I'm not going to kill you, Chuck. We had an agreement. I keep my word. I will have to knock you unconscious, however."

Chuck swallowed. "Fair enough."

Without further adieu, Juris swung at Chuck, connecting with his cheekbone. Chuck dropped to the floor like a sack. Juris felt around on his neck for a pulse. The guard was still alive. That was fine. He had no apprehensions about leaving Chuck alive. By the time someone found him, Juris would be long gone. Besides, Chuck had laughed at his jokes.

Juris stepped around the carnage as he made his way to the door of the dusty little room. He was expecting more guards to be standing just outside, but when he opened the door, there was no one. He was in some sort of empty warehouse. He crept quietly through the place until he found an exit. Running a hand over his head, he felt wetness, and realized that his hair was sprinkled with flecks of Stanley's blood. He turned to examine a pile of junk left on a rickety set of shelves. He grabbed a discarded baseball cap. Pulling the cap onto his head, he opened the door, stepped out into the early evening air and breathed deeply.

He had to get to Shep, but first, he had some unfinished business of his own. He did not like being held captive. In fact, it was his least favorite thing. He had been imprisoned once before, and it had lasted for over two thousand years. Somebody was going to pay for putting him through it again.

Tucking his tell-tale blond curls up under the baseball cap, he made his way down the city street, blending in with the pedestrians. He scowled as he read the signs. He was not within walking distance of his destination. He hailed a cab, something he'd never done before. The driver smelled like onions, and Juris realized that he was hungry. His stomach could wait.

"Where to?" The cab driver asked him.

"Saint Mary's Parish," he said, and gave the man the street address.

Chapter Forty-Nine

Copie cut the vegetables on a wooden carving board while Father Carbone cranked the handle of his pasta-making machine. Tiny tubes of the starchy white substance oozed through the holes, forming thin strands of spaghetti. The priest glanced over at Copie where he sat at the opposite counter. "You have to dice those onions very fine, Copie," he advised.

"Yes, I know how to dice onions, your holiness. I may not be an Italian goomba like you, but I have done some cooking in my time."

Carbone raised his hands. "Hey, I'm just trying to help. I didn't know if you'd made sauce before."

Copie gave him a look. "You think I don't know how to make sauce because I'm black. Is that it?"

"Yes, Copie. You figured me out. I believe you to be culinarily challenged because of your racial origins."

"Yeah, that's what I thought."

The conversation was lighthearted. Their spirits were up for the first time in weeks. The meal was in celebration of a call they had received from Agent Litner. If Litner's predictions were correct, then they would all have their lives back soon. Though they were still worried about Patrick and Robin, they had faith in Agent Litner's abilities to get them out safely. Or rather, Father Carbone had faith. Copie merely took the priest's word for it.

Copie pushed the diced onions to the side of the cutting board with the long knife and gathered the garlic cloves that Carbone had set out for him. "Are you sure you want me to press all this garlic? It looks like an awful lot."

Father Carbone shook his head, grinning. "Oh, my dear boy. Lesson of life; you can never have too much garlic."

A metal clanging sound echoed from somewhere outside, like a barrel knocked over. The two looked at each other. "What the hell was that?" Copie asked, wide-eyed.

Father Carbone put down the scissors. "It's probably just a raccoon. 'Tis the season."

"I just put those veal scraps out in the barrel," Copie said. "Maybe they're after those."

"Did you wrap them in plastic like I asked you to?" Carbone asked him. Copie looked down, whistling. "Copie?" Carbone snapped.

"Well, I might have forgotten to wrap them up."

Carbone shook his head. "I'd better go clean up the mess and chase away the varmints. There's probably trash all over the lawn by now. I don't think our parishioners would be too thrilled to find the house of God looking like a garbage dump."

Father Carbone grabbed a broom and a rubber glove and disappeared out the screen door. Copie hopped off his stool and danced around the kitchen to the Italian music playing on the stereo. He sang, inventing his own words. *"Chela luna caciatore Goomba uses too much garlic...la la la la la la la la he's a chasin a raccoon!"* The phone rang. It was the secured line Agent Litner had installed. Copie jumped for it enthusiastically. Answering the private line was one of the few privileges Copie had. It didn't sound like much, but when you were supposed to be dead, any contact with the outside world was a treat. Even if it was the FBI.

"Hello? Carbone's kitchen."

"Copie, it's Litner. Listen to me very carefully. I want you and Father Carbone to stay inside the house with the doors locked. I'm coming by to pick you up."

"Why? What's going on?"

"Juris has escaped."

Copie's hands went numb and he almost dropped the phone. "Es-es-caped?" he whispered.

"Yes, and he has some sort of weapon. I've got one dead guard and another who took a blow to the head and won't wake up. Now don't panic, Copie. I honestly don't believe he would risk going back to Saint Mary's, but we can't be sure. Where's Carbone? Put him on the phone."

"Father Carbone just went out side to chase a raccoon...oh shit!"

"Call him back inside!" Litner yelled. "Call him back in the house now. If he doesn't answer you after a couple of calls, close the door and lock it. Do you hear me, Copie?"

Copie dropped the phone and ran to the door in a panic. "Carbone!" he yelled out through the screen. He paused then shouted again. "Father Carbone! Where are you?" Still no response. His eyes scanned the yard fearfully. It wasn't full dark yet. He should have been able to see the priest. He glanced over at the trash barrels. They were upright and covered as he had left them. Father Carbone was nowhere in sight. Copie closed the inner door and locked it, panting now. He ran and picked up the phone where it still dangled from the cord. "Litner?"

"Copie what's going on?" Litner's voice asked frantically.

"Carbone's not answering. He's not answering, man! Where the hell did he go? You've got to come over, Litner! I'm scared!"

"Take it easy, Copie. Just stay put. Do not answer the door, and stay away from the windows. I'll be there in ten minutes."

Litner hung up on him and Copie let the phone drop out of his hand. He backed up into the center of the kitchen, his eyes darting around at the windows. "Sure. I'll just stay put," he said, trying desperately to calm himself. "Just stay put. Yeah. Litner will be here in ten. Everything's fine. It's cool."

The front door burst inward in an explosion of wood and glass, as though it had been hit with an atomic battering ram. Copie dropped to the floor and covered his head. When the debris stopped falling, he looked up through a haze of wood dust.

Juris stood in the shattered hole where the door had been. He looked surreal as a wind whipped at his hair and clothing while he remained perfectly still. His platinum curls were dotted with tiny red flecks that looked like blood. Copie swallowed hard, frozen where he crouched. Juris grinned down at him. "Hello young one. How have you been?"

Copie grimaced as he forced out a squeaky answer. "Fine. You?"

"Never better. What do you say we go for a little ride? We have some...catching up to do."

Chapter Fifty

It was the evening sermon. Robin looked on in horror at the slack faces of the star-struck followers as Joey spewed his emphatic ramblings of meaningless rhetoric. Patrick watched her, silently amused as her eyes darted from Joey's face to the faces of the crowd who stood huddled before him in awe. Joey was a priest, a rock star, a teacher, and a god. He was the king of bullshit.

"And now the time has come, that the words which have fallen on us alone will be made to pass. You, children of the time to come and the passing of the old world, will see from thy hands the storm that passes like a wind of truth."

The followers shouted "Amen."

Robin leaned in to Patrick and whispered in his ear. "What the fuck is he talking about?"

Patrick leaned in. "Nobody knows. Not even Joey. Amusing, isn't it?"

Robin gaped at the followers. "He's like Obiwan Kenobi or something."

"It's the power to enchant. Remember? Father Carbone told us about it."

Robin looked at Patrick. "You mean that shit is for real?"

Patrick looked at the followers, who gazed at Joey with adoring hunger. Some of them had tears in their eyes. "Is it for real?" Patrick said. "Just look at them. What do you think?"

"I think I have seriously underestimated just how badly Shep has fucked Joey up," she whispered.

Shep looked over at them from where he stood on the right side of Joey. Robin leaned back away from Patrick, but Shep's suspicious gaze lingered on them momentarily. Shep's gaze didn't rattle Patrick as it had when he'd first arrived. In fact, he'd gotten used to a lot of things out here at the Forest Bluffs home for wandering lunatics. But now he had a new fear. Margol had scared the living shit out of him. Margol knew. So on top of everything else now, Patrick had to worry about getting his intestines pulled out. He had a flash image in his mind of Margol sitting comfortably on a deck chair while he delicately picked apart Patrick's corpse. Patrick squeezed his eyes shut and willed the image away.

There was a tension in his and Robin's faces, an extra stiffness to their shoulders. They were waiting for the sound of Agent Walsh's gunshots. They had come up with a half-assed plan to get Joey to go out to the guest house with them when the time came. It was not a good plan, but neither of them could think of a better one. When the gunshots sounded, Patrick would tell Joey that he needed to go out to the guest house for safety's sake. He would be persistent and incorrigible, acting desperate and pained as though it was the blood pact guiding his decision. Joey would have no choice but to take Patrick's word for it.

The followers formed their now familiar line and came forth to have Joey touch each of their heads. Regardless of Kelinda's suspected coup, the followers did not seem any less enchanted with Joey than they ever had. The evening sermon was almost over. With any luck it would be the last one Patrick would ever have to witness. Patrick felt a shiver of fear. He held Agent Litner in very high regard, to the point of near worship in his admiration of the seemingly unstoppable tough guy, yet he was still skeptical as to whether or not the stoic agent could outsmart Shep.

The sermon was over and the company of six, minus Klee, walked back up toward the house. Shep had left Klee behind, ordering him to 'practice his strengths' while they were gone. Russell had also missed the sermon, claiming to have a headache. Shep had agreed, but under the condition that Russell prepare dinner for them while they were gone. He scolded Russell for spending too much time in his room and not contributing to the household enough as of late.

It was almost full night, but the sun's glow clung to the earth in a lavender twilight that was neither darkness nor light. Klee came bounding out of the back door and ran like a crippled deer toward the group. His hair was like a white beacon shining through the falling darkness as he galloped in seeming desperation. "Zirub! I mean Shepherd!" he screamed across the field.

Patrick and Robin risked a quick glance at each other. A chill ran down Patrick's spine. Though they had claimed to be convinced that Shepherd was this legendary Zirub, Klee's slip of the tongue had just confirmed it. Patrick felt the vile weight of that truth crash over him like a wave. Little did he know that what was to come in the next few moments was a far worse truth.

"Shepherd!" Klee's voice was a high-pitched squeal. He was delighted about something. He came stumbling up, stopping in front of them and doubled over with his hands on his knees. Margol held him up as he struggled to catch his breath.

"What is it Klee?" Shep asked.

Still panting, Klee looked up at Shep and smiled, his childish face lit with joy. "It's Juris. He is back. My brother Juris is back!"

The coldness that had settled in Patrick's legs now spread to his entire body. Robin went very still beside him. Shep dropped the book he'd been holding as a smile spread across his lips. "What?" he said, and began running toward the house. Allisto and Margol followed behind him.

"Juris!" Allisto screamed in delight as he chased up to the house.

Klee turned to Patrick and Robin, his face lit up with pure joy. "Come Patrick! You will meet my brother Juris! You will love my brother Juris!"

Klee took off then like a drunken deer across the lawn, leaving Patrick and Robin cemented in their tracks. "Oh, joy," Joey said sarcastically and moved off more slowly toward the house.

Robin grabbed Patrick's arm. "We have to get out of here! We have to run! Now!"

Patrick took her by the shoulders. "I can't leave, Robin. It's physically impossible for me to leave without Joey. You go. Find Litner and tell him what's happened."

She shook her head, her voice rising to a level of panic. "No! I'm not going by myself! They'll kill you!"

"Robin, you have to! Find Agent Litner! Tell him!"

She shook her head adamantly. "No. If Juris has escaped then Litner already knows about it. He'll come for us! He'll come for us right away, Patrick! Won't he?"

Patrick looked at her terrified pale blue eyes and knew that he'd give his life to keep her from harm. The thought quieted his fear for his own safety, and a strange calm fell over him. "You have to go Robin. I'll be fine."

She shook her head. "No. I won't leave you. We're in this together."

"Juris is going to tell Shep about us. He's going to tell Shep everything."

Robin took in a breath. "Well then. I suppose we'd better go face the music."

"Robin please!"

She put a finger over his mouth. "We can stall, Patrick. You know Shep. It will take him a while to digest the information. Then he'll spend hours trying to figure out what to do with us. It will buy us some time. Agent Litner will come for us! He promised to get us out of here! You heard Agent Walsh! He promised!"

"That was before this, Robin! They didn't figure on this!"

"I have faith in Agent Litner," she said.

Patrick did not share that faith, not fully, but he could see that it was all she was clinging to. "Okay. Let's go," he said.

It was a crazy scene in the kitchen when Patrick and Robin walked through the back door. All of the brothers, Shep included, were huddled in a sort of pig pile on the kitchen floor, hugging, squealing and crying. All Patrick could see was a montage of limbs, tie-dyed shirts and different colored curls. Russell stood to one side with a spatula in his hand. He looked at Patrick and raised a questioning eyebrow. Joey watched the spectacle with crossed arms, looking bored. Finally, the little huddle started to break apart and Patrick spotted Juris in the mass. Klee clung to him like a tiny clone with his matching platinum hair. "Now we are five!" Klee said.

"As it should be," Juris answered, taking Klee's head in his hands lovingly. He kissed the tears on Klee's cheeks.

Having regained his composure, Shep brushed himself off and backed away from the little group. Juris stood as well and approached Shep, standing at attention before him like a loyal soldier awaiting a command. He was clearly subordinate to Shep, yet Juris had a confidence that surpassed the other brothers. Patrick understood something then that he hadn't before. Juris was second in command. If Shep were to ever remove himself from this little group, Juris would surely be the boss. But now he faced Shep with open respect, his chin stiff and humble. "Where were you, Juris?" Shep asked.

"I see that you got Klee through unharmed," Juris said. "My compliments. I've been so worried."

"Klee is fine. Where were you, Juris?"

Juris didn't seem at all pressured to answer Shep's question until he was damn good and ready. He looked away from Shep and his bulbous green eyes scanned the company of the room, finally coming to rest on Patrick and Robin. He smiled coldly. "Well. Hail, Hail. The gang's all here," he said. Patrick's stomach did a flip.

Frustrated, Shep took Juris by the shoulders. "Listen to me when I speak to you, Juris! Have you been gone so long that you've forgotten your place?" Shep leaned his forehead against Juris's. It was an odd gesture that Patrick had seen the brothers do often, as though they were directly driving their thoughts into the other's skull. Shep's dirty blond curls looked nearly brown next to Juris's white ones.

Juris pushed Shep off of him. Patrick was shocked, having never seen one of the brothers dare to even look at Shep with defiance. Shep did not react. Apparently Juris was allowed such luxuries. "You know not what I have been through! I was a prisoner! I was held captive! I was restrained and kept from my freedom!"

Shep's face softened. "A prisoner? Oh my poor dear." He reached a hand out and Juris flinched, thinking perhaps that Shep was going to strike him. Instead, Shep took Juris's face in his hands and gently cradled it. "My poor, poor dear." Shep leaned in and kissed Juris on the mouth. Tears streamed down Juris's cheeks as he kissed Shep back. There was nothing sexual about this kiss, but there was such love and feeling behind it that the room went still.

Shep took a step back then, his face serious. "Who did this to you, and please tell me that they no longer breathe this earth's air."

"It was a priest," Juris said.

"I knew it!" Shepherd said. "I saw it in a vision. Tell me, who was this priest? Was it Father Bello of Saint Christopher's parish?"

Juris shook his head. "No." He walked over to Margol and reached out, brushing a strand of red hair back from his face. "I felt it when he baptized you. I felt it, Margol, but I could offer you no help. I was trapped." Margol nodded, falling back into his trademark silence. Juris turned back to Shepherd. "It was Father Carbone of Saint Mary's. The one you said was so harmless when we began this. The one whose church you chose for the project."

Shep stepped forward. "Father Carbone? That little Italian fireplug? You've got to be kidding me! Is he dead? Please tell me he's dead."

Patrick heard Robin suck in her breath. Juris heard it too. He looked directly at Robin and said, "No, he is not dead. He is in the basement. His freedoms are restrained. I wish for him to experience what I did."

Shep's jaw dropped and he shoved Juris. Juris slammed against the back wall of the kitchen. "You brought a priest into this house? Have you gone mad, Juris? You know what that could bring! It could bring the Schlarr or worse! Idiot!"

Juris looked up at Shep with rage in his eyes. "He needs to be punished slowly! At my will!"

Shep came at Juris again. Juris flinched but did not turn his head as Shep slapped him. Klee ran to the corner and began to cry. "Juris, have you lost your mind?"

Allisto piped up now. "You know better than to bring a priest here!"

Juris threw his head back. Placing his hands on the side of his face, he shrieked that reptilian sound that made Patrick's flesh crawl. He turned on Allisto now, a finger pointed at his chest. "They held me captive under a church, Allisto! A Schlarr came for me! A Schlarr came!"

There was a group sound then, all the brothers sucking in their breath. Juris nodded. "That's right! A Schlarr came! It attacked me! It scratched my face!" Juris trailed his fingers along a thin, fading mark along his cheek. Margol, Allisto and Klee gazed at Juris with a newfound awe.

Shepherd stormed forward. "You brain dead fuck. A Schlarr came to his church to protect this priest! And knowing this, you bring him into this house! You threaten us all! I want you to get that priest out of here right now! Kill him if you have to, but get him out."

Patrick took a step forward but Robin grabbed his forearm, holding him back. Juris turned and looked at Patrick. "We have much more to discuss, Zirub," he said.

Shep gaped at Juris. "Do not call me by that name. Have you lost all of your senses?"

"The boy is alive," Juris said, turning back to Shep.

Shep froze. "What boy?"

"The boy who had the photographs."

Russell stepped forward now, looking like he was going to vomit. "What?" he whispered.

Patrick felt a tangible energy building in the kitchen. Juris was taking his time exposing them, savoring the moment, toying with them. Patrick could feel the chaos getting ready to erupt like a volcano, and he was right in the line of fire. Shep grabbed Juris by the wrist. He glanced at Patrick and Robin. "Obrien," Shep said, "Could you and Robin go upstairs? My brother Juris is confused about things. I need to speak to him in private." Juris began to laugh. Shep spun to face him. "Is something funny, Juris?"

Juris looked Shepherd in the eye. The moment had come. "You need not send these two away, and you need not censor your conversation for their sake," Juris hissed. "Patrick and Robin know everything."

Shep shook his head, a deep crease forming between his eyebrows. "What do you mean?"

Juris turned and pointed a long bony finger at Patrick. "Here are your betrayers, Zirub! They mean to destroy you! They plot against you as we speak!"

Shep turned and stared at Patrick and then at Robin. His face was a combination of surprise and disbelief. He laughed and looked back at Juris. "Not possible," he said. Juris just nodded. Shep turned back and stared at Robin, his mouth dropping into a frown.

Robin laughed forcefully. "Shepherd, what is he talking about?"

Patrick caught her vibe. Maybe, just maybe, they could convince Shep that Juris was off his rocker. Could Powers become insane? Sure they could. Just look at Shep. Juris continued to point and scream. "These two are your enemies, Zirub! Your lover and your best friend! They were at the church where I was held! They have spoken with the FBI! They were even in the cave the night that Klee was born!"

Allisto gaped at them. Margol smiled smugly at Patrick. There was another group gasp and the room fell silent. Shep walked slowly toward Patrick as though in a dream. His face was masked in shock. He came within an inch of Patrick's face and looked into his eyes. Patrick looked down his nose into the green emeralds that stared up at him.

"Obrien? Is Juris telling me the truth?" he said and his voice cracked. Patrick's heart sank. He'd expected a reaction of anger, not tears. He tried with all his might to make his mind go blank.

"I don't know what he's talking about, Shepherd," Patrick said emphatically. "Your brother Juris is quite obviously insane."

Shep's eyes narrowed as though trying to read a message written on Patrick's pupils. He took a step back, staring at Patrick with intense concentration. Then his eyes flickered with something, as though he had gotten the answer he was looking for. His mouth opened and he gasped. He almost fell, but Margol came forward and steadied him. Shep let out a short laugh, a shocked angry sound, then he shook his head. His voice was choked with sadness as he spoke. "Do you know what, Obrien?"

"What's that Shep?"

Shep's lower lip quivered. "When you lie, your aura gets little green spots."

Patrick said nothing. He had never seen a look quite like the one Shep now wore on his face. Shep shook his head at Patrick, then quickly shook it again, as though he could make it all go away. "How could you?" he asked. "How could you?" Then Patrick understood how Wesley could have begged for Shep's forgiveness even after Shep had murdered his aunt. Shep's shattered expression was almost more than he could bear. Patrick did not beg for forgiveness, however. He looked directly at Shep, and found his voice.

"You didn't leave me any choice," he said.

He was waiting for Shep's anger, but it didn't come. He was waiting for a blow, but it didn't come either. A tear ran down Shep's cheek, then his eyes went hard, so hard that Patrick took a frightened step back. That one tear fell from Shep's chin and shattered onto the floor, like the final drop of friendship left between them. Then the sadness was gone from Shep's eyes, replaced with a hatred that chilled Patrick's soul.

Shep tore his horrible gaze away from Patrick and walked over to Robin. He leaned in and sniffed her hair. She flinched, and he pulled back and stared at her. He looked over at Patrick and a light of realization flickered in his stony green eyes. "I see. I see what's going on here now. You really can't find your own girls, can you Obrien?" Patrick said nothing. Shep turned back to Robin. He clenched Robin's face between his fingers. "This is what you have forsaken me for? Obrien? This is what has turned your heart cold toward me?"

"No," she answered, her face twisted. "You turned my heart cold!"

Shep's lips curled back from his gums, making him look feral. "I was going to offer you eternity! I was going to offer you immortality! Now! In this lifetime!" He shoved her. "But you'd rather fuck this stray dog." He pointed to Patrick. "My own dog!"

Patrick had never heard Shep's voice sound the way it did at that moment. It vibrated with an unnatural volume that echoed over the walls of the spacious kitchen. Russell dropped the spatula and began backing out of the room. "What the fuck, Shepherd?" he asked in a high pitched quiver. "What the fuck?"

"Go upstairs Russell," Shep said calmly, his gaze still on Robin. Russell happily complied.

Shep paused a moment longer, then looked away from Robin. "I knew I smelled something in that cave," he said with disgust. He turned to Juris. "Get them out of my sight. I need time to think."

Juris, with Margol alongside him, closed in on Patrick and Robin. Joey jumped in front of Robin suddenly. "Wait a minute! What are you doing? Robin hasn't done anything wrong!"

"Step aside Joseph," Shep said. His voice was perfectly calm, as if all emotion had been drained from him and he now felt nothing.

"You're not touching my cousin," Joey persisted. "You're the one who broke your promise by involving her! I'll throw in the towel, Shep. I'll blow the whole thing!"

Shep grabbed Joey by the collar. "She is trying to destroy us! Don't you get it? Haven't you been listening?"

He released Joey. Joey looked at Robin, his brow furrowed. "That's not true. You don't want to stop us. Do you, Robin?" Robin dropped her eyes. Joey's face fell. "Oh, no. Robin, why?"

She met his eyes. "Jesus, Joey. How can you even ask me that?"

"Take them!" Shep yelled. "Get them out of my sight before I fucking snap!"

Margol and Juris were on them immediately. Allisto went to console Klee, who was curled up in the corner like a frightened animal. Patrick and Robin went with Margol and Juris willingly. They knew the brothers could break them in half if they resisted. They were led toward the basement, stopping only once at a closet for rope. Juris tied their hands behind their backs as Margol stood by like a bodyguard. When Juris finished binding their arms, Margol shoved Patrick. "Now move! Down the stairs!" Patrick complied, remembering Margol's threat to remove his intestines. He hoped Margol didn't offer that up to Shep as a suggestion for their punishment.

Father Carbone sat on the basement floor with Copie beside him. They each had their hands tied behind their backs, and their ankles bound together with rope. They had been listening to the sound of yelling and commotion coming through the floor above them. Copie looked at the priest. "Do you think Litner knows we're here?"

Father Carbone desperately wanted to tell Copie what he wanted to hear. The problem was his faith that everything was going to be all right had all but disappeared. His head still throbbed from the blow Juris had given him when he'd gone outside to check on the trash barrels. He'd never even seen it coming. The next thing he knew he was waking up next to Copie in the back of a taxicab. Juris was driving. He had stolen Carbone's cassette tape of Italian songs from the kitchen and popped it into the taxi's cheap stereo. Juris sang joyously in perfect Italian as he drove, oblivious to the dead cabby still slumped in the passenger seat with his head wobbling on a broken neck.

He'd thought so much about these brothers, rejected from a higher realm and left in stasis indefinitely. He lay awake many a night trying to imagine what it had been like for them. He'd pictured them floating in a watery darkness, the brothers curled up asleep in fetal position while Shep searched the darkness for what must have felt like infinity. "Copie, you had a direct confrontation with him. What is he like?"

Copie frowned at him. "What is who like?"

"Shepherd. Zirub. What is he like?"

Copie scrunched up his face. "What is he like? Father Carbone, Shep was trying to kill me at the time. We didn't sit down and have tea together."

"Just tell me this, is he like Juris?"

Copie shrugged. "Sort of. He's more civilized though. I mean, he doesn't spit or anything."

The door opened at the top of the basement stairs. Their eyes turned in frightened anticipation. The first thing they saw was Patrick and Robin. Their wrists were bound behind their backs. Soon after came Juris and a man that looked very much like him despite a fiery red cascade of curls. They led Patrick and Robin down into the basement and sat them along the wall next to Copie and the priest. Robin gave Carbone a small smile and he nodded.

Juris stepped back and looked at them all. "Well. This little party is almost complete. All we need now is your FBI Agent. He should be arriving soon. Don't you think?"

It was Father Carbone who spoke up. "Don't be so smug, Juris. If Agent Litner does come, he won't be alone."

Juris grinned at him. "Yes. He is coming with a party of sixteen men."
Father Carbone flinched. "Oh come now, Father Carbone. Did you really think

you could outsmart Shepherd? He's already gotten into Litner's computer." Juris leaned in to Father Carbone and touched his face. "Why, you look pale, Father. Don't you like being held captive? I know what you need. Some chocolate!"

Juris pulled a bag of chocolate Kisses out of his pocket and began whipping the tiny pieces of candy at Father Carbone. "Here you go priest! Have some chocolate! Have some chocolate!" Father Carbone ducked his head, trying to dodge the incoming candies.

"Stop it Juris!" Patrick screamed. "You're being a baby!"

Margol gave Patrick a kick in the shin and Patrick doubled over in pain. "You mind your business, Obrien," he said.

Father Carbone looked up as a third set of footsteps came down the stairs. Yet another curly-topped stranger rounded the corner at the bottom of the stairs. This one had platinum curls and looked nearly identical to Juris, despite a smaller frame and a few minor discrepancies in his facial features. He looked frightened and unsure of himself. "Juris?" he called out softly.

Juris stopped pelting Father Carbone with candy and turned around. "What is it Klee?"

"Shep wants to see you upstairs."

"I'll be right there," Juris said.

"He said *now*, Juris." This one had soft, innocent eyes and a babyish chub to his cheeks and mouth. He looked like a true angel, Carbone thought. As if feeling the weight of his stare, Klee looked over at Father Carbone. The pretty young man-thing winced at the sight of him, as though the priest was some sort of threat.

Juris threw the entire bag of candy at Father Carbone in a frustrated tantrum. "Fine," he said to Klee. "I'm going." Juris stormed up the stairs with Margol following behind. Klee stood where he was, staring at the captives who sat like a row of ducks against the wall. He came forward and kneeled in front of Patrick. His babyish face drew into an angry pout. "How could you betray us, Patrick? Juris says that the FBI is coming. Now there is going to be a war! You were supposed to be Shepherd's friend. You were supposed to be his friend!"

Patrick leaned forward until his lips were nearly touching Klee's. "And you were supposed to keep away from Russell, weren't you, Klee?" Klee drew back like he'd been slapped. Patrick winked at him. Klee turned and ran up the cellar stairs, slamming it shut behind him. The prisoners were alone.

"Why are you taunting them?" the priest asked.

"Because it's fun," he said. Patrick was aware that he was beginning to lose it. It was bound to happen sooner or later.

"Priorities, Patrick," Father Carbone said. "We need to stay alive long enough to get out of here. Purposely angering our captors is not going to help."

Patrick nodded. "I know. I'm sorry. I'm just so sick of them though! And where the hell is Litner anyway? He said he was going to help us! He said he was going to get us out of here! Look at us now!"

Robin leaned in close to him. "We are going to get out of here, Patrick. You just have to hold it together a little bit longer. Okay?"

He nodded. "Okay. What the hell. There isn't much left of my mind, but whatever's there, I'll hold together." He looked over at Father Carbone. "Shouldn't you be praying or something?"

Father Carbone looked down at the ropes that bound his legs. "Yes, Patrick. I suppose I should be. I'll get right on that."

Patrick nodded. "See that you do."

Chapter Fifty-One

Joey sat out on the deck, sipping a brandy. Let the others celebrate Juris's homecoming. Joey didn't care. Something caught his eye at the edge of the woods, a flash of pink. At first he thought it was Kelinda, then the figure stepped out into the clearing. It was Carlos. His pink Mohawk shone in the moonlight as he slowly approached. "Carlos? What are you doing up here? You're supposed to be guarding the guest house."

Carlos took a few steps closer to the deck. "Hello Joey."

Joey gave an exasperated sigh. He stood up and walked to the edge of the deck. "Yes, hello Carlos. Maybe you didn't hear me. Shep wants all of you guarding the guest house and the perimeters. Did you forget?"

The boy shook his pink head. "No, I didn't forget. I've found something. You need to come take a look at it."

Joey walked toward Carlos. "What have you found?"

Carlos smiled. "It's amazing. You have to see it for yourself."

Joey stared at him for a long time. He sighed. "All right Carlos, I'll come with you for a minute. But this better be good! Shep has us on high alert right now and he'd be none too pleased if he knew you left your post."

Carlos smiled. "Come quickly!"

Joey hopped off the deck and followed Carlos into the woods. Branches snapped against his bare legs and he cursed. He wasn't used to trucking through the woods in his shorts. They walked for close to ten minutes and Joey was getting aggravated. They had nearly reached the end of one of the property lines when Carlos stopped and turned around.

"Well? What is it Carlos? What did you find?"

"I found Kelinda," Carlos said.

"Kelinda?" Joey said wrinkling his nose. "Where is that crazy bitch?"

Kelinda stepped out from behind a tree, along with eight of the male followers. "The crazy bitch is right here, Joey," she said. Joey looked at the followers that now surrounded him. They gazed at him with a mixture of adoration and hunger.

"What the hell do you guys want?"

"You need to come with us Joey," Carlos said.

Joey laughed. "I don't think so. I need to get back to the house and you guys need to get back to your posts. This has gone far enough."

Kelinda stepped forward. She wore the black lace nighty from the night she disappeared. She walked toward him seductively. He took a step back. She noticed and a grin spread across her face. "What's the matter Joey? Do I make you nervous?" She looked at the two men to either side of him. "Grab him," she said.

They each took one of Joey's arms. He struggled against them. "Hey! What the hell are you doing? You don't listen to her! You listen to me! I am your Messiah!"

Kelinda leaned in close. "That's right Joey. You are our Messiah," she whispered. Joey tried to get away but the two men held him tight. The others formed a circle around him. Kelinda laughed, a mad sound. "You see, Joey," she said, "we've been thinking. Jesus gave his body and blood for his follow-ers." Her smile dropped. "We expect no less of you."

Chapter Fifty-Two

They all grew frustrated as an hour passed and there was no sign of Agent Litner. There were no gun shots from the abandoned house next door, and no dramatic rescue attempts. Just the four of them, tied up and helpless, left alone to contemplate their fate. Patrick wondered exactly how much Juris was telling Shep up there. But more urgently, he wondered what exactly Shep was going to do about it.

As if in response to his thought, the door opened at the top of the stairs with a crash. They heard Shep's voice before they saw him. As he stomped slowly down the stairs, he spoke in a loud, somber voice. "From the time The Vessel was conceived, he was hunted. He would be hunted all the days of his life by those who would question his rule and ask for his death."

Shep's feet appeared, then his legs, then he himself rounded the corner at the bottom of the stairs. He was freshly showered, dressed in a pair of faded jeans with a purple and white tie- dye tank top. He looked sweet and harmless as a kitten. Father Carbone's eyes widened at the sight of him. Shep walked slowly forward, now directing his little speech to Patrick alone.

"From the time The Vessel was conceived," he repeated, "he was hunted. He would be hunted all the days of his life by those who would question his rule and ask for his death."

Shep crouched down before Patrick. "Do you know who it was, Obrien? Do you know who it was who finally succeeded in bringing about the death of the Messiah, The Vessel?" Patrick sat still as a stone. "It was the government, Obrien. The government. And what do you do? You lead them to my door. You lead them right to my fucking door!" he screamed into Patrick's face. His voice bellowed through the empty basement.

Patrick began to shake. Shep was radiating with the same energy he'd exhibited the day he told Patrick he couldn't leave the property. It was like an electric current tingling in the air of the dank basement. His green eyes held an unnatural gleam. Energy spilled off of him like a wave of fury. And to make matters worse, Patrick was beginning to feel the tingling in his temples that told him Joey was in trouble. This was probably a bad time to bring it up. "Please, Shepherd. Be reasonable. Joey is not the Messiah," Patrick said.

Shep punched him in the cheekbone so hard that Patrick saw stars. Patrick swooned from the pain as he struggled to keep consciousness. "Joey is whatever I say he is."

In all the years Patrick had known Shep, Shep had never hit him. Sure, they'd fought before, but they were silly scuffles that usual involved wrestling in the dirt. And Shep had never, ever used his full strength. This time he had.

Patrick heard a ringing in his ear, and he was fairly sure his cheekbone was fractured. Patrick felt his terror mounting, overwhelming even the pain in his face.

Shep shook out the hand he'd used to administer the punch, gave Patrick one more look of disgust, then he moved on, inching his way down the line. He tossed his hair back almost seductively, and kneeled down in front of Copie. Copie's brown skin paled to ash. "So," Shep said. "You're alive."

"It would seem so," Copie whispered.

"And the photographs?"

"Destroyed in the fire," Copie said.

Shep nodded, and stood up. "Well, at least we accomplished that much."

Father Carbone had his head bowed, whispering softly in prayer. Shep reached out and waved his hand in front of Carbone's face. The priest looked up. "Could you stop that please, Father Carbone? Thanks."

Carbone was staring up at Shep with something like awe. Carbone's expression worried Patrick. He was counting on the priest to be their backbone in this mess. He hoped Carbone wasn't about to go soft on him. Shep paced back in forth in front of them. He pulled a stone out of his pocket and began to toss it from one hand to the other. "Where is Special Agent Steven Litner, and when is he going to try to steal my crop?" he said to no one in particular.

The room fell silent. Shep looked over at them. He placed a hand to his ear. "Huh? I can't hear you! Maybe you didn't hear the question. Where is Special Agent Steven Litner, and when is he going to try to steal my crop?"

Again none of them spoke. Shep strode casually down to Father Carbone and knelt in front of him. "You're Agent Litner's buddy, aren't you, priest? According to my research, which I admit was a rush job, you and Litner went to school together." Carbone nodded slightly, still staring at Shep the way a child would a twinkling Christmas tree. Shep reached out and ran his hands over Father Carbone's body without actually touching his skin. He scanned his hands over his head, down to his feet as though feeling some invisible energy. "Your faith is strong. No wonder that stinking Schlarr came. I can feel it like a sting against my soul."

"Do you still have a soul?" Carbone asked.

Shep laughed. "When is your friend, Agent Litner, coming to pay us a visit? Will it be tonight? Tomorrow? The next day?"

"I'll tell you nothing," the priest answered sharply.

Shep moved in very close to him and Carbone pushed himself back against the wall. "What's this?" Shep said. "So brave in your words yet you're afraid to touch me. That's all right I suppose. I'm afraid to touch you too, Father."

"Leave him alone, Shep!" Robin quipped.

Shep pointed a warning finger at her. "You be quiet. You don't exist to me anymore, so I don't want to hear your voice." He turned his attention back to Father Carbone. With eyes still on the priest, he reached over and trailed a finger down Copie's cheek. Copie let out a small whimper and squeezed his eyes shut. "Are you fond of this child, Father Carbone?"

"Leave the boy alone. You almost killed him once, isn't that enough?"

"Is it enough? Well obviously not. He's still here, isn't he?" Shep smiled at Copie. "Have you risen from the dead my boy? I'm familiar with the concept. Impressive if you can pull it off. The thing is no one's ever done it twice.

Shall we give it a try?"

"Leave him be!" The priest hissed.

Shep glared at him. "Then tell me what you know!"

"I don't know where Agent Litner is, and I don't know exactly when he is coming," Carbone said. "That's the truth."

Shep studied Father Carbone, looking unsure. "I find that hard to believe," Shep said. "He's confided in you thus far. Why would he stop now?"

"I told you I don't know! Patrick said you could sense a lie. Can't you see that I'm telling you the truth now?"

Shep crossed his arms. He looked vaguely uncomfortable. Patrick thought he knew why. "You can't, can you?" Patrick said. His jaw hurt when he spoke. "You can't read his aura, can you?"

"No," Shep said.

"Is it because he's a priest?"

Shep stood up and brushed his pants off. "Something like that. Anyway, it doesn't matter. When your hero Litner comes, we'll be ready for him."

A small pain ripped through Patrick's head, small enough to hide, but sharp enough to make him wince. Joey was definitely in some sort of danger. He only hoped it didn't escalate. If there was a positive side to his bond with Joey, it was that it enhanced his physical strength when Joey was in crisis. If Patrick could hide the reaction until Shep left the room, he was sure he could bust out of the ropes. He might even be able to do it now, but he wouldn't risk it. One punch from Shep convinced him that he could never win in a physical altercation.

Shep, however, did not seem to be planning on leaving them any time soon. He sat down in front of them and pulled his knees up to his chest, resting his chin on his arm. "Do they know what it does?" he asked Father Carbone.

"Excuse me?"

"My crop. Do they know what it does?"

"No," Father Carbone lied. The priest catches on fast, Patrick thought. Unfortunately, Shep catches on faster. He looked at Patrick.

"Obrien, I'll ask you, since you can't lie to me. At least not very well. Does the FBI know what the crop does?"

Patrick sighed. It was futile to lie to Shep, so he told him what he knew. "The FBI believes you intend to use it for human sterilization."

Shep looked surprised, then angry. "How did the stupid sons of bitches figure it out?"

"Agent Litner tested it on himself," Father Carbone answered.

Shep shook his head. "Slippery bastard."

"That's just what he said about you," Carbone said. Shep raised his eyebrows and nodded, looking somewhat intrigued. His anger had momentarily subsided.

"Why are you doing it Shep? I mean, you can't possibly sterilize everyone," Patrick said.

"I don't want to sterilize everyone. What the hell do you think? That I'm out to eliminate human life?"

"Well, aren't you?"

"No you dumb Mick. I'm here to improve humanity, not to destroy it."

"Then why do you want to sterilize people? Why would you do something so monstrous?"

Shep laughed, throwing his head back. "Monstrous? Personally, I think it's exquisitely humane. It's not like I'm wiping them out with a nuclear bomb. I'm just preventing a portion of them from ever being born."

"But why, Shep? Why are you doing this at all?"

"Come on, Obrien! You're a businessman. Surely you understand the need for downsizing as a result of any corporate takeover."

"But we're talking about the world here. It's not a corporation."

"Isn't it? Just because you can't see the top of the ladder, doesn't mean it's not there."

Patrick chewed on that for a moment, but couldn't figure out what the hell it was supposed to mean. He'd never been good with Shep's metaphors. "Enough with the riddles already. Just tell me why!" Patrick insisted.

Shep lifted himself to his knees and glared at him. "You are in no position to be making demands, Obrien! And you might want to stop worrying about the little details so much. You're going to be dead soon."

"Why? Because I betrayed you?"

"Yes!" Shep bellowed and the basement windows rattled.

Patrick felt terror, but it was laced with frustration and anger. "How the hell can you sit there and scream about my betrayal after everything you've done to me? You used me, Shep. You used me for ten God damned years!"

"Oh, you're breaking my heart," he said.

Patrick stared at Shep and wanted to cry. After all that had happened, Patrick was still hurt. He was hurt that Shep had never cared about him. "You know something Shep? Even when I found out the truth about you, I still hoped that you would let this all go, and move on. I know what you are, you know."

"Yes, I kind of figured that out after Juris told me you were in the cave the night Klee was born."

"I'm aware of your...origins. I know now that you were never really my friend and you chose me for a purpose and all that crap, but I didn't know that. You were my friend! I would have accepted anything about you."

Shep seemed disturbed by the sentiment. He looked down at the floor. "Obrien, with all due respect to that touching rhetoric, this is not a minor character flaw I have here. This isn't like, 'hey buddy, I'm an alcoholic and a cross-dresser, thanks for understanding'. I'm from another realm! The two of us don't exactly have a lot in common. I have existed for longer than the earth. Do you understand that?"

"I think so, yes."

"No! No you don't!" Shep yelled. "Do you think that because you watch the Sci-fi channel that you can begin to know a damn thing about this? Moving from one realm to the next is a violent, unnatural, scorching experience! Those that don't die trying it usually go insane and that is a death all its own. Do you get it? I was left for dead! Now I have to sloth around in the mud with the rest of you swine!"

"If God wanted you dead, you would be dead," Father Carbone said.

Shep turned to face the priest. "Well. Listen to Father know-it-all over here. You didn't even believe in us until a Schlarr came and showed you its lovely pointed teeth."

"And I would love more than anything to go back to that ignorance. I don't want to know about you. I wish I'd never heard of you. You, Zirub, are not supposed to be here."

Shep went very still. "What did you call me?"

"Zirub," Father Carbone said.

Shep nodded. "Oh, I see. You've learned Rumplestiltskin's name. I didn't realize there was literature about me out there."

"There isn't much," Carbone said. "We only came up with one source. A book of folklore."

Shep sneered. "Well isn't that appropriate. My life in a fairy tale book. What does it say?" Shep moved over toward the priest, looking vaguely intrigued. Father Carbone seemed to be developing some sort of rapport with Shep. Shep was still being cautions, but Carbone was slowly drawing him in. "Don't be shy, Father. I'm curious."

"Well," Carbone said in his fatherly tone, "Your name is Zirub and you are a level four in the celestial hierarchy. Your main duties are to act as a patrol between the material and the immaterial worlds. You are the border guard. How am I doing so far?"

Shep hunched his knees to his chest. "Impressive. Go on."

"Legend has it that you went against the wishes of your superiors and made an emergency pilgrimage to earth, taking the other four members of your band with you. Before you reached your destination, your exit path was blocked. You could neither proceed to earth, nor return from whence you came. You were trapped."

Shep fiddled with the lace of his sneaker. He no longer looked amused. He looked shattered. "It says all of that in this...fairy book?" A small frown had formed between his eyes. Father Carbone remained placid, his face unreadable.

"Is that a correct interpretation of your plight, or has history muddied the facts?"

"Close, Father Carbone. Pretty damn close." Shep stared at the priest. There was pain visible in his large green eyes, as though hearing the tale had awoken something deep inside of him. It was only a slight waver in his resolve, but it was there. Father Carbone seemed to see it, for he pressed on.

"There are still one or two things I don't understand, however," Carbone said.

"Ask away, Father," Shep said, hostile now, "I don't mind telling you. You are, after all going to die here."

Carbone didn't flinch. "What was so urgent? Why did you risk so much to come to earth? To become flesh, as the Son of God did?"

Carbone had struck a nerve, and if Patrick had to guess, he'd say the priest knew exactly what he was doing. Shep stood up suddenly and put his hands on his hips. He threw back his head and let out a strained laugh. "Hah! You think I wanted to be like him? Is that what you think this is all about? That's irony. If you only knew! But of course you would think that. I've read your bible. I laughed at every page! I hate to bust your little Catholic bubble, but you and your brothers in the clergy are not playing with a full deck!"

"Enlighten me, then," Carbone said. "Why the urgency? And why after the death of Christ? Was the timing significant, or was it a coincidence?"

Shep began pacing back and forth. His eyelids fluttered. He was chewing on his thumbnail and muttering to himself quietly. Shep's agitation visibly escalated and his mutterings got a little louder. "Ich lew wosh sole lagfa..."

Father Carbone interrupted. "Mr. Shepherd?"

Shep turned abruptly and pointed at Father Carbone. "It was my idea! It was my idea! Mine!"

"What was your idea, Shepherd?"

"To speed things up! To teach the morons that all of the answers were around them! Oh you humans have always been fuck-ups, but back then it was so much worse. We could go to earth and teach them the way. It was the only logical thing to do! They needed guidance! They were worshipping cows!"

Carbone nodded. "I see. It sounds reasonable."

Patrick made a mental note. Encourage Father Carbone to become a therapist. Shep began to pace again, running his fingers through his dark blond curls and muttering. "Ebwana tuhflara ich flana tu mala!"

Copie looked at Patrick, wide-eyed. Shep stopped abruptly again and looked at the priest. It was as if the rest of them were no longer in the room. "It could have been any one of us. We all had the knowledge. But no. The Light was put into a human vessel! The Light, in a human vessel! Imagine! Well, I knew it was a mistake from the beginning. I knew it wouldn't work."

"I don't understand," Carbone said. "You are talking about Jesus, right?"

Shep spun round with his hands in his hair. "I'm talking about The Vessel!" he raged. "The Vessel is The Vessel, no matter what name you call him by."

Carbone shook his head. "What do you mean, then? That plan did work. His words and deeds are still being taught today, world wide."

"He got himself killed!" Shep screamed. "He wasn't finished yet! That's why the world is still such a mess! But I suppose you're one of those ignoramuses that believe that The Vessel's death was meant to happen. It was all part of the plan right?"

Carbone nodded. "Right. He was given up to death, a death he freely accepted."

"Wrong!" Shep yelled, shaking a fist. "Freely accepted? Wrong!"

Carbone shook his head. "He sacrificed himself for us," he said.

"Bullshit!" Shep screamed. "That's just something the Catholic Church teaches morons like you so that the stunted little microcosm you live in makes sense. It was not meant to happen that way, Father Carbone. The Boy Wonder fucked up."

"He was part human, Shepherd. We all fuck up sometimes."

"He was too human! That is the point. He got himself killed!"

"Jesus knew that he was to sacrifice himself. It was his destiny," the priest said, beginning to sound a bit agitated himself.

Shep shook his head, smiling patronizingly at the priest. He sighed deeply and leaned over. "Father Carbone, do you know what 'Eli, Eli, lama sabachthani' means?"

Father Carbone bowed his head and paused. "Yes. I know what it means."

"Say it!" Shep ordered.

"They are the words that Jesus called out in the ninth hour of his crucifixion. It means, My God, My God, why have you forsaken me?"

Shep stood up and pointed at Father Carbone. "My God, My God, why have you forsaken me. A cry for help. A plea for mercy. A cry of outrage! Now tell me something, Father Carbone. Do those sound like the words of a man who had volunteered to die? Do those sound like the words of a man who knew that his death was, as you say, 'meant to be'?"

There was utter silence in the room. Father Carbone's confidence looked slightly shaken. It seemed the tables had momentarily turned. Shep could see the questions forming on Father Carbone's face. He was beginning to doubt his own point of view.

"It makes sense now, doesn't it?" Shep said, smiling and nodding. "The Messiah wasn't supposed to die. It was a bad plan gone terribly wrong. Bad planning, my friend. The way he went around, healing those idiots, telling them who he was before he had control! He had twelve to protect one man! Well, we all know how that turned out. Humans are incapable of sacrificing themselves to save another. The survival instinct gets in the way. He needed someone who was bound by blood to protect him. He needed a Shield. He needed my plan. My plan! I should have been in control of the project!"

Father Carbone met his eyes. "That's why you tried to come to earth. When you found out that He had been killed, you were going to try and do it your way."

Shep shrugged, almost coyly. "Somebody had to clean up the mess. If they had just listened to me in the first place I wouldn't have had to break the rules. Not that you would understand. You don't get it. Your kind will never get it."

Father Carbone shook his head. "No, Zirub. It is you who doesn't get it."

Shep stepped forward, looking like he was going to strike the priest, then curiosity won out and he stopped. "What do you mean?"

"The Messiah appeared to several people after his death. He showed them his risen body. Can I assume that this actually happened, and is not more Catholic ignorance?"

Shep shrugged. "So what?"

"So what? These post death appearances are what made his teachings endure! It is not his remarkable life that is responsible for his teachings lasting for two thousand years. It is his remarkable death! Don't you see, Shepherd? Without the resurrection, people would have forgotten him. Without the resurrection, Christianity falls."

Shep laughed. "You speak as if the world lives in harmony, Father Carbone. Have you looked around lately? Your precious Christianity is not doing squat. It's time for a new Messiah. One who will be prepared. One who will be protected. One who will endure."

"Who? Joey?" Patrick said, unable to hide the cynicism in his voice.

Shep gave Patrick a dirty look. "Yes, Joey. Just as God put part of himself into The Vessel, so I have put part of myself into Joey."

"But Joey's an asshole!" Patrick said.

"No, Obrien you are an asshole. Joey is the new Messiah."

"But you suppressed his soul!" Father Carbone jumped in. "The only reason he does your will is because you've doused him with your blood!"

Shep shrugged. "So what?"

"So what? Shep, you've cheated! You've cheated with Joey and you've cheated with those followers out there. That's not leading. That's not teaching. It's brainwashing. You've taken control of their minds. At least The Vessel gave the people a choice."

Shep laughed. "Yes, look what good that's done the world. At least Joey won't be killed. I've found a way to design a perfect Shield for the Messiah. Humans may not be able to sacrifice themselves to save another, but they can be made to, as Patrick has. He is bound by blood to protect Joey. He would die for him without a second thought."

Patrick felt the throbbing getting worse at his temples. Would this be a bad time to bring up that Joey may actually be in trouble right now? Probably.

Father Carbone was shaking his head. "So that's what the crops are for. You're trying to get the population back down to what it was when Jesus walked the earth."

Shep shook his head. "That is incorrect, Father Know-it-all."

Patrick looked up, surprised. "Why then? Why sterilize people?"

Shep moved over and sat in front of Patrick. A sinister grin curled across his mouth. "Do you know what's going to go through the minds of everyone on earth when the babies stop coming? There's nothing like the smell of extinction to turn the masses toward religion. Of course, the human race won't really be becoming extinct. They'll just think they are because of the sudden widespread onset of fertility problems. They'll go into a panic. They'll think that the human race is being gradually snuffed out. They'll think it is the beginning of the end. They'll be begging for answers. And then, we will be there. Ready to show them the way."

"I'm almost afraid to ask, but how are you going to do that?" Patrick asked.

Shep grinned. "Cast your mind, Obrien. Thirty odd years into the future. You all remember Joey Duvaine, the Yuppie Prophet from years back who refused to divulge secrets given to him by the Blessed Virgin when she appeared to him on the church? Well folks, Joey's back. You see, it seems that this little extinction problem was exactly what the Virgin spoke to Joey about on that fateful night. She predicted it, and blessed him with the knowledge that when the time came, he would be the new Messiah. She gave Joey the key to saving the human race. If the masses follow Joey's way and listen to his truths, then the fertility problems will stop. If they do not, then the human race will stop reproducing until they become extinct. That is what we will tell them, and that is what they will believe. And why will they believe it? How did the Blessed Virgin give Joey the power to prove this truth?"

Patrick swallowed hard. "By stopping him from aging."

Shep grinned. "Give the dumb Irishman a prize! Good old Joey emerges from the shadows, and guess what? He hasn't aged a day in thirty years. Nothing short of a miracle can stop aging, right? Oh, besides my blood but they don't know that. Seeing Joey, this miracle of nature, they are convinced of his authenticity. They flock to Joey like good little sheep and we lead them toward enlightenment. Mission accomplished."

"Holy shit," Patrick said, his wounded jaw dropping.

"That is..." Robin struggled for the words. "That is evil. It's..."

"It's hell," Copie said.

They all turned toward Father Carbone, awaiting his response. He looked up at Shep and raised an eyebrow. "Then what?" he said with a shrug.

Shep tilted his head. "Excuse me?"

"What happens next? You lead the poor miserable masses toward enlightenment. Hooray. What happens then? You're a celestial being. Or at least you were once. Don't you expect any retribution for your actions since you arrived on this planet?"

Shep shrugged. "I'm going to bring world peace, Father Carbone. When I pull it off, I will have proven that my plan was right all along. When I prove that, The Light will see. The Light will want to take me back."

The room fell completely silent. It was such a childish statement, yet Shep seemed one hundred percent, assuredly serious about it. Father Carbone let out a shocked laugh. "Take you back? Take you back!"

Shep frowned at the priest. "I was obviously let loose from prison to accomplish my mission. I was given a second chance. The Light will see that I have done so. Then The Light will let me back in."

Father Carbone shook his head. "Um, Shepherd, or Zirub, or whatever you like to be called..."

"Shepherd is fine."

"Okay, Shepherd then. Do you honestly think that The Light is going to take you back after all you've done? You've committed multiple murders! You've committed atrocious sins!"

Shep shook his head. "The murder commandment was written for humans, not celestial beings. I know that when someone dies by my hand that they are going to a better place. You're supposed to believe that too. Yet you weep for your dead. I've never understood that."

"We weep for the dead out of love and loss," Father Carbone said angrily. "Have you thought of the families and loved ones of your victims? They must now endure a lifetime of pain and loss!"

"Well, that's their weakness. Weeping for the dead is silly. This place is a toilet compared to where most of them are going."

"You have caused pain and suffering to innocent people. The Light will not take you back."

Shep stormed over to Father Carbone and pointed in his face, "The Light will take me back! Or I will take this world and I will crush it! It belongs to me now!"

Father Carbone got very still. "This world does not belong to you, and you do not belong in this world."

"Shut up, priest! I know I don't belong here. Is that supposed to be some sort of startling revelation for me? Coming here was the only option for me outside of spending eternity in a shapeless void. I had to get my brothers out! What did you think? That I chose to pop out in the middle of some fucking cave in East Redneck, Massachusetts? I mean, the entire earth is a toilet but it would have been a little better if we'd landed somewhere in the tropics. At least then it would have been warm. God, I despise this state! It's cold, it's dirty, it's boring and I hate the fucking Kennedys!" Shep panted, winded from his rant, and ran a few fingers through his hair, brushing it out of his eyes.

"I have a practical question," Father Carbone replied after a short silence. "Your abhorrence of the Commonwealth and the Kennedy family aside, is there anything about this world that you do like?"

"No. Not a damn thing."

"Then why would you work so hard to save it?"

Shep gave Father Carbone a contemptuous look. "To prove a point! Have you not been listening?"

"You are completely full of shit," Patrick said through his swollen lips.

Shep looked so shocked that he gazed over at Patrick as though he must have heard him wrong. "I beg your pardon, Obrien?"

"I said you are completely full of shit. All of this profound talk about hating this earth and blah blah blah, it's a bunch of bullshit. You're more human than I am. I've known you for ten God-damned years. Don't try to tell me that there's nothing on this earth you like."

"Go to hell, Obrien. There isn't a damn thing on this earth that I would classify as redeemable."

"Chickpeas," Patrick said.

Shep scratched his head, and walked over to stand in front of Patrick. "Chickpeas?"

"Yes, Shep. You like chickpeas. When we were in college, you'd go to the salad bar every day for lunch. You always put three huge scoops of chickpeas on your salad. You'd eat every last one of them, even if you had to dig through the forest of lettuce and shredded carrots to get at the last chickpea."

"I'm a vegetarian, Obrien. I eat chickpeas for protein, nothing more. Besides, I wouldn't call chickpeas a world redeeming value."

"I'm not finished yet," Patrick said. "You like tie-dyed tee shirts. You have like thirty of them in all different colors. You like to smoke weed. You like to drive across rich people's lawns in your Jeep. You like having a fireplace in your house. You start lighting it in late September, as soon as the temperature starts to drop a little. You like listening to opera music at an obscene volume while you're cooking. You like sex. You like ancient swords. You like really bad thunder storms."

Shep rolled his eyes. "Is this coming close to a point any time soon? Because if I have to listen to much more of this, I'm going to crawl back into the void."

"My point is Shep, that there is no single redeeming quality to this world. There are lots of little ones. Alone, they're just chickpeas, but when you put them all together, you get…"

"Hummus?" Shep said cynically.

"You get life, Shep. This world is far from perfect, I'll give you that. We have to find the things that are redeeming to us, as individuals. We learn to overcome the bad things and seek out the good. It's what makes us human."

Shep laughed. "I've been crawling around in human skin far longer than you have Obrien, and I certainly don't need to listen to you lecture me on what I do and do not like. In fact, I don't need to listen to you at all. I'm in control here!"

Patrick laughed then, and though his jaw screamed in pain, he made the laugh as long and contemptuous as he could. "You're in control?" Patrick said. "You can't even control what's going on in your own house."

"What the hell are you talking about? I'm in control of everything that happens here!"

"Oh really? Let's take Kelinda for instance. Do you know why the followers are so taken with her? It's not just because she sleeps with Joey."

Shep's face twisted. "I suppose you're going to tell me."

"How can I put this eloquently? She takes her new improved blood on out to visit your guests in the fields. She then cuts her hand and they mix her blood with the wine you've so graciously provided for them. So you see the followers are even more jacked up on Joey than you thought. Did you know that?"

Shep's eyes narrowed. "Kelinda will be dealt with. If what you are saying is true, and the followers have been contaminated, they can be replaced. I'm nearly done with them anyway. Was that your big secret?"

Patrick smiled. "That, and then there's Russell." A pain ripped through Patrick's head and he gasped.

Robin leaned in to him. "Patrick, what's wrong?"

He saw flashes of Joey. He was being restrained. Patrick could hold in his pain no longer. "Something is wrong with Joey. Shep, you have to untie me."

Shep laughed. "Yeah, right Obrien. I'm not falling for that. What were you going to say about Russell?"

The pain subsided to a dull throb, but it was constant now, as was the tingling. "Shep, I'm serious. Joey's in trouble."

Shep jerked Patrick forward by the neck of his shirt. "Joey is on the deck drinking brandy. The only thing that could have possibly happened is that he fell off of his chair. Now tell me what you were saying about Russell, before I give you a matching bruise on the other side of your face!"

Patrick took a deep breath. "All right. You want to know just how much of your precious control you've lost? Not only do you not know what's going on under your roof, you don't even know what's going on with your own family. Did you notice that Russell is not wearing his glasses anymore?"

Shep glared at him. "What's your point?"

"Let's just say that Russell is seeing the world in a new light these days," Patrick said.

Shep slammed Patrick hard against the wall. "Damn you, Obrien! What are you trying to tell me? Is Kelinda sharing her blood with Russell as well?"

Patrick was suddenly afraid to tell Shep. He should have never brought it up. Russell was an asshole, but he didn't deserve this. Oh well. Too late. "Russell got to Klee," Patrick blurted out.

Shep blinked at Patrick, clearly not understanding. "Got to Klee? What do you mean he got to Klee?"

When in doubt, be blunt. "Russell gave Klee a blow job."

Shep shook his head. "No he didn't. Don't be sick, Obrien." Patrick said nothing further. He just let Shep look into his eyes. Shep drew back, his face a mask of horror. "You're telling me the truth!"

Patrick nodded. "So much for being king of the castle, eh Shep?"

Shep went very still, his eyes shifting about rapidly as they did when he was thinking many things at once. He looked at Patrick again. "Klee? He put his filthy hands on Klee?"

"More than his hands actually. If it's any consolation, Russell deeply regrets the whole thing."

Shep straightened up. "Not as much as he's going to regret it." Patrick didn't like the look on Shep's face. He smiled, but it was a dark smile. "I'll show you king of the castle." He walked to the bottom of the stairs. "Allisto?" he screamed up.

"What is it Shepherd?" Allisto called down from above.

"Send Russell down here, will you?"

"Yes, Shepherd."

Shep circled the room rubbing his hands together. The rest of them sat in silent anticipation of what was sure to be an unpleasant display. Russell came down the stairs looking frightened. He still wore no glasses, and his naked eyes darted fearfully over at the company who sat restrained along the wall. His eyes rested on Patrick, and Patrick looked away.

"You wanted to see me Shepherd?"

"Come here, Russell." Russell looked at Patrick again, then walked slowly over to Shep. "Russell, why aren't you wearing your glasses?" Shep asked. Russell tried to look at Patrick again but Shep grabbed his chin and turned it to face him. "Look at me, not Patrick. Tell me, Russell. Why aren't you wearing your glasses?"

Shep let go of his face and waited with his arms crossed. Russell began to cry and he looked down at Patrick. "You told him, didn't you!" he whispered to Patrick. Patrick looked back at him but could not find his voice. "You said you wouldn't tell him! Do you have any idea what you've done?" Russell shrieked at Patrick through his tears. "Do you have any idea what you've done?"

Patrick hung his head. He had sold Russell down the river, and now he felt terrible.

Russell finally turned back to Shep. His entire body was trembling. "I'm sorry, Shep! I'm sorry!"

Shep looked at him sweetly. "Sorry for what, Russell?"

Russell shook his head and began to sob. "You owe me, Shep! I saved your ass! If it weren't for me there would be photographs of your phony Virgin all over the city! You owe me!"

Shep remained calm. "That's funny Russell, because the thing is, Copeland is still alive. He's sitting right over here. See him?" Shep waved to Copie. "Hi Copie! Wave to Russell."

"My hands are tied behind my back," Copie said.

"Oh, right. At any rate, Russell, I owe you nothing."

"I did it because I love you!" Russell sobbed to Shep.

Shep put a finger to his chin. "Ah, I see. You sucked my innocent brother's cock because you're so in love with me. That makes sense."

"I wanted to punish you! You were so cruel to me! I loved you so much and you wouldn't give me the time of day! All I wanted was a little of your attention!"

Shep grabbed Russell by the neck and tossed him across the room, where he slammed into the back wall and fell in a crumpled heap onto the floor. "Well you've gotten my attention now, Russell."

Robin leaned forward as Patrick did, both trying to determine if Russell was still alive. Then he shifted a little, and whimpered in pain. Patrick sighed relief. But the show was not over. Shep went back to the bottom of the stairs and called up to Allisto again, ordering him to fetch Klee this time. Less than a minute later, Klee came stomping haphazardly down the steps, a huge chocolate stain across the front of his shirt and on his chin.

Klee glanced at Russell's wounded form with disinterest, then trotted over to Shep, awaiting instructions. Shep smiled at Klee lovingly. "Hello Klee."

"Hello my brother," Klee said sweetly.

"Do you know what's been happening here tonight, Klee?"

Klee nodded.

"Tell me," Shep urged.

"Patrick betrayed us to the government. There is going to be a war. Am I right, Shepherd?"

"Yes Klee. There is more than likely going to be a war. Now the question is, do you feel ready?"

Klee looked at him seriously. He stiffened his pretty lips in an attempt to look tough. "I am ready," he said.

"Are you sure?"

Klee looked hurt. "You don't have faith in me. You don't think I am strong enough yet. I have been practicing my strengths, Zirub!"

"I know you have, Klee. And now we are going to test those strengths." Shep walked over to Russell's limp body and yanked it up by the shirt. Russell cried out in pain. Klee watched with growing discomfort. Shep dragged Russell's body over to the other side of the basement. He propped Russell against the wall in a sitting position. Russell's hand was hanging off of his wrist at an unnatural angle. His eyes fluttered, struggling to open, but he seemed in too much pain. Robin looked at Patrick, who had beads of sweat pouring down his forehead.

"What's wrong with you? Is it really Joey?" she asked.

Patrick nodded. "Yeah," he whispered. "But this isn't helping much either," he said, nodding toward the charade unfolding before them.

"What's he going to do to him?" Copie whispered to Father Carbone.

The priest shook his head, his face pinched in anguish. "I don't know, Copie."

Shep took Klee by the hand and guided him forward until he stood directly in front of Russell, then Shep stepped off to one side. "Okay Klee. Consider this practice. We are in a war, and Russell is the enemy."

Klee looked terribly nervous. He glanced at Shep with uncertainty.

Shep nodded. "Go on Klee. You can do it. I have faith in you."

Klee nodded at Shep, then took a deep breath. He stared at Russell and narrowed his eyes. His cheeks flushed red with blood and his hands began to tremble. Then he brought his fingers to his temples, and Robin gasped as a tingling of electricity filled the room. Then it was gone, as though sucked back from whence it came. The air in the dusty basement seemed to grow warm, then it retreated, as though some unseen door had been opened, sucking the warm air out.

Then Russell's head exploded. Pieces of blood-covered brain and bone splattered onto the wall behind him, leaving a shard of naked spine sticking up out of what was left of his neck. A few droplets of brain landed on Patrick's shoe, and as he turned his head away, he saw that Copie's legs were splattered with a sizeable spray of blood and one dislodged eyeball.

"Jesus Christ!" Copie's scream echoed through the basement. "Jesus Christ!" he repeated, his voice filled with horror. Father Carbone tried in vain to calm Copie. Copie squirmed and twisted his rope-bound legs until the eyeball rolled off of his thigh and onto the floor. Copie kicked it away from him. "Jesus Christ! Jesus Christ!" he screamed.

Klee turned around and stared at Copie with interest, then approached him. Copie stopped screaming and looked up at the cherubic blond. Klee shook his head innocently. "The Christ is dead," he said, as though offering Copie a fact that he must not have been aware of.

Two consecutive gunshots rang out from somewhere outside. Shep and Klee both turned toward the stairs. *Oh thank God,* Patrick thought. He never thought he'd be so happy to hear the sound of gunshots.

"Allisto!" Shep wailed.

Allisto came stomping down the stairs in a panic. "Shot's fired!" Allisto said, then another three shots could be heard.

"Is it on the property?" Shep asked.

Allisto shook his head. "No. It's coming from that house next door. There are lights on in the windows and we saw shadows moving inside. Somebody is over there."

Shep scowled. "Yeah and I'll bet I can guess who. That crazy old redneck is back, and this time he won't be leaving again."

"Do you want Margol and me to go?" Allisto asked.

"No," Shep said. "I want to take care of this myself. Just keep the perimeters guarded while I'm gone."

Patrick's body jerked forward against his will and he cried out in pain.

In his mind he had a clear image of Joey's head being slammed into a tree. Shep glanced over at him, then looked back at Allisto. "Where is Joey, Allisto?"

"The last I saw him he was taking a walk with Carlos."

Patrick looked up from where he had fallen over. "Untie me Shep! Damn it! I need to go check on Joey."

Shep shook his head. "I'll send someone else to check on Joey. I'm sorry Obrien, but I promised Juris I'd keep you all tied up down here. Be thankful that's all I promised him. You should have heard what he wanted me to do with you." Shep turned toward the priest. "For future reference, Father Carbone, never take a being that has been held captive for twenty five hundred years and tie him up in your basement. It tends to stir up bad memories."

Father Carbone did not respond, for he was praying. He had been ever since Russell's head had popped like a balloon. Shep waved Allisto and Klee on and headed for the door. "I'll be back," he said to the group. "Try not to miss me too much."

Yes, go, Patrick thought. Go check out the house next door and walk into Agent Walsh's trap. As soon as the door at the top of the stairs slammed shut, Patrick screamed, arching his back.

"Patrick!" Robin screamed.

Patrick's body convulsed once and he screamed again. "It must be the blood bond," Father Carbone said. "Something must really be happening to Joey."

"Are you serious?" Copie asked, speaking for the first time since the Russell incident. "I thought he was just faking that shit to try and get Shep to untie him!"

"Not...faking!" Patrick squeaked out, then he threw himself onto the floor and strained against the ropes until his face turned red. The ropes popped and he was free.

"Holy shit!" Copie said. Patrick threw the ropes off of him and stood up. He looked at the others, his eyes wild. "I have to go help Joey. I don't want to, but I have no choice."

"Untie us first!" Copie yelled frantically.

Still pumped with whatever odd power was pulsing through him, Patrick tore at their ropes until they were all free. "That gunshot was a signal that Agent Litner is here. We need to get Joey and meet Litner at the guest house. But now I'm not so sure we can pull it off. It's going to get messy out there. You all might be safer staying here."

"Fuck that!" Father Carbone said, standing up and shaking off his ropes. The rest of them turned, startled by the profanity. He looked at them. "What? You actually expect us to stay in this house? Gee, should we stay upstairs with the demented murdering brothers, or downstairs with the decapitated corpse? I'll say it again. Fuck that! I'll take the messy outside crap, thank you very much."

Patrick smiled at the priest. "Okay, Father Carbone. It's your choice."

"Good. Now show us the way out of this loony bin."

Chapter Fifty-Three

Shep decided to enter the big brown house through the front this time. There were too many places to hide back in that overgrown garden, and he wasn't about to let himself be ambushed by the crazy jungle rat. He stood before the front steps and looked up at the second floor windows, brightly lit from inside. A figure walked passed the upper window, and it was so unexpected that Shep actually jumped. He took a step back and waited. Then he saw him again, the kook with the long gray hair. He walked past the second window, in plain sight. Then he stopped and looked down. He seemed to be looking directly at Shep, then he turned and disappeared from view.

Waiting for me. The thought came to Shep as clear as if he'd read it on a page. Klee's power surge in the basement had awakened Shep's own abilities. He was like a raw nerve, his mental perception at a peak. He urged his mind to enter the house and find the veteran, who skulked about upstairs, seeming to...*waiting for me.* The thought came again and Shepherd winced.

Something was not right here. Shep had the distinct sense that he was being lured in. But for what reason? *Waiting for me. He's waiting for me. Waiting to trap me.* The thought began to form more substance as Shep concentrated on the windows above on the second floor. He got a hold of himself and focused. He needed to see the man again. He needed to look into his eyes, even if it was from a distance. His heart pounded at the feeling of danger, a natural warning urging him to flee. But he did not flee. He waited, and watched the windows.

Finally the man with the long gray hair passed the window again. Again, he stopped briefly, letting Shep see him. He turned his head for a moment and looked down at Shep. For that brief moment Shep locked onto his thoughts, then the man moved out of sight again. At this distance, Shep was only able to receive a jumbling of impressions from the man, but he did pick up one crucial piece of the puzzle. He gasped, taking a step back. *FBI*, was what rang in his mind now. *FBI. Waiting for me. The FBI is waiting for me.*

"Shit!" Shep said aloud. Of course. It made perfect sense now. This was no half-wit redneck. This guy was a federal agent. He'd probably been spying on them since they'd moved to Forest Bluffs. "Shit!" Shep said again, angered by his own stupidity. He should have known. He should have figured it out sooner. Then a grin spread across his face. They were expecting him to enter the house. They were trying to lure him away from the crop, or perhaps even to restrain him somehow. Well, he would just have to give them a little surprise of his own.

He examined the windows on the first floor, then he scurried off to the

shed. He unlocked the shed and stepped inside, examining the explosive de-
vices stacked along the floor. After filling the wheelbarrow with the appropriate items, he returned to the big brown house. First he looked to see if the
stranger was still inside, and soon saw his silhouette, purposely walking in
front of the upstairs windows. He began to douse the exterior of the house
with gasoline. He stayed close to the house, flattened up against it so that the
agent lurking above would not see him.

When he had saturated the perimeter, he lifted one of the explosive de-
vices out of the wheelbarrow. He opened a rear window and tossed the container of gasoline into the house. It landed on its side just in front of the stair
well, and the remainder of the gas began to spill in a steady stream onto the
floor. The gas can triggered some sort of booby trap and a net fell from the
ceiling onto the floor, covering the gasoline canister. Shep grinned at what
was to be his capture net. Then he tossed the explosive device through the
window as well, and he walked away. He scrambled around front and tossed
the second device in through the front door, then he ran for the woods. He
was whistling when he pressed the detonator and heard the explosion.

"Ashes to ashes," he said. He looked back over his shoulder and saw the
flames shoot up the back side of the house with a loud *whoof* sound. He
pressed the second detonator. "And dust to dust." The front of the house
exploded and began to roar with flames. Satisfied, he turned toward home.
"Fuck with me, will you," he said. "Think you're so smart. Look at you now."

When he got back to the house the brothers were waiting for him in the
basement, having sensed his urgency from across the wooded sprawl. He
noticed that Obrien and the others were gone, but could not make himself
care at the moment. He had bigger fish to fry.

"They are here, aren't they?" Allisto asked. "The government?"

"Yes," Shep said calmly, hoping to instill his sense of focus into them. If
the brothers panicked, they would lose.

"Then our Messiah is hunted, just as The Vessel was," Margol said.

Shep walked over to the back wall and pulled the lever that lay hidden
alongside the fuse box, and the wall slid to the right with a mechanical whir,
revealing the arsenal that lay concealed behind it. The weapons shone in the
dim basement light. There were all manner of guns, grenades, and assorted
explosives. The brothers stared at the arsenal with stoic awe. Shep turned to
them, his eyes set. "The Vessel didn't have one of these."

Chapter Fifty-Four

Joey was tied to a tree. He had ropes around his chest, his waist and his ankles. His arms were free but the tree was so thick that he couldn't reach the back side where the ropes were knotted. His lip hurt, the metallic taste of blood tainting his mouth. He had fought so hard that one of the followers had to punch him in the face, knocking him unconscious. He remembered as the darkness fell, the young man gripping his shoulders and pleading for forgiveness. Joey's entire following seemed to have gone stark raving mad. He looked over at the bonfire that blazed in the center of the field.

There was music coming from somewhere nearby. A few shadowy bodies danced rhythmically around the fire, while the rest of the followers made preparations. They had a long table set up, and two of the women were busy de-corking bottles of wine. Joey squinted as he tried to make sense of what was going on around him. He thought he heard a gunshot from somewhere in the distance. What the hell was happening? Then Kelinda was there suddenly, standing before him. Her pink hair shone from the firelight, giving it an orange halo, as if it was also made of fire. Her blue eyes twinkled with hostility.

"Kelinda? What's going on? Why are you doing this to me?"

She reached up and ran a finger along his lip. The finger came away with blood and she put it to her mouth, licking the blood determinedly, making sure he saw it. "You see, Joey, we're going to have a little party tonight. You're the guest of honor."

"That's kind of you, Kelinda, but I'm very busy. Maybe you could just let me down and we could make it another night."

"There is a power in you," she said, ignoring his plea. "You've given a portion of it to me, but of course, you already know that. I heard you and Shep talking about it one night. About how you could always kill me if I got out of hand. Do you remember?" Joey remained silent. "Well, Joey, I think I may have gotten out of hand. You gave me so much of your wonderful essence that I decided to share it. Why be selfish, right? Now the followers share in my essence. But it's not enough. My source is not pure and I can only give them so much. They want more."

"What are you saying?"

She smiled, and it was edged with ice. "You are going to sacrifice yourself like a good little Messiah. We will drink of your blood and be healed."

"The fuck you will! Get me down from here!" Joey struggled against the ropes.

"Don't bother fighting, Joey. It's your destiny."

Joey realized that the strange jingling music had stopped. He looked up to see the followers forming a single file line in front of him. They each held an open bottle of wine. Kelinda looked behind her, then she turned to Joey and pulled a glittering silver knife out from under her dress. She held it up to the sky as if in ceremony, then she brought it down and made a cut along the palm of Joey's hand. Joey screamed, but his voice sounded small and seemed to get lost in the trees.

Kelinda took his hand and lifted it up, showing the wound to the followers. Sounds of awe ran through the crowd. "This is his body!" she called out. "Which will be given up for you!"

The crowd cheered and Joey looked on in horror. All of those eyes were focused on him. Their usual looks of awe and admiration had been replaced with a maniacal hunger. Joey screamed again but his voice was lost in the cheers of the crowd. Kelinda leaned in and licked the blood off of his palm. The followers quieted, waiting anxiously behind her with the wine bottles. Kelinda leaned in close to Joey with a demented grin. "You know what's ironic, Joey?" she whispered. "I never wanted to share you before. I guess I've become more secure in our relationship."

"You're a crazy bitch!" he hissed.

"Yes, Joey. I am crazy. And who made me that way?"

He didn't argue. It was he who had done this to her. There was no denying it. "I'm sorry," he said.

"Not half as sorry as you're going to be!" she whispered. Turning to the crowd, she lifted her arms over her head. "Bring forth the wine!" she screamed.

"Great party. Mind if I crash?" a male voice behind her said. Kelinda spun furiously around to see Patrick standing there. Robin stood behind him with a young black man and a priest.

"Patrick! Leave this place now! You don't belong here, you stupid Mick!"

He took a step forward. "You know, I'm getting really tired of hearing that. Not only am I not stupid, I'm also part French."

Joey looked down at Patrick and smiled. "Obrien! Hey! Buddy! Listen, I've been meaning to tell you how sorry I am about that whole lying to you for ten years thing. No hard feelings, right?"

"Don't worry Joey. I'm still bound to your lying ass. Are you all right?"

"Do I look all right?"

He did not. He looked pale and kind of beaten up, but he still had his sense of humor, which was a good sign. Kelinda stepped toward Patrick, waving a thick silver knife in front of her. "Do not challenge me, Patrick. I have not yet shown you my full strength."

Patrick took a step toward her, closing the gap. "And I have not yet shown you mine."

Kelinda lunged at him with the knife. He ducked to one side and she stumbled, dropping the knife. Patrick stepped on the knife and she hit him in the chest with startling force. He was thrown backward, but was quickly on his feet again. She stampeded toward him and he caught her by the arm, hurling her to one side. She hit the ground with a thud, but was on her feet again and facing him within seconds. Adrenaline coursed through him.

He was about to run toward her when six of the followers were on him. He fought them furiously. He tossed one aside and punched another in the face. Kelinda looked nervous for a moment, but then more followers came at him. They kept coming. Even with his heightened strength, he could not hold all of them off. He was vaguely aware of Father Carbone and Copie trying to aid him by pulling off the ones on the outer circle.

With Kelinda distracted watching the struggle, Robin hurried over to the tree where Joey was. "Untie me!" he said.

"First drink this." She held the tiny vile up to his mouth.

"What is that?" he asked.

"It's blood. The blood of your true family. The blood of those who love you for yourself, not for spells or trickery or because of some phony miracle, Joey."

Joey sneered at the vial. "You want me to drink blood?"

Always the actor, Robin thought. "Give me a break, Joey. It's not like it's something you've never done before," she said, giving him a knowing look. He stared at her for a moment, then dropped the phony disgust.

"What will it do?" he asked.

"It will free you."

"Are you sure?"

"No," she said honestly.

He looked wary, but finally he nodded and opened his mouth. Robin poured the red liquid into his open mouth, making sure that it went down his throat. She spoke the simple, somewhat hokey words Aunt Betsy had given her. "Dissolve this bind and make thee whole, by heart and blood I call thy soul."

Joey finished swallowing the liquid. He gasped. His eyes rolled back in his head and he began to convulse. "Oh shit! Joey!" Robin cried. "What have I done?" Joey continued to thrash as all the muscles in his body simultaneously contracted. A strand of drool ran down the side of his lip and Robin was afraid he was dying. Then he stopped twitching. His head hung limply and his eyes fluttered. Robin leaned in and felt his face. He was breathing.

Two pairs of hands grabbed her and pulled her back away from Joey. Kelinda stood in front of her. "Keep your hands off of him, Robin!"

"Kelinda, please. You need help. Just forget all this and help me cut Joey down. We'll get you to a hospital."

"No! You back off, Robin. Joey is ours. We are going to absorb him."

Robin tried to run to Joey but the two men gripped her arms more tightly. She looked up at Joey. His head still hung limply but she could see the rise and fall of his chest. His eyes blinked occasionally. Kelinda took a step toward him.

"Touch him and I'll kill you," Robin said.

Kelinda looked at her and laughed. "It doesn't look to me like any of you are in a position to stop me," she said. Robin followed Kelinda's gaze, where no less than twelve men had Patrick pinned to the ground. Copie and the priest had also been restrained. Kelinda walked over to Joey and lifted his bloody hand. "Bring the wine!" she ordered. The followers retrieved their bottles and lined up again.

Kelinda took the bottle from the first in line. She held it under Joey's bleeding hand and began to squeeze droplets into the bottle. She went to hand the bottle back to the follower, and stopped suddenly. She sniffed the top of the bottle, then looked quickly up at Joey. She grabbed his hand again. She sniffed his palm and her head jerked back as though she had smelled something foul. She ran one finger across the wound on his palm and touched the blood to her tongue. She looked confused. She then leaned in and licked the entire palm. She paused, then turned and spit the blood out onto the ground.

She spun around, her faced contorted with rage, and pointed a blood-stained finger at Robin. "What did you do?" she screamed.

Robin froze. "I don't know what you mean."

Kelinda sniffed the wine bottle again, then threw it against a neighboring tree in a rage. It smashed loudly and red wine spilled down the bark. "His power is gone! I can't taste it anymore!" She took a step closer to Robin. "It was you!" she hissed. "You took it out of him, didn't you? You took it out of him! You bitch! I'll kill you!"

Kelinda ran at Robin in a blind rage. Confused, the two men that held Robin let go of her. Robin dropped to the ground just as Kelinda made contact. Using her legs for leverage, she tossed Kelinda over her head. Kelinda tumbled to the ground. She got up, and made as if to strike again. She looked around her suddenly and saw that some of the followers were walking away. "Hey! Where are you going? We'll get it back! Why are you leaving?" They ignored her as they meandered off in all directions. "No! Don't leave!" Several of the followers dropped their wine bottles and shuffled like zombies away from Kelinda, and away from Joey. Then Kelinda fell to the ground. She sobbed into the earth, clawing at the grass and mumbling.

The followers that had Patrick pinned down let go of him. Slowly, they all walked toward Joey where he hung on the tree, sniffing his palm and sniffing the stains of wine splattered on the neighboring tree. They appeared disjointed and confused. A good portion of them wandered off of the property, looking as though they had just woken up from a dream. Others retreated to their tents. Some cried.

Patrick pushed his way through the crowd, shoving the zombie followers out of the way. None of them stopped him this time. He and Father Carbone worked to untie the ropes that held Joey. Robin found the knife that Kelinda had dropped and handed it to Patrick. Patrick sawed at the ropes until finally they let go. They eased Joey to the ground. He immediately curled up into fetal position and began to weep. Robin ran to his side. "Joey? Can you hear me?"

Joey looked up at her with a grimace. "What did you do to me, Robin?"

"Tell me what you're feeling," she said, stroking his head.

"Pain!" he screamed. "I feel pain and guilt and remorse! Something's wrong. Shepherd! Shepherd, help me!" he screamed into the night sky. Patrick put a hand on him, struggling to calm him. "Shepherd!" he screamed again.

"Stop it Joey. Just calm down," Patrick urged. "Tell me what you're feeling."

"I want to die. Please let me die." He curled into a ball again and began to shake.

"Joey, you're safe now," Patrick said. "It's going to be all right."

Joey shook his head as he lay crying in high squeaky jerks. "It's not all right," he said, sounding like a frightened child. "Not all right. Not all right. Not all right," he chanted as he rocked back and forth.

Patrick looked at Robin. "I want you to take him up to the house. Take Father Carbone and Copie with you. I'll be there shortly."

"What if Shep and the brothers are up there?" Copie asked fearfully.

"I don't believe they are. I'd guess that they've gone over to the guest house by now to try and protect the crop supply. I'm going to go try to find Agent Litner and warn him, that is if it's not too late. I think something has gone terribly wrong here."

"Why?" Copie asked.

Patrick looked off in the distance and the rest of them followed his gaze. "Because burning that house down was not part of the plan." They all stared at the blazing house up on the hill.

"Shepherd!" Joey called out again.

Robin stroked his hair. "Forget about Shepherd for now, Joey."

"Oh no. Oh no. He killed them. Shep killed them!"

"Who did Shep kill, Joey?" Patrick asked.

Joey looked up now, his eyes wet with tears. "My family. My mother. My father. Jeffrey. He killed them all! He needed their blood to get the brothers out. It's my fault! Oh God, it's all my fault!" Joey sobbed loudly.

Patrick and Robin exchanged a quick shattered stare. Robin looked down at the sobbing Joey, then leaned in and hugged him. "It wasn't your fault, Joey. It wasn't your fault."

He looked at her with a heartbreaking grimace. "You don't understand. I gave him permission! He killed my family, and I gave him permission! I gave him permission!" Joey fell to the ground again and rocked back and forth whimpering. "You don't know what he is," he said so softly it was almost a whisper.

Father Carbone placed a hand on Joey, closed his eyes and began to mutter a prayer.

"We do know what he is Joey," Patrick said, looking at Father Carbone.

"We'll take care of him," Carbone said. "You go ahead and find Litner. Be careful, Patrick."

They carried Joey off to the house. Patrick watched them grow smaller with distance until he saw them climb up onto the back deck and go into the house through the sliding door.

Two quick gunshots rang out in the night, only this time they were close by. Patrick turned with a start. The few remaining followers in the field went scrambling off in all directions. Another shot rang out. The shots were coming from the direction of the guesthouse. Patrick took a deep breath and headed across the field.

Chapter Fifty-Five

Three of Agent Litner's men were wounded and they'd barely seen what attacked them. A glimpse of blond curls here, a fleeting shape there. The brothers were hidden in the trees somewhere. They were all around them now, circling like phantom wolves, taking little bites out of the team, wearing them down gradually. Litner looked down at the three melted guns on the ground and scowled. He looked over at the three agents sitting on the edge of the truck, with their bandaged hands and wincing faces. One of the men had seen something in the trees, so Litner had sent him to check it out. When he returned, he was screaming.

Agent Rourke came scurrying over now. The big blond agent was dressed in full fatigues with a variety of weapons strapped to his body. "We finished setting the charges. All of the trucks are wired, along with the rest of the barrels inside the guesthouse. The detonator is here."

Litner took the tiny box from Agent Rourke. He surveyed the area around him. The followers had given up the guesthouse without a fight. Most of them didn't even seem to care that the FBI was there. Some of them tried to wander off toward the road, but they were subdued and loaded into one of the FBI trucks and taken off the property. They would be needed later for questioning.

Litner's team had begun loading the crop into the trucks, but with the brothers stalking them, the task had nearly come to a stop. They had only succeeded in transporting about a quarter of the stuff into their own trucks. The rest was still in the guest house and locked in some of the Arcania Foods trucks. He hoped they wouldn't have to blow the lot of it, but things weren't looking good. He stuffed the detonator into his coat pocket.

Now Agent Litner and the remaining unharmed agents sat huddled, boxed in alongside the guesthouse, surrounded by their own vans and trucks. Litner looked back at Agent Coleman, who was trying hard not to cry despite the pain in his burned hands. The former Navy seal had been the first to come running from the edge of the woods, screaming that something had attacked him. He said the attacker came out of nowhere, then disappeared in a flash. Coleman's hands were blistered with third degree burns. When Litner asked him what had burned him, he claimed it was his own gun. It had melted in his hands when the assailant briefly stood before him.

Litner had then sent four men out to retrieve Coleman's gun and search for the assailant, who was most likely one of the brothers. They returned carrying two of the men, both of them with burns identical to Coleman's. They too claimed to have only caught a glimpse of their assailant. He was described as a thin redhead with chin length curls and eyes like saucers.

Agent Rourke had managed to retrieve the guns. Litner looked down at the weapons again. On each of them, the barrel had melted like wax until it was nothing more than a distorted glob of steel. If this continued, Litner wouldn't have enough men functioning to transport the crop once they finished loading it. He supposed that was the whole idea. He was not comfortable huddling in a circle like sitting ducks, but he couldn't risk putting any more of his men on guard at the woods. He knew that eventually Shep and the others would come forth for a direct confrontation, but it was a chance he had to take.

Crouched down on one knee now, he scanned the perimeters with his gun out. Half of the team stood guard with him, while the other half resumed loading the crop with record speed. He glanced over at the blazing house next door. So Shep had outsmarted him again. Litner only hoped that Walsh had not gotten trapped inside the burning house. Walsh had not returned to base, so chances were the worst had happened. He couldn't dwell on that now. "Where are those night vision goggles?" Litner asked Rourke.

The enormous blond agent retrieved the goggles and handed them to Litner. Litner put them on and scanned the edge of the woods and the surrounding fields. "Why can't I see them?" he said.

"I don't know, but the guys are loading as fast as they can, and we haven't even made a dent in the guest house supply. The place is stock full of those barrels. I'm a little skeptical that we're going to get this stuff out of here before they attack again. Our guys are good, but they're not superhuman," Rourke said.

"No, you're right," Litner said, still peering through the goggles. "Only our opponents are superhuman."

A twig snapped behind him and he spun about with his weapon up. Rourke did the same. Patrick Obrien stood there with his hands over his head. "Don't shoot. It's me."

Litner let out a sigh and lowered his gun. "Obrien! How did you get out here?"

"I walked. Why?"

Litner waved him over. "Come on. Come in close to me and stay down. Did you see Father Carbone and Copie? Are they dead? Did Juris kill them?"

Patrick walked over and crouched down alongside Litner. "No, I was just with them. They're okay. Nice goggles."

"This is no time for jokes, Patrick. We're under attack."

Patrick looked over at the agents who were systematically loading barrels of the crop into the black government trucks. "It doesn't look like you're under attack," he said. Then he glanced over at the three agents who sat propped up in the back of a truck with their hands wrapped in bandages. "What happened to them?" he asked.

Litner gave him a humorless smile. "Tell me something, Patrick. Shep's brothers, can they also...melt things with their minds?"

Patrick shifted uneasily. "Well, um, yes. Yes I believe they can."

"Well that's just great!" In a rare show of emotion, Litner kicked the pile of guns on the ground. He picked one of the melted guns up and held it out for Patrick to see. "Are there any other little tidbits I'm unaware of? Can they turn invisible? Do they transform into giant mechanical robots?"

Patrick had never seen Litner lose his temper before. It was unnerving. "Take it easy, Agent Litner."

"Take it easy? I'm down to thirteen men. Agent Walsh has probably been barbecued, and our weapons..." Litner tossed the melted gun at Patrick's feet. "Our weapons are apparently useless!"

"Yes, but ours aren't." They barely had time to turn and see the source of the voice when Juris shot Agent Rourke in the forehead. The big blond agent dropped like a rock. Litner had his gun up immediately but was not quick enough. Juris dove through the air, went about fifteen feet and hit the ground in a summersault. Agent Litner's bullet missed him by several feet. When Litner turned to take another shot, Juris was gone, sprinted off like lightning into the darkness.

"Fuck!" Litner yelled, tossing his goggles onto the ground. He leaned down and examined Agent Rourke's body. The bullet had hit him in the direct center of his forehead, a perfect death shot. The blond agent's eyes stared lifelessly up. Litner put his hand on Rourke's face and gently closed his eyes. Looking up at Patrick, he said, "Have you ever fired a machine gun before?"

Patrick nodded. "Once. Back in high school at the shooting range."

"Good." Litner ripped the gun out of Agent Rourke's dead hands and thrust it at Patrick. Patrick took it reluctantly. "Congratulations. You've just been made an honorary agent. What size jacket do you wear?"

Patrick looked down. "I, uh, I'm not sure."

"Extra large? Good. I just happen to have something in your size." Litner maneuvered Agent Rourke's body, pulling the camouflage jacket off of his limp dead bulk. He brushed a couple of flecks of blood off of the jacket and handed it to Patrick. "Put this on."

Patrick complied, though he was reasonably sure that Litner was losing his mind. "Are we going somewhere, Agent Litner?"

"We're going out into those woods and we're going to find those freaks. When we find them, we're going to kill them. Do you have a problem with that, Obrien?"

"Well, no sir. But—"

"But what?"

"It's just that I'm not sure if Klee deserves to be killed."

"Why? Because he's cute?" He looked down at Agent Rourke's body. "Did you know that Agent Rourke has a three year old daughter? She's cute too."

Litner got down on his elbows and began to crawl outside the line of trucks and toward the woods. Patrick crouched down and followed, trying to imitate Litner's motions. It was awkward with the machine gun. "This is a bad idea," Patrick said.

They had only crawled twenty yards across the field when Shep came walking out of the woods with his hands over his head like a phantom in the moonlight. Wind whipped his curls and tugged at his clothing. No, Patrick thought. This is too easy. Shep give himself up? Never.

Litner stopped crawling and stood up. Pointing the gun at Shep, he yelled, "Stop where you are!" Shep smiled and stopped in his tracks. Patrick stood up and poised his weapon. Litner inched slowly forward and Patrick followed. He stopped in front of Shep. Shep was still smiling, his hands over his head in a surrender that they all knew was false. Patrick looked around uneasily at the empty darkness.

"Where are the rest of them?" Litner asked.

"The rest of who?" Shep asked innocently.

"You know damn well who. Your brothers. Where are they?"

Shep shrugged. "Gee, I just don't know. I must have gotten separated from them."

"Sort of the way Jeffrey Duvaine got separated from his friends on that hunting trip?" Litner seethed.

Shep's forehead furrowed in exaggerated confusion. "I'm sure I don't know what you mean."

"Yeah right." Litner said. "Turn around slowly."

Shep complied, turning slowly, giving his back to Litner. Litner moved in and frisked him, patting down his jeans and up under his arms. He pulled the purple tie-dyed tank top out and his eyes lingered on Shep's horseshoe shaped scar for a moment, then he let the shirt go. "All right. Turn around slowly, and don't try anything." Shep complied.

"So, this is Special Agent Steven Litner," Shep said. "Your record is quite impressive. Obrien, you didn't tell me he was so handsome."

Litner stared back at Shep. It seemed that now that he had him, he didn't know quite what to do with him. "Maybe you should handcuff him," Patrick said, trying to shake Litner out of his stun.

Litner nodded. "Right. Of course." Shep held his hands out politely and Litner cuffed them at the wrist. "Walk back toward the trucks. Slowly."

"Whatever you say, Agent," Shep said, and began walking toward the cluster of FBI vehicles near the guesthouse. Patrick could sense something was wrong as soon as they rounded the side of the guesthouse where the FBI's little makeshift bunker was set up. It was too quiet. Then he saw it. In the center of the field just in front of the guesthouse were the rest of the federal agents. There were twelve of them. They were tied together, back to back in a human circle and they had all been gagged with handkerchiefs. Litner stared at them, unable to speak. Then he and Patrick felt the guns against their backs.

"Put your weapons down please." It was Margol's voice. Litner lowered his weapon and Juris snatched it out of his hand. It was Klee who took Patrick's as he pointed a handgun at his temple.

"I don't want to hurt you, Patrick," Klee said.

Patrick turned and faced him. Klee's innocent eyes had turned cold and feral. "But you will. Won't you Klee?"

"Yes. If I have to."

Shep came forward grinning and stood before Litner. He held his hands out for Litner to see, then he snapped the handcuffs apart effortlessly, as though they were made of plastic. "Now I get to frisk you, Agent. What fun." Litner held his hands over his head while Shep went through his pockets and felt up along his pant legs. Patrick looked on, amazed as Shep pulled out weapon after weapon. Patrick couldn't believe the amount of hardware Litner had concealed on his body. There were three more guns, four knives and a grenade. The last thing Shep pulled out was a small black box with a red button on it. "Well. What do we have here?" he asked.

In a swift movement, Agent Litner kicked his leg out and his foot connected with the little box. It flew through the air, back over his head and Patrick caught it. He almost dropped it, until Litner yelled, "Patrick, it's the detonator! Don't let them take it!"

Shep looked over at Margol. "Go to the guest house and the Arcania trucks. Remove any explosives and attach them to the FBI trucks."

"I wouldn't do that Shep," Patrick said, waving the little box in his hand. His eyes flitted over to the guesthouse, and to the fleet of white Arcania truck's that stood ominously behind. His eyes glanced over to the four boxy black FBI trucks to his right.

Patrick knew that part of the crop had already been loaded into FBI vehicles, a fact that Shep seemed unaware of. If Patrick pushed the detonator button, he still would not be destroying the entire crop. He glanced at Litner, who seemed to read his thoughts. Litner gave him a slight nod. Litner did not want Shep to know about the barrels that had been loaded into the FBI trucks. He did, however, want the rest of the crop destroyed. That meant Patrick had to push the button.

"Do it, Patrick!" Litner yelled. Juris punched Agent Litner and he fell to the ground. He was hurt, but still conscious.

Shep grabbed Litner's handgun off the ground and came toward Patrick, his lips pursed in angry determination. He stopped in front of Patrick and pointed the gun at his forehead. "Give me that detonator, Obrien."

Patrick held it up over his head. "No. No, stay back or I'll blow up the crop."

"Not before I shoot you," Shep said.

Shep cocked the gun, his lower lip trembling in fury.

"You can shoot me, Shep. But not before I can blow up the crop."

Shep braced the gun firmly with his second hand. "I mean it, Obrien. I will shoot you."

"Go ahead. Do it, Shep."

Shep hesitated. "Give it to me, Obrien. I know you want to live, so just stop fucking around. You're no hero. You're no federal agent either. You're just a dumb accountant, so give me the detonator and maybe I'll let you live."

"Kiss my ass!" Patrick said and pressed the little red button.

The explosion knocked them all off their feet as the hub of the guesthouse and fleet of Arcania trucks shared a simultaneous explosion. There were minutes of panicked confusion, then the smoke and dust began to clear. Tiny flakes of ash fell out of the sky like a delicate black snow flurry.

Shep got up first, still clinging to the gun, and gaped at the flames that engulfed the guesthouse and the white box trucks. It was a giant ball of fire, the biggest Patrick had ever seen. Nothing inside could have survived it. The roof of the guesthouse was already starting to give way under the heat. The crops were gone. At least the ones Shep knew about. The Black FBI trucks were parked out of the line of fire. They remained unscathed. Klee began to cry. "Zirub! The crops are burning! Zirub! Zirub what are we going to do?"

Shep reached out and punched Klee hard in the face. Klee dropped to the ground, unconscious. The other brothers looked at Shep with disbelief. "What?" Shep said. "He doesn't need to see any more of this. He's too new. Don't worry. He'll be fine." Shep then turned the gun on Patrick. "But you won't!"

"Yes, I suppose you're going to kill me now," Patrick said. He marveled at how fearless he had become. It was most likely some by-product of the weirdness overload he'd been exposed to over the past weeks. He was too tired to be scared. He had exhausted his fear reserve.

"That's right, Obrien. You've just ruined fifteen years of planning you dumb fuck! You were a mistake from the beginning. Now you're going to die."

"So kill me already!" Patrick squawked. "Please, just shut up and kill me. I am so tired of listening to your bullshit, Shepherd. I've been listening to your crap for ten years. Please, spare me from having to hear another word!"

Agent Litner gave him a warning look from where he sat on the ground. Juris had a gun pressed against Litner's temple. "Oh don't worry," Shep said through clenched teeth. "You've got your wish. You won't have to listen to me anymore, Obrien. Ever." Shep sounded serious enough but here was a hesitation in his eyes. He lifted the gun higher. A gust of warm heat blew through the air from the direction of the burning house and trucks. They were all sweating now.

"What are you waiting for then? Come on Shep! I mean nothing to you! I'm just the Shield, remember? You can make another one. I'm nothing. You don't care about me. So shoot me! What are you waiting for?" Patrick's voice had elevated to a hysterical scream.

Margol looked over at the wall of flames that engulfed the guesthouse, then back at Shep. "Shepherd!" he said. "What *are* you waiting for? Kill him already!"

"Oh I will, Margol. I will." But he didn't. He just stood there, his face a tortured mask of indecision.

"I'll do it then!" Margol said and pointed his own gun at Patrick. Shep spun and pointed his weapon at Margol. Margol froze, looking shocked and hurt.

"No, Margol!" Shep snapped. Margol lowered his gun. Shep got a hold of himself and turned his gun on Patrick again. "It has to be me. I have to be the one to kill Obrien," he said.

"Yes, Dr. Frankenstein," Patrick said. "You created me, so you must destroy me right?'

"Oh, I'm going to destroy you."

"You keep saying that. Pull the trigger!" Patrick was screaming at the top of his lungs now. He paused, panting as he waited for death to come. Everything around him seemed to go still. Litner looked up from where he sat. Margol looked at Shep with a combination of surprise and disappointment. Allisto watched patiently with his gun pointed at the cluster of agents tied in a circle a few yards away, Klee lay on the ground like a sleeping child. Patrick and Shep stood five feet apart, staring intensely into each other's eyes.

Shep's face twisted in frustration as he tried to muster the courage to shoot. Patrick saw the conflict behind his green eyes. It was surprising really. Patrick never expected Shep to have any trouble killing him. He certainly didn't have any trouble killing any one else.

"Do it, Shepherd!" Margol urged.

Shep nodded and took a deep breath. "Okay. I'll do it. Here we go."

"Put the gun down, Zirub!" a voice called out from the darkness. All eyes turned to the right, where a thin young man with short yellow hair was walking toward them, seemingly from out of the flames. As he got closer, his features became clear.

"Wesley!" Agent Litner whispered.

Shep watched the handsome young blond approach. Even in the dim fire lit night, Patrick could see Shep's face go pale. He looked like he was seeing a ghost. Wesley stopped when he got to them and stood alongside Patrick, directly in front of Shep.

"You!" Shep hissed, and that one word held more hatred than Patrick had ever heard.

"Still won't say my name, huh Zirub?" Wesley said sadly.

"What are you doing here? This does not concern you! Go back to your mountain home or I promise you there will be hell to pay!" Each of Shep's words he spat out through clenched teeth. Patrick had never seen Shep with so much hate. Even Patrick and Robin's betrayal did not elicit this. It was a hate so intense that Shep's yes brimmed with hot tears as he glared, wide-eyed at Wesley. His entire body began to tremble with rage.

"Oh, Zirub," Wesley said, his voice a soft quiver. "There already has been hell to pay. Still trying to take over the world I see. You'd think you'd get the point by now. It's not going to happen. They won't allow it. What are you going to do, Zirub? Keep trying time after time until we're into the next millennium? Hell, the real Messiah will probably be back by then."

Tears of rage fell down Shep's cheeks. His lips trembled as he glared at Wesley.

"You know nothing about this! I don't need you this time! I've formed a new plan and it doesn't concern you. How dare you come to me like this! How dare you show your face here?"

Wesley was an odd sight amongst this crowd, with his pale yellow polo shirt and green pleated shorts. He looked over at the burning house and trucks. He looked at Rourke's dead body, at the Agents tied in a circle, then back at Shep, and at the gun in his hand. "Oh yes, Zirub," he said. "I can see that your plan is working out far better this time. Things have gone off without a hitch, have they? Drop the gun, Zirub, and let Patrick go."

Shep turned and stared at Patrick. "How does he know your name?" Patrick felt a little rush of the hate that was in Shep's eyes. It was scalding. Patrick didn't dare answer. Shep turned to Wesley then and screamed, "How do you know his name!"

"Patrick is a friend of mine," Wesley said.

Shep shook his head frantically. "No! No! You cannot possibly know him. You no longer exist. Patrick is my Shield! He's mine!"

"Yes," Wesley said, "And I can see that you're looking out for his well being, just as you did with Rollie."

Shep bared his teeth at Wesley and uttered what sounded like a dog's growl deep in his throat. It scared Patrick more than the gun. Wesley jumped a little, but stood his ground. Patrick stole a glance at the wispy blond. Wesley was shaking. He was clearly terrified, but he stiffened his jaw and met Shep's stare. "I am so tired of being afraid of you," he said.

Shep's eyes gleamed like a cat's. "How dare you bring up Rollie? That wasn't my fault. Rollie was weak! He made a terrible Shield. I have created a better one. Patrick is far stronger and more effective than Rollie ever was!"

"Really?" Wesley said. "Then why are you about to put a bullet into him?"

Shep glanced at Patrick and his face pulled back with emotion. Then he looked back at Wesley, and he closed his eyes, slapping his palm to his forehead repeatedly. "Shut up!" he screamed. "Shut up, shut up, shut up! I can't think!"

"Let this end, Zirub. This is twice your plan has been foiled. Can't you read the signs? Your plan is not meant to be!"

Shep pointed the gun in Wesley's face. "You are not supposed to be here. You do not exist," he said.

Wesley swallowed hard and took a daring step toward Shep. "You can pretend I don't exist all you want, Zirub. I even tried to pretend I didn't exist. For forty years I've hidden myself away from the world, and before that, I lived only for you. Only for you. I'm sixty-two years old, Zirub, and I haven't even lived yet. I want my freedom. I want to be free of you, and free of my fear."

"No!" Shep said. "You will never be free. You tried to push me back into the void!"

"I was still a child, Zirub! You murdered my aunt!"

"I don't care! You tried to push me back into the nothingness! And as punishment you will live with nothing. You will live *as* nothing until you die. And since you no longer age, that could be a very long time. An eternity. You have two choices. Kill yourself, or go back to your mountain home and live as

I instructed you to live!"

Wesley's eyes leaked tears now. He shook his head. "I'm leaving that house, Zirub. And I'm leaving this property. But I'm taking Patrick with me."

Shep pointed the gun at Patrick again. "Really? You can take him, but you won't take him alive." Shep held both hands on the gun, now pointed directly at Patrick's head. His arms trembled as he tried to steady the weapon. He met Patrick's eyes, teeth clenched in determination. Patrick waited for death to come, but again there was only the silent stillness of anticipation. Finally, Shep grunted angrily and lowered the gun.

"Damn it!" he screamed. "It seems I can't kill you, Obrien." He said the words with disappointment. He looked confused, like he couldn't comprehend his own failure to kill Patrick. Patrick didn't know quite what to say to Shep's announcement that he could not murder him. He didn't think 'thanks' would be appropriate.

He was shocked out of his pondering when Shep suddenly turned the gun on Wesley. "But YOU! You I can kill...Wesley Jackson Shepherd!"

Patrick had a microsecond to think, *Hey, he finally said his name!* Then Shep pulled the trigger. In that instant before he was absolutely sure that Shep was going to do it, Patrick made a decision. It was not a decision born of blood or bonding spells, it was a decision made of his own free will. Patrick dove in front of Wesley and caught the bullet in his side, just below his chest. He actually felt one of his ribs shatter, and then the side of his body exploded with the worst pain he'd ever felt. As he fell to the ground, his only thought was, *this hurts a lot more than it looks like on TV.*

Someone was screaming "Noooo!" and it took him a moment to realize that it was Shep. He was vaguely aware of Litner shouting, trying to get to Patrick. Wesley knelt down and grabbed Patrick's shoulders. "Patrick! Patrick can you hear me?"

"I hear you Wesley," he whispered through the pain.

Wesley looked at him through tears. "Why did you do that? Why, Patrick? You are not my Shield. You're not bound to me."

Patrick winced in pain. "Wanted to," he squeaked out. "You haven't lived yet. You said it yourself. You can't die here. Not like this."

"Neither can you! I'm going to get you some help!" Wesley lifted his hands from Patrick's side, and they were covered with blood. Patrick dared a glance down and saw the thick dark blood seeping out of his rib area. Then a hand came in and shoved Wesley roughly aside. It was Shep.

"Get away from him!" Shep hissed. Wesley tumbled over in surprise. Shep leaned over Patrick and pressed his hands down on the wound. "Obrien, you dumb Mick! What the hell were you thinking?" Shep opened Patrick's jacket and lifted his tee shirt up, examining the wound. Margol came forward and knelt down.

"What are you doing, Shepherd? Just let him die! He betrayed us!"

Without looking up, Shep said, "Get away from me Margol, or I'm going to get angry."

Margol retreated. Shep looked down at Patrick's wound, his eyebrows knitted in confusion. "This isn't right. You're supposed to be healing!" He pushed his hands down on the wound and Patrick winced. "It doesn't make any sense! Heal damn it!" he yelled. "Heal!" Patrick was astonished to see that Shep's concern was genuine.

"What do you mean he's supposed to be healing?" Wesley asked.

Shep gave Wesley a dirty look, but then he answered. "There was an attachment I added to his blood bond with Joey. I gave him extraordinary healing power when I made him The Shield, so that he could take hits for Joey and still live. The bleeding should have stopped by now!"

Patrick remembered now that Robin had administered the little vial of blood to Joey. It seemed to have succeeded in undoing the bonds Shep had instilled. Patrick grinned.

"Not the Shield," he said, in a painful voice.

"What did you say?" Shep asked.

"I'm not the Shield anymore. The bond has been broken."

"What?" Shep paused, then leaned in close to Patrick, running his hands over his body without touching him. He pulled abruptly back and looked at Patrick with shock. "You're right! How the hell did you manage that? Shit!" Shep turned around and looked at Agent Litner. "Hey, Agent Fuckhead, get over here!"

Agent Litner looked up at Juris, who waved him on. Litner scurried over to where Patrick lay. "I need to get him to a hospital," Litner said.

"I know," Shep said. "But if we don't do something else first, he'll bleed to death on the way there."

Litner gave Shep a wary look. "What are you suggesting?"

Shep used the bottom of his tank top to wipe the blood away from the wound. "Call it a Band-Aid."

"A Band-Aid?" Litner said, frowning.

"Give me your hand," Shep said.

Litner shook his head. "No."

"He's going to die, Agent Litner."

Patrick laughed, delirious with pain and blood loss. "You were wrong, Shep. Human beings can sacrifice themselves. You were wrong."

"Yes, Obrien, I was wrong. Now shut the fuck up so I can save your life." Shep looked at Litner. "Quickly, Agent Litner. Do you care about him?"

Litner shrugged. "What do you mean?"

"Do you speak English, man? Do you care about Patrick?"

"Yes. Very much."

"Then give me your God-damned hand, you government fuck!"

Litner offered his hand to Shep, palm up. He met Patrick's eyes. "Is he always this complimentary?" the white-haired agent asked.

Patrick grinned. "Pretty much."

Shep asked Margol to bring him a dagger, which he did. He made a small slice in Agent Litner's hand, and led it over Patrick's wound, letting it drip directly onto Patrick's own blood. He released Agent Litner's hand, then made a cut in his own hand, and went to do the same. Agent Litner grabbed Shep's wrist. "No. Not your blood."

"I can stop the bleeding for at least an hour this way. You do want him to live, don't you?"

Reluctantly, Litner let go of Shep's wrist. Shep dribbled some of his own blood over Patrick's wound, and closed his eyes. He began to whisper. "Uhl jetra pleffar, uhl jetra ongs." Shep repeated the phrase several times, smearing the blood across the wound, mingling it with Patrick's. Then he took a deep breath and pulled his hands back.

Litner's eyes widened in shock as he reached in to examine Patrick's wound. He pulled a handkerchief out of his pocket and cleared the blood off of Patrick's rib area. "The bleeding has stopped! That's amazing! How did you do that?" Shep smiled. Litner remained focused on Patrick's ribs. "Unbelievable!" he gasped.

Shep stood and wiped his bloody hands on his pants. "Yeah, well it won't be unbelievable in another hour or so. He'll start to bleed again, just like before, so you'd better get him to a hospital. You can take my car."

Litner frowned. "Take your car? Why?"

Shep smiled coldly. "Because I will be taking those FBI trucks over there, Agent Litner. You know, the ones that are filled with what's left of my crop?" Litner's face dropped and Shep laughed. "Oh, I see. You thought I didn't know about them. My goodness Agent Litner, you continue to underestimate me."

"Yes, I do," Litner said, with the slightest tone of respect.

The flames engulfing the guesthouse had all but died down, but suddenly they shot upward as though doused with a giant canister of lighter fluid. All eyes turned to look. The flames died back down gradually, and everyone looked away, until one of the restrained agents began to scream. Patrick was able to sit up with Wesley's help, and he looked over at the cluster of agents who sat tied together a few yards away.

"Uhhnk!" one of them was trying to yell through the gag. "Uhhnk! Uhhnk!" The gagged agent was motioning his head toward the guesthouse. It took Patrick a moment to realize that the agent was trying to say the word 'look'. Everyone else seemed to catch it too, because they all turned their eyes toward the flaming guesthouse.

Patrick sucked his breath in so hard that his gunshot wound stung with fresh pain. In the center of the wall of flame was an enormous circle where the color had gone pure white. And in that white flaming circle was a figure. Patrick blinked at the apparition several times, trying to make sense of what he was seeing. It was huge, about the size of four men. It did seem to have legs and human hands, but that's where the similarity ended. It had four heads, one on top of the other. Two of them looked vaguely human, but the other two were beast-like. One of the bestial heads resembled a lion, and the other some sort of bird. It had four large wings, two on either side of its torso, and each wing was covered with eyes. The eyes seemed to turn together in whatever direction the heads would. It glowed with a soft white light that seemed to pulse and move through its form.

"What in the name of hell is that thing?" Patrick said softly, as if afraid to disturb the strange apparition.

"Impossible," Wesley said. "It can't be."

Patrick and Litner both looked at him. "What is it, Wesley?" Patrick asked.

Wesley's blue eyes gazed hypnotically at the freakish vision. "Cherubim!" he said with a whisper. "Cherubim!" he said again. "But it can't be! It's not possible!"

"Cherubim?" Patrick said. "I thought Cherub's were fat little toddler-looking things with butterfly wings."

Wesley shook his head. "No. That's a common misconception spawned by the interpretations of popular artists. That thing right there is what a Cherubim is really supposed to look like. Four heads, human hands, four wings with eyes on them. "

"Well, shit!" Patrick said. "That's a pretty big misconception! There's a slight difference between fat winged babies and that...thing!"

"It's a hoax, right?" Litner said, his eyes darting back and forth nervously. "Patrick, who's doing that?" Litner looked behind him toward the field, as though expecting to see someone projecting the apparition from somewhere. Litner looked crazed. "It's another hoax, right Patrick? Who's projecting it? Is Russell doing it?"

Patrick shook his head. "All I can tell you, Litner, is that it sure as shit isn't Russell."

The thing hung there, translucent yet solid, like a watery photograph within the flames. Patrick looked up at Shep, and the look on Shep's face told him that this was no hoax. Whatever that thing was, it was real. Shep grabbed Juris and shook him. "I told you not to bring that priest here!" he said. "I told you!"

Juris's lip quivered as he glanced fearfully at the apparition. "I'm so sorry, Shepherd!"

Patrick tugged on Wesley's arm. "Hey! What else do you know about that thing? Why is it here?"

Wesley crouched down to where Patrick sat with Agent Litner. He leaned in close, keeping his voice low. "Cherubim are very high up in the hierarchy, second only to Seraphim. They are so high up in fact, that I doubt even Zirub and the other Powers have ever seen one, in person so to speak." Wesley raised his eyebrows. "Supposedly, they carry the Light of God with them. They never visit the material world unless it's for something outrageously important. This is highly unusual."

"Define outrageously important," Patrick said.

Wesley shrugged. "Well for instance, it was supposedly a Cherub who evicted Adam and Eve from the Garden of Eden."

"Oh," Patrick said. "That kind of important. What the hell is it doing in Forest Bluffs?"

Wesley shrugged. "I don't now. Somebody must have been very naughty."

Patrick looked over at Shep. "Gee, I wonder who that could be."

"How do you know so much about this stuff?" Litner asked Wesley.

Wesley smirked. "Let's just say I have a special interest in celestial beings, and I've had a lot of time to catch up on my reading."

The apparition was not looking at Shep, however. It turned slightly, gliding gracefully, and all of its eyes, including the multitude on its wings, focused on something to its far left. Tiny bolts of electricity, like heat lightning was sparking out from the white fire that encircled it, as though it was building energy. Then a larger bolt shot out from the fiery circle and crashed into the first black FBI truck. The bolt seemed to go right through the truck and connected with the other three trucks. It remained there, feeling around like a fiery tentacle. Then it pulled back suddenly, and all four FBI trucks exploded in a ball of fire.

Well, Patrick thought, at least now we know why it's here. Apparently the Feds weren't the only ones who didn't like Shep's little sterilization plan. Shep gazed at the apparition fearfully, and then he turned to the brothers. "We have to get out of here. Now. Go. All of you. Go to the safe place we talked about. I have to get Klee. I'll catch up with you. Go to the safe place. Go now!"

Margol and Juris sprinted off toward the road, faster than any human should have been able to run. Shep turned back to look for Allisto. Allisto was walking toward the apparition. All four faces of the thing watched Allisto calmly. "Allisto no!" Shep cried and ran over, grabbing him by his tank top and pulling him backward. Allisto tried tugging away from his grasp, but

Shep held tight.

Allisto faced Shep then, and looked into his eyes as if in a dream. "Did you see it, Zirub? It has The Light! Did you see it?"

"The Light is not for us anymore, Allisto!"

Allisto's face pinched in anger and he shoved Shep away from him and began walking toward the fire again. The being still hung in the flames, motionless except for the gentle pulsing of its four wings. Shep grabbed Allisto again, and Allisto spun on him. "It has The Light, Zirub! The Light!"

"You can't go to it, Allisto! It's dangerous! Get out of here now! Go to the safe place and wait with your brothers!"

"No!" Allisto screamed. "I don't want this flesh anymore!" Allisto's yells were laced with tears. "I don't want to stay here anymore! I want to go back!"

"Get a hold of yourself, Allisto! You can't go back!"

"I never wanted to be flesh! It's disgusting! I want my wings back!"

Shep grabbed him by the shirt and gave him a hard shake. "You agreed to this, Allisto! You consented to come here with me!"

Allisto tried twisting away from him. Tears streamed down his cheeks. "I agreed to come here with you, Zirub. I never agreed to staaaaaay!" he shrieked.

Shep looked like he'd been slapped. "You said you didn't blame me," he whispered. "You swore it."

Allisto's lip quivered, his eyes tightened in emotional agony. "We shouldn't have left our posts, Zirub. I told you it was a bad idea back then, so long ago. Do you remember? I told you it was a bad idea. We shouldn't have left our posts!"

"You blame me!" Shep said, his voice as anguished as Allisto's now. "All these years, you've blamed me for what became of us!"

Allisto shook his head. "I don't blame you, Zirub." Allisto's voice had become high and squeaky. "I just want my wings back. That's all, Zirub. I just want my wings back." Allisto broke free of Shep then and darted full speed toward the apparition. "Hey!" he squealed, in a maddened fury. "I want my wings back!"

Fifteen pairs of eyes shifted eerily and focused on the figure of Allisto running toward it. Allisto looked vulnerable in its shadow, a tiny lithe figure with dark bouncing curls, running toward the mountain of fire like a lost child. He was maddened now, delirious. "I want my wings back, I want my wings back, I want my fucking wings back!"

"Allisto no!" Shep screamed in horror. All four mouths of the being opened, and a sound came out that was a combination of a shrieking bird and a lion's roar. A white light shot out and bathed Allisto in a glowing beam. Allisto fell to his hands and knees as if he'd been struck down. He climbed clumsily to his feet, then his head and arms whipped back and he howled in pain.

Something was happening to him. Patrick, Wesley and Agent Litner all froze, unable to believe what they were seeing. Out of the scar on Allisto's back sprouted two black lumps, pulsing like living things. Then they began to grow and change. His tank top tore free and hung in shreds off his arms. Allisto shrieked and fell to his knees as the black things on his back seemed to unravel from him until they were complete. Spread out behind him were two, black leathery looking wings the likes of which should have belonged to a reptile. They looked vulgar there, sprouting out of Allisto's soft, smooth flesh.

Allisto stood up and looked behind him. He fanned the wings twice, then looked back toward the creature with confusion. "These are not my wings," he said. Then the confusion on his face turned to rage, and he charged at the thing. "These are not my wings!"

Shep went running after him. He caught up with him and dove forward, taking Allisto down by tackling him around the ankles. Allisto fell to his belly and began clawing at the earth, trying to get at the apparition. "These are not my wings! I'll kill you! I'll kill you!" he screamed at the bizarre thing that loomed over them.

Shep struggled with all his might to pull Allisto back away from the apparition and out of the beam of light, but Allisto clawed and kicked his legs where Shep pulled on them. The beam of light that engulfed Allisto fell onto Shep now, as he was practically on top of him. Shep's tank top split open and a pair of black leathery wings, identical to Allisto's, sprouted grotesquely out of his back. Shep continued to struggle to retrieve Allisto, even as the reptilian wings grew and spread, erupting from the scar on his back. A trail of blood ran down Shep's back, making a red stain at the top of his jeans.

He had managed to drag Allisto back several feet, but then Allisto caught Shep square in the nose with the heel of his shoe. Shep let go of Allisto for a second, and Allisto was out of his grasp and sprinting full speed toward the Cherubim, vowing to kill it. When he finally made contact with the apparition, his body simply exploded in the flames and a shower of sparks that looked like fairy dust puffed out into the air. Allisto was gone. The human faces on the Cherubim looked sad. The lion head roared, and the sound was also somehow sad.

⁊ ⸂

Shep lay on the ground, face down on his hands and knees. The horrible black wings seemed to be bouncing on his back, and that was when Patrick realized that Shep was sobbing. He watched as Shep raised himself to his knees, took in a deep breath, then let out an echoing howl. "Allistoooo!" he cried. It was the most heartbreaking sound Patrick had ever heard. "Allistooo!" he cried out again. Shep dropped his head into his hands then and cried with unspeakable sorrow.

"I have to go get him!" Patrick tried to get up and found that his ribs would not hear of it. He winced painfully and looked at Agent Litner. "He's right in front of that thing. You have to go get him!"

Litner shook his head. "No way!"

Patrick's eyes filled with tears as he looked out at Shep, sobbing into his hands, the two leathery wings gliding up and down gently in the breeze. "He saved my life."

"He's the one who shot you!" Litner snapped. "It was the least he could do! And he killed Agent Rourke!"

"Juris killed Rourke," Patrick said.

"Under Shep's command!" Litner screamed. "It's the same difference!"

"I'll go," Wesley said, and both Patrick and Agent Litner looked at him with shock. After all, Shep had just attempted to kill him. The young-looking blond with his Bermuda shorts and Polo shirt jogged out into the field toward Shep. He glanced briefly up at the fiery apparition, then leaned down, reaching around Shep's new black wing to take his arm. Shep did not fight Wesley as he lifted him up and swung one arm over his shoulder. Shep hung his head miserably as Wesley led him back to the shadows where the rest of them waited.

The apparition then lifted its four wings up high, clasped its human hands to its chest, and faded until it was gone. The white fire faded too, and now there was only a slowly burning guesthouse again. It was over. Except that Shep now had a less than savory pair of wings on his back.

Wesley eased Shep to the ground where he sat with his face pressed to the earth, weeping sorrowfully into the grass. No one dared speak. Patrick glanced over at the cluster of agents still tied together. They looked like they were going to need some serious therapy. Their eyes were huge and haunted. Agent Litner grabbed the dagger off the ground and went over to cut their ropes, untying them all and removing the gags from their mouths. None of them moved, though they were free of restraints now. They just sat, their heads all turned toward Shep. Their mouths hung slack as they gazed with wonder at this strange, weeping creature.

Klee began to stir on the ground, coming out of his unconsciousness. This got Shep's attention, and he lifted his head. His green eyes were swollen and bloodshot. He wiped his tears, and assumed a responsible air. Like a grieving parent who had lost one child, yet still had another little one to look after, he stood up, brushed himself off and regained his composure. Ignoring the rest of the company, he walked over and knelt down to Klee, easing his hands underneath his body and lifting him up like a baby in his arms. Klee hung there, his legs dangling, and looked up at Shep. "Zirub. Are we all right?"

"Yes, Klee. Everything's fine."

"My head hurts. Why are you wearing those wings?"

"We have to go now, Klee. We can talk later."

Klee seemed to accept this, and closed his eyes, docile and secure in Shep's arms. Shep looked up at the others then, as though just remembering they were there. He looked directly at Patrick, who gaped at the image of his former best friend with his new appendages. Shep saw the look, and seemed slightly embarrassed. "My other wings were much nicer," he said.

Patrick nodded. "I'm sure they were beautiful."

Shep smiled sadly and started to turn away, then he looked back at Patrick. "Oh yeah. Obrien, you were right, you know."

"About what, Shep?"

"The chickpeas. I love those damn things."

Shep turned away then and the ugly black wings spread out. Still holding Klee like a child in his arms, he took flight, and it was the most disturbing sight any of them had ever seen. People weren't supposed to fly, and it grated against all that their minds were willing to accept. Patrick watched him until he was very high up and far off in the distance, becoming a small speck, indecipherable from a bird.

Then a gun shot rang out and Shep's distant form went spiraling downward like a damaged fighter jet. Patrick screamed as the shadowy form in the sky fell earthward and disappeared somewhere off in the distance. He turned and saw Agent Walsh standing behind him with a shotgun. Walsh limped forward on what looked like a broken leg. Half of his long gray hair had been singed off, and his skin was covered with blistering burned patches all over his body. He stumbled forward again, then fell to the ground. Litner ran to him.

Patrick felt the wound in his side burst open, and warm blood began to spread across the front of his tee shirt. Wesley saw it too, and ran to him. Patrick heard somebody screaming for an ambulance, then he passed out.

Chapter Fifty-Six

Patrick drifted in and out of a haze of painkillers. During his brief bouts of consciousness, he was aware that he was in the hospital, and that he was alive, but that's about as far as his thoughts progressed. There were swimming images of Robin there sometimes, the smell of her hair as she kissed his cheek, the softness of her hand on his. A couple of times he awoke to see Father Carbone praying at the edge of his bed, and where he should have been comforted, he found it unsettling. Nurses came in and out, changing his bandages and checking his blood pressure.

He came awake one time and Agent Litner was sitting silently next to him, tapping his gold pen to his temple. He leaned forward when Patrick opened his eyes. "How do you feel?"

Patrick scratched his face. "Drunk," he said.

"They have you pretty doped up. Do you remember anything?" Patrick shook his head and tried to scratch an itchy spot on his abdomen. Agent Litner stopped his hand. "You had surgery to get the bullet out. You're going to be fine but you're still healing."

A rush of memories came charging into Patrick's mind then like an army of panicked horses. He sat up and grabbed Litner's arm. "Is he dead?"

Litner tried to ease Patrick back down on the bed. "Now Patrick, there's plenty of time for talk after you've fully recovered."

Patrick grasped weakly at Agent Litner's collar. "Litner, is he dead? Tell me, damn it!"

Litner sighed and Patrick fell back, too weak to hold the threatening pose. "All right. We think Agent Walsh's shot caught Shep just as he was heading out over the ocean cliffs near the bluffs. We found some blood on one of the rocks, as well as a lock of blond hair, and um...a piece of wing. We assume that he and Klee smashed into the cliff and then tumbled into the ocean. Their bodies were not recovered, but they are both presumed dead." Patrick rolled over onto his side, giving his back to Litner. "Patrick?"

"Go away, Agent Litner. I need to be alone."

The next time he saw Litner he was in less of a haze. He'd lost track of time but guessed it had been three days. The doctor informed him that they had lowered his pain meds and that he was recovering nicely. Patrick expressed concern about paying his medical bills since he was currently unemployed. The doctor assured him that the Federal Government was covering all of his medical expenses.

As the doctor opened the door to leave, Agent Litner came in carrying a basket of flowers. "Now that is a rare sight," Patrick said humorously.

Litner smiled. "Ah, you're feeling better. These are from Wesley."

"Wesley? Is he here?"

"No. He's not quite ready for civilization yet, but he's working his way out of hermit-dom, slowly. I took him into Boston the other day."

"You're kidding me!"

Litner place the flowers on top of the television and took the seat next to the bed. "No bullshit. Wesley and I went to the museum, then we drove around. He couldn't believe the changes. The crowds started to freak him out, so I took him back home. It's a start though. He's agreed to actually read a newspaper this weekend."

"Imagine that," Patrick said. "And Agent Walsh?"

Litner looked uncomfortable. "He's still in the burn unit but he's making progress. He was lucky to get out of that house. The last thing he remembers is jumping out of the second floor window. He has no recollection of making his way back over to us. Or of..." Litner paused.

"Shooting Shep out of the sky like a Christmas goose?" Patrick said.

"Patrick, I am sorry that you feel badly."

Patrick waved him off. "Don't worry about it, Litner. It hurts, but I'm certainly not blaming anyone. Shep was the bad guy. I get it. Did you, um, find Russell?"

Litner nodded, his lip tightening "Yes. We found what was left of him. His parents have been told that he died in a fire. His brother Craig isn't buying it. He's raising holy hell and making all sorts of accusations. We'll deal with it though." Litner stared at the floor for a moment, then changed the subject. "Joey isn't doing so well."

Patrick flinched. He'd been dreading this conversation. "I can't feel him anymore."

Litner nodded. "He said the same thing about you. I guess that bond is really broken."

"Is he still crying a lot?"

"Only when he's awake," Litner said, and Patrick laughed. "He is doing better than he was. He's been able to talk to us and his appetite has increased a bit. The other day he even asked if anyone had any marijuana. We of course had to remind him that it's still illegal."

Patrick laughed. "I guess he is feeling better." There was an awkward silence. Patrick adjusted his bed so that he was in a sitting position. "They're going to prosecute him. Aren't they?"

Agent Litner brought the pen to his temple and began to tap. "Patrick, when Joey was going through his emotional awakening, he spilled his guts to anyone that would listen, including several of my superiors. Even if I wanted to help him, I'm not sure that I could at this point. He has admitted being an accessory to three murders. He knew that Shep was going to kill his family, and he didn't do a damn thing to stop it."

"But you know that's not fair. You know there are special circumstances, Litner."

"So what do you suggest, Patrick? That we start talking to the FBI about magical blood? I had a hard enough time covering up what happened at Forest Bluffs that night."

"Joey cannot go to jail. You know it wasn't his fault. Shep did something to him!"

"Yes, he calmed his soul. I'm aware Patrick, but last I heard the 'I had no soul' defense did not hold up in a court of law."

Patrick pointed at him. "You are a very resourceful person, Litner. I know there is something you can do!"

"Patrick, I'm sorry. I'm just not sure I'm ready to jump on this, 'Joey is innocent' bandwagon. I profile people for a living. I don't get a good feeling about Joey. Even now that he has his...soul back."

Patrick sighed. "When I was under the spell of that blood bond, I did things that I would never have done, could never have done under normal circumstances. I know the power that Shep had. I'll say it again. It was not Joey's fault. You have to get them to set him free."

Litner shook his head. "I don't know, Patrick."

"You owe me," Patrick said.

Litner snapped his head up. "Excuse me?"

"You owe me, Agent Litner. You promised to get me out of Forest Bluffs safely."

"You're out. You're safe." Litner said.

"Yes, but not because of you. If I hadn't jumped in front of that bullet, Shep wouldn't have needed you. He would have let Juris kill you eventually. So you see, in effect, you didn't get me out safely. I got you out safely." Patrick grinned smugly.

Litner scowled at him. "I think I liked you better when you were on morphine."

"So you'll help him? I'm vouching for his character, Litner. I take full responsibility. I'm begging you."

"I'll see what I can do, Patrick. I'm not promising anything."

Joey was being held at a special medical ward at the main FBI offices so he could be watched closely, yet kept hidden at the same time. The FBI had prevented all manner of sensationalism from leaking to the press by saying that the fire at Forest Bluffs was merely an out of control brush fire, caused by airborne debris from the house fire next door, which in turn had been caused by benign electrical problems. The fire did make the news, but with some careful spin control it was reported that all was fine at the well-known church, and that Joey Duvaine was unharmed.

Now Joey lay in a secured room behind a thick wall of glass, curled up on his side. He seemed to be asleep, but his lips continued to mutter and he cried out occasionally. Litner glanced at the two bullish guards at the door and flipped his identification at them. They stepped out of the way and let him in the room.

He was surprised to see Agent Michaels seated in the chair near the bed, sipping coffee and staring at the sleeping Joey. "Litner. Just the man I've been looking for. Why don't you come on down to my office with me. We need to talk."

Litner looked over at Joey. His black hair had been cut back into the corporate style he'd once worn. Litner stared at the perfect bones in his face, the tanned skin and the long black lashes. Joey's perfect face grimaced then and he cried out incoherently in his sleep. His shoulders trembled. Whatever good fortune had graced this young man in the past, he was miserable now. Michaels stood up and stared at Joey as well. "It's the damndest thing I've ever seen. I ask him the simplest questions, like where he went to high school, and he starts to cry."

"Well, he's been through quite an ordeal," Litner said.

Michaels stared at him for a moment. "Come on, Litner. We need to talk."

When they got to Agent Michaels's office, he told his secretary to hold his calls. After they both sat down, Michaels began to yell. "Do you think I'm a fucking idiot, Litner?"

"I'm sorry?"

"Don't give me that 'who me' look. This report you gave me is so full of holes I can't believe you expected me to buy it. Why don't you tell me what really happened out there?"

"It's as I stated in the report sir. If you have further questions, I'd be happy to try and answer them."

Michaels gave him a cynical grin. "Really. Well I do have further questions, Agent. I want to know why six of my men came back from that siege requesting leaves of absence for 'personal reasons'. All six of them suddenly need time off. That's a little strange, wouldn't you say?"

Litner made his face blank and said nothing. Michaels continued. "I would also like to know why I have three agents with third degree burns on their hands, who claim that they don't know how they got them. Can you tell me about that?"

"I'm sorry sir, I cannot. There was a lot of—"

"A lot of confusion," Michaels said, finishing his sentence. "Yes, you said that in your report. It must have been damn confusing out there for three people to have their hands burned without their knowledge. I'm not buying that. I see the scared looks on their faces. They're hiding something. You're all hiding something. Tell me the truth, Litner. Are you withholding facts from me?"

"I want you to cut Duvaine loose," Litner said, using the shock value of the statement to avoid answering the last question. It worked.

"What did you say?"

"I said I want you to cut Duvaine loose. I have reason to believe that he was not in his right mind during the time his family was murdered. That is, if they were murdered. There is still no proof of that."

Michaels was literally thrown by the statement, and he tilted back in his chair, nearly tipping over. "No proof? No proof? How about a full confession from Duvaine himself? Is that not proof enough for you?"

"As I said sir, I believe that Duvaine was not in his right mind."

"Hold on Litner. Just hold on a minute. All I've heard from you and Agent Rourke, God rest his soul, for the past year, is that Joey Duvaine was involved with his family's deaths. You insisted on it. You argued about it. You begged me not to close the case. So now Duvaine has confessed to having prior knowledge of these murders, which he claims his friend Shepherd committed. This is no innocent young man we're dealing with here."

"But sir, as I was saying—"

"Have you heard some of the things he's confessed to? He's admitted, among other things, to dressing his friend Shepherd up as Captain Morgan before sending him off to murder his father. You know, Captain Morgan from the rum bottle? Complete with pirate costume and theatre make-up. Why would he do such a thing? I'll tell you why. In order to, and I'm quoting here, 'mess with his father's mind' before Shep killed him. Should I go on, or is that disturbing enough for you?"

"As I explained, sir, I believe there were extenuating circumstances."

"See, that's just the thing, Litner. You've explained shit. You've told me nothing. Until you can do better than that, the answer is no. Duvaine is going to fry. End of story."

Litner drummed the side of his head with his pen. "What if I were to offer you something in return for Joey Duvaine's freedom?"

Michaels frowned. "I'm afraid that you haven't got anything that good, Litner. This case is in the can."

"What if, for arguments sake, I did have something that good. Would you consider trading Joey's freedom?"

He could see that he'd sparked his boss's curiosity, though he struggled to make his face blank. Michaels was not as practiced at hiding his feelings as Litner was. "Again, for argument's sake," Michaels said, "if you did in fact have a piece of information that valuable, then yes, I would consider it."

"Duvaine goes free from prosecution?"

"Tell me what you've got, and I will consider it. I'm not promising anything."

Litner grinned. "What if I were to tell you that I know where there is a Cripulet."

Michaels looked up in surprise, then he shook his head. "Yeah, I know where a Cripulet is too, Litner. It's out in India, sitting underground in the bowels of the earth. It's been dry and inactive for decades. So what?"

Litner shook his head. "I'm not talking about that Cripulet. I'm talking about a Cripulet that we have right here."

Michaels shrugged casually, but Litner saw his black skin pale just a little, a flicker of excitement in his eyes. "Here? Here meaning in the United States?"

"No. Here, meaning in Massachusetts," Litner said.

Michaels stared at him for a moment. "Bullshit. Don't fuck with me, Litner. There is no damn Cripulet in Massachusetts."

"Have you ever known me to lie?" Litner asked.

Michaels's face changed then, and he leaned forward. "A Cripulet in Massachusetts? Are you shitting me?"

"Sincerely. Oh, and it's active."

Michaels almost fell out of his chair again, only this time it was from leaning too far forward. "Active? How active?"

"It was just opened last month."

Michaels swallowed hard and his voice dropped to a whisper. "You know this for sure?"

"I wouldn't joke about something like this. I have eyewitness accounts."

Agent Michaels got very quiet then. He stood up and locked his door, then returned to his seat. He looked across the desk at Litner, his brown eyes wide. "Where is it?"

"You give me Joey Duvaine and I'll give you the location of the Cripulet," Litner said. He decided to leave out the small fact that the Cripulet needed the blood of the newly dead in order to open. Or that it led into some shapeless void of nothing on the outskirts of heaven. He'd save that information for when he needed another favor in the future. The location of the Cripulet was enough of a bargaining chip for now.

Michaels went still as stone. "Take the murdering little bastard. He's yours."

"Thank you."

"Don't thank me. Tell me."

Litner took a deep breath. He knew that what he was about to do could be a grave mistake. He was taking a terrible chance. But he owed Patrick this. Even if he did not agree that Joey was innocent. Finally, he spoke. "Do you know where Pearl Chasm is?"

Agent Michaels smiled.

Litner stopped by Joey Duvaine's room again on his way out. Robin was there now, sitting by his side, reading. She looked up and waved at him through the glass. Joey was still sleeping. They had him on large doses of sedatives. They were the only things that seemed to calm him. He stared at the sleeping man, the would-be god. "I hope you're worth it, kid," he muttered and walked by the room, giving Robin a final wave as he left.

Inside the room, Joey opened his eyes. "Robin."

She put her book down. "You're awake. Are you feeling better today?"

His pale blue eyes stared at her intently. He did not bother to sit up. "No. I am not feeling better today. I was not feeling better yesterday, and I will not be feeling better tomorrow. What did you do to me?"

Robin sighed. "Oh please, Joey. Not this again."

"I'm miserable."

"You're free. The pain will lessen over time. Give it time, Joey."

"Time? And just how much time would it take you to live down fact that you'd allowed the murder of your entire family?"

Robin looked into those wolf-like eyes and saw the hostility apparent every time she visited him now. She brushed the thought out of her mind. Joey would get better. He would. It would just take time. Between worrying about Joey and Patrick and grieving Shep's death, she hadn't slept in days. "Joey, you can't possibly prefer to be what you were. Do you want to live your life without feeling? Do you want to go back to that...madness?"

Joey studied her for a moment longer, then the hostility was gone and he sighed. "Of course not. I'm sorry, Robin."

His face broke then and he buried his head in his pillow. "Oh, no," Robin said. "Don't start crying again, Joey. I can't take it."

He lifted his head and the tears streamed down his face. "I'm sorry. I can't help it! Do you see what's happened to me?"

"I know it hurts now, Joey, but look at it this way. You've been saved from something evil."

"Have I? Then why do I feel like I'm already in Hell?"

He buried his face in the pillow and wept. Robin frowned. The door opened and one of the bullish guards came in. "Joseph Duvaine?"

Joey did not lift his head. Robin answered for him. "Yes, this is Joey Duvaine. What is it?"

"Agent Michaels wants to see him."

Robin scowled. She knew they wanted to put Joey in jail. "Tell him that he's upset right now. What the hell does Michaels want now?"

"He wants to discuss his release."

Robin blinked. "His release?"

"Yes. Joey's free to go. When he's feeling better, that is."

Joey sat up abruptly. He wiped his tears and looked at the guard. "I've never felt better," he said. "I'd like to go home now, please."

Chapter Fifty-Seven

Three weeks later.

Patrick sat on the train, trying to figure out who smelled so bad. All he really knew was that it wasn't him. He was wearing a new suit and some very expensive cologne. His first day on the new job had been tough. Agent Litner had pulled some strings to get him the job, and he was grateful. The job itself was not tough. It was just hard getting back into the swing of things. As much as he'd loved the routine of working for a living, he felt differently now. He was not that same regimented, docile guy he had been before the nightmare. It did feel in a way that it had all been a bad dream. Except that Shep was no longer with them, a reality that would not go away. He had not been prepared for how hard that would hit him. He'd spent a couple days at his brother Ryan's house when he got out of the hospital. Ryan had comforted him, listened to him, and let him cry.

Copie had gone to work as well, as a photographer for a small local paper. It wasn't CNN, but it was a start. Copie didn't mind. He was just happy to be alive, physically and legally. Patrick had heard through the grapevine that Father Carbone was leaving Saint Mary's and going to serve at Saint Christopher's church with Father Bello. It seemed the two scholars had a new common interest; celestial folklore.

The train stopped and Patrick got off. It was odd walking up the familiar street toward Joey's apartment. He would miss Joey terribly, but he understood why he needed to get away for a while. Joey was packing his bags and going to spend a few months up in Canada, where he claimed with dark humor that there may still be a few Duvaine's left that he hadn't killed. Joey's family had originally come from Montreal. The two of them had gone out for beers at Monty's earlier in the week with Calvin White as a bon voyage party for what Calvin called Joey's 'temporary leave of his senses'. It had been strange being back at the bar as though nothing had happened. It would have been all too familiar, but again, there was no Shep. He left a large and obvious hole. The other major difference was that Joey was now a celebrity of sorts, and he still got a lot of attention regardless of his attempts to quietly enjoy a beer with friends.

Patrick had bid Joey farewell that night, but he could not resist stopping by the apartment one last time. Joey was scheduled to leave that night for Montreal. When Patrick rounded the corner, he saw the new mini-van sitting outside. He'd never imagined Joey to drive a mini-van, but then again a lot of things had changed. Patrick grinned at the van, pleased that Joey was home.

He had to at least have one last beer with him. It might be months before they saw each other again.

Joey had the door open at the top of the stairs and was peeking out before Patrick got half-way up. "Obrien! You didn't have to come by again."

"I wanted to. Are you all packed?"

"Pretty much. Come on in."

Patrick followed Joey into the house just as the telephone rang. "Oh, I have to get that. It might be Aunt Betsy. She's supposed to give me a list of relatives to look up when I get to Montreal. Grab a beer, I'll be right out. "

Joey went down the hallway to answer the phone in his bedroom. Patrick wandered into the familiar living room and looked around with nostalgia, remembering all the Saturday mornings he had spent here. He glanced over at the suitcases piled up on the couch and felt a pang of sadness. Moving into the kitchen, he grabbed a beer out of the fridge. Stuck to the fridge was a yellow post-it with the name and number of a mental health center nearby. Patrick had the same number at his apartment. It was the place where Kelinda was currently residing. They had tried to get in to visit her earlier in the week, but she had refused to see them. Her mother was there, and proceeded to inform them that if either one of them ever went near her daughter again, she would remove their testicles.

The new, emotional Joey had been particularly disturbed by Kelinda's mother's comments, and Patrick had had to calm his sobbing on the way home. Talk about a role reversal. Patrick heard Joey's laughter from down in his bedroom, and he smiled. He'd been to see Aunt Betsy himself earlier that week. She'd tried to hide the fact that she was proud of her little potion, but Patrick had called her on it. She was pleased, to say the least, and felt that she had done something worthwhile to honor her dead brother and his family.

He meandered back into the living room and plunked down on the recliner, taking a long swill of his beer. The apartment had a funny smell. At first Patrick assumed it was because the place had been shut up all spring. But there was something familiar about the smell. It smelled like, well...Forest Bluffs. Like burned rubber. Patrick looked down at the chair he sat in. It was Joey's favorite recliner, the one he'd brought out to Forest Bluffs with him. The smell was probably coming from the chair. But it was so damn strong.

Patrick stood up and walked around the room. The smell was stronger near the couch. He shook his head and started to walk back to the chair when something caught his eye. There was a clump of material rolled up and tossed off in the corner of the room. Patrick took a few steps toward it. It was a tie-dyed tee shirt. Joey did not own any tie-dyed tee shirts. Patrick supposed he could have ended up with some of Shep's clothing. It was eerie to see it though, knowing that it must have been Shep's. Patrick walked over and picked up the shirt. He recognized it. It was a turquoise and orange one with tiny dancing bears that spiraled into a point in the center. He could even smell Shep's shampoo as he shook out the shirt, and he found that his heart was breaking.

He tossed the shirt back onto the floor, and was about to walk away, when he saw it. The shirt had blood on it. He froze, his stomach turning to ice. Somewhere down the hall, Joey cackled on the phone. Patrick bent over and slowly lifted the tee shirt up again. He turned it around and looked at the back. It was soaked with blood. The stain had a slight curve to it, like an upside down horseshoe. And it was fresh. The blood was fresh.

Patrick dropped the tee shirt in horror and began walking backwards as his mind spun. He found that he was gasping for air. He stopped moving when he bumped into the couch and fell backward onto Joey's suitcases. He paused, listening for Joey's voice. After a few seconds, he heard it. Joey was still on the phone.

On a whim he opened one of Joey's suitcases. He wasn't sure what he expected to find. He lifted the lid of the case and the smell wafted up, accosting his nostrils. He looked down at the contents of the case. "No," he said quietly. "No."

He shook his head, unable to believe his eyes. Now he knew what he'd been smelling. There in the suitcase, were hundreds of clear plastic zip bags full of reddish brown seeds. He knew that smell. It was the smell of the crop. He grabbed another suitcase and unzipped it. More seeds. He tore through the bags now, ten suitcases piled up on the couch. Patrick opened every one of them, and every one of them was full of seeds.

He put his hands to his head. "No," he whispered. Words he'd said to Wesley echoed in his mind. 'So that's it? He screws up with you and this Rollie guy, and he just starts over again?'

Patrick looked over at the telephone extension on the end table next to the couch. Slowly, he reached his hand over and picked up the receiver. He was sweating when he brought it to his ear. There was a dial tone.

He heard the click of a gun behind him and he spun around. Joey stood on the other side of the couch. He had a small black handgun pointed at Patrick's head. "Step away from the seeds, Obrien."

Patrick stayed frozen in place. "Joey, what are you doing?"

"I said, step away from the seeds."

Patrick put his hands up and took two steps back from the couch. "So," he said, his voice trembling. "Who did he get to cut his wings off this time? I know it wasn't Dr. Lichtenstein."

Joey took a step toward Patrick. "I cut his wings off. That's what friends do."

Patrick shook his head. "Who the hell are you, anyway?"

Joey grinned, but his eyes were dark and hostile. "You know who I am. I'm Joey Duvaine."

Patrick shook his head. "I know a character played by an actor named Joey Duvaine. Have I ever really known you, Joey?"

Joey held the gun on Patrick. His blue eyes danced with anger. "He told me what happened that night. About how he couldn't kill you. It's ironic, really. All these years he was afraid that I would be the one to get attached. The way Wesley got attached to Rollie. But that never happened to me. I never gave a shit about you."

"Who are you, Joey?"

"Oh please, Obrien. You've gotten so dramatic lately. I liked you better before. You were so...simple. That's why we picked you. You ask me who I am. Well let me tell you who I'm not. I am not Shep. I have no soft spot for you that will prevent me from pulling this trigger. I am also not Wesley Shepherd. I don't intend to hide away for the rest of my life in some cabin, shivering with guilt and self-loathing."

"When did he get to you?" Patrick asked in a low voice.

Joey laughed. "Get to me? He didn't get to me. I sought him out. I went looking for him. I know you want to place all of the blame on Shep, Obrien. You need to believe that he's the one who corrupts and controls me. But that's not the way it is. It never has been."

Patrick shook his head. "No. No I won't believe it. Shep calmed your soul. He made it so that you couldn't feel remorse."

"Yes. If it will make you feel any better, that blood Robin gave me really did break the blood bonds I had with you and Shep. Kudos to Aunt Betsy, that fruity fucking witch. I didn't think she had it in her."

"So the pain you were experiencing was real. The remorse was real. Then why are you doing this now?"

"I don't want to feel the pain! I don't want to, as the therapist said, 'explore my feelings'. I can't live with that kind of guilt. Why would I want to? So I found Shep. I knew he was alive, I could feel it. I found him and I had him do me again. I had him give me his blood and calm my soul. It wasn't as easy this time. He's in pretty rough shape after that fall he took. He was barely able to save Klee from drowning. I still can't believe you brought the FBI to our door, Obrien. I've been wanting so badly to tell you that you make me sick, you piece of shit. You make me sick for what you did to us."

Patrick shook his head. "No. You don't know what you're saying, Joey. Please, come with me. We'll go see Aunt Betsy."

"I don't want to go see fucking Aunt Betsy! Don't you get it? I am not a victim here! I volunteered to this when I was fifteen, and I volunteered to it again this time. This was my choice!"

"I don't believe you. You were an innocent boy back then. Shep took advantage of you. He manipulated you. You didn't know what you were getting into."

"You're wrong, Obrien. Shep told me everything before he ever calmed my soul. I know you don't want to believe that. You want to make him the bad guy, but you don't understand. All of those years ago, he gave me a choice. I could have said no and he would have walked away and found somebody else."

Patrick shook his head. "God, Joey. Why? Why would you choose this?"

Joey laughed. "You mean why didn't I want to be normal? Normal like you? Let me tell you something, Obrien. I was never normal. Do you have any idea what my I.Q. is?"

Patrick shrugged. "I've heard it's quite high."

Joey threw his head back and laughed. "Yes, Obrien. It's quite high. That's putting it mildly. It's the highest I.Q. ever recorded. I'm a fucking freak."

Patrick coughed sarcastically. "Oh yes. I'm sure it's been rough on you, being a drop dead gorgeous genius and all."

"It has!" Joey screamed so loud that his cheeks flushed red. The deadpan stare was gone and now Joey's face was pinched with true emotion. Patrick was startled by the reaction. Joey stepped a little closer, the weapon still pointed at Patrick.

"You have no idea. You think everything is peaches and cream for a kid that smart? When everyone around you has average intelligence? It's a nightmare, Obrien. Nobody could relate to me. I needed more sensory input than my so-called normal life could offer. And when the teachers wanted to move me up three grades in school, my mother declined. She wanted me to be with the morons my own age. I was restricted, Obrien. I was trapped, in a world without stimulation. I died of boredom every day. All of my relationships seemed so shallow and false, even those with my family. And I had all of these thoughts. These brilliant thoughts that nobody else could understand! I had ideas, and nobody to discuss them with. My own thoughts bombarded me until I felt like I was going insane. I was the most depressed nine-year old you ever saw."

Joey paused and looked off into the distance. "By age ten I was contemplating suicide. By age eleven, I had attempted it twice."

Patrick was shocked, and it showed on his face. Joey smiled coldly. "That's right, Obrien. My parents swept that little tidbit under the rug. We can't have the neighbors knowing that the great Charles Duvaine has a nutcase for a son, now can we? The first time, I jumped off of the roof of the house. Unfortunately, I only broke my leg. The second time, my mother found me in the bathroom with a razor blade in my hand. I'd started to slice one of my wrists. They never even got me a doctor. They never even got me professional help. They decided that they could deal with me themselves. They were ashamed of me. They didn't want anyone, even a doctor, to know what a freak I was."

Patrick stood in shocked silence, understanding that he was now meeting the real Joey for the very first time. "Is it beginning to make sense to you now, Obrien?" Patrick nodded. Joey continued. "I became an actor, because I could at least pretend to be someone else for that short time that I was on the stage or in front of the camera. I could be someone else, someone without my problems. The down side was that it always ended. Then I'd have to go back to being me again. The real world was slow and stagnant. It was like a vacant repressed hell. I hated my life. I hated the world."

Joey's white eyes looked off into the distance, remembering. Then his face warmed, and his lips tilted into a grin. "Then one day, that all changed. Someone came along who offered me the role of a lifetime. He offered to make me someone else for as long as I lived. He offered to give me an extraordinary life, where the rules did not apply and I'd be free to explore stimuli and power that went beyond the eternal dulling numbness of this world."

"Shepherd," Patrick said softly.

Joey smiled. "The one and only. Melvin Eugene Shepherd, otherwise known as Zirub of Ilch Chlana Quonst."

Patrick looked confused. "Ilch what?"

"Ilch Chlana Quonst. That was his designated area when he was in the other place."

"You mean heaven?"

"It's more complicated than that, Obrien. But as I said, he told me everything from the beginning. He was amazing. His intelligence exceeded my own, tenfold. You can imagine how thrilled I was to have met him, to have someone so above average to converse with."

Patrick shrugged. "So you're saying that from day one, Shep offered to...what?"

"Make me a god," Joey said. "I know how narcissistic that sounds, but it was more than that. He offered me a life beyond the mundane confines of this world. Don't you see? He really did give me life. I'd be dead now if it weren't for him, I'm sure of it. He is my best friend. He is my brother. He is my everything."

"But Joey, he's not right. He's mentally unstable. He's hell-bent on revenge and control of something he will never have! Did he tell you about that thing that appeared the night Allisto was killed?"

"Of course."

"Well for Christ sakes, Joey! Doesn't that make you a little wary of him? Of his authenticity?"

"You don't know anything about it, Obrien."

"Well I know that I wouldn't put my trust in someone who God clearly is not pleased with!"

Joey howled with laughter. "God? Do you really think that that Cherubim was sent by God? Do you honestly believe that God the almighty would send one of His minions down to fucking Forest Bluffs, Massachusetts to destroy a few trucks full of grain? That thing you saw was there of its own free will, Obrien. That and things like it have been stalking Shep for years. For their own reasons!"

"Why? For what reason?"

"To sabotage Shep's plan! That was one of his so-called superiors. They twisted Shep's plan from the beginning and kept him from being involved in executing it! It was Shep's idea, and he never even got credit for it. Don't you see? Shep has the chance to prove himself now. They know this. If Shep executes his plan now and succeeds in turning the world toward enlightenment, then they will be proven wrong. In simple terms, he makes them look bad. That, Obrien, is why that thing showed its ugly faces and destroyed those crops. It's part of an age-old pissing contest. Everything that crawls out of that realm is not on a holy mission."

Patrick shook his head. "I don't believe it. You're as crazy as he is. You actually buy into all his paranoid bullshit. My God, Joey. You really do worship him."

"Shep gave me life. Don't you understand that? I am nothing without him. He is the most beautiful thing I've ever known. How could you have possibly thought that I would give him up? You should have joined us, Obrien. You could have been part of it. But it's too late for that now."

Joey lifted the gun, and Patrick didn't like the hostility he saw in his face. "You know, Joey, I've had a lot of guns pointed at me lately. It's really getting tiresome."

"I'm not going to kill you. That would displease Shep, although I can't quite understand why. But he's still heartbroken about losing Allisto and I don't want to add any pain to that. I'll have to subdue you until I'm safely out of here. Then I'll send someone to free you."

"Subdue me?" Patrick said warily

Joey smiled. "Oh don't worry. You won't feel a thing." Joey moved toward him, and Patrick backed up defensively. When he was backed against the wall, Joey grabbed him by the shirt with one hand and lifted him up over his head. Patrick looked down in amazement. "Oh, right. I forgot to tell you. Since you're not the Shield anymore, Shep gave me your strength. I hope you don't mind. After all, you weren't using it." Joey slammed Patrick's head into the wall and everything went dark.

Chapter Fifty-Eight

Robin still wasn't sleeping. Sure, Patrick was better, and Joey seemed to be getting back to normal, but she still couldn't seem to get through a night without waking every two hours. Each time sleep started to take her under, she'd be jolted awake with disturbing images, such as Russell's eyeball rolling off of Copie's leg. She knew that if she didn't get some uninterrupted sleep soon she would lose her mind. She'd already started hallucinating a bit in the car, imagining a bug crawling up her arm, only to jump and discover there was nothing there. That's when she decided that the sleeping pills were in order.

It was only six o'clock at night when she put on her nightshirt, swallowed the two pills and settled down on the couch. She was drawn down into a dreamless sleep almost immediately. It was not even full dark yet when she opened her eyes a crack. "I'm not done sleeping yet," she said groggily to whoever had touched her face. Her eyelids felt like they had weights tied onto them, but she forced them to open fully, sensing that she was not alone.

She glanced at the clock on the coffee table. It read 7:15. She'd only been asleep an hour. She lifted her heavy head and glanced around the room. The apartment was quiet and empty. She decided she must have been dreaming. Her eyes fell like cement and she began to drift into sleep again.

That's when she felt the weight shift on the couch and the soft curls fall onto her face as Shep kissed her. It had to be Shep. No one else smelled like that. I'm dreaming, she thought. "You're dead," she whispered through the haze of sleep.

"I'm not dead. I'm right here," the familiar voice said. Part of her was aware that this was real, and she started to cry.

Eyes closed, she said. "No. Not this. I can't take anymore. I just can't."

He stroked her face. "Shhh. It's all right." She felt his full weight lean over on her then, and smelled his skin as he trailed his lips along her cheek. "Do you love Patrick?" he asked.

"Yes," she slurred.

"Does he love you?" the voice asked.

"Yes," she whispered. "He loves me."

There was a long pause and she thought that Shep's voice was going to go away and let her sleep. "Do you love me?" the voice asked after a long silence.

She didn't answer. She was beginning to come awake now and fear was starting to arise in her heart. Shep in her apartment? Shep lying on the couch with her? Impossible. Shep was dead.

"Robin?" Her body jerked at the sound of her name. "You didn't answer me. Do you love me?"

She felt his hair brush against her face, felt his weight pressing down on her and she wanted him there. Of course, he was only a dream. "Yes," she whispered, even softer this time.

"Then you'll come with me." It was a statement, not a question. His voice had stopped being soft and dream-like. It was louder and more commanding. "You'll come with me, if you love me."

She came fully awake now. Her eyes sprang open and she started to sit up. Shep was there on the couch. She gasped when she saw him, and the condition he was in. This was no dream.

"Shepherd!" she said as she struggled to get up. He gently held her down. He had cuts and horrible bruises all over his face. Broken blood vessels trailed like a purple spider web down the right side of his cheek. His left eye was swollen completely shut, and one of his wrists had a cast on it.

"Be still," he said.

"You're alive!" she said in amazement.

He nodded. "Did you mean what you said?" he asked, touching her hair. She couldn't stop looking at his swollen eye. "Do you love me, Robin?"

She sat up then and he allowed her to do so. She took in his entire appearance. He had long gray cotton pants on and a black sweatshirt with a hood. On his feet he wore black high-topped sneakers. In his right hand, he held a pair of dark sunglasses. On the coffee table next to him was a black baseball cap. He's in disguise, she thought. He looked at her pleadingly, waiting for her to respond to his request that she go with him. Go with him where? She knew that she should have been running for the door but she was still pleasantly hazy from the sleeping pills.

"I do love you, Shep, I'll always love you. But I can't go with you."

He looked down then, nodding.

"You understand. Don't you?" she asked.

He sighed deeply, fiddling with the bottom of his wrist cast. He looked up at her with one green eye, the other swollen shut in a black and blue bruise half the size of a golf ball. "No," he said. "I don't understand."

He covered her mouth and nose with a wet rag. She tried to pull away but he pressed it down harder, forcing her to breathe through it. It smelled like the gas she'd gotten at the dentist's office as a child. She tried to scream, to speak, to strike out, but then the euphoria came over her and she fell back onto the couch. She was vaguely aware of Shep carrying her toward the door, then there was nothing.

Chapter Fifty-Nine

Someone was pounding on the door and calling his name. Patrick awoke and found that he could not move. His head was throbbing. He looked around in confusion. He was in Joey's apartment. The events preceding his blackout came back to him. He looked down at himself. He was on the recliner, bound with bungee cords. He looked over at the couch. Joey's bags were gone, and so was Joey.

"Patrick! Are you in there?"

It was Agent Litner's voice. "I'm in here!" His voice cracked. "I'm in here, Litner!"

"Can you open the door?"

"No. You'll have to break in."

There were a couple of thuds, and then the door flew open. Litner came storming into the apartment with his gun drawn. He stopped dead when he saw Patrick tied to the chair. "Oh no," he said, re-holstering his gun. "What now? What is this?"

Patrick winced. "Could you untie me please?"

Litner went to him and began to struggle with the bungee cords. "Who did this to you?"

"Joey did." Litner stopped moving and looked at Patrick. Patrick shook his head. "Don't say it. I know you told me so. How did you know I was here?"

Litner sighed and finished untying Patrick. "Joey left me a message. He said that you were at his apartment and that you needed my help. What the hell happened here?"

"Shep is alive," Patrick said.

Litner's mouth went rigid. "What?"

Patrick moved from the recliner to the couch, which still smelled like Forest Bluffs. He told Litner about what had happened. Litner sat down on the recliner and tapped his temple. "So we really have no proof that Shep is alive, then."

Patrick looked him in the eye. "He's alive, Litner."

"Are you sure? Did you see him with your own eyes?"

"Joey said—"

"You just told me that Joey is a lunatic. But you're going to take his word that Shep is alive? Did it ever occur to you that Joey could have bloodied that shirt?"

Patrick sat silently, rubbing the back of his head where a nice egg was forming. Litner stood up. "What's wrong with Robin anyway?"

Patrick perked up. "Robin? What do you mean?"

"Well, on Joey's message, he told me to make sure we stopped by Robin's place."

Patrick stood up. "Shit."

Litner had Patrick drive the car so that he could use his laptop computer. He sat in the passenger seat tapping away at the keys while Patrick hammered the car up the narrow streets toward Robin's apartment. Litner shook his head. "Son of a bitch," he said, staring at the computer screen.

"What is it?" Patrick asked frantically.

"Shep is alive."

Patrick glanced at him. "How do you know for sure?"

Litner sighed. "Because Joey Duvaine's FBI file has been wiped clean. I only know one person who could have accomplished that. Also, he left me a...greeting."

Patrick glanced at him frowning. "A greeting?"

Agent Litner turned the computer toward Patrick. "My login has been changed to Agent Fuckhead."

They reached Robin's apartment. Patrick had a key now, which he dropped twice upon storming up the narrow stairway to her door. Finally, they reached the door and the two of them stepped inside. The apartment was empty. Patrick stormed through the place calling Robin's name, to no avail. Litner stepped into the bedroom behind him. "I've found something," he said. Patrick turned and saw the candy necklace he'd given Robin, dangling from Litner's fingers. There was an envelope pinned to it. "It's addressed to you," Litner said.

Patrick sat down on the bed and put his head in his hands. "You read it. I can't. I just can't."

Litner opened the envelope, pulling out a piece of lined paper. He looked up at Patrick. After a moment's pause, Litner began to read the letter.

"Dear Obrien, although I still think you are a..." Litner paused, frowning. He cleared his throat and continued. "Although I still think you are a stupid fucking scumbag for what you did to me, I guess I can understand why you did the things you did. I tried to do my best with you, and believe it or not, everything I did was for your own safety. Now I need to go away and re-think things. Please do not try to find us, because it won't do you any good. We will succeed in our endeavor. We will endure. You merely slowed us down a bit. Forget about us. Forget about Robin. She was too extraordinary for you anyway. Be ordinary, Obrien. It's what you always wanted. It's what you always were. Good luck with your life. I'm sure you will meet a nice, normal woman and raise a bunch of little potato eating Irish kids. P.S..."

Litner paused and looked warily at Patrick. "What is it Litner? Damn it, just tell me! What does the P.S. say?"

Litner resumed reading. "P.S. I'm sorry that I had to take Robin away from you, but let's face it, she was never really yours to begin with."

Patrick stood up and snatched the candy necklace from Litner's hand, seething. Litner handed him the letter as well. He took it and crumpled it into a ball without reading it. "He's kidnapped her."

Litner looked at him sadly. "There is no evidence that Robin has been kidnapped. She could have gone of her own free will."

Patrick glared at him. "How can you say that? Or do you also think that I'm too ORDINARY for her!"

Agent Litner sighed. "Let me do some checking. I want you to stay out of things this time."

"Stay out of things? No way! I love Robin, and I am the one who is going to find her."

"I don't think that's such a good idea. And neither do you, deep down inside."

Patrick studied Litner. "Don't try to mind-fuck me. If you have something to say, just say it."

Litner frowned apprehensively. "All right. I saw what Shepherd did that night of the siege. In the midst of a self-initiated killing spree, he stopped everything to save your life, Patrick. There are only two types of people to Shep; people he loves, and people that are dispensable. You are obviously one of the people he loves, something that came as a surprise even to him. And for the people he loves, he will go to the greatest lengths to keep them with him. Just look what he did for the brothers. Staying awake in the void for all that time just to get them out. Then once he was out he stopped at nothing until he could bring them through that Cripulet. Did you really think he was going to just let you walk away?"

"I'm not one of the brothers," Patrick said.

"No, but in some ways you are equally important to him. I saw the look in his eyes when he thought you were going to die. His claims of wanting you to go off and live an ordinary life are bullshit. He even used the right words, the words he knew would anger you the most. He called you ordinary, something he knew always plagued your ego when you were friends with them. That letter, and taking Robin is all part of his plan to get you back."

"He's a lunatic," Patrick said. "He's a—"

"Now let's talk about you."

Patrick raised his eyebrows. "Me?"

"Yes, you, Patrick. In the midst of trying to disassociate yourself with your friends, you chose to fall in love with, of all people, Shepherd's girlfriend. You have clung to Robin like a life-line ever since you've been out of the hospital."

"Because I love her."

"Perhaps. Or is it because you still thought Shep was alive? Just as Shep knows that holding on to Robin will lead you to him, so you knew that holding on to Robin would bring him to you."

Patrick stood up. "Oh, I see. The neurotic pen tapper is going to psychoanalyze me. The big bad criminal psychologist. I should feel flattered. I suppose you've developed a profile of me after all this time we've spent together."

"It's what I do, Patrick. It's nothing personal. Please don't be angry, I'm trying to help you see things clearly."

"Oh! Now I'm not seeing things clearly?"

"Please, Patrick."

Patrick spread his arms out wide. "Go ahead, Litner. Take your best shot. I can handle it. Tell me about myself. Enlighten me."

Litner walked over to the window, giving Patrick his back. "All right. You, Patrick Obrien, are basically a good man who wants to do good things. However, you are also one of the most insecure people I have ever met." He turned to face him. "I don't know enough about your childhood to lay blame, but if I had to make a guess, I'd say that you have a disapproving mother who degraded you at every turn. Your father most likely pretended to be the strong silent type, but you always knew that this was an act. He just didn't want to take on any of the responsibility for raising you, so he hid behind his silence. Should I go on?"

Patrick was amazed by the accuracy of Litner's conclusions. They made him feel like he was standing there naked. He refused to let Litner see his discomfort. "Go ahead Litner. Why stop now?"

Litner shuffled over to the bed and sat down. "You grew up thinking that you had to give something of yourself away in trade in order to be liked. There was no unconditional love from your parents. You had to earn their approval at every turn. This spilled over into your social life. That's where the sports hero thing came from. You're athletic and well-built. It was the most obvious route. And with the sports came instant friendships. Friendships with popular people. But to maintain those friendships, you had to look like them, act like them, and perform for them. That's why you clung so hard to Joey and Shep. Joey and Shep gave you something unique. They gave you something that in hindsight you must know does not really exist."

Patrick snickered coldly. "And what's that, Dick Tracey?"

"Unconditional love. Unconditional friendship. No matter what you did, they were there. No matter how you acted, they were there. It didn't matter how smart or popular you were. You could have done anything to them and they still would have been there, loving and supporting you. It was the answer to your dysfunctional childhood prayers. The only problem, Patrick, is that it wasn't real. And that is something I'm afraid you still don't understand."

"Bullshit. That's crap. I know it wasn't real. I know they never cared for me."

"Then why do you still seek them?"

"I don't!"

"I saw you that night in the field, Patrick. You can verbally condemn Shep all you want, but when you thought you were really going to lose him, to lose that unconditional friendship for good, you lost your mind. You screamed for me to save him. Just minutes after you had seen him order the death of Russell and of Agent Rourke. Just minutes after he shot you. You pleaded for someone to save him. Of course it was Wesley who did so, but I won't even tap into his issues. The point is that you haven't gone out that door to find Robin yet, because you are afraid."

"Afraid of what?"

"You're afraid of yourself. You know that Shep is going to leave you a trail of breadcrumbs. You know that if you go after Robin, you're going to find the rest of them. Only this time, you're afraid that you won't stop them. You're afraid you'll join them."

"Fuck off!"

Litner shrugged, twirling his pen like a baton. "Think about it, Patrick. You weren't just fighting Joey and Shep when you went undercover. You were fighting yourself. Part of you agreed to go undercover at Forest Bluffs, not because you wanted to stop them, but because you wanted to be with them."

Patrick sat perfectly still as the breath leaked out of his lungs. What Litner said stung. He had had feelings of wanting to throw in the towel, to throw himself onto the mercy of Joey's court. But he hadn't. He hadn't, damn it. With all of the conflicting emotions and twisted loyalties he had to endure, he had done the right thing, and he had fought them. He had stopped them. Or had he? He began to second-guess himself then. Had he indeed done the best job he could? Or had he been subconsciously hoping that Shep would escape? He remembered the desperate call to save Shep. Patrick had been terrified that Shep would be destroyed, just as Allisto had been. The feeling he'd had at that moment was one of sheer panic. All he could think was, what would he do without Shep?

But regardless, it certainly didn't mean he was about to up and join the little imp in his quest to take over the world. "You're wrong," he said.

Litner stared at him, looking pained. "Don't go after her yourself. It will only lead you to Shep."

"You think I'm so weak as to join him?"

Litner said nothing, but his expression spoke the truth. That was exactly what he thought.

Patrick stood up. "I see," he said. "Thank you Agent Litner for all of your help. Thank you for finding me a job, but I'm afraid I'll have to take a leave of absence. I'm going to find my girlfriend. Because I love her. Then I am coming home with her, and we are going to live an ordinary life together. Without Shep. And that is all that is going to happen."

Litner stood up. "Patrick please. I'm begging you."

"You've underestimated my strength, Agent Litner. Good bye."

Patrick stormed out of the apartment. Litner heard the door slam. Sighing, he lay back on Robin's bed and began to tap his pen against his temple. "I haven't underestimated your strength, Patrick," he said. "I've overestimated it."

Chapter Sixty

Joey and Shep sat in the front seats of the wholesome-looking minivan, letting the fresh mountain air cleanse their senses as they cruised up interstate 89 toward Vermont. The brothers were already up north getting the new property ready. Robin lay in the back seat, snoring. She had begun an angry rant, promising to kill both Shep and Joey; Shep for abducting her yet a second time and Joey for recklessly squandering the soul she'd worked so hard to get for him. Apparently she hadn't slept in a few days, because in the middle of the rant she just ran out of steam and lay down on the seat. She was asleep within seconds.

Shep looked out the passenger side window at the plush green mountains that surrounded them like a trusted guardian. The giant yellow moon shone down like a beacon, just for them, leading the way. Shep took a long swallow of the beer he held. Joey glanced over at him. "Hey Popeye, give me a sip of that."

Shep handed the beer over to Joey. "Enough with the Popeye jokes already. My face will heal."

Joey laughed. "Sorry. I'm just not used to seeing you all banged up. Why didn't you just whip up some of that herbal balm and heal yourself?"

Shep looked at him, smirking. "I did."

Joey looked at him, then back at the road. "Holy shit! What did you look like *before* you healed yourself?"

"I slammed into the rock face of a cliff, Joey. You don't want to know what I looked like before."

Joey nodded. "You're probably right." He took a sip of the beer and handed it back to Shep. "That's the best beer," Joey said. "Do you think we can really make ours as good?"

Shep grinned. "Well after you enchanted the owner into giving us the recipe, it should be damn close. But we have to start our own brewery, with our own name."

"How can we be sure our beer will sell well enough to spawn a wide enough distribution for the crop?"

Shep leaned back in his seat and took another sip. "Because that's what you do Joey. Remember? You sell things."

"Oh, yes. So I do. Hey are you going to give me one of those beers or do I have to keep getting warm swill off of yours?"

Shep pulled a beer out of the cooler, opened it and handed it to Joey, who took a long sip. "Damn this is good beer. We have to make our beer at least this good."

"Yes, well we'll do the best we can. We have to add certain ingredients as a prerequisite to mask the crop. The substance must be undetectable. As far as anyone will know, it's just going to be another microbrew to take storm of the market."

Joey laughed. "Yeah. Except contrary to the other microbrews, ours will be able to sterilize a suds-swilling college student with one sip."

Shep smiled, looking dreamy as he gazed off into the night. "Yes. It's going to be beautiful. This time it's going to work. This time, everything will go as planned."

They were silent for several moments, with only the soft whir of the engine and the whistle of the night wind as it passed through the open windows. Then Joey glanced over at Shep. "What about Obrien?" he asked.

Shep continued to stare dreamily out the window. "Obrien will come around," he said.

Joey nodded. "Yeah. He'll come around." After another extended silence, Joey turned back to Shep. "How can you be sure he'll come around?" he asked.

Shep glanced over his shoulder at Robin, where she lay slumbering in the back seat, then he looked back to Joey. "Because he doesn't have a choice. Does he, Joey?"

Joey chewed on his lower lip for a moment, then he nodded. "No. I guess he doesn't."

The End

About the Author

Author of the acclaimed novellas *Gypsies Stole My Tequila* and *Temple of Cod*, Adrienne Jones is known for her unusual clashing of genres, with an inclination towards Science-Fiction, Fantasy, and Humor.

The Hoax is her first full-length novel.

Printed in the United States
67989LVS00003B/58